D1272965

The Undivided Self

By the same author

Fiction

Liver
The Butt
The Book of Dave
Dr. Mukti and Other Tales of Woe
Dorian
How the Dead Live
Tough, Tough Toys for Tough, Tough Boys
Great Apes
The Sweet Smell of Psychosis (with Martin Rowson)
Grey Area
My Idea of Fun
Cock & Bull
The Quantity Theory of Insanity

Non-fiction

Psycho Too (with Ralph Steadman)
Psychogeography (with Ralph Steadman)
Feeding Frenzy
Sore Sites
Perfidious Man (with David Gamble)
Junk Mail

The Undivided Self

— Selected Stories —

Will Self

Introduction by Rick Moody

BLOOMSBURY

New York • Berlin • London

Published by Bloomsbury USA, New York

All papers used by Bloomsbury USA are natural, recyclable products made from wood grown in well-managed forests. The manufacturing processes conform to the environmental regulations of the country of origin.

LIBRARY OF CONGRESS CATALOGING-IN-PUBLICATION DATA

Self, Will.
The undivided self : selected stories / will self ; introduction by Rick Moody—1st U.S. ed.
p. cm.
ISBN-13: 978-1-59691-297-7
ISBN-10: 1-59691-297-9
I. Title.
PR6069.E3654U53 2010
823'.914—dc22
2010017365

First U.S. edition 2010

1 3 5 7 9 10 8 6 4 2

Typeset by Westchester Book Group
Printed in the United States of America by Quad/Graphics Fairfield

Contents

Introduction

On Will Self

Will Self, short story writer, as indicated in the volume you have in your hands, has among his many awesome talents two that make him the singular writer that he is, at least according to this reader. These are his ear and his imagination. A disquisition on these subjects follows herewith.

By *ear*, of course, I mean his preternatural ability to ape the dulcet voices of citizens of the United Kingdom (likewise, occasionally, Americans) of every class, accent, dialect, and intoxicant. Not just the Oxbridge eggheads of his own university years, but Jamaican drug dealers, fox-hunting lords, middle-class shopkeepers, self-inflating novelists, you name it. As regards this perfection of *audition*, it's almost as if there is no Will Self. It's as if London and its environs are speaking through him.

It's not only this ear for voices that I find so beguiling and which you will too in *The Undivided Self*. There's also Self's love of and facility with the twists and turns of language. His affection for old Anglo-Saxonisms is something that has long been apparent—*ullage*, *thirrup*, *toff*, *hawcubite*, *gibber*, *flotch*, *spillikins*, *swingeing*—though he is not above the odd Latinate gem if it is germane to his purposes. Accordingly, on each and every page, we find *le mot juste*, dozens, in fact. Leaving aside Martin Amis, with whom Self shares a love of the scabrous and satirical, there is no other flourisher of English (or American) who is quite so spectacular. Permit me to quote: "His socks had peristalsized themselves down into the ungy, sweaty interior of his boots." ("Fly-topia") Such a blunt sentence and yet so great! And not only for the forcible use of *peristalsis* as a verb, but also for the juxtaposition of *ungy* and *sweaty*, the former of which occurs in no dictionary of American usage that I can lay my hands on, but whose slang appropriateness cannot be denied, especially if one has suffered—and who has not?—from the existential woe of boots and inelastic socks.

Or how about:

> And by the walls of the abandoned shop premises they were skirting was a frozen wave of detritus, a fully evolved deco-system, where the squashed spine of an old vacuum cleaner was preyed on by the strut of an umbrella, which in turn was ensnared by a shred of gabardine, upon which suckered last night's discarded condom, which for its part was being eaten away by the white acid of bird shit. ("The Five-Swing Walk")

The Will Self ear, naturally hard-wired into a keen capacity for caustic observation, here finds its perfect evocation in the neologism *deco-system*, which, once employed, permits a great luxury, a torrent, a viaduct of trash, Rube Goldbergian in its aspect.

And even one further example:

> Then the large, velvet-robed woman started to cough. It was . . . a particularly hoarse and rattling cough, with an oil-drum resonance to it, admixed with something like the sound of fine shingle being pulled this way and that by breakers on a beach. ("Grey Area")

The foregoing will serve for the moment as a celebration of Self's ear, and his ear leads naturally and inevitably to the next register of success I wish to address. As to Self's imagination, it is, since *Cock & Bull* was first published in this country, legendary. Of the more fanciful examples contained in the book you are holding, we might single out: a British council flat in which a colony of silverfish arrange themselves so as to give advice to the tenant holder; a race of supersized pals called Emotos whose only purpose is to make each and every one of us Americans *feel good about ourselves*; an incredibly dull indigenous tribe who refer to themselves as the kind of people you would *avoid at a party*, and so on.

These two preternatural strategic weapons, *ear* and *imagination*, are impossible to acquire by dint of longing or, even, in most cases, through hard work. This I can assure you as a fellow engineer in words. Where, you therefore ask, does such a talent come from? Self's early life was not unusual, though not without intellectual privilege. He was born of an academic father, a citizen of the UK, and a Jewish-American mother from Queens. He was raised mainly in North London, though he did spend a little time here in the States. He was educated at Exeter College, Oxford, where he studied politics and philosophy rather than literature, and he works, in addition to writing novels and stories, as a journalist for a plethora of publications. He has served, on occasion, as both television critic and food reporter. He's been twice married, in the current instance to a newspaper editor who is a firebrand and a steadying influence. He has four children, two from the prior marriage. He lives in a middle-class neighborhood that once spawned the likes of Roger Daltrey. Self appears on British television occasionally, as an astringent commentator. In all things, the author works assiduously, as even a cursory examination of his list of publications will indicate. His rate of production, as with many other aspects of his professional life, is much to be admired.

Of the author's youth as *enfant terrible*, a fair amount is known, and I will not belabor this introduction with the inclusion of falling-off-barstool nights at the Groucho Club, nor accounts of high jinks on John Major's airplane. However, few people, and especially few Americans (I accord him honorary status), are given second acts in their lives, as others have noted. Self, unlike other literary reprobates (of whom we could compile a long list), made a clean break over a decade ago, and to this reader you can see the revolution in the work.

He was, from the first, a great short story writer, whose longer works were conceptually catchy but sometimes unruly. He has since become a very great novelist *and* a great writer of stories. *The Undivided Self* (the title, besides being a pun that he must have saved up, is a backhanded homage to that social thinker of the late sixties, R. D. Laing) collects stories from each of Self's five volumes of stories, of which two, it seems to me—*Tough, Tough Toys for Tough, Tough Boys* and *The Quantity Theory of Insanity*—are indisputable masterpieces of shorter prose. Each of these books is excerpted here liberally, as are a few stellar selections from the other three collections, *Grey Area*, *Dr. Mukti and Other Tales of Woe*, and *Liver*.

As there are any number of Will Selves, there are also many kinds of stories in this sampling. Biographically speaking, I would argue that Self is a restless person in the second act of his life, a man full to bursting with ideas. When he has learned enough about a particular idiom to excel, he puts it aside to try something else entirely. If the template here generally involves a Swiftian presupposition, we can also discern echoes of other great dystopian comic voices such as Laurence Sterne, Flann O'Brien, Roald Dahl, Anthony Burgess, and William S. Burroughs. Self is not content to make comic misery the *sine qua non* of his accomplishment. There are quite heartfelt stories tucked into this collection, though Self, as is his tendency, might deny it. For me, the relationship between mother and son in "The North London Book of the Dead," which sketches out themes later expanded in his novel *How the Dead Live*, is genuinely heartbreaking. The fumbling, hapless attempts of a father to look after his children in the "The Five-Swing Walk" are equally tender. No short story collection, according to the argument I'm constructing here, is a success without use of the complete color wheel of human affinities, and *The Undivided Self* is no exception. Those who come in search of the traditional humanist epiphany are liable to get a kick in the ass for their trouble—deservedly, I might add. Still, that doesn't mean that there isn't something deeply passionate running in the gutters of Self's tragicomic United Kingdom.

Exile, Joyce famously noted, is a necessary precondition for art. If so, Self must feel himself abundantly exiled. He's half American, but writes as sublimely and mercilessly about London as anyone in his generation. He's half Jewish but has a keen eye for the hypocrisies of organized Christian religion. He's a merciless skeptic about the sacred cows of liberal humanism, who occasionally writes with considerable tenderness, and who is also loyal to his friends and family in ways few tender people are. You are about to reap the rewards of this abundance of Selfish exile. Whether *The Undivided Self* investigates the crack trade or the banalities of contemporary psychology, it is inexhaustible, and no matter your cherished beliefs or hidden prejudices, there will be work here that alarms you, dazzles you, makes you laugh out loud. This, therefore, is the ideal volume in which to test the waters of Self. But don't stand at the water's edge getting your toes moist. Dive right in.

—Rick Moody
New York City, 2010

The Rock of Crack as Big as the Ritz

A building, solid and imposing. Along its thick base are tall arches, forming a colonnade let into its hard hide. At the centre are high, transparent doors flanked by columns. There's a pediment halfway up the façade, and ranged along it at twenty-foot intervals are the impassive faces of ancient gods and goddesses. Rising up above this is row upon row of windows, each one a luxuriant eye. The whole edifice is dense, boxy, four-square and white, that milky, translucent white.

Over the central doors is a sign, the lettering picked out in individual white bulbs. The sign reads: THE RITZ. *Tembe looks at the luxury hotel, looks at it and then crosses Piccadilly, dodging the traffic, squealing cabs, hooting vans, honking buses. He goes up to the entrance. A doorman stands motionless by his slowly revolving charge. He too is white, milky, translucent white. His face, white; his hands, white; his heavy coat falls almost to his feet in petrified folds of milky, translucent white.*

Tembe stretches out a black hand. He places its palm against the column flanking the door. He admires the colour contrast: the black fading into the yellow finger flanges and then into the white, the milky, translucent white. He picks at the column, picks at it the way that a schoolboy distresses a plaster surface. He picks away a crumb of the wall. The doorman looks past him with sightless, milky, translucent eyes.

Tembe takes a glass crack pipe from the pocket of his windcheater and fumbles the crumb into the broken end of Pyrex piping that serves as a bowl. Setting the pipe down on the pavement, at the base of the white wall, from his other pocket he removes a blowtorch. He lights the blowtorch with a non-safety match, which he strikes on the leg of his jeans. The blowtorch flares yellow; Tembe tames it to a hissing blue tongue. He picks up the crack pipe and, placing the stem between his dry lips, begins to stroke the bowl with the blue tongue of flame.

The fragments of crack in the pipe deliquesce into a miniature Angel Falls of fluid smoke that drops down into the globular body of the pipe, where it roils and boils. Tembe draws and draws and draws, feeling the rush rise up in him, rise up outside of him, cancelling the distinction. He draws and draws until he is just the drawing, just the action: a windsock with a gale of crack smoke blowing through it.

'I'm smoking it,' he thinks, or perhaps only feels. 'I'm smoking a rock of crack as big as the Ritz.'

When Danny got out of the army after Desert Storm he went back to Harlesden in north-west London. It wasn't so much that he liked the area – who could? – but that his posse was there, the lads he'd grown up with. And also there was his uncle, Darcus; the old man had no one to care for him now Hattie had died.

Danny didn't like to think of himself as being overly responsible for Darcus. He didn't even know if the old man was his uncle, his great-uncle, or even his great-great-uncle. Hattie had never been big on the formal properties of family – precisely what relation adults and children stood in to one another – so much as the practical side, who fed who, who slept with who, who made sure who didn't play truant. For all Danny knew, Darcus might have been his father or no blood relation at all.

Danny's mother, Coral, who he'd never really known, had given him another name, Bantu. Danny was Bantu and his little brother was called Tembe. Coral had told Aunt Hattie that the boys' father was an African, hence the names, but it wasn't something he'd believed for a minute.

'Woss inna name anyways?' said the newly dubbed Danny to Tembe, as they sat on the bench outside Harlesden tube station, drinking Dunn's River and watching the Job Seekers tussle and ponce money for VP or cooking sherry. 'Our 'riginal names are stupid to begin wiv. Bantu! Tembe! Our mother thought they was kind of cool and African, but she knew nothing, man, bugger all. The Bantu were a fucking *tribe*, man, and as for Tembe, thass jus' a style of fucking *music*.'

'I don' care,' Tembe replied. 'I like my name. Now I'm big –' he pushed his chest forward, trying to fill the body of his windcheater '– I tell everyone to call me Tembe, so leastways they ain't dissin' me nor nuffin'.' Tembe was nineteen, a tall, gangly youth, with yellow-black skin and flattish features.

'Tcheu!' Danny sucked the inside of his cheek contemptuously. 'You're a fucking dead-head, Tembe, an' ain't that the fucking troof. Lucky I'm back from doing the man stuff to sort you, innit?'

And the two brothers sat passing the Dunn's River between them. Danny was twenty-five, and Tembe had to confess he looked good. Tough, certainly, no one would doubt that. He'd always been tough, and lairy to boot, running up his mouth whenever, to whoever.

Danny, many years above him, had been something of a hero to Tembe at school. He was hard, but he also did well in class. Trouble was, he wouldn't concentrate or, as the teachers said, apply himself. 'Woss the point?' he used to say to Tembe. 'Get the fucking "O" levels, then the "A" levels, whadjergonna do then, eh? Go down the Job Centre like every other fucking nigger? You know the joke: what d'jew say to a black man wiv a job? "I'll have a Big Mac an' fries . . ." Well, I'm not going to take that guff. Remember what the man Mutabaruka say, it no good to stay inna white man's country too long. And ain't that the troof.'

So Bantu, as he was then, somehow got it together to go back to Jamaica. He claimed it was 'back', but he didn't exactly know, Aunt Hattie being kind of vague about origins, just as she was about blood ties. But he persuaded Stan, who ran the Montego Bay chippie in Manor Park Road, to get him a job with a cousin in Kingston. Rootswise the whole thing was a shot in the dark, but in terms of getting a career Bantu was on course.

In Kingston Stan's cousin turned out to be dead, or missing, or never to have existed. Bantu got all versions before he gave up looking. Some time in the next six months he dropped the 'Bantu' and became 'London', on account of what – as far as the Jamaicans were concerned – was his true provenance. And at about the same time this happened he fetched up in the regular employ of a man called Skank, whose interests included buying powder off the boat and cooking it down for crack to be sold on the streets of Trenchtown.

Skank gave London regular pep talks, work-incentive lectures: 'You tek a man an' he all hardened, y'know. He have no flex-i-bil-ity so he have no poss-i-bil-ity. But you tek de youth, an' dem can learn, dem can 'pre-ci-ate wa' you tell for dem . . . You hearing me, boy?' London thought most of what Skank said was a load of bullshit, but he didn't think the well-oiled M16s under the floorboards of Skank's house were bullshit, and clearly the mean little Glock the big dread kept stuck under his arm was as far from being bullshit as it was possible to be.

London did well in Skank's employ. He cut corners on some things, but by and large he followed his boss's orders to the letter. And in one particular regard he proved himself to be a very serious young man indeed: he never touched the product. Sure, a spliff now and then just to wind down. But no rock, no stones, no *crack* – and not even any powder.

London saw the punters, he also saw his fellow runners and dealers. Saw them all getting wired out of their boxes. Wired so they saw things that weren't there: the filaments of wire protruding from their flesh which proved that the aliens had put transmitters in their brains. And hearing things as well, like non-existent DEA surveillance helicopters buzzing around their bedrooms. So London didn't fuck with the stuff – he didn't even *want* to fuck with it.

A year muscling rock in Trenchtown was about as full an apprenticeship as anyone could serve. This was a business where you moved straight from work experience to retirement, with not much of a career in between. London was getting known, so Skank sent him to Philadelphia, PA, where opportunities were burgeoning, this being the back end of a decade that was big on enterprise.

London just couldn't believe Philly. He couldn't believe what he and his Yardie crew could get away with. Once you were out of the downtown and the white districts you could more or less fire at will. London used to get his crew to wind down the windows on their work wagon and then they would just blast away, peppering the old brown buildings with 9-mm rounds.

But mostly the hardware was just for show. The Yardies had such a bad reputation in Philly that they really didn't have to do anyone much. So, it was like running any retail concern anywhere: stock control, margins, management problems. London got bored and then started to do things he shouldn't. He still didn't touch the product – he knew better than to do that – but he did worse. He started to go against Skank.

When the third key went missing, Skank grew suspicious and sent an enforcer over to speak to his errant boy. But London had headed out already: BIWI to Trinidad, and then BA on to London, to cover his tracks.

Back in London, London dropped the name, which no longer made any sense. For a while he was no-name and no-job. Floating round Harlesden, playing pool with Tembe and the other out-of-work youth. He lived on the proceeds from ripping off Skank and kept his head down way low. There were plenty of work opportunities for a fast boy who could handle a shooter, but he'd seen what happened in Trenchtown and Philly, he knew he wouldn't last. Besides, the Met had a way with black boys who went equipped. They shot them dead. He couldn't have anything to do with the Yardies either. It would get back to Skank, who had a shoot-to-kill policy of his own.

Without quite knowing why, he found himself in the recruitment office on Tottenham Court Road. 'O' levels? Sure – a couple. Experience? Cadet corps and that. He thought this would explain his familiarity with the tools, although when he got to training his RSM knew damn well it wasn't so. Regiment? Something with a reputation, fighting reputation. Infantry and that. Royal Green Jackets? Why not?

'Bantu' looked dead stupid on the form. He grinned at the sergeant: 'Ought to be "Zulu", really.'

'We don't care what you call yourself, my son. You've got a new family now, give yourself a new name if you like.' So that's how he became Danny. This was 1991 and Danny signed on for a two-year tour.

At least he had a home to go to when he got out of the army. He'd been prudent enough to put most of Skank's money into a gaff on Leopold Road. An Edwardian villa that was somewhere for Aunt Hattie, and Darcus, and Tembe, and all the other putative relatives who kept on coming around. Danny was a reluctant *paterfamilias*, he left all the running of the place to Aunt Hattie. But when he came home things were different: Hattie dead, Darcus almost senile, nodding out over his racing form, needing visits from home helps, meals on wheels. It offended Danny to see his uncle so neglected.

The house was decaying as well. If you trod too hard on the floor in the downstairs hall, or stomped on the stairs, little plumes of plaster puffed from the corners of the ceiling. The drains kept backing up and there were damp patches below all the upstairs windows. In the kitchen, lino peeled back from the base of the cooker to reveal more ancient layers of lino below, like diseased skin impacted with fat and filth.

Danny had been changed by the army. He went in a fucked-up, angry, potentially violent, coloured youth; and he came out a frustrated, efficient, angry black man. He looked different too. Gone were the fashion accessories, the chunky gold rings (finger and ear) and the bracelets. Gone too was the extravagant barnet. Instead there were a neat, sculpted flat-top and casual clothes that suggested 'military'. Danny had always been slight, but he had filled out in the army. Darker than Tembe, his features were also sharper, leaner. He now looked altogether squared-off and compact, as if someone had planed away all the excess of him.

'Whadjergonna do then?' asked Tembe, as the two brothers sat spliffing and beering in front of Saturday afternoon racing. Darcus nodded in the corner. On screen a man with mutton-chop whiskers made sheepish forecasts.

'Dunno. Nuffin' criminal tha's for sure. I'm legit from here on in. I seen enough killing now to last me, man.'

'Yeah. Killing.' Tembe pulled himself up by the vinyl arms of the chair, animated. 'Tell me 'bout it, Bantu. Tell me 'bout the killing an' stuff. Woss combat really like?'

'Danny. The name's Danny. Don' forget it, dipstick. Bantu is dead. And another fing, stop axin' me about combat. You wouldn't want to know. If I told you the half, you would shit your whack. So leave it out.'

'But . . . But . . . If you aren't gonna deal, whadjergonna do?'

'Fucking do-it-yourself. That's what I'm gonna *do*, little brother. Look at the state of this place. If you want to stay here much longer with that fat bint of yours, you better do some yersel' as well. Help me get the place sorted.'

The 'fat bint' was Brenda, a girlfriend Tembe had moved in a week after his brother went overseas. Together they slept in a disordered pile upstairs, usually sweating off the effects of drink, or rock, or both.

* * *

Danny started in the cellar. 'Damp-coursing, is it?' said Darcus, surfacing from his haze and remembering building work from four decades ago: tote that bale, nigger; Irish laughter; mixing porridge cement; wrist ache. 'Yeah. Thass right, Uncle. I'll rip out that rotten back wall and repoint it.'

'Party wall isn't it?'

'No, no, thass the other side.'

He hired the Kango. Bought gloves, goggles, overall and mask. He sent Tembe down to the builders' merchants to order 2,000 stock bricks, 50 kilo bags of ballast, sand and cement. While he was gone Danny headed down the eroding stairs, snapped on the yellow bulb and made a start.

The drill head bit into the mortar. Danny worked it up and around, so that he could prise out a section of the retaining wall. The dust was fierce, and the noise. Danny kept at it, imagining that the wall was someone he wanted done with, some towel-head in the desert or Skank, his persecutor. He shot the heavy drill head from the hip, like an action man in a boys' comic, and felt the mortar judder, then disintegrate.

A chunk of the wall fell out. Even in the murky light of the cellar Danny could see that there wasn't earth – which he had expected – lying behind it. Instead some kind of milky-white substance. There were fragments of this stuff on the bit of the drill, and twists like coconut swarf on the uneven floor.

Danny pushed up his goggles and pulled down his mask. He squatted and brought a gloveful of the matter up to his face. It was yellowy-white, with a consistency somewhere between wax and chalk. Danny took off his glove and scrunged some of it between his nails. It flaked and crumbled. He dabbed a little bit on his bottom lip and tasted it. It tasted chemical. He looked wonderingly at the four-foot-square patch that he had exposed. The swinging bulb sent streaks of odd luminescence glissading across its uneven surface. It was crack cocaine. Danny had struck crack.

Tembe was put out when he got back and found that Danny had no use for the stock bricks. No use for the ballast, the cement and the sand either. But he did have a use for Tembe.

'You like this shit, that right?' Danny was sitting at the kitchen table.

He held up a rock of crack the size of a pigeon's egg between thumb and forefinger.

'Shee-it!' Tembe sat down heavily. 'Thass a lotta griff, man. Where you get that?'

'You don' need to know. You don' need to know. You leave that to me. I found us a connection. We going into business.' He gestured at the table where a stub of pencil lay on top of a bit of paper covered with calculations. 'I'll handle the gettin', you can do the outin'. Here –' he tossed the crack egg to Tembe '– this is almost an eightf. Do it out in twenties – I want a oncer back. You should clear forty – and maybe a smoke for you.'

Tembe was looking bemusedly at the egg that nestled in his palm. 'Is it OK, this? OK, is it?'

'Top-hole! Live an' direct. Jus' cooked up. It the biz. Go give the bint a pipe, see how she like it. Then go out an' sell some.'

Tembe quit the kitchen. He didn't even clock the brand-new padlock that clamped shut the door to the cellar. He was intent on a pipe. Danny went back to totting up columns of figures.

Danny resumed his career in the crack trade with great circumspection. To begin with he tried to assess the size of his stock. He borrowed a set of plumber's rods and shoved them hard into the exposed crack-face down in the cellar. But however many rods he added and shoved in, he couldn't find an end to the crack in any direction. He hacked away more of the brickwork and even dug up the floor. Every place he excavated there was more crack. Danny concluded that the entire house must be underpinned by an enormous rock of crack.

'This house is built on a rock,' he mused aloud, 'but it ain't no hard place, that the troof.'

Even if the giant rock was only fractionally larger than the rods indicated, it was still big enough to flood the market for crack in London, perhaps even the whole of Europe. Danny was no fool. Release too much of the rock on to the streets and he would soon receive the attentions of Skank or Skankalikes. And those Yardies had no respect. They were like monkeys just down from the fucking trees – so Danny admonished Tembe – they didn't care about any law, white or black, criminal or straight.

No. And if Danny tried to make some deal with them, somehow imply that he had the wherewithal . . . No. That wouldn't work either. They'd track him down, find him out. Danny had seen what men looked like when they were awakened at dawn. Roused from drugged sleep on thin mattresses, roused with mean little Glocks tucked behind their crushed ears. Roused so that grey patches spread out from underneath brown haunches. No. Not that.

Danny added another hefty padlock to the cellar door and an alarm triggered by an infra-red beam. Through a bent quartermaster at Aldershot who owed him a favour he obtained an antipersonnel mine in exchange for an ounce of the cellar wall. This he buried in the impacted earth of the cellar floor.

At night Danny sat in the yellow wash of light from the streetlamp outside his bedroom. He sucked meditatively on his spliff and calculated his moves. Do it gradual, that was the way. Use Tembe as a runner and build up a client list nice and slow. Move on up from hustling to the black youth in Harlesden, and find some nice rich clients, pukkah clients.

The good thing about rock – which Danny knew only too well – was that demand soon began to outstrip supply. Pick up on some white gourmets who had just developed a taste for the chemical truffles, and then you could depend on their own greed to turn them into gluttons, troughing white pigs. As long as their money held out, that is.

So it was. Tembe hustled around Harlesden with the crack Danny gave him. Soon he was up to outing a quarter, or even a half, a day. Danny took the float back off Tembe with religous zeal. It wouldn't do for little brother to get too screwed up on his profit margin. He also bought Tembe a pager and a mobile. The pager for messages in, the mobile for calls out. Safer that way.

While Tembe bussed and mooched around his manor, from Kensal Green in the south to Willesden Green in the north, Danny headed into town to cultivate a new clientele. He started using some of the cash Tembe generated to rent time in recording studios. He hired session musicians to record covers of the ska numbers he loved as a child. But the covers were percussive rather than melodic, full of the attacking, hard-grinding rhythms of Ragga.

Through recording engineers and musicians Danny met whites with a taste for rock. He nurtured these contacts, sweetening them with bargains, until they introduced him to wealthier whites with a taste for rock, who introduced him to still wealthier whites with a taste for rock. Pulling himself along these sticky filaments of drug-lust, like some crack-dispensing spider, Danny soon found himself in the darkest and tackiest regions of decadence.

But, like the regal operator he was, Danny never made the mistake of carrying the product himself or smoking it. This he left to Tembe. Danny would be sipping a mai tai or a whiskey sour in some louche West End club, swapping badinage with epicene sub-aristos or superannuated models, while his little brother made the rounds, fortified by crack and the wanting of crack.

It didn't take longer than a couple of months – such is the alacrity with which drug cultures rise and fall – for Danny to hit human gold: a clique of true high-lowlife. Centred on an Iranian called Masud, who apparently had limitless funds, was a gaggle of rich kids whose inverse ratio of money-to-sense was simply staggering. They rained cash down on Danny. A hundred, two hundred, five hundred quid a day. Danny was able to withdraw from Harlesden altogether. He started doling out brown as well as rock; it kept his clients from the heebie-jeebies.

Tembe was allowed to take the occasional cab. Darcus opened an account at the betting shop.

The Iranian was playing with his wing-wang when Tembe arrived. Or at any rate it looked as if he had been playing with it. He was in his bathrobe, cross-legged on the bed, with one hand hidden in the towelling folds. The smell of sex – or something even more sexual than sex – penetrated the room. The Iranian looked at Tembe with his almond eyes from under a narrow, intelligent brow on which the thick, curled hair grew unnaturally low.

Tembe couldn't even begin to think how the Iranian was getting it up – given the amount of rock he was doing. Five, six, seven times a day the pager peeped on Tembe's hip. And when Tembe dialled the number programmed into his mobile, on the other end would be the Iranian, his voice clenched with want, but his accent still that very, very posh kind of foreign.

Supporting the sex explanation there was the girl hanging around. Tembe didn't know her name, but she was always there when he came, smarming her little body around the suite. Her arrival, a month or so ago, had coincided with a massive boost in consumption at the suite. Before, the Iranian had level-pegged at a couple of forties a day and half a gram of brown, but now he was picking up an eighth of each as soon after Tembe picked up himself as he could engineer it.

After that the Iranian would keep on paging and paging for what was left of the day. Now, at least three nights a week, Tembe would be called at one a.m. – although it was strictly against the rules – and have to go and give the two of them a get-down hit, to stop the bother.

Tembe hated coming to the hotel. He would stop at some pub and use the khazi to freshen up before taking a cab up Piccadilly. He didn't imagine that the smarmed-down hair and chauffeured arrival fooled the hotel staff for a second. There weren't that many black youths wearing dungarees, Timberland boots and soiled windcheaters in residence. But they never gave him any hassle, no matter how late or how often he trod across the wastes of red carpet to the concierge and got them to call up to the Iranian's suite.

'My dear Tembe,' Masud, the Iranian, had said to him, 'one purchases discretion along with privacy when one lives in an establishment such as this. Why, if they attempted to restrict the sumptuary or sensual proclivities of their guests, they would soon have vacant possession rather than no vacancies.' Tembe caught the drift below the Iranian's patronising gush. And he didn't mind the dissing anyway – the Iranian had sort of paid for it.

The girl let Tembe in this time. She was in a terry-towelling robe matching the Iranian's. The dun blond hair scraped back off her pale face suggested a recent shower, suggested sex.

How could the Iranian get it up? Tembe didn't doubt that he got the horn. Tembe got the horn himself. Got it bad. But the stiffie was hardly there, just an ice-cream, melting before there was any chance of it getting gobbled. Not that Tembe didn't try it on, far gone as he was. If he had a pipe at Leopold Road he'd make his moves on Brenda – until she shoved him away with lazy contempt. If he was dropping off for one of the brasses who worked out of the house on Sixth Avenue – who he still served without Danny's knowledge – or even the classier ones at the Learmont, either they would ask, or he would offer: rock for fuck.

It was ridiculous how little they'd do it for. The bitch at the Learmont –

who, Tembe knew for a fact, regularly turned three-ton tricks – would put out for a single stone. She stepped out of her skirt the way any other woman took off her coat and handed him the rubber from the dispenser in the kitchenette drawer like it was a piece of cutlery.

Usually, by the time they'd piped up together Tembe was almost past the urge. Almost into that realm where all was lust, and lust itself was a grim fulfilment. He'd try and push his dick into the rubber rim, but it would shrink back. And then he'd just get her to un-pop the gusset of her sateen body. Get her to stand there in the kitchenette, one stilettoed foot up on a stool, while he frigged her and she scratched at his limpness with carmine nails.

Tembe tried not to think about this as the Iranian's girl moved about the bedroom, picking up a lacy bra from the radiator, jeans with knickers nesting in them from the floor. The Iranian was taking a smoke of brown from a piece of heavily stained foil a foot square. Tembe watched the stuff bubble, black as tar dripping from a grader. The girl slid between him and the door jamb. Wouldn't have been able to do that a month ago, thass the troof, thought Tembe. She's that fucking gone on it. Posh white girls don't eat any, and when they're on the pipe and the brown they eat even less. Despite that, skinny as she was, and with those plasticky features like a Gerry Andersen puppet, Tembe still wanted to fuck her.

The Iranian finished off his chase by waving the lighter around hammily, and said, 'Let's go into the other room.' And Tembe said, 'Sweet,' keen to get out of the bedroom with its useless smell of other people's sex. The Iranian moved on the bed, hitching up his knees, and for a second Tembe saw his brown dick, linked to the sheet by a pool of shadow or maybe a stain.

The main room of the suite featured matching Empire escritoires that had seldom been written on, an assemblage of Empire armchairs and a divan that had seldom been sat on. In front of the divan there was a large, glass-topped coffee-table, poised on gold claw feet. On top of this were a crack pipe, a blowtorch, a mirror with some smears of rock on it, cigarettes, a lighter, keys, a video remote, a couple of wine-smeared glasses and, incongruously, a silver-framed photograph of a handsome middle-aged woman. The woman smiled at Tembe forthrightly over the assembly of crack-smoking tools.

The room also featured heavy bookcases, lined with remaindered hardbacks, which the hotel manager had bought from the publishers by the yard. The carpet was mauve, the walls flock-papered purple with a bird-and-shrubbery motif worked into them. On the far side of the coffee-table from the divan stood an imposing armoire, the doors of which were open, revealing shelves supporting TV, video and music centre. Scattered around the base of the armoire were videos in and out of their cases, CDs the same.

Somewhere inside the armoire Seal was singing faintly: 'For we're never going to sur-vive/Un-less we go a little cra-azy . . .' 'Ain't it the troof?' said Tembe, and the Iranian replied, 'Sorry?' but not as if he meant it.

'For we're never going to sur-vive/Un-less we go a little cra-azy . . .' Tembe warbled the words, more falsetto than Seal, but with a fair approximation of the singer's rhythm and phrasing. As he neared the end of the second line he did a little jig, like a boxer's warm-up, and wiggled his outstretched fingers either side of his face, his head chicken-nodding. '. . . You know, man, like cra-azee.'

'Oh, I see. I get you. Yeah, of course, of course . . .'

The Iranian's voice trailed away. He'd put himself down in the centre of the divan and was using the flap of a matchbook to scrape up the crack crumbs on the mirror, sweeping them into a little vee-shaped pile, then going over the same surface again, creating a regular series of crack smears.

Tembe looked at the pipe and saw the thick honey sheen inside it. There was plenty of return there, enough for five or six more hits. Tembe wondered why the Iranian had called him back so soon. Surely the return alone would have lasted the pair of them another couple of hours? But now Tembe saw that the Iranian had got down on his hands and knees behind the coffee-table and was methodically combing the strip of carpet between the table and the divan with a clawed hand. The Iranian's starting eyes, hovering six inches above the carpet, were locked on in the hand's wake, crack-seeking radar.

Thass it, Tembe realised. The fucker's so fucking far gone he's carpet-cruising. Tembe had seen it enough times – and done it himself as well. It began when you reached that point – some time after the tenth pipe – where your brain gets sort of fused with crack. Where your brain *is* crack. Then you start to see the stuff everywhere. Every crumb of bread on the carpet or grain of sugar on the kitchen lino looks like a fragment of ecstatic potential. You pick one up after the other, checking them with a touch of wavering flame, never quite believing that it isn't crack until the smell of toast assaults your nose.

The Iranian had turned in his little trench of desperation and was crawling back along it, head down, the knobbles of his spine poking up from behind the silvery rim of the coffee-table. He was like some mutant guard patrolling a perverse check-point. His world had shrunk to this: tiny presences and gaping, yawning absences. Like all crackheads, Masud moved slowly and silently, with a quivering precision that was painful to watch, as if he were Gulliver, called upon to perform surgery on a Lilliputian.

The girl wandered back in, tucking the bottom of a cardigan into the top of her jeans. She fastened the fly buttons and then hugged herself, palms going to clutch opposing elbows. Her little tits bulged out.

'Fuck it, Masud,' the girl said, conversationally, 'why have you got Tembe over if you're just gonna grovel on the floor?'

'Oh, yeah, right . . .' He slid his thin arse back up on to the divan. In one hand he held a lighter, in the other some carpet fluff. He sat and looked at the ball of fluff in his hand, as if it were really quite difficult to decide whether or not it might be a bit of crack, and he would have to employ his lighter to make absolutely certain.

Tembe looked at the blue hollows under the Iranian's almond eyes. He looked at the misnamed whites of those eyes as well. Masud looked up at Tembe and saw the same colour scheme. They both saw yellow for some seconds. 'What . . . ? What you . . . ?' Masud's fingers, quick curling back from exploded nails, bunched the towelling at his knee. He couldn't remember anything – clearly. Tembe helped him. 'I got the eightf anna brown.' He took his hand from the pocket of his jacket, deftly spat into it the two marbles of clingfilm concealed in his cheek and then flipped them on to the table. One rolled to a halt at the foot of the portrait photograph of the handsome woman, the other fetched up against the video remote.

This little act worked an effect on Masud. If Tembe was a cool black dealer, then he, Masud, was a cool brown customer. He roused himself, reached into the pocket of his bathrobe and pulled out a loose sheaf of purple twenties. He nonchalantly chucked the currency on to the glass pool of the table top, where it floated.

Masud summoned himself further and resumed the business of having his own personality with some verve, as if called upon by some cutting-edge *auteur* to improvise it for the camera. 'Excuse me,' he stood, wavering a little, but firm of purpose. He smiled graciously down at the girl, who was sitting on the floor, and gestured to Tembe, indicating that he should take a seat on the divan. 'I'll just throw some clothes on and then we must all have a big pipe?' He cocked an interrogative eyebrow at the girl, pulled the sides of the bathrobe around his bony body and quit the room.

Tembe looked at the girl and remained, rocking gently from the soles to the heels of his boots. She got up, standing in the way young girls have of gathering their feet beneath them and then vertically surging. Tembe revised his estimate of her age downwards. She sat on the divan and began to sort out the pipe. She took the larger of the two clingfilm marbles and laborious unpicked it, removing layer after layer after layer of tacky nothingness, until the milky-white lode was exposed and tumbled on to the mirror.

She touched a hand to her throat, hooked a strand of hair behind a lobeless ear, looked up and said, 'Why don't you sit here, Tembe? Have a pipe.' He grunted, shuffled, joined her, manoeuvring awkwardly in the gap between the divan and the coffee-table.

Masud came back into the room. He was wearing a shirt patterned with vertical stripes of iridescent green and mustard-yellow, sky-blue slacks in raw silk flapped around his legs, black loafers squeaked on his sockless feet, the froth of a paisley cravat foamed in the pit of his neck. What a dude. 'Right!' Masud clapped his hands, another ham's gesture. Upright and clothed, he might have been some motivator or negotiator freeing up the wheels of commerce, or so he liked to think.

The girl took a pinch of crack and crumbled it into the bowl of the pipe. 'I'm sure,' said the Iranian, his tone hedged and clipped by annoyance, 'that it would be better if you did that over the mirror, so as to be certain not to lose any –'

'I know.' She ignored him. Tembe was right inside the bowl of the pipe now, his boots cushioned by the steely resilience of the gauze. The lumps of crack were raining down on him, like boulders on Indiana Jones.

Tembe mused on what might be coming. Masud had paid for this lot, but could he be angling for credit? It was the only explanation Tembe could hit on for the welcome in, the girl's smiles, the offer of a pipe. He decided that he would give Masud two hundred pounds' credit – if he asked for it. But if he was late, or asked for any more, Tembe would have to refer it to Danny, who would have the last word. Danny always had the last word.

The girl lit the blowtorch with the lighter. It flared yellow and roared. She tamed it to a hissing blue tongue. She passed Tembe the pipe. He took the glass ball of it in the palm of his left hand. She passed him the blowtorch by the handle. 'Careful there . . .' said Masud, needlessly. Tembe took the blowtorch and looked at his host and hostess. They were both staring at him fixedly. Staring at him as if they wouldn't have minded diving down his throat, then swivelling round so they could suck on the pipe with him, suck on it from inside his lips.

Masud hunched forward on the divan. His lips and jaws worked, smacking noises fell from his mouth. Tembe exhaled to one side and placed his pursed lips around the pipe stem. He began to draw on it, while stroking the bowl of the pipe with the tongue of blue flame. Almost instantly the fragments of crack in the pipe deliquesced into a miniature Angel Falls of fluid smoke that dropped down into the globular body of the pipe, where it roiled and boiled.

Tembe continued stroking the pipe bowl with the flame and occasionally flipped a tonguelet of it over the rim, so that it seared down on to the gauzes. But he was doing it unconsciously, with application rather than technique. For the crack was on to him now, surging into his brain like a great crashing breaker of pure want. This is the hit, Tembe realised, concretely, irrefutably, for the first time. The whole hit of rock is to want *more rock*. The buzz of rock is itself the wanting of *more rock*.

The Iranian and the girl were looking at him, devouring him with their eyes, as if it was Tembe that was the crack, their gazes the blowtorch, the whole room the pipe. The hit was a big one, and the rock clean and sweet, there was never any trace of bicarb in the stuff Danny gave Tembe, it was jus' sweet, sweet, sweet. Like a young girl's gash smell sweet, sweet, sweet, when you dive down on it, and she murmurs, 'Sweet, sweet, sweet . . .'

It was the strongest hit off a pipe Tembe could ever remember taking. He felt this as the crack lifted him up and up. The drug seemed to be completing some open circuit in his brain, turning it into a humming, pulsing lattice-work of neurones. And the awareness of this fact, the giant nature of the hit, became part of the hit itself – in just the same way that the realisation that crack was the desire for crack had become part of the hit as well.

Up and up. Inside and outside. Tembe felt his bowels gurgle and loosen, the sweat break out on his forehead and begin to course down his chest, drip from his armpits. And still the rocky high mounted ahead of him. Now he could sense the red-black thrumming thud of his heart, accelerating through its gearbox. The edges of his vision were fuzzing black with deathly, velvet pleasure.

Tembe set the pipe down gently on the surface of the table. He was *all*-powerful. Richer than the Iranian could ever be, more handsome, cooler. He exhaled, blowing out a great tumbling blast of smoke. The girl looked on admiringly.

After a few seconds Masud said, 'Good hit?' and Tembe replied, 'Massive. Fucking massive. Biggest hit I ever had. It was like smoking a rock as big as . . . as big as . . .' His eyes roved around the room, he laboured to complete the metaphor. 'As big as this hotel!' The Iranian cackled with laughter and fell back on the divan, slapping his bony knees.

'Oh, I like that! I like that! That's the funniest thing I've heard in days! Weeks even!' The girl looked on uncomprehendingly. 'Yeah, Tembe, my man, that has a real ring to it: the Rock of Crack as Big as the Ritz! You could make money with an idea like that!' He reached out for the pipe, still guffawing, and Tembe tried hard not to flatten his fucking face.

At home, in Harlesden, in the basement of the house on Leopold Road, Danny kept on chipping, chipping, chipping away. And he never ever touched the product.

Flytopia

'Ending up as I am with animals and alcohol, one of her last friends, when she was losing her faculties, was a fly, which I never saw but which she talked about a great deal and also talked to. With large melancholy yellow eyes and long lashes it inhabited the bathroom; she made a little joke of it but was serious enough to take in crumbs of bread every morning to feed it, scattering them along the wooden rim of the bath as she lay in it, much to the annoyance of Aunt Bunny, who had to clear up after her.'

–J.R. ACKERLEY
My Father and Myself

In Inwardleigh, a small, Suffolk town which had been marooned by the vagaries of human geography, left washed up in an oxbow of demography, run aground on the shingle of a failing economy, and land-locked by the shifting dunes of social trends, the landlords in the three desultory pubs on the main street (the Flare Path, the Volunteer and the Bombardier) drew pints for themselves in the cool, brown, afternoon interiors of their establishments. The landlords stretched across the bars, from where they sat – feigning custom – tipped the handles of the pumps down with the heels of their hands, and then brought the glasses to their lips before the yellow foaming had subsided, before head had been separated from heart.

In the Volunteer a lone young lad, who was skiving off from the harvest, played pool against himself. He made risky shots, banging the balls off the cushion, hazarding tight angles. He felt certain he could win.

Jonathan Priestley, an indexer by profession, came bouncing on balled feet, out from the mouth of Hogg Lane and into the small council estate flanking the village. He savoured the anonymous character of the place, the semis' blank, concrete-beamed façades; the pebble-dashed lamp standards; the warmed gobs of blue-black tarmac in the dusty, spore-filled gutters. Savoured it, and thought to himself how it was that while in turning in on themselves some places achieve character, Inwardleigh had been visited only with anonymity.

In the windows of Bella's Unisex, Jonathan observed a young woman. She wore a blue, nylon coverall, elaborately yet randomly brocaded with the abandoned hairs of a sector of the population. She was sitting in one of the battered chairs, head tilted back against the red vinyl headrest, and as Jonathan passed by he saw her reach up to pluck, pull and then deftly snip at a lock of her own. He sighed, shifted the strap of the small rucksack he carried from one arm to the other, tried whistling a few notes through gummy lips, abandoned the attempt, proceeded.

Jonathan tripped on down the main street. His socks had peristalsized themselves down into the ungy, sweaty interior of his boots. He passed flint-knapped houses kneeling behind low walls, with peeling paint on their lintels, window frames and doors. The shutters on the windows of the small parade of shops were mostly rolled down. It was Wednesday, early closing in Inwardleigh. Have to buy everything in Khan's, thought Jonathan.

He passed by the window of Ancient Estates. The photographs which depicted properties for sale or rent were curling up like the eaves of pagodas. Jonathan sighed. Some of the asking prices were ridiculously low, Mars Bar money really. But then no one much wanted to live in Inwardleigh and its environs, where self-abuse was rife and the vet shot up his own horse tranquilliser.

Some way to the north and east of Inwardleigh a vast nuclear power station crouched on a lip of shingle and dune abutting the North Sea. The station hummed both sub- and ultrasonically. Its very size made it paradoxically invisible, as if its presence were quite simply too monumental to be apprehended.

Almost daily Jonathan would drive up there and walk out along the beach below the power station. The thing was so vast as to defy human scale, or even purpose. The reactor hall, a great dome coated in some ceramic material, was scored into so many panels, or cells, like the compound eye of Moloch. It sat on a murkily iridescent plinth. The whole was frequently wreathed in tissuey steam, sea mist, even low-hung cloud. At night the place was orange floodlit, and at all hours it echoed and crackled with amplified announcements. Announcements for whom? And by whom? He never saw any of the workers. Perhaps there weren't any; and the place was talking to itself, soliloquising while the brown waves slapped the shingle, the violet butterflies tumbled on the tips of the dune grasses and the geese honked overhead.

Inwardleigh was outflanked by the two mighty pylon lines which leapt from the power station, marched over the gorse and scrub and passed either side of the town, giving it a wide berth as if anxious to avoid being netted in for a quiz night at the Flare Path, or a cake-bake at the Methodist Hall.

These behemoth lyres, strung with lethal strings, sang the life out of the town and its environs, made them feel scorched, irradiated, scarious and desiccated. And so the working-class trippers and the middle-class weekenders steered clear of Inwardleigh, heading for the twee villages further up the coast.

Yet for Jonathan the pylon lines were part of the district's appeal. They provided what little relief the countryside possessed, for this was an area of low, rolling farm land, studded with dense copses and gouged with gravel pits dug from the sandy soil. It was a landscape of ingress and of repose: a tired body lying down on an old, horsehair mattress.

In Khan's Jonathan moved up and down the aisles putting bits of stuff in his wire basket. Joy had been gone two days and there were two more before she would return. Could he be bothered to cook something proper for himself, or would he go to the pub for fish and chips again that evening? He stood, hand hovering over a small freezer full of eugenic vegetables and macerated, frozen beef, lost in thoughts of the kitchen at the cottage.

If he cooked and didn't vigorously clean afterwards he could be guaranteed an invasion of insect life. Should he bother therefore? But to not cook was to counsel defeat, to acknowledge the unsustainability of life at the cottage. That, or maybe only its unsustainability without Joy.

The cottage was small. The summer heat percolated it entirely, forcing its way through the gaps in the dusty, velveteen curtains. Even if

Jonathan kept them drawn throughout the day, it was still hot enough in his study for the sweat dripping from his fingers to gum up the keyboard of the Macintosh. And then there were the flies. Jonathan didn't think of himself as squeamish or phobic about insects, but this long, hot summer had brought the six-legged kind out in force.

Every room in the cottage had its own, buzzing pavane; which revolved ceaselessly, with unsettling inertia, usually beneath the light fitment. There were other species as well. Daddy-long-legs which fluttered and thirruped in the evenings, skipping up the Artex pinnacles in the bathroom, then abseiling down them, like spindly climbers. Wasps also frequently diverted into the cottage. As he worked, Jonathan would become teased into awareness of them by their doodle-bug droning, which undercut the higher whine of the houseflies. This noise was insistent and somehow predatory in its very essence. He would abandon work on the index, grab whatever magazine or journal was to hand and hunt out the hunters. He would not be satisfied until he had created another pus-like smear, another shattered tangle of broken legs and wings, of mashed thorax, head and abdomen.

When Joy was staying the insects barely bothered Jonathan. She did the annoyance and upset for him. But since she had gone they had begun to irritate him more and more. He tipped back in his chair and contemplated them from under furrowed brows. How to kill? Why to kill? What the killing meant? The insects – and in particular the flies – were becoming an object of study, a platform for obscure games in virtuality.

Jonathan was compiling the index for a scholarly work on ecclesiastical architecture – or meant to be. Normally the whirrings and clickings of the Macintosh soothed him, as he moved from application to application, working in symbiosis with the mechanism. But now he found himself listening the whole time, listening for the other whirrs and clicks of his fellow residents. It occurred to him that perhaps they were learning to imitate the noises of the computer; that through some quantum, phylogenetic leap, the insects were becoming computer-like. An outrageous act of Batesian mimicry, akin to that with which the undistinguished wasp beetle jerkily pretends to the status of its more dangerous namesake.

The heat. The fucking heat. He was broiled in vexation.

Mr Khan manifested himself by Jonathan's elbow. A dun pyramid of a man who multiplied his chins to acquiesce with his customers, and divided them to dissent. 'Was there anything else?' he said. Jonathan flailed, he had been lost in the fugue, staring sightlessly at the frozen vegetables. 'Garden peas, French beans?'

'No, no, silly of me . . . I don't – all I can think of that I really need is some of those Vapona thingies. I'm convinced the ones I've got at the moment must be losing their effectiveness.'

'They're meant to last at least a month.' Mr Khan regarded Jonathan quizzically, from out of an eye with a bruised ball.

'That's as may be, but the house is still full of flies.'

'We-ell, that's the summer we've been having, isn't it? And with the harvest on now, you'll be lucky if you don't get a lot of mice and rats coming into your place as well. So how many will it be?'

'Give me another five, Mr Khan, and I'll take a box of fly-papers as well please.'

Inwardleigh was stretching and yawning as Jonathan came back up the main street. A knot of teenagers was gathered outside the public toilets, opposite the defunct Job Centre. They were smoking, hands cupped around fags, bodies cupped around hands. A couple of cars stood by them, doors open so that the techno which blared from their stereos was clearly audible from well down the road. It was, Jonathan reflected, not exactly music at all; more like a sound effect devised by a radiophonic composer to accompany a film featuring giant, mechanical cockroaches.

The teenagers ignored him. He walked on by, conscious of the weight of the rucksack, parasitic on the small of his back, and the damp partings and clammier marriages of his nether limbs. Reaching the end of the estate, Jonathan dropped back into Hogg Lane. Two gossamer lines wavered some three feet above the track, each one following the line of the rut below. They were comprised of many many thousands of tiny midges, which hovered, tumbling over and over and over. Why would the midges gather in this way? Jonathan thought as he pushed on into the tunnel of greenery, his waist cresting the wave of life-forms. Could it be an attraction to the moisture latent in the rut? Or animal droppings? Or was it some new behaviour? Certainly the summer had been doing things to the insects, gingering them up, pushing the hot air faster through their spiracles, so that they were able to fly faster, feed faster, and reproduce in even greater numbers.

The haunch slathered with infective matter. Bulging from within, the fact of decay possessing and altering it, changing it from organism to environment. Delicately, methodically Mustica Domestica *goes about her business of insertion.*

Almost every week there were irruptions of silverfish or ants into the kitchen. Usually Joy was first up in the morning, so it would be her cry that awoke Jonathan: 'Ayeee!' she would bellow, and the sound would yank him from sweat-impacted sheets, pull him down to where she stood, her nightdress clutched up in folds around her belly by one hand, while the other flapped in the air. Did she imagine they were intent on accessing the pit of her body? 'What! What!' he would cry, angry with her and hating the little kitchen as well, despising its linoleum confines, the ruched, muslin, pseudo-curtain in the tiny window over the sink. She would gesture to one or other of the wooden, Melamine, or stainless steel surfaces, where the invaders were boiling up from crack or join.

Were silverfish insects? Jonathan bent down low to examine them. They flowed as much as crawled, each wriggling driblet of a creature adopting a piscine undulation. Were they recently hatched, or fully mature? On these occasions he sent Joy back up to bed, boiled the kettle, located the break-out point and poured down libations of exterminatory water into the navel of the silverfish world.

Ants didn't bother him as much. It was like a racial prejudice. The ants carried things. Teams of them would move crumbs with an orderly sideways shuffle; or one would roll a nugget of sugar on to another's back. They were like the Japanese: small, efficient, manifesting an unknowable, collective mind.

Back upstairs Jonathan would reassure Joy. Roll her on to her carapace and investigate the damp portions of her thorax and abdomen. Then the two humans adopted peculiar, mating postures, their limbs outlined against the pink, vernal riot of the flower-patterned wallpaper. Jonathan nuzzled her and struggled not to think of the insects nuzzling all about them, the pillowy dust mites labouring below the pillows as they laboured above them, carrying away the dead epidermal portions of Jonathan and Joy.

And in the primal, physical contortions of sex, Jonathan laboured as well not to think of the earwigs. The earwigs bothered him the most of all the insects. These prehistoric beasts, with their excremental bodies both shiny and somehow unclean, made it their business, their *métier* even, to seek out the dampest and most intimate portions of the cottage. Were they parodying Jonathan and Joy's efforts to keep the cottage clean, keep it as a viable, human-supporting environment? Whenever he picked up a dishcloth, a mug, a cake of soap even, one of the earwigs would emerge, moving unsteadily, antennae and forceps waggling, and mooch off across the allegedly clean surface. It was the insouciance that did it. Jonathan would take the offender between thumb and forefinger, crush the life out of it.

Don't think of the earwigs as she lifts my balls. Don't think of them as her pink triangle of a tongue traces the brown crinkles of my perineum. Don't think of them as I palp the gristle between her legs; gristle beneath hairs as insubstantial as frass. Don't think of earwigs emerging from beneath labia or foreskin. Don't think of earwigs, don't think of her. Gone.

So the insects whirled in front of and behind Jonathan's grey eyes; and he walked on unseeing. Beyond the thick hedging bordering the lane, the pylons kept pace with him, their cables thrumming in the late-afternoon heat.

The cottage reposed at the bottom of what passed for a combe in this relaxed landscape. A stream-cum-drainage ditch ran alongside the garden hedge. When there was any rain it burst its confines, flooding lane and field. On all sides of the cottage the fields swept up at a modest angle for some hundreds of yards, on two sides meeting the pylon lines, on the third a liner-shaped copse, and on the fourth the paddock of tumbledown jumps and dried-out pits where his landlord's tinkly-voiced daughters rode their ponies.

Jonathan's cottage pinioned this awning of fieldscape, weighed it down at its centre. He debouched from the lane and walked the hundred yards of his landlord's drive to the cottage gate. Arbuthnot – the landlord – was away. Jonathan could tell this from the pile of black plastic bags set at the end of the drive. As he passed by them, the black bucklers the bags formed palpably radiated heat, and then a cloudlet of scintillating flies, gold and blue, arose from them to dance on the tiny thermals.

Jonathan entered his cottage, went through the breakfast room to the kitchen and unloaded his rucksack on the work surface by the fridge.

The fly-paper dangling by the window was full. So full that the gooey corpses of its victims entirely covered it, like an advanced chancre on a tongue. As he watched a fly homed in on the thing, circling, dipping and finally alighting on the back of one of its conspecifies. Jonathan watched, only slightly sickened, as the fly applied its nozzled proboscis to the chink betwixt the head and thorax of the corpse and began to feed.

Then the repulsion did come, and Jonathan found himself moving from room to room, fetching chairs so that he could rear upwards, prise out the drawing-pins in the ceiling and take down the tacky mausoleums. Such was his hurry over this loathsome work that on two occasions the fly-papers came down on top of him, gifting him a head-dress repellent in the extreme. He ran from the house, hunched over, head and arm angled as if he were a Pompeian, about to receive a lava bath; and then ran back in again, mewling; there was no succour abroad. He had to wash his hair before he could resume work on the index.

In the study a gold beam lanced down from a chink in the curtain, to spotlight a patch of wear on the carpet. On the screen of the Macintosh, small pellets ricocheted about like insects in a killing jar. Jonathan sat down in his swivel chair and clicked on the Anglepoise. He flicked the mouse and the screensaver dissolved into a body of text.

Jonathan had reached the term 'nef' before going out to do the shopping. It was an obscure term meaning the nave of a church. He plugged the three letters into the word-search and hit the control key. The computer went about its work, chomping through the text, looking for instances. He felt himself relax into the machine's labour. It made its clicks and whirrs companionably, this clean thing, this ergonomic thing. Jonathan honed his appreciation, concentrated, tried to ignore the deeper zzzing undercutting them . . . the deeper, more organic, more moribund zzzing.

A fly was dying in the lea of his mouse mat. As Jonathan watched it span out from the thin, hard-edged shadow and into the full glare of the Anglepoise. The fly was on its back. Must be propelling itself with its wings, thought Jonathan, as it span to a halt like a minuscule merry-go-round, the wings, the hairs, the compound eyes, returning from blur.

Was the fly a victim of Vapona? Jonathan had erected the little venetian-blind slatted units, one to each room, but done it in the spirit of magic, not really believing that they worked. How could the poison affect the flies – and not me? Or the earwigs for that matter? It started up twirling again, buzzing again. The upside-down fly moved top-like across the desk, batted off the edge of a piece of paper and came to rest among some breadcrumbs. How long, Jonathan wondered, will it take to die?

And this query sent his febrile mind spinning into an orbit of twisted, insect supposition. Why? Why were flies' bodies full of what appeared to be pus? From where Jonathan sat he could see the smear paths of two of his earlier executions. Was it perhaps an adaptive response to parasitising humans? Making sure that the act of killing was an unpleasant, if marginal activity? And why did killing flies need to be unpleasant at all? Why couldn't it be made into some kind of pastime, or sport even. That's it! A solution to the need for blood sports and the need to kill flies. Perhaps miniature needle-guns could be developed, able to achieve the pin-point accuracy necessary for targeting flies?

Jonathan tilted back in his chair, imagining the ramifications of his new idea. A fully functioning hunting field contained within the compass of a single Axminster carpet. Beaters – or rather beetles – moving through the pile, flushing out the grazing flies. The huntsmen sitting motionless at their workstations, needle-guns at the ready. The quarry has broken from behind its cover of lint and fluff. It's in the air! And the guns lead the flies, their muzzles moving sharply up, down, obliquely, tracking the erratic paths. A slight pressure on the trigger and the needle flies fast and true, skewering the droning bluebottle precisely through one wing and its bulbous abdomen. Crunch! It falls to the twistpile, bounces, settles down into death, like a slo-mo film of a wildebeest dropping on the veldt. Small wicker cages are opened by the guns, and specially trained wasps fly out. They bank, right themselves, lose altitude to the carpet, move in to retrieve the quarry.

Outside the summer afternoon droned on. The sun drummed on the hard, cracked earth. The cicadas, crickets and grasshoppers chafed and stridulated, rubbing leg on leg, wing-case on wing-case, or else popping a rigid tegument of their bodies, so as to produce noises like a child's toy. The land pulsed, as a woman's vagina does in the aftershocks of orgasm: holding the hot air to itself, and releasing it; holding the hot air to itself, and releasing it.

Jonathan's head fell back, jerked forward, rolled some, righted itself, fell back. His eyelids fluttered, then fell. He slept. In his dream Joy returned to the cottage. The taxi from Saxmundham station dropped her in the lane. She looked tremendous, her high, pointed shoulders enveloped in clear, veined wings. She had – he was amused and titillated to see – three, dear little pairs of hands. Her hands, so small, he found the thought of their childish grip on his thickening penis insistently erotic, even as he pitched and yawed in sleep, and the computer's screensaver enveloped the recondite text.

'Look,' Joy said, gesturing with three hands towards her lower body, and twitching the drapery of wings to one side, 'I bought it at Harvey Nick's, it's the very latest in abdominal sacking,' 'Darling!' he exclaimed. 'It's tremendous.' And it was. Alternate filleted panels of silk and satin, in two shades of blue, ran from her thorax, down in smooth and sensual slickness, to where a simple tassel hinted at the delights within.

In the bedroom Jonathan stripped nervously, like an adolescent, hunching up to remove his trousers and pants, as if he could somehow hide his ravening erection. She stood by the window to disrobe, and as she removed epidermis after epidermis, the sun streamed through her wings, creating a jalousie pattern on the ceiling. Her six hands moved rapidly, speeded by her own, insistent appetite. Then they were one writhing thing on the sheet. She arched above him, her multifaceted eyes capturing and scattering the light. He groaned – in awe and pleasure. Out of the line of his sight, her modified ovipositor pushed smoothly from the tip of her abdomen, each one of its barbs dripping with Cacharel. She arched still more, bending herself back underneath him. The ovipositor nuzzled his anus; and then the sting oozed up, killing him at the moment of climax.

Jonathan awoke, his mouth full of glutinous, mucal crud. It was ten thirty in the evening, and he was now living in Flytopia.

This he realised on entering the kitchen. Silverfish boiled up from the crack at the back of the sink and spread out over the draining-board. Their myriad bodies formed some comprehensible design. Jonathan leant down to see what it was. It was writing; the silverfish had formed themselves into a slogan: WELCOME TO FLYTOPIA . . . it said, the leader dots being, as it were, the fifty or so stragglers who couldn't make it into the final leg of the 'A'. Jonathan rubbed his eyes and exclaimed, 'Well, this is a turn up. Tell me – if you can act in this fashion presumably you can understand my speech – what does being in Flytopia entail exactly?'

The swarm of silverfish fused into a single pullulating heap and then fissioned back into readable characters, spindlier this time, which ranged across the corrugations of the draining-board, as if they were lines on a sheet of paper:

IN FLYTOPIA HUMANS AND INSECTS LIVE TOGETHER COOPERATIVELY. WE HAVE UNDERSTOD YOUR ANXIETY AND REVULSION FROM US, BUT WISH NOW TO LIVE AT PEACE WITH YOU. YOU ASSIST US – WE WILL ASSIST YOU.

'That should be "understood",' said Jonathan, 'not "understod".' The silverfish rearranged themselves to correct the living typo. 'Hmm,' Jonathan continued to speak aloud as he got a beer from the fridge and opened it, 'I suppose you want some kind of quid pro quo then?'

IT WOULD BE KIND IF YOU GOT RID OF THE VAPONAS AND THE FLYPAPERS – INCIDENTALLY, SINCE YOU WERE WONDERING, THE VAPONAS EMIT A KIND OF NEUROTOXIN THAT PARALYSES US. IT'S NOT A NICE DEATH.

'I'm sure . . . I'm sure . . . but you must appreciate, I don't want to relax my campaign against you until I have more evidence of your goodwill.'

WE UNDERSTAND THAT. IF YOU CONTINUE ABOUT YOUR DAILY EXISTENCE, WE WILL DO OUR BEST TO ACCOMMODATE OURSELVES TO YOUR NEEDS. I THINK YOU WILL FIND THAT WE CAN BE SURPRISINGLY USEFUL. YOU ARE TIRED NOW, WHY NOT GO AND SEE WHAT WE'VE DONE IN THE BEDROOM?

Jonathan went upstairs and snapped on the overhead light in the bedroom. The bed, normally a slough of damp and disordered sheets, was not only neatly made, but peculiarly clean in appearance, clean as if burnished from within. A four-inch-wide rivulet of mites was flowing off the plumped-up pillow, down to the floor, across the intervening strip of carpet, up to the window-sill, and out the window itself. 'What's going on here?' Jonathan asked, taking a slug of his beer. The back end of the stream of tiny insects quivered, detached itself from the larger body of its kine and began to form characters on the pillow. Within seconds a slogan arranged itself:

WE ARE THE DUST MITES WHO HAVE BEEN LIVING IN YOUR BEDROOM. IN THE MATTRESS, THE PILLOWS, AND THE CARPET. AS A GESTURE OF GOODWILL FROM OUR ORDER WE HAVE THOROUGHLY CLEANED YOUR BEDDING AND NOW WE ARE DEPARTING. SWEET DREMS.

'That should be "dreams",' said Jonathan pedantically, but the dust mites, paying no attention, had already reformed their column and were completing their ordered withdrawal.

It was the first night of dreamless and undisturbed sleep that Jonathan could remember having in weeks. But when he awoke the following morning the bedroom was humming with insect life. As he opened his eyes he saw that the ceiling immediately above him was carpeted with flies. DO NOT BE ALARMED! The flies quickly and quiveringly arranged themselves into the words: WE WISH TO ASSIST YOU WITH YOUR TOILET.

'Fair enough,' said Jonathan, heaving himself blearily up on to his elbows.

A beautiful flight of cabbage white butterflies then came winging into the room, for all the world like a host of angels. Before Jonathan could react they had blanketed his face with soft, faintly damp wings. He felt their tiny mandibles pluck, and nibble at the crusted matter on his lips and eyelids. He lay back on the pillow and let the insects give him what amounted to an entire facial. When the butterflies lifted off, regrouped and flew out the open window, he arose, refreshed and ready for the day.

All morning the insects proved as good as their command of words. Whenever Jonathan needed something, a pencil or a computer disk, he had only to point to it for an insect formation to arrange itself in the air, lift the required object, and port it to where he sat, labouring at the Macintosh. Once their task was completed, the flies quit the room, leaving him with blissful quiet. No noise of miniature timpani, as tiny heads butted giant panes.

The sight of a clump of blue-black flies, holding within their midst such quotidian human artefacts, was also, in and of itself, a kind of displacement activity. Jonathan found that with these little breaks in the work to entertain him progress on the index was effortless. He was on to 'rood' before the end of the morning.

At lunch he had a protracted dialogue with the draining-board. 'OK,' he told the silverfish, 'I accept that so far you have acted in good faith. I will throw the Vaponas away!'

HOORAY! wrote the silverfish.

'I will also remove the spiders' webs I have allowed to be established around the cornices and the architrave.'

THANK YOU! THANK YOU! WE WILL CONTINUE TO SERVE YOU.

Jonathan was using the broom to knock out the last of the webs in the spare bedroom when Joy rang. 'Everything all right?' she asked.

'Fine, fine.' For some reason he found the very sound of her voice, vibrating in the receiver, intensely irritating, as if she were somehow trapped there, her nails rap-rap-rapping against the Bakelite.

'Insect life not getting to you then, is it?' She laughed, another tinkly, irritating noise.

'No, no, why should it?'

'Well, it's been bothering you all summer. And frankly I can't tell you what a relief it is to be in London, away from all of that bloody nature . . .' She paused, and Jonathan bit his lip, restraining himself from pointing out that 'bloody nature' could just as well do without her. '. . . Still, I'm sure I'll be longing for it by Friday. I'll be on the three-forty train, would you get a cab to pick me up from Sax?'

Jonathan filed this request away, but as soon as he hung up, Joy vanished from his mind. He was finding Flytopia an exhilarating place to live in. They left him well alone in the study, but whenever he emerged he found orderly teams of insects going about their business of assisting him elsewhere in the house. Neat phalanxes of beetles trundled across the carpets, their mandibles seeking out whatever detritus there was. Similar teams of earwigs were at work in the bathroom, and in the kitchen all signs of his breakfast, right down to the ring of coffee powder he had left by the jar, were eradicated by the industrious ants.

At lunch he took down the remaining fly-papers, and had a more protracted dialogue with the silverfish on the draining-board. AS YOU ARE NO DOUBT AWARE . . . they began, to which Jonathan expostulated: 'I'll thank you not to adopt that high-handed tone with me!' The insects immediately reformed into a demurral:

SORRY! WHAT WE WANTED TO SAY WAS THAT WE DON'T LIVE IN YOUR COTTAGE OUT OF CHOICE. WE COME INSIDE BECAUSE IN THE NORMAL COURSE OF THINGS THERE IS USUALLY SOME CARRION WITHIN WHICH WE CAN DEPOSIT OUR EGGS, SO THAT OUR LARVAE MAY GROW AND BECOME FULLY FUNCTIONING AND WELL-ADJUSTED MEMBERS OF FLYTOPIA.

'I see.'

HOWEVER, IF WE ARE CLEANING EVERYTHING UP FOR YOU, WE'RE RATHER DOING OURSELVES OUT OF A KEY COMPONENT IN OUR OWN ECOSYSTEM.

'I understand that, of course.'

WHAT WE WONDERED WAS WHETHER YOU MIGHT CONSIDER TURNING THE SPARE BEDROOM OVER TO US EXCLUSIVELY. IN WHICH CASE WE WOULD BE MORE THAN HAPPY TO ABANDON THE REST OF THE HOUSE TO YOU –

'– But I'm rather pleased by the way you've been helping me –'

– APART THAT IS FOR THE WORK WE NEED TO DO TO HELP YOU.

'I see. Well, I'll give it some thought.'

And he did, but really Jonathan's mind was already made up. The insects were proving such capable little friends. He no longer found them revolting at all, and when he saw them at work on the carpet he would bend down so as to catch whatever expressions might be contained in their alien faces. He also found their assistance in his toilet not simply helpful, but peculiarly sensual.

At night the moths tapped at the panes of the bathroom window until he allowed them access, and then they would blanket him with their softly pulsing wings. They tenderly licked away the encrusted sweat and dirt of the day, before drying him off with teasing flutterings of their wings. He didn't bridle when the silverfish on the draining-board suggested that he might like some of the beetles and earwigs to seek out the more intimate portions of his body and give them a thorough scouring as well.

Jonathan wondered if he had ever felt in more harmony with his environment. Not only that, but wondered if the grosser manipulations of human intercourse weren't becoming altogether more alien to his nature than these subtlest of digitations. In the morning he walked into Inwardleigh and bought ten pounds of pork sausages at Khan's. 'Barbecue?' asked Mr Khan, quadra-chinned today. 'Not exactly,' Jonathan replied.

He laid them out in the spare bedroom on the white plastic trays he had taken from the fridge. He left the door open for most of the day, but when evening came the silverfish told him that there was no need for this. So he shut the door and fell asleep in his voluntarily insect-free cottage.

The next morning, when Jonathan peeked inside the spare bedroom he felt a rush of paternal pride to see the bulging, bluing aspect of the rotting sausages, each one stippled with the white nodules that indicated the presence of maggots. Maggots chewing, maggots growing, maggots that he had gifted life to. A group of female flies who had been methodically working their way across the last five pounds or so of sausages, injecting their eggs into the putrefying meat, rose as he entered the room, and executed what looked to Jonathan like a gay curtsey, acknowledging his assistance and his suzerainty.

He worked steadily all morning. One particularly faithful fly proved the most adept of wordfinders, shuffling over the open spread of the *OED* until it found the correct entry, and then squatting there, gently agitating its wings, so as to act as a living cursor.

MORE MEAT? queried the silverfish on the draining-board, when he went in to make a sandwich at lunch. 'I'll think about it,' Jonathan replied, tossing them a sliver of ham to be getting on with. Then he retreated to the study, to phone for a cab to pick Joy up from the station.

Jonathan was so engrossed in the index that he didn't hear the squeal of brakes as Joy's cab pulled up outside the cottage. 'I'm home!' she trilled from the front door, and Jonathan experienced the same revulsion at the sound of her voice as he'd had on the phone. Why must she sound so high-pitched, so mindlessly insistent? She came into the study and they embraced. 'Have you got a fiver for the cab, darling?'

'Um . . . um . . . hold on a sec.' He plumped his pockets abstractedly.

'Sorry, not on me. I think there's a pile of loose change up in the spare bedroom . . .'

Jonathan listened to her feet going up the stairs. He listened to the door of the spare bedroom open, he heard the oppressive, giant, fluttering hum, as she was engulfed, then he rose and went out to pay the cab.

Caring, Sharing

When Travis came out of the side door of the Gramercy Park Hotel – avoiding the guy who ran the concession stall, because earlier on he'd been embarrassed by his failure deftly to marshal the correct change – he felt pretty hollow. Brion was right behind him, and although Travis thought he really shouldn't need to, he couldn't help reaching back and clutching the emoto's forty-inch thigh.

Brion's response was immediate; he stooped down and grasping Travis by the generous scruff of his tweed suit, lifted him right up, drew him into his arms, and planted a series of wet kisses on Travis's face, while all the time patting his back and muttering soothing endearments.

Travis felt all the knotted tension in his neck and shoulders begin to ebb away. It was a palpable sensation, just as if the emoto had been rubbing some balm into his exposed skin. Travis sighed deeply and snuggled further into the warm-smelling gap between the brushed cotton collar of Brion's shirt and the prickly tweed of his suit collar. Travis always dressed his emoto the same as himself. He knew that some people found it intolerably gauche, like putting twins in matching sailor suits, but he loved Brion so much – the emoto wasn't *just* an emoto, more an aspect of Travis himself.

And Brion smelt good. He smelt of Imperial Leather soap and Ralph Lauren aftershave. He smelt of sweat and cocktail fish. He smelt of flannel and cigarette smoke. He smelt – in short – very much like Travis himself. Even Brion's kisses smelt good; Travis could feel a slick patch of the emoto's saliva on his upper lip, but he had no urge – as he might with any other individual's secretions – to wipe it off. Instead, he gently scented the enzymic odours, while idly considering whether or not emotos had the same chemicals in their bodies as other humans. They couldn't be exactly the same, because emotos couldn't drink alcohol – or smoke for that matter; and that implied some different oils, boiling in the pullulating refineries of their massive bodies.

Travis didn't like thinking about the inside of Brion's body – it made him distinctly queasy. So he cancelled the observation and snuggled still deeper into the sheltering arms. The emoto's vast hands smarmed over Travis's back, over his shoulders, smoothed down his hair, so gentle, yet so firm. Travis heard Brion's voice rumble in his chest before the words reached his muffled ears, 'Are you worried about the date tonight, Travis?'

Travis stiffened. The word 'date' – how he hated it. It put him in mind of the fruit, not two adults enjoying each other's company. 'You don't even like the word, do you?' The comforting hand almost completely encapsulated Travis's head, as if it were a helmet of flesh and tendon and bone. The voice was beautifully modulated, sonorous even. The emoto's words seemed to come zinging straight to Travis's heart, each one with a top spin of sympathy.

'It makes me think of the fruit . . .' he muttered. Brion chuckled in a rumbly sort of way and hugged him still harder. Hugged Travis and lifted him high up in the early evening air, twisting the grown-up's body as he did so gifting Travis a few seconds of Gramercy Park upside-down. Travis noted an old douche bag, clanking with jewellery, walking her miniature Schnauzer on the roof of the world. Then Brion deftly lowered him, and bestowing one, final drooly kiss on Travis's forehead, set him back neatly on his feet.

'You shouldn't worry so much,' Brion admonished Travis. 'I'm sure Karin is just as anxious about the whole thing as you are. She probably thinks of the fruit too. Now come on, we better get going if we've got to head uptown.' Brion's armchair hand descended once more and cupping Travis's back, the emoto pushed his grown-up gently in the direction of Madison Avenue. As they walked under a canopy tethering a townhouse to the sidewalk, Brion had to duck down, but then he straightened up, and the two tweed-suited figures, one about six feet tall, the other closer to fourteen, ambled away and were presently engulfed by the croaking roar of Manhattan.

Three miles to the north, in the West Seventies, Travis's date for the evening, Karin, *was* feeling just as uneasy. She was even on the verge of cancelling altogether. Karin had met Travis a couple of weeks ago at a wine tasting arranged by her friend Ariadne. The event was a pure snob thing – Ariadne wanted to show off her wine cellar and her new SoHo loft apartment-cum-studio; which was big enough – Karin had reflected – to enable Auguste Rodin, Henry Moore and Damien Hirst to work alongside one another, with little danger of them muddling up tools, or materials. Really, an exorbitant waste of space when you considered the further fact that Ariadne herself was a miniaturist.

Ariadne's friends were mostly the usual *faux* bohos who congregated in the environs of SoHo, Greenwich Village and Tribeca; affecting the style of penniless, fifties, *rive gauche* students; while living on the income from vast tranches of AT&T stock. These types were always on the verge of exhibiting, publishing, constructing, filming or presenting *something*, but never actually managed it. At one of Ariadne's soirées, a young man with pigtails had even deliriously informed Karin that he was about to present a presentation. 'What do you mean?' Karin politely queried. 'Y'know, make a pitch for a pitch, I guess . . .'

'And if you get the pitch?'

'Aw, hell, I dunno . . . I dunno if I want to follow through that far.'

Karin wandered away from this absurd reductivism. Later, she was pleased to see that the pigtailed pitcher had had to be carried out by his emoto, dead drunk, more incoherency falling along with the drool from his slack mouth.

But on the night of the wine tasting nobody much got drunk – and Karin met Travis. Travis, who seemed initially a little creepy in his immaculately cut English-retro tweed suit. Travis, who smoked, which meant he had to stand out on the fire escape, engaging her in flirtatious conversation through the window. Karin couldn't really approve of the smoking, but nor could she condemn it. In fact, she found something faintly racy and daring about Travis on that first encounter, certainly in comparison to the posing *rentiers*, who were swirling their wine glasses around in the studio as if to the château born.

Travis, it transpired, knew a great deal about wine; or 'fine wine' as he invariably referred to it. He could tell a Chareau-Carré Muscadet from a white Bordeaux by bouquet alone. He knew the names of all the varieties of phylloxera, their life cycles and their effects. He had once rafted down the Rhône, stopping for a bottle of wine in every vineyard he passed. But there was nothing overbearing or self-satisfied in the way he retailed all of this knowledge and experience. Rather, it seemed to be an essential mannerism of the man to be tirelessly self-effacing, albeit with such an ironic inflection to his voice, that it was clear he had a perfectly healthy opinion of his own wit and talents.

'I'm basically a wealthy dilettante –' He paused, his long upper lip twitching with self-deprecation. 'And not a very good one at that.'

'How d'you figure that?' Karin thought she sounded like some whiny co-ed – his diction was so studied.

'Because I can't really settle to anything, the way you have. I just flit from one hobby to the next. But I enjoy my enthusiasms – if that isn't something of a contradiction in terms.'

Karin had told Travis all about the small dress-making business she ran. How she had turned her two-room apartment in the twenties into a miniature atelier, staffed by six deft Filipino seamstresses. How she had made a considerable name for herself selling near-couture to wealthy Manhattanites. And how she had now been offered, by an enormous fashion business, a *prêt-à-porter* range of her own.

Travis listened to all of this intently, nodding and gifting polite noises of encouragement in the correct places. When Karin finally faltered he asked exactly the right question: 'D'you also make clothes for emotos?'

'Oh sure, actually I'm really best known for my fashion wear for emotos. Some people, y'know, some people find it easier to do a bias cut using a bigger expanse of cloth –'

'I guess that's to do with the weight and tensility of the fabric,' Travis replied, in his rather tense, weighty fashion. Karin couldn't believe it – a presentable, youngish man in Manhattan who knew what a bias cut was.

'Is your emoto here?' Travis asked after a short while.

'Yeah, Jane, she's the one with the long blonde hair over there.' She pointed to the section of the loft that had been set aside for the emotos. Suitably enough this was in the highest section, where a trapezoid skylight formed a twenty-foot-high roof space. A table had been set up for the emotos – a table that was to their scale, about six feet high – and on it were five litre jugs full of Kool-Aid and root beer and cherry cola, the kind of sweet, sickly drinks that emotos preferred. The emotos were supping these and engaging in the slightly infantile banter that passed for conversation among them.

There were about ten emotos, and they were of all types: black, white, old, young. But Travis's and Karin's were easy to spot, for, naturally, they were both dressed identically to their grown-ups. Travis laughed. He turned first to Karin and then to Jane. He compared the trim, thirtyish blonde in front of him to the lissom, twelve-foot emoto at the far end of the loft. Both wore the same well-cut jackets that flared from the hip; and the same velveteen leggings tucked into snakeskin ankle boots. Both had their straight blonde hair cut into bangs, and Travis was even more amused to note that Karin had equipped her emoto with a heavy, scalloped silver choker necklace, the same as her own. This must have cost a great deal of money.

'And that's . . . ?' Karin pointed at the chunky, fourteen-foot emoto in the immaculately cut, English-retro tweed suit.

'Brion – yeah, that's my emoto. We've been together a long, long time. In fact, he's the same emoto that I had when I left group home –'

'Snap!' Karin cried. 'I've been with Jane since I was sixteen too.'

At this point the emotos concerned came over to give their grown-ups a much needed cuddle. Jane, coming up behind Karin, leant down and draped her flawless white hands over the grown-up's shoulders. Then she pulled Karin backwards, so as to nuzzle the grown-up's entire body against her crotch and lower belly. Brion did pretty much the same thing to Travis; so that the two grown-ups continued their conversation from within the grottoes of these massive embraces.

Perhaps it was the security of Jane's arms around her, or that Travis was – in his own eccentric fashion – almost alluring, which made the idea of them meeting again, perhaps enjoying a meal, a movie or a gallery visit together, seem a good one. Jane took Karin's organiser out of her shoulder bag – which for reasons of convenience also held her grown-up's shoulder bag – and Karin exchanged numbers with Travis. Brion had an outsize, Smythe's of Bond Street, leather-bound address book, in which he noted down Karin's numbers with an outsize, gold propelling pencil. 'Wow!' Karin exclaimed. 'Can your emoto *write*?'

Brion laughed. 'No-no, Karin, I don't need to write – Travis does that for me – but I like to make the shapes of numbers!' Both the grown-ups laughed at this typical display of emoto naivety – and that too cemented their acquaintance.

They had both left the wine tasting shortly after this; and the last Karin had seen of her new friend was Travis's face, blooming, like some tall, orchidaceous buttonhole, above the solid tweed ridge of his emoto's shoulder, as Brion bore him off in the direction of Riverside Drive.

That had been a fortnight ago. Travis called Karin a week after the wine tasting and with commendable dispatch suggested they have dinner together. 'What? You mean like a date?' She couldn't keep the incredulity out of her voice.

'Erm . . . yuh . . . well . . .' It was oddly reassuring to hear how discomfited he was. 'I guess it would be a date, sort of.'

'Travis, I haven't been on a date for four years –'

'Snap!' He almost shouted down the phone, and that bonded them with laughter once more. 'I haven't been on a date for four years; and I'll tell you something else, I can't stand the very word – it makes me think of fruit –'

'Fruit?'

'Y'know – dates . . .'

This last little revelation hadn't struck such a chord with Karin, but she still agreed to meet Travis on the evening of the 29th April at the Royalton Hotel. 'You're in the seventies,' he'd said. 'I'm in the twenties – we'll split the difference. Then if things are going well we can head downtown for dinner.' He sounded a great deal surer on the phone than he felt. It was true, Travis hadn't been on a date for four years, and he hadn't slept over with anyone for nearing a decade.

Karen had had a sleepover more recently. About two years ago she'd met a man called Emil at a weekend beach party out on Long Island.

Emil was small, dark, Austrian, in his forties. He'd been living in New York for eight years, and had an emoto – Dave – for the last five. Emil admitted, frankly, that he'd been a procro in Salzburg, where he'd run a fashionable restaurant before deciding to emigrate. Karin took this in her stride. Emil was very charming, seemed absolutely sincere, and his relationship with Dave was unimpeachable – the big black emoto cradled his little grown-up with obvious affection. Lots of grown-ups had started out as procros and then decided that the whole messy business of sexual and emotional entanglement wasn't for them – there was no shame, or obloquy in that. And just as many procros had found, after getting on in life a bit, that what they wanted more than anything else in the world was the absolute reassurance that an emoto would provide them with. If these procros were lucky the awakening would coincide with children growing up, leaving home, and they could slide without too much disruption from their procro-union to a proper, grownup relationship with an emoto.

Emil led Karin to understand that this had been the case with him: 'My ex-wife and I met and married when we were very young, you know. We both came from poor families, the kind of background where there were very few grown-ups, very few emotos. I suppose we were happy in a way – we knew no better. But slowly, over the years, the relentlessness of being with someone the whole time . . . someone who you touch intimately' – his voice dropped lower – 'touch sexually . . . Well, you know the terrible things that can happen.' He shuddered, snuggled deeper into his emoto's firehose-thick arms. 'Eventually, after our daughter had gone – at her own request, I must say – to a group home, we were both able to become grown-ups. We're still good friends though, and I see her whenever Dave and I go back to Salzburg – which is a lot. Dave and I even have four-way sleepovers with Mitzi and her emoto, Gudrun.'

They had spent most of that day chatting, both of them cuddled by their emotos; the childlike giants standing waist deep in the ocean swell, cradling their respective grown-ups in their arms. 'There is nothing more sensuous,' Karin had said to Emil in an unguarded moment, 'than the smell of wet emoto skin, wet emoto hair, and the great wet ocean.' Emil gave her a peculiar sideways look.

But Jane had taken to Dave, and encouraged Karin to see Emil. Jane had dinner with Emil twice; and he'd taken her once to the Met, to see *Don Giovanni.* On all three occasions he was charm itself, courtly and leisured; as if, Karin had thought, the Habsburgs were the patrons of taste, rather than Texaco. If later, Karin felt awful for not paying proper attention to the subtext of Emil's charms, it was because she blamed herself. Blamed herself for not paying attention and for putting her trust in Jane's emoto intuition. After all, emotos weren't meant to protect you from others – only from yourself.

On their fourth date Emil suggested that Karen and Jane might like to sleep over at his apartment. Dave nodded his great cropped head vigorously. 'It'll be great!' he said to Jane – and the rest of them. 'We can play together in the morning!' The grown-ups laughed, but it was really Jane who sealed the deal, crying out, 'Yes! With pillows too!'

'Isn't that typical of an emoto!' Emil exclaimed when he and Karin were at last alone together. 'They really can be just like kids –'

'But they aren't.'

'I'm sorry?' Emil was momentarily querulous, shocked by the intensity of her reaction.

'They aren't children. They don't grow – they're big already. They don't make demands on you – you make demands on them. They don't have to be dressed, fed, wiped or groomed in any other way. They have good intuitions – and good dress sense if you trouble to develop it . . .' Karin tailed off, realising that she was beginning to sound oddly impassioned. She was, also, already missing Jane, although the two emotos had only left their grownups a few minutes before.

Emil's apartment was on the Upper East Side, and the last thing Karin had seen before going to bed that fateful night were the soaring piles of the Van Eyck Expressway legging over the river's rumpled pewter, so solid, so supportive, so emotolike.

Karin was sleeping in the main bedroom, Emil in the spare. The emotos were closeted in the old water tank on top of the block, which Emil had tastefully converted – like many other financially clever Manhattanite grownups – for emoto use. But during the night, despite the friendly locks on the door of the bedroom (friendly because they were bolts), Emil managed to get into the room. Presumably he had a secret passage, or some even stranger means of entry . . .

These thoughts were thumping with awful inconsequence through Karin's mussed mind as she stared at the dapper little man who was sitting beside her, on the edge of the bed, entirely self-possessed, wearing black silk pyjamas, and with his dumpy, manicured hands arranged neatly in his lap. At least he never actually touched her – that was something. But the violation of his presence was enough. To have him, at night, alone, this close to her, this *able* to touch her was – terrifying.

Karin didn't so much know that she wanted Jane – as scream it. The scream was the knowledge. Karin screamed and screamed and screamed; at the same time she groped for the emotopager she had slung to one side of the bed a couple of hours before. The first scream chopped off what Emil had been trying to say to her: 'All I want's a little cud –' For ever afterwards Karin wondered what exactly it was that he'd wanted, 'a little cud', it was strangely enigmatic, unlike the man himself, who had been revealed as no grown-up – but a potential rapist.

There was that odd, shadowing memory of the sexual assault, and there was another discrepancy which Karin kept stuffed to the back of her mind, lest it rock too much the frail boat of her own sanity. Karin knew that Jane and Dave had to have been asleep – that's what emotos did at night, just like other humans. What's more, the emotos were sleeping three storeys up, on top of the building – so it couldn't have been Karin's screams that had woken them; and at the time, even through the fog of fear, she had, with bizarre clarity, appreciated that it might take Jane many minutes to reach her. But in fact Jane was there in seconds. There, and cradling Karin to her massive breast. There, and palming off Emil. There and admonishing Emil in that peculiarly affecting way that emotos – creatures devoid of any vestige of aggression-promoting sexuality – have: 'You've scared, Karin, why did you do it? Oh Emil – this ruins everything. Oh Emil! If you touched her we shall have to call the police –' In the corner Dave cowered, unsure of whether it was safe for him to go and comfort his own emoto. Emil looked inscrutable – altogether beyond cuddling. Dave was naked – another anomaly Karin filed in a bottle.

'It's OK,' Karin nearly shouted, she was so relieved to be able to respond, to react, not to be just a *thing* under the Austrian's bland brown eyes. 'He didn't touch me.'

Jane gave her a searching look and adjudging that this was the truth, scooped up Karin, her clothes, her bag, and before her grown-up had had a chance to respond in any other way, she found herself being borne north towards the corner of the park: 'We can get a taxivan there,' said the willowy emoto, still holding Karin tightly to her. Jane never said anything more about the assault – and nor did Karin.

Not until tonight, that is. Karin sighed again. It was too late to call it off now – Travis would be on his way; and he didn't look like the kind of man who carried a phone with him, more the type to use a liveried servant, porting a missive on a salver. Thinking of this aspect of Travis, his unforced anachronism, made Karen smile. With such an innately gallant man, surely nothing could go wrong? There was this sense of security and there was the tangible security of Jane's arms. As ever, the emoto had sensed her mood perfectly, sashayed across the room and taken the grown-up in her arms. Karen marvelled anew at the grace of the giantess, and her physical perfection. Some emotos were so gross: the genetic effect of pumping the human frame up to two or three times its normal size could have bizarre consequences. Some emotos had hair as thick as wire on their bodies; and if they got bad acne it was truly something to behold, like the Grand Canyon at sunset.

But Jane was perfection. Her skin a delicate honey shade; the down that covered it universally white-blonde; and soft, so soft. Karin relaxed back into the down, allowed herself to be enfolded by the honey. She felt the lower belly and pubic mound of the emoto nuzzle between her shoulder blades. Funny how an emoto's touch was so intimate, so comforting, and yet so utterly devoid of sexuality – let alone eroticism. The idea of Jane's vast vagina being employed in the nonsensical, animal jerkings of copulation was unthinkable, like imagining Botticelli's Venus squeezing a blackhead, or a chimpanzee addressing both houses of Congress.

Karin relaxed. Jane went on squeezing her in just the right way, swaying gently the while. New effusions of greenery on the trees lining the block below struck Karin's eye with a fresh intensity. It was a beautiful spring evening, she was young, she was secure, perhaps she was even ready for some experimentation, for some fun. Karin broke from the embrace and turned to face Jane, her arms outstretched. 'Carry?' she asked.

The evening went far, far better than either grown-up could have hoped for – and as for the emotos? Well, they rubbed along pretty well, much as they always do.

Travis hadn't only seized on the Royalton for reasons of mutual convenience – it also made a good talking point. Well past its fashionable sell-by date, the hotel's décor retailed a series of dazzlingly crass decadences, which Travis knew provided salience for his own sepia image. To go anywhere more established, or timeless in its own right, would only set his own fuzzy grasp on contemporaneity off to lesser effect. But in the large, modernist lobby bar of the Royalton, with its primary curves and aerodynamically sound light fitments, he would be thrown into sharp relief, and he would be able to entertain Karin with his pointed remarks about the waxing and waning of status, of money, of beauty, of all things human.

Brion and Travis arrived about twenty minutes early. The emoto ducked down to enter, and then gratefully stretched when they entered the airier purlieus of the bar. 'D'you want to join me, Brion?' Travis asked him as the emoto set him gently down, Church's brogues meeting deep pile with the merest of kisses.

Brion seemed to think for a moment, and a shadow of near-reasoning crossed his ample, freckled brow. 'No, that's all right, Travis, I'll set myself down here.' He gestured to the emotos' portion of the bar. 'You get yourself a dry martini – you deserve it for getting this close to the fruit.'

Was there a trace of irony in Brion's remark? Travis wondered as he walked to the other end of the bar, where he waited to be seated. That was impossible; emotos might have highly developed emotional intelligences – that's what made them so good at caring, at sharing; but irony demanded an ability to realise dramatically situations that was far beyond their mental age, hovering as it did at around seven. Some grown-ups – Travis knew one or two – had emotos with higher mental ages, but they were regarded askance by the majority, almost as if they were engaging in a peculiar form of abuse.

All this weighed heavily on Travis while he waited to be seated. He didn't want to be thinking about emotos in this way, at this time, he had to concentrate on the fruit. However, once he'd been deposited by the graceful waiter in the elegant chair, and had a dry vodkatini the size of a vase deposited with him, Travis began to unwind. He was amused to see a new piece of status style-slavery at the Royalton. The bar seats for grown-ups had always been colour coded, so as to reflect the relative importance of their tenants. High rollers were placed in the purple thronelets, less important ones in the red, and so on, all the way down to the gawking hicks in from the boonies, who were stacked unceremoniously in a distant gulag of far smaller, white-covered chairs. Now the management had taken it upon themselves to do the same with the chairs in the emoto portion of the bar. However, as there were fewer of these, and they were much larger, it was impossible to create proper sections. Instead, the waiters in this area had to wait and see where the emoto's respective grown-up was sitting, then seat them accordingly – if possible.

Travis was pleased that Brion had got the purple, and he was just thinking how he might frame this latest bit of Manhattan lunacy as an anecdote for Karin, when she was there in front of him. Travis leapt up, seated her, and without preliminary small talk, launched straight into his Royalton riffs. Karin, far from being discomfited, roared with laughter as he deconstructed the trappings of the luxury hotel. Travis was getting ready to vouchsafe a genuine indiscretion, concerning a certain film star and her football team-sized posse of emotos, when he caught himself. 'But I'm rambling on, I haven't let you get a word in edgeways, and worst of all I haven't told you how radiantly beautiful you're both looking tonight.'

The effect was as instantaneous as it was desired. Karin blushed and tilted her head in a disarming, almost girlish way, turning in the process so that she was angled in the direction of Jane. Although the female emoto was over fifty feet away, and deep in chatter with Brion, she looked up and smiled as well. Clearly, Travis thought, they have a high level of tele-empathy, a good sign. Of course, Travis's compliment hadn't been paid out of any other account but that of The Truth. He wasn't a shameless flatterer, and anyway, Karin just *was* looking fantastic. She was wearing a black silk sheath dress, cut in an interesting, asymmetrical way across the bodice; her thick blonde hair was up, and her sole accessory was the heavy silver necklace, which Travis remembered from the wine tasting in SoHo. Turning to Jane, he observed how well the same dress hung on her far larger frame. He turned to Karin once more. 'Tell me, was this pattern originally cut for Jane or you?' and was rewarded with another peal of joyful laughter.

If things went well at the Royalton, once they got in the taxivan and headed downtown, they began to go – as Travis himself might have said – swimmingly. There was something about these situations that was almost instinctively memorable, something that both grownups and emotos intuitively understood: the two grownups, intelligent, rational, foresighted; and their two emoto charges, who might be physically larger, warmer and more responsive, more caring; but who wouldn't last for five minutes alone on the scabrous city streets.

The four discovered such ease in each other's company, that within minutes they were developing the syntax and grammar of a cliquey argot. Brion, staring as he always did, out of the back window as the darkened streets and lit blocks strobed past, had spotted a rollerblader coursing through the cars on the far side of the avenue. 'Wow!' he exclaimed – as he always did. 'Those high heels sure let that man go zippy!' Both Karen and Jane laughed, and the emotos high-fived, which is all the physical contact they ever seemed to have with one another. From then on in 'Go zippy!' was one of their gathering number of catch phrases, to be rolled around and then expelled with gusto, as if it were an assayed sip of one of Travis's 'fine wines'.

The restaurant Travis had initially chosen for the evening, Chez-Chez, with its heavy Lyonnaise cuisine, didn't really suit the fruit he was engaged on; so after laboriously rethinking the whole nature of the event, running over his slender stock of Karin intelligence, and even going so far as to ring up Ariadne and ask some circumspect questions, he opted instead for the twin pillars of idiocy: the Royalton and the Bowery Brasserie. He wouldn't be able to smoke there – which might make him a bit nervous, but that there would be plenty to joke about and lots of noise and colour would compensate.

They quit the taxivan. The night was clear, stars wheeling over the jagged cityscape, its stanchions and aerials, fire stairs and emoto-housing converted water tanks. The Bowery Brasserie, like many of the more fashionable Manhattan eateries, had its own sub-restaurant specifically catering to emotos. This was simply called 'The Emoto Hole'. Brion grinned hugely when he realised where they were – like most emotos he had hardly any capacity for effective orientation – and turning to his rangy companion said laughingly, 'You'll love this place, Jane, they've even got root beer on tap!' Once again the grown-ups joined in the effervescent, conspiratorial merriment that the mature traditionally share with the immature.

When they had got their emotos settled next door, Travis and Karin entered the Brasserie and were shown to their table. Travis ordered a bottle of Montrachet and asked Karin, 'D'you mind being apart from your emoto? Because personally I'd rather eat with Brion all the time.'

He was delighted when she replied, 'I feel pretty much the same way,' and then amazed as she told him why.

Karin had made the commitment to tell Travis about what had happened with Emil, when she made the final decision not to stand him up at the Royalton. What was the point, she reasoned, in even going on a date if she wasn't – at least in principle – prepared to consider the possibility of a sleepover? And if Travis couldn't handle it? Well, Jane made the point that he couldn't be worth a great deal.

Travis sat rapt while she told the awful story, nodding and muttering the occasional 'Omigod' in the right places. When she had finished he said very simply, 'Karin, that is hellish, you're a very brave woman,' then went on to amaze her still more than she had amazed him, by fully identifying. Moreover, it wasn't only that the same thing had happened to Travis, but that it had been far far worse. The woman who invited him home for an innocuous sleepover actually *touched* Travis, and intimately, before Brion had managed to come to his rescue. Travis played it down, but Karin could tell that he was massively relieved to get the whole thing off his chest, for he had, naturally, told no one about it.

Which explained his diffidence, and also the very close relationship with his emoto. It also helped to explain his dilettantism; for Travis revealed, *en passant*, that at that time he was assaulted he had been a vastly successful antique dealer, and the abuser one of his clients. Karin understood perfectly that after such an experience he had had to retire.

But while the confessions had been risky on both sides, and the chasms of intimacy they had opened up would've appeared impossible to traverse with the slender bridge of conversation alone, Travis and Karin were after all grownups, and so they passed on to other subjects. By the time the entrée had been and gone, the date had swum its way into becoming a veritable whale of a time.

There was no awareness on either side as to who had suggested the idea of coffee and brandy at Travis's house, but both understood what would happen when Karin agreed. Travis said, 'To be frank I'm really gasping for a Havana; and things being still as they are . . .' He shrugged. 'But anyway,' he continued, paradoxically in a breezier fashion, 'if we need either Jane or Brion we can always page them!' and with a flourish he showed her his miniature emotopager, which was concealed beneath the boss of his signet. In return Karin mutely displayed her purpose-built necklace emotopager. They both understood that this was a profound event.

It was a pleasant night, on the cusp of being balmy, so the foursome walked uptown from the Bowery. The grown-ups took the lead, while the emotos followed on behind in their shambling fashion. Glancing back at them Karin remarked, 'It's funny, isn't it, Travis, how when it comes to giving a grown-up a cuddle, or carrying us, or kissing us, emotos are so graceful and deft, but any activity outside of that seems to give them such difficulty.'

'That's why they're emotos,' he replied with finality.

Karin knew plenty of wealthy people, but had never had a friend who actually owned an entire brownstone; let alone one in Gramercy Park. The house was beautiful from the outside, the delicate wrought-iron balconies just beginning to froth with the wisteria that would enmesh them as the summer progressed. Inside the house was furnished in such a way as to suggest both opulence and austerity. Travis hadn't cluttered the rooms, but in each there were a couple of extremely good pieces culled from his antique-dealing days. He showed Karin around the place from top to bottom. 'It's amazing how big these houses are . . . Oh! Gee! Is that what I *think* it is?'

'Hepplewhite, yeah; and that's a Frank Lloyd Wright chair, Chicago 1907.'

He showed her the master bedroom, which had its own emoto room *en suite*. 'That's neat,' said Karin, who was now so relaxed she was content to mouth banalities.

Travis smiled gently. 'I'll show you what's neater.' They continued on up the switchback staircase. On the next floor there was another grown-up-emoto suite, and there was the same on the storey above. 'I guess it's something I thought of after the . . . y'know . . . I thought really I'd rather Brion were on hand during the night, should I need a bit of reassurance, a cuddle, whatever. I know a lot of people prefer to have their emotos closeted up on the roof for the night, but . . . well . . .'

'I understand,' Karin said – and she really did.

They drank a brandy that had been distilled in the year of the Wall

Street crash. Travis puffed a Patargas Perfecto. On an antique Victrola Chaliapin creaked and groaned his way through 'The Song of the Volga Boatmen'. They sat facing one another in matching art-deco armchairs, which had semicircular backs inlaid with tortoiseshell. In the shadowy periphery of the room the emotos slouched on a scaled-up divan, drinking Slush Puppies and exchanging the shy glances of overgrown youngsters.

Karin wished the evening could go on for ever. As it was she drank three brandies – and that on top of the two bottles of wine they had shared at the restaurant, *and* the paddling pool of vodkatini she'd supped at the Royalton. Yet she didn't feel drunk – if anything the reverse. It was as if, having cracked the whole hideous problem of dating again, she was liberated, set free into a new kind of intimacy. Karin thought that, as long as she always had Jane with her, always there to care for her, she could cope even with the intimacy of a sleepover.

'You look tired,' said Travis after Chaliapin had creaked and groaned up and down the Volga several times, and Ma Rainey had ululated 'Titantic Man Blues' at least three. 'Would you like Brion to show you and Jane up?'

Karin gathered herself together, Jane came over louring – after all she couldn't help it. Their combined bags were dangling from the emoto's – proportionately – slim wrist. 'No, it's OK, I think we can find our own way.' Karin stood and looked down levelly at Travis, noticing for the first time what a very sky shade of blue his twinkling eyes were. 'Travis.' Her voice dipped into sincerity. 'I just want to thank you for everything, the drinks, the meal, your lovely house . . . It really has been . . . peachy!' They all laughed at this – the fruit gag was well on its way to being iconic.

For a long time after Karin and Jane had left the room Travis sat, silently sipping his brandy and drawing on his Perfecto. Eventually he cleared his throat to summon Brion, and when the big Celtic emoto was beside him, he reached up his arms and uttered the command that ended all of their days: 'Carry!'

Brion gently lifted Travis up, one massive arm behind his back and the other tucked neatly under the grown-up's legs; and porting him thus like some giant baby, he smoothly exited the room, climbed the angled stair and entered the master suite. Setting Travis down, upright, next to the Second Empire bed, with its curved footboard, and extravagant, overarching pediment, Brion started to undress him, efficiently stripping off the lineaments of Travis's anachronism to reveal first Calvin Klein underwear, and then latterly the robust, healthy body of a fit man in his middle thirties. 'Pjs?' the emoto queried, and his grown-up nodded acquiescence.

At last Brion had Travis settled in bed. The grown-up lay, arms outside the covers, pyjama top neatly buttoned, looking like some old-fashioned illustration; to complete the engraving the pocket Gargantua sat by him, one atlas hand ever so softly smoothing Travis's sand-blond hair. Travis sighed, 'Night-night, Brion.'

'Night-night, Travis,' the emoto sighed back at him. And in due course the grown-up was asleep.

As was Karin in the suite of rooms upstairs. Jane looked down into her already flickering eyelids with an expression that changed, as she realised her grown-up was definitively unconscious, from cloying compassion to decided relief. She rose from the bedside and shook herself down, as some great mastiff or indeed any other fine, healthy, unneurotic creature might shake itself down after a dousing.

Jane strode to the window, her six feet-long legs divinely scissoring apart the hip-length slash in her dully scintillating silk dress, and picked up her bag. She drew out a five-litre catering bottle of Stolichnaya vodka, sheathed in a coolant sleeve, and holding it to the light from the window, sighed appreciatively to see that the bottle was still frosted. The emoto reached into the bag again and drew out a pack of twenty regular Marlboro and a disposable plastic lighter. These items might have appeared queer in such large hands had they been actual size – but they weren't; they too were scaled up for the use of the emoto, the Marlboro pack the size of a paperback, the lighter as long as a pencil. Holding the long lighter aloft, like a cheap beacon, Jane made her way with ginger grace to the door, opened it, ducked down and withdrew her mighty trunk and endless limbs from the room.

Jane encountered Brion on the half-landing a floor below. The male emoto was backing out of his grownup's bedroom in much the same way as Jane had: retracting his body in a series of phased movements as he squeezed under the dwarfish lintel. He straightened up to his full, magnificent height. Even in the wan light of the stairwell – provided by two unusual baroque electroliers Travis had snapped up in Venice – Jane could see the shadows of intelligence and amusement pass across Brion's handsome countenance. Jane held the long lighter to one side of her face and the frozen Stoli to the other. 'Party?' she mouthed. Brion grinned hugely and indicated with a series of significant head jerks that they should go downstairs.

Back in the main sitting room of the house, the antique Victrola was curled on the floor, casting its analogous, auricular shadow. The light – orange street stuff – cast itself in splashes on the rich patterning of the Persian rug, working up a beautiful palette. Jane went to the window, while Brion carefully shut the double doors leading to the stairs. She undid the cap of the bottle of vodka and took a long, shuddering pull on it. The great female's throat pulsed and in four large gulps she had managed to decimate the contents. She set the bottle down on the windowsill, and taking out one of the mutant Marlboros, lit it with a flourish of the long lighter. Jane expelled the smoke in a series of hisses and pops: the Morse code of satiation.

Brion had finished securing the door. He hit the lights and the golden oldie tones of the room sprang back up. 'So,' Brion said, 'despite her terrible experiences, and her terrible nerves, she managed to fall asleep in someone else's house for the first time in years?' His voice wasn't just freighted with irony – it was sinking under the weight of it.

'Yup, that's about it – of course that Tylenol/Nytol/Valium combo helps no end.' The babyish lilt was excised from Jane's voice; and in its place were the definite tones of a woman of the world.

'Poor old Travis.' Brion shook his big, Roman senatorial head. 'He adds Prozac to that downbeat cocktail, sad fucker. I don't think he knows whether he can sleep naturally or not any more, he's been necking them for such a long time.'

'So there's no chance of him waking?'

'None at all – and Karin?'

'Nix. The only thing that could wake the beauty up would be what? A kiss? She'd die!'

'Which leaves us.'

'Indeed. Us. Drink?'

Brion accepted the vodka tank and drained a further tenth of it. He then took a pituitary-case Marlboro from the proffered pack and lit it by pressing its dead end against her live tip. For a few moments the two emotos experienced ignition, then he broke. 'My God!' he guffawed. 'What a nerd – "I do hope you wouldn't mind joining me . . . If it's not too much . . . That would be lovely . . ." Never saying what he fucking means – never meaning what he fucking said.' The male emoto's voice was below basso; it had ultrasonic undertones which caused the glass of the window they were standing by to vibrate. But now there was no irony in that voice, nor sarcasm, but a genuine – if hideously patronising – concern.

Jane took another hefty draught of vodka before answering – between them they'd now dealt with a quarter of the five litres; then she drawled through a hedge of blue curlicues, '*Fucking* would hardly be the operative word, now would it?'

He snorted, 'No, I guess not, the poor little etiolated mice –'

'Which leaves you – and me.'

'Indeed.' Jane studied Brion a bit more, he really was the most astonishingly handsome male, and freed of the soppy expression he adopted to deal with his grown-up's puling anxiety, he had a countenance of nobility and gravity, tempered by a wild humorousness. Jane found herself saying – rather than said, 'Brion, would you show me your body – please?'

He stripped the foulard tie from his neck with one swipe; he shrugged his shoulders and his suit jacket fell like a theatre curtain; the shirt ballooned away from him; the trousers unsheathed; the underpants were kicked; and finally the socks – and attendant garters – were shot by Brion into the corners of the room, like kids fire off elastic bands. They were both laughing, but she was marvelling, marvelling at the great slab-sided length of him; marvelling at the marbled skin with its endearing rash of brown moles; marvelling at the flames of hair that burned in his crotch; marvelling at his beautiful, two-foot cock. It was curved up prominently; symbol and reality priapically nailed together.

Jane bent down so that her long hair swept the floor. She grasped the hem of her dress with crossed hands and, with a movement not unlike a nursery-school pupil impersonating the growth of a tree, she shed her silken foliage. Then she too was resplendent in the night light and it was Brion's turn to marvel. But before long they were locked in passionate, needful, delirious and athletic congress. The emotos were so large that they could simultaneously brace themselves against either wall, so as to achieve exciting contortions. It would have been fearful – this orgiastic clash of the Titans – were it not for the fact that they were both so beautiful, and so clearly in love with the moment.

When at last they were spent, and lay wrapped demurely in the Persian rug which had been yanked from the floor by their thrashings, Brion lit a Meta-Marlboro with the lanky lighter and turning to Jane, cupped her big face in his big hand. 'Just remember,' he winked at her, 'don't say a word to the grown-ups.'

Tough, Tough Toys for Tough, Tough Boys

Bill saw him about five miles after he had powered past the Dornoch turning. The hitchhiker was walking with one foot in the newly minted road, and one on the just-born verge. He was wearing some kind of cheap plastic poncho, which didn't really cover the confused pack on his back. There were no road markings, as yet, on this fresh stretch. Two hundred metres before he saw the hitchhiker, Bill had passed one of the road workers holding a lollipop sign with GO written on it in white-out-of-green capitals. The traffic was thick – solid files moving at twenty miles an hour in both directions. The cars were kicking up spray, and from out of the sharp blue sky, big, widely spaced drops of rain descended.

The hitchhiker was trying simultaneously to turn and give the car drivers a come-hither grin, keep his footing on the uneven surface, and shelter himself under his plastic poncho. It was, Bill thought, a pathetic sight. There was that, and also an indefinable something about the hitch-hiker's bearing – Bill thought later, and then thought that he had thought so at the time, in the precise moment foot slipped from accelerator to brake – which he recognised as being not that of a tourist, but someone going somewhere with a purpose, not unlike Bill himself.

Bill had spent the night at Mrs McRae's bed and breakfast, at Bighouse on the northern coast of Caithness. In the blustery evening, after a poorly microwaved pie – there was a chilly nugget in its doughy heart – he had stumped to the public phone, the half-bottle of Grouse in his jacket pocket banging against his hip, and called Betty. Once his fingertips had been digitised and resolved into connection the line sounded dead in Bill's ear. He could recognise the tone of Betty's phone – he knew it that well; but the phone was at the bottom of a galvanised metal dustbin. Then Betty was in the dustbin as well, and he was calling down to her: 'Betty? It's me, Bill.'

'Bill, where are you?' She sounded interested.

'Bighouse, I'm at Mrs McRae's –'

'Bill – why are you there, why did you backtrack?'

'I could only get the four o'clock ferry from Stromness, and I wanted to stay between Wick and Tongue . . .' This was an old joke, and Betty didn't laugh. Anyway he was lying – and she knew it.

'What's it like then between Tongue and Wick?' She owed it to the history of the old joke to sustain the repartee – a little.

'Oh, you know, furry, an odd bit of lint here and there, some sweat, a smear of soap, perhaps later some semen –' He broke off – preposterously there was banging on the door of the phone box.

A white face bloomed out of wind and darkness: 'Will you be all night? The wind's bitter.'

'I've only just got through.' He held the receiver out towards the old woman's scarf-wrapped face. She looked at it. Bill thought of Betty on the other end of the line, listening to the gale, participating in this non-conference call.

'The wind's bitter,' the old woman reiterated – she would say nothing more.

Bill jammed himself back inside the phone box, but didn't allow the heavy door to close completely. Pinioned thus, he called down into the dustbin, 'Betty, there's an elderly lady here who needs the phone – I'll call back later.' He heard her faint valediction and hung up. He hadn't called back later.

In the morning the storm that had hung over Caithness and Orkney for the past week had cleared. The sun was chucking its rays down so hard that they exploded off all glass and metal. Looking out from the window of the kitchen, where he sat at Formica dabbling rind in yoke,

Bill saw that the aluminium trim around the windows of his car was incandescent. He paid Mrs McRae with wadded Bank of Scotland pound notes – eleven of them. 'Will you be back soon, Dr Bywater?' she asked.

'Y'know, Mrs McRae,' he replied, 'when I'm next up to Orkney.'

'And any idea of when that'll be?'

He shrugged his shoulders and held his hands out, palms uppermost, so as to indicate the maximum possible mixture of doubts and commitments.

Bill threw his bag in the boot of the car and picked up the CD interchanger. He inserted the restocked cartridge of CDs into the rectangular aluminium mouth, and listened with satisfaction as the servomotors swallowed it up. He set the interchanger back in its housing and slammed the boot. He walked round to the front of the car and undid the bonnet. He checked the oil, the water and the windscreen reservoir. He checked the turbo cooling unit pipe that had burst while he was in Orkney, and which he'd welded himself. He did this all quickly and deftly, his blunt fingers feeling the car with unabashed sensuality. Bill was proud of his hands – and his skill with them.

Inside the car he wiped the hands on a rag. He started the engine of the car and listened carefully to the note of the engine. He stashed the rag and inserted the CD-control panel into its dash mounting. He dickered with the servos that automatically adjusted the driver's seat. He gave the windscreen a few sweeps of soapy water. He programmed the CD to play randomly. Finally, he lit one of the joints that he'd rolled while he was shitting after breakfast. Exhaling the first blast of smoke made the interior of the car seem like a fantastical van de Graaff generator, the lights on the fascia sparking through the haze.

Bill reached behind him, pulled up the bottle of Campbelltown twelve-year-old from under the stack of professional journals he kept on the back floor. He glanced about at the roadway, but there was nothing, only the slate roof of Mrs McRae's, with a bank of grass swaying in front of it. Bill took a generous pull on the whisky, capped the 'car bottle' as he jocularly styled it – to himself – and re-stashed it. He checked his rearview, then planted his foot on the accelerator. The big car shook itself once before plunging along the road. The inertia pressed Bill into the worn leather of the seat, releasing tiny molecules of good smell. He heard the turbo-charger kick in with its pleasing whine. John Coltrane's sax burst from the four seventy-watt speakers, the long flat sheets of sound spooling out like algorithms of emotion.

Bill managed the twenty miles into Thurso in about half an hour, ridiculously good going for this twisting stretch of road, the camber of which constantly surprised with its adversity. But the rain was gone and the visibility good. Bill kept his foot down, feeling the weight of the big saloon slice through the fresh air. The car was so long that if he drove with one arm cradling the headrest of the passenger seat – which he often did – in his peripheral view he could see the back of the car turning, gifting him a peculiar sense of being a human fulcrum.

As he drove Bill looked at the sky and the land. He didn't love Caithness the way he did Orkney. Orkney was like Avalon, a mystical place where beyond the rampart cliffs of Hoy a shoal of green, whale-like islands basked in the azure sea. But this northern coast of Britain was composed of ill-fitting elements: a bit of cliff here, a green field there, a stretch of sand and dunes over there; and over there the golf-ball reactor hall of Dounreay, the nuclear power station, waiting for some malevolent god to tee it off into the Pentland Firth. Caithness was infiltrated with a palpable sense of being underimagined. This was somewhere that nobody much had troubled to conceive of, and the terrain bore the consequences in its unfinished aspect.

It was one of the things Bill loved most about the far north. Professional, middle-class friends down south would have no sense of the geography of these regions. When he told them that he had a cottage in Orkney, they would insistently confuse the islands with the Hebrides. It allowed Bill to feel that, in a very important way, once the *St Ola* ferry pulled out of Scrabster harbour, he was sailing off the face of the earth.

Thurso. A grey, dour place. The council housing hunched, constrained, barrack-like; and pushing its closed face into the light of day, as if only too aware that this sunshine was the end of things, and that soon the long, long, windy nights would be back. Bill stopped at the garage, on the rise from where he had the best possible view of Orkney, sixteen miles away to the north. The day was so clear he could make out the crooked finger of the Old Man of Hoy, where it stood proud of the great sea cliffs. There was a light coping of snow on top of the island, which flared in the sunlight. With a wrench in his heart Bill pulled off the forecourt, and wheeled right.

Once he had left Thurso, and was accelerating up the long gradient out of the town, Bill settled down to think about the drive. Into this mental act came the awareness that he hadn't, as yet, really relaxed into it. The Bighouse to Thurso stretch had required the wrong kind of concentration; Bill needed to sink into the driving more. He liked to trance out when he was driving, until eventually his proprioception melded with the instrumentation of the car, until he *was* the car. Bill conceived of the car at these times as being properly animate: its engine a heart, its sump a liver, its automated braking system a primitive – but engaging – sentience.

The car supported Bill's body in its skin-coated settee, while he watched the movie of the road.

Bill thought about the drive and began to make wildly optimistic estimates of the time each stage would take him: two hours to Inverness, an hour and a half on through the Highlands to Perth, then another hour to Glasgow. Maybe even make it in time for lunch. Then on in the late afternoon, down the M72 to Carlisle. Then the M6 – which felt as if it were a river, coursing downhill all the way to Birmingham. He might be in time to stop off in Mosely for a balti. Penultimately the M40 in the dead of the night, ghostly tentacles of mist shrouding the road as the big car thrummed through the Midlands towards London. And then finally the raddled city itself; the burble of the exhaust reverberating from the glass façades of the car showrooms and office-equipment suppliers along the Western Avenue.

Placing himself in London at 1 a.m. after seven hundred miles of high-pitched driving, Bill could anticipate with precision the jangled condition of his body, the fraying of his over-concentrated mind. He might – he thought – let himself into Betty's flat, then her bed, then her. Or not. Go to the spieler instead. Get properly canned. Ditch the car. Reel home.

The car was lodged behind a glowering seven-ton dump truck. Mud bulged above its grooved sides, the occasional clod toppled off. They were on the long straight that heads down to Roadside, where the A882 pares off towards Wick. There had been rain more recently here and long puddles streaked the road; in the sunlight they were like mirror shards, smashed from the brilliant sky. Without thinking, Bill checked the rearview mirror, the side mirror, flicked on the indicator and rammed his foot to the floor. The car yanked forward, the turbo-charger cutting in with an audible 'G'nunngg!'. Bill felt the wheels slide and skitter as they fought for purchase on the water, mud and scree strewn about the surface. He was two hundred metres past the truck and travelling at close to ninety, before he throttled back and pulled over to the left once more.

The first pass, was, Bill reflected, the hardest. It represented an existential leap into the unknown. If car and man survived they had made their compact for the journey. There were only two ways to do this mammoth run: slowly and philosophically, or *driving*. Bill had opted for the latter. He celebrated by lighting the second of the joints he had rolled at stool. The Upsetter came on the CD, awesome bass noise transforming the doors into pulsing wobble boards, the whole car into a mobile speaker cabinet. Bill grinned to himself and hunkered down still further in his seat.

The car bucketed through the uneven terrain. The landscape was still failing to distinguish itself. From the road a coping of peat bog oozed away into the heart of Caithness, a caky mush of grasses and black earth. In the distance a single peak raised its white-capped head. It was, Bill considered, a terrain in which a few triceratops and pterodactyl wouldn't have looked altogether out of place. He'd once had an analysand who had a phobia about dinosaurs – not so much their size, or possible rapacity, he could handle that – but the notion of those vast wartinesses of lizard hide. Bill had cured the phobia, sort of. He grinned at himself in the rearview mirror at the memory; he hoped ruefully. But the herpetophobe became correspondingly more erratic in almost every other area of his life. Eventually, psychotic, he ended up being sectioned after ripping the heads off hundreds of model dinosaurs in a spree through South London toy shops.

Bill didn't psychoanalyse anybody any more. He could no longer see the virtue in it – or so he told himself. In truth, he found it easier to sign on with agencies and do various psychiatric locums. He could pick and choose his shifts, and he got a variable case load. Bill had a peculiar affinity for talking down the real crazies; people who might become fork-wielding dervishes. The cops called him a lot nowadays, when they had a berserker in the station and didn't want to get body fluids on their uniforms. Bill wouldn't have said he fully entered into the crazies' mad mad world – that kind of Laingian stuff had gone the way of non-congenital schizophrenia – but he could fully empathise with these extruded psyches, whose points of view were so vertiginous: one minute on the ceiling, the next on the floor.

Bill also liked to live a little dangerously. To swing. He used to seduce women – but tired of it, or so he thought. In truth he had simply tired. He still drove fast and hard. Up and down to Orkney five or six times a year. At the croft on Papa Westray he mended walls and fences, even built new outbuildings. He had five longhorns – really as pets. And of course there was drinking. He had Betty, sort of. A relationship based on sex on his part, and sex and anticipation on hers. Bill didn't think about his ex-wife. Not that he couldn't bear to acknowledge the truths surrounding her – insight was, after all, his profession – but because he really didn't feel that he needed to harp on it any longer. It was the past.

Bill had a thick leather car coat. Bill had a turbo-charged three-litre saloon. He liked single malts and skunk. He liked boats; he had an Orkney long liner skiff on Papa. He was a blunt-featured man with rough-cropped blond hair. Women used to stroke his freckled skin admiringly. He liked to climb mountains – very fast. He'd often done three Munros in a day. He wasn't garrulous, unless very drunk. He liked to elicit information. He was forty this year.

At Latheron, where the North Sea reared up out of the land, and the low cliffs collapsed into its silver-blue beauty, Bill checked his wrist-watch – a classic chronometer. It was just shy of eleven. The dash clock said five past, the LCD on the CD control panel winked 11 dead on, and as he looked back from the road, winked 11.01. The Portland Arms at Lybster would be opening; after such a tough morning's driving there was a good case for a pint – and a short. Bill lazily circled the steering wheel to the left and headed north up the A9.

In the wood-panelled bar lounge Bill was the only customer. The barking of his leather jacket against the vinyl of a banquette summoned an elaborately courteous man in the Highland toff's – or wannabe toff's – uniform of tweed jacket, waistcoat with horn buttons, flannel trousers, brogues. His Viyella shirt absorbed his tartan tie into its own slight patterning. He sported in addition a ridiculously flamboyant ginger handlebar moustache, which cancelled out his weak-featured face as surely as a red bar annuls smoking. Bill didn't recognise the man, and thought that he must be the winter manager; new to Caithness and perhaps not yet aware of how bleak his allotted four months of erratic pint-pulling would prove.

'Good morning sir,' said the absurdity, 'and it is a fine morning, isn't it?'

'It is.' Bill replied curtly – and then, feeling he had been too curt, 'I've had a clear run all the way from Bighouse; not so much as a shower.'

'Well, they say the gales will be up again tonight . . .' He picked up a half-pint glass from the draining board beneath the bar and began, idly, yet with skill, to wipe it. Bill walked to the bar, and the absurdity took his cue: 'What'll you be having then?' Up close Bill saw brown crap on the man's teeth, and lines of burst blood vessels, like purple crow's feet around his eyes.

Bill sighed – no need to account for his choices with this one: 'Is that a Campbelltown there?' He stabbed a finger towards the bottles of malt brooding on the shelves.

The absurdity got the bottle down without further ado. 'This is the fifteen-year-old?' His tone indicated that this was a request.

'A double,' said Bill.

Bill had brought yesterday's paper with him from the car, but he didn't bother to open it. He knocked back the whisky, and then chased it with a bottle of Orkney Dark Island. The whisky gouged more warmth into his belly, and the ale filled his head with peat and heather. Really, Bill thought, the two together summed up the far north. He was sitting back on the banquette, his feet propped on a low stool. His back and shoulders were grasped by the thick leather of his jacket. It was an old leather jacket, of forties cut. Bill had had it for years. It reminded him of a jacket he'd once seen Jack Kerouac wearing in a photograph. He liked the red quilted lining; and he especially liked the label on the inside of the collar that proclaimed: 'Genuine Leather, Made from a Quarter of a Horse'. Bill used to show this to young women, who found it amusing . . . seductive. Bill used to rub saddle soap into the thing, but recently had found he couldn't really be bothered, even though the leather was cracking around the elbows.

While Bill had been drinking, the absurdity was pottering around the vicinity of the bar, but now the pint glass was empty, and plonked back on the bar mat, he was nowhere to be seen. Bill pictured him, padding along the chilly corridors of the old granite hotel, like a cut-rate, pocket-sized laird. Impatiently, he rang a small bell – and the ginger moustache appeared instantly, directly in front of him, hoisted by its owner through the cellar hatch, like some hairy standard of rebellion.

'Sir?' came from behind the whiskers.

'The damage?' Bill countered.

'That'll be . . .' He turned to the cash register and played a chord. '. . . Four pounds and seventy-eight pence.' While Bill fought with his jeans for the cash, the absurdity had produced – from somewhere – a printed card. This he handed to Bill in exchange for the money, saying, 'You wouldn't mind, would you, filling out this card. It's a sort of survey we're doing, y'know, marketing and such, trying to find out who our clientele are . . .' He trailed off.

Bill looked at the card: 'Where did you first hear about us? 1. In the media 2. Personal recommendation 3. As part of a package holiday . . .'

'Of course,' he told the deluded hotelier, 'but if you don't mind I'll fill it out later and post it, I'm in a bit of a hurry.'

'Not at all, not at all – here's an addressed envelope for you. Make it easier.'

As he marched across the car-park to the car, Bill crumpled the card and the envelope into a ball and tossed it into a convenient bin. He also abandoned himself to unnecessarily carping laughter – the idea that this isolated spot would ever attract anything much besides passing trade, and the occasional shooting, fishing and drinking crew was as ridiculous as the ginger moustache.

Feeling the wind rising at his back impressed further how far Lybster was from anywhere – save the North Sea. Bill took off his jacket and chucked it on the back seat of the car. Then he swung himself into the front. He rammed the key into the ignition, turned it, and the car thrummed and pulsed into life. The CD chirruped – then some John Cage came on. With another negligent circling of his hand, Bill scraped the big saloon around a hundred and eighty degrees, and shot back up on to the A9, this time heading south.

For the next hour, until he saw the hitchhiker, Bill drove hard. There was something about the man in the pub at Lybster, the whole episode in fact, that unsettled him. There was that, and there was the sense that as the car plunged south – switch-backing over spurs, and charging down hillsides – it was taking Bill out of the underimagined world and into the world that was all too clearly conceived of, fixed in its nature, hammered into banality by mass comprehension.

Not that you'd know it thus far: the road still leaping and twisting every few yards, the gradients often one in ten or better. In mist, or rain – which was almost always – the A9 was simply and superficially dangerous, but shorn of its grey fleece it became almost frolicsome. So Bill thought, chucking the car in and out of the bends.

In rain you had little opportunity to pass even a car, let alone any of the grumbling lorries that laboured up this route to the far north; and there were many of these. It could slow the whole trip if you got caught behind one. Slow it up by as much as a half again. Even in fair conditions the only way to pass their caravans – they tended to travel in naturally occurring clutches, equally spaced – was to get up to about ninety on the straight, then strip-the-steel-willow of the oncoming traffic and the lorries themselves.

It was exhilarating – this headlong plunge down the exposed cranium of Britain. After twenty miles or so Bill had a spectacular view clear across the Moray Firth to the Grampians. The mountains pushed apart land, sea and sky with nonchalant grandeur; their peaks stark white, their flanks hazed white and blue and azure. Not that he looked at them, he looked at the driving, snatching shards of scenery in the jagged saccades his eyes made from speedometer to road, to rearview mirror, to wing mirrors, and back, over and over, each glance accompanied with a head jerk, as if he were some automated Hasidic Jew, praying as he went.

In a way Bill was praying. In the concentration on braking and accelerating, and at these speeds essentially toying with life and death – others' as well as his own – he finally achieved the dharmic state he had been seeking all morning: an absorption of his own being into the very act of driving that exactly matched his body's absorption into the fabric of the car; a biomechanical union that made eyes windscreens, wheels legs, turbo-charger flight mechanism. Or was it the other way round?

The wands of memories interleaved themselves with the sprigs of scenery, and then the whole hedge of impressions was further shaped and moulded by the music which poured from all four corners, before being flattened by the mantra of impulsion. Last night at the pub – the local doctor, Bohm, drunk – mouthing off about miracle cures for dipsomania – psychedelic drug rituals in West Africa, mystical twaddle – the walk home in the stiff wind, rain so hard it gave his cheeks and forehead little knouts. Now, on the road ahead, a passing opportunity, slow-moving old Ford Sierra, ahead of it two lorries and another two cars slightly further on, doing about sixty – a good seven hundred metres to the next bend. A bend beyond that allowed a view of more open road, but what of the hidden stretch? Calculate how much there was. Count: one, two, three seconds. Chance it. Rearview, Bam! Accelerator floored, wheel wrenched, back pressed back into seat. Leather smell. Vague awareness of oceanic chords playing – perhaps Richard Strauss. Indicator popping and tocking. Past the Ford. Past the first lorry. Up to eighty now. Bam! Shift rammed into third. Eighty now, nearing the bouncing butt of the second lorry. Fuuuck! There was a car. Now about a hundred metres off. Moving fast. Deathly fast. Check wing mirror. Dance the one-step of shock. Slide between the two lorries. Receive a fusillade of flashing and honking. Then – Bam! Back out again. Two hundred metres left of the straight – no view of the next stretch, just green tussocks, grey-green wall, strident black-and-white cow – keep it in third, will it back up . . . eighty . . . ninety . . . the ton. Fifty metres left – and the second lorry was cleared, evacuated, left behind as surely as a shit in a toilet in a motorway service centre. Left behind like the past, like failure, like regret.

Bill felt this marvellous sense of freedom and release as he cheated death and unslipped the surly gravity of the lumpen lorries. He felt it ten times between Borgue and Helmsdale, fifteen between Helmsdale and Brora, then more and more as the road opened up and the hills retreated from the road, leaving it to flow and wiggle, rather than twist and turn.

A glimpse of Langwell House, gothic on its promontory, as he zigzagged through Berriedale; a proscenium framed shot of Dunrobin Castle as he wheeled past its gates and cantered down into the long spare main street of Golspie, And still the sun fell down, and still the road glimmered, and still Bill thought – or perhaps only thought he thought – of nothing. Past the Highland Knitwear Centre. How many sweaters had Bill bought in a lifetime of blandishment? Too many perhaps. One purple cable knit at this very shop – for a girl called Allegra. A diminutive blonde – too young for Bill. Then twenty-two to his thirty-five. She was all chubby bits, a dinky little love handle, who when stoned on dope became psychotic, fanatically washing her hands in the air like some method-trained obsessive.

Bill had to talk her down every time it happened – and he didn't like taking his work to bed with him.

She gave head like a courtesan – like a goddess of fellation. She pushed down the prepuce with her lips, while her tongue darted round the root of his glans. One of her childlike hands delved in the lips of cloth that sagged open over his crotch, seeking out the root of him, juggling the balls of him. And this as the car motored along the banks of the Cromarty Firth, past the outcropping of cranes and davits at Invergordon. Even at the time Bill had recognised the automotive blow job as a disturbing concomitant to Allegra's manic laving. It was her way of placing him back under her control; he might have the steering wheel – but she was steering him, gnawing the joy stick.

It was Allegra's first and last trip to Orkney with Bill. Their relationship didn't so much split up as shatter some weeks later, when, at a dinner party given by middle-aged friends of Bill's, Allegra, drunk, had screamed, 'Why doesn't he tell you all that he *loves* going down on women, but can't stand to have them go down on him!' then thrown her vodka tonic in Bill's face, then attempted to ram the solid after the liquid. A lunge that Bill deflected, so that the crystal shattered on impact against the invitation-encrusted mantelpiece. The friends had plenty to talk about after Allegra and Bill had left.

As the car tick-tocked along the bleak street, Bill imagined the grey houses to either side populated with his past courtesans, his myriad lovers. It would be like some Felliniesque dream sequence. No, come to think of it, better to house the past lovers – there had to be at least a hundred of them – in Dunrobin Castle itself. It was so big there would be a room each for the more mature, and convenient dormitories for the young girls. Bill smiled at the thought of this perverse seraglio. But hadn't Fellini been right? Wasn't this the only possible psychic solution to the sense of hideous abandonment that the practice of serial monogamy imparted? To get them all in one place. It wasn't that Bill wanted them all sexually available – quite the reverse. But he wanted them in a context that made what existed between him and them, if not exactly important, at any rate viable. He wanted to feel that it had all mattered, that it wasn't simply animal couplings, mechanistic jerkings, now forgotten, now dust.

Taken with the fantasy, Bill allowed it to occupy him as he pressured the big car through the long avenue of trees that led from Golspie to

Loch Fleet. Dunrobin Castle populated by all of his lovers, all of the women he'd ever had sexual relations with. The younger ones would handle the bulk of the domestic work. There was Jane, who was a professional cook, she could run the kitchens, with the assistance of Gwen, Polly and Susie. There would be enough women in their twenties to handle all the skivvying, leaving the more mature women free to spend their time in idle conversation and hobby-style activities. Why, come to think of it, there was even a landscape gardener in Bill's poking portfolio; perhaps there was a case for not simply maintaining the grounds of the castle, but redesigning them?

Even as Bill entertained this notion of a comforting castle, cracks began to appear in its façade. *All* of his former lovers . . . That meant not just Allegra, coming at him time after time with vitrified daggers, during the fatal attraction of cocktail hour, but other, still more unstable lovers, howling and wafting around halls and stairways. Worse than that, it meant his ex-wife; where would she come to roost? No doubt in an outhouse, from where, on dark nights, the sounds of screamed imprecations could be heard, blown in with the wind, and echoing around the drawing room where the others sat sewing, and Bill himself grimaced over another whisky.

And if there was to be room for the ex-wife, there would have to be room for other unsavoury characters as well. Despite himself, Bill urged the conceit to its baleful conclusion. The tarts – there would be room at Dunrobin for the tarts, the brasses, the whores. Bill imagined trying to keep them out – this delegation of tarts. Meeting them at the gates of the Castle and attempting to turn them back. 'But you fucked us!' their spokesmadam would abjure him. 'We demand room in the Castle!' He would have no choice but to admit them – and then the fragile concord of the seraglio would be shattered. The other lovers might have been prepared to accept sorority as a substitute for monogamy, but the tarts? Never. The tarts would swear and drink. They would smoke crack in the billiard room, and shoot smack in the butler's pantry. They would seduce the younger lovers and outrage the older. On cold nights Bill would find himself desperately stuffing his head beneath covers, beneath pillows, trying to shut out the sounds of their wassailing, as they plaited with the moan and screech of the wind.

On the long straight that bounced up the other side of the loch, Bill clocked the signs requesting assistance from the coastguard in the fight against drug smugglers: If You See Anything Suspicious . . . The image of gracious polygamy faded and was replaced by one of Bill beachcombing, prodding at shells with a piece of driftwood, his jacket collar turned up, its points sharp against his chilled ears. The oiled tip of his makeshift shovel turns up a corner of blue plastic bag. He delves further. Six rectangular blocks, each sealed in blue plastic and heavily bound with gaffer tape are revealed to be neatly buried. Bill smiles and gets out his penknife . . .

Another sign whipped by at the top of the rise: Unmarked Police Cars Operating . . . Spoilsports. No seraglio and now no mother lode of Mama Coca; no white rails for the wheels of the big car to lock on to; no propulsive, cardiac compression to take Bill's heart into closer harmony with the rev counter . . . He hunkered down once more, gripped the steering wheel tighter, concentrated on the metallic rasp of John Lee Hooker's guitar, which ripped up the interior of the car. Then came the roadworks. Then came the hitchhiker.

Bill braked, and looked for somewhere to pull over. About fifty metres further on there was a break in the earth-soft verge where blue-grey gravel puddled on to the roadway. Bill aimed for it, indicated, and then crunched the car to a halt. In the rearview mirror he could see the hitchhiker running towards the car, his pack bouncing, his poncho flapping, an expression of gap-toothed desperation on his face, as if he were absolutely certain that this offer of a lift was a taunt or a hoax, and that as soon as he was level with the car Bill would drive off guffawing.

The hitchhiker yanked the car door open and the fresh air and moisture and sunlight streamed in. 'Thanks, mate –' He was clearly going to converse.

'Get in!' Bill snapped. 'I can't stop here for long.' He gestured at the roadway, where the cars were having to pull over the centre line in order to pass. The hitchhiker threw himself into the front passenger seat of the car, his pack still on. Bill glanced in the rearview, indicated, lazily circled the wheel to the right, and rejoined the traffic.

For some seconds neither said anything. Bill pretended to concentrate on the driving and observed his captive out of the corner of his eye. The hitchhiker sat, his face almost against the windscreen, the backpack – which Bill now saw had a tent bag and roll of sleeping bag tied to it – was like a whole, upper-body splint, designed so as to force its wearer into closer contemplation of the road. A Futurist's corset.

'I'll stop as soon as I can,' Bill said, 'and we can put that in the back.'

The hitchhiker said, 'Thanks very much.'

He was – Bill guessed – in his late twenties or early thirties. His accent was Caithness, the sharp elements of a Scottish brogue, softened and eroded by a glacial covering of Scandinavian syllables. His black, collar-length hair was roughly cut. He wore the yellow nylon poncho, and under it a never-fashionable, fake sheepskin-lined denim jacket. From behind the distempered non-wool, poked the collar of a tartan shirt. The hitchhiker's breath smelt foully of stale whisky. His eyes were bivouacked in purple bags, secured by purple veins. He was unshaven. His teeth were furred. He had an impressive infection in the dimple of his strong chin – he wasn't bad-looking.

'Are you going far?' he asked.

'All the way,' Bill smiled, 'to London, that is.'

The hitchhiker grinned, and attempted – insofar as the pack allowed him – to settle more securely in his seat. It was the last question he asked Bill for the whole journey.

They were across the Cromarty Firth causeway and on the Black Isle before Bill found a proper layby to stop in. They both got out of the car and Bill rearranged the things on the back seat so that the hitchhiker could stash his pack. They were rolling again in a couple of minutes. Bill pushed the car up to seventy and then idled there, the index finger and thumb of his right hand holding the lower edge of the steering wheel as if it were some delicate surgical instrument. The rain ceased and the roadway shone once more. The muted CD played the current single by a hip guitar band. The hitchhiker drummed chipped, dirty nails on frayed, dirty denim.

'So,' said Bill after a while, 'where are you headed?'

'I'm going all the way too.' He hunched round to face Bill, as if they were casual drinkers striking up a conversation at the bar of the car's dashboard, 'I stop in Poole, Dorset, but I've a mate in Glasgow I want to see for tonight.'

'Well, I can drop you outside Glasgow, I'm heading straight on through and south.'

'That'll be grand.' The hitchhiker smiled at Bill, gifting him a sight of peaks of plaque. It was a smile that should be given at the conclusion of such a trip – not the beginning. 'Nice car,' the hitchhiker said, still smiling.

'Yeah,' Bill drawled, 'it motors. So, where're you from?'

'Thurso.'

'And what's the purpose of the trip?'

'I'm studying down in Poole, got myself on a computer course like. I had a reading week so I thought I'd get up to see my kiddies –'

'They're in Thurso?'

'Aye, right enough.'

The old 'fluence was still there, Bill thought. A couple of miles, a few questions insinuated in the right vulnerable places, and like some cunning piece of Chinese marquetry – a box with hidden compartments subtly palped – the hitchhiker's psyche would begin to open out, to exfoliate. They swung over the ridge of Isle and the car caromed on down, on to the dual carriageway. They emerged from a forest of scattered conifers and there, hunkered around its cathedral spire, Inverness gleamed.

'Inverness,' said the hitchhiker.

He even states the obvious! Bill snidely exulted.

'Did you come from Thurso this morning?'

'I did. After a bit of a session – if you catch my meaning.'

'Some mates saw you off then?'

'They couldna' exactly see me off – they were all pished malarkey. Five of the fuckers, all inna heap. So I tiptoed out. Got a lift right away across to Latheron, then down to Dornoch. Then I was walking in the bloody rain for four miles before you stopped for me –'

'It was difficult to stop. The roadworks –'

'Aye, right enough.'

'You've got a tent and stuff there?'

'In case I get caught short like – and have to spend the night on the road. I had to do that on the way up. I slept by the side of the road near Aviemore.'

'Wasn't that a drag?'

The hitchhiker snorted. 'I'll say. Come five in the morning the rain starts coming down holus-bolus, and then a fucking cow starts giving a horn to ma' flysheet. I was back on the road before dawn, with my thumb stuck up like a fucking icicle . . .' He trailed off and gave Bill another grimy grin. His stubble was blue.

Bill was emboldened to ask, 'So, you're fond of a drink then?'

The hitchhiker pressed the ball of his thumb into one eye socket, the middle joint of his index finger into the other. He kneaded and scrunched his features, answering from within this pained massage, 'Oh well, I suppose . . . perhaps more than I should be. I dunno.'

Bill grimaced. He looked for a turning on the left – the carriageway was still dual – when he saw a forestry track. He dabbed the brakes, indicated, lazily circled the wheel and pulled in. 'Slash,' he said.

They both got out. Bill left the car running. They both pissed into the edge of the woodland. Through steam and sun Bill examined his companion's urine. Very dark. Perhaps even blood dark. There was a touch of jaundice in the hitchhiker's complexion as well. Maybe kidney infection, Bill thought, maybe worse. Not that this would be necessarily pathological in any way. They drank like that in Thurso – as they did in Orkney.

Bill knew ten men under thirty-five on Papa alone who had stomach ulcers. In Dr Bohm's surgery there were forty-odd leaflets urging parents to check their children for symptoms of drug abuse. Absurd, when about the only drugs available on the island were compounds for ensuring the evacuation of bovine afterbirth. Bohm also had one small tattered sticker near the surgery door, which proclaimed: Drinkwise Scotland, and gave a help-line number. This lad was, Bill reflected, quite possibly addicted to alcohol, without necessarily being an alcoholic.

When they were back in the car Bill reached back behind the young man's seat and pulled up the car bottle. It was half-full. 'Will you have a dram?' He sloshed the contents about; they were light and pellucid – as the stream of urine ought to have been. Bill appreciated the exact battle between metabolic need and social restraint that danced with the young man's features. He broke the spell by uncorking the bottle and taking a generous swig himself. Then he passed the bottle to the young man who was saying, 'Sure . . . Yeah . . . Right.'

The whisky went off like an anti-personality mine somewhere in the rubble-strewn terrain of Bill's forebrain. He flicked the shift into reverse and crunched backwards. He took the bottle from the young man and re-stashed it. He hugged the headrest and sighted down the road. Nothing. He banged the accelerator and the car twisted backwards, pivoting at the hips, rested on its rubber haunches for a second while Bill flicked the shift into drive, then shook itself and plunged back up the long hill. Twenty, thirty, forty . . . the turbo-charger 'gnunng'ed!' in . . . fifty-five, seventy, eighty . . . to either side the rows of orderly conifers strobed back; the gleaming road ahead twanged like a rubber band; the sky shouted 'Wind!'; the reggae music welled like beating blood: 'No-no-no-oo! You don' love me an' I know now –' Bill was feeling no pain. The young man was shouting something, Bill hit OFF.

'– arked cars –'

'What was that you said?' Bill's voice was precise and dead level in the instantaneously null environment of the car. It sounded like an aggressive threat.

'Y'know the police, man . . . the pigs . . . They have unmarked cars on this road.'

'I know.' Bill poked at the speedometer. 'Anyway I'm only doing eighty-five, they won't pull you till you get within a whisker of ninety – d'you smoke?' Without so much as twisting the thread of conversation, Bill had filched another joint from his inside pocket.

The whisky and the skunk opened the young man up. He skewed himself further in his seat, imposing more intimacy, and Bill began to feed him questions. His name was Mark. His father had been a marine engineer. Much older than the mother. The father was Viennese – Jewish. A wartime refugee, he designed some of the early SONAR systems. The mother died of cancer when Mark was eight, the father four years later. The father had had money but the estate was mismanaged by uncaring trustees. Mark and his brother ended up in children's homes. They were separated. Mark left school, got a job with a carrier's. Married, had two children and . . .

'Fucked up, I s'pose, right enough.'

'What's that?'

'With the kiddies like. Fucked up. Y'know, I was young – didn't know what I wanted. Still don't, I s'pose.' He gifted Bill another smile that had once – no doubt – been charming.

Bill had been waiting for this; this descent into the cellar of Mark's mind. The kids – his relationship with his kids – would have to be the trapdoor, the way down. Bill had pegged Mark as a bolter almost immediately. There was an aspect of bruised dejection about the young man which suggested someone who was willing to wound but afraid to strike. Someone who would say the unsayable and then attempt retraction. Someone whose capacity for self-love would only ever be manifested through attitudinising and narcissism.

Bill thought that he quite hated Mark already. He hated the young man's willingness to be drawn out. His self-absorption. His tiresome lack of cool – he had told Bill four times while they smoked the joint how good the dope was in Poole, and how adept he and his pals were at obtaining it. Bill resolved to pump Mark for all he was worth. To gut the man's past, quarter his present, and draw a bead on his future. It was a game Bill had often played before – trying to find out as much as he could about someone he encountered by chance. Find out as much as he could, and – this was crucial – not give away anything about himself. Once the mark began asking questions themselves the game was over.

'It's difficult bringing up kids –'

'Specially with no dosh. Specially with no space, y'know. Space to think. I always thought there was more to me than just a driver. My father was a brilliant man. I couldn't find myself. Couldn't in Thurso – nothing there. And my wife . . . she didn't, sort of, get it . . .'

'Understand?'

'Right.'

'And it's better down in Poole? Did you go there directly?'

'Well, no. I bummed around the country, sort of, for a while. I mean, I set off aiming for Glastonbury that year – and then just sort of kept on. Got, well, ended *up* in Poole because of the Social –'

'Easier to claim?'

'Aye.'

They were well into the mountains and the clouds had come down. To the right the Monadhliaths, to the left the Grampians. The valley was a mile or so wide. Beyond the rough summer pasture the mountains did what they did best: mounting. Either the furred flanks of forestry, or the abrasive architecture of scree. Up and Up, until the indefinite, thrusting peaks made contact with the cloudy massifs lowered from above. Bill noted that the car was almost out of petrol. They would have to run into Aviemore.

'I'm going to run into Aviemore,' he said to Mark, who was humming along with the music, 'but we won't be stopping, we'll just grab some sandwiches and head on – have you eaten?' The young man was hitching. It was plain that he'd spent all of his money on booze the night before. This was Bill's opportunity to do him a real turn. Feed him up.

'Nah, really . . . nah . . . I'm all right.' The suitable case for charity suitably hung his face. Bill said nothing – he was looking for signs. Eventually one ran along the road towards them – it was a mile to the turn. The sign – as did most in this part of the Highlands – showed a turnoff diverting from the main road, lancing a boil destination, and then rejoining it. Bill mused on how like life this was; the temporary diversions that you attempted to make, which were always cut off, subsumed once more to the ruthlessly linear, the deathly progression. Bill thought of sharing this observation with Mark, but then thought better of it. Then he did anyway.

Mark pondered for a while, then factored himself in: 'Yeah, I feel that my whole life's been like that up till now. I haven't been doing what I should – I've been marking time.'

'Neat.'

'What?'

'Neat.'

'What?'

'Nothing.' They sat silent as Bill piloted the car through the outskirts of Aviemore. The place was still tatty despite the money that had recently been poured in. Most of the buildings were chalet-style, with steeply pitched roofs running almost to the ground. But the materials were synthetic; concrete and aluminium; asbestos and perspex. Every surface seemed to be buckling; every edge rucking up. 'Shit hole,' Bill said.

Seeing a biggish Texaco station, set back off the road, Bill lazily circled the steering wheel to the left and the car oozed on to the forecourt. He pulled up to the pumps, was out of the door with the petrol-cap key in one hand and a tenner in the other, before Mark had a chance to plan his arrival. The air here was a sharp embrace. Bill still vibrated with the road. The outside world was warped. It felt like leaving a cinema after a matinée, and coming out into the inappropriately bright afternoon.

'I'll fill the tank – could you go and get us three or four of those crappy plastic sandwiches they do – tuna, chicken, whatever . . . And some drinks, Coke, Irn Bru – yeah? And some fags. Regal blue. OK?'

Mark slouched off to the shop. If I give him enough things, Bill thought, he'll have to ask me about myself. He'll have to evince some curiosity about his benefactor. Bill wanted this. He didn't like his dislike of the young man, didn't like the way it was curdling in his gut – curdling it with still more bilious, watery gripes. If Mark would only ask him about himself the inquisition could be called off. They could chat normally, instead of this ceaseless interrogative chatter. Eventually silence would fall – not companionable, but not alienated either. In due course he would drop the young man off, on a slip road, about ten miles outside Glasgow. They would part and forget.

Spasmodically, Bill clutched the handle of the pump, until the attendant hit the flashing button on his console and the petrol began to glug. Perhaps Mark had done a flit, a new bolt, Bill couldn't make him out in the shop. It wouldn't be a bad score for the lad; a bit of whisky, some dope, a tenner, a ride, why not duck out now while he was ahead? Then Mark appeared from the back of the shop, where the customer toilets were, and Bill allowed himself the luxury of feeling a little guilty, imagining that he had misjudged human character.

Back in the car Mark struggled with his seatbelt while they rolled back out on to the road. 'They'd no tuna, but I got a bacon one, and chicken with corn . . . and . . . smoked ham.' He displayed the plastic-packed chocks of sandwich to Bill, as if he were about to be asked to perform some visio-spatial test with them.

'Have you got a Coke?'

'Aye.' Mark passed it to Bill, but not before thoughtfully opening it.

Bill drank the Coke and drummed the wheel. They puttered between more, mutant chalet-style blocks of tourist flats, then past a shopping parade, then out into the country again. Bill didn't say anything until they were heading south on the A9 once again. Then he sighed, cranked the big car up to eighty-five, overtook a convoy of Finnish campervans which were struggling up a long gradient, and said, 'So, did you see much of the kids when you were up this time?'

'It was . . .' Mark was struggling with a recalcitrant piece of ham; gristle in a tug-of-war between bread lips and flesh lips. 'It was . . .' Bill decided to ignore the appetitive recovery. 'Difficult, y'know. I've nowhere to take them, and I'm not happy hanging around her place – not that's she's keen or anything. I took them to the park a couple of times . . . and for tea.'

Either the clouds were descending, or the road was still rising, because turbulent clumps of vapour were falling down from the dark passes, and scudding a couple of hundred feet above the road. Bill put on the headlights, full beam. 'Was it a long time since you were up before then?'

'I hadn't been back before.' Mark let this fall from between chomping jaws, then grimaced. 'Ach! It's not like me.'

'What's that?'

'To be saying so much.'

'Really?'

'Ach ye-es, well, I dunno . . . I was always a bit of a tearaway, y'know –'

'I gathered.'

'Nothing grievous, but this and that, y'know, telling a few tall ones to the Social, doing a few chequebook and card jobs. So I was always good at . . . y'know . . .'

Y'know, y'know, y'know? What could this young man imagine about Bill? That he knew everything? That such a nonce word had become Mark's asinine catch phrase, begged the very question the answer to which it assumed. The more 'y'know's filled the car, the more Bill felt certain that he did know – and bridled from the truth: 'Lying?'

'Yeah, I s'pose. There's a way of doing it –' He grinned. 'A technique almost. It's like job interviews –'

'Job interviews?'

'Yeah. If you don't want the job, you tend to do well in the interview. It's the same with lying. People always make the mistake of trying to make someone believe what they're saying – but that's not the way. You've got to not care whether they believe – and they will. I'm pretty good at it, if I say so myself. Not that I lie now though.' He was gabbling. 'I don't have to any more – don't need to . . .'

But he had lost Bill, who was no longer listening to the content of what Mark said – only its form. Bill was listening to the emotional shapes that Mark was making. In the rising and falling of tone, the bunching and stretching of rhythm, he was able to discern the architecture of Mark's past history: the outhouses of unfeeling and evasion; the vestibules of need and recrimination; the garages of wounding and abuse. All of it comprehensively planned together, so as to form a compound of institutionalisation and neglect. Bill honed his ears, concentrating on this shading in of a sad blueprint. The young man's actual *pride* in his mendacity – that would have to be one part bravado, one part a lie and one part the truth. Nasty little cocktail. Nasty little dilemma for the two of us, imprisoned in a car, speeding through a mountain pass. Bill hunkered down more against the comfortable padded extrusion of the door, letting his weight rest on the inside handle. He scanned Mark out of the corners of his eyes; a series of quick penetrating glances, as ever interleaved with shards of scenery, fragments of road. He really was rough. The fingers nicked and burnt: pus-ridden here – browned there, the knuckles fulsomely scabbed. He might not be altogether *compos mentis* – this hitchhiker, awarded to Bill by the journey, like an idiotic prize – but that made him all the more potentially dangerous.

'Potential for people, like me, to do all sorts of things . . .' Mark had veered on to the subject of the Internet. It appeared to verge most of his discourse. 'Don't you think?'

'Oh definitely,' Bill replied, surfacing, and used the hiatus to ask for the chicken sandwich, before getting back down to the drive, getting back down to the questioning.

Past the turning for Kingussie, past the A86, forking away to the west coast and Fort William, the big car bucketed on along the darkening road, as the autumn afternoon curled about the mountains. Bill kept the speed up – because he had no speed. The last of the Dexedrine had been used for the drive north. It was unwise for him to blag any more for a while. More than unwise – fucking foolhardy. So, on this mammoth drive Bill would have to depend on caffeine and ephedrine pills. Hideous shit he hadn't scoffed since revising for school exams. Feeling himself flag and sopor welling up from the road, Bill scrabbled in the pocket of his jacket, located a couple of the bitter little things, washed them down with a mouthful of flat Coke. Mark was talking about what served him as a love life.

'If you've had bad experiences it affects you. I dunno – maybe I'm not so good on the trust end of things . . .' Bill realised he was referring, preposterously, to his capacity for trust – not his trustworthiness. 'So I keep my distance. Jennifer' (that was the new girlfriend) 'did move in for a bit, but I felt crowded. We couldn't see eye to eye. The place was too small. She wouldn't give me my space – like my wife. Always crowding me, getting on my case about . . . stuff. We're still seeing each other though . . . though it's not quite so full-on . . .'

Bill thought he could probably decipher this completely now. Mark was abusive – like many of the abused. Back in Thurso was a wife who had cowered when one of those barked hand-battens was raised; and in Poole it had been the same. Bill heard hysterical flutings of heterosexual discord in his inner ear: Mark and the nameless women, pleadings and beratings like vile duets. The hitchhiker harped on about the harpies.

By now they were coming down off the mountains. The land turned a greener, tawnier hue by the mile. The isolated shuttered lodges were being replaced by scattered habitations, farms carved out from the heathery hillsides. But as if to taunt the occupants of the car, who were, after all, coming in from a kind of cold, the rain now recommenced. Bill flicked the stalk, the wipers did their thing intermittently, then steadily, then rapidly. And by the time they were passing the turning for Pitlochry the land, the road and the sky had been boiled up into a vaporous stock. Turner, Bill thought, would have painted this greying haze, had he been alive to suck the butt-end of the twentieth century.

Mark was talking about the Internet again. About how a friend of his – an acquaintance really, had set up a small service provider and software technical-support company. The friend was letting Mark spend time on his equipment, learn his way around it. The friendship, Bill surmised, was actually just as virtual as a Windows window. Mark was there under sufferance – if there at all. But Bill wasn't really thinking about this, he was remembering a woman he'd bedded in Pitlochry. A wannabe thesp, up for the summer theatre festival. Bill had motored through and caught her in an execrable production of *Lady Windermere's Fan.* Funny that – a bad production of Wilde. Funny how bad direction, bad acting, bad sets and costumes were the dramatic equivalent of monkeying with the controls on a television, so that the picture became over-contrasted, or too dark. In this case the effect of the monkeying was to produce leaden vulgarity, rather than frothy and sophisticated farce.

After desultory applause he had cornered her in her cubbyhole dressing room. The smell of silk, satin, crinoline and powder was sharp, overpowering. She'd giggled as he pushed up her skirts . . .

'We didn't realise he had a stash in there. We just went in to get these tapes back, but we found it in his room, so we took it. It turned out it was his whole stash. He paid us upwards of two hundred to get it back – a decent score.' Mark was, Bill realised, talking about another rip-off. He'd slid from contemplating that mundane world of electronic encoding, to the airily fascinating world of Poole bedsits.

'So.' Bill lit a Regal with the lighter he now held, permanently crushed, between palm and steering wheel. 'Did you take any of the smack?'

'God, no! I wouldn't do that! Bit of puff, fine – bit of whizz when it's about, but I don't want to fuck up – I've seen what that shit can do to people.'

Bill inwardly grinned. What more could a heroin addiction have done to this young man? Make him leave another family? Make him lie more than he had already? Make him a more self-satisfied and still less reflective petty thief? Bill doubted it.

They were past Perth and heading down the long valley towards Gleneagles and Stirling. The country was still green here, with the stubbly residue of crops catching, with a shimmy of light, the occasional burst of sun from between cloud banks. The hills had pushed back still further from the road, and the farmhouses were trimmer, better kept, more on show. The changed landscape dampened the mood in the car; the evocations of domesticity, whipping by in the slipstream, reminded both Bill and Mark of the queer accommodations they had made with life. Bill felt like a drink.

He could visualise – quite clearly – the slopping level of whisky in the car bottle. He wanted to stop and have a piss and then a decent pull. Tramp down the memories that his cross-examination of Mark was dragging to the surface. But Bill didn't trust Mark at all now. He wouldn't feel safe leaving the car running while he splattered on the verge. He could all too clearly imagine the sound of the door slamming at his back, the car's wheels crunching, spattering gravel. His own anguished cries as he turned, and ran up the road, his cock still spluttering pee as he contemplated loss of car and everything else. And he wasn't even insured for theft. Bill really hated Mark now. Hated him for being pathetic – and a threat; at one and the same time.

A layby came by. Bill dabbed the brakes, lazily circled the wheel. The car ground to a halt. Bill yanked up the bottle of Campbelltown from its sleeve of medical journals. He unscrewed it, took a deep pull and passed it to Mark, who looked at him warily, took a slug and passed the bottle back. 'You're not bothered by the pigs then?' he asked.

'Of course I am,' Bill replied tartly, 'who isn't? But that's the last before Glasgow – I'll not risk going head-to-head with them.' He checked the rearview and side mirrors, lazily circled the wheel to the right, then pushed home the accelerator, like the plunger of some 300 cc hypodermic. The big car summoned its inertia and banged back up on to the crown of the road. Bill felt the bladder of mistrust push its toxic cargo back against his pelvis. He resigned himself to the sensation. Better score more distraction.

'So, what'll you be doing with this mate in Glasgow then?'

'I dunno, not too much. We certainly won't be drinking single fucking malts.' He grinned at Bill in a way he hoped was rueful. 'More like single fucking pints. He's on the sick – my mate. But I've got a few quid, I promised him a bit of a night. It'll be the same as our normal routine. Do a few cans at home. Down to the pub for a few. Then a carry-out; and then the racing –'

'Racing?'

'We-ell, not racing exactly. It's just a thing we do – we've always done – when I'm in Glasgow. My mate – he's got these old Tonka toys, y'know?'

'Yeah.'

'Not the little one – the jeeps and that. But the big ones, the ones kids can sit on and push along wi' their feet. Y'know, the big earth movers and that?'

'Yeah.'

'Once we're right bladdered we get them out. There's one each – an earth mover and a dump truck, but we always have a little scrap over who gets which. The dump truck's faster, but it has a dicky wheel – comes off at speed. Anyway, we get 'em out, like I say, and we go racing down Sauchiehall Street. Y'know Sauchiehall Street?'

'Yeah.'

'Aye – well, you'll know it's got a good long slope to it then, just right. Like a sort of ski-jump effect, y'know. Anyway, it's a right good laugh. All the folk coming out of the pubs cheer us on; and if one of us runs into a feller, there's always a ruck of some sort. Good laugh – great *craic*!'

Mark was clearly gingered up by this, this prospect of a drunken race seated on toys long since outgrown. His eyes were wide – so that Bill could clock all the yellowed rim of them. His grin gaped; his sour mash breath blanketed the car. Bill lit the last of his pre-rolled joints and took a big pull of flowery smoke. Mark was still puffed up, but Bill's silence about the Tonka-toy trials was clearly unnerving him.

Eventually Bill spoke: 'Tough, tough toys for tough, tough boys,' he said.

'Whassat?'

'You remember – don't you? Or are you too young? It was the advertising slogan for Tonka toys. The telly advert was all set in a sand-pit and there would be this drumming – tom-toms, I suppose – and the various Tonka toys would come into view, all of them self-propelled. No drivers – of any scale at all. Then the drumming would go to a kind of peak, while one of the Tonka jeeps bounced over the terrain, and a voice would say "Tough, Tough Toys for Tough, Tough Boys!" in *very* stentorian tones – you remember?'

'No, I can't rightly say I do.' Mark was downcast.

Perhaps, Bill thought, I shouldn't have upstaged his anecdote, or maybe he's embarrassed because he doesn't know what stentorian means. They drove on in silence, passing the joint between them.

They were leaving Dunblane behind on its promontory of green, when the rain, which up until then had been confining itself to irregular bursts, clamped down in earnest. As Bill pushed the big saloon up on to the M9 motorway, curtains of near-solid precipitation were pulled to around them. The world disappeared into an aqueous haze. Bill sat forward in his seat and concentrated hard on the driving. There was so much water on the road that any sudden braking would result in an aquaplane. And the skunk – which never troubled him in clear weather – seemed to slick his brain, so that an injudicious thought might result in a psychic aquaplane. He tried a few more conversational forays with Mark, a few more insinuating questions, but the hitchhiker had clammed up. He'd shot his wad with the Tonka toys anecdote. Either that, or – and the apprehension of this made Bill peculiarly uneasy – Mark was coming to an awareness of the extent to which he'd been filleted; of how much Bill had managed to get out of him, while rendering nothing of his own in return.

What must it feel like, Bill considered, to have given that much of yourself and got so little in return? It was a version of psychic rape. It was a dishonest employment of his own neglected analytic abilities. It was an abuse of someone who had never agreed to be a patient. It was like trying to get a whore to come. It was an obscenity – a violation. Bill kept silent, piloted the car through its new, turbulent element.

Past Stirling with its folly wavering through the rain. Every time Bill went by he swore that one day he would stop, climb the tower, preferably with a woman. It looked like the tower's summit might be a good place to make love. Or at any rate fuck. The rain was worse now – almost solid. And the traffic was heavier – in every respect. Enormous articulated lorries pummelled the carriageways. Bill began to bite the insides of his cheeks. By the time they passed Falkirk, and joined the A80 for a spell, the conditions were truly dangerous, and the big car was wallowing along at between thirty and forty.

'There won't be much racing tonight if this keeps up,' Bill said, trying to leaven the atmosphere. But all he got from Mark was a grunt.

Bill couldn't get the Tonka-toy racing out of his head. He could picture it only too well: the drunk ragamuffins at the top of the road, their outsize toys clutched between their tattered bejeaned legs. The knots of men and women spilling on to the pavements from pubs and clubs. And then the bellow to begin. The acrylic wheels skittering and scraping on the paving. The sense of accelerating on nothing as the stabilising legs retract. A biff here, a bash there, and all the time picking up speed. The racers' jerky perspectives disclosing only the onrush of the street . . . How will it all end, if not in tears? Tough, tough toys – for tough, tough boys.

'I can't drop you right in Glasgow –'

'Whassat?' Mark had to shout over the drumming of the downpour and the thrumming of bass. Bill killed the CD.

'I can't drop you right in Glasgow, I was going to let you off when I got on to the M73, but –' Bill remembered the confused pack, the cheap plastic poncho. 'I couldn't do that in this rain – you'd be soaked.' Mark gave him a look as if to suggest that this was all that people like Bill ever did to people like him. 'What would you say to my dropping you in Motherwell and then you can get the train in from there – it'll only be a few quid . . .'

Mark looked at Bill, his expression heavily freighted with the lack of a few quid more than the very few quid he had; and the eternal recurrence of people's assumption that he might be capable of making good the deficiency. Bill thought of Mark's night out, the cheap drinks scrounged; the dregs drained; a crumb of hash on a pin head trapped beneath a milk bottle; perhaps solvents or fights towards dawn. Bill ambivalently relished the opportunity to say, 'Look, it's no bother to me – a few quid. I'll stump it up . . . and well, who knows, maybe you'll have the chance to pay it back in the future.' Bill presented Mark with the grin of an inverted Cheshire cat – it was gone long before Bill was.

'I wouldna' want to impose –' said Mark, with the easy non-assurance of someone who had been doing just that for years.

'It's no problem – no worry.' Bill wanted to go on with this mini litany of reassurance, to say that there would be no *pain*, no *poverty*, no *want* of any kind. That Mark and he would be reunited after the storm had spluttered to a finish. That they would find themselves in a field, verdant with opportunity, growing with cash; and that the two of them would smoke skunk and drink whisky. Make fiscal hay while the sun shone.

But instead Bill said nothing – simply drove; and as the prow of the big car parted the downpouring waves he envisioned Sauchiehall Street, the tough, tough toys, their tough, tough riders. Surely with this offer of money Mark would ask him something – his *name* even. But no.

They splashed past the slip road for the M8 and central Glasgow. By the time they reached the Motherwell exit of the M74 the rain hadn't simply thinned – it had gone altogether. The road ahead was mirror-bright once more; the verges painfully green. Even the outcrops of housing in the middle distance appeared sluiced into cleanness. See The Difference With Flash-floods. If only this will hold, thought Bill, knowing full well it wouldn't. He began making those same, implausible calculations of hard driving he had made on the road out of Thurso that morning. It was four-thirty now, drop the hitchhiker by five. He might be in the region of Manchester by eight, Birmingham by ten, home by midnight – wherever that was.

They were puttering up the hill into Motherwell, then they were channelled into the switchbacks of the one-way system. The inhabitants of the old steel town had taken the break in the rain as a signal to sally forth. There was a preponderance of wheeled shopping bags and thick overcoats among the precincts. Eventually Bill found the entrance to the station and pulled in. He twisted sideways in his seat, while Mark, galvanised by arrival, yanked open his door, swung out, opened the back door and commenced reassuming his confused backpack. Bill managed to extract a tenner from his tight pocket; a tenner so worn and soft that it felt like the pocket lining. 'This should do it,' he said to Mark. The hitchhiker looked at the money as it were no more than his due – a reasonable prophylactic, Bill tacitly agreed, to the shame occasioned by receiving charity.

'Are you sure?'

'No problem, really, no problem at all.'

'Well, thanks for that, really, thanks . . .' Mark dried, perhaps conscious of a hole in his gratitude; a hole where a name should have been inserted – but it was too late for that now. 'I dunno – maybe some time –'

'Whenever, really – whenever.' Bill did his negative Cheshire cat act again.

'And thanks for the lift, and the smoke . . . and the dram –'

'Really, no problem, good to have company. I wish you luck with all of your endeavours. A bright young man like you – you'll come through.' Sounding portentous no longer seemed to matter. It was better to pull out this Capraesque bullshit, rather than allow Mark to wallow in the gathering realisation that he was an unthinking, unfeeling drone. That he could take a lift from a man, smoke his dope, eat his food, drink his whisky, and then take his money, all without even asking him his name.

The hitchhiker stood, one foot on a newly laid kerb, the other on the wet asphalt of the roadway. His pack was back on his back, his poncho caught the wind and billowed: the spinnaker for a solo yacht on a round-the-life race.

Bill leaned across and addressed him through the lowered passenger-door window. 'And as for the dosh – don't worry about it. I hope there's a couple of quid left over – you'll need some oil for the racing tonight –' Bill heard Mark try and cut across this final imprecation, but the big car was already rolling, and the blunt hand was already circling, and the bloodshot eyes were already checking, and the bored ears were already adjusting to the thrum of bass.

In the rearview mirror Bill saw Mark jerk the pack into a more comfortable position and head towards the station entrance. It wasn't until he was back on the M74 and rolling south, at speed, that Bill considered what it might have been that the hitchhiker was trying to say.

Food, who needed it? It just made you shit more on these sedentary migrations. Best not to bother. Best not to think about rest either. Those signs that whip by in the already hazy periphery of vision:

T...A...K...E......A......B...R...E...A...K...
T...I...R...E...D...N...E...S...S......K...I...L...L...S.

And what would rest be like anyway? Bill had tried that option, sagged across the wheel like a human air bag, in some forlorn service-station car-park. Or Welcomed Inn to seven hours of thrashing in thin duvets, then tea-making in the chill dawn, rearranging individual plastic cups of UHT milk on a little ledge, before putting on his pants, his jacket, driving again.

No, stopping was out of the question – there had already been an unscheduled halt at Mrs McRae's. But that was only to be expected . . . by the time the *Ola* got into Scrabster it had already been eleven . . . and there was no point in pushing on with that savage headache . . . or that savage tremor. Did he perhaps have a savage tremor now? Bill held one hand free of the steering wheel and watched its level, relative to the horizon of the windscreen itself, which, as he honed in on it, gulped up a hundred metres of road and a chunk of hillside. No, no tremor in particular. Bill groped for a couple more Pro-Plus pills in his jacket pocket. He lit another cigarette. He boosted his speed, overtaking a lorry, undertaking a panel van in the fast lane, ratcheting the big car up to ninety-five as he hovered back to within sideswiping distance of the central barrier. Strip-the-steel-willow!

Bill liked this section of the drive. To have slipped away from Glasgow so surely, and now to bucket down Clydesdale with the last of the afternoon sun bouncing over his shoulder, and the hills of the Ettrick Forest opening up to the south-west. It was also an entrance to another hinterland – the Borders – and suitable that night should meet day here as well.

But, Christ! Bill was tired. And ever since he'd dropped the hitchhiker in Motherwell, dropped him back into his own particular sink of anonymity, he had felt troubled. It was a mistake to have picked up the hitchhiker. *He* certainly hadn't appreciated the gesture. No, not a gesture – actually an *altruistic act.* Or was it that the hitchhiker had got his measure all too well? He wasn't that stupid. He had been genuinely affronted by the inquisition, resolved to give nothing real at all – spun Bill a line. 'Genuinely affronted'! What an asinine expression. Bill laughed at the asininity and then tried to surf a little more on his own hilarity. He tried to imagine that he was high – and lighthearted. It didn't work.

Darkness was welling up from the road; to the west it flowed from the valleys. Bill switched the lights back on to full beam. I'll be cosy in my little light tunnel, he joked. He had stopped at Mrs McRae's because he was sick with drink. He had more or less gone up to Orkney this time because he was sick with drink. He didn't like doing locums – he couldn't hold any other kind of job down. Not any more. He knew what genuinely affronted him – Bill did. What genuinely affronted him was the vigour of his fingernails. They kept on growing despite everything. Even now, the pallid fingers wrapped around the steering wheel each had their own dear little crescent of new life – and new dirt. Only something as dumb as a fingernail could go on growing in this hellish environment. Take skin, for example. Take the skin on Bill's ankles – Bill had. Bill had picked and plucked and even strummed the ulcerating skin on his ankles, and it had rewarded him by generously suppurating. That was skin for you – very intelligent stuff. Didn't go on growing after death, like hair or nails.

The hitchhiker had had this information encoded in his own lousy, drink-raddled body. In that they were alike – in that and perhaps a lot else as well. Bill thought of how workable, how trustworthy, his denial of his own drink problem usually was. It was like a handy, movable bulwark that he could position in front of any one of the dark corridors leading away from his self-awareness. The hitchhiker – Bill shouldn't have picked him up. He'd broken the rhythm of the journey; he'd made Bill late. He'd fucked with the bulwarks. Ha! Late for his own funeral. No – his own *cremation.* In Hoop Lane, opposite the Express Dairy. When Bill was young he thought that everyone had died here, that everyone was burnt here – at Golders Green Crematorium – their essence disappearing in the form of charcoal smoke issuing from a red-brick tower, into a grey sky. Now Bill knew he had been right.

And now, in the gathering gloom, Bill felt all pushed out of shape. His method of dealing with himself depended on carefully negotiated transitions from being alone to being among others. Hence Mrs McRae – who didn't, of course, count. Hence also Anthony Bohm, who was no threat to anyone; least of all – with his swollen liver more or less *propped* on the bar – to Bill, or any other physic-fond physician for that matter.

The encounter with the hitchhiker had turned Bill about. He had mentally castigated the hitchhiker for his abusive relationships – but what constituted such an abuse? He knew what constituted such an abuse. The 3 a.m. rows that cranked up and then cranked down and then cranked up again; the siren song of emotional fracture. He knew all about them, just as he had full cognisance of the serial, parallel monogamist's lifestyle. No, no socialese, call a fucking spade a spade. He fucked around – like a spade. Grasped his haft and planted it where he would. At the Felliniesque conversion of Dunrobin Castle it wouldn't simply be a case of wassailing whores causing trouble – the whole emotional Utopia, the whole fantasy of inclusion was just that – a fantasy.

Bill's life was now – and he realised this groping in the dark for the car bottle, as the big saloon whipped through the roundabout and on to the A74 – based, established on exclusion. Every hysterical evasion, every late-night session rubbing up the whisky bottle, until Mr Blubby, the drunken genie, emerged – it was all coming back to him. He took a slug, and in his hurry to get the bottle up and down without leaving go of the wheel, managed to slop several measures on to his chest. He was tired – and yes, perhaps it would be worth admitting it to himself – just a little drunk.

No time to consider that now. Heads down, no nonsense, mindless boogie. Hone in on the music – ignore the background screech of the Furies, who pursued him: 'Bill! Bill! Why did you do it/say it/go there/lie/come back/treat me like this!' He pumped up the CD. He bit down on another caffeine lozenge, hoping the bitterness alone might make him alert. It wasn't working. The road was doubly blurred. He rubbed one ulcerated shin against the other. He chomped the inside of his cheek. He pinched the fat on the inside of his thighs with his unabashed fingernails. Eventually he took to slapping himself. Big, open-handed clouts. First one with the left, then one with the right. Left to left and right to right. Each blow gave him a few seconds of clarity, another hundred metres of onrushing progress.

And as the big car bisected the night, drumming past Lockerbie, ignoring the blue signs that blazoned: Carlyle's Birthplace, and eventually gaining the M6 – which was lit for its first few miles, a tarmac chute – Bill gutted the carcass of his own life. He pulled out the entrails of neglect, and the gall bladder of resentment; he removed the engorged liver of indulgence, and excised the kidneys of cynicism. He fumbled in the cavities of his body for his heart – but couldn't find it.

The big car plunged on. No longer a chimera, a meld between man and machine, but merely a machine, with a ghost loose in it somewhere. Desperately Bill shuffled his pack of shiny memories, of *al fresco* lovemaking, of dramatic hill scenery, of . . . his son. Who would be what – around five now. Not very clever that. Not clever at all – to have not seen your own child for two years. Three years. It had been three years.

That had been the shabbiest of the accusations he had laid against the hitchhiker – the one of neglect. Bill knew all about neglect. He knew all about unanswered phone calls, crumpled-up letters, torn postcards. People said they didn't want children because they didn't want the responsibility. But if you didn't take responsibility for them – how could you have it for yourself?

About forty minutes later, at Shap in the Lake District, at the point where the M6 really did begin to feel as if it were plunging inexorably downhill, down to the south, down to London, the ghost that was piloting the machine took a long final look in the rearview mirror, before lazily circling the steering wheel to the left and turning into an inexistent layby.

Design Faults in the Volvo 760 Turbo: A Manual

'. . . bearing in mind the fact that everyone hides the truth in matters of sex . . .'

—SIGMUND FREUD,
'My Views on the Part Played by Sexuality in the Aetiology of the Neuroses'

1. Instruments and Controls

Welcome to the terrifyingly tiny world of the urban adulterer. Bill Bywater has been snogging with a woman called Serena. Giving and receiving as much tongue as possible – exactly at the point where Sussex Gardens terminate, and the streams of traffic whip around the dusty triangular enclosure of trees and grass, before peeling away in the direction of Hyde Park, or Paddington, or the M40.

Bill has been snogging – and the adolescent term is quite appropriate here – in a way he remembers from youth. Not that the palpings of lip-on-lip, tongue-on-lip, and tongue-on-tongue have been any less accomplished, or plosively erotic, than we have come to expect from the man. It's just that Serena has recently had an operation on a benign cyst in her cheek. Bit of Lidocaine. Slit and suck – two stitches. Bosh-bosh. 'Perhaps it would be wise' – the surgeon had said, admiring the creamy skin of her cleavage, the standing into being of her ever-so-slightly large breasts – 'if you were to avoid using your mouth for anything much besides eating over the next week or so?'

He was right to make this statement interrogative – almost verging on the rhetorical, because Serena hardly uses her mouth for eating at all, preferring dietary supplements and cocaine to get by on. Serena used to be an 'it' girl – but now she's 'that' woman. A socialite – she went to a finishing school in Switzerland where they taught her to fellate. She'd set her cap at Bill months ago. Not that he wasn't ripe for it.

Serena says, 'I've had a small operation on my cheek . . .' The eyelashes perturb the polluted air, monoxide and burnt rubber. 'Try and be gentle with this side –' She caresses her own elastoplasted cheek. Their bodies marry. Her thighs part slightly to receive the buttressing of his thigh. Her lips begin to worry at his mouth – so adept Bill wonders if they might be prehensile. He allows his hands to link in the region of her coccyx. A thumb lazily traces the rivulets and curves between her arse and the small of her back. She moans into his mouth. The traffic groans into his ear. He concentrates on stimulating the side of her which isn't numb.

As he is snogging, Bill is acutely aware of the time: 6.30 p.m.; the place: Sussex Gardens, W2; and the implied logistics: his wife, Vanessa, cycles home every evening along Sussex Gardens, at more or less this time. It is not unlikely that Vanessa will see Bill snogging with Serena, because Bill is – he acknowledges with a spurt of dread – at least sixty feet high. He bestrides the two lanes of bumpy tarmac, his crotch forming a blue denim underpass for the rumbling traffic. Vanessa will be able to see him – this Colossus of Roads – the very instant she jolts across the intersection of the Edgware Road, and commences pedalling down Sussex Gardens.

Caught bang to rights, caught snogging with this slapper . . . His only defence, the fact that she's a little dolly of a thing compared to him. He's holding her aloft in one hand, clutching her wiggling torso to his huge, bristly cheek. He's having to be so damn gentle, tasting with his forty-inch tongue the sweetness of her two-inch bud. Her white satin shift dress has ridden up over her hips. She isn't wearing any tights – her pants are white, with an embroidered panel over her pubis.

'Bill!' Vanessa shouts up from below – she's ramming her front tyre against his foot, the knobble of uncomfortable bone protruding above the edge of his moccasins. 'Bill – what are you doing!?'

'Doing?' He squints down at her, as if she's caught him in an inconsequential reverie – stagnantly considering the cost-effectiveness of double glazing, or fully comprehensive insurance. 'Doing?' He looks at the writhing, half-stripped woman in his hand, and then sets her down, gingerly, on the far side of the road from his wife. 'Oh *her*, or rather – *this.* It's just a doll, my love – you can't possibly be jealous of a *doll.*'

Couldn't be jealous of a doll, but might well be jealous of Serena who is not only a doll, but who has also, predictably, been a model. Bill, feeling the laser beams of his wife's gaze burning through buildings, fences, filing cabinets, people, had broken the embrace – which was getting nowhere. Or rather, it was getting somewhere only too fast. What could he do with Serena, short of hiring a room in the Lancaster Hotel for half an hour? No, that would show up on his credit card statement. They were too old for Hyde Park bushes, and the Volvo 760 Turbo was out of the question on account of various design faults.

Serena had been having a session with her therapist, who had his consulting rooms on Sussex Gardens. Bill had arranged to meet her by her car. A metal rendezvous. Serena had a Westminster permit – Bill didn't. He couldn't find a meter for aeons – he imagined her growing old, her face wizening, an old apple on a draining board. When he did eventually find a space – by the needle exchange Portakabin on South Wharf Road – he had neither pound coins nor twenty-pence pieces. He wanted to ejaculate and die – simultaneously. He stopped one, two, three passers-by – got enough to pay for twenty minutes' snogging. Park up the Volvo – and grab a vulva. Pay for space – space to live.

The minutes tick away in her wounded mouth. Until – confident that at any minute he'll get a ticket – Bill breaks from Serena. 'Call!' they call to each other as he staggers back across the road and disappears in the direction of Paddington Station.

Not that he's out of danger yet. Bill starts up the Volvo and savours its clicking, ticking and peeping into life. But when he pulls away he realises – given that he has absolutely no justification for being in this part of London, on this day, at this time – that the car is grotesquely elongated. When he turns right out of London Street and on to Sussex Gardens, the back end of the vehicle is still in Praed Street. When he reaches the lights on the corner of Westbourne Street, his tail end is still blocking the last set of lights, causing traffic in all four directions to back up, and engendering a healthy tirade of horn-accompanied imprecations: 'Youuuu fuuuucking waaaanker!'

Deciding that the only way he can escape detection – given that he's driving an eighty-foot-long vehicle – is to head for the Westway flyover, Bill turns right. As he circles the triangular enclosure where he snogged with Serena, he is appalled to see that the back end of the Volvo is passing by on the other side. He looks through the rear windows of his own car and can see sweet wrappers and medical journals scattered around on the back seat. Jesus! Astonishing how ductile these Volvo chassis are – they know what they're about over there at the Kalmar Plant. Know what they're about when it comes to building an eighty-foot extrudomobile like this, that can be seen clearly from a mile away . . .

Bill Bywater, feeling the Volvo concertina back to its normal length, as he gains the anonymity of the motorway flyover, scrabbles in the breast pocket of his shirt for a cigarette. He lights it with a disposable gas lighter. The dash lighter has long since gone. Bill airily lit a fag with it a year or so ago, waved it gently in the air, and then threw it out the car window. One of the design faults – although hardly limited to the Volvo 760 Turbo – was this lack of a tether.

Another was the ashtray itself. This was accommodated neatly enough, in the central housing of the dash, but it was impossible to pull the tray out at all unless the shift was in drive; and fully out only if it was in first gear. The implications of this stagger Bill anew as he struggles to insinuate his ash-tipped fag into the small gap. Could it be that the car *cognoscenti* at Kalmar intended this as an anti-smoking measure? It hardly made sense. For the ashtray couldn't be opened at all when the shift was in park – implying that you should only smoke, and even empty the ashtray, when the car was in motion.

The Volvo is passing Ladbroke Grove tube station, doing around seventy. Bill can see commuters tramping the platform. And anyway – even if the operation was technically difficult – he did at least know how to empty the ashtray. The manual expressed it quite succinctly: 'Empty ashtrays by pulling out to the limit and pressing down the tongue.'

Bill was masterful at this – he could even avoid the cyst.

2. Body and Interior

Bill has arranged to meet Serena at a pub in Maida Vale. It's a barn of a gaff on Cunningham Place – so prosaic it might even be called The

Cunningham. It's the night of a vital World Cup qualifier for England, and the city soup is being insistently thickened by cars, as the spectators head for their home terraces. The driving is stop-start – and so is the parking. Eventually, he finds a tight space on Hamilton Terrace. He cuts in well enough the first time, but the space is so confined that he has to turn the steering wheel in the other direction, then back, then reverse again, each time gaining just a few inches more of the precious, temporary possession.

With each rotation the power steering 'Eeeeeeyouuuus' – a fluid, pleasurable kind of whine; and with each dab on brake, or plunge on accelerator, the rubber limbs buck, receiving pressure or its release. 'In-Glands! In-Glands! In-Glands!' his pulse chants in his temples. Bill feels exposed – in this act of taking the space; worries that he may be observed, censured. When he's finally got himself and the car properly berthed – no more than six inches to front and aft – he lunges out the door, giddy in the hot, sappy, fume-tangy evening air. But there's nothing; only an old woman with secateurs in a front garden; the roar of traffic from the Edgware Road; a Tourettic man – gnome-like with a spade of grey beard – who high-steps it over the domed camber of the road, legs smiting his chest, whilst he expels a series of sharp 'Papp-papp-papp!' sounds.

Bill is reassured. In a London uncaring enough to ignore such blatancy – the Tourettic looking as if he were on a run-up to jumping clear of his own nervous system – Bill's own peccadilloes *not even consummated, as yet*, can hardly be of any interest at all. Still, it takes him five minutes of walking up the road, patting his pockets, retracing his steps to see if he has forgotten anything, or dropped anything, or illegally parked the car – only too easy to do in a city where the controls of adjoining zones are radically different – before he resigns himself to the concrete reality of the rendezvous. He is going to meet Serena – this time he might fuck her.

Serena is sitting on one of the four trestle-table-and-bench combinations that occupy the dirty oblong of paving in between The Cunningham itself, and the low brick wall that borders it. A very believable terrace – for London. There are metal ashtrays with beer spilt into them, there are crisp packets wedged in the tabletop cracks, there are sunshades poking through two of these tabletops. One advertises

Martini – the other is in tatters. The compression of boozing bodies within the cavernous boozer is already considerable; the baying of the clientele and the baying of the Wembley crowd – relayed by a giant-screen television suspended from the ceiling – are echoing one another. The beery exhalations surge from the double doors of the pub; which are propped back, so as to allow the T-shirted multi-lung to draw in another great gulp of exhausted air.

Bill considers that this rendezvous is taking place within a spatial gap – the Edgware Road/Maida Vale hinterland – and, more importantly, a temporal one. 'I can't stand all this nationalist sporting triumphalism' – he has been priming Vanessa the five days since he avoided Serena's cyst – 'it's going to reach a hideous climax . . . And then what – when they lose there'll be a national depression for days. I can't stand it. I want to opt out.'

Of course, what Bill really wants to opt out of is any situation of *bonhomie*, of excitation, that might embrace them – and tighten up the vice of fidelity. Bill has been working on his dissatisfactions with Vanessa for weeks now – building up a comprehensive dossier of her awfulness. Without this adulterers' manifesto Bill knows he'll be incapable of being remotely serene – with Serena. It would only take one embrace, one shared apprehension, for him to have to abandon his plans. Therefore, why not excise this possibility *and* use the time available.

'Shit! It's all shit!' he had cried an hour or so before. 'I can't stand it – I'm off out. I've got to find somewhere – anywhere where nobody's concerned about this fucking football match!' He then grabbed his car keys from the hall table, performed an uninteresting arabesque in the process of snatching up the CD face-off and his mobile phone, before slamming the door and sprinting off up the garden path. Vanessa, who was sat marking spelling tests, wondered what the hell her husband was on about – she wasn't remotely interested in the football international; and their two-year-old son was, somewhat proleptically, already at his grandmother's.

'Hi!' says Serena – who cares nothing for Bill's predicament, who indeed positively savours it. 'I thought you wouldn't make it.'

'Traffic – parking.' He fobs her off with his key fob. 'Have you got a drink?' She downs the rest of her sea breeze and downs the glass.

'No.'

He shuttles in and out of the bar over the next half-hour. Serena has four more sea breezes – a nicely paradoxical drink for this landlocked Saragossa. Bill struggles to keep his alcohol intake down; tonight has undoubtedly seen the inception of a special Metropolitan Police Task Force to deal with adulterous drunk drivers. Every time he thinks she isn't looking – he checks his watch. The seconds are ticking by towards half-time. In the meantime they edge closer as well.

Serena is wearing a black suede miniskirt. It has six brass buttons to fasten it at the front – but the three bottom ones are undone. Serena is wearing a cream silk blouse and no bra. Serena never wears tights in summer – her legs are too good. Each time she leans forward Bill sucks her nipples; each time she leans back he runs his bent-back index finger up the front of her pants. Not.

Bill dives into the public bar of The Cunningham and edges through the crowd of passive dribblers. 'Awwwww!' they cry – awed by some feat of failure. It takes several such 'awws' and accompanying pokes in the ribs for Bill to gain the far side of the public bar, and the stairs down to the toilets. In the toilet he releases the trap of his flies and the grey hound of penis comes out frothing. Painful – peeing with an erection – Bill has to force himself into alarming postures in order to lend his urine to the giant ceramic ear. While he's doing this he reflects on the paradoxical sense of control offered by reckless driving.

That's what he needs – to get Serena away from the pub, get her in the Volvo, take her for a spin. There's a vanity mirror set into the passenger-seat sunshade – she'll like that. And there'll be no chance of being observed by anyone who knows either of them – or Bill's wife. Even if Bill's wife were to suddenly manifest herself in the Volvo – Serena could hide in the glove compartment, as any other adulterer might hide in a cupboard. She really was a doll.

3. Starting and Driving

It takes the same brake shoe-shuffle to extract the Volvo (overall length four metres and seventy-nine centimetres) from the parking space. Bill, as he circles the steering wheel back and forth, wishes he were coming rather than going – because he could then make some crack to Serena, analogise the parking space and *her* space.

They pop up on to the crown of Hamilton Terrace and Bill turns the big car to the north. He is conscious of Serena on the seat beside him, her thighs slightly parted, her trunk slightly tilted in his direction, a tip of pink tongue between her scarlet lips. 'How's the cyst?' he forays – they have yet to snog.

'Better!' she laughs, a horrible, expensive, phone-your-divorce-lawyer kind of laugh. She is – Bill reflects – an awful, venal, unprincipled and deeply alluring woman.

Bill turns right into Hall Road and then left into Abbey Road. He's driving fast – the decision to leave the pub had been mutual. He had said, 'It's getting insane in there – looks like they'll be going to a penalty shoot-out. Let's get out of here, go somewhere where there's neither sight nor sound of football, hmm?' And she had said, 'If you like.'

The streets are emptied of traffic – the whole city is inside, watching the match. Bill banks to the right, to the left, he feels the weight of the car shift beneath him like a body. He concentrates on the whine of the transmission and the thrum of the engine. He pokes at the CD and a track with a suitably heavy bass line begins to underscore the tense atmosphere in the car. 'Drive smoothly, avoid fast starts, hard cornering and heavy braking . . .' What the hell do they think anyone wants a Volvo 760 Turbo for, if, as the manual suggests above, it's inadvisable to drive the car with any alacrity?

At Kalmar – where Bill knows from his careful reading of the manual, the Volvo 760 Turbo is built by dedicated teams of workers, rather than by an unconscious and alienated assembly line – they presumably have no need of the car's maximal performance capability. In the sexually tolerant atmosphere of Sweden, the Volvo has evolved as a highly safe vehicle in which to transport the promiscuous. If you're about to start an affair with a fellow worker at the Plant, you simply say to your wife, 'Bibi, I've decided that I must make love to Liv. I shall take the estate today – and a clean duvet!' Whereupon she replies, 'Of course, Ingmar, but remember, "Protective bags should be used to avoid soiling the upholstery" . . .'

'You seem preoccupied?' Bill wouldn't have believed that anyone could actually say this whilst toying with her silken *décolletage* – but Serena just has.

'Mmm . . . s'pose so, work, y'know –'

'Yes! Your work.' Serena stirs her languor into an animated whirl. 'What's it like being a shrink? Have you got any really weird, disturbed patients? D'jew think I'm crazy?'

Bill tilts the car up on to Fitzjohn's Avenue before replying, 'Which of those questions do you want me to answer first?'

'Oh, the last, I suppose . . .'

Christ! The woman knows how to toy – she's a world-class toyer. 'Why on earth do you imagine that you're crazy?'

Serena takes her time answering. She chafes her thighs together so slowly that Bill cannot forbear from imagining the minute accommodations of flesh, hair and membrane that are going on behind the three-buttoned curtain covering her lap. Eventually, when they are level with Lindy's Pâtisserie on Heath Street, she comes back with, 'Bluntly, I find I have to have a really good orgasm every day,' and gives him an amazing smile, her teeth so white and vulpine, her gums so pink.

Bill feels the sweat burst from his armpits like spray from a shower fitment. He grips the wheel so tightly that as the Volvo bucks across the junction with Hampstead High Street, he feels he might wrench it clear off and twist the O of metal, foam and plastic into an involved pretzel shape. Kerrist! He's thinking about adultery in Hampstead – it's gone this far, he keens inside; my life has plunged into a prosaic – prolix even – vanishing point.

At Whitestone Pond they stop in order to allow a man with black-and-white striped trousers to traverse the zebra crossing. Serena doesn't appear to notice this – but Bill does. Bill finds he is noticing everything: the golden micro-fleece on the nape of Serena's neck; a model yacht on the pond, tacking neatly around a floating Coke can; to the right of the road the Heath, and beyond it, collapsing waves of concrete and glass and brick and steel – maritime London. 'When you say "a really good orgasm" ' – Bill chooses her words carefully – 'do you mean good in a moral sense?'

Serena breaks into trills and even frills of laughter – if that's possible. 'Tee-hee-hee, oh no – not at all! *I* mean a ripping, snorting, tooth-clashing, thoroughly cathartic orgasm, one that makes me feel as if every individual nerve ending has climaxed. *That* kind of good orgasm.'

'Oh, that kind.' Bill feels certain he's damaged the turbo unit. He habitually does everything to the Volvo's engine that – according to the manual – he shouldn't. He races it immediately after starting, before the cold oil has had a chance to reach all the lubricating points. Worse than that, the engine has also been turned off when the turbocharger was at high speed – with the risk of seizing or heat damage – although, admittedly it wasn't Bill who'd done it.

It was Vanessa. She managed to lean right across Bill, tear the keys out of the ignition and throw them out the window of the car and clear over the parapet of the Westway, as the Volvo was ploughing along it at seventy. When they had coasted to a halt, Vanessa threw herself out as well. No one likes to be made a fool of.

Bill parks the car in the small car-park off Hampstead Lane, diagonally opposite to Compton Avenue. They walk out on to the Heath. A light breeze is blowing up here and within seconds it's dried their sweaty brows, cooled their sweaty bodies. They embrace and Bill feels Serena's hair being blown about his chops. It's the closest he's ever been, he realises, to a shampoo commercial.

They walk on, stopping every few yards for more snogging and groping. Bill is certain he has never had a more turgid erection in his life. If he flung himself forward on to the macadamised path, his resilient member would simply bounce him back up again. If he took his trousers off and scampered across the grass he would, to all intents and purposes, be indistinguishable from the famous statuette of Priapus, his penis as large and curved as a bow. Good orgasm, ha! Great orgasm, more like.

On top of Parliament Hill they take their bodies to a bench that faces out over the city, and sit them there to listen to its peculiar silence. From the direction of Gospel Oak a man comes running up the hill. Even from three hundred yards away Bill can see that he's wearing an England football shirt. The man is clearly in some distress; as he nears Bill becomes aware of labouring breath and pumping arms. He comes up to them like someone about to deliver news of a bad naval defeat by the Persians. But instead of collapsing he props himself against their bench saying, 'Iss gone to penalty shoot-outs – I couldn't cope any more.'

He's a small plump man, with a bald pate fringed by a neat horseshoe of grey hair. Clearly football is his life. 'I got meself this fucking big Havana – to celebrate wiv.' He displays the stogie to them, clamped in his humid paw. 'But now I dunno, I dunno, I can't cope –'

'We came here to get away from the football,' says Serena.

'Me too, me too,' the man puffs back.

'Actually' – Bill takes a certain delight in this savage betrayal – 'I bet we'll be able to hear the result from up here.' On cue there's an enormous roar from the city below. 'There we go, that was one goal.'

The three of them wait for two minutes, then there's a second eruption of roaring from the metropolis. They wait another two minutes and . . . nothing. Worse than nothing – a negative roar, a sonic vacuum in which a roar should have been. 'They've missed one . . . the fuckers . . . they've missed one . . .' The little man is destroyed, ripped asunder. He grinds the Havana into the grass with his training shoe, then he heads off back down the hill.

Five minutes later Bill and Serena are rutting in a copse.

4. Wheel and Tyres

It is four days later and Bill Bywater sits at the desk which occupies most of the half-landing in his Putney house. Vanessa likes to be by the river; Bill rather wishes she was in it. Bill thinks it suitable that his study should occupy this in-between place, neither up nor down, because he has an in-between kind of psyche – especially at the moment. This is now the terrifyingly tiny house of the urban adulterer and Bill moves about it with incredible subtlety, acutely aware that every movement – from now on and for the rest of his natural life – will constitute a potential, further violation.

Bill sits at the desk and contemplates the Volvo 760 Owner's Manual for the year 1988 – perversely enough the year of his marriage. He has reached the section entitled 'Wheels and Tyres'. Bill smiles manically – he's lost his grip – and reaches for the Tipp-Ex. On the opposing page there's a neat pen-and-wash drawing of a 1957 Volvo Amazon, captioned accordingly. With great deliberation Bill applies the little brush with its clot of liquid paper to the word 'Volvo' and smiles, satisfied by its deletion. It is approximately the hundredth instance of the word that he has dealt with, and soon the manual will become an opaque text, the arcanum of a vanished religion.

As he leafs back through the pages, Bill is deeply satisfied by the small white lozenges of Tipp-Ex smattering them. They look like the results of pin-point accurate ejaculations. Bill, like Freud, has never repudiated or abandoned the importance of sexuality and infantilism, and with this unusual action he is attempting to reorient his sexuality through infantile handiwork. Bill is working hard to convince himself that by eradicating the word 'Volvo' from the manual, he will also annul his obsession with Serena's vulva, which has got quite out of hand.

In the copse she made Bill take off all of his clothes – and all of her own. At last his hands got to go on stage and open her curtain skirt. He shivered despite the summer heat and the close, dusty rot of desiccated shrubbery. 'What's the problem?' she laughed at him, cupping her own breasts, stimulating her own nipples. 'No point in worrying about the cops – we're in it already.' Their clothing made an inadequate stage for the performance that ensued. Bill could never have guessed that such a sexual Socrates would prove so satisfied a pig; she snorted and truffled in the musty compost. They had fucked five times since – top 'n' tailing each other at the top 'n' tail of each day.

Again and again Bill scans the preamble to the section, which admonishes him to 'Read the following pages carefully', but his eyes keep sliding down to the subheading 'Special Rims', what can it mean? On page 67 there are directions for changing wheels, and a photograph of a young woman doing just that. The caption reads: 'Stand next to body.' Bill finds this distracting, but not as much as he does the boldface line further down the page which reads: **'Make sure that the arm is lodged well in the attachment.'**

Bill sighs and throws down the Tipp-Ex brush. It's no good, it's not working. Instead of the deletion of the word 'Volvo' cancelling out thoughts of Serena's vulva, it's enhancing them. The firm, warm, lubricious embrace of living leather; the smell of saliva and cigarette smoke; the twitter and peep of the CD – a soundtrack for orgasm. Perhaps, Bill thinks, perhaps if I get to the very root of this I'll do better. Perhaps if I delete the word 'Volvo' from the car itself it will do the trick?

Serena has mastered a trick. She can apply ever so slight pressure to

Bill's indicator levers and she can effortlessly flick his shift into drive. Serena has undoubtedly read and absorbed the manual. Bill wouldn't be at all surprised to learn that she knew exactly how to grease the nipple on the retractable-type towing bracket. That's the sort of woman she is, as at home in a family car like the Volvo 760, as she would be in a sportier model.

Bill crouches by the radiator grille. The tarmac is so warm on this summer evening that his feet subside a little into the roadway. In his right hand Bill holds a pot of Humbrol metal paint, in his left a brush. He is carefully painting out the word 'Volvo' on the maker's badge of the car. He hears a riffle of rubber wheels and the fluting of a toddler, and turns to see that Vanessa has come up beside him, pushing their son in his buggy.

'Bill' – how can a voice be so cram-packed with wry irony (or 'wife-ronry' as Bill awkwardly compounds it – to himself) – 'what on earth are you doing?'

'Whaddya' think?' he snaps.

'I don't know – that's why I asked.' The toddler's eyes are round with anxiety; his life is already characterised by these tonal conflicts between giants, Gog and Magog smiting his Fischer-Price bell.

'I'm getting rid of all the instances of the word "Volvo" on this fucking car – that's what I'm doing.'

'Dada said the F word.' The toddler doesn't lisp – his voice is high and precise.

'Dada wants to rid himself of the F word,' Vanessa pronounces sententiously.

'How true, how true . . .' Bill mutters.

When the buggy and its cargo have disappeared inside the house Bill straightens up; he has arranged to meet Serena in the pub in St John's Wood, and more importantly – he's covered. He holds a seminar at the Middlesex Hospital every Wednesday evening at this time, so Vanessa won't be curious about his absence. Bill stashes the paint and brush in the cardboard box of car impedimenta that he keeps in the boot of the ex-Volvo. He strolls up the path and opening the front door with his key shouts into the crack, 'I'm off!' and at the same time snatches up the CD face-off, his mobile and a sheaf of lecture notes he has to drop off for Sunil Rahman – who is giving the seminar. To Vanessa, who is feeding the toddler in the kitchen, this irruption of sound is just that – an odd kind of effect, as of a train window being opened while passing through a tunnel at speed.

In the ex-Volvo, waiting at the lights by Putney Bridge, Bill dickers with the servos that alter the angle and rake of the driver's seat. One of the servos is on the blink, and if he presses the button too much the seat tilts forward and to the left, threatening to deposit him face down, dangling over the steering wheel, in a posture all too reminiscent of how Bill imagines a suicide would end up after making with a section of hose and watering the interior of the ex-Volvo with exhaust fumes. 'Jesus!' he exclaims out loud as the lights change. 'I've got to stop this!'

Proceeding up Fulham Palace Road Bill faffs around with nodulous buttons until he manages to get Serena's number. He clutches the purring instrument to his ear and hears her recorded pout. When the time comes he leaves a plaint in place of himself: can't make it, lecture, car trouble . . . later. This isn't, of course, the first time that Bill's bailed out of this kind of situation, nor, he suspects, will it be the last.

The lecture notes dropped in reception at the hospital, Bill wheels the big car up on to the Westway and heads out of town. There's only one place for him now, Thame, and only one person he can speak to, Dave Adler, proprietor of the Thame Motor Centre – Repairs and Bodywork Our Speciality. Dave has worked on Bill's Volvo for many years now – ever since he gave up psychiatry. Dave sees no intrinsic design faults in the Volvo 760 Turbo itself, rather he is inclined to locate them in the driver.

Conversations between the two men usually go something like this:

Dr Bill Bywater: Dave? It's Bill.

Dr Dave Adler: Yeah.

Dr BB: There seems to be something wrong with the transmission . . .

Dr DA: Yeah.

Dr BB: The car isn't changing up smoothly, it sort of over-revs and then – well, *surges*.

Dr DA: Have you checked the automatic transmission fluid?

Invariably Bill hasn't checked it, or the windscreen reservoir, or the oil, or the brake fluid, or indeed any of the seething, bubbling liquids that course through the car's blocky body. This will provide Dave Adler with an entrée for a sneer about how ridiculously cavalier Bill is about his car, and how if he would only pay attention to maintenance he wouldn't run into this trouble.

While Bill smiles to himself at the thought of the unscheduled lecture he will receive this evening when he turns up in Thame, the ex-Volvo rumbles down off the flyover and heads west into the soft heart of Britain.

Forty minutes later the car rolls to a halt in a dusty lane that snakes away from the market square of the small Oxfordshire town. The high wooden doors of Dave Adler's garage are shut and chained. Dangling from the hasp of the lock is a peculiar sign which Dave uses in lieu of a more conventional one. The sign reads:

'BEARING IN MIND THE FACT THAT EVERYONE HIDES THE TRUTH IN MATTERS OF SEX – WE'RE CLOSED.'

Bill guffaws to himself, albeit a little wearily.

Meanwhile, in Putney, Dave Adler lowers himself carefully into the inspection pit of the Bywaters' marital bed. He has the necessary equipment and he's intent on giving Vanessa Bywater's chassis a really thorough servicing. As far as Dave Adler is concerned a car is a means of transport, nothing more and nothing less.

The Nonce Prize

1.

Danny and Tembe were standing in the kitchen of their house on Leopold Road, Harlesden, northwest London. It was a cold morning in early November, and an old length of plastic clothesline was thwacking against the window as the wind whipped it about. The brothers were cooking up some crack cocaine; Danny worked the stove while Tembe handled the portions of bicarb and powder. On the kitchen table a deconstructed boom box – the CD unit, speakers and controls unhoused, connected only by a ganglion of cabling – was playing tinny-sounding drum 'n bass.

Tembe had heard an item of gossip when he went to buy the powder off the Irishman in Shepherd's Bush three hours before, gossip he was now hot to impart. 'Yeah-yeah-yeah,' he said, 'sheeit! Those fuckers jus' sat in the fuckin' house an' waited for the punters to come along –'

'Issat the troof?' Danny cut in, but not like he really cared.

'I'm telling you so. The filth were smart, see, they come in an' do the house at aroun' eleven in the morning – like the only fuckin' down time in the twenty-four. Bruno and Mags was washing up an oz in the kitchen – Sacks was crashed out with some bint in the front room. They got one of them jackhammer things, takes the fuckin' door to pieces, man, an' then they come in with flak jackets and fuckin' *guns*, man, like they've got the fuckin' tactical whatsit unit out for this one –'

'Tactical firearms unit,' Danny snapped, 'thass what they call it – but anyways, wasn't Bruno tooled?'

'Yeah – and some. The blud claat had a fuckin' Saturday night special, .22 some motherfucker built from a fuckin' starting pistol. You recall I tol' you that Bruno shot that nigger Gance and the bullet bounced off his fuckin' rib – that was this shooter. Anyways he didn't have no time nor nuffin' for that cos' they was on 'im in seconds, gave him a good pasting, nicked his fuckin' stash, nicked about a grand he had in cash, an' then tol' 'im he had to front it up while they nicked all the fuckin' punters.'

'And did he?'

'Yeah, man. Solid. He had no choice. He sat there by the fuckin' door an' greeted them all in. Jus' imagine it, man, you fink you're goin' to score a nice rock, you're all didgy about it, all worked up an' that, pumping, right, an' you get to the fuckin' door, in a right state, only to get fuckin' nicked! Silly motherfuckers! The filth got twenty of them – that's that Bruno out of the fuckin' crack business –' and Tembe, no longer able to contain himself at the thought of this busted crack house, like a ship of fools grounded off the All Saints Road, burst into peals of unrestrained laughter; a laughter that to Danny's over-sensitive ears sounded peculiarly harsh and insistent.

To cut the flow Danny waved the bottle he'd been cooking the crack up in in front of Tembe's face. 'Lissen,' Danny said, 'now you've tol' me hows about I get to have my fuckin' get up an' that – yeah?'

'Yeah, all right, no fussin', yeah. Keep it mellow like . . .' Tembe fumbled around in the mound of crack that sat drying on a wad of kitchen towelling, his finger picked a peck and he passed it over. 'There you go – thass at least three hits, bro', get it down you an' then fuck off an' that.' Danny wasn't paying any attention to this, he'd already fumbled out his stem from where he kept it, tucked in the top of his right boot, and was crumbling a pinch of crack into its battered end. Once the stem was primed he lit the blow torch and commenced smoking.

Tembe regarded him with quizzical contempt. 'Y' know I mean it,' he said, putting on his most managerial of tones for this troublesome employee. 'I want you doin' those City drops like *now*, man. Those boys want their shit nice an' early. If you're done by one, you can pick up another 'teenth – do the bitches at the Learmont. I'll sling you some brown in all –'

'How much?' Danny snapped, he was still holding down the hit of crack.

'A bag – whatever.'

'In that case,' he spoke through the gust of exhalation, 'you do the fuckin' portioning – and I'll' – he snatched up a roll of clingfilm from the work surface – 'do the fuckin' wrapping.'

Two hours later Danny was limping down Aldergate. It was raining and he was soaked through. About the driest things he had about his person, Danny reflected bitterly, were the rocks of crack housed in his cheeks, each one snugly wrapped and heat-sealed in plastic.

'Do the City,' Tembe impatiently ordered and off Danny had to go, clanking down the Bakerloo Line to Oxford Circus, and then clanking on along the Central Line until he reached Bank. On the fucking tube, the *tube*, not even a cab to ease his lot. And when he got to Bank it was the fucking foot slog. Up to Citibank, the stupid plastic jacket he had to wear flapping in the wind and rain, the defunct radio attached to its lapel banging against his collar bone. Then get the fucking Jiffy-bag out in the vestibule. Spit a couple of rocks into it. Seal it. Up to fucking reception: 'Delivery for Mistah Fuckin' Crack-Head Banker.'

'Fine, if you leave it right here I can sign for it –'

'Sorry, it's a special whatsit thingy – he's gotta sign himself, yeah?'

'Oh right – sure, I'll ring his extension.' She looks through Danny at a Monet reproduction while he waits, finger-drummingly bored. And then here he comes, Mistah Fuckin' High Wire Act, tripping across the quarter-acre of carpet tiling without a care in the world, on his own little personal conveyor belt, which is carrying him straight to a seventy-quid Nirvana.

'Is that for me? Thank you. Where can I sign – there?'

You can sign wherever you fucking please, asshole, because this biro doesn't work and this bit of paper is just that.

'Thanks again – and do give my regards to Mr Tembe.' He rolls away again.

Fucking pin-stripe suit, fucking old school tie. He won't be looking so fucking dignified in five minutes' time, Danny internally sneers as he slops his way back to the lift, sitting in a fucking toilet stall, pretending to do a shit while he sucks on a pipe made from a crushed Coke can. Silly cunt.

In Aldergate Danny paused to envy a dosser. The young white guy sat in the doorway of a travel agent's, surfing to nowhere on a piece of old packing case. His blue nylon sleeping bag was pulled up to his armpits, leaving his arms free for entreaty. He looked, Danny thought, like some enormous maggot that had crawled into this niche in order to metamorphose, possibly into a crack-head banker. Danny gave the dosser a fifty-pence piece, and savoured the shock on the young man's face when he realised he had successfully begged from a black guy not much better off than himself.

Good karma, Danny thought to himself as he slopped on down the road. Give to those worse off than yourself and the Fates will look kindly on you. Nowadays Danny was increasingly drawn to consider the attitude of the Fates to almost anything he did. The Fates had to be consulted as to which sock he should put on first when he got up; which boot he should tuck his stem into before leaving the house; and which side of Leopold Road he should walk down on his way to the tube.

Danny appreciated – with a deep, almost celestial clarity – the fact that the Fates were very much a product of the ten or so rocks of crack he was smoking every day. For one thing the Fates often appeared in his mind's eye as tall, wispy, indeterminate figures, their forms actually *composed* by gossamer wreaths of crack smoke. However, if Danny honed in on them, their miasmic covering fell away to reveal truly terrifying, djinn-like figures – the towel-heads from hell. Bearded, turbaned, wearing long grey-and-black robes, and carrying mutant, nine-foot-long Kalashnikovs.

The Fates kept him company – they were the bears that would savage him if he stepped on the crack. But if he maintained those good high stimulant levels, the Fates would keep counsel with him, warn him of the filth round this corner, or some Yardie cunt Danny had stolen from round the next. Of course, Danny didn't really *believe* in any of this, it was simply a magical soundtrack to his life; but then the Fates were very similar in their manifestation to Danny's crack habit itself – both were paradoxical addictions to something intrinsically frightening and unpleasant. He shifted the wads of plastic in either cheek, with a motion akin to rinsing with mouthwash; then he delicately palped each one with the tip of his tongue.

Danny conducted this internal stock-taking at least a thousand times a day. In his left cheek was his own stash – in his right was the merchandise. Usually, when Danny set off from the house in the morning, the right-hand cheek would have around twenty-five rocks in it, and the left five. Five rocks to take him through five hours of tube rides and walking around the City pretending to be courier, a cowboy without a horse. Ducking into a khazi, or an alley, or a fucking hole in the wall, every quarter-hour on the quarter-hour to smoke the poisoned flour. Out with the stem; out with the lighter; crumble finicky crumble as the Fates gather at the periphery; crowding in, a press of dirty beards and muttering; the recitation of arcane fundamentalist texts, decrying the existence of Danny; dirty grey nails reaching out to rend him – then blown away, extinguished, blanketed by the first rich gush of smoke from his nozzled mouth.

Five rocks equalled twenty pipes – one every fifteen minutes. Enough time while the gear was still doing its thing for him to slop to another financial institution, make his drop, slop on. Enough time – if he eked it out righteously – for Danny to avoid a clanking comedown on the Central Line, seated sweating in a strip-lit cattle truck, along with the rest of his hetacomb. All too often, however, Danny's lop-sided chipmunk visage began to balance itself a little early in the day, the right-hand cheek getting delved into a little more than it should. And on those occasions Tembe would withhold the bag of brown at the end of the shift; or even – if he was feeling particularly managerial – even a measly taste. And Danny would have to accept this – accept the rack of shit his life had become.

How had it come to *this*? Danny bit down on the cyanide capsule of the past as he turned into London Wall, heading for London Bridge and the offices of Barclays De Zoete Wedd. How had he ended up being a runner for his dumb little brother Tembe – or 'Mr Tembe' as he was apparently known to the denizens of the Citibank futures department? Dragging his drenched carcass around these terrifying caverns of commerce, feeling his life blood, his manhood drain away, and with only the Fates to keep him company. Danny knew, of course, the answer: he had touched the product.

Whether this had occurred before or after the exhaustion of the seam of crack Danny had discovered in the basement of Leopold Road, he did not wish to acknowledge. The mother lode of crack had certainly been too good to be true – and now it no longer was. Whether Danny's estimates with plumbers' rods had been inaccurate at the outset, or the bulk of the crack had simply been washed away, corrupted by drainage and seepage, was besides the point. All that mattered was that after a couple of years of very high living the seam was gone, and at around the same time Danny, feeling wrung out by the experience, had taken his first pipe of crack and discovered what he had always suspected; that, in this most unnatural of pursuits, he turned out to be a natural.

Corresponding mysteriously to an episode in their childhood, the two brothers now found themselves on a seesaw, Tembe coming down to the ground, while his older brother shot up into a psychotic sky. For, as Danny cranked up the go-go candy, doing first three, then five, then sixty pipes a day, so Tembe decided that enough was enough and stepped on the shit once and for all.

In fairness to Tembe, contrary to the expertise of a thousand counsellors, psychiatrists, politicians, churchmen, and the parents of teenagers who had died from ecstasy overdoses, he found it astonishingly easy to step back through the door of non-perception. 'Never did like the shit anyways,' he explained to members of the posse, hanging out on the traffic island by Harlesden tube, drinking Dunn's River and riding the dossers. 'I jus' did it cos it was like *there*. Gimme a spliff anna beer any day; I can do up a ton of sensi a day an' all it do to me is to make me more righteous, more irie an' that.'

Being more righteous and more irie for Tembe largely consisted in a switch from unbridled crack consumption to quite remarkably efficient production and distribution. As Danny gibbered his way through the peaks and troughs of the crack storm, no longer the master puppeteer – merely a puppet on a pipe, so Tembe took up the strings that fell from his numb fingers. Little brother grabbed the clientele and set big brother – once so fucking arrogant, so high and mighty – to work.

Whereas Danny the non-user had always felt at worst indifferent, and at best friendly towards the munificent mannequins, Tembe the former user felt nothing but contempt for them – especially if they were white. 'They have every opportunity, every fuckin' break an' all they do is smoke this shit. They have no respect for themselves – I tell you, they actually *deserve* to be crack-heads, they should give me their money an' that, because they're really *donatin'* it, donatin' it to a righteous cause.'

The righteous cause was Tembe's black Saab 9000, with full skirts, fairing, personalised number plate etc., etc.; and feeling irie for Tembe was equivalent to feeling silk shirts between his shoulder blades, and the weight of an entire wardrobe of American, gangsta rap-style suits hanging from them. Tembe brought a fervour to his materialism that was almost messianic, as if, having pissed thousands of pounds up the wall, he was determined to wring out bricks and mortar until he got it all back again.

'You're too fuckin' fly, boy,' Danny had admonished him, as they sat, Tembe beering and spliffing, Danny piping and cracking, in front of the Saturday-afternoon racing. With Darcus long gone – all that was left of him was a hair-oil stain on the ancient antimacassar of his armchair – Danny, preposterously, was adopting some of the old man's avuncular manner 'You go strutting roun' the fuckin' town, making out like you're some big mutha-fuckin' dude. Thass the way you bring the heat down, man; all the fuckin' heat – an' not just the filth, the Yardies, the Turks, the Essex boys, the Chinese . . . even the fuckin' *Maltese*. You need to maintain a low fuckin' profile, look respectable an' that –'

'Yeah, yeah, yeah, t'chew!' Tembe sucked his cheek disdainfully. 'You taken a decco at your fuckin' profile recently. It ain't just *low*, big brother – it's in the fuckin' gutter.'

Danny had had to admit that his terminally stringy vest, caked dungarees, and flip-flop footwear that wasn't flip-flops was hardly the acme of respectability. He shut up and applied himself to the business of acquiring more blow-torch burns on his hands. And now, replaying the conversation in his echoing inner ear as he slopped through the oppressive, grooved runnel of Lothbury EC2, it occurred to Danny that the Fates were undoubtedly responsible for this bizarre vice versa, and that even these intimations of doom and destruction – which were nothing if not routine – were, on this particular day, awfully germane portents.

Poor Danny – as he crouched in a service entrance of the Bank of England, servicing his own entrance – he couldn't possibly have known which, precise, words had been portents (they were, as it happens, 'Maltese' and 'low profile'). And although the Fates were temporarily routed in the direction of Aldgate – stashing their AKs, pocketing their false

Korans, gathering their ghostly robes about them as they went – at the precise moment, some five minutes later, when Danny flotched into the lobby of Barclays De Zoete Wedd, his head uncluttered by magical thinking, his nemesis was touching down at Heathrow.

Skank, who for the purposes of this business trip had sensibly adopted the work name 'Joseph Andrews', had certain inflexible views about air travel: it was against the law of God, and it terrified him. 'You tek de bird,' he would lecture his fear-hobbled audience, 'de bird have feathers, it have light bones. Pick a bird up – feel it weight in your hand. Feel how *sui-ta-ble* it is for flyin' – because God made it that way. But you tek de plane. De plane is made of metal, it shaped like a bullet. It may go up high in the sky, but one day it falls back to eart'.'

Skank dealt with his fear of flying by coshing himself insensible for the duration with a Rohypnol; but as the wheels bumped and then glued themselves to tarmac, he was wide awake, and clutching the hands of the two small children who were sitting either side of him so tightly that they did his screaming for him.

The children came courtesy of one of Skank's employees, as did their mother, who was, purely recreationally, the wife of the real Joseph Andrews, a Pentecostalist minister who had absolutely no idea that she was in so deep with crack, that she was in still deeper with the Yardies; and that it followed they'd pay her to take a little holiday to her sister's in London. After Dorelia had gone, Joseph had no idea where his passport was either.

Joseph Andrews, a.k.a. Skank, entered the immigration hall with his two pseudo kids still tightly clasped. His 'wife' walked demurely a few paces behind him carrying the hand luggage. When he reached the counter he put the two green Jamaican passports directly into the officer's hand. The officer scanned the face in the photograph – same celluloid dog collar, same v-neck pullover, same serviceable black jacket – then scanned the face in front of him once more. Skank bore an expression of bleak sanctimoniousness, utterly befitting a man who believed in the full weight of the Lord's Providence.

'Is this the address you'll be staying at during your stay, Reverend Andrews?' asked the officer.

'Thass right, my sister-in-law's in Stockwell.'

'And the purpose of your visit, Reverend?'

'Y'know, catching up with the family, friends –'

'But you won't be doing any work?'

Skank fixed the officer with an inquisitorial eye. 'I don't consider the Lord's work to be work as such, but since you ax' I will be preaching at the Stockwell Temple –'

'Of course, of course, that's quite all right, Reverend.' And with a cursory glance at the children and their mother, and then at their passport photographs, he waved the party on. The next entrant in line came to the desk and proffered his passport.

A young man had been circling the arrivals' pick-up zone for some time in a Mercedes saloon, when Skank and the Andrews emerged from the terminal. He pulled up to the kerb and they got in. As the car sped down the exit ramp Skank yanked off the stiff dog collar, and in one fluid motion removed the Glock which was stashed in the glove compartment. He checked the magazine and put the automatic in his jacket pocket, then turning to the driver said, 'So, what de word, Blutie?'

'The word is good, Skank,' the young man replied, flashing a gold 'n gap grin.

'Then *drive* blud claat.'

Skank dropped the Andrews in Stockwell and went on, heading for the East End. As the big merc. splashed through the low-rise high density of South London, the big dread carefully removed what remained of his hairy finery from beneath a wig and a flesh-coloured bathing cap. Turning to Blutie, Skank said, 'De blud claat gone done make me shed me locks, y'know. It's not enough for him to steal – he have to mek a man shed 'im locks. And for why? Jus' to pay some fucker – jus' to pay him!'

'It's the way here, Skank. The Chinaman said he'd happily farm the contract for you – but you gotta come in person to hand over the dosh – shows good faith an' that.'

'T'chew! I call it rank stu-pid-ity, boy. If de chink knew we was settlin' a hundred thousand-dollar score mebbe he'd want more for hisself.'

'Undoubtedly,' said Blutie – who liked the sound of the word.

'As is, wa' he charge for us to rub out dis piece of shit?'

'Two hundred quid.'

'Two hundred pounds! Sheeit! Life is cheaper than fuckin' Trenchtown in this place.'

'You ain't tellin' no word of a lie, Skank, but see here.' Blutie shifted in his seat and spread his hands wide on the steering wheel. 'You've got to 'preciate that the Chinaman isn't taking out a contract on London for us, it's more like he's selling on the debt. The enforcer we're going to meet *wants* the contract. He thinks he can extract a fair wadge out of Danny – thass London's moniker now – before he does the how's your father –'

'But he gua-ran-tee to kill 'im, right? He gua-ran-tee to shoot the little fucker, yeah?'

'He's solid – the Chinaman says so.'

It was unfortunate for Skank that he didn't know as much about the Chinaman as he did about revenge. Skank's revenge on Danny wasn't a dish eaten cold – it was well nigh frozen. It had been five years since the three keys had gone missing in Philly, and all that time Skank had bided, waited. He picked up bits of information here and there and husbanded them; he put irons in the fire and sended them. Eventually the poisonous tree bore fruit, the Chinaman, a long-time associate of Skank's, told him that a black crack-head from Harlesden, who smoked regularly in his house, had told him in turn, about a crew on his manor who were outing much better than average product.

The Chinaman found this interesting enough in itself – it was always wise to keep abreast of the competition. But more interesting still was the thumbnail c.v. the crack-head supplied of the two brothers who ran the operation. Apparently, the older brother, who went by the name of Danny, had been in the army. But more than that, he had gone into the army after a trip to Jamaica. A trip to Jamaica in the late eighties.

It was the only down time in the twenty-four when the big merc. bearing the big dread pulled up in front of the old house on Milligan Street, in back of the Limehouse Causeway. 'Wa' de fuck's *that*?' enquired Skank, seeing the Canary Wharf Tower for the first time in his life as he got out of the car.

'Offices,' Blutie replied. 'I'll park the motor.'

Skank was ushered into the mouldering gaff by a child, who might have been the Chinaman's granddaughter, or even his great-granddaughter. They picked their way through the warren of interconnected rooms and found the old man in what could have been a kitchen, had it not been for the presence of a large steel desk and two filing cabinets, in addition to sink, fridge and vomit swirl-patterned lino tiles. 'Please!'

he exclaimed, getting up from behind the desk. 'Please to be welcome to my office, Mistah Skank!'

'Please,' Skank countered, 'jus' Skank is suff-ic-ient. So iss all offices roun' hereabout now?'

'Oh yes, oh yes, plenty change, big new dewelopment. Plenty offices. Plenty office workers. Plenty office workers who need help –'

'So, busyness is good then?'

'Busyness is excellent! This is an enterpwise zone –'

'Issatso.' Skank couldn't help feeling that the Chinaman's efficiency and zeal was undercut by his working apparel, a dirty terry-towelling bathrobe, but he hadn't come to talk about that. 'I've got de two hundred – have you got my man?'

'No problem, no problem –' He broke off and called into the next room, 'Mistah Gerald, would you come through, the Jamaican gentleman has arrived.'

Certainly the Chinaman liked to think that Gerald was a run-of-the-mill enforcer. But the Chinaman's mind was not unlike his place of business, a bewildering agglomeration of different spaces housing deeply incompatible contents. And as in each of the rooms of the Chinaman's bizarre den – one set aside for opium smoking, the next for crack, a third for ecstatic gibbering – each of the compartments of his mind featured a different belief system, an incompatible truth, another story.

Even Skank felt a chill run down the back of his neck when Gerald walked into the room. He was a small man with hardly any shoulders; his face wasn't so much warped as entirely twisted to one side, as if the wind had changed at the precise moment Gerald had been hit with a hard right cross. He had on a blue nylon anorak of the kind children wore in the sixties; set on his head was an obvious toupee. Set beneath the toupee, and shining forth despite the violent moue was a visage of absolutely uncompromising vapidity and bloodlessness; a face like the belly of a toad. This was not a man with ordinary feelings – or perhaps any feelings at all. Accompanying Gerald was a boy of about fifteen, the same height as his master – for clearly, that's who Gerald was – pipe-cleaner thin, ginger-haired, freckled, and wearing an identical blue anorak. They both had flesh-coloured rubber gloves on.

Skank cleared his throat, 'Errm . . . Gerald.'

'Yes.' The voice was blank as well.

'Dis man 'ere say you can deal with my prob-lem.'

'Yes.'

'Do you know where de fellow lives?'

'Not necessawy,' the Chinaman interjected. 'The man who told me about him – he'll bring him here tonight. He's had a little twouble with the police – it wasn't hard to persuade him.'

'Good. Den what?' Skank had folded his arms and was regarding Gerald critically. The blank man unzipped his anorak without speaking and flipped it open. A shotgun, cut down so that there were only three inches of the barrel and half the stock left was dangling from a hook inside it. Skank said nothing. Gerald zipped the anorak up again.

Blutie came into the room and handed Skank an envelope, which the big dread handed to the Chinaman. The Chinaman handed it to Gerald. Skank shook hands with the Chinaman, nodded to Gerald and he and Blutie left the room. Skank didn't take a full breath until they were back in the street.

2.

Bruno and Danny sat on the stairs of the old house in Milligan Street husbanding the last crumbs of Bruno's crack. It was around midnight. Bruno had sworn to Danny that he'd be generous with the shit – even though he was buying. But inevitably, now that they were down to the penultimate hit they were beginning to squabble. 'Sheeit!' Bruno exclaimed. 'Thass loads more than my last – take a bit of it off, man!'

'No way!' Danny replied. 'You said I could have a big one to finish on – then there's that for you.' He pointed at the crumb of white stuff that remained lying on a piece of plastic on the dusty stair. 'Iss no help that we've only got this poxy fuckin' bottle.' Danny gestured with the pipe they were using, which had been crudely fashioned out of a miniature Volvic mineral-water bottle.

'You should've brought your fuckin' stem, man,' Bruno retorted.

'*You* should've brought *your* fuckin' stem 'n all.' And to put an end to the pathetic quarrel, Danny sparked his lighter, applied it to the heap of fag ash and crack set in the tin-foil bowl, and commenced drawing on the biro stem.

At that moment a large party of people – perhaps six in all, entered the hallway at the foot of the stairs. The Chinaman met them himself, ushering in their leader – a large, heavy-set man wearing an expensive 'crombie – with much bowing and scraping. The four other men who shuffled in behind were clad in various degrees of fashionable suiting, and together with them was a quite beautiful young woman in a very short skirt. Danny wasn't paying any attention, but Bruno pegged them as West End media types, out for a night's drug slumming.

The party, led by the Chinaman, commenced tramping up the stairs past the crack smokers. They all ostentatiously averted their eyes from the spectacle of Danny, drawing for all he was worth on his final pipe of the day, except for the last man to pass, a fat type with oval glasses smoking a cigar, who squinted down at the pipe in Danny's hand and sneered, 'I prefer Evian myself.'

Danny stopped drawing on the pipe, and together with a plume of crack smoke spat at the man, 'Whassit t'you, cunt!' but Bruno laid a hand on his arm and muttered, 'Safe, Danny.' And he let it lie.

Not for long though. After ten minutes had elapsed and together with them the last vestiges of Danny's hit of crack, he began to appreciate the full awfulness of his position. He was hideously strung out. He'd done three rocks more than he should have during his morning's sodden tramp around the financial institutions. He managed to deliver twenty rocks to the bitches at the Learmont and the ones in Sixth Avenue, but it hadn't been quite enough to mollify Mr Tembe, who had cut his evening hit of brown to a mere smear. So Danny now had the rumbling beginnings of heroin withdrawal to contend with, as well as the hideous trough of a crack comedown. He hated sitting on this filthy staircase, waiting to summon the energy to stagger down, stagger to the tube, clank all the way back to Harlesden, face the derision of his squeaky-clean little brother: 'Thass whappen when you smoke the shit, man, give it a rest . . .' And all the way the Fates walking with him, whispering and cachinnating, ordering him to tread there, breathe here, spit there, unless he wanted to be eviscerated by destiny. But what Danny hated most of all, right here and now, was the dissing the fat white cunt had given him.

Danny leapt to his feet, ran up the stairs, barged through the door of the room the party had disappeared into. He didn't take any time to register the occupants – who were smoking opium, contorted by the sloping ceiling of the attic room into various cramped postures – he merely picked out the fat ponce and gave him a smack in the mouth. Then it was back down the stairs and straight out the front door, to where Vince, the Chinaman's Maltese minder, who had witnessed Danny's sudden departure, was waiting.

Vince delivered a deft karate chop to the back of Danny's neck which felled him instantly. Crack had winnowed away the muscle that Danny had put on in the army – the huge Maltese could lift him by the scruff of his jacket using only one hand. Vince carried Danny as if he were a kitten, down the area steps. At the bottom he pressed him up against the wall, and when Danny began to come round – his flickering eyes providing him a view of Vince's repugnant nose, which had been sliced in two during a knife fight and crudely sewn back together again – Vince began, almost tenderly, to press down on his cartoid artery.

Two minicabs pulled up to the kerb and the West End slummers emerged from the house. The party got into the cars and they drove off. Shortly afterwards a vomit-coloured Austin Maxi pulled up and Gerald and his boy got out. Gerald was about to go up the short flight of steps to the front door when he saw Vince and his unconscious kitten in the basement area. Gerald jerked his head significantly in Danny's direction, and Vince, enjoying the conspiratorial silence of the very ugly, wordlessly did his bidding. By the time he'd carried Danny back up to the street, the rear door of the Maxi was open Vince slid the body on to the seat and without even giving Gerald so much as a backward glance, reentered the house.

Gerald and the boy got into the Maxi. The boy was driving. They drove off to the north, heading for Clapton.

Sixteen hours later, at around three in the afternoon, Danny regained consciousness. He was lying on dirty linoleum. The first sensations he had on awakening were the smell of the stuff, and the thrumming weight of his head, mashing his cold cheek into the floor. Danny groaned, coughed, spat and sat up. The room he was in might once have been an office – there were a couple of cheap wooden kneehole desks set against one wall, a battered filing cabinet against the other. The office must have also been a shop of some kind, because there was a large front window.

However, this had been completely boarded up on the inside and the only light in the place came from the chinks between the planks.

Following one of these wavering beams to its destination on the back wall, Danny saw that this was entirely covered with a papering of posters. He squinted at them through the gloom. They all featured photographs of children. The photos were obviously family snaps that had been blown up and reproduced in black-and-white – Danny could see the individual dots composing the images. Then he read the lettering and realised, with an access of dread, what they were. They were posters appealing for help in the search for missing children.

Danny scrambled to his feet. He felt an awful thickening and distortion in the already unpleasant atmosphere of the room. He could smell something sickly, yet faecal. A dollop of vomit came into the back of his mouth. He could see a tartan blanket thrown over something in the dark corner, only three paces away. Danny knew what the thing was before he lifted the blanket – and then he knew for sure.

It was the mutilated corpse of a six-year-old white boy. Danny registered blond hair, pulped features, cut throat. There was a lot of blood. The child's hands and feet had been severed and left beside the corpse, which was naked from the waist down. The last thing Danny took in before he began, simultaneously, to puke and scream, was that the little boy was wearing a bright sweatshirt, featuring a decal of the character Buzz Lightyear from the film *Toy Story*.

Yes, Gerald, who by this time was heading west, to Bristol, was no ordinary enforcer, as the Chinaman well knew. Just as his accompanying boy – whose name was Shaun Withers – was not really a boy at all, but a twenty-year-old violent retard. Gerald and Shaun had met each other on the treatment course for sexual offenders at HMP Grenville. Day after day they had sat together in group-therapy sessions where sincere psychiatrists urged them to give voice to their most keenly desired fantasies of rape, abuse, torture and murder, in the hope that this would enable them to gain the merest sliver of objectivity about their conditions.

Gerald and Shaun managed to achieve very considerable objectivity about their favourite shared fantasy – the abduction, buggering, torture, mutilation and eventual murder of a young boy, the younger the better. They resolved to join forces and make it a reality as soon as they were released. Gerald got out first – he had been serving a two-year stretch for indecent assault – and went back to his home town of Bournemouth. But the local paper there had already published a picture of him the day before, and printed the address of his house. Gerald found that the constant posses of vigilantes screaming abuse outside, and the flaming, petrol-soaked rags shoved through his letterbox, rather cramped his style.

Gerald left Bournemouth and headed for London where he lost himself in the immemorial city's stygian underworld. He worked sporadically for the Sparks family in Finsbury Park, collecting debts for them and when necessary inflicting a beating. But generally he kept quiet, moved his digs every month, and bided his time. Six months passed before Shaun was released after completing his three-year stretch for rape. In London he joined Gerald, who already had the elements of a plan in place.

Shaun had spent the last year of his sentence, at Gerald's behest, cheerfully allowing himself to be buggered by the ex-cop who was the boss of the nonce wing. The ex-cop had gone down for corruption and was desperate not to be sussed as a queer. Shaun guaranteed to keep this information to himself in return for a little assistance with getting back on his feet once he got out. The assistance he most required was a reasonably roomy set of premises where he and his good buddy Gerald could resume their activities. The ex-cop had to oblige. It transpired that he had the lease on the offices of a defunct minicab firm on the Lower Clapton Road. The place was boarded up and had no electricity or water, but it had several rooms, and most importantly a back entrance that wasn't overlooked. Gerald and Shaun took the keys while making sincere expressions of gratitude.

They found the boy in a playground a mile away in Stoke Newington; his name was Gary. It took only minutes for the two men to persuade the six year old to accompany them to their house for some sweets and videos. He got into the Maxi almost gaily and chattered away as they drove carefully back to the cab office. For Gary was not simply neglected and unwanted – he was also being abused already. Shaun and Gerald found this out when they got him inside and took his clothes off – his little arse was cratered with cigarette burns. The burns were the work of his mother's sadistic boyfriend. The same boyfriend who had bought him the *Toy Story* top.

Still, despite this, Gary was blond and slim and almost pretty. Gerald and Shaun managed to have plenty of fun with him over the next ten days or so, but then he became a bit of a drag. He was incontinent, he wouldn't eat, he'd lost his freshness, and the two men began to argue about who should have the task of washing him in between sessions. And Gary didn't even struggle satisfactorily any more, he just whimpered. Worse than that, Gerald had already clocked the profusion of missing-child posters that had gone up in the area, and he'd read in the local paper that the police were conducting exhaustive house-to-house questioning. It could only be a matter of time before the knock on the door came.

Gerald decided that what they needed was another body, someone to take the rap. Then, through the Sparks, he heard about a Chinaman in Limehouse who had a contract that needed enforcing. 'Just the ticket,' Gerald said to Shaun. Gerald never spoke much, but when he did he invariably retailed such hackneyed turns of phrase. When the two men came to heaving Danny's unconscious body into the office, and stuffing the downers down his throat, and removing the semen from his seminal vesicles with a long hypodermic, Gerald referred insistently to him as the 'thingummyjig'.

And that's how the thingummyjig came to be in the boarded-up cab office in Lower Clapton Road, screaming and puking on a cold November afternoon. But he didn't have to suffer his terror and revulsion alone for long. Gerald and Shaun had thoughtfully phoned the local constabulary, shortly after quitting the premises.

Three months later, and ensconced on the nonce wing of Wandsworth Prison, Danny had plenty of leisure with which to reflect on the awesome apathy that had gripped him during those few minutes in which he waited with dead Gary for the door to the cab office to be kicked in by the police. Granted, he still had enough downers in his system to make a polar bear sluggish; and granted he had the smack withdrawal and the crack come-down underlying this fateful torpor, but even so there was a genuine acceptance of his fate – or rather his Fates.

They thronged the corners of the dark room, their gloomy robes brushing against the missing-children posters, their grimy turbans scratching the polystyrene ceiling tiles. The Fates muttered and chuckled over the child's corpse, and for the first time since they emerged from the cracks in the corners of the world to keep him company, Danny could clearly understand what they were saying. The words 'low profile' and 'Maltese' and 'set-up' and 'Skank' were there; along with 'fool' and 'crack-head'. And in the dark room, perfumed by psychopathy, Danny acknowledged that his nemesis had come back to haunt him.

It was just too smooth – and too inexplicable otherwise. Bruno offering to front him an evening's rocking in the East End. The big, ugly Maltese who had given him a careful twice-over when they arrived at Milligan Street, and then the same fucker, choking the sense out of him after Danny had given that lairy git a smack. Now he was here, obviously many hours later, and there was blood on his hands. Danny, unlike anything else graphic in the room, had been neatly framed.

For, there was not only blood on his hands, it was under his nails and in his hair as well. Some of it was his own – some was Gary's. This, when it was also neatly catalogued at the trial, was damning enough; as were Danny's dabs on assorted implements: knives, hacksaw blades, screwdrivers etc., revolting etc. . . . But worse, far worse, was Danny's semen in the little boy's anus, Danny's semen in the little boy's throat. These were facts that thankfully weren't published in the newspapers, although they remained in Danny's deposition papers, when the corridor was frozen and he was hurried down it on his way to the nonce wing.

The police were amazed by Danny's quietism when they arrested him. Since he put up hardly any resistance, they administered a minimal beating. It was the same as he was shuffled from one nick to the next over the next nine weeks. It didn't matter what they screamed at him, or how they slapped him – he wouldn't rise to it. Eventually they gave up – it was no fun punching a bag.

Danny's lawyer, a young white woman, was perfectly prepared to attempt a proper defence of her client. She may have been inexperienced, and have had as little knowledge of Danny's world as she did of the dark side of the moon, but she could see that none of it added up. Danny had no form as a sex offender, and was too old to have suddenly blossomed into such an evil flower. He might have no alibi, and no willingness to go in search of one, but there was no effective circumstantial evidence against him either. This was an organised killing, but the police could find no signs, other than forensic, that it had been Danny who'd organised it. And anyway, why organise a murder so comprehensively, then fail to remove yourself from the crime scene in time?

None of this mattered though. None of this could fly in the face of that semen, which Gerald had so artfully extracted, then inserted. And none of it could be challenged if Danny remained, as he did, listless, silent, surly, showing no indication that he wanted to substantiate his – purely formal – plea of not guilty.

For Danny the trial was a series of unconnected, almost absurd, impressions. At the Crown Court in Kingston, the police who had arrested him stood about in the lobby, smoking heavily in their short hair and C&A suits. Danny mused on how peculiar it was that they always looked more uniformed when they weren't. The gold-painted mouldings of fruit bordering the ceiling of the large hall jibed with the freestanding, cannister-shaped ashtrays that pinioned its floor. The court usher was black, and had more than a passing resemblance to the late Aunt Hattie. The prosecuting QC was white; he affected a large signet ring, a watch chain and a clip-on bow tie. He reminded Danny of one of the punters he used to serve in the City. As he waited each morning with the Securicor guards for the expensive charade to begin, Danny would look for sympathy in the eyes of a large portrait of Queen Caroline – and find none.

Sitting in the dock for day after day, Danny was acutely conscious of the need not to look at anyone. The jury were ordinary people, who, in the struggle to appear mature at all times, ended up seeming far more childish. Especially childish in the way that they beamed hatred at Danny given half a chance. The public gallery was, of course, out of the question. Instead Danny concentrated on the peculiar, double-jointed ratchets that were used to open the high windows in the courtroom. And for hours he would lose himself in the texture of the vertical louvres that covered those windows.

Danny came to during the judge's summing up: It was for the jury to decide what they believed; it was up to them to assess whether the witnesses were telling the truth; it was important that they accepted the judge's direction in matters of law, but it was for them to decide in matters of fact. The judge was careful to acknowledge that they might decide to believe *this*; but on the whole he thought it far more likely that they would prefer to accept *that*. So he cut up the cake of justice and handed out a slice to everyone saving Danny.

The jury were out for such a short time that it was difficult to believe they'd done anything save walk into the jury room, chorus 'He's guilty as hell' and walk straight back out again. Even the judge was impressed by their alacrity – and the prosecuting QC positively glowed. It was three in the afternoon when the scrap of paper was passed by the foreman to the clerk, and then by the clerk up to the bench. All morning the court had been directly under the Heathrow flight path, and each damning summation by the judge was accompanied by the roar of another 747, bearing another six hundred people and escaping earthly confinement at six hundred miles an hour. As the judge took the scrap of paper Danny heard an almighty boom, and peering through the gap in the louvres behind the judge's shoulder, he saw the white needle of Concorde lifting off into the grey sky.

Danny's sentence was life. With a minimum recommendation that he serve twenty years.

His solicitor managed to grab a few minutes with him in the holding cell. 'You'll have to ask for protection,' she told him. 'With your offence and sentence you have no choice – otherwise you'll get a pasting. But do everything you can to get off Rule 43. If you come to your senses and want to fight this, want to appeal, it will go far better for you if you've protested at your sentencing all along, and the best demonstration of that is that you refuse to admit you're a nonce. Never admit you're a nonce – you're not a nonce, are you, Danny?'

Danny gave the young woman a long, level look for the first time since he'd met her, then tonelessly replied, 'No.' Then two Securicor men came into the cell, cuffed him and led him out.

For Danny the next two weeks were as confused as the last two weeks before his rendezvous with Gerald. With its elision of day and night, its muddling of time and distance, and its random acts of senseless departure, the Prison Service did its best to replicate the lifestyle of the drug addict. Outside the court Danny was bundled into a blacked-out category 'A' Securicor van. The inside of the van was divided into sixteen individual cell-lets, eight each side. Once he had been locked into his cell he was there for the duration of an eighteen-hour day, every day, for a fortnight. The cell window was blacked out, so that the outside world was doused in permanent night-time; and the door was solid to the ceiling. Inches in front of Danny's face there was a metal grille which ran from waist-height to the roof of the van. Should Danny have chosen to do so he could have communicated, through this grille, with his fellow traveller in front. And if he'd been prepared to twist around in his seat he could have done the same with the prisoner behind.

Danny chose to do neither. He sat still, listening to the catcalls of the inmates and the imprecations of the guards. When the van stopped he heard the slop and slurp of the shit and piss in the covered bucket between his shins. It didn't feel like any kind of an indignity – this; after all Danny was a nonce. A nonce, a sickening, shitty, pissy nonce. The lowest of the low. Danny had been around enough to hear the stories about what happened to sex offenders inside. He knew about juggings and shivings and socks full of pool balls. He had heard tell of how the 'normal' offenders plotted to get their hands on nonces; how even a fairly lowly crim' – a crack-head, a larcenist, whatever – could vastly improve his status by doing a nonce. Behind those high walls slathered with anti-climb paint there was only ever one season; an open one for nonces.

So Danny kept silent, lest he give himself away, and listened to the constant yammering of his fellow prisoners. Every time they stopped at another nick and there was an exchange of personnel, the questioning would start up: 'Who're you?'; 'What're you in for?'; 'Have you got anything bottled?'; 'D'jew know Johnnie Marco?' and so on.

Every day, late, the van would halt for the night and the shackled prisoners would be led into another shower block, ordered to strip, doused, and then locked away for a few hours in holding cells. Then, with dawn still far off in this winter wonderlessland, the cell door would be whacked open, they'd be shackled again, marched out to the van, loaded, and driven off.

After a few days Danny became conscious of the fact that almost every prisoner in the van, at some point during the day, would realise that he knew one of the other prisoners in the van. Further, all the prisoners in the van seemed to take this for granted: 'Issat so-and-so?' they'd call out, and when it was confirmed that it was, they'd try and ascertain what it was that had happened to so-and-so. Had he done a screw? Had he been on the block? Had he been nicked for drugs? Gradually it dawned on Danny that this snail's-pace progression in the jolting miniature cell actually was a form of incarceration for these men; and that the prison van itself was a special kind of institution. The prisoners who were moved so relentlessly were the troublemakers, the bolters, the ex-barons, and presumably those like Danny himself who required rigorous sequestration.

Danny began to wonder whether he would serve all of his twenty years being shunted around the country in this fashion, with nothing to read save his deposition and no one to talk to at all. Along with this creeping suspicion came another, curiously ambivalent intimation. The Fates had gone – or perhaps they'd never existed at all. No longer did Danny have to indulge in peculiar twists of magical thought in order to protect himself from the malevolent djinns, there was no point – his fate was worse than death already. Not only had the Fates gone, but his stomach had ceased to gurgle and void itself, his armpits had ceased to drip cold sweat and his appetite had – grossly inopportunely – returned in force. Danny was clean.

With cleanliness came an indignation that burned inside Danny like a whole body dose of clap. Granted he'd ripped off Skank, and granted that he'd been due a comeuppance, but this? This! To be framed as a nonce! No, it couldn't be, Danny would do anything, adopt any stratagem to clear his name. He remembered what the solicitor had said after the trial; that he should do all he could to avoid getting stuck on the nonce wing – that would have to be his first priority. He would tell the governor – he remembered that every new inmate had an interview with the governor – that he didn't want protection, he didn't want to be segregated.

All of this Danny firmly resolved on the thirteenth day of the van. But the following morning, when the van pulled up for the fifth time, and to his blinking surprise Danny found himself standing outside the high brick wall of HMP Wandsworth, his resolve began to drain away.

It continued to drain away as Danny was inducted into the prison. The screws who showered him, printed him, issued him with his kit, and then led him through the curiously empty reception block seemed so uncustomarily unaggressive that they were almost solicitous. Danny, of course, didn't say anything to them save for 'Yessir' and 'Nossir', but when he was ready to go on to the wing, one of them muttered 'Poor fucker', and he couldn't forbear from asking, 'What's up?'

The screw, who was white moustachioed and close to retirement, shook his head and looked straight at Danny before answering, 'You'll see.'

There was no enigma to this arrival. Danny was led across a yard, in through one gate, across another yard and in through the end door of A Wing, the first of the five 'spokes' that comprise the Wandsworth panopticon. It's possible – but unlikely – that had Jeremy Bentham, the originator of the panopticon prison design, seen Danny's welcome at Wandsworth, he would have felt that his ideas had reached an effective fruition.

Bentham conceived of the panopticon, with its five spoke-like wings, projecting from a hub-like central hall, as an evocation of the all-seeing eye of God. He had hoped that the inmates of the five wings, constantly aware of their observation from the central hall, would apprehend within the architectonic of their own imprisonment the true nature of the relationship between God and Man. Certainly, Danny felt the presence of an all-seeing eye as he walked down A Wing, a screw to his rear and another in front, and then walked through the central hall and on down E Wing to his final destination. But this was an all-seeing eye made up of many hundreds of other eyes, an all-seeing eye that also possessed hands, hands which were all banging cutlery against the bars of their cells. And there were all-shouting mouths as well, row upon row of them. They kept pace with Danny as he marched through the gauntlet of hatred. 'Nonce! Nonce! Fucking nonce!' they all screamed, and every ten shaky paces Danny heard a more personal, targeted remark like: 'We'll get you – you fucking nonce!'

By the time Danny reached his allotted cell, on F Wing, he was blanched with the sweat of terror. 'We thought we'd put you two together,' said the screw, gesturing through the doorway of the cell he'd just unlocked, 'given that you're both black geezers and that.'

Inside the cell a fat black man was sitting on a bunk. He looked up from something he was writing on a pad of paper, gave a broad grin and said, 'So, you're the famous Clapton cab killer.'

And that's how Danny came to meet Fat Boy, the mentor from hell.

3.

'Yah man!' said Fat Boy, 'I've got it on damn good authority – you're gonna get jugged, an' right here, on the fuckin' nonce wing, tomorrer –'

'B-but this is – I mean we're *all* fuckin' the same here, how can anyone think they have the right.'

'The right! Ha-ha-ha! Rights he talks about. That's real fine; you, the fuckin' Clapton cab killer, talking 'bout rights. You – a fuckin' monster who tortured and sexually abused a six-year-old child for days before killin' 'im and cuttin his fuckin' hands and feet off! Sheee!' Fat Boy ran his finger around the omega sign he had shaved into the hair at the back of his neck before continuing. 'You've got a nerve, man. Right here, right now, you're regarded as one of the badarsed of the badarsed in the whole fuckin' nick. And, since this wing is the fuckin' clearing house for every single fuckin' nonce in the whole country – it means you're one of the baddest arseholes there is.' And Fat Boy went back to running his finger around the furry groove of his omega sign; a nervous tic, which, in a few short hours had driven Danny closer to distraction than anything else he'd experienced since going down.

Danny slapped the linoleum with the soles of his shoddy canvas shoes. 'So,' he asked after a while, 'who's gonna do the sodding jugging, then?'

'Waller, he's gonna do it. He's an ex-cop, see, an' he's the fuckin' baron in here right now. He an' another bent copper, name of Hansen, between 'em they've got the whole fuckin' wing sewn up. Any given time they've got five hundred and forty Rule 43 prisoners on 'ere. That's five hundred and forty to tax. They've got the drugs, they've got the money, they say who goes on an' who goes off the wing, an' naturally they organise the fuckin' juggings.' Fat Boy snuggled into the bunk a little more, drawing his chubby legs up into a tenth-lotus position, before continuing to impart wisdom, like some grotesque sadhu. 'See, yer nonces are basically a law-abiding lot, an' cowardly to boot. It comes natural to them to do whatever a copper says – whether 'e's bent or not, see? And anyways these coppers are 'ard fuckers, man, real 'ard fuckers –'

'Well, I'm no fuckin' battyboy myself,' Danny spat. 'An' I'm no nonce neither. I'm gonna see the fuckin' governor today, right? They've gotta let me, right? An' I'm gonna say I don't want no protection nor nothing –'

'Yeah-yeah-yeah-yeah,' said Fat Boy, as if he'd seen it all before – which he had, 'an' I'm no nonce neither – leastways not a fiddler or a fucker – but let me tell you, man, as a favour like, there's only one fuckin' way of doing *your* stretch an' thass right here. Forget going over there, you wouldn't last seven seconds. An' anyway, he won't let you, not until you build up some trust wiv' 'im, then he might let you go, but only as a fuckin' *tout*, mind. No, you've got a jugging coming, man, an' the only fuckin' hope in hell you have of avoidin' it is sittin' right here in front of you in the shapely shape of yours truly, Mistah FB, the moderator, the negotiator, the secretary general of the United Nations of Nonce.'

Fat Boy relaxed his legs and swung himself up. He waddled to the door, poked his jug head out and checked the landing in either direction, then he waddled back to the sink in the far corner and removed one of the tiles on the splash back; behind it there was a stash of – among other things – chocolate bars. Fat Boy took one out and replaced the tile, securing it with shreds of Blu-Tac. Turning back towards Danny he held the chocolate bar up and said, 'Snickers?' Danny ignored the offer. 'Whadd'ya' mean *you're* not a nonce?'

'I'm not.' Fat Boy bit deep into his Snickers.

'Well, are you filth then?'

'Nah! Course not! I'm doing a fuckin' "nyum-nyum" five for supplying child porn, right? It's not my kick, you understand, but where there's a market . . . "nyum-nyum" . . . I could probably get away wiv' being over there – I've got friends an' that, but it suits me well enough to be on the nonce wing on account of the business opportunities, see? I'm on to a good "nyum-nyum" earner here an' thass why I can help you out, stop you getting a fuckin' jug of boilin' water and fuckin' sugar poured over your fuckin' nonce bonce.'

'What's the earner then?' Danny asked, seemingly contrite.

Fat Boy saw Danny was in earnest and sat down on the opposite bunk again, brushing fragments of peanut, chocolate and toffee from his ludicrously inappropriate, loudly patterned Hawaiian shorts. 'You know what's it that envelope you carry everywhere wiv' you?' His voice was queasily intimate and lubricious.

'W-what? My deposition, you mean?' Danny reached instinctively for the brown envelope – he had been told that it was a disciplinary offence not to know where it was at all times.

'That's the one – wass innit?'

'I dunno, my statements, trial evidence an' stuff –'

'Trial evidence, right, trial evidence!' Fat Boy snatched the envelope from Danny's hand, and before he could protest had opened it and scattered the contents on top of the bunk. Fat Boy sorted through the slew of paper with both hands. 'See, here's your original statement, here's the filth's, here's psych' reports an' bullshit, an' here's bingo!' He had a smaller manila envelope in his browner hand, from which he pulled a sheaf of photographs. As he examined each one and tossed it on to the blanket, Fat Boy gave a helpful commentary: 'Mug shot of you, 'nother one . . . ah, here we go, crime scene, exterior, day – worth a few bob; crime scene interior – worth a few bob more; and here's the real spondulicks, victim at crime scene – one, two, three, four of 'em. Oooh! Ugly man, ugly – good angles as well – *and* the fuckin' icing, an' old shot of the victim, ahhh! Ain't he sweet, lovely *Toy Story* top – !'

'Gimme that!' Danny snatched the photo from Fat Boy and grabbed the rest of them as well. He began stuffing them all back into the envelope, whilst almost shouting, 'You sick fuck! You sick fuck! Thass your earner is it, is it?' Fat Boy recoiled, his new cell mate might have looked skinny and run down but the boy's reflexes were damn fast. Danny ranted on: 'You sell this shit, do you? Issat it? You sell this shit to the nonces, oh man! Seen I caan't believe it. Blud claat!'

'An' the fuckin' address.' Fat Boy acted unperturbed.

'What?!'

'The address, some fucker will pay well for little Toy Story's address. They get a kick out of it – the nonces do, sendin' tapes an' shit out to the victim's family. Yeah, they get a real kick out of it. You could cut it either way, man – a package deal, address, shots, the lot, or parcel it off. Given your rep' man, *half* your bag will get you off the jugging, an' then there's a bit of a profit to be 'ad. Bit of puff, bit of brown, I can even get you a rock if you fancy one, whaddya' say? If you want to cut a deal wiv' Waller – I'm your man. I'm the deposition king of F Wing an' thass the troof.'

Danny had finished packing the envelope. Still holding it he stood and walked the two paces to the end of the cell. There was a foot-square, heavily barred window set near the top of the wall. Danny gripped the bars with one hand and dangled there for a while, allowing the strong currents of nausea that were passing through his mind gently to twist his body this way and that. He tilted his face over the sink in the corner and didn't so much spit into it, as allow the saliva to fall from his mouth. Christ! He'd known he was going to encounter men who would revolt him, men who had done unspeakable things, but Fat Boy's parasitism on the nonces' perverted desires was even worse. To think that he might be banged up in here with the omega man – who was at it again as Danny dangled, his fat finger rasping through the nappy hair – for hours, then days, then months, then years. The two of them sleeping and shitting only inches apart, their breath, their farts, their very thoughts commingling. Danny retched and a cable of phlegm tethered him to the plughole.

There was a cough and a rasp of boot outside the cell. The screw who had escorted Danny on to the wing was standing there. He clicked his heels, wiped his moustache with the back of his hand and intoned, '7989438, O'Toole, the Governor will see you now.'

'O'Toole! Hahaha! O'Toole, that's your *handle* is it, man.' It was inevitable that Fat Boy would appreciate a feeble pun. 'O'Toole! Not enough you should be coon and nonce, you're a Mick into the bargain –'

'Shut it, Denver,' snapped the screw at Fat Boy; then he jerked his head at Danny, who disentangled his fingers from the bars, wiped his mouth and shuffled out of the cell. Before heading off along the landing Danny poked his head back into the cell and sang in a reasonably tuneful falsetto, 'You fill up my se-enses like a night in a forest/Like a sleepy blue ocean –' and then he was gone, leaving the omega man without the last word.

The screw marched Danny along the iron catwalk of the landing; one pair of feet banging with boot-shod authority, the other slapping ineffectually. In the awful, silent drum of the nonce wing theirs were the only beats. To their left and twenty feet below, the ground floor of the wing was more or less empty, no association going on in this least sociable of areas. Bats were neatly aligned on the ping-pong table, balls racked on the pool table. To their right, cell doorway after cell doorway presented a vignette of a nonce standing, a nonce sitting, a nonce writing, a nonce obsessively brushing his teeth. There was no soundtrack save for their footfalls on the landing; it was like a black-magic lantern, or the advent calendar of the Antichrist.

When they reached the grey-painted iron stairway Danny cleared his throat and rasped, 'Sir?'

'Yes, O'Toole.'

'Will we have to go right up those two wings, sir, the way we came like – I mean to get to the Governor?'

The screw pulled up and faced Danny, giving him a proper screwing out – it was his trademark. 'No, son, we won't. That was your initiation; every inmate who's going into protection is led through those two wings. It satisfies the inmates who aren't protected.' The screw was still screwing him out. Danny couldn't believe it, the old fucker was for real; he was talking to Danny as if Danny were a human being.

'An' you don't hold with it . . . sir?'

'No, I don't. This is meant to be a showcase nick now, run by the POs, but don't believe it, lad, the cons still have a big hold here. Mind yourself.' And they descended.

The Governor of HMP Wandsworth, Marcus Peppiatt, was considered a high-flyer in a hierarchy that positively thrived on Icaruses. Since his graduate entry Peppiatt had fully justified his rapid ascent through the ranks. While Assistant Governor at Downview he had nobbled a skunk-growing operation in the prison infirmary. At Blundstone in Norfolk, where he assumed the gubernatorial position, he had put a stop to a situation where the bulk of supervisory visits was supervised by the inmates themselves. Then came the appointment to Wandsworth, in theory a great step up.

But Peppiatt was only too aware that the old Victorian panopticons such as Wandsworth remained the dark-star ships of the prison fleet. It was an irony screaming into an eternal void that these five-winged whirligigs, built to embody an ideal, were the very real centres of eruption in a volcanic system. Peppiatt's appointment came in the wake of fifteen inmates seizing a JCB that had been brought into an inside yard for construction work. They'd battered nine prison officers and seriously assaulted three civilian workers. The only thing that prevented them from ramming their way through the gates and taking off across Wandsworth Common, batting promenading matrons to either side as they fled, was their inability to get the earthmover into reverse gear. The Home Office could manage reverse gear; they fired the then governor.

Marcus Peppiatt was a liberal – in a strong sense. He believed in a prison system that embodied rational, utilitarian principles, not that far removed from those enjoined by Jeremy Bentham himself. Indeed, Peppiatt had gone so far as to set his ideas on these matters down in a book entitled *Rational Imprisonment*. Several copies of this tome were stacked in a shelf behind the Governor's desk. The spines of the books were blue, with the words 'Rational Imprisonment' picked out in a particularly virulent yellow. When, as now, the Governor was seated behind his desk, his head became aligned with the shelf in just such a way that, to a viewer in the position of 7989438, O'Toole, he appeared to be ensnared by his own slogan.

'7989438, O'Toole, sir,' said the old human screw with the white 'tache.

'Thank you, Officer Higson.' The Governor hunched forward over his blotter. 'Could you wait in the outer office to escort the inmate back, please, I don't think we'll be long. Deposition?' This last was aimed at Danny, who passed across the envelope. The Governor extracted the folder inside and began to scan the contents. So this was the Clapton cab killer. He scrutinised the original mug shot of Danny; one that displayed to full effect the vapid, lost expression which had led the prosecutor at Danny's trial to descend to the banality of evoking the banality of evil. To the Governor it contrasted remarkably with the alert, tense, angry expression on the face of the young black man who stood in front of his desk.

The Governor placed both his hands palm down over the contents of Danny's deposition, as if he could staunch the blood of the victim inside. 'Well.' He regarded the psycho. 'You're on F Wing now, O'Toole, and if you behave you'll stay there indefinitely.'

'Sir?'

'Yes.'

'I don't want no protection, sir, I want to be on an ordinary wing.'

'Is that so, O'Toole.' The Governor got up from behind his desk – a standard-issue, large-scale, dark-wood, gubernatorial item – and began to pace the office like the public-school headmaster he so closely resembled. Danny's eyes paced it along with him: over to the window (bars on the outside, mesh on the inside, people don't realise that it's the staff as much as the inmates who're in jail). 'I expect you got a worse initiation on your way from Reception to F Wing than most, O'Toole . . .' Wheels away from the window, hand scrabbling in wire-wool hair. 'You're a convicted sex killer, O'Toole, and your victim was a child; there are at least a thousand men in this prison who, given the chance – left alone with you in this office, for example –' Moves over to the smoked-glass door, grey-flannel legs scissoring, shuts the door eliminating the riffle of computer keys in the outer office. 'Would happily wring the life out of you with their bare hands.' Moves back behind the desk and sets himself down, steeples his fingers erecting a small church over the deposition and addresses Danny from this fleshly pulpit. 'I'm not so sure that I'm not one of them.'

Danny wasn't impressed. The army had taught him how to square up to authority in the right way, directly but without any attitude. They didn't like attitude. 'But, sir, if I'm on F Wing for my own protection how can you explain the fact, yeah, that the man I'm banged up with has jus' tol' me I've gotta sell him that' – he stabbed a finger at the deposition on the desk – 'if I don't want to get jugged.'

At this the Governor sat up straight and was rationally imprisoned once more. 'I see, yes, your deposition. And what's the name of your cell mate, O'Toole?'

'The PO called him Denver, sir, but he styles 'imsel Fat Boy.'

'We know about Denver, O'Toole –'

'It's bloody sick, sir, sick, the man's floggin' the pictures of victims an' that, floggin' them to the nonces. He say they even get the victims' addresses and send tapes and shit to them. It's *bad*, sir, it's n-not r-right.' Danny stuttered to a finish, and took a step back, aware of having overstepped a mark and attempting practically to correct it.

The Governor was quite beautifully perplexed, 'I see, sick, is it.' He'd heard of the righteous lack of conscience of paedophiles; he'd even witnessed plenty of it, but this was ridiculous. 'I suppose it's sicker and *badder* than what you've been convicted for?' He'd tapped the barrel. Danny commenced gushing.

'I didn't do nothing, Governor. Nothing. I'm not a nonce – I've never interfered with no kiddies, no way, not ever, man. No, man – you gotta believe me, sir, I been set up. I was a crack dealer, see? For years like, an' I worked for this man in Trenchtown. He sent me the powder an' I had a crew in Philly, US of A. We'd cook the shit up and flog it, see? But I nicked a couple of keys off of him, this Yardie called Skank. It's him what done this, framed me up. You gotta believe me, I can't be with those nonces, I'll lose all respect, man, respect for myself, whatever –'

'Appeal, O'Toole.'

'Whassat?'

'You will be wanting to appeal.'

'Yes, sir, of course, but first off I gotta get off of the nonce wing.'

The Governor looked at a pair of crossed miniature sculls that had been left on the far wall by his predecessor. Next to them was his own Plexiglass-encapsulated Mission Statement. He could just about make out bullet point four: 'Inmates should be regarded as potentially viable economic contributors, even while in a punitive environment.' Next to this was a photograph of the Governor's freshman year at Loughborough; a long, pale, spotty swathe of humanity, curiously vague at one end because twenty of them had run round behind the stand while the camera was panning, so as to appear in the picture twice. The Governor's eyes returned to Danny's. 'Anything is possible, O'Toole.'

'Sir?'

'It's not impossible for you to get off F Wing – if you really want to.'

'Yeah, but Fat Boy says only as a tout – an' I believe him . . . sir.'

'Tout's an ugly word, O'Toole, but anyway that's not the point. You're in it up to here; even if you don't get attacked because you're a sexual offender it would appear more than likely that this man Skank will still want you dead, right?'

'Even so, sir, even so, I ain't no nonce, I need my respect, my self-respect –'

'You need a friend, O'Toole, and a very well-connected one at that.'

'I've gotta get off the wing, Governor.'

'You've *got* to listen – are you prepared to listen?'

'Course.'

'Good. Well, for now do just that. Do *only* that, and we'll see what we can do, and, O'Toole.'

'Sir?'

'Do something useful while you're here. It's quiet enough on F Wing, there's work available, there are courses available. Show me you can make something of yourself; show me you're worth it. Got it?'

Danny nodded. The Governor signalled that the interview was at an end and was about to call for the PO when Danny butted in. 'Sir?'

'Yes, O'Toole.'

'What about the jugging, sir, what about Fat Boy, he says it's this ex-copper, Waller, he's the one that's gonna do me.'

'I see.' The Governor shuffled Danny's deposition together on the blotter, and handed it to him with a smile the bitter side of wry. 'Well, everybody has to save their skin, don't they, O'Toole?'

'Sir?' Danny couldn't tell if this was fuckwit racist dissing or what.

'I'll leave it to your conscience.'

Back on F Wing Danny cut a compromise deal with Fat Boy. All the shots, even the one of the boy's corpse, but no address. The boy was dead now – and he didn't even know he was; but the living knew everything.

In prison, in the English winter, the word crepuscular acquires new resonance, new intensity. You thought you knew what permanent dusk was like – you knew nothing. For here and now is an eternity of forty-watt bulbs, an Empty Quarter of linoleum, and a lost world of distempered walls. It's an environment of corridors and walkways, a space that taunts with the idea of progression towards arrival; then delivers only a TV room full of modular plastic chairs and Styrofoam beakers napalmed by fag ends. In this sepia interior the nonces move about reticently, unwilling to trouble the gloom. There's even a certain modesty in their demeanour, a modesty that flowers in the exercise yard, where their efforts to avoid one another and create zones of inner protection within their non-fraternity become almost courtly.

Danny was absorbed into this mulch of humanity with barely a ripple. It was as Fat Boy had said: the nonces were a law-abiding lot. Indeed, abiding was their main strength. While the idiots over in the panopticon lost their heads, hung from the bars ranting, disdained pork, took up Rastafarianism, went on dirty protests and generally fought time's current, the nonces abided in their isolated gaol, shat out from the body of the prison, marooned in the desert of its own perversion.

The nonces abided, trading photographs of their victims like soccer stars. They were largely family men, community-charge payers. Many had had travelling occupations – salesmen and such. They saw themselves as avuncular – and had often introduced one another to children as 'uncle'; they were generous, and had frequently been apprehended by the police, carrying toys, looking for a child to give them to. The nonces abided and contemplated the sick society that denied its own desires and by extension theirs. They were big fans of *The Clothes Show*, and would be found in the TV room in silent ranks on Sunday afternoons, muttering about the obscene thinness of the teenage couture models, and how it shouldn't be allowed. They also enjoyed *Children in Need.*

The nonces abided, plotting certain revolutionary acts that would enable them to advance the cause of noncery. They factored in social hypocrisy, but on the whole still considered that things would have changed by the time they got out, attitudes would have matured. Their 'liberation' of certain youthful citizens would be seen as just that: the freeing of tender souls into the warmth and *bonhomie* of a full relationship with someone older. Much older.

There were some malcontents. A small posse – perhaps twenty in all – who gathered along with Waller and Higson outside the POs' office on the ground floor. Here, the tough, bent ex-cops would swagger, showing their nonce acolytes the most effective way to punch out a screw. It worked – everybody was suitably intimidated.

But Danny found he could cope. He cultivated sleep when lock-up came round. He would withstand an hour of Fat Boy's vapid, con-man blether, before pointedly wrapping the anorexic pillow round his head and diving for the bottom. Fat Boy still came on to him, of course. There were the endless wheedlings over the address, and the ceaseless exhortations for Danny to apply for a visiting order: 'When yer gonna get a fuckin' VO, O'Toole?'

'When is never, Denver.'

'Come on, O'Toole, one good bottler and we'll be flush for months. Come on. They say you can't bottle at Wandsworth – but that's bullshit, I done it loads of times. All you's gotta be is blatant like – just shove it up your jacksie right in front of the screw, all nonchalant like –'

'I'm not getting a VO, Denver – I don't want no fuckin' visitors.'

'I know *you* don't want a fuckin' visitor, but there's friends of *mine* that might like to visit you, get acquainted an' that. Come on, O'Toole, you tol' me you used to like a bit of smoke . . .'

'Used to' were the post-operative words. No longer was this the case. The inmates of F Wing were subjected to random drug testing as much as those in the rest of the prison. A smoke of dope would get you a positive test result after two weeks; although, with hoe-downing, honking irony, smack or crack would be out of your system in hours. It was as if the authorities were doing everything in their power to inculcate a vicious, hard-drug culture in the prison system.

Danny took the long view and eschewed the puff. He didn't want to lose his remission, even though he was scheduled for release in 2014. And with the smack and crack evacuated from his body, and the Fates exiled, no more potent now than the dust balls which blew along the corridors, Danny knew that class As were off the menu as well. He began to work out again, stretching and slamming his body back into high tensility. He lobbied for work and got a cushy number: eight hours a week turning the poles for birdhouses. The work was pernickety, repetitive and economically useless; the birdhouses were shoddy and barely paid for the materials used to make them. It reminded Danny, in its very essentials, of the way he, in the depths of his crack addiction, had ceaselessly combed the carpets of Leopold Road on the lookout for lost bits of rock.

But the work and work-outs got him away from Fat Boy and the cell. Because after lock-up, when he plunged into sleep, the Terrors were waiting for Danny. The Fates had always had a certain sang-froid, a certain disdain for their own haunting, but the Terrors were hams, pure and simple. They screamed at Danny, ringed him round with their gaping mouths, tier upon tier of them, like the landings of the wing, and every single one ejaculating nothing. The nothing of imprisonment, the nothing of a dead life, the nothing of a millennial come-down. Towards dawn Danny would usually awake, wrung out, more exhausted. He would essay an unambitious wank – two score tugs and a plash against the sheet – then wait for the darkness of the cell to be infused with the darkness of another day.

Danny was waiting for the Governor to be in touch, to give him his break. He remained scrupulously low-profile, muttering 'sir' to the screws if they spoke to him, and shuffle-slapping out of trouble whenever he saw it coming at him, along a rumbling walkway, or around a distempered corner.

One day, about two months after he'd arrived on the nonce wing, having taken receipt of a compartmentalised lunch tray mounded with mashed potato and little else, Danny found himself scrutinising the list of educational courses pinned up outside the POs' office. It was a tatty little codification of tatty little opportunities. There was a carpentry class, if you wanted to brush up on birdhouse construction; and a music appreciation course, if you felt that Albinoni might soothe your soul. All in all there were eleven different classes offered. Danny sucked the inside of his cheek and considered the possibilities. Presumably this was what the Governor had meant went he talked of Danny 'making something' of himself; perhaps if he undertook one of the courses the Governor might hear of it and moderate his attitudes accordingly. Best to do a vocational course – that would go down well. At the very bottom of the list there was a course called 'Creative Wiring', taught by a Mr Mahoney. That sounded OK to Danny – it must, he thought, be to do with electrics and stuff. If he could add a few more skills to what he already knew about DIY, Danny would have the beginnings of a trade. The course kicked off that week on the Thursday afternoon, an hour before lock-up. Danny resolved that he would be there.

4. The Nonce Prize

Danny got permission from Officer Higson to go up to the Education Room. He walked along the ground floor of the block, eyes down, avoiding any eye contact with his fellow prisoners. Not that Danny worried about the nonces any more, and he certainly didn't perceive them as a sexual threat. The first few days he'd been on the wing, he'd been certain that every second he was on association, or in the exercise yard, or in the queue for food, the perverts were eyeing him up from behind, assessing his potential role in some deviant playlet. Danny could swear he felt their corkscrew gazes, like static electricity on the nape of his neck. But Fat Boy disabused him of this notion, as he had of so many others. 'Na, na, you're wrong there. You gotta look at it this way, O'Toole; even yer rapist is incapable of any real straight sex, and yer nonce is doubly incapable. For a nonce to want to butt-fuck you, well! It wouldn't really be a perversion, as such, you'd 'ave to say that 'e was cured!'

At the end of the block Danny took the stairs up to the Education Room. F Wing, although built later than the panopticon, was still constructed along the same severe lines. However, at either end of the landings there were several storeys of miscellaneous rooms, piled up higgledy-piggledy. Here the noxiousness of Victorian architecture, unconstricted by utility, burst forth into duff mouldings and depressing finials. This was Gormenghast Castle converted into an old people's home.

Danny spiralled his way up glancing into rooms as he went. Here was a therapy group – there an early-release group. Knots of nonces sat about reassuring each other that everything would be all right – for them. Danny climbed on. At the very top of the staircase he found the Education Room. He paused outside and glanced through the window set in the door. Inside there were four battered desks; three of them had old manual typewriters set on them, and the fourth an equally primitive word processor. Two of the desks were tenanted, one by Sidney Cracknell, the other by Philip Greenslade.

These were a couple of the most reviled nonces on the wing – nearly as reviled as Danny himself. They were both serving life, Cracknell for running a children's home in the way he thought best; Greenslade for a Clapton cab office-style abduction, torture, rape and murder of an eleven-year-old girl. They were physically diverse types. Cracknell was so warped and wizened, it was difficult to imagine anybody entrusting a gerbil to his care – let alone a human being; whereas Greenslade had the affable, open-featured countenance, the white hair, and twinkly blue eyes of a gregarious West Country publican. Which he was. Danny thought it a coincidence, if not an especially remarkable one, that they should both want to be electricians.

Together with them in the room was a third man, who had to be the teacher. He was big, at least six feet four, and standing with his back to the door. He had a hip-length leather jacket on and black jeans. When he turned, Danny was confronted by a face that was the essence of Ireland: two big pink ears; full, sensual red lips; a blob-ended Roman nose and a knobbly forehead. The man's waxy complexion suggested that his potato-shaped head had been buried in a field for some months; while his broad shoulders and solid stance implied that he might have dug it up himself. He was probably around forty. He had deep-set, curious grey eyes which radiated intelligence and ferocity in equal measure from beneath an overhang of thick brown quiff. As he watched him, the man trained these eyes on Danny, then crooked his finger. Danny entered the room.

'And you are?' The man's voice was quite high, but crisp and assured, with the merest whiff of an Irish accent.

'O'Toole, sir.'

'No sirs here, *Mister* O'Toole. I prefer the title "Mister". I am *Mister* Mahoney – I assume you know *Messrs* Greenslade and Cracknell?'

'Err, well, yeah, sort of . . .' Danny wanted to say 'by reputation', but didn't think it would go down well. As it was Cracknell was already tittering at him.

'Please, Mister O'Toole, be so good as to take a seat. We are a small convocation, but I hope we'll prove a productive one.' While Danny shuffled behind a desk the Irishman ran on. 'I myself hold with the Alcoholics Anonymous dictum regarding these things – wherever two students of creative writing are gathered together, it's possible to hold a class.'

Cracknell tittered some more at this quip, and Greenslade managed an amiable-sounding grunt, but Danny chimed up, 'Mister Mahoney?'

'Mister O'Toole, how may I assist?'

'Did you say creative *writing*?'

'That's right.'

'Thass like stories an' that?'

'Stories, short or otherwise, that are part of cycles or standing alone; novellas of all kinds and genres; novels even – although for the beginner I would counsel against attempting the longer narrative form; in a word: a tale, and you, Mr O'Toole, the teller. Hmm?'

Danny thought carefully before answering. The wiring/writing mix-up would make him a laughing stock for weeks, the running gags on the nonce wing had incredibly weak legs. And anyway, writing was a proper thing to do, writers – Danny thought – could make good money, especially if they wrote ads and stuff like that. The Governor might well look kindly on Danny's burgeoning writing career, let him off the nonce wing and give him protection from Skank's associates, one of whom would undoubtedly be waiting for Danny in the main prison.

'Mister Mahoney, this course, I mean, does it like . . .' Danny struggled to find some new words, Mahoney forbore from assisting. 'I mean will it like look *good* . . . I mean so far as the Governor's concerned.'

Cracknell was openly laughing now, but Mahoney silenced him with a glare. 'Mister O'Toole, I cannot speak for the Governor in this matter, or the Home Office in general. I don't believe they have an espoused position on writing as an aspect of rehabilitation. What I can tell you' – he slapped the desk in front of Danny to emphasise his easy articulation – 'is that *every single one* of the inmates who has completed my creative writing course has obtained a positive benefit from it. I'm not claiming to have produced an Henri Charriere, who after twenty years on Devil's Island had the singular success of publishing two bestselling novels, and having himself portrayed in the film version of one of them by Dustin Hoffman, but I've had my modest successes. One of my students last year is now being regularly published, and the year before we had a runner-up in the Wolfenden Prize for Prison Writing. That got a lot of good publicity for Wandsworth, and the then governor certainly looked very kindly on *that* inmate, got him the transfer he wanted to a cat. B, integrated nick, hmmm?'

Danny was convinced – he said, 'Will Smith.'

'I'm sorry, Mister O'Toole?'

'Will Smith. I mean, he'd have to play me in a film based on my prison experience – leastways I never seen that Hoffman blacked up nor nothing – in a skirt, granted, but never done up as a black geezer. A few years ago it'd have to be Wesley Snipes, but now it's gonna be Smith. The man's got more 'umour an' that, more sex appeal.'

There may have only been three students in Gerry Mahoney's creative-writing course, and they may have all been sex offenders, but despite that they managed to exemplify the three commonest types of wannabe writer. Greenslade was the relentless, prosaic plodder. Mahoney had read a story of his already, while they waited for other aspirants. It was suitable for a fourth-rate Lithuanian women's magazine, with its contrived characters, mawkish sentimentality and anachronistic locutions: 'And so it was . . .', 'The pale fingers of dawn . . .', and 'Deep in his heart . . .' all featured on more than one occasion. The only thing to indicate that this story was written by a man with an unconscious as dark as a black hole was the peculiar absence of affect. The author might have felt for his creations in the abstract, but on the page he manipulated them like wooden puppets, like victims.

Then there was the warped Cracknell. He was another stereotype – the compulsive scrawler. Once Cracknell got going, he couldn't rein it in. He'd been the first to arrive at the Education Room, dragging up the stairs with him – he walked with a particularly convoluted fake limp, the substance of ongoing and unsuccessful petitioning to the European Court of Human Rights – two heavy shopping bags full of hideous manuscript. 'My novels,' he'd puffed as he came in the door. 'I mean, I say novels, but really they're all part of the same big thing . . . like a . . . like a –'

'Saga?' groaned Mahoney, who had seen the like of this many times before. Cracknell positively beamed.

'Yeah, *saga*, that'd be the word, although it's not like there are a lot of Vikings and trolls and what have you in my novels; these are more sagas of the distant future – Oh! I like that, that's good, "Sagas of the Distant Future", that could be on the spines of all of them, with the individual titles on the covers, or perhaps the other way rou –'

'And what would you like me to *do* with these sagas, Mister Cracknell?' Mahoney had his hands on his hips and was observing Cracknell unpack his literary load, with such a baleful expression that his brows were not so much knitted as knotted.

'I'd be much obliged, Mister Mahoney – given that you're a published writer and that – if you'd give me your opinion.'

Mahoney flipped open the cover of the first of the eighty-five narrow feint exercise books Cracknell had piled up. Inside there was a furious density of manuscript: thirty words to the line, forty lines to the page. The handwriting was viciously regular, backward-sloping, and utterly indecipherable. Doing a quick calculation, Mahoney reckoned there had to be five million words in the exercise books – at least.

'You see,' Cracknell continued, 'these books here – one through twenty-seven – deal with the first three thousand years of the Arkonic Empire; and books twenty-seven through to forty cover the thousand-year rise to power of its arch rival, the Trimmian Empire. What I'd like is some gui –'

'Do you like writing, Mister Cracknell?'

'Pardon?'

'Is it the writing itself you enjoy, Mister Cracknell; or is it merely a way for you to fill your time?'

'Well, it certainly does fill my time. The bloke I share my cell with, he gets a little irritated now and then, because after lock-up it's out with the latest exercise book, open it up, and I may end up writing all night! By torchlight! I find it restful y'see –'

'That's as may be, Mister Cracknell, and I'm sure there is considerable merit in your sagas of the distant future, but as far as here and now is concerned, I'm not going to read them.'

Cracknell was dumbstruck, appalled. He nearly left the class forthwith, taking his literary tranche with him. He muttered about inmates' rights, about requests to the Governor, and finally about the possible envy of a certain Irish writer who might not be quite as fluent as Cracknell himself. Mahoney was unmoved. When, following Danny's arrival, he came to address the class as a whole, Mahoney set out his curriculum in a series of bold emphatics:

'Gentlemen, I appreciate Messrs Greenslade and Cracknell bringing me their work to read, but in my class we shall start from scratch, from the beginning, and proceed in an orderly fashion to the end. During this course you will write one short story, gentlemen, of between four and six thousand words. That's it. That's what we will focus on. Writing a story is deceptively easy – and deceptively hard. I don't want you to run before you can walk. I'm not going to be looking for fancy timescales, unusual settings, or stories that take place entirely within the mind of a stick insect.' He paused and gave Cracknell a meaningful look. 'And nor will I be satisfied with stories which feature unbelievable characters in unreal settings.' The look was directed at Greenslade. 'Your stories should be about something you *know*, they should be written in *plain* language, and they should have a *beginning*, a *middle*, and an *end*.'

These last assertions were punctuated by Mahoney turning to the clapped-out whiteboard at the front of the room, and writing the three words on it, each with an eeeking flourish of a marker pen. 'Beginning, middle, end,' Mahoney reiterated pointing to the words in turn, as if he half expected the three nonces to sing along. 'When I'm at the beginning I should know where I am, and the same goes for any subsequent point in the story. A story is a *logical progression* like any other. For the next twenty minutes or so I should like you to think about a subject for your story and write me a single paragraph about it.' As he said this Mahoney moved between the three of them depositing pieces of paper and biros. 'A single paragraph' – Crackell got the look again – 'that tells me *who, where, what, why*, and *when*. That's all, no fancy stuff. Got it?'

And with this the big Irishman plonked himself down in a chair, put his feet up on another, pulled a small-circulation left-wing periodical out of his jacket pocket, and commenced reading.

Twenty minutes later Mahoney identified the third stereotypic wannabe in his creative-writing course: the writer who can't write. Danny had just about managed a paragraph, but the sentences composing it infrequently parsed, and the individual words were largely spelt phonetically. Mahoney, however, did find to his surprise that Danny had genuinely fulfilled the assignment. His projected story had a beginning, a middle and an end, it had recognisable characters, and it was set in a milieu Danny clearly knew well. Mahoney looked down sympathetically at his newest recruit to the fount of literature. 'This isn't too bad, Mister O'Toole. I like the idea, although I'm not so sure how you're going to handle the triple cross over the coke deal, but you can get to that later. Are you serious about giving this a try?'

'Well, yeah, s'pose,' Danny muttered – Mahoney hadn't taken this trouble with the other two.

'In that case I would be obliged if you'd stop behind for a couple of minutes.'

When the repugnant duo had shuffled off down the stairs, each secretly satisfied that *he* was the most talented writer in HMP Wandsworth, Mahoney turned to Danny with a new and more serious expression on his broad pink face. 'You've got to get your spelling and grammar up to speed,' he said. 'It's no good having good ideas – and I can see you've got those – if you can't express them. I don't want you to take this the wrong way, but I've got two course books here designed to help adults with their literacy – with their reading and writing, that is. I'd like you to have at look at them. If we're going to make a writer of you, Mister O'Toole, you need to have a good command of basic grammar, hmm?'

Danny didn't take it the wrong way; he had decided a while before something quite momentous – he liked Mister Mahoney and wanted to please him. And within a matter of a fortnight Gerry Mahoney discovered something rather momentous as well – Danny O'Toole had genuine talent as a writer.

Danny chewed up the adult literacy course and digested it with ease. By the time the next class came round he was able to hand in to Mahoney all of the completed exercises. Mahoney gave him another book for a higher standard. Danny also began to read – and read at speed. He invested all of his birdhouse earnings to date in a torch and a supply of batteries. Then, after lock-up each afternoon, he proceeded to read his way through every single book available in the meagre nonce-wing library.

In the army Danny had read Sven Hassel, and on the outside he'd occasionally toyed with a thriller, but he'd never devoured print like this. He read historical romances and detective stories; he chomped his way through ancient numbers of the *Reader's Digest*; and he scarfed vast quantities of J.T. Edson westerns, with titles like *Sidewinder*, and *Five Guns at Noon.* As he read more and more Danny found himself essaying more difficult texts – the old dusty linen-bound books with the oppressively small type that were crowded on the bottom shelf of the library cart. So he came to read Dumas and Dickens, Twain and Thackeray, Galsworthy and – and an especial favourite – Elizabeth Gaskell.

Reading, for Danny, triggered an astonishing encephalisation. Not that he was stupid before – he was always sharp. But the reading burst through his mental partitions, partitions that the crack had effectively shored up, imprisoning his sentience, his rational capacity, behind psychotically patterned drapes. The alternative worlds of nineteenth-century novels enabled Danny to get a hard perspective on his own world, and to interpret his own life honestly. And there was more, much more. Danny, it transpired, also had an ear for prose. He could assay a line of English for its authenticity – the effectiveness with which the writer had psychically imprinted it – at the same time as he could parse it. As it was to crack addiction, so it was to literature – Danny was a natural.

After a month Gerry Mahoney began to bring books in for his favourite pupil, augmenting the tattered basics of the trolley with selections from his own library. Mahoney thought that Danny, being black, might prefer black literature. So he lent him James Baldwin ('Queer anna' coon – thass a turn up!'); Ralph Ellison ('That brother is *angry*, man – he's feelin' it all the time!'); Toni Morrison ('Yeah, yeah, yeah – but I did fill up a bit at the end.'); and Chester Himes ('Wicked! The man's a contender, funny, sharp, and he knows his shit – the fucker did time!'). Contemporary black writers appealed to Danny as well. He particularly admired the coolness of Caryl Phillips's prose and the quiet, lyrical anger of Fred D'Aguiar, but to Mahoney's enduring astonishment, the literature that Danny really liked was altogether different.

Danny liked the Decadents. To be more precise he adored tales of unnatural pleasures and artificial worlds. He devoured Maldoror; he cantered through *À Rebours*; and he spotted that *Dorian Gray* was sadly derivative. Within four months, with Mahoney's prodding, Danny was seriously translating *Paradis Artificiel* – and enjoying it. Not that any of this leaked into the story that Danny was writing himself; here he remained very much Mahoney's own acolyte. The story was set in Harlesden; it featured a protagonist not unlike Danny himself; it had the mandatory beginning, a middle Danny was attempting to slim down into an elegant waist, and an end that both of them agreed was an absolute stonker.

Already, even before the spectre of the prize came to haunt them, there was an exacting rivalry between the members of the writing class. Greenslade, who had once had a poem about his cat ('Oh beautiful cat/That makes me happy/Why can't you use your flappy . . . ?') published in the *Rainham Advertiser*, considered himself streets ahead of the other two when it came to the actual business of being a writer. 'Professionalism' was his watch word; and he would interrupt Mahoney's discourses on dialogue, or description, or development, to share his latest information on available grants, or royalty scales, or subsidiary rights. In fairness to Greenslade it has to be admitted that he *did* actually conform to most of the attributes of a British writer of his age (late fifties), without having had to go through the tedious business of actually publishing books, and then seeing them fade out of print, like dying stars.

Living stars were Cracknell's preoccupation. Mahoney had bullied him into attempting a short story, because that's what the class was all about, but Cracknell's subject matter – five thousand years in the history of the Printupian Empire – proved difficult to manage effectively in the abbreviated form. Rather than taking this personally – something he was incapable of, along with ordinary sympathy – Cracknell saw the whole thing in terms of genres. Science fiction – as its name implied – was the way forward, the way of the future. Anyone who continued to write sublunary tales was dealing in the worn coinage of mundanity. Not that

Cracknell could have put it that well himself, he simply interrupted Mahoney's flow from time to time in order to observe that this or that sci-fi writer had long ago exemplified the point the teacher was making, and could they move on?

Moving on remained in the forefront of Danny's mind. His new-found absorption into literature wasn't about to sway him from his course. Danny still burned with a fervour; he wanted off the nonce wing, then he could appeal, clear himself, get free. Fat Boy, who was quite happy where he was, thought the piles of paper that trailed though their cell were quite ridiculous. 'You wanna get a transfer, right?' he wheedled Danny.

'You know that, Fat Boy, you know that damn well.'

'An' you fink that all this reading and writing's gonna get it for you?'

'Maybe – I dunno.'

'One good bottler, my man, one good fucking bottler. Half an ounce of gear – a quarter even; and you'd be out of here. That old man Higson, yeah?'

'Principal Officer Higson?'

'Yeah, yeah, yeah, *Principal* Officer Higson, that's the one. He's an old-style PO, knows the form, right? Now, a couple of years ago it would've taken a poxy grand, but given inflation an' that, and given that you're near the beginning of your sentence – which always makes it look a bit fishy – he says he can manage it for two.'

'Manage what?'

'Your fucking transfer, you moody little git, your fucking transfer!'

'Two grand?'

'Wake up, will you, O'Toole? I can't make it any clearer; you come up with two K for old Higson an' he'll recommend your transfer to the Governor. You'll be in a fully integrated, cat. C nick before you can say knife. And the only fucking writing involved is one poxy letter – instead of all this bollocks.'

But Danny stuck with the bollocks and then Mahoney announced the prize. It was another Thursday afternoon in the Education Room, and the three grown men were leaning – cheeks cupped in hands, elbows jammed below – on their desks like adolescents. 'Gentlemen,' said Mahoney in his high, faintly mocking tones, 'I think I mentioned to you at the outset of this course the existence of a competition for prison writing. It's called the Wolfenden Prize, it brings the winner guaranteed publication in an anthology, five hundred pounds, and considerable esteem.' Mahoney pulled some entry forms from his briefcase and handed one to each of them, whilst continuing. 'It's awarded for the best submitted story of between four and six thousand words. So, gentlemen! You can see that there was method in my madness; that there was a reason why I was so insistent on beginnings, middles and ends. I think all of you have the ability to be potential winners.' Mahoney fixed all of them in turn with his gimlet gaze, and each of them thought he was referring to them alone. 'And entering the competition will bring our course to a natural, effective end, by enabling you all to learn the absolute importance of' – he began eeeking on the whiteboard – 'deadlines!'

Greenslade, preposterously, accused Danny of nicking his ideas. Cracknell, ludicrously, imagined Danny was appropriating what passed for his style. Tensions ran high. There were two weeks to go before the entries were due in, and during that time the three men studiously avoided one another. This wasn't easy, given that they all had to type up their manuscripts in the same room. Danny was acutely conscious that he'd managed to avoid any trouble on the nonce wing until now; but he sensed that Greenslade wouldn't hesitate if he thought that a strategic jugging was all that lay between him and the literary laurels.

Mahoney attempted to defuse the rivalry: 'I'm aware that the three of you feel very competitive about this, but I urge you to remember that there are at least ten men in this prison who will be entering for the Wolfenden, let alone the tens of others that will be entering in other nicks. And anyway, when you write you are competing only against yourself and posterity – there can be no living rivals.'

Mahoney certainly believed this, but he also believed that Danny was a genuinely talented young man who really deserved a break. He'd read Danny's story and it was streets ahead of most of the stuff currently being published. He'd never discussed Danny's crime, or sentence, to do so was taboo, but Gerry Mahoney didn't believe for a millisecond that he was a nonce.

Cal Devenish had agreed to judge the Wolfenden Prize for Prison Writing in the way that he agreed to do so many other things – without thinking. It sounded like a worthy cause, and there was something sexy about the whole notion of prisoners writing. Perhaps Cal would discover another Jack Henry Abbott, and become tied up in an infamous correspondence like Norman Mailer? What Cal hadn't factored in was the actual reading of the entries, set against his own fantastic indolence.

The shortlisted entries had arrived about three weeks before. Cal signed the courier's docket and leant them against the radiator by the front door. They were still there, a bulbous Jiffy-bag full of unimaginable pap. Cal groaned. It was a sharp, cold morning in early April, and he was scheduled to present the prize the following afternoon. He'd been awoken at nine sharp with an apposite alarm call: it was the secretary of the visitors' board at Wandsworth Prison, where the prize giving was to be held: 'Mr Devenish?'

'Yeah, what? Yeah, right?' Cal was gagging on consciousness.

'I'm sorry, I didn't wake you or anything?'

'Naw, naw!' Cal had been having a dream of rare beauty and poignance. In it, he had awoken and tiptoed downstairs to discover that the novel which he had been procrastinating over for the past two years had been completed during the night and lay, neatly word-processed on the desk. On picking it up and beginning to read, Cal was delighted to find that it was just as he had conceived of it during the long hours of not writing – but far far better.

'It's John Estes here, I'm the secretary of the visitors' board at Wandsworth.'

'Oh – yes.'

'We're very much looking forward to seeing you tomorrow –'

'Me too.'

'I wondered if it might be possible at this stage, Mr Devenish, for you to give me some idea of your decision regarding the winner – and the runners up?'

'Decision?' Cal floundered in his slough of irresponsibility.

'As to who's won the prize?'

'Is there any particular reason, Mr Estes?'

'Well, the thing is, as you may be aware, Mr Devenish, a lot of prisoners get transferred, and we wanted at least to be sure that the winner would be actually in the prison when you came tomorrow.'

'Oh I see, that does sound reasonable . . . the thing is, I was about to reread my short shortlist when you called. I should have an idea about that before the end of the day; may I call you then?'

Cal took the secretary's number down and hung up. Christ! It wasn't as if he didn't have enough other things to do today. He swung himself out of bed and, naked, stamped down the stairs of the mews house into the main room where he worked. Cal's desk was thatched with an interesting rick of unpaid bills, unanswered letters, notes for unwritten articles and unwritten books. As if to garnish this platter of ennui, almost all the sheets of paper, the desk itself, the computer and the fax machine had Post-it notes stuck to them recording never answered phone calls. Cal groaned and headed for the Jiffy-bag; at least with the formidable excuse of judging the short-story competition he could hold the rest of the obligatory world at bay for another day. He headed back up the stairs and dived into bed with the entries.

Cal Devenish had won a prestigious literary prize himself about five years previously. It was for his third novel, and the previous two – which had barely been in print – were yanked back into favour as well. The glow had been a long time fading, but now, along with the advance for a further novel, it had. Cal told himself that he was marking time, allowing himself the creative liberty of genuine abstraction. But on days like these, when he was confronted with other potential contenders' work, he was worse than rattled.

It didn't matter that about ten of the fifteen shortlisted stories were barely literate – at least their authors had managed to get the words down on paper. And anyway, reading bad writing was like playing against a bad opponent – your game suffered as well. Every duff sentence Cal read convinced him that he himself would never write another good one; every feeble plot he speedily unravelled hammered home the fact that he himself would never contrive another interesting one; and every wooden character's piece of leaden dialogue left him with the chilling intimation that he lacked any human sympathy himself.

The stories ran the whole gamut of predictable awfulness. There were chocolate-box romances, and dead-pet dramas; there were 'it was all a dream's, and Stephen King copycat nightmares. Naturally, there was also a whole sub-genre of justification, stories about honest crims who would do a bank and give the proceeds to a charity; or else save kiddies from unspeakable nonces. The stories were so terrible overall that Cal decided to order them in terms of being least bad, because he had such difficulty in judging any of them to be good.

That's until he got to the last three in the batch – these definitely had something, although exactly what it was difficult to say. One was a kind of spoof space opera about an intergalactic empire called Printupia. The writer had attempted to compress five thousand years in the history of this enormous state into the six thousand words allowed, and the result was an astonishingly compacted, near meaningless prose. Cal wondered if it might be a satire on the ephemerality of contemporary culture; narrative itself characterised as a non-biodegradable piece of packaging, littering the verge of the cosmos.

The second story was a piece of well-sustained, naturalistic writing about two young black guys dealing crack in north-west London. The writer had done well with all the orthodox conventions of the short story, but then he'd got carried away and added magical realist elements that jibed. There was that, and there was the uneasiness of his spelling – he could never quite decide whether to come down on the side of phonetic transcription of non-standard English, or not. The result was far less accomplished than Cal hoped for when he began reading.

The third story was the strangest in the whole batch, the most unsettling. Ostensibly a description of a man's intense love for his dead wife's cat, 'Little Pussy' was written with a close absorption into the minutiae of a solitary man's life that reminded Cal of Patricia Highsmith's style. There were other Highsmithian elements: the sense the writer imparted that awful things *were* happening – both physically and psychically – a little bit outside the story's canvas. The story was told in the first person – but the narrator wasn't simply unreliable, he was altogether non-credible as a witness to his own life. Nothing dramatic happened in the story – the man adapted his routines to those of the feline, and so mitigated his mourning for his wife – but when Cal tossed the typescript to one side, he realised it was one of the cleverest and most subtle portrayals of the affectless, psychopathic mind that he had ever read.

At five that afternoon Cal called John Estes back. 'Mr Estes? Cal Devenish here.'

'Ah, Mr Devenish, any decision in the offing?'

'Yuh – I think so. There's a short shortlist I have in mind – the stories by Cracknell, O'Toole and Greenslade – but I haven't decided on an overall winner as yet.'

'That's not necessary – I only needed to know that the winner would be able to attend –'

'And he will?'

'Oh yes, no problem there.'

At two o'clock the following afternoon Cal Devenish, wearing an unaccustomed suit and carrying a superannuated briefcase, met the secretary to the visitors' board in the reception area of Wandsworth Prison. Estes was carrying a large bunch of keys; he was a small, dapper man who radiated considered concern. 'It's a pleasure to meet you,' Estes said proffering his manicured hand, 'I enormously enjoyed *Limp Harvest.*'

'Thank you, thank you,' Cal blustered – he hated references to his past success. 'You're too kind.'

'The inmates are also very much looking forward to talking with you –'

'How many of them will be here?'

'Ah, well, there's a thing.' Estes paused to unlock a door and they passed out of reception and into a high walled yard. 'By a great, good coincidence, the three inmates on your short shortlist are the only ones left here at Wandsworth – all the others had been transferred.'

'That's lucky.'

'Isn't it.' Estes broke off again to unlock a gate, and they passed into a second high-walled yard.

They were crunching across this expanse of gravel, under the slitted eyes of the cell windows in E Block, when Estes halted and turned to Cal. 'Mr Devenish,' he began hesitantly, 'I don't want to confuse in any way, or unsettle you, but I did wonder if you noticed anything special about the three stories on your short shortlist?'

Cal was nonplussed. 'I'm sorry?'

'If there was anything the authors seemed to have in common?'

'Well.' Cal mused for a few seconds, scrabbling to recall the stories he'd hurriedly flipped through in bed the previous day. 'There was an element of err . . . how can I put it . . . sort of *distance*, almost a remoteness in all of them –'

'I'm glad you noticed that,' Estes cut in, 'you see the thing is all three were written – purely coincidentally – by inmates who're under protection.'

'Protection?'

'Erm . . . yes, prisoners who're . . . erm . . . convicted sex offenders.'

'I see.' Cal began internally to rewrite his speech as they crunched on across the yard.

'I thought I err . . . ought to tell you, because the prize giving is being held on F Wing. It's the block over there, outside the main prison, that's why we have to go through all these yards . . .' Estes unlocked another gate with one of his lolly-sized keys. 'F Wing is the clearing house for all protected inmates in Britain –'

'Jesus!' Cal blurted out. 'You mean where we're headed is the biggest concentration of sex offenders in the country?'

'Five hundred and forty, to be precise,' Estes said with a limp smile, then he unlocked the door to the nonce wing.

Gerry Mahoney came by Danny's cell to pick him up and take him to the prize giving. He already had Cracknell and Greenslade in tow. All three prisoners had done their best to spruce themselves up for the occasion, and Greenslade had, optimistically, starched creases into his prison-issue denims. The Wing was uncharacteristically busy today, knots of prisoners hung over the railings on the upper landings, and there was a large number of suited men milling around by the POs' office.

'Wass goin' on?' Danny asked Mahoney.

'You're going on – those are all AGs come for the prize giving. You see, the actual cheque will be handed over by Judge Tomy, the Chief Inspector of Prisons, and all the staff here are expecting him to make a speech that isn't entirely focused on literature.' The creative-writing class walked to the end of the wing, then began climbing the spiral stairs to the Education Room.

Upstairs the desks and equipment had been tidied away and about forty chairs had been crushed into the room. By the time the four of them had taken their seats, near to the back, the rest were fully occupied. As well as the twenty-odd assistant governors, in regulation middle-management suitings, there were about fifteen uniformed POs and the Governor himself, who was accompanied by a white-haired, elderly man sporting a loud bow tie and a cashmere overcoat.

'Tomy,' Mahoney whispered to Danny 'don't be fooled by his appearance – he's one of the most outspoken critics of the Home Office there's ever been. You wait – he'll give this lot a lambasting.'

As if prompted by Mahoney, Judge Tomy now stood and took control of the proceedings. He welcomed them all to the Wing and then gave a fifteen-minute speech outlining every single thing that was wrong with the prison administration, from failure fully to end slopping out, to food lacking adequate nutrition. The Governor, the assistant governors and the prison officers all sat tight, sinister smiles on their thinned lips. They could do nothing – Tomy was the Inspector of Prisons, he was merely doing his job.

Cal Devenish, who was sitting beside Judge Tomy at the front of the room, was amazed by the elderly man's combative vigour. This was an Inspector who took his remit seriously. But Cal was far more concerned about his role in things. It was easy to spot the three men who he'd shortlisted for the Wolfenden Prize – they were the only prisoners in the room, crushed in between the rows of their jailers. The young black prisoner was obviously the writer of the story about the crack dealers. He looked intelligent, but his expression was on the aggressive side of fierce. Cal felt threatened whenever this gaze fell on him.

Next to the black guy sat an amiable-looking, white-haired man in his late fifties. Cal knew better than to be taken in by such superficial considerations, but it was really very hard to conceive of this man as being a *serious* sex offender. He might have been a flasher of some sort, Cal hypothesised, but not a truly revolting nonce. Anyway, by contrast, the man who was sitting next to him was so obviously the real McCoy that he made everyone else in the room look like Peter Pan by comparison. This individual's hideous countenance was the fleshly equivalent of a wall in a public urinal, the individual tiles grouted together with shit. He was terrifying. Cal pegged him as the science-fiction satirist.

Danny sat staring at Cal Devenish. So this was the man who was going to decide his fate? This lanky, bearded thing in a black suit, who so resembled a white equivalent of . . . the Fates. They were back. They lingered in the corners of the room. They hissed and cackled, updating Danny's doom on this of all days. Danny was paralysed. He looked at the Governor, willing him to look up and see this model prisoner, this aspirant writer so worthy of transfer. The Governor remained staring abstractedly at a broken lampshade which dangled above his head.

Cal Devenish got up to make his speech. He voiced some platitudinous – but for all that heartfelt – observations on the liberating, empowering capabilities of writing, especially for those who're in jail. Cal was going to analyse the three shortlisted stories in considerable detail, but the nonce revelations had put him off his stride. He confined himself to mentioning the strong points of all three, before concluding limply that 'Little Pussy' exhibited all the hallmarks of a compelling moral ironist. Cal had no hesitation therefore in awarding the Wolfenden Prize for Prison Writing to . . . Philip Greenslade.

Cal Devenish almost gagged when Philip Greenslade was within a few paces of him – the rot of the man's corrupt soul was that strong-smelling. Cal felt even sicker when he had to shake Greenslade's hand – it felt like the clamp of a laboratory retort stand, only thinly upholstered with flesh.

'Thank you so very much.' Greenslade's tone was wheedling, despite there being nothing to wheedle. 'I can't tell you how much I value your judgement . . .' He gripped Cal's hand a little tighter, and Cal thought he might scream. 'I so look forward to having a proper discussion with you about literature when all of this is over.'

Cal realised that he'd given the prize to the wrong man – there hadn't been a particle of ironic distance in 'Little Pussy': the author *was* a psychopath.

The Governor turned to his deputy who was sitting beside him. 'Is that the Greenslade who's always petitioning for a transfer to a cat. C? The sickening nonce who did that murder?'

'Yes, Governor, that's the man.'

'Well, since he's won this bloody prize, let's use it as an excuse to get shot of the tedious bugger. Prepare the papers for his transfer when we get back to the office.'

Danny was very nearly in tears – he simply couldn't believe it. How could this twat Devenish have chosen Greenslade's story over his own, it made no sense at all. The only way Danny could prevent himself from crying out was by staring straight ahead and gripping the back of the chair in front of him as tightly as he could.

Gerry Mahoney tried to bank down Danny's distress. 'I've no idea what got into Cal Devenish,' he said. 'I know him slightly and I've always respected his literary judgement. Mind you, if it's any consolation I've heard it rumoured that he has a bit of a drug problem. Perhaps that's what queered it – he couldn't cope with the realism in your story . . .'

But Danny wasn't in the mood for a post-mortem. He got up and began to shoulder his way to the front of the room. His cell was preferable to this shit hole full of screws. At the door, in his haste to get out, he collided with a tall suit, which turned to reveal that it was owned by the Governor. 'Sorry, sir,' Danny muttered.

'That's all right – ah! It's O'Toole, isn't it?'

'Yes, sir.'

'Well, well done, O'Toole, it seems you took my advice on committing yourself to a useful course of study. Mr Mahoney tells me you have a genuine talent – see that you cultivate it.'

'I will, sir.' The Governor turned to depart, but once he'd gone a couple of paces he turned back to face Danny.

'And O'Toole.'

'Yes, sir?'

'Better luck next year.'

Conversations with Ord

I was down to one friend, Keith, a former bank robber. We never talked about his bank-robbing days, just as we never discussed the fact that, although he'd long since said he would, he never got round to decorating his flat. A bucket, ladder, roller, tray and drip-stained cans of emulsion had stood in the hall for years, for so long, in fact, that arguably they now constituted the decorative scheme.

There was a dark, unpalatable truth hunched behind the unused decorating gear. Keith's flat was furnished with what had been the acme of modernity in 1973. An oval glass-topped dining table with steel legs like an inverted coat tree dominated the main room, the six matching high-backed chairs were too scary to sit on. A seating area had been contrived around a vinyl kidney of coffee table, and here a three-seater divan upholstered in vomit-coloured, oatmeal-textured fabric formed a right angle with a two-seater divan upholstered in fluffy electric-blue fabric. In the neglected portions of the poorly converted flat – its queered corridors and unnecessary half-landings – yuccas loitered, like the urban cousins of absentee triffids, willing to wound but afraid to strike. In the bathroom dusty, slatted cabinets harboured old liniment and when opened disgorged silvery tongues lumpy with aspirin. I never dared to enter the bedroom.

Keith, presumably, had thought his furniture, when he bought it in the early 1980s, to be amazingly futuristic, quite simply out of this world. And it was out of his world, because he had – as he quietly reminded me when I made some unthinking aside about glam rock, Camden Lock, or Pol Pot – missed the 1970s altogether.

Keith and I had a certain rapport – we were both formidable mnemonists. Keith was the first man I've ever been able to play mental Go-Chess with. Mental Go-Chess is a game of my own invention in which, at any point during an orthodox mental-chess game, either opponent can suddenly change the game to Go. Both players must then transform the sixty-four-square internalised chess board into a three-hundred-and-sixty-one-intersection Go board, substitute the appropriate number (ten for a queen, eight for a castle, etc, etc) of Go stones for each of his remaining chess pieces, and then congruently configure them. Obviously, if you were black in the chess game you remain so in the Go game.

Keith was dead good at mental Go-Chess, something I couldn't help but put down to his many years of solitary confinement.

'Did you do a lot of systematised abstract thinking and memory exercises when you were in solitary?' I asked him after he'd beaten me at mental Go-Chess for the third time in succession.

'No,' he replied flatly and limped on along Battersea embankment – we invariably played while strolling – a great broken bear of a man, with a full beard and shoulder-length hair. I suspect that Keith thought his coif made him look like a rock star from the unnameable decade, but the truth was that he closely resembled a late-nineteenth-century patriarch, deranged by sexual repression and successful imperialism.

If we were tiring of mental Go-Chess we'd invent imaginary dialogues. One Keith and I particularly liked was entitled 'Conversations with Ord'. Ord was a general, in his eighties, who had fought in every important campaign of the first fifty years of the twenty-first century. Flamboyant, openly homosexual, violent, brilliant, Ord had something to say about anything and everything. He had invented and then marketed his own range of militaristic skin-care products; he had synthesised all the Eastern martial arts into an exercise regime suitable for the fattest of Western veal calves, then sold millions of DVD manuals. During Ord's most savage and protracted campaigns he'd hung a sign on the flap of his self-invented, self-erecting tent HQ, which read 'I am ninety-nine per cent fit, are you?' His staff officers entirely grasped the meaning of this, and just as they surrendered themselves to his aggressive sexual attentions, so they also recognised his profound asceticism and radical scholarly bent. Ord had translated the Upanishads into the street language of Los Angeles's black ghettos. He saw himself standing in a long line of learned warriors, stretching back through Wilfred Thesiger, T.E. Lawrence and Count Tolstoy, to Frederick the Great, Akbar, King Alfred and even Marcus Aurelius.

I liked being Ord, but Keith was masterful. When he was being Ord and I played the role of Flambard – his reticent biographer and amanuensis – we could often stay in character as far upriver as Teddington Lock, or as far downriver as the site of the Millennium Dome.

But no matter how far we walked, these lateral journeys were the only relief we ever had from the suffocating confines of South London. Not for Keith and me were the cultured salons of the moneyed and the creative, where the high Regency ceilings opened out into an international atmosphere of sustained invention. Nor did we have access to the roof gardens of the beautiful people, where the platinum-plated pelvises of the rich paraded as purple parakeets trilled, each species mimicking the other.

No, we were confined to the horizontal. Keith and I inhabited a city of dusty parks, 1930s blocks built round scraps of park, 1950s blocks built behind oblong strips of park, and 1960s, '70s and '80s blocks built over-toppling, or actually within, parks. Degenerate parks with piddling water features and knock-kneed, demented loggias. Victorian parks, their faded imperial grandeur and once exotic plantations replicating the pattern of shoddy trade with former dominions. In Vauxhall Park – which was particularly favoured by street alcoholics – there was a crappy row of miniature buildings – house, church, cinema – done up crudely but durably with emulsion-slapped-on-concrete. Yet some way into our second season of walks I noticed that these had been subjected to miniature vandalism, the church's spire bent, the house's roof bashed in, the cinema's façade sprayed with a giant graffiti tag. Of course, this was as nothing to Ord, who in 2033 (and again in 2047) had seen the mud flats of the Dhaleswari turn to lava as his jet-helicopter gunships took out the shanty towns of Dacca. Nothing at all.

As for so many others the pretext for our park life was a dog, Dinah, Keith's shambolic Dalmatian. No one likes to admit that they like London parks pure and simple, so thousands have traditionally relied on a canine alibi. A few even go so far as to have children, in order to justify hanging out by the swings or feeding the ducks. Ord had trenchant things to say on the subject of dogs. His own genetically modified South African Ridgeback-Poodle cross had lived to the age of fifty-seven and reputedly killed as many men. Ord had doted on Robben, and after the hound died he became distinctly cynical about the species, viewing them as little more than effective parasites.

'Isn't it bizarre,' Keith said, in character as Ord, 'that you two – allegedly intelligent – grown men have gone even further than most dog owners of your era. With no significant livelihood, appreciable interests, or even viable relationships of your own, you've become the parasites of this parasitical creature. It would take a complete collapse in the social order to release you from your bondage.'

'Maybe . . .' I acknowledged, then donning Flambard's mantle I continued, 'Ord, presumably you've been in many war zones where dogs have reverted to their natural savagery, hunting in packs and so forth?'

But cruelly, Ord was not to be drawn. 'Dog's done a shit, Flambard,' he snapped. 'Best pick it up.'

I gloved my hand in a Salisbury's bag and did the necessary, smearing runny faeces on the asphalt. What was Keith feeding her on?

'Perhaps you two should become faggots and hang out at the Hoist,' Ord sneered. 'You couldn't be more ensnared than you are already.'

Bondage of all kinds preoccupied Ord, although he professed to have no taste for it himself. Leaving Vauxhall Park we would pass by the Hoist, a club in the arched arse-end of the battered old railway viaduct. On a couple of occasions we did go in for a drink, and ended up sipping Red Bull and vodka, while watching the sado-masochists assess one another's heft. Epicene opera critics stood with us at the bar, awaiting the arrival of Jean-Paul Gautier and discussing the novels of Théophile Gautier. But it hardly mattered whether we swung in the Hoist or not, for it was almost always constricted and dark in this city of ours. It made no difference if we trolled around Battersea Park, or ranged along the underside of the Power Station, and the badlands of the Thames littoral, there was no escaping the bondage of our own claustrophobia.

Even in high summer the clear sky seemed particulate, as half-visible droplets of heavy metals drizzled down on us. To walk the dry ski slopes of Lavender Hill was like struggling into unfamiliar underwear. Everything grated. Sometimes, stopping for a meat patty at an Afro-Caribbean takeaway, and feeding a few scraps of virulent yellow pastry to Dinah's wet black maw, I would despair of myself. Why had I found it necessary to exile so many people I had once been intimate with, to the very periphery of my acquaintance?

To begin with the outer circle had been easy to abandon. A few unanswered phone calls, a flannelled date – not exactly a stand-up but almost – and these seedling friendships would shrivel then die. There were more established relationships which had required persistent neglect. It could take as long as nine months of evasions, unspoken intimacies, unshared items of gossip, and unattended parties for these to wither by the roadside of life. But they did, eventually. And then there was the tangle of close connections that had to be actively hacked away at. So it was that I insulted those I had formerly embraced, I traduced those I had once exalted, and I resolutely failed to recognise former lovers in the bakery aisle of Nine Elms Salisbury's. This went on until the awful ullage had occurred, and all that remained was bitter salt.

It was arrogance, naturally, an arrogance that was so solid within me I could feel it. I actually *felt* superior to myself – let alone others. I would hunch on the corner of the tilting heap of old mattresses which served me as a bed and pinch the slack flesh on the insides of my knees, whilst muttering, 'Not good enough . . . Not good enough . . .' like a child who has yet to appreciate the raw vulnerability of his own anatomy. I scrunched up my ears, bending their cartilage until it creaked. I popped my eyelids inside out, and pulled my scrotum up and around until it encased my penis in its hairy basket. On an average morning, as I was actually performing this ritual of superiority, my landlady, Mrs Benson, would call me from downstairs. 'It's Keith on the phone for you! He's wondering whether you'd fancy a walk.'

Ord had uncomfortable observations to make about my new living arrangements, for all that they amused him. 'Once you had too much space, a large house and an accommodating wife. Now look at you, the lodger of another family!'

I deserved his contempt – when my marriage broke up I rented this attic at the Bensons', a Tetra-pak of space, close in summer, distant in winter, in which the possessions salvaged from my former life looked like precisely that. As I lay on my springy, sleepy slab, fat-bellied planes wallowed in the muddy cloud overhead, threatening time after time to plop through the skylight. Even Keith was a relief.

'What d'you think of the balloon?' Keith said, one day in late summer when we were on our way to another MI6 cook-out. The balloon had been up for some weeks, tethered four hundred feet above Vauxhall Cross. But although it was on our beat we'd yet to visit its moorings. From where we currently were, crossing Battersea Park in a south-easterly direction, we could see its stripy awning of a belly nudging against the defunct cooling towers of the Power Station. Foreshortened London.

'Pssht! Dunno. It's a balloon, I s'pose. Can you go up in it?'

'Course you can; what would be the fucking point in tethering a balloon four hundred feet over London if you couldn't go up in it?'

'Dunno. Observation of some kind – I mean it's right next to MI6.'

'You have distinctly primitive ideas about the secret state,' said Keith in Ord's camp, fruity and yet severe voice. 'Neither cloaks nor daggers are necessary at all when there are many many men – and women – who regard proximity, loyalty and even fealty as the mere small change of historic arbitrage. When I was suppressing the anarcho-narco warlords of Grand Cayman in '31, my death squads were penetrated to the very apex of their command structure. If I executed one of my traitorous officers another one immediately took his place and fed vital intelligence to the other side. Eventually I realised that the swine had penetrated us so deeply that I myself must logically fall under suspicion.'

'B-but what,' Flambard stammered obsequiously, 'd-did you do?'

'Simple, I too swapped sides. Taking control of the anarcho-narco forces I attacked the government and seized control of the State. With my hand thus massively enhanced' – Ord clenched his meaty fist and hit out towards the balloon – 'I could turn on the terrorist scum and finally eliminate them. Victory as usual!'

Still, whatever Ord said, the idea that the balloon was an observation platform didn't seem such an absurd notion to me. After all, if the not-so secret service could flaunt itself in a ludicrous postmodern wedding cake of an office building immediately abutting Vauxhall Bridge, then why shouldn't they have a hot-air-powered eye in the sky? Besides, I liked the MI6 building, its beige concrete façade and cypresses for finials suggested a kindlier apparatus than Ord's brutal vision, and there was also the tiny roomlet of riparian beach next to it, a notch of the way we were. The oddest driftwood and trash got snagged by the notch, then, at low tide, Keith and I would build little fires out of it. As dusk fell we'd sit toasting marshmallows and staring moodily across the ruched brown river to the Tate Gallery on the opposite shore, while Dinah frolicked leadenly on the compacted silt.

Sometimes, when night had all but closed in, the Frog Tours amphibian would come pitching and yawing upriver from Westminster. Going half-about in the ebb tide, its way-off-road tyres would skitter and then gain purchase on the concrete ramp which angled down from our beach. With a throaty roar of its diesel engine the bizarre vehicle mounted towards us, until with a splutter and a gasp it freed itself from the heavier element. Keith grabbed Dinah, and the three of us flattened against the vertical dunes of our refuge. Bemused tourists stared down at us from the cabin of the amphibian as it headed for the Albert Embankment. A terrified Dinah would howl, and once or twice Keith lost his cool, chucking shingle against the garish landing craft as it established its commercial beachhead. Then I had to assume the role of Ord and restrain him.

But on this particular day it wasn't the Frog Tour that concerned him. 'Nah,' said Keith as we circled the ornamental lake, 'the balloon's a tourist thing. It's a tenner to go up – maybe we should do it. We could leave Dinah with that nice Australian lad in Majestic Wine –'

'But why – why would we want to go up in it?'

'To see the city, you pillock. To orientate ourselves. Jesus, we spend most of our waking hours trudging round this bit of London – why not see it from the air?'

'No thanks, I feel hideously orientated already . . .' I felt a surge of anger and when I continued it was as Ord. 'About the only thing I could think of doing in that balloon is holding a debate –'

'A debate? Whaddya mean?'

For the first time in weeks I'd both grabbed the role of Ord and caught all of Keith's attention. I could tell this because it was his habit, when his massive Difference Engine fell properly into gear, to call Dinah over, put her on the lead, then walk with her closely to heel, as if he were a blind man entering his seeing-eye dog for Cruft's. Some baggy-clad adolescents stared at us as we worked our way over the Queenstown Road roundabout: big, little and spotty, side by side by side, was that what they were thinking?

'So, General, this balloon debate,' Flambard enquired as we marched under the railway bridge which spans the appendix of Prince of Wales Drive, 'would it be like a parachute debate?'

How I loathed Flambard's mock humility. He was like all biographers of the living, a ghoul standing by the road his subject was due to drive along, waiting for the inevitable crash so he could gawp and then write it down.

'Quite so,' Ord snapped.

'The loser would . . . what? Be thrown out?'

'I'd rather hoped they would have the decency to jump, but yes, if necessary they would be thrown. I well remember the balloon debate I had in '42 with Dickie Heppenstall and the Maharaja of Rawlpindi. That was during our pole-over-pole circumnavigation of the globe, and we had very little to do for weeks on end as our capsule was batted about the stratosphere by the trade winds. Madness to attempt such a journey, but then madness was always my forte . . .'

Ord paused, Dinah was straining at her leash, responding to the chorus of anguished barks from the canine rejects banged up in the Dogs' Home. Flambard got her under control, and then as we went on he remained respectfully silent.

'We were up there for so long that I was able to interest both men in certain practices, but inevitably that led to pettishness, jealousy and eventually a terrible falling out as they vied for my affections. A fight of some kind was looking increasingly likely, so in order to appeal to both men's intellectual vanity I proposed we debate the motion: "This capsule believes that the man of action has more to contribute to the world than the man of learning." We all spoke . . .'

We turned the corner into Kirtling Street, and the dun peaks of sand and aggregate in the yards of the Tideway Works loomed into view, arid urban alps.

'And our contributions were judged from the ground by the then Professor of Metaphysics at Oxford, and Stig Öbernerdle, the powerboat-racing wunderkind of the interwar years.

'To give the Maharaja credit, when he realised he'd lost he went as quietly as a lamb. We dropped the balloon down to five thousand metres and he climbed out of the porthole. It was a dramatic scene, the sun rising over the Weddell Sea, the towering bergs throwing long shadows, and if I craned up I could see the tiny figure of the Maharaja crawling up the massive curve of the balloon above me, like a fly on a wine glass. Over it all scudded the cloud cover – awesome.'

'But tell me, General, what about this rather more lowly balloon debate. Had you a motion in mind?'

'Mmm.' Damn! Keith had wrong-footed me. Getting Ord back from the future was always tricky, and I felt my Ord mask slipping.

'And what about the participants?' Keith wheedled.

'Err, you – me, obviously; and . . . and . . . Sharon Crowd.'

'Ha-ha! I see, back to that, are we, Sharon-bloody-Crowd.'

'There's no need for you to get narked –' The Ord mask came right off; my face felt nude without it.

'Oh-no,' Keith snorted, 'not when you have so conspicuously already.'

There it was, out in the open, the nub of our friendship, and perhaps also the root of our dreary common isolation. Keith had an affair with Sharon Crowd. They broke it off, and, without knowing the whys and wherefores, I then had an affair with Sharon Crowd. In due course this ended and she went back to Keith. Hence the bloody between Sharon and Crowd. Tmesis, it's called, one word shoved between the legs of another. Months later, at about the last party I ever attended, a louring bear of a man came up and prodded me in the back while I was plopping guacamole on a paper plate, then he bellowed loud enough for the other guests to hear, 'Why don't you just put your prick up my arse and cut out the middle-fucking-woman!'

This was Keith, who was, by now, once more without Sharon Crowd. I never discovered whether he felt genuinely aggrieved about the loss of Sharon Crowd. If, like some true romantic, his flesh crawled from the wanting of her, his belly gurgled at the thought of her belly, and his eyes watered when he glimpsed the future stretching out ahead of him without her. I didn't want to believe that Keith was so sentimental – not about Sharon Crowd at any rate. It hardly fitted in with his background in violent crime, or his formidable reasoning powers, especially given the way she'd unceremoniously shafted him.

Bax, an ageing, hairy, dwarfish, and onetime very successful novelist, also knew Sharon Crowd, carnally and otherwise. Bax said of Sharon Crowd, 'You've got to admire her style. In the 1960s when you'd see girls weeping on the stairs outside parties, because they'd had some man do them wrong, you'd also see the odd smattering of doleful, lachrymose boys – they were Sharon's.'

'But Bax,' I'd objected, 'you can't champion a woman solely on the basis that she's a cruel deceiver.'

'Can, and do. Also she's clever and still remarkably handsome, which counts for something.'

At this juncture he'd leant forward to apply himself to rolling up a little turd of a cigarette, and dislodged the perilous quiff of hair that perched atop his head, so that it fell like a curtain over his puckish face. This was Bax's way of showing that a subject was closed.

But Bax had never been one of Sharon Crowd's lachrymose boys. Bax didn't do lachrymose, except – as he once confided in me – when he finished one of his novels, although whether this was because he felt keenly the loss of his intellectual companion, or he was already anticipating the indifference of the reading public, he never vouchsafed. Keith too had once had a promising little career – albeit his second – as an academic. But then Sharon Crowd had exposed the delicate embroidering of some of his research and Keith lost his job. What was it with Sharon Crowd? Professional jealousy didn't seem likely, even though she was a chalk-pusher herself. Why was it that she had so little respect for pillow talk? Because for me, well, there was the small matter of ten years' marriage down the tubes. I lost sleep with Sharon Crowd three times – we have no need of euphemisms here – and it felt worth it at the time. Hell, it still seems worth it now I'm accelerating at 32 feet per second per second. Her lovemaking was a peculiar combination of the tender and the athletic; frequently, having engendered a bruise, she'd lay her thin lips on it.

At a Christmas party in Clapham, given by friends with a mortgage the same size as our own, Sharon Crowd sidled up to Maeve, my then wife. The interval between our third bout and what I fervently hoped would be our fourth was already far longer than that separating the second from the third. At a punch-in-the-gut level I knew time out had already been called between us.

'Your husband's penis really is most astonishing,' was her opening. And when Maeve failed to respond to this sally, unable to recognise any connection between said organ and this stringy, washed-out, fiftyish blonde, Sharon Crowd continued: 'I mean the way that when erect it bends so exaggeratedly to the left, then tips up at the end. In a nose you'd call this aspect retroussé.'

Comprehension soaked into Maeve's face like spilt milk into kitchen towelling. 'You mean to say you've been fucking my husband?' Maeve made a fisheye lens of her wine glass through which to exaggerate the truth.

The conversation I'd been having near by with the host about free-range chickens was decapitated. It ran around for a few seconds then died.

'Yup. I've stopped now though . . . he isn't . . . he isn't very *versatile*, is he?'

That hurt. I'd fed it to her in every conceivable position. We'd copulate with her on top, with me on top, side-by-side, standing up, sitting down, leaning to and falling over. I thought I'd been leading this, but it turned out to be Sharon Crowd's merry dance.

'Face it,' she said to me months later when the lawyers' letters had stopped coming, 'if the marriage had been any good it would've survived my intervention – so you'd have to say what I did was for the best. After all it's not as if there were children involved.'

Even at the time this struck me as the most Stalinist application of logic, allowing for the possibility of such alarming moral propositions as: If I hadn't killed you, you would've died anyway. Keith took an even more robust view. He was extremely fond of Maeve, admiring both her capability and her sociability. As far as he was concerned there was a child in the marriage, me, and this was my way of showing that it was time I left home and let my mummy get on with her life. In Keith's eyes Sharon Crowd remained mysteriously pure, apart from this little matter of destroying his career.

Two days after Ord had proposed the balloon debate, Keith and I went for one of our regular lunches with Sharon Crowd. Despite – or perhaps because of – her betrayals, the three of us remained close. One argument for this was that her flat was a convenient staging post on our walks. The other was that Sharon made us delicious meals. Pasta with ginger and tomato, fresh sardines swimming in lemon juice, artichoke hearts in melted butter, peppers stuffed with peppery stuff, and so on. White bourgeois woman tapas. She prepared the food in Le Creuset dishes, in her tiny galley of a kitchen, and brought it to Keith and me, where we sat, looking down the Wandsworth Road towards Nine Elms.

Sharon Crowd's flat was in a block next to her place of work, South Bank University. Ever since the balloon had arrived, and was winched into the municipal heavens, Sharon Crowd's dining area was the place to be if you wanted a spanking view.

'Have you been up in it?' Keith queried, poking a fork laden with bruschetta at the balloon, which from this vantage was well clear of the surrounding city, and motionless in the typically pewter sky.

'No, why should I?' Sharon poured me another glass of Côte Rotie – there was no faulting her as a hostess.

'He and I are holding a balloon debate.' The bruschetta wavered round to me.

'What's that – like a parachute debate?'

'Sort of, but instead of the winner getting the parachute the loser jumps from the balloon.'

'And what's the subject?'

At this Keith clammed up. It was one thing to disrespect Sharon Crowd in the privacy of our mournful promenades – quite another to do so to her face. I, however, felt a rush of delirious irresponsibility, a carefree loss of all self-protective instincts, and said, 'You.'

'I'm sorry?' Sharon Crowd's bone-china brow cracked.

'We're going to debate your conduct towards us – Keith and me, that is.'

'Conduct?' Her incredulity curdled the atmosphere. 'Let me get this straight, you troglodytes –'

'That isn't, "nyum-nyum", fair . . .' said Keith. The long years of imprisonment meant he was able to do indignation and tomato salad simultaneously.

'Nomads then. Yes, you two nomads are going to debate – to the death – my conduct towards you?'

'If Bax is to be believed' – having taken on the challenge I was determined to push this as far as it would go – 'many many hundreds of similar offences should be taken into consideration.'

Shaping words suddenly seemed too hard for our mouths and they regressed to munching, squidging, cracking and lunching. From where I sat Sharon Crowd's sharp profile was etched against the painful concrete portico of South Bank University, which jutted out with brutal certitude. The two façades were not dissimilar, and Sharon Crowd's chin, although small, was impressively cleft, like facial buttocks.

'You never had any academic prospects to speak of, Keith.' Sharon Crowd's tone was brusque. 'Your research capabilities were negligible, and your ability to teach was severely compromised by the fact that the majority of your students were born in a decade of which you have no direct knowledge. I was doing you a fav –'

'What!?' Keith couldn't suppress this yelp.

'A favour. You don't know your own mind, you would've been humiliated. Publicly humiliated. You'd have found yourself worse off than you were already' – again the Crowd counterfactual – 'and certainly worse off than you are now.'

Keith hung his big head, bruised with the bumpy passage of the years. He had no ability to resist her. It was the same tactic she'd applied to me; by proposing an alternative – and still more negative – future, Sharon Crowd completely extirpated Keith's free will. He'd told me that on occasion she still came to his place and 'did things'. His imprecision matched my own unwillingness to imagine what such things could be, and I hoped my refusal to comment was interpreted by Keith as evidence that she still did things with me as well.

Now Sharon Crowd was the convenor of the business studies department at SBU, she undertook many lucrative consultancies and even appeared on late-night current affairs programmes, debating matters of public import. Her burnish, once merely institutional, was now digital and televescent. Her suits had always been severe but now they were mannish. Her tits were non-existent. When we'd lost sleep together her nipples had been astonishing, smooth pink cones of erectile tissue rising straight from the grille of her ribcage, but perhaps they were gone now? I certainly couldn't visualise them any more – all I saw beneath her tailored breastplate was smooth, nippleless skin.

'And you, you're the originator of this motion?' She looked at me as if I were very small, a long way away and falling fast.

'You're a tyrant, Sharon,' I pronounced. 'You may even be corrupt.'

Her eyes zeroed in on the level of wine in my glass. 'You're probably drunk, and therefore not worth talking to – but let's say you are, you think I mistreated you, do you?'

'Sharon, given the benefit of hindsight, the passage of the years, after many a summer – and all that jazz . . .' I inhaled more wine, chiefly to wind her up. 'I can say with some authority, and all due respect, that at the end of the day you righteously fucked me over. Did it to me up the arse with a fucking telegraph po –'

'You *are* drunk – offensive as well. Get him out of here, Keith.'

Late that afternoon we were back at the MI6 beach and I was winding up the security cameras which sat on poles and the tops of walls. If I paused behind a pillar, the camera, which was tracking my movement, became paralysed, wavering in the place I should've been. 'Like me and Sharon Crowd!' I shouted over to Keith who was dabbling in the tidal wrack with Dinah, their six legs tangled up in nylon twine, sodden newsprint, and water-smoothed wood.

'What?'

'The security camera – it thinks it knows where I ought to be – but of course I'm not. Anyway, what I know – and it doesn't – is that it's only a machine . . . Well . . . I blew that, didn't I?'

I climbed over the fence, descended a flight of five concrete steps, crunched across the shingle to where man and dog stood.

'Not necessarily.' Keith sounded gnomic, he was in a serious mood, like when I accidentally referred to the unnameable decade.

'She's never going to go up in the balloon now, is she?' I felt teary carpets unroll on my cheeks. 'Not now she knows we want to chuck her out.'

'There are several considerations.' Ord picked up a length of old curtain rail from the beach; he used its tip to inscribe his battle plan in the silt. 'Firstly, she may not think we're serious.' His militaristic boot descended on a tessellated pane of glass set in a ruptured frame. 'Secondly, she may be so proud she wishes to defy us, and the third – and I think strong – likelihood is that she'll do it because Bax wants her to.'

'Bax?'

'I've dealt with people like Sharon Crowd, y'know. In the 2050s when I was stationed in Dar es Salaam, there was a very proud woman – a cult priestess – who became overly attached to my adjutant –'

But I wasn't in the mood to play Flambard, 'Bax?' I reiterated.

'Yes.' I couldn't tell if it was Keith or Ord speaking. 'I have considerable sway with him, y'know.'

I looked over my shoulder, through the defile between MI6 and Tintagel House, then across four carriageways to where the balloon crouched behind the Vauxhall viaduct. It was moored for the night, a cumbersome woman in a loud sundress who'd been mugged by gravity. It was hot all right, and it was bright enough still, but the light came welling up from an unidentifiable place, like the blood from an internal injury.

After a very long while Keith said, 'Come on then, let's play Go-Chess.'

'I don't *want* to play Go-Chess.' Why couldn't he acknowledge my pain?

'Let's have a dialogue then, I'll be Ord –'

'I don't want to do Flambard!'

'OK, OK, keep your fucking hair on, you don't have to, just let me be Ord and I promise I'll amuse you.'

So we passed on along Lambeth Walk and Ord regaled me with his tales of how he suppressed the Dog-Headed Jockstraps of Minnesota, the most feared motorcycle gang of the 2030s.

I met Bax in the Beer Engine, a pub in Stockwell. It was an awful dive, yet Bax frequented it so much that they kept his tankard hanging behind the bar. This was a ghastly miniature stein, with a witch's face bulging from the green glaze. Bax drank light and bitter from it, he was a one-man preservation league. I was having a particularly arrogant day. My arrogance was so palpable that my belly bulged uncomfortably, inflated by my superiority. Bax noticed the odd way I was canted on the leatherette bench.

'Whass the matter?' he slurred through smoke and beer.

'Arrogance.'

'Flatulence?'

'Arrogance. I've an inflated opinion of myself.'

'Whichever it is they're both calculated to drive people away.'

'I know that.'

Bax fell to building another roll-up behind his safety hair curtain and I fell to examining the wristlets he always wore. These protruded from the cuffs of his denim shirt and extended as far as his knuckles. They looked as if they were made of either very pale leather, or some peculiar rubber. It was impossible to tell whether they were a fashion accessory or an orthopaedic brace. A bit like Bax's novels really.

'Whassat?' He was sharp – horribly so.

'I didn't say anything.' I brazened it out.

'Sharon says' – he pooted the words out, together with irritating little dribbles of smoke – 'that she'll go up in the balloon with us on Sunday, this Sunday.'

'Really? And she'll take part in the debate?'

'Of course, that's why she's going. We'll debate the motion "This balloon considers Sharon Crowd to be thoroughly immoral". I assume you'll be proposing and Keith seconding?'

'S'pose so.'

'Sharon will reject the motion – obviously – and I'll support her. If you win, one of us takes the dive. If we win, the reverse will be the case.'

'I see . . .' This was a turn-up. I wasn't at all sure about Keith's reaction if his life was weighed in the balance with mine. 'And who did you have in mind to deliberate?'

'Why, whoever's operating the balloon, I s'pose, and whoever else is taking the trip with us, tourists and suchlike.'

I found Keith at the Vauxhall city farm. Dinah was tied up outside, but her master was down at the far end from the animal enclosures, past the new straw-brick pigsty, crouching in the small allotment section. I'd like to be able to say that with his beard and his weathered features Keith had a peaceful appearance in this bucolic – if diminutive – setting, but he didn't. Not even the three small children, who frolicked about him throwing handfuls of straw in the air, could lighten his mood.

'Bax says that whoever's operating the balloon, together with any others who're there at the time, should deliberate. On the matter of Sharon, that is –'

'Or you.'

'Or me, or you, or Bax.'

'Ah, but it isn't necessarily Bax or you, or Sharon or me, now is it?' His big boot rolled a small pellet of sheep shit around on the earth with surprising delicacy. 'It's me or you in the final analysis.'

I thought of big tie knots, droopy moustaches, the Rubettes, the Winter of Discontent and the death of Blair Peach. It was a lot for someone to have missed out on, and while I was thinking this Keith was gathering himself together and moving off.

'Yeah, yeah,' he flung over his shoulder, 'well, that's that then.'

'They'll never cooperate,' I called after him, 'the people in the balloon. They'll freak out.'

'I'll handle it.'

'Really?'

I caught up with him by the exit as he was untying Dinah. The Dalmatian had managed to wriggle inside and was straining at the leash so hard that her collar disappeared in the folds of her neck. Keith and I took a look at the doggy porn as well, a glass tank of ferrets scrabbling and flowing through sections of plastic piping.

'I'll *handle* it.' Keith rounded on me – I was reminded of Ord.

'Are you in character . . . ? As Ord, I mean.'

'No, of course not, you prat.'

Off he went, Dinah's nails clicking behind him, as he traversed the cracked lozenge of paving beside the Vauxhall Tavern. Even at this early hour there was a scrum of bare-chested, bald-headed clones outside the grotty old rotunda. They goosed one another, snapping braces, nipping necks, while the techno broke over them in waves and the traffic roared past. The balloon was coming down for the night; from where I stood, it appeared to be settling in a giant egg cup of masonry. Foreshortened London – there was never any escaping it. Respectfully, I asked Ord if he had any comment to make on the clones, but for once he was silent.

The week before the balloon debate they began demolishing the Nine Elms Cold Store. This huge concrete box – which closely resembled a beehive of the cubic kind – had dominated the messy confluence of Nine Elms Lane and the Wandsworth Road for the last twenty years, shouting solidity and radiating chill. Presumably advances in refrigeration had done for it, the encroaching entropy. They bashed a big hole in its side and the wound festered as epidermal layers of asbestos swelled and the steel maggots squirmed out.

It was easy enough to get on to the demolition site, which, of course, Keith, Dinah and I did. We'd always got on to the Battersea Power Station site as well, dodging hard hats in order to wander, like post-apocalyptic communicants, into the towering chancel of red brick. Now the two massive structures were both being flung down, like the victims of summary war-time executions. At least the Cold Store was being dealt with with some dispatch, but the city had decided to make an example of the Power Station. The nave of the building, open to the dank sky, was profaned by abandon. Where once erg upon erg had been burnt into being, there were only pigeon droppings, and the strange cries of bungee jumpers, falling from a crane erected over the Thames, and shitting themselves as they plunged.

Ord had penetrating observations to make about London, its future and its fabric. During that last week he dismissed Flambard and gave me the full benefit of his long-term view.

'Let me say' – his voice was as clipped and peremptory as ever, radiating discipline and ferocity – 'that from the perspective of 2073 all your concerns about the removal of this building, or the implanting of that structure, seem trifling in the extreme. Take this stretch of the Thames littoral,' and he did just that, cupping the shimmering oxbow of the river in his callused hand. 'Apartment blocks with gull-wing roofs will rise up on the site of the Cold Store, then soar down again, a mighty Ferris wheel will dominate the Central London skyline for decades and then roll away. Some commentators may see the city as a peculiar entity, with its hillside suburbs and inner-city marshes as phrenological bumps and depressions, each revealing an enduring aspect of the metropolitan personality, but frankly this is bolderarckshifucklenoo.' Ord lapsed into the profane slang of the mid-future. 'London hasn't had any personality to speak of since the tube system, like some mighty course of electroconvulsive therapy, linked node to neighbouring node and shorted them out with hundreds of thousands of volts.

'That being the case –' He stopped to observe a queue of Somalians – golf-ball heads, golf-club bodies – waiting to send money orders from a small chemist's. 'You can't imagine what the Central Spike erected in 2035 will be like. Over a thousand storeys high, shaped like an immense termites' nest, its interior hollowed out into thousands of offices and apartments, hundreds of atria and gardens, and the whole mighty structure a permanent home and workplace for half the city's population, its many different streams of power, air and information both generated and regulated by newly developed bio-force.'

'No I can't.' I tried not to sound bitter. 'I can't imagine.'

In between walks I did my best to put my affairs in order. My will was a thin document: to Mrs Benson my pile of old mattresses, an envelope stuffed with foreign currency for a brother I'd neglected, boxes of old paperbacks and worn-out clothes to charity stores. Any money I'd once had had long since been frittered away. In an office crackling with static electricity and insulated with the papery record of the lives of others, I frittered away the rest.

'It's hardly worth your while to make out this will,' the solicitor said. 'It costs to have me write it, it costs to deposit it. To be frank – this stuff is near worthless.' Sweat plastered her white blouse to her white bra.

'I don't like the idea of the State getting hold of anything, anything at all.'

A desk fan creaked back and forth, ruffling the fates of men and women.

'I see.'

The water-cooler bubbled, perhaps it was boiling?

'I would scream in eternity if I thought a single battered paperback or mismatched sock was contributing in its material essence to the power of the State.'

'I see.' The solicitor was looking at me with mounting suspicion. 'Tell me, is there any particular reason why you should be making a will now?'

'No, no reason. Mortality bears down on us all though – doesn't it?'

It was clear but gusty for late summer on the Sunday morning appointed for the balloon debate. A pebble pinged against my attic skylight. Standing unsteadily on my princess's bed, I poked my head through and looked down to see Keith and Sharon Crowd standing on the pavement.

Keith called up to me through cupped hands: 'Get a move on!'

They reminded me of schoolkids come to fetch one of their mates for a morning's skiving. I hurried down, grabbing the parcel I'd spent the previous night preparing. This I slung over my shoulder as I came out of Mrs Benson's front door, but neither Sharon Crowd, nor Keith, appeared to notice. One of the Benson kids shouted after us, but his words were caught up and mangled by the passage of an early lorry. We walked across Albert Square and down the Clapham Road towards the Oval. At the mouth of Fentiman Road, Bax fell in beside us and we walked on, in silence, line abreast across the pavement, like band members in a pop video, or urban Samurai. There was silence between us, a malevolent, brooding silence.

As we marched around the curve of the Oval, then down the grimy stretch of Harleyford Road to Vauxhall Cross, the tension began to mount.

'Where're you gonna leave Dinah?' I asked Keith, who I could hear inside my head, grinding his dentures.

'With the Australian lad in Majestic – obviously.'

'Oh yeah, yeah, sorry.'

'Why don't you leave him with the doorman of the Hoist,' said Bax – they were his first words of the day – 'it's still open.'

It was. A metre or so of satiny fabric was attached to a hot-air blower in the doorway of the club. Its simulation of fire led me to picture a hell in which the torments were quite as ersatz. But Keith didn't deign to answer Bax, and the four of us trudged on as doggedly as Dinah.

The wind was smearing sheets of paper, strips of packing tape and dead leaves in broad brushstrokes across the stretched and primed sky, but the ulterior element remained daubed with its own plenitude. As ever, full of itself. It wouldn't be such a bad thing to leave this behind, this thick brick viaduct, these ancient pubs, these silent showrooms full of cacophonous motorcycles, these leprous squeegee merchants, and those Sunday saloons stacked with life-size Playmobil figures, on their way to shop in Croydon. The whole pasta mash of Vauxhall Cross, with its myriad transport conduits noodling through the city.

While Keith and Dinah nuzzled one another under the kindly eye of the wine warehouse assistant, Sharon Crowd, Bax and I waited on the false hillock that runs along Goding Street. This was a barrow of scurvy grass, speared by sticks planted in wire baskets, and garnished with sweet shit. The balloon was being unlimbered for the day, its securing cables untethered by New Zealander travellers and Canadian postgraduate students. They worked efficiently.

'It seems fairly windy,' I said to Bax. 'Maybe they won't go up.'

'That would be a shame,' he replied distractedly, his yellow nails scrabbling at one of his wristlets. Sharon Crowd was looking magnificent. She'd elected to wear a brown Nehru jacket and matching brown trousers. The ensemble did her every compliment available. Her hair was scraped back severely, her lips were barely there at all. She and Bax went on ignoring my parcel.

When Keith returned we advanced down the hillock and crossed the park to the balloon enclosure. A Portakabin stood at a gap in the wire fence. Inside they were selling tickets and souvenirs to a clutch of tourists. I couldn't really take them in. I was getting very antsy. We all paid for our tickets separately, then filed out of the hut and along a plank walkway to the balloon's giant basket. It was not a basket as such, but an open square of walkway, the sides made of metal posts linked by five double strands of cable from waist to shoulder height, and below waist-level there were metal panels. It was Wright Brothers rather than Mongolfier, and when I saw it I realised I'd been hoping for a gondola with silk-embroidered panels, and in it a few show goats and a vicuña for company on our experimental ascent. But there was little time for quibbling, because one Kiwi took my ticket and tore it, another ushered me on board, then a third cast off.

The ascent was phenomenally fast, as quick as a lift.

On the far side of the platform from me, across a fifteen-foot gap, a child squirmed and protested in her mother's arms: 'Mummy, I'm scared aoooh! Mummy – I don't want to go up! Mu-uuummy!'

Fucking abuser, I thought to myself. 'Sadist,' I said aloud.

Then I noticed that Sharon Crowd and Bax weren't on board. I checked the other passengers: together with the abusing mother and abused child there were a couple of teenagers in white anoraks, while to my right there was a young Middle Eastern couple, and next to them was Keith. The Antipodean balloonist was isolated by the gate; he held a length of chain attached to the burner which he yanked from time to time, sending a great tongue of flame licking and roaring into the ever-tautening belly of the canopy. I looked down: framed in the square of the walkway was a rapid, reverse-zoom shot of the patch of Vauxhall Cross Park. It grew to encompass the Portakabin, the barrow, the Hoist, some boys having a kick-around, then the stand of vetch growing on top of the Vauxhall Tavern, and eventually the figures of Sharon Crowd and Bax, both equally tiny now, who arm in arm were striding towards the tube.

I was down to one friend, Keith, a former bank robber, although we'd never talked about his bank-robbing days. He was wedged into the corner of the platform, and as I looked on, awed, Brockwell Park disappeared below his shoulder, only to reappear beneath his feet. We were two hundred feet up and still rising.

'So,' Keith called over, 'no debate. Didn't think they'd go through with it. We may as well just enjoy the ascent.'

His knuckles were white, his arms bent back to brace him, his purple windcheater snapped in the stiff breeze. I was shocked by how precipitate the balloon trip was turning out to be – the platform bucked and heaved in the wind as if it were a crow's nest surmounting a flexible mast.

'Or perhaps you'd like a game of Go-Chess to distract you – how like a Go board London is, from this elevation.'

Keith turned to survey the city falling away beneath us, and I turned as well. The Antipodean chatting, the gas burner roaring, the Middle Eastern couple hand-holding, the child whimpering, all were as nothing when set beside its warty enormity. Already I could make out the burst boil of the Millennium Dome to the east and the greenery of Teddington Lock to the west. As we rose still higher, the streets of the city eerily unknotted themselves, straightening out to form a grid of many many poignant intersections, places where I'd laid the wrong stone.

'It is peculiarly like a Go board!' I shouted over to Keith, who was faint against the sharp sky. 'So we'll have to begin with –'

'Go!' shouted Ord, and I took this to be an order, as I'm sure it was intended. We understood our secret mnemonics – Ord and I.

I unslung the linen parcel from my shoulders. The Middle Eastern couple backed away from me muttering. The man tried to look me in the eyes, attempting the command of me with his own inner Ord. I evaded his control beams just as I ignored the woman's suitable beak and her black flapping chador. I unpopped the poppers of the duvet cover and took out the fitted-sheet parachute. The Antipodean called to the couple to move back towards me, they were unbalancing the platform. Ord gave a single bark of cruel laughter. How like the man. I got one foot up on the taut cable and swung myself over. The horizon tipped like a giant grey swell and I fell, screaming, towards the periphery of my own acquaintance.

The Five-Swing Walk

'It is through children that the soul is cured.'

– FYODOR DOSTOEVSKY

Stephen awoke to find himself lying in a cold damp roadway. His knees were drawn up to his chest, his cramped hands implored the tarmac. His cheek and chin were jammed in a gutter full of sodden, unclean leaves, which had been tossed into a salad with a few handfuls of polystyrene S's, the kind used for-bulk packaging. Near by lay the dead body of his six-year-old, Daniel. Stephen levered himself up on one elbow; the driver of the black cab that had struck and killed his son was standing over the child's corpse. Stephen noticed that they were both wearing shorts, Daniel's were denim, the cabbie's khaki. The cabbie was scratching his head in a perplexed way.

'Is he dead?' Stephen asked.

'Oh yeah, 'e's dead.' The cabbie was friendly, if a little solemn. ''e didn't stand a chance, the bonnet hit his bonce like a fucking 'ammer.'

'It doesn't seem right,' Stephen spluttered on the sweet saliva of grief, 'a little boy dying in this filthy place.'

He rose and floated over to where the cabbie stood. He gestured about at the junction, at the freshly cladded council blocks, the tubular garages and workshops slotted into the railway arches, at the traffic lights and the twisted safety railings. Just how twisted could a railing be, Stephen pondered, before it ceased to be one at all?

'No, it doesn't seem right.' The cabbie stroked his mono-jowl. 'You'd far prefer 'im to be all tucked up in a nice fresh bed, yeah, wiv nurses an' doctors an' his mum to look after 'im, yeah?'

'Oh, absolutely.'

'Tell you what –' The cabbie was clearly the kind of man for whom a good turn is a good deal. 'St Mary's isn't too far from 'ere. What d'you say to giving the lad a jolt with the jump leads, and seeing if we can get 'im up and running for twenty minutes? That'll be long enough to take 'im down there an get 'im admitted before 'e snuffs it again.'

They weren't exactly jump leads, they were long thick cables coated with yellow rubber. The plugs were the kind used to link up a portable generator. Stephen was surprised to see – when the cabbie smoothed back his fringe – that Daniel had the requisite three-pin arrangement on his forehead. The cabbie made the connection and walked back to his cab, which stood, engine still stuttering, like a big black hesitation.

'Right,' he called over, 'tell 'im you love 'im.'

'I love you, Daniel,' Stephen said, crouching by his son, taking in for the first time the unnatural angle of the boy's neck, the blood and brain matter puddling beneath his head.

The cabbie gunned the engine, the cables pulsed, Daniel's eyes opened: 'Dad?' he queried.

'It's OK, Daniel,' said Stephen, feeling the vast inexplicability of loss. 'We're going to take you down to the hospital.'

'But I'll still be dead, won't I, Dad.'

'Oh yes, you'll still be dead.'

The cabbie came back and handed Stephen what was either a large pellet or a small canister. It was the same yellow as his jump leads.

'This thing is pretty amazing, mate,' he said. 'If it has any contact wiv water it expands to ten thousand times its own size.'

'Like a seed?'

Stephen looked at the plastic cylinder and felt the all kinds of everything packed up inside it, amazing, bio-mechanical energy. He could feel a tear struggling to detach itself from the well of his eyelid, fighting the tension of this greater surface with its own need to become a moment. Then it was. It rolled down his cheek, dripped on to the cylinder. All hell broke loose.

And resolved itself into an idiotic collage of tissues gummed up with snot, a clock radio, a lamp, a book, the moon face of a toddler confronting him from a few inches away.

'Bissa – bussa,' said the toddler, and then, 'Gweemy.'

Stephen levered himself up on forklift arms. The dream was still exploding in his head, smattering everything he saw with its associations, simultaneously lurid and tedious. Were dreams always this prosaic? he wondered, or had they become so through over-analysis? The collective unconscious now seemed to be expertly arrayed for merchandising, like a vast supermarket, with aisle after aisle of ready-made psychic fare. Still, his kid . . . dead . . . it didn't bear thinking about.

'Currle,' the toddler broke in, butting his arm with a mop of black ringlets.

Stephen snaked an arm around small shoulders and pulled the child up on top of him.

'Hiyah,' he said, pressing his lips into the thicket.

The toddler squirmed in his grasp, butted the underside of his chin, which nipped his tongue between his teeth.

'OK!' Stephen snapped. 'Getting up time!' And he deposited the child back on the floor, followed by his own feet.

A broad little base of squished nappy and brushed-nylon pyjama bottom supported the eighteen-month-old, an expression of stolidity was painted on to the smooth face. Stephen stood, teetering, a pained grimace pasted across his own rough one. Casually yet deliberately, he knocked the small torso sideways with his flaky foot, and it toppled over, curly head clonking on the mat. Too surprised to protest, the child lay there mewling softly. Stephen scrutinised bubbles of saliva forming on perfect pink lips, each one reflecting in its fish eye the bright grids of the bedroom windows. He couldn't say its name, its absurd name. After all, a name was an acknowledgement – and he'd had no part in its naming.

'This bedroom looks like a fucking bathroom!' he cursed, then added, 'while the bathroom looks like a fucking bedroom!'

And they did. She'd put bathroom mats either side of the bed, a festoon of netting by the window had dried starfish and sea horses caught up in its ratty folds, the walls were papered in vertical stripes of blue and white. But there was never any rowing at this regatta, only vigorous rowing.

Stephen stomped into the adjoining bathroom, and here white, lace-fringed pillows were plumped up on small carpeted surfaces; there was a stripped-pine shelf of swollen paperbacks over the bath itself, and the mirror above the sink had a gilt picture frame. Stephen grasped the cool sides of the sink and thought about wrenching it out of the floor. He stared at his face in the mirror. 'No oil painting!' he spat. And it was true, with two days of greying grizzle and the sad anachronism of pimples and wrinkles on the same cheeks, he looked like an ageing slave rather than an old master.

A turd floating in the toilet caught his eye – one of hers. Smooth, and brown, and lissom – like her. He hitched up an invisible robe and hunkered down over it.

'I shit on your shit!' he angrily proclaimed, while at the same time, in a feat of bizarre moral tendentiousness, he felt satisfied to be saving two gallons of water.

In his mind's eye a video clip of emaciated Third World women was reversed, and they walked jerkily backwards from a distant dusty well to an encampment of battered huts. The toddler came crawling into view.

'I shit on your mother's shit,' Stephen addressed it conversationally, but then, as he strained, he thought, I can't go on behaving like this, these casual kicks, these slipshod remarks. None of it is harmless. But why had she left the kid with him on this of all days?

When he rose to wipe himself, and involuntarily looked back, he saw that his turd had been married with hers, that they were entwined, with a lappet of his shit curled around hers like a comforting arm. Intimacy, it occurred to Stephen, is highly overrated. In the middle of the night she had kicked out at him hard, her heels drumming on his sleep-softened thighs. Kicked him and cursed him, and at the time he'd been inclined to give her the benefit of the doubt – doubting that he was awake at all. Now she was gone.

Over a soft pap of cereal that the toddler made free with, Stephen thought about how he had come to be here, in a tatty kitchenette way across town. Still, two years after the move, he awoke with this sense of disorientation, wanting to go back to the home that was no longer a home, from this, which was no kind of home at all. He looked at the kitchenette, at the sharp flaps of melamine detaching themselves from the surfaces, at the Mesopotamian outline of the electric jug, at the nodular malevolence of a mug tree, and he grasped how all the lines of his life had unruled themselves. He wouldn't – he couldn't – take responsibility for this . . . He wouldn't own these other, bonded lives, this bewildering emotional dovetailing. He felt only a monumental sense of self-pity for his own self-piteousness.

'Zyghar,' said the toddler.

On the radio a weathered voice spoke of cloudiness. Stephen had heard how they held up a grid to the sky and counted the cloud cover in each square. There was such a crude calculation – he understood – as average cloudiness. Squinting up through the tiny flap window, Stephen saw, between tapering walls of London brick, a sky of more than average cloudiness, grey on grey on greyer, shapeless shoals of grey slipping over and under each other. It was always gloomy on these, his days off. Off from what? He remembered yesterday morning, and the ugliness that occurred beside the Sasco year planner when he reminded his boss that he wouldn't be coming in tomorrow. 'But what about –' and 'Didn't you realise – ?' and 'Couldn't you have – ?' When it was all there already on the board, his days off, meted out in felt-tip strokes. And anyway, Stephen's job, what did it consist of? Save for saying on the phone the valediction 'See you' to people who, in fact, he had never seen.

'H'hooloo,' toodle-ooed his breakfast companion.

Stephen tried to wrench it out of the high chair too fast; chubby legs were caught under the rung and he swung the entire edifice – a tower of metal and plastic, a penthouse of flesh – aloft. Then set everything down, disentangled the feet, tried again. He did a nappy change, wiping the grooves around its genitals with careful uncaring. He taped up the little parcel of excrement with its Velcro tabs. In due course, he mentally carped, this would be added to tens of thousands of others, and deposited in a landfill in the East Midlands, where it would wait for ten thousand years, to confront the perplexed archaeologists of the future with yet more evidence of their shit-worshipping ancestors.

Stephen dressed his charge, his fingers feeling like bloated sausages, as they grappled flaccidly with the fiddly straps and clasps. In its nylon all-in-one, the toddler looked to Stephen like some dwarfish employee of a nuclear inspectorate, ready to assess the toxicity of the Chernobyl that lay in wait outside. Backing and filling in the awkward confines of the flat – where bedroom, bathroom, kitchenette and living room all opened on to a hall the size of a mouse mat – Stephen manoeuvred the buggy with one hand while grasping glabrous scruff with the other. The borrowed buggy – what a risible, lopsided contraption. The buggy, with its collapsible aluminium struts, like a tragicomic boxing glove on an extendable arm, made to smack him in the face again and again and again. He could fold it up, but never put it away. Now it half-opened and jammed a door, and while he closed it up the prisoner escaped. But at the moment of recapture the double buggy fell open once more.

In the street Stephen married child and conveyance in a union of plastic clips and nylon webbing, then he sat on a low wall bounding a hedge and, feeling the sharp twigs scratch him through his thin clothing, he wept for a few minutes. It was here that Misfortune – that ugly, misshapen creature – saw fit to join him. And, when he rose and pushed the buggy off up the pavement, Misfortune went along for the ride.

'Inquitty,' said the toddler, registering the tinkle-thud of a falling putlock on a building site they passed by, and Stephen pondered how it was that, while everything had gone perfectly well with the child's development, now it was beginning to speak he found that it was he who was becoming autistic.

There was a bad thing waiting in the wings. There was an awful event struggling to happen. It was maddened already, battering against the windowpane of reality with its dark wings, like a bird caught in a room. I should never, Stephen thought as he pushed the buggy, have driven my wife insane by slowly increasing the duration of the car journeys we took together. I knew she had no sense of orientation, and yet I tormented her. If we had to go to friends' houses, or even to the supermarket, each time I'd take a different route, each time slightly longer. Naturally she'd protest: 'Stephen, I'm sure we didn't go this way last time.' And to derange her still more, I'd say, 'It's a short cut.' Now there was no car and no wife. Or rather, there was an ex-wife, and instead of circling each other like boxers in the confinement of their own home, the ring had expanded to fill the city, while they were still stuck in the same bloody clinch, mauling each other with short jabs to the belly.

At the bus stop Stephen waited with an old woman drinking a can of Special Brew and a dapper old man who leant against his cane at a jaunty angle. The old man sported a feather in his porkpie hat, his tweed suit was immaculately pressed. He looked as if he were watching for a field of runners and riders to round the corner and come galloping up the high street in a breaking wave of pounding sinew and frothing silk. He looked happy. Stephen sank down on one of the narrow, tip-tilting rubber seats; his misery stung him like heartburn. Misfortune, seizing the opportunity, played with the child.

Misfortune tickled its feet and the toddler chuckled, 'Chi-chi-chi.' Misfortune stroked a cheek and accepted the nuzzle of the frizzy head. Misfortune sympathised entirely with the child and took on its hallucinogenic impression of a sharp-smelling trough, full of toy cars, and bounded by neat piles of building blocks. Behind these were grey walls too high to touch, and over it all unfurled haunting skirls. The toddler, too young to know Misfortune, felt it to be an outgrowth of the parental absence slumped at its side, and accepted its distorted presence willingly.

'Fulub,' it said.

But the old woman, who knew Misfortune for what it was – who felt it congealed in her hair, smeared on her neck – cried out, hands shaking to ward it off, 'Gerariyer-gera –'

Lager beaded the little brow, Stephen jerked the handle of the buggy to roll it back a couple of feet and reached in his pocket for a tissue. The bus came.

In the time it took for the obtuse old man to pay for his ticket and climb up the bus to his seat, Stephen was able to load the human cargo, fold the buggy and stack it in the luggage rack. Misfortune, under the cover of the hiss of compressed air and the slap of the automatic door, slid on board too, and took up the seat behind the driver, the one allocated for elderly people or those accompanied by children. The old woman – if you can call fifty-three old – stayed on the bench, and watched, awestruck, as the bus stop slid away down the road, leaving the bus behind.

On the other side of town Stephen's ex-wife kept up a large detached Edwardian villa on maintenance. Stephen didn't know whether she had lovers – she hadn't vouchsafed – but if she did there was plenty of space for them in the generous rooms. The walk-in cupboards alone could've housed five or six closet Lotharios and, when Stephen wanted to make himself feel particularly bad, he imagined them in there, sitting comfortably in the close darkness, her dresses rustling around their shoulders, as they waited for her to select one of their number. Stephen's ex was beautiful. She was trim, raven-haired and sharp-profiled. She despised sexual incontinence in specific men – this he knew to his cost – but mysteriously, admired it in the generality of mankind. And so it was easier to imagine her with lovers than with a boyfriend.

Misfortune dogged his footsteps as he clunked the buggy over paving stones ridged with virulent moss. From the bus stop they went up the hill between flat-faced semis, then around the playing field at the top, with its stark goalposts like gallows. Then past the gasometer, down the short street walled with poky terraced houses, and finally along the parade of shitty little shops, each one apparently devised for public inconvenience. A grocer with only two kinds of fruit and three of vegetables; a butcher selling just sausages and mince, who counted on three boxes of dried stuffing as a tempting window display; an ironmonger's that never had anything you wanted. Stephen recalled asking for thirteen-amp fuses in it, for eggshell paint, for clothesline, for grout, but all of these were unavailable. Preposterously, the ironmonger's had been refitted in the last year, yet still sold nothing that anyone needed. Perhaps, Stephen thought, the ironmonger's existed solely to refit itself – not so much a retail concern as an evolved play on the whole notion of doing-it-for-yourself.

They turned the corner into Tennyson Avenue and passed by the Hicks' house (elderly bedridden mother, son on drugs), the Fakenhams' house (he a closet paedophile, she a pillar of the local church), the Gartrees' house (no human children but many cat babies). How could it be that he, Stephen, was exiled from this poisonous Eden, while so many serpents retained their tenancies? It occurred to him – not for the first time, not for the thousandth – that he should fake his own suicide, utilise the handy wreckage of a train he'd never caught, or the immolation of an office building he'd failed to enter, or simply leave his clothes, for once neatly folded, on a rock, and walk away from the CSA, from the children, from the pain.

Bending down to unlatch the front gate he caught the tang of urine emanating from the toddler. Best not to leave it – it would lead to a rash, and then he'd have to face its mother's wrath. Inside the gate he unbuckled the child and laid it down on the patch of grass behind the bins. He glanced up at the blank windows of the house, each with its cataract of net curtain, but saw nothing twitching.

'Anurk'a,' the toddler protested, as he ripped open the front of its all-in-one, yanked out its chubby legs, then held them open, spatchcocked, as he removed the absorbent wad.

While Stephen was groping for a clean nappy in the compartment underneath the buggy he heard the front door swing open, and looked up to see his ex-wife standing, radiating contempt. Behind her slim shoulders the hallway receded, lined on either side with hummocks of school bags, rows of shoes, stooks of sports equipment and piles of books.

'Huh!' she exclaimed, arms crossed, and Stephen, observing her quick-bitten fingers clutching at her elbows, and the anger that semaphored from her lantern eyes, could not forbear from remembering the exact quality of her rage.

'I've got fucking head lice!' Those same hands in frenzied agitation, as she sits on the side of the bed. 'Fucking nits! Fucking nits!'

He leaps from his side of the marital bed, in that instant grasping that he'll never lie down there again. His eyes search across the carpet for any certain object that they might anchor on in this suddenly fluid, frightening world. But he sees only a nude Barbie doll, pushed overboard by a passing child, its feet up beside its head, its pink plastic pubis a disturbing juncture. How can this thing be – he's floundering in stormy irrelevance – a toy?

'Kids!' Stephen's ex bellowed back into the house, and then again, still louder. 'Kids!'

Stephen finished parcelling up the toddler and placed it back on its side of the double buggy.

Now he has so few things he tries to treat them with the respect others deserve. In the small flat on the other side of town he washes up the toddler's plastic bowl with care, then dries it and puts it away in the cupboard. He no longer has the detached villa, with its innumerable corners, all of them slowly silting up with the materiality of years of family life.

The six-year-old and the eight-year-old came down the stairs to the hallway like surprised conspirators, reluctant to admit their involvement with each other. Taking their anoraks from the pegs in the hall they put them on with an orderliness and efficiency that struck Stephen as overwhelmingly pathetic. Then they winkled their feet into wellingtons, and he wanted to go forward and help them but knew he really shouldn't. They came out of the house and shuffled down the path to where he stood.

''lo, Dad,' said the older one, the girl, while the boy said simply ''lo.'

They both nodded to their half-sibling in the buggy, as if this were a working situation, and they were all being formally introduced for the first time. ' 'lo,' they said again.

'Lorol,' said the toddler.

Stephen hunkered down and shuffled forward to encompass all three children with his outstretched arms. He smelt Ribena on their breath, conditioner in their hair. Looking at their pale faces he saw yet again the way his ex's incisive features cut out his weak ones.

Stephen's ex-wife reappeared in the hallway, dragging a protesting two-year-old by its arm.

'I'm not wanted it!' the two-year-old was complaining. 'I'm gonna' stayere, I'm gonna –'

'Doesn't he want to come?' Stephen called, half hoping.

'Oh no, he's going with you,' she replied, expertly stuffing the little boy into his anorak, then tripping him backwards over her foot, so that he sat on the floor. While she inserted his feet into wellingtons, she kept up an incantation of irritation: 'If you think I'm going to miss out on the only two bloody hours of the week when I have the house to myself . . . the only time I have to make a call, or even wash my bloody hair . . . You've no idea, have you? No bloody idea at all . . .'

While the boy, for his part, kept on dissenting. 'I gotta having this to show Daddy, 'cause . . . An' Daniel says I wasn't gonna 'cause . . . He tooken it, he-he –'

'Josh wants to bring his driving thingy,' Daniel explained.

'I told him it would be in the way,' his older sister, Melissa, explained.

'But I has to!' Josh cried out from the doorway.

'Then take the bloody thing! Take-the-bloody-thing!'

On 'take' she picked up the toy dashboard with steering wheel and gear stick attached; on 'the' she shoved it in Josh's arms; on 'bloody' she picked him up and placed him outside the door; and on 'thing' she slammed it.

In the frozen moment before Josh began to bawl in earnest, Stephen turned and looked away. On the opposite side of the road two nuns were passing by. They were both bespectacled, both wearing blue wimples and blue raincoats. From beneath their hemlines extended a foot or so of white nylon. The whole outfit, thought Stephen, gave them a look at once ecclesiastical and medical, as if they were on their way to nurse their Saviour in a specially equipped crucifixion unit. They flashed their lenses in his direction, and Stephen wanted to cry out, 'Suffer these little children to come unto you! You won't find a group of people more in need of help than us . . .' But instead he turned back to Josh who was keening, 'Erherrr-erherrr-erherrr,' his way into hysteria, 'waaaa!'

'ComeonowJosh, noneedt'cry, here we go, here we go . . .'

Stephen kept up a prayerful murmur as he lifted the roaring boy and his toy up, carried him down the path to where the others were clustered around the buggy, strapped him into his side, balanced the driving toy on his knees, got the buggy out through the gate, got the older ones positioned on either side, small hands on handles, and with his shocked progeny four abreast, started off back up the road. Misfortune took up its position to the rear.

'It's OK, Josh, it's OK. We'll have a good time – you'll see . . .'

Melissa had taken over from him and although he was grateful to her, Stephen couldn't forbear from feeling sick with inadequacy, his own paternal dereliction melting into his shoulders like an irreversible jacket of napalm.

'So, kids,' he said cheerily. 'What're we going to do this afternoon? Museum? Zoo? Film? What's it going to be – you decide.'

'We wented to a film –'

'Went,' Stephen corrected Daniel – the six-year-old's grammar was always the first casualty of these emotional firefights.

'We went to a film yesterday.'

'Good?'

''s' OK.'

'How about the zoo or a museum then?'

'Nah, boring,' the older children chorused.

'What then? It's a bit gloomy for the park, isn't it?'

Their silence said they didn't agree.

'D'you want to go on the four-swing walk then?'

'Yes, and you'll push us up an' up an' up –'

'So high, so high we'll go over the bar –'

'Or fly into space pasted the moon an' Mars an' everything –'

'To another galaxy –'

'Another universe, you mean.'

'OK, the four-swing walk it is then, but I can't promise you space exploration.'

Another universe – that was a good idea. Stephen didn't doubt that Daniel and Melissa wanted to go on the four-swing walk because they connected it with the time before he'd left. The older children had come into consciousness on these four sets of swings: two in the local playing field, then one in an adjoining patch of overgrown park, and the last, tucked away in a playground on a council estate. Perhaps they hoped that if they swung high enough they could describe a perfect parabola into the past.

'Swush,' said the toddler on the left-hand side of the buggy, and it was only then that Stephen realised it was autumn, for the child was mimicking the sound of feet and wheels sweeping leaves along the pavement.

Autumn, which explained this damp, oppressive sky, like a dirty grey clout waiting to be squeezed. Autumn, which located this sense of irretrievable loss in its appropriate context. Autumn, hence Stephen's aching weariness. He would've given anything to be able to lie down underneath that scarified hedge until spring. Autumn, which made sense of the silage beneath his feet, a mulch of lolly sticks, ring pulls and macerated paper cups, laid down during the long harvest of the school holidays. Autumn, when it had all happened.

'Come here! You come here! You come here and sit down by me. Sit here!' Her belly rounded and plumped up amidst the squashed pillows, her nightdress rucked up in angry folds.

'Melissa hasn't had them for months – for months! I comb her every day – every day! You sit here, you let me look in your hair. In your fucking hair!'

And so, like half-naked apes, they engage in a savage grooming that destroys all social cohesion. She scrabbles and yanks at his hair.

'There! There! You've got them too! And eggs – and fucking eggs! What is this, Stephen? You're fucking someone, aren't you?! Someone with fucking head lice. Who is she, Stephen? A schoolgirl?'

No, not a schoolgirl. At the time, still fixated on the disturbing juncture of Barbie's thighs, Stephen had considered that perhaps, had she been a schoolgirl, the truth would've been easier to acknowledge, because it would've been so grotesque, so singular. But of course it's lies that are singular; the truth – that she was Melissa's teacher – was merely prosaic.

At the shopping parade Stephen's engine, with its double-buggy cow catcher, clattered over invisible points and turned to the left, back up the hill towards the playing field. Misfortune was in the guard's van.

'Whoo-whoo!' said the toddler, and Josh, who sat beside it yanking on the orange plastic steering wheel, beeped his horn.

'So, how's school?' Stephen asked Melissa, because he thought he ought to.

''s' OK,' she replied.

'Good OK or bad OK?' he probed.

'OK. OK.'

And that was that, that was the full extent of his input into her education.

As soon as they reached the playing field the two older children broke from the sides of the buggy like swing-seeking missiles and headed off across the scummy grass. Seagulls lifted off in advance of them, crying unpleasantly. Stephen pushed the buggy along the path, past a zone of crappy benches where two adolescents were nuzzling. He felt an intense physical sympathy for the little goatee of pus and scab on the boy's chin. He wanted to touch it, but cancelled the feeling by staring at his feet as they negotiated the blobs and dollops of dog shit, some brown, some black, some desiccated white, some livid yellow. It was interesting the way that the two toddlers managed to ignore each other. Maybe in a few months' time Josh would turn to the other one and say, out of the blue, 'Are you capable of holding a conversation yet?'

At the playground Melissa and Daniel were already on two of the big swings. Daniel was kicking his feet out and leaning back, he'd gained quite a bit of height, but Melissa couldn't manage it, and merely dangled, twisting from side to side. Stephen got Josh out of the buggy and put him in one of the small swings, tucking his feet through the holes. Then he did the same with the other toddler and got them both swinging.

'Hold on to the front!' he ordered them.

'Come and swing *me*, Dad!' Melissa called over. 'I can't get going.'

'She can't swing!' Daniel cried out, delighted. 'She doesn't know how to, doesn't know how to!'

'Shut up, Daniel! Shut up!' Immediately Melissa was close to tears.

'She's eight and she can't swing!' he crowed as he swooped above her.

'Shut up – I mean it!'

'Now then,' said Stephen, leaving the two toddlers swinging. 'I'll swing you both.'

He got Melissa swinging using both hands, then shifted to shove the boy with one hand and the girl with the other. He pushed the seat one time and their backs the next. He felt their backs, the curvature of their spines, the warmth of their small buttocks. At the apex of the swings' curve he felt their bodies hover in his hands. And yet he felt no physical sympathy for these children – his children. Melissa and Daniel left themselves behind as they swung, left behind their preternaturally aged selves, they travelled in time – if not space – to a place of fun, that was simply and physically now. Stephen tickled them under the arms on the upswing and they giggled. He ran in front and like a crazy matador just avoided their feet-for-horns on the downswing and they screeched. He ran over to the toddlers on their little swing and got them going again, then ran back to the big kids and pushed them still higher. Back and forth Stephen shoved, round and round he ran. Now all four were laughing – even the stolid little toddler. Misfortune picked up a lost mitten someone had stuck on top of a railing and tried it on for size.

Then they stopped. Daniel squeaked himself to a halt, his rubber soles buffing the rubber tiling. He sprung off the swing before it came to a halt and walked over to the static roundabout. He knelt on the edge and leant his dark little head against one of the metal stanchions, as if praying. In that instant the whole desolation of the scene returned: the louring sky, the scuffed surface of the playground, rubber peeling away from bitumen, bitumen rubbing off concrete; the two-decade-old climbing frame like a garish steel pretzel for a metal-eating giant; the swings themselves, some of which had their chains twisted around the crossbar, evidence of adolescent mayhem, or maybe children genuinely catapulted into orbit. There was broken glass by the enclosing railings, there were lopsided crash barriers grouped around a depression in the concrete, which was filled with water and leaves, there was a bin all buckled in its bandolier of wooden struts. That such a rigid thing could have been vandalised at all was evidence, Stephen thought, of the most extreme population explosion.

Melissa got off her swing as well. The two toddlers were hanging, barely moving in their little swings.

'Come on, everyone!' Stephen injected enthusiasm into his voice as if it were a stimulant drug. 'Let's go to swing two.'

'Two!' the toddler cried out, loudly, distinctly, with perfect enunciation. They all ignored it.

Swing two was in the smaller, recently constructed playground next to the one o'clock dub. The little army marched there across the playing field, a direct route that took them sloshing between the gibbet goalposts, each set erected in mud. The older two ran on ahead, the younger toddler rode in the buggy, Josh trudged carrying his plastic dashboard. Stephen remembered how Melissa and Daniel had clung to him so ferociously, demanding to be carried until they were well past Josh's age. But this two-year-old just plodded on, hunched up, clearly no keener to be touched by his father than his father was anxious to touch him.

It was the weekend so the one o'clock club was closed, steel shutters pulled down to the ground, and each horizontal line filled in with sloppy graffiti. The small playground was yet to be vandalised, its black rubber tiling was inviolate. Each beautifully appointed piece of equipment stood on its own inset carpet of green-rubber tiling. The sandpit was covered and padlocked. The climbing frame-cum-slide had a neat gabled roof, and ramps leading up to it with firm wooden treads, each one edged with more black rubber. Clover-leaf-shaped platforms stood about on coils of giant spring. The whole assemblage was so new and neat and padded. It defied the outside with its evocation of a safe domestic interior.

'It's so fucking claustrophobic,' Stephen muttered aloud, putting Josh and the toddler into another duo of swings. He felt this inside-out playground to be outside in the playing field, and the outside playing field in turn to be inside the city, and the city to be enclosed by the country, and the country to be jumbled together with other countries inside the world. A world like a vast and messy playroom, strewn with the broken and discarded toys of an immature humanity, who had been having an awful tantrum for decades. The terrible two millennia. Like the security camera atop its red pole in the corner of this playground, God observed it all from his own distant enclosure, a child-lover passively watching for paedophiles.

Stephen got the two toddlers swinging again, and then went over to the bigger swings and got the bigger kids going. The two sets of swings were facing, so four pairs of wellingtons were aimed at Stephen as he scampered around the red safety bafflers, desperate to keep the swingers all up in the air.

'I like this swing best,' said Melissa.

'I like swing three best,' said Daniel.

'This swing is faster,' said Melissa.

'Yeah.' Daniel cultivated the conversation as if he were attending an aerial cocktail party. 'But swing three is fastener – I can go fastener.'

'Sinee!' the toddler sang out.

'I'm thursday,' said Josh.

'You mean you're thirsty,' Stephen puffed.

'I'm very thursday,' the child reiterated.

They left the playing field through a short alley that became a cul-de-sac. Parked along the kerb were an abandoned car and two toppled motor scooters. The car had been both seared and eviscerated. All the windows were caramelised, the seats were cut into slices of burnt foam rubber. The dashboard had been cut out so that the electrical guts spilled all over the floor. All the wheels were gone, making it just the right height for Josh, who crunched towards it through the debris hefting his own dashboard. 'My car,' he said. 'My car.'

'No it's not!' Stephen snapped. He snagged him too hard and, picking him up, slammed him into his side of the double buggy. Josh began to cry, and the other three children turned their frightened faces towards him.

'I'm sorry, Josh, I'm sorry.' Stephen knelt down to bring comfort within Josh's range. 'Really I am. Look –' He peered at the accusatory faces. 'Look, you can all have drinks and sweets. How's that?'

There was silence save for sniffles for three beats, and then Daniel said, echoing the performance of some fifth-rate American actor which had become lodged in his own repertoire, 'OK, then, sure, whatever.'

They trundled on.

The four-swing walk wasn't going well – Stephen knew that. He had to stop stumbling through his life, he had to take all these children in hand – but how? How could he practise emotional hygiene in this filthy city? The scooters lay like the corpses of animals, each in a tacky pool of its own oil. The petrol stench of decomposing machinery was overpowering. And by the walls of the abandoned shop premises they were skirting was a frozen wave of detritus, a fully evolved deco-system, where the squashed spine of an old vacuum cleaner was preyed on by the strut of an umbrella, which in turn was ensnared by a shred of gabardine, upon which suckered last night's discarded condom, which for its part was being eaten away by the white acid of bird shit. Stephen checked his watch, although he'd promised himself he wouldn't. Misfortune bided its time.

Down on the main road men stood about in Saturday afternoon poses outside the bookie's. One was throwing an empty lager bottle into the air and catching it again by the neck, another was savagely and methodically shredding betting slips, then letting the fake snowflakes flutter around his shaken-up world. Traffic coursed and thumped along the uneven surface of the road. After the stunned silence of the playing field, the way these vehicles honked and beeped seemed almost companionable. Stephen pushed the buggy right inside one of the shops, and the older children tagged along.

They were all the same – these shops – the same in their heterogeneity. They all sold small stocks of random supplies. Many shelves were empty – others bulged with useless plenitude. One shop would offer booze, fags, yams, ten-kilo bags of rice, cassava, sweets, fans and ex-rental videos; while right next door you could purchase seat covers, disposable barbecues, monkey nuts, sink plungers, aubergines, booze, dog chews, fags, sweets and sixteen-inch black-and-white TVs. One shop would be entirely sealed by an inner sleeve of steel mesh, so that customers had to transact their business in a sort of dog pen; while right next door it was all wide open, soda crystals and incense holders there for the taking.

In this one, a man with a V-necked cashmere pullover, blue stains beneath his brown eyes, sat behind a counter piled high with foreign-language newspapers, picking his teeth with a biro cap. Stephen let the children have what they wanted: Cokes and sweets. He even let the little toddler hold a big red can in its little brown paws. So much sugar – it wouldn't do any of them any good. Sweet guilt. Gummy, granulated, one hundred per cent refined shame.

'All right, boss,' said the man when Stephen paid him.

'Thank you, sir,' Stephen countered.

Neither of them knew if the other was being ironic.

Swing three was behind this parade, in a little misshapen scrap of park, a dumb-bell shape of overgrown grass and shrubbery, even more littered than the street. Stephen hated swing three most of all. It felt diseased here, with the backs of the shops exhaling their awful humours over a loose rank of overflowing wheelie bins, and five or so distempered chestnuts moping up above. But the children didn't mind, they were caught up in their sugar rush, rushing ahead, Josh hard on the heels of his older siblings, the toddler in the buggy screeching between slugs of Coke, 'Weeee!' Then they all pulled up short.

Sitting on the run-down swings that were their objective, kicking their feet and sharing a cigarette, were three teenagers. Two girls and a boy. They didn't look remotely threatening, but set beside the swings – which were small anyway – they were completely out of scale. Three teenagers. One of the girls was pretty in an over-made-up way, her lips a brilliant pink, her hair oiled and smarmed down into a series of precise curlicues across her coffee brow. The other girl was much more heavy-set and darker, her big breasts a veritable shelf, her large arse cut into by the swing's chains. She wore stretchy black clothing. The lad was in blue denim, a hip-length jacket buttoned to the neck, wide-legged trousers, the crotch of which was located in the region of his knees. A Los Angeles Raiders baseball cap was crushed down on his head, so hard that his hair formed frothy earphones. The pretty girl had a mobile phone in her lap, the hands-free set plugged into her delicate, gold-studded ear. She was toying with the keyboard of the phone, while the lad swung himself towards her and away, pretending to try and grab hold of it. The big girl ignored them, stared at her feet, smoked.

They didn't notice Stephen and the children for some moments. Moments during which he weighed up their timeless triangle, the priapic pipsqueak importuning the pretty one, while being silently warned off by this bulky black chaperone. The three of them, come here to the overgrown playground in an attempt to recapture an innocence that they'd probably never had. Then the pretty one saw Stephen and his kids. She stood, and trailing the lad by the flex – he'd snatched the mobile – she walked over to the seesaw. The big girl got up and followed them, goosing the lad with her hefty haunch. The pretty girl snatched back the mobile, the lad hitched up his mainsail trousers and sat on the middle of the seesaw, the big girl moved off to one side and stood, staring into a thicket.

Stephen's kids took their places. He helped Josh up on to the swing and began pushing him, the older two kicked and leaned, kicked and leaned. The other toddler still sucked on its Coke, buckled into the buggy like a fitful pilot, the whites of its eyes sharp in the mounting twilight. The rusty eyelets of the chains grated in their corroded bolts, 'ear-orr-ear-orr'.

Melissa gave up, and dropping to the ground walked towards the teenagers. She stopped a few feet away and examined them intently, then said, 'Hello.' They ignored her. 'Hello,' she said again, this time louder. The teenagers went on ignoring her, Stephen wanted to stop pushing Josh and go and pull her away, but he couldn't. 'Hello, my name's Melissa.'

'Y' all right, M'lissa,' said the lad.

'Y' all right,' the pretty one echoed him, and the big girl snickered, an oddly high-pitched 'tee-hee-hee'.

Melissa walked over to the buggy and stood there regarding the toddler for a while. She stooped, slid her hand inside the hood of its all-in-one and rubbed the curly mop of hair. The toddler, said, 'Lissl.'

Then she came back to where Stephen was pushing Josh and, looking up at him with an expression minted by her mother, said, 'Dad, why's Setutsi black?'

The teenagers paid attention now, their six eyes sought out Stephen's pale face, the pale faces of the three older children, then wavered over to take in the pretty black eighteen-month-old girl in the buggy.

'Yeah, black right,' the lad exclaimed to no one in particular. 'Black like me innit.'

And as if responding to some hidden signal, or perhaps to express a mutual disapproval of this miscegenation, the three teenagers gathered themselves into a little posse and strolled off. The last that was heard of them was the 'delaloodoo-delaloodoo-doo' of the mobile ringing.

Stephen stopped pushing Josh. He went over to the buggy and began unstrapping Setutsi. For something to do he got the changing mat and spread it on the damp grass. He got the wipes and a clean nappy. He undid the poppers of Setutsi's all-in-one, and pulled down the elasticated waist of her velveteen trousers. Her nappy was swollen with pee. He got it off, cleaned her with a wipe, then put a hand under her small, sweaty back and lifted her up so he could position the new nappy. As he fastened the Velcro tabs he looked up to see the three palefaces grouped around his shoulders.

'Isn't Setutsi toilet-trained, Dad?' asked Melissa.

'Well, she is really, but as we were out all day I put a nappy on her.'

'Josh is toilet-trained.'

'I know.'

'Mum says people don't toilet-train their kids 'cause they're lazy.'

'Well, maybe I am a bit lazy, but Setutsi's very good at going to the toilet by herself when we're at home.'

'D'you and Miss Foster sleep in the same bed?' Daniel asked, and before Stephen could reply he went on, 'Miss Foster doesn't teach at our school any more.'

'Can we come to your flat, Dad?' Melissa asked. 'Can we have supper there?'

'Have you got a video, Dad?' Daniel added. 'Can we watch TV while we have supper?'

Josh had knelt down by Setutsi and was half tickling her, half trying to do up the poppers of her all-in-one. Setutsi giggled obligingly. And even though his head was swarming with the ugliest of images – the bedroom like a bathroom where they spat and shouted and writhed – and his nostrils were full of her coconut conditioner – which had once aroused, but now nauseated him – he knew that this was a momentous breakthrough. That this rapid-fire inquisition was the beginning of an acceptance – for them, for him – of all that had happened. Of course Melissa and Daniel knew full well why Setutsi was black and exactly what that meant. But up until now Stephen had only offered instalments of this reality to them, randomly cut up, just as Setutsi herself had been a fleeting visitor, seen in blurred longshot through car-window screens. Now the older children had taken it upon themselves to construct a proper narrative, a story that involved them.

The questions kept on coming as he helped Josh to pee in a bush, then kissed him and set him on his side of the buggy. The enquiries continued as they left the grotty park and headed in the direction of swing four. And Stephen did his best to answer them truthfully, while observing the necessary economy of truth: Yes, he and Miss Foster did share a bed, and yes, he would ask their mother if they could come to the flat, but they mustn't be angry if she didn't want them to. And yes, he knew that Setutsi looked like him, even though she was black. And yes, she even looked like them, because she was their half-sister.

The leaden weight of Stephen's depression was lifted. He felt the physical sympathy he'd longed for for months course through him like electricity. He felt tears prick his eyes. He wanted to cuddle them all simultaneously. He pushed the two little ones in the double buggy, and felt the uneven tug of Daniel and Melissa hanging on at either side. He felt the joyful freight of his paternity. He paid no attention to the boarded-up windows of the flats on the estate they were walking through. He didn't notice the travesty of a recycling bin, which had been set on fire, so that its plastic bowel prolapsed on to the pavement. And he most definitely failed to register Misfortune, who, having taken a detour through the estate – to close the eyes of an overdosing addict, to clutch the aorta of a heart-attack victim, to clout the fontanelle of a suffering baby – chose this moment to rejoin them.

Swing four was floodlit by the time they arrived. A tiny quadrangle of black rubber under bright white lights. The wind was getting up and the cloud cover was breaking up. Most of the equipment here was still smaller than that at the one o'clock club, so small that the children of the estate disdained to use it, preferring to ride their scaled-down mountain bikes in the surrounding roadway, taking it in turns to jump off a ramp that one of them had propped against a speed bump. But there was one larger set of swings, and these were tenanted. A fat black boy, a year or so older than Daniel, dangled listlessly on one. He wore a green tracksuit several sizes too big for him, and assuming this was a hand-me-down, or a garment chosen by his parents to disguise his weight, Stephen pitied him.

As soon as they were all inside the gate the boy became galvanised and began talking at them. 'My name's Haile,' he said. 'I'm seven an' I'm big for it, yeah, an' I go to Penton Infants yeah, an' I like football an' I like Gameboy 'cept I ain't got one but I got my cousin's some of it, yeah. What's your name?' He asked Daniel first, but then he wanted to know all their names and their ages.

'I'm forty-six,' Stephen told him, laughing, although close to there was a disquieting air to Haile – his eyes bulged and he was sweating. Perhaps, Stephen thought, he has an untreated thyroid condition. It was only too likely.

Haile kept on harrying them, darting about the place, while Stephen got Josh and Setutsi out of the buggy, lifted them into the little swings. Haile then took it upon himself to push Daniel, staggering forward, his hands pressed hard into the younger boy's back.

Daniel said, 'You're hurting me!'

And Haile suddenly stepped clear so that the swing dropped and rattled on its chain. 'I gotten stay here most days, but also I get sweets from up by there.' Haile gestured towards the main road. 'D' you like sweets or chocolate?' He addressed Melissa, but before she could answer he embarked on a nauseating inventory: 'I like Snickers an' Starburst an' Joosters an' Minstrels an' all them little fings, an' chews an' lollies . . .'

But even though Haile was a bit crazed none of his lot seemed fazed. It's the new dispensation, thought Stephen, it's going to be like this from now on, my big multiracial family absorbing all and sundry, like a mobile melting pot.

He stopped turning every now and then to see what Haile and the older two were doing, and concentrated on the little ones, pushing them and tickling them, touching first Josh's nose and then Setutsi's, as if conjuring with their consanguinity. He looked over towards the flats where a couple of black guys the same age as Setutsi's mother's brothers were jump-starting a car; one of them was attaching the leads, while the other was gunning the engine of a second car which was drawn alongside. Yeah, thought Stephen, it's all going to be different now. I'm going to get along with Paul and Curtis, I'll go to the pub with them, stand them drinks, smoke a little weed. He lost himself in this new vision of familial accord, seeing the three of them, brothers-in-law, arms around each other's shoulders, full of mutual respect and amity despite their differences.

'Hey! Don't do that!' Melissa's voice cut through his reverie.

Stephen turned and couldn't believe what he saw. In the few seconds that had elapsed, Daniel had begun to swing so high and so vigorously that his swing was now twisting and plunging at the top of each arc, in a jangle of chain links. But Daniel seemed powerless to stop the violent motion, he kept on leaning back and plunging forward, the better to see what Haile was doing. The fat kid sat astride the crossbar of the swings, his plump legs hooked around them. He must've shinned up there, Stephen realised, although he didn't look at all capable of such gymnastics, and now he was there he was swaying dangerously.

'Daniel!' Stephen shouted, starting towards the swing. 'Stop swinging now! Stop swinging!'

Melissa had got off her swing and was standing well clear. Daniel began braking himself with his wellingtons.

Stephen walked below the crossbar. 'Hey, Haile,' he said, 'that's a hell of a dangerous thing to do, you should come down right away.'

'No bother if it is,' Haile said, ' 'cause I do it all times, see, t'pull the swings up.' And he began drawing one of the swing seats up by its length of chain.

'It's not a good idea, Haile,' Stephen pleaded with him. 'You could lose your balance.'

'Leave it, mister!' Haile shouted back, pulling up whole arm-lengths of chain now, looping first one about his shoulders and then a second around his neck, like some grotesquely chunky piece of jewellery. 'It's not fucking business, is it? It's not *your* fucking bloody business, you cunt!'

The final expletive propelled him backwards, the child rocked, then rolled, then fell. The chain loop rattle-yanked around his soft neck. Haile's head bulged. The neck snapped. His legs in the green tracksuit bottoms kicked once down towards Stephen's upturned face, then twice, taking the five-swing walk. Stephen, even in the mad numbness, could feel a tear struggling to detach itself from the trough of his eyelid, fighting the tension of this greater surface with its own need to become a moment. Then it was. It rolled down his cheek, dripped on to the rubber tiling. All hell broke loose. Misfortune expanded ten thousand times to fill the void.

Scale

Prologue

(to be spoken in conversational tones)

The philosopher Freddie Ayer was once asked which single thing he found most evocative of Paris. The venerable logical positivist thought for a while, and then answered, 'A road sign with "Paris" written on it.'

Kettle

Some people lose their sense of proportion; I've lost my sense of scale. Arriving home from London late last night, I found myself unable to judge the distance from the last exit sign for Junction 4 to the slip road itself. Granted it was foggy and the bright headlights of oncoming vehicles burned expanding aureoles into my view, but there are three white-bordered, oblong signs, arranged sequentially to aid people like me.

The first has three oblique bars (set in blue); the second, two; and the third, one. By the time you draw level with the third sign you should have already begun to appreciate the meaning of the curved wedge, adumbrated with further oblique white lines, that forms an interzone, an unplace, between the slip road, as it pares away, and the inside carriageway of the motorway, which powers on towards the Chiltern scarp.

The three signs are the run-in strip to the beginning of the film; they are the flying fingers of the pit-crew boss as he counts down Mansell; they are the decline in rank (from sergeant, to corporal, to lance corporal) that indicates your demotion from the motorway. Furthermore, the ability to co-ordinate their sequence with the falling needles on the warmly glowing instrument panel of the car is a sound indication that you can intuitively apprehend three different scales at once (time, speed, distance), and that you are able to merge them effortlessly into the virtual reality that is motorway driving.

But for some obscure reason the Ministry has slipped up here. At the Beaconsfield exit there is far too long a gap between the last sign and the start of the slip road. I fell into this gap and lost my sense of scale. It occurred to me, when at last I gained the roundabout, and the homey, green sign (Beaconsfield 4) heaved into view, that this gap, this lacuna, was, in terms of my projected thesis, 'No Services: Reflex Ritualism and Modern Motorway Signs (with special reference to the M40)' – an aspect of what the French call *délire*. In other words that part of the text that is a deviation or derangement, not contained within the text, and yet defines the text better than the text itself.

I almost crashed. By the time I reached home (a modest bungalow set hard against the model village that is Beaconsfield's principal visitor attraction), I had just about stopped shaking. I went straight to the kitchen. The baking tray I had left in the oven that morning had become a miniature Death Valley of hard-baked morphine granules. The dark brown rime lay in a ruckled surface, broken here and there into regular patterns of scales, like the skin of some moribund lizard. I used a steel spatula to scrape the material up and placed it carefully in a small plastic bowl decorated with leaping bunnies. (After the divorce my wife organised the division of the chattels. She took all the adult-size plates and cutlery, leaving me with the diminutive ware that our children had outgrown.)

I have no formal training in chemistry, but somehow, by a process of hit and miss, I have developed a method whereby I can precipitate a soluble tartrate from raw morphine granules. The problem with the stuff is that it still contains an appreciable amount of chalk. This is because I obtain my supplies in the form of bottles of kaolin and morphine purchased in sundry chemists. If I leave the bottles to sit for long enough, most of the morphine rises to the top. But you can never eradicate all the kaolin, and when the morphine suspension is siphoned off, some of the kaolin invariably comes as well.

Months of injecting this stuff have given my body an odd aspect, as with every shot more chalk is deposited along the walls of my veins, much in the manner of earth being piled up to form either an embankment or a cutting around a roadway. Thus the history of my addiction has been mapped out by me, in the same way that the road system of South-East England was originally constructed.

To begin with, conscious of the effects, I methodically worked my way through the veins in my arms and legs, turning them first the tannish colour of drovers' paths, then the darker brown of cart tracks, until eventually they became macadamised, blackened, by my abuse. Finally I turned my attention to the arteries. Now, when I stand on the broken bathroom scales and contemplate my route-planning image in the full-length mirror, I see a network of calcified conduits radiating from my groin. Some of them are scored into my flesh like underpasses, others are raised up on hardened revetments of flesh: bloody flyovers.

I have been driven to using huge five-millilitre barrels, fitted with the long, blue-collared needles necessary for hitting arteries. I am very conscious that, should I miss, the consequences for my circulatory system could be disastrous. I might lose a limb and cause tailbacks right the way round the M25. Sometimes I wonder if I may be losing my incident room.

There's this matter of the thesis, to begin with. Not only is the subject matter obscure (some might say risible), but I have no grant or commission. It would be all right if I were some dilettante, privately endowed, who could afford to toy with such things, but I am not. Rather, I both have myself to support and have to keep up the maintenance. If the maintenance isn't kept up, my ex-wife – who is frequently levelled by spirits – will become as obdurate as any consulting civil engineer. She has it within her power to arrange bollards around me, or even to insist on the introduction of tolls to pay for the maintenance. There could be questions in the bungalow – something I cannot abide.

But last night none of this troubled me. I was lost in the arms of Morphia. As I pushed home the plunger she spoke to me thus: 'Left hand down. Harder . . . harder . . . harder!' And around I swept, pinned by g force into the tight circularity of history. In my reverie I saw the M40 as it will be some 20,000 years from now, when the second neolithic age has dawned over Europe.

Still no services. All six carriageways and the hard shoulder are grassed over. The long enfilades of dipping halogen lights, which used to wade in concrete, are gone, leaving behind shallow depressions visible from the air Every single one of the distance markers 'Birmingham 86' has been crudely tipped to the horizontal, forming a series of steel biers. On top of them are the decomposing corpses of motorway chieftains, laid out for excarnation prior to interment. Their bones are to be placed in chambers, mausoleums that have been hollowed out from the gigantic concrete caissons of moribund motorway bridges.

I was conscious of being one of these chieftains, these princelings of the thoroughfare. And as I stared up into the dark, dark blue of a sky that was near to the end of history, I was visited by a horrible sense of claustrophobia – the claustrophobia that can come only when no space is great enough to contain you, not the involution that is time itself.

I have no idea how long I must have lain there, observing the daily life of the simple motorway folk, but it was long enough for me to gain an appreciation of the subtlety with which they had adapted this monumental ruin. While the flat expanse of the carriageways was used for rudimentary agriculture, the steeply raked embankments were left for aurochs, moufflon and other newly primitive grazers.

The motorway tribe was divided up into clans or extended families, each of which had made its encampment at a particular junction and taken a different item of the prehistoric road furniture for its totem. My clan – Junction 2, that is – had somehow managed to preserve a set of cat's eyes from the oblivion of time. These were being worn by the chieftain, bound into his complicated head-dress, when he came to see how I was getting on with decomposing.

'You must understand,' he said, observing the *Star Trek* convention, whereby even the most outlandish peoples still speak standard English, 'that we view the M40 as a giant astronomical clock. We use the slip roads, maintenance areas, bridges and flyovers azimuthally, to predict the solstices and hence the seasons. Ours is a religion both of great antiquity and of a complexity that belies our simple agrarian culture. Although we are no longer able to read or write ourselves, our priesthood has orally transmitted down the generations the sacred revelations contained in this ancient text.' With this he produced from a fold in his cloak a copy of 'No Services: Reflex Ritualism and Modern Motorway Signs (with special reference to the M40)', my as yet unwritten thesis.

Needless to say, this uncharacteristically upbeat ending to my narcotic vision left me feeling more melioristic than usual when I awoke this morning. Staggering to the kitchen I snapped on the radio. A disc jockey ululated an intro while I put on the kettle. The sun was rising over the model village. From where I sat I could see its rays reflected by a thousand tiny diamond-patterned windows. I sipped my tea; it tasted flat, as listless as myself. Looking into the cup I could see that the brown fluid was supporting an archipelago of scale. Dirty grey-brown stuff, tattered and variegated. I went back to the kitchen and peered into the kettle. Not only was the interior almost completely choked by scale, but the de-scaler itself was furred over, transformed into a chrysalis by mineral deposits. I resolved that today I would visit the ironmonger's and purchase a new de-scaler.

It's on my route – the ironmonger's – for I've burnt down every chemist in Beaconsfield in the last few months, and now I must head further afield for my kaolin and morphine supplies. I must voyage to Tring, to Amersham and even up the M40, to High Wycombe.

Relative

'Can I pay for these?'

'Whassat?'

'Can I pay for these – these de-scalers?' Time is standing still in the ironmonger's. Outside, a red-and-white-striped awning protects an array of brightly-coloured washing-up bowls from the drizzle. Inside, the darkness is scented with nails and resinous timber. I had no idea that the transaction would prove so gruelling. The proprietor of the ironmonger's is looking at me the same way that the pharmacist does when I go to buy my kaolin and morphine.

'Why d'you want three?' Is it my imagination, or does his voice really have an edge of suspicion? What does he suspect me of? Some foul and unnatural practice carried out with kettle de-scalers? It hardly seems likely.

'I've got an incredible amount of scale in my kettle, that's why.' I muster an insouciance I simply don't feel. Since I have been accused, I know that I am guilty. I know that I lure young children away from the precincts of the model village and subject them to appalling, brutal, intercrural sex. I abrade their armpits, their kneepits, the junctures of their thighs, with my spun mini-rolls of wire. That's why I need three.

Guilt dogs me as I struggle to ascend the high street, stepping on the heels of my shoes, almost tripping me up. Guilt about my children – that's the explanation for the scene in the ironmonger's. Ever since my loss of sense of scale, I have found it difficult to relate to my children. They no longer feel comfortable coming to visit me here in Beaconsfield. They say they would rather stay with their mother. The model village, which used to entrance them, now bores them.

Perhaps it was an indulgence on my part – moving to a bungalow next to the model village. It's true that when I sat, puffing on my pipe, watching my son and daughter move about amongst the four-foot-high, half-timbered semis, I would feel transported, taken back to my own childhood. It was the confusion in scale that allowed this. For if the model village was to scale, my children would be at least sixty feet tall. Easily big enough, and competent enough, to re-parent me.

It was the boy who blew the whistle on me, grassed me up to his mother. At seven, he is old enough to know the difference between the smell of tobacco and the smell that comes from my pipe. Naturally he told his mother and she realised immediately that I was back on the M.

In a way I don't blame him – it's a filthy habit. And the business of siphoning off the morphine from the bottles and then baking it in the oven until it forms a smokable paste. Well I mean, it's pathetic, this DIY addiction. No wonder that there are no pleasure domes for me, in my *bricolage* reverie. Instead I see twice five yards of fertile ground, with sheds and raspberry canes girded round. In a word: an allotment.

When my father died he subdivided his allotment and left a fifth of it to each of his children. The Association wouldn't allow it. They said that allotments were only leased rather than owned. It's a great pity, because what with the subsidies available and the new intensive agricultural methods, I could probably have made a reasonable living out of my fifth. I can just see myself . . . making hay with a kitchen fork, spreading silage with a teaspoon, bringing in the harvest with a wheelbarrow, ploughing with a trowel tied to a two-by-four. Bonsai cattle wind o'er the lea of the compost heap as I recline in the pet cemetery . . .

It was not to be.

Returning home from High Wycombe I add the contents of my two new bottles of kaolin and morphine to the plant. Other people have ginger-beer plants; I have a morphine plant. I made my morphine plant out of a plastic sterilising unit. It would be a nice irony, this transmogrification of taboo, were it not for the fact that every time I clap eyes on the thing I remember with startling accuracy what it looked like full of teats and bottles, when the children were babies and I was a happier man. I think I mentioned the division of chattels following the divorce. This explains why I ended up, here in Beaconsfield, with the decorative Tupperware, the baby-bouncer, sundry activity centres and the aforementioned sterilising unit. Whereas my ex-wife resides in St John's Wood, reclining on an emperor-size bateau-lit. When I cast off and head out on to the sea of sleep my vessel is a plastic changing mat, patterned with Fred Flintstones and Barney Rubbles.

It's lucky for me that the five 'police procedurals' I wrote during my marriage are still selling well. Without the royalties I don't think I would be able to keep my family in the manner to which they have unfortunately become accustomed. I cannot imagine that the book I am currently working on, *Murder on the Median Strip*, will do a fraction as well. (I say that confidently, but what fraction do I mean? Certainly not a half or a quarter, but why not a fiftieth or a hundredth? This is certainly conceivable. I must try and be more accurate with my figures of speech. I must use them as steel rulers to delimit thought. Woolliness will be my undoing.)

In *Murder on the Median Strip* (henceforth *M on the MS*), a young woman is raped, murdered and buried on the median strip of the M40 in between Junction 2 (Beaconsfield) and Junction 3 (High Wycombe). As shall become apparent, it is a howdunnit, rather than a whodunnit. The murder occurs late on a Friday evening when the motorway is still crowded with ex-urbanites heading for home. The police are patrolling, looking for speeders. Indeed, they have set up a radar trap between the two principal bridges on this section of road. And yet no one notices anything.

When the shallow, bitumen-encrusted grave is discovered, the police, indulging in their penchant for overkill, decide to reconstruct the entire incident. They put out a call on *Crimewatch UK* for all those who were on the motorway in that place, at that time, to reassemble at Junction 2. The public response is overwhelming, and by virtue of careful interviewing – the recollection of number plates, makes of car, children making faces and so forth – they establish that they have managed to net all the cars and drivers that could have been there. The logistics of this are immensely complicated. But such is the ghastliness of the crime that the public demands that the resources be expended. Eventually, by dint of computer-aided visualisations, the police are able to re-enact the whole incident. The cars set off at intervals; the police hover overhead in helicopters; officers in patrol cars and on foot question any passers-by. But, horror of horrors, while the reconstruction is actually taking place, the killer strikes again – this time between Junction 6 (Watlington) and Junction 7 (Thame). Once more his victim is a young woman, whom he sexually assaults, strangles, and then crudely inters beneath the static steel fender of the crash barrier.

That's as far as I've got with *M on the MS*. Sometimes, contemplating the *MS*, I begin to feel that I've painted myself into a corner with this convoluted plot. I realise that I may have tried to stretch the credulity of my potential readers too far.

In a way the difficulties of the plot mirror my own difficulties as a writer. In creating such an unworkable and fantastic scenario I have managed, at least, to fulfil my father's expectations of my craft.

'There's no sense of scale in your books,' he said to me shortly before he died. At that time I had written only two procedurals, both featuring Inspector Archimedes, my idiosyncratic Greek Cypriot detective. 'You can have a limited success,' he went on, 'chipping away like this at the edges of society, chiselling off microscopic fragments of observation. But really important writing provides some sense of the relation between individual psychology and social change, of the scale of things in general. You can see that if you look at the great nineteenth-century novels.' He puffed on his pipe as he spoke, and, observing his wrinkled, scaly hide and the way his red lips and yellow teeth masticated the black stem, I was reminded of a basking lizard, sticking its tongue out at the world.

* * *

A letter came this morning from the Municipality, demanding payment of their property tax. When I first moved here, a man came from the borough valuer's to assess the rateable value of the bungalow. I did some quick work with the trellises and managed to make it look as if Number 59, Crendon Road, was in fact one of the houses in the model village.

To begin with, the official disputed the idea that I could possibly be living in this pocket-sized dwelling, but I managed to convince him that I was a doctoral student writing a thesis on 'The Apprehension of Scale in *Gulliver's Travels*, with special reference to Lilliput', and that the operators of the model village had leased the house to me so that I could gain first-hand experience of Gulliver's state of mind. I even entered the house and adopted some attitudes – head on the kitchen table, left leg rammed through the french windows – in order to persuade him.

The result of this clever charade was that for two years my rates were assessed on the basis of 7ft 8in sq. of living space. I had to pay £11.59 per annum. Now, of course, I am subject to the full whack. Terribly unfair. And anyway, if the tax is determined by the individual rather than by the property, what if that individual has a hazy or distorted sense of self? Shouldn't people with acute dissociation, or multiple personalities, be forced to pay more? I have resolved not to pay the tax until I have received a visit from the borough clinical psychologist.

The Ascent

'Affected as well as asinine' *TLS*

Some of my innovations regarding the new genre of 'Motorway Verse' have been poorly received, both by the critics and by the reading public. My claim, that what my motorway verse is trying to do represents a return to the very roots of poetas, an inspired attempt to link modish hermeneutics to the original function of oral literature, has been dismissed *sans phrase*.

I myself cannot even understand the thrust of this criticism. It seems to me self-evident that the subconscious apprehension of signs by motorway drivers is exactly analogous to that act whereby the poets of primitive cultures give life, actually breathe reality into the land.

Taking the M40 as an example of this:

> Jnctn 1. Uxbridge. Jnctn 1A. (M25) M4.
> Jnctn 2. Slough A365. No Services.
> On M40 . . .

would be a very believable sample of such a 'signing up' of the country. Naturally, in order to understand the somewhat unusual scansion, it is necessary that readers imaginatively place themselves in a figurative car that is actually driving up the aforementioned motorway. Metrical feet are, therefore, to be determined as much by feeling through the pedals the shift from macadamised to concrete surfaces, and by hearing the susurration produced by alterations in the height and material construction of the crash barrier, as by the rhythm of the words themselves.

Furthermore, a motorway verse that attempts to describe the ascent of the Chiltern scarp from the Oxfordshire side will, of course, be profoundly different to one that chronicles the descent from Junction 5 (Stokenchurch) to Junction 6 (Watlington). For example:

> Crawling, crawling, crawling. Crawler Lane
> Slow-slow O'Lorry-o. Lewknor. 50 mph max.
> 11T! Narrow lanes, narrowing, narr-o-wing,
> na-rro-wing.

as opposed to:

> F'tum. F'tum. F'tum.
> Kerchunk, kerchunk (Wat-ling-ton) . . .

Well, I'm certain no one reading this had any difficulty in divining which was which!

On the Continent they are not afflicted by the resistance to the modern that so entirely characterises English cultural life. In France, '*Vers Péage*' is a well-respected genre, already making its way on to university syllabuses. Indeed I understand that a critical work is soon to be published that concerns itself solely with the semantic incongruities presented by the term 'soft vierge'.

It has occurred to me that it could be my introduction of motorway symbology itself, as if it were an extension of the conventional alphabet, that has hardened the hearts of these penny-ante time-servers, possessors of tenure (but no grip), and the like. But it seems to me that the white arrow pointing down, obliquely, to the right; the ubiquitous '11T' lane-closing ideogram; the emotive, omega-like, overhead '[X]'; and many many others all have an equal right to be considered capable of meaningful combination with orthodox characters.

On bad days, days when the tedium and obscurity of my life here at Beaconsfield seem almost justified, I am embarrassed to say that I console myself with the thought that there may be some grand conspiracy, taking in critics, publishers, editors and the executives in charge of giant type-founders such as Monotype, to stop my verse from gaining any success. For, were it to do so, they would have to alter radically the range of typefaces that they provide.

Is it any wonder that I look for consolation – partly in draughts of sickly morphine syrup (drunk straight off the top of bottles of kaolin and morphine), and partly in hard, dedicated work on my motorway saga, entitled *From Birmingham to London and Back Again Delivering Office Equipment, with Nary a Service Centre to Break the Monotony*?

There's that, and there's also the carving of netsuke, at which I am becoming something of an expert. I have chosen to concentrate on rendering in ivory the monumental works of modern sculptors. Thus, I have now completed a set of early Caros and Henry Moores, all of which could be comfortably housed in a pup tent.

The ebb and flow of my opiate addiction is something that I have come to prize as a source of literary inspiration. When I am beginning a new habit, my hypnagogic visions are intricate processions of images that I can both summon and manipulate at will. But when I am withdrawing, I am frequently plunged into startling nightmares. Nightmares that seem to last for eons and yet of which I am conscious – at one and the same time – as taking place within a single REM.

Last night's dream was a classic case of this clucking phenomenon. In it, I found myself leaving the bungalow and entering the precincts of the model village. I wandered around the forty-foot-long village green, admiring the precision and attention to detail that the model makers have lavished on their creation. I peeked first into the model butcher's shop. Lilliputian rashers of bacon were laid out on plastic trays, together with sausages, perfect in every respect, but the size of mouse droppings. Then I sauntered over to the post office. On the eight-inch-high counter sat an envelope the size of a postage stamp. Wonder of wonders, I could even read the address on the envelope. It was a poll-tax demand, destined for me.

Straightening up abruptly I caught sight of two model buildings that I was unfamiliar with. The first of these was a small, but perfectly formed, art gallery. Looking through the tall windows I could see, inside, on the polished wooden floor, a selection of my netsuke. The Caros rather than the Moores. Preposterous, I thought to myself, with one of those leaps of dream logic; a real village of this size would never have an art gallery. Let alone one exhibiting the works of an internationally renowned sculptor.

The second building was my own bungalow. I couldn't be certain of this – it is after all not that remarkable an edifice – until I had looked in through the kitchen window. There, under the dirty cream melamine work surface surrounding the aluminium sink, I could see hundreds of little kaolin and morphine bottles, serried in dusty ranks. That settled it.

As soon as I had clapped eyes on them, I found myself miraculously reduced in size and able to enter the model bungalow. I wandered from room to room, more than a little discomfited at my phantasmagoric absorption into Beaconsfield's premier visitor attraction. Stepping on to the sun porch I found another model – as it were, a model model. Also of the bungalow. Once again I was diminished and able to enter.

I must have gone through at least four more of these vertiginous descents in scale before I was able to stop, and think, and prevent myself from examining another model bungalow. As it was I knew that I must be standing in a sun porch for which a double-glazing estimate would have to be calculated in angstroms. From the position I found myself in, to be 002 scale would have been, to me, gargantuan. How to get back? That was the problem.

It is fortunate indeed that in my youth I spent many hours tackling the more difficult climbs around Wastdale Head. These rocky scrambles, although close to the tourist tramps up the peaks of Scafell Pike and

Helvellyn, are nevertheless amongst the most demanding rock climbs in Europe.

It took me three months to ascend, back up the six separate stages of scale, and reach home once more. Some of the pitches, especially those involving climbing down off the various tables the model bungalows were placed on, I would wager were easily the most extreme ever attempted by a solo climber. On many occasions, I found myself dangling from the rope I had plaited out of strands of carpet underlay, with no apparent way of regaining the slick varnished face of the table leg, and the checkerboard of lino – relative to my actual size – some six hundred feet below.

Oh, the stories I could tell! The sights I saw! It would need an epic to contain them. As it is I have restrained myself – although, on awakening, I did write a letter to the Alpine Club on the ethics of climbers, finding themselves in such situations, using paper clips as fixed crampons.

The final march across the 'true' model village to my bungalow was, of course, the most frightening. When contained within the Russian-doll series of ever diminishing bungalows, I had been aware that the ordinary laws of nature were, to some extent, in abeyance. However, out in the village I knew that I was exposed to all the familiar terrors of small-scale adventuring: wasps the size of zeppelins, fluff-falls the weight of an avalanche, mortar-bomb explosions of plant spore, and so on and so forth.

My most acute anxiety, as I traversed the model village, was that I would be sighted by a human. I was aware that I could not be much larger than a sub-atomic particle, and as such I would be subject to Heisenberg's Uncertainty Principle. Were I to be in any way observed, not only might I find the direction of my journey irremediably altered, I could even cease to exist altogether!

It happened as I picked my way over the first of the steps leading up from the village to my bungalow. The very grain of the concrete formed a lunar landscape which I knew would take me days to journey across. I wiped the sweat that dripped from my sunburnt brow. Something vast, inconceivably huge, was moving up ahead of me. It was a man! To scale! He turned, and his turning was like some geological event, the erosion of a mountain range or the undulation of the Mohorovicic Discontinuity itself!

It was one of the maintenance men who works in the model village.

I knew it because, emblazoned across the back of his blue boiler suit, picked out in white as on a motorway sign, was the single word 'maintenance'. His giant eye loomed towards me, growing bigger and bigger, until the red-and-blue veins that snaked across the bilious ball were as the Orinoco or the Amazon, to my petrified gaze. He blinked – and I winked out of existence.

I don't need to tell you that when I awoke sweating profusely, the covers twisted around my quaking body like a strait-jacket, I had no difficulty at all in interpreting the dream.

To the Bathroom

'Like, we're considering the historic present –?'

'Yeah.'

'And David says, "I want to go to the bathroom.' "

'Yeah.'

'So, like we all accompany him there and stuff. Cos in his condition it wouldn't like be a . . . be a – '

'Good idea for him to be alone?'

'Yeah, thassit. So we're standing there, right. All four of us, in the bathroom, and David's doing what he has to do. And we're still talking about it.'

'It?'

'The historic present. Because Diane – you know Diane?'

'Sort of.'

'Well, she says the historic present is, like . . . er . . . like, more emotionally labile than other tenses. Yeah, thass what she says. Anyways, she's saying this and David is, like, steaming, man . . . I mean to say he's really plummeting. It's like he's being de-cored or something. This isn't just Montezuma's revenge, it's everyone's revenge. It's the revenge of every deracinated group of indigenes ever to have had the misfortune to encounter the European. It's a sort of collective curse of David's colon. It's like his colon is being crucified or something.'

'He's anally labile.'

'Whadjewsay?'
'He's anally labile.'

Labile, labile. Labby lips. Libby-labby lips. This is the kind of drivel I've been reduced to. Imaginary dialogues between myself and a non-existent interlocutor. But is it any surprise? I mean to say, if you have a colon as spastic as mine it's bound to insinuate itself into every aspect of your thinking. My trouble is I'm damned if I do and I'm damned if I don't. If I don't drink vast quantities of kaolin and morphine I'm afflicted with the most terrifying bouts of diarrhoea. And if I do – drink a couple of bottles a day, that is – I'm subject to the most appalling undulations, seismic colonic ructions. It doesn't really stop the shits either. I still get them, I just don't get caught short. Caught short on the hard shoulder, that's the killer.

Say you're driving up to High Wycombe, for example. Just out on a commonplace enough errand. Like going to buy a couple of bottles of K&M. And you're swooping down towards Junction 3, the six lanes of blacktop twisting away from you like some colossal wastepipe, through which the automotive crap of the metropolis is being voided into the rural septic tank, when all of a sudden you're overcome. You pull over on to the hard shoulder, get out of the car, and squat down. Hardly dignified. And not only that, destructive of the motorway itself. Destructive of the purity of one's recollection.

That's why I prefer to stay home in my kaolin-lined bungalow. I prefer to summon up my memories of the motorway in the days before I was so afflicted. In the days when my vast *roman-fleuve* was barely a trickle, and my sense of scale was intact. Then, distance was defined by regular increments, rather than by the haphazard lurch from movement to movement.

This morning I was sitting, not really writing, just dabbling. I was hunkered down inside myself, my ears unconsciously registering the whisper, whistle and whicker of the traffic on the M40, when I got that sinking feeling. I hied me to the bathroom, just in time to see a lanky youth disappearing out of the window, with my bathroom scales tucked under his arm.

I grabbed a handful of his hip-length jacket and pulled him back into the room. He was a mangy specimen. His head was badly shaven, with spirals of ringworm on the pitted surface. The youth had had these embellished with crude tattoos, as if to dignify his repulsive skin condition. His attire was a loose amalgam of counter-cultural styles, the ragged chic of a redundant generation. His pupils were so dilated that the black was getting on to his face. I instantly realised that I had nothing to fear from him. He didn't cry out, or even attempt to struggle.

I had seen others like him. There's quite a posse of them, these 'model heads'. That's what they call themselves. They congregate around the model village, venerating it as a symbol of their anomie. It's as if, by becoming absorbed in the detail of this tiny world, they hope to diminish the scale of society's problems. In the winter they go abroad, settling near Legoland in Belgium.

'Right, you,' I said, in householder tones. 'You might have thought that you'd get away with nicking something as trivial as those bathroom scales, but it just so happens that they have a sentimental value for me.'

'Whadjergonna do then?' He was bemused – not belligerent.

'I'm going to put you on trial, that's what I'm going to do.'

'You're not gonna call the filth, are you?'

'No, no. No need. In Beaconsfield we have extended the whole principle of Neighbourhood Watch to include the idea of neighbourhood justice. I will sit in judgment on you myself. If you wish, my court will appoint a lawyer who will organise your defence.'

'Err –' He had slumped down on top of the wicker laundry basket, which made him look even more like one of Ali Baba's anorectic confrères. 'Yeah, OK, whatever you say.'

'Good. I will represent you myself. Allow me, if you will, to assume my position on the bench.' We shuffled around each other in the confinement of tiles. I put the seat down, sat down, and said, 'The court may be seated.'

For a while after that nothing happened. The two of us sat in silence, listening to the rising and falling flute of the Vent-Axia. I thought about the day the court-appointed officer had come to deliver my decree nisi. He must have been reading the documents in the car as he drove up the motorway, because when I encountered him on the doorstep he was trying hard – but failing – to suppress a smirk of amusement.

I knew why. My wife had sued for divorce on the grounds of adultery. The co-respondent was known to her, and the place where the adultery had taken place was none other than on these selfsame scales. The ones the model head had just attempted to steal. At that time they were still located in the bathroom of our London house. After the decree absolute, my ex-wife sent them to me in Beaconsfield, together with a caustic note.

It was a hot summer afternoon in the bathroom. I was with a lithe young foreign woman, who was full of capricious lust. 'Come on,' she said, 'let's do it on the scales. It'll be fun, we'll look like some weird astrological symbol, or a diagram from the *Kama Sutra.*' She twisted out of her dress and pulled off her underwear. I stood on the scales. Even translated from metric to imperial measure, my bodyweight still looked unimpressive. She hooked her hands around my neck and jumped. The flanges of flesh on the inside of her thighs neatly fitted the notches above my bony hips. I grasped the fruit of her buttocks in my sweating palms. She braced herself, feet against the wall, toenails snagging on the Artex. Her panting smoked the mirror on the medicine cabinet. I moved inside her. The coiled spring inside the scales squeaked and groaned. Eventually it broke altogether.

That's how my wife twigged. When she next went to weigh herself she found the scales jammed, the pointer registering 322 lb. Exactly the combined weight of me and the family au pair . . .

Oh, *mene, mene, tekel, upharsin*! What a fool I was! Now fiery hands retributively mangle my innards! The demons play upon my sackbut and I am cast into the fiery furnace of evacuation. I am hooked there, a toilet duck, condemned for ever to lick under the rim of life!

The model head snapped me out of my fugue. 'You're a Libra,' he said, 'aren't you?'

'Whassat?'

'Your sign. It's Libra, innit?' He was regarding me with the preternatural stare of a madman or a seer.

'Well, yes, as a matter of fact it is.'

'I'm good at that. Guessing people's astrological signs. Libra's are, like, er . . . creative an' that.'

'I s'pose so.'

'But they also find it hard to come to decisions –'

'Are you challenging the authority of this court?' I tried to sound magisterial, but realised that the figure I cut was ridiculous.

'Nah, nah. I wouldn't do that, mate. It's just . . . like . . . I mean to say, whass the point, an' that?'

I couldn't help but agree with him, so I let him go. I even insisted that he take the bathroom scales with him. After all, what good are they to me now?

Lizard

Epilogue. Many years later . . .

If you want to walk round the Lizard Peninsula, you have to be reasonably well equipped. Which is not to say that this part of Cornwall is either particularly remote (the M5 now goes all the way to Land's End) or that rugged. It's just that the exposure to so much wind and sky, and so many pasties, after a winter spent huddled on the urban periphery (somewhere like Beaconsfield, for example), can have an unsettling effect. I always advise people to take an antacid preparation, and also some kaolin and morphine. There's no need any more to carry an entire bottle, for Sterling Health have thoughtfully created a tablet form of this basic but indispensable remedy.

One other word of warning before you set out. Don't be deceived by the map into thinking that distances of, say, eight to ten miles represent a comfortable afternoon's stroll. The Lizard is so called because of the many rocky inlets that are gouged out of its scaly sides, giving the entire landmass the aspect of some giant creature, bound for the Atlantic vivarium. The coastal path is constantly either ascending or descending around these inlets. Therefore, to gain a mile you may have to go up and down as much as six hundred feet.

I myself haven't been to the Lizard for many years, in fact not since I was a young man. Even if I felt strong enough to make the journey now, I wouldn't go. For those younger than I, who cannot remember a time before the current Nationalist Trust Government took power, the prospect may still seem inviting. But personally, I find that the thought of encountering the Government's Brown Shirts, with their oak-leaf epaulettes, sticks in my craw. I would bitterly resent being compelled by these paramilitary nature wardens to admire the scenery, register the presence (or even absence) of ancient monuments, and propitiate the wayside waste shrines with crumpled offerings.

Of course, we aren't altogether immune from the depredations of the Trust here in Beaconsfield. Last month, after a bitterly fought local election, they gained power in almost all of the wards, including the one that contains the model village itself. There have been rumours, discreet mutterings, that they intend to introduce their ubiquitous signs to the village. These will designate parts of it areas of (albeit minute) 'outstanding natural beauty'.

But I am old now, and have not the stomach for political infighting. Since the publication of the last volume of my magnum opus, *A History of the English Motorway Service Centre*, I have gained a modest eminence. People tell me that I am referred to as 'the Macaulay of the M40', a sobriquet that, I must confess, gives me no little pleasure. I feel vindicated by the verdict of posterity. (I say posterity, for I am now so old that hardly anyone realises I am still alive.)

I spend most my the days out on the sun porch. Here I lie naked, for all the world like some moribund reptile, sopping up the rays. My skin has turned mahogany with age and melanoma. It's difficult for me to distinguish now between the daub of cancerous sarcoma and the toughened wattle of my flesh. Be that as it may, I am not frightened of death. I feel no pain, despite having long since reduced the indulgence of my pernicious habituation to kaolin and morphine to a mere teaspoonful every hour.

With age have come stoicism and repose. When I was younger I could not focus on anything, or even apprehend a single thought, without feeling driven to incorporate it into some architectonic, some Great Design. I was also plagued by lusts, both fleshly and demonic, which sent me into such dizzying spirals of self-negation that I was compelled to narcosis.

But now, even the contemplation of the most trivial things can provide enough sensual fodder to last me an entire morning. Today, for example, I became transfixed, staring into the kettle, by the three separate levels of scale therein. First the tangible scale, capping the inverted cradle of the water's meniscus. Secondly, the crystalline accretions of scale that wreathed the element. And thirdly, of course, the very abstract notion of 'scale' itself, implied by my unreasoned observation. It's as if I were possessed of some kind of Escher-vision, allowing me constantly to perceive the dimensional conundrum that perception presents.

I am also comforted in my solitude by my pets. One beneficial side-effect of the change in climate has been the introduction of more exotic species to this isle. But whereas the *nouveaux riches* opt for the Pantagruelian spectacle of giraffes cropping their laburnums, and hippopotamuses wallowing in their sun-saturated swimming pools, I have chosen to domesticate the more elegant frill-necked lizard.

This curious reptile, with its preposterous vermilion ruff, stands erect on its hind legs like a miniature dinosaur. When evening comes, and the day's visitors have departed, I let it out so that it may roam the lanes and paths of the model village. The sight of this pocket Godzilla stalking the dwarfish environs, its head darting this way and that, as if on the look-out for a canapé-sized human, never fails to amuse me.

However, not every aspect of my life is quite so easeful and reposed. The occasional dispute, relating to a lifetime of scholarly endeavour, still flares up occasionally. It is true that my work has a certain status here in England, but of course all this means in practice is that although many have heard of it, few have actually read any of it.

In the ex-colonies the situation is different. A Professor Moi wrote to me last year, from the University of Uganda, to dispute the findings of my seminal paper 'When is a Road Not a Road?'*, in which – if you can be bothered to recall – I established a theory that a motorway cannot be said to be a motorway unless it is longer than it is broad. I was inspired to this by my contemplation of the much maligned A41(M), which at that time ran for barely a mile. Moi took issue with the theory, and after I had perused the relevant Ugandan gazetteer it became clear to me why.

The ill-fated Lusaka Bypass was to have been the centrepiece of the Ugandan Government's Motorway Construction Programme. However, resources ran out after only one junction and some eighty feet of road had been built. Faced with the options of either changing the nomenclature or

* *British Journal of Ephemera*, Spring 1986

admitting failure, the Ugandans had no alternative but to take issue with the theory itself.

But such episodes are infrequent. Mostly I am left alone by the world. My children have grown up and disappointed me; my former friends and acquaintances have forgotten me. If I do receive any visitors nowadays, they are likely to be young professional couples, nascent ex-urbanites, come to enquire whether or not the bungalow is for sale.

It is a delicious irony that although when I first moved to Beaconsfield the bungalow was regarded as tacky in the extreme, over the years it has become a period piece. The aluminium-framed picture windows, the pebbledash façade, the corrugated-perspex carport: all of these are now regarded as delightfully authentic and original features. Such is the queer humour of history.

And what of the M40 itself, the fount of my life's work? How stands it? Well, I must confess that since the universal introduction of electric cars with a maximum speed of 15 mph, the glamour of motorway driving seems entirely lost. Every so often I'll take the golf buggy out and tootle up towards Junction 5 (Stokenchurch), but my motives are really rather morbid.

Morbid, for it is here that I am to be buried. Here, where the motorway plunges through a gunsight cutting and the rolling plain of Oxfordshire spreads out into the blue distance. Just beyond the Chiltern scarp the M40 bisects the Ridgeway, that neolithic drovers' path which was the motorway of Stone Age Britain. It is here that the Nationalist Trust has given gracious permission for me to construct my mausoleum.

I have opted for something in the manner of an ancient chamber tomb. A long, regular heap of layered stones, with corbelled walls rising to a slab roof. At one end the burial mound will tastefully elide with the caisson of the bridge on which the M40 spans the Ridgeway.

It is a fitting memorial, and what's more, I am convinced that it will remain long after the motorway itself has become little more than a grassed-over ruin, a monument to a dead culture. The idea that perhaps, in some distant future, disputatious archaeologists will find themselves flummoxed by the discovery of my tomb, together with its midden of discarded motorway signs, brings a twitch to my jowls.

Will the similarities in construction between my tomb and the great chamber tombs of Ireland and the Orkneys lead them to posit a continuous motorway culture, lasting some 7,000 years? I hope so. It has always been my contention that phenomena such as Silbury Hill and the Avebury stone circle can best be understood as, respectively, an embankment and a roundabout.

And so it seems that it is only by taking this very, very, long-term view that the answer to that pernicious riddle 'Why are there no services on the M40?' will find an answer.

In conclusion, then. It may be said of me that I have lost my sense of scale, but never that I have lost my sense of proportion.

Repeat this exercise daily, or until you are thoroughly proficient.

Chest

The pavement outside Marten's the newsagent was streaked with sputum. In the outrageously dull light of a mid-afternoon, in midwinter, in middle England, the loops and lumps of mucus and phlegm appeared strangely bright, lurid even, as if some Jackson Pollock of the pneumothorax had been practising Action Hawking.

There was an incident – of sorts – going on in the entrance to the shop. A man in the middle of his middle years, dressed not so much warmly as tightly in a thick, hip-length jacket, corduroy trousers, brogues, and anaconda of woollen scarf, was upbraiding the shop manager. His voice – which was in the middle of middle-class accents – would start off at quite a reasonable pitch, but as he spoke it would creep up the scale until it was a melodramatic whine. The shop manager, blue-suited, nylon-shirted, with thinning hair and earnest expression, kept trying – albeit with appropriate deference – to break in, but without success.

'I can't put up with this any more, Hutchinson,' said the man, whose name was Simon-Arthur Dykes. 'I've two sick children and an invalid wife, as well as other dependants. God knows how many times I've told your boy to bring the paper to the door and knock, but he still won't do it. The paper is vital for my work – it's useless to me if it's damp and soggy, but every single day it's the same, he just chucks it over the fence. What the hell does he think it's going to do, grow legs and scamper up to the house?'

'But Mr Dykes –'

'Don't "but" me, Hutchinson, I'm paying you for a service that I don't receive. I'm a sensitive man, you know, a man who needs some caring and consideration. My nerves, you see, they're so very . . . so very . . . stretched, I feel that they might snap. Snap! D'you appreciate that? The nerves of the artist –'

'I'm not un –'

'You're not what? Unaware? Unsympathetic? Unaffected? All of the above? Oh, I don't know – I don't know – it's all too much for me. Perhaps my wife is right and we need a redeemer of some kind, Hutchinson, a reawakening . . .' And with this, Simon-Arthur Dykes's voice, instead of climbing up towards hysteria, fell down, down into his chest where it translated itself into a full-bodied coughing. A liquid coughing, that implied the sloshing about of some fluid ounces of gunk in his lungs.

The shop manager was left free to talk, which he did, fulsomely. 'No, Mr Dykes,' he began, sounding placatory, 'I'm not unsympathetic, I do feel for you, really I do. I can imagine what it must be like only too well. Out there at the Brown House, isolated, with the wet, exposed fields all around you, damp and encompassing.' His fingers made combing motions, ploughing dismal little furrows in the air. 'I can see what a torment it must be to receive a wet newspaper every morning' – now the manager's own voice had begun to quaver – 'knowing that it may be the only contact that you will have with the world all day, the only thing to touch your sense of isolation. I don't know. Oh Christ! I don't know.'

And with that the manager's voice cracked, and he began to weep openly. But the weeping didn't last for long, for having given way to the flow in one form, the manager's will to resist the ever present tickling in his own chest was eliminated. Soon, both of the men were hacking away, producing great caribou-cry honks, followed by the rasping eructation of tablespoon-loads of sputum, which they dumped, along with the rest of the infective matter, on the pavement fronting the newsagent's.

A group of adolescents was hanging about outside Marten's, for this was where the buses stopped, picking up passengers for Oxford, High Wycombe and Princes Risborough. They wore padded nylon anoraks, decorated with oblongs of fluorescent material and the occasional, apparently random, selection of letters and figures: 'ZX – POWER NINE', was written on one boy's jacket; and 'ARIZONA STATE 4001' on his girl companion's. With their squashy vinyl bags at their rubber-ridged feet and their general air of round-shouldered indifference, the adolescents gave the impression of being a unit of some new kind of army – in transit. Part of a pan-European formation of Jugend Sportif.

None of them paid any attention to the two men, who were now reaching the rattling end of their joint coughing fit. They were all focused on one of the older boys, who held a small red cylinder attached to a valved mouthpiece. Mostly he kept the mouthpiece clamped in his teeth and breathed through the double-action valve with a mechanical 'whoosh', but every so often he would pass it to one of the others, and they would take a hit.

Straightening up the manager said, 'What's that you've got there, Kevin-Andrew?'

'It's oxygen, Mr Hutchinson,' said the lad, removing the mouthpiece.

'Well, give us both a go, Kevin, for the love of God. Can't you see the state poor Mr Dykes and I are in?'

'I don't know if I can, Mr Hutchinson . . .' The lad paused, looking shamefaced. 'You see, it's the family cylinder. I just got it recharged at the health centre and it's got to last us till the weekend.'

'If that's the case, why are you giving it out to your pals like a tube of bloody Smarties!' This was from Simon-Arthur Dykes. He too had straightened up, but was still gasping and visibly blue in the face. He shouldn't really have expostulated with such vigour, for it got him wheezing again, and he began to double over once more, one hand clutching at the doorjamb, the other flopping around in the air.

'Come on, Kevin-Andrew,' said the manager, 'give him the mouthpiece, for heaven's sake. Tell you what, you can all have a belt off of my Ventalin inhaler, if Mr Dykes and I can just get ourselves straight.'

Grudgingly, and with much shoulder-shrugging and foot-shuffling, the youth handed over the small red cylinder. In return Hutchinson passed him the angled plastic tube of the Ventalin inhaler.

For a while there was a sort of calm on the wan stage of the pavement. The two men helped one another to take several much needed pulls from the oxygen cylinder, while the group of adolescents formed a circle around which they passed the inhaler. There was silence, except for the whirring whizz of the inhaler and the kerchooof! of the oxygen cylinder.

All the parties began to look slightly better than formerly. Their pale cheeks acquired an ulterior glow, their eyes brightened, their countenances took on the aspect of febrile health that only comes to those who have temporarily relieved a condition of chronic invalidism.

Simon-Arthur Dykes drew himself up in the doorway, passing the oxygen cylinder back to Kevin-Andrew. 'Thank you, Mr Hutchinson, really I thank you most sincerely. You are a man of some honour, sir, some Christian virtue in a world of ugliness and misery.' Dykes clutched the manager's upper arm. 'Please, please, Mr Dykes, don't upset yourself again – think of your poor chest.' The manager gave Dykes his copy of the *Guardian*, which he had dropped during the coughing fit.

Dykes looked at the paper as if he couldn't remember what it was. His rather protruberant grey eyes were darting about, unable to alight on anything. His thick brown hair was standing up in a crazy bouffant on top of his high, strained forehead.

He took the manager by the arm again, and drew him back into the shop a couple of paces. Then he leant towards him conspiratorially saying, 'It's Dave Hutchinson, that's your name, isn't it?'

'Ye-es,' the manager replied uneasily.

'And your patronymic?'

'Dave as well.'

'Well, Dave-Dave, I want you to call me Simon-Arthur. I feel this little episode has brought us together, and I stand in debt on your account.'

'Really, Mr Dykes –'

'Simon-Arthur.'

'Simon-Arthur, I don't think it's at all –'

'No, I do. Listen, I've just picked up a brand-new nebuliser in Risborough. I've got it in the car. Why don't you come around this evening, and give it a try – bring your wife if you like.'

This invitation, so obviously felt and meant, softened the manager's resistance, broke down his barriers of social deference and retail professionalism. 'I'd like that, Simon-Arthur,' he said, grasping the artist's right hand firmly in both of his, 'really I would. But I'm afraid my wife is bed-bound, so it would only be me.'

'I am sorry – but that's OK, just come yourself.'

'I've got a few mils of codeine linctus left over from the monthly ration – shall I bring it with me?'

'Why not . . . we can have a little party, as best we can.'

The two men finished, smiling broadly, in unison. Simon-Arthur took

Dave-Dave Hutchinson's hand warmly in his and gave it several pumps. Then they parted; and whilst Dave-Dave Hutchinson turned back into the interior of the shop, Simon-Arthur Dykes crossed the road to where his car was parked in the middle of the town square.

As he gained the herringbone of white lines that designated the parking area, Simon-Arthur felt a whooshing sensation behind him. He turned to see the 320 bus bearing down on the stop outside Marten's. Observing the way the rows of yellow windows shone through the murky air, he jolted into greater haste. Darkness was coming; and with it the great bank of fog, that had hung two hundred feet above the ground all day, was beginning to descend, falling around the shoulders of the grey stone houses like some malodorous muffler.

Simon-Arthur kept his mouth clamped shut, but sniffed the fog judiciously with a connoisseur's nose. Lots of sulphur tonight, he thought, and perhaps even a hint of something more tangy . . . sodium, maybe? He turned on the ignition. His headlights barely penetrated the thick fog. As he pulled out and drove off down the road Simon-Arthur avoided looking at the fog too closely. He knew from experience that if he peered into it for too long, actually concentrated on its twistings, its eddies, its endless assumptions of insubstantial form, that it could all too easily draw him down a darkling corridor, into more durable, more horribly solid visions.

But halfway home he had to stop. A heavy mizzle was saturating the air. The A418 was a tunnel of spray. Heavy lorry after heavy lorry churned up the fog and water. Simon-Arthur was jammed between two of these grunting beasts as he gained the crest of the hill at Tiddington. The vacuum punched in the air by the one ahead was sucking his flimsy 2cv forward, whilst the boil of turbulence pushed up by the one behind propelled him on. The wheels of the car were barely in contact with the tarmac. He dabbed the brakes and managed to slide off the road into a lay-by.

Sort of safe, Simon-Arthur slumped over the Citroën's steering wheel. He felt more than usually depleted; and the thought of facing his family produced a hard, angular sensation in his gorge. Without quite knowing why he opened the door of the car and got out. If he had felt unsafe in the car – he was now totally exposed. Lorry after lorry went on slamming by, throwing up clouds of compounded gas and liquid.

Simon-Arthur lurched round to the other side of the car and stood transfixed by the hard filthiness of the verge. The bank of grass and weeds was so stained with pollutants that it appeared petrified. It was as if the entire lay-by had been buried in a peat bog for some thousands of years and only this moment disinterred.

Simon-Arthur stood, lost in time, ahistoric. He looked along the A418 towards his house. The road manifested itself as a serpent of yellow and orange, winding its way over the dark country. Each ploughing vehicle was another muscular motion, another bunching and uncoiling in its anguiform body. But if he turned away from the road he was enclosed in his lay-by burial ship. A Sutton Hoo of the psyche. The armour of mashed milk cartons and crushed cans, the beadwork of fag butts, the weaponry of buckled hub caps and discarded lengths of chromium trim. They were, Simon-Arthur reflected, entirely useless – and therefore entirely apt – funerary gifts, for his sustenance in this current afterlife.

He would have stayed longer, savouring this mordant feeling, but the fog was seeping into his chest, producing acute sensations of rasp and tickle that grew and grew until he began to cough. When he was underway again he had to drive with the Citroën's flap window open so that he could spit out of it. And by the time he turned off the main road, up the track to the Brown House, he was as blue as any Saxon – chieftain or otherwise.

The house stood about twenty yards back from the track, in an orchard of diseased apple trees; their branches were wreathed in some type of fungus that resembled Spanish moss. The impression the Brown House gave was of being absolutely four-square, like a child's drawing of a house. It had four twelve-paned windows on each side. As its name suggested, it was built from brown brick; atop the sloping brown-tiled roof was a brown brick chimney.

As Simon-Arthur got out of the car, he looked up at this and noted with approval that it was gushing thick smoke. The fog was so dense now that he could barely make out the point at which this smoke entered the atmosphere; it looked, rather, as if the Brown House were sucking in the murk that wreathed it.

He took a tightly sealed cardboard box from the back of the Citroën, and tucking this under one arm and his *Guardian* under the other he struggled over the buckled wire fence. There was a gate, but it was awkward to open and as Simon-Arthur was the only member of the family who how left the immediate purlieus of the Brown House, he hadn't bothered to fix it. The fence and the gate had been Simon-Arthur's stab at being a countryman. It was summer when he built it and Simon-Arthur, stripped to the waist, spent a sweaty afternoon hammering in the stakes and attaching the netting. He imagined himself like Levin, or Pierre, communing through labour with the spirit of Man. It was a vain delusion.

Even then the fog had been in evidence – albeit as a shadow of what it later became. That afternoon it gave the air a bilious tint. It made everything seem disturbingly post-nuclear, irradiated. When Simon-Arthur had finally finished and stood back to admire his work he saw an aching disjunction between what he had imagined he had achieved – and what was actually there.

The fence zigged and zagged and sagged its way along the track's tattered verge. It looked like a stretch of wire looming up across the shell-holed sludge of no man's land in an old photograph of the Somme.

For as long as the children had played in the garden the fence had acted more as a psychic barrier than a physical one. While it prevented them from getting on to the farm track, it also turned them in on themselves, in on the sepia interior of the Brown House. The fog came. Now it had been over two years since any of them had even ventured out of the house for more than a few minutes. Every time Simon-Arthur contemplated the fence he thought of pulling it down, but to do so was to counsel defeat on too many different levels.

Simon-Arthur opened the front door and stepped into the small vestibule. The first sound that met his ears was of some child plainting in the sitting room. He ignored it and kicking off his muddy boots went into the parlour and set the nebuliser box down on the table. He was unpacking it when his wife's cousin, Christabel-Sharon, came wafting in.

'Is that the nebuliser?' she said, without preamble. He grunted assent. 'Well, as soon as you've got it up and running we'd better put Henrykins on it for a while – the poor child is panting like a steam engine.'

'What about Stormikins?'

'Stormikins is fine, she can have second go. It's Henrykins who's really acting up.' Christabel-Sharon pulled one of the cane-backed chairs out from the table and slumped down on it with a sigh. A sigh that turned into a choke, a splutter and then a full-blown rasping cough. A bronchitic cough that was of such sub-sonic, juddering intensity that Simon-Arthur, as always, could hardly believe her narrow chest capable of producing – or containing – it.

He watched her out of the corner of his eye, whilst continuing to ready the nebuliser. Christabel-Sharon was very thin – almost anorectic. Her ginger-blonde hair was done up in a chignon, revealing what once must have been a graceful swoop of pale, freckled neck, but what was now a scrawny shank of a thing with greaseproof skin stretched over a marbling of vein. She had once been very pretty, in a sylphlike way. Her grey eyes were deep-set, like Simon-Arthur's own, although he could no longer remember whether they had always been so. They glittered under her brows, sending out a coruscating beam with each heave of her chest. Her breasts, fuller than the rest of her, moved under the stretchy fabric of her pullover; the nipples were erect and to Simon-Arthur they betokened nothing more than an autonomous and involuntary sexuality, parasitic on its hacking host.

He had the nebuliser assembled now and he plugged it in to the mains and switched it on. The rubber suction pads moved up and down in the glass chambers of Salbutimol and steroid. He turned on the stopcock of the oxygen cylinder and pressed the mask to his mouth. The sense of relief was overpowering. He could feel the electric engine adjusting itself to the motion of his ribcage, so that with each of his trembling and ineffectual inhalations it pushed more drug-laden oxygen into him.

It was bliss – like breathing normally again. The sensation marched at the head of a procession of memories: windows flung open and deep gouts of ozone-flavoured air drawn in unimpeded; running up hills and gasping with joy – not pain; burying his head in the bosom of the earth and drawing its warm fungal odour in through flaring nostrils. These pneumo-recollections were so clear that Simon-Arthur could visualise each molecule of scent and gas burying itself in the pinkness of his membranes.

Christabel-Sharon's woollen bosoms came into the corner of his eye. 'Come on, Simon-Arthur, don't you think you're being a little selfish with that thing?'

'Selfish! What the hell do you mean?' As suddenly as the gift had been bestowed it was snatched away. Simon-Arthur's anger rose up in him unbidden. 'Listen, Christabel-Sharon, I'm the person in this house who has to go out, to engage with the brutal commerce of the world. I come back after a gruelling trip, blue in the face, on the verge of expiring, and just because I dare to take a few breaths – a few trifling puffs – on this nebuliser, this nebuliser which I abased myself to get . . . you call me selfish. Selfish! I won't stand for it!'

Christabel-Sharon had recoiled from him and was pressing herself up against the side of the tiled Dutch stove that stood in the corner of the parlour. Simon-Arthur noted through stinging tears of self-pity and frustration that she was doing something he found particularly disgusting: jettisoning sputum from her full lips into a pad of gauze that she had pressed against her mouth. She had quantities of these fabricated pads hidden about her person, and after use, deposited them – together with their glaucous contents – in a bucket lined with a plastic bag that she kept in her room. The dabbing practice further erased her beauty. For Simon-Arthur could never look at her without seeing little parcels of infective matter studding her body.

Simon-Arthur's wife, Jean-Drusilla, came hurrying into the kitchen. In her arms she carried Henry-Simon, their son, a child of about eight.

'Simon, thank God, thank God! The nebuliser. Praise be to the Father and to the Son. Praise be to the Mother of God especially, for granting us this deliverance.' She set the child down on a chair and attached the mask, which was still giving out little 'poots' of oxygen, to his pallid face. Then she fell to her knees on the cold stone flags. 'Simon-Arthur, Christabel-Sharon . . . You will join me.' It was a command, not a request.

Looking sheepishly at one another Simon-Arthur and Christabel-Sharon knelt on the flags. The three adults joined hands. 'Oh merciful Mother,' Jean-Drusilla chanted, 'giver of all bounty, repository of all grace, we thank you for this gift of a nebuliser. Be sure, oh Blessed One, that we will employ it solely in furtherance of your Divine Will. So that our children and ourselves might breathe freely, and so that my dear husband might create beautiful art, the greater to glorify your name.'

Simon-Arthur had knelt grudgingly, and cynically observed the way that this spiritual intensity shaped his wife's rather homely features. Her thick black hair was cut so as to frame her broad brow and firm chin, but the flesh hung slackly on her and there was a yellowish tinge to the whites of her eyes when she rolled them up to stare beatifically at the fire-resistant tiles. Even so, the effect of her measured chanting, which adapted itself to the background chuffing of Henry-Simon and the nebuliser, was mesmeric.

Perhaps there is a Redeemer, Simon thought. Perhaps He will come in a cloud of eucalyptus, freeing up all our passages, gusting through us with the great wind of the Spirit. And before he knew it tears were coursing down his cheeks. Jean-Drusilla, seeing this, leant forward and, taking his head, cradled it against her breast. Christabel-Sharon leant forward as well and stretched her thin arms around the both of them, and for quite a while they stayed like that, gently rocking.

When Dave-Dave Hutchinson, the manager of Marten's the newsagent, arrived at the Brown House about three hours later, the *ecstasis* had somewhat subsided. He knocked, and waited on the metal bootscraper, treading gingerly from one foot to the other. After a few minutes Simon-Arthur himself came to the door. 'My God, it's you,' he said. 'I didn't think you'd make it over tonight, the fog's ridiculously thick.'

'I've got the new radar in the car. It's a bit tricky but once you've got the hang of it you can drive well enough.'

'Come in, come in.' Simon-Arthur almost yanked Dave-Dave in off the doorstep. 'The children aren't quite in bed yet and I don't want them getting a lungful of this.' He grabbed at the air outside the door and brought a clutch of the fog inside, which stayed intact, foaming like a little cloud on the palm of his hand for some seconds.

'I brought this along with me.' Dave-Dave pulled a small brown bottle from the side pocket of his sheepskin jacket.

'Is that the codeine?'

'Yeah, I'm afraid I've only about sixty mils left, but I pick up tomorrow.'

'Sixty mils!' Simon's face lit up. 'That's splendid, that'll bring us some warm cheer, but' – and here his face fell – 'what about your poor wife?'

The newsagent's face adopted a serious expression. 'I'm afraid she gets Brompton's now.'

'Oh, I see. Well, that's too bad. Anyway, come in now, come in here to the drawing room, where it's warm.'

Simon-Arthur ushered Dave-Dave into a long room that took up half of the Brown House's ground floor. Dave-Dave could see at once that this was where the family spent the bulk of their time. There were two separate groupings of over-stuffed armchairs and sofas, one at either end of the room. Mahogany bookcases went clear along one of the walls, interrupted only by two windows in the centre and a door which presumably led to the garden.

On the other wall there was a vast collection of icons set on a number of shelves that were unevenly spaced, giving the impression that the icons were somehow radiating from the smouldering fire in the grate. Everywhere in the room, set on little tables – occasional, coffee and otherwise – on the arms of the chairs, and even the floor itself, were votive objects: crucifixes, incense burners, hanks of rosary beads, stat-uettes of the Blessed Virgin. The long room vibrated with the hum of so many patterns flowing into one another: wallpaper into carpet; carpet into seat-cover; seat-cover into cushion; cushion into the gilded frame of an icon. It was like a peacock's tail under the glass dome of a taxidermist's collation.

The overwhelming clutteredness of the room so impressed itself upon Dave-Dave Hutchinson that it wasn't until Simon-Arthur said, 'Jean-Drusilla, I want to introduce Mr Hutchinson, he manages the newsagent's in Thame,' that he realised there was anyone in it besides the two of them. A rather gaunt woman with severely chopped black hair and a prominent, red-tipped nose rose from behind the moulting back of a horsehair armchair where she had been seated.

'I am so pleased to meet you, Mr Hutchinson,' she said, holding out her hand. Dave-Dave Hutchinson advanced towards her, picking his way between the outcroppings of religionalia. She was wearing a crushed velvet, floor-length dress. Both the lace at her throat and that of her handkerchief broadcast the caramel smell of Friar's Balsam.

He kissed her hand, and releasing it looked up into her eyes, which were deep brown. There, he caught a glimpse of her graphic religiosity: circling the two diminutive Hutchinson heads, reflected in her pupils, hovered imps, satyrs, minor demons and hummingbird angels. 'A-and I you, Mrs Dykes,' he stammered.

'Simon-Arthur told me about the help you gave him this afternoon – and the concern you showed him as well.'

'Really, Mrs Dykes, it was nothing, nothing at all.'

'No, not nothing, Mr Hutchinson, far from it. It was a truly Christian act, the behaviour of a man of true feeling. A Samaritan casting aside the partisan claims of place, people and estate, selflessly to aid another.'

She was still holding his hand and she used it to draw him round and pilot him into an armchair that faced her own. 'I fear my husband was asthmatic even before the fog, and he will let his emotions run away with him. Like all artists he is so terribly sensitive. When he gets upset . . .' She tailed off and shrugged expressively, both of her hands held palm-upwards. Dave-Dave Hutchinson stared at the many heavy gold rings, studded with amethysts and emeralds, that striped her fingers.

'What exactly is it that you paint, Mr Dykes?' Dave-Dave Hutchinson asked, turning in his chair to face Simon-Arthur, who was still hovering by the door. Even as the newsagent said it, he felt that the question was both too prosaic and too forward. He was painfully aware that his own social position was quite inferior to that of the Dykeses, and while it didn't matter when he and Simon Dykes had formed that spontaneous bond of friendship at Marten's – which was after all his own preserve – here at the Brown House he felt awkward and gauche, on guard lest he commit some appalling gaffe, or utter a solecism that would point up his humble origins.

'Oh, I don't paint much besides icons nowadays. These are some of mine around the fireplace.'

The newsagent rose from his chair and walked over to the wall. The icons were really very strange indeed. They featured all the correct elements of traditional icons, but the Trinity and the saints depicted were drawn not from life, nor imagination, but from the sort of photographs of public personages that are printed in the newspapers. These bland faces and reassuring eyes had been done in oils with total exactitude. The artist had even rendered the minute moiré patterning of coloured dots that constituted the printed image.

'I can see why you're so concerned to get your newspaper in good condition each day, Mr. Dykes,' he said – and immediately regretted it, it sounded so trite, so bourgeois a comment.

'Ye-es,' Simon-Arthur replied, 'it's very difficult to get that level of detail if you're working from a soggy paper.'

'Is there much of a demand for icons at the moment?'

'A huge demand,' said Jean-Drusilla Dykes, 'a vast demand, but

Simon-Arthur doesn't sell his. He paints them for the greater glory of our Saviour, for no other client.'

Just then the door of the room swung open and Christabel-Sharon came in, carrying her three-year-old daughter Storm in her thin arms. The little girl was feverish. She was murmuring in a distracted way and had two bright, scarlet spots high up on her cheeks. Christabel-Sharon herself was in tears. 'Henry has thrown Storm out of the oxygen tent again, Simon-Arthur; really, you must do something about it, look at the state she's in.'

Simon-Arthur didn't say anything, but left the room immediately. Dave-Dave Hutchinson could hear heavy feet thudding up the stairs and then voices raised in the room above, one deep, the other reedy.

'Christabel-Sharon,' said Jean-Drusilla Dykes when her husband had gone, 'this is Mr Hutchinson who manages the newsagent's in Thame. Mr Hutchinson, this is my cousin Christabel-Sharon Lannière.'

'I'm delighted to meet you, Ms Lannière,' said Dave Hutchinson, and waited for her to put the child down somewhere so that he might kiss her hand. She dumped the little girl quite unceremoniously on a *chaise-longue*, and advanced towards him smiling broadly, hand outstretched, the tears already drying on her cheeks, like snail trails in the morning sun.

And as he took the hand, and noticed how small and fine it was, Dave-Dave Hutchinson decided that she was unquestionably the most beautiful woman he had seen in a very long time. He was, after all, so conditioned to accepting emaciation as a body-type, that he could dwell on the hollow beneath a woman's clavicle, even if it threatened to bore through her thorax. Christabel-Sharon must have sensed this silent homage on his part, for, as she curtsied, she gave an extra little bob, as if acknowledging this new allegiance to her attractions.

They stood like that for a while, looking at one another, whilst Jean-Drusilla Dykes tended to the little girl, propping her up on some cushions, finding a coverlet for her, and eventually placing the nebuliser mask over her whispering mouth and turning the machine on.

'Oh, is that the nebuliser?' Dave-Dave Hutchinson asked. 'It looks absolutely fantastic.'

'Isn't it,' said Christabel-Sharon, with equal enthusiasm. 'We've been on the waiting list for one now for months, but somehow Simon-Arthur managed to get priority –'

'We don't talk about that, Christabel-Sharon,' Jean-Drusilla Dykes cut in. 'It isn't seemly.'

'I'm dreadfully sorry,' Dave-Dave Hutchinson said hurriedly. 'I didn't mean to seem intrusive.'

'No, no, Mr Hutchinson, it's not your fault, but the truth of the matter is that Simon-Arthur did use connections to get hold of the nebuliser; and even though I'm delighted to have it I can't help feeling that the way in which it was obtained will tell against us eventually. Oh Mr Hutchinson, what a shoddy, cheap world we live in when a fine man like my husband, a moral man, a just man, has to resort to such expedients merely in order to aid his suffering family –' Her voice broke, quite abruptly, and she began to sob, screwing the handkerchief soaked with Friar's Balsam into her eye.

Then the large, velvet-robed woman started to cough. It was, Dave-Dave Hutchinson noted – being now as adept at judging the nature of a cough as any doctor – a particularly hoarse and rattling cough, with an oil-drum resonance about it, admixed with something like the sound of fine shingle being pulled this way and that by breakers on a beach.

'Now there – there, Mrs Dykes, please don't upset yourself, please . . .' He pulled the little brown bottle of codeine linctus from his pocket and showed it to her. 'I have some linctus here – that'll help us all to stop coughing for a while.'

'Ach-cach-cach-cach-Oh Mr ach-cach- Hutchinson, you are too kind, too kind. Christabel-Sharon, kindly fetch the linctus glasses.' Christabel-Sharon exited. The two of them were left regarding one another over the *chaise-longue*; on which the child lay, her laboured breath wheezing contrapuntally to the choof-choof of the nebuliser.

'Did you say,' asked Dave-Dave Hutchinson, by way of making polite conversation, 'that you had an oxygen tent?'

'It's nothing really,' she replied, 'hardly a tent at all, more of an oxygen fly-sheet.' They both laughed at this, and it was a laughter that Dave-Dave Hutchinson was profoundly grateful for. It ruptured the rather fraught atmosphere of the room, earthing the static sheets and flashes of his hostess's spiritual intensity. But his gratitude didn't sustain for long, because even this trifling response to her witticism, this strained guffaw, was enough to give him a coughing fit – this time a bad one.

He sat back down on the armchair, both hands clasped against his mouth. Dave-Dave's lungs heaved so, they threatened to turn themselves inside out. He laboured to retain some element of composure, or at any rate not to void himself on the Dykes' Persian carpet. The edges of his visual field turned first pink, then red, and eventually purple. He felt himself losing control, when a cool, white hand was placed on his arm and he heard a voice say, 'Here, Mr Hutchinson, pray take one of these, it looks as if you could do with one.' It was Christabel-Sharon. She had materialised back inside the room and was proffering him a neat pad of gauze. 'You'll doubtless need it for the –'

'Buh, buh –' he laboured through his hands to express his shame and embarrassment.

'Now, now, Mr Hutchinson, you musn't worry about a bit of sputum with us,' said Jean-Drusilla Dykes firmly. 'We know how it is, we understand that the normal proprieties have had to be somewhat relaxed during the current situation.' He gratefully seized the pad and as discreetly as he was able deposited several mouthfuls of infective matter into its fluffy interior. When he had finished Christabel-Sharon passed him a bucket lined with a plastic bag.

Simon-Arthur Dykes came back into the room. 'Did you sort the children out, Simon-Arthur?' asked his wife.

'Ye-es,' he sighed wearily. 'Henry and Magnus are back in the small room, so Storm can go up to the oxygen tent whenever she's ready; and then Dave-Dave can take a turn with the nebuliser. He obviously has need of it – and I'm not surprised, coming out on this vile night.'

'Is the humidifier on in the boys' room?'

'Yes, of course.'

'And the ioniser in ours?'

'Yes, yes, dear Jean-Drusilla, please don't trouble yourself.' He crossed the room to where his wife stood, and taking her arm, bade her sit beside him on a divan covered with brocade cushions. Their two heads leaned together and the four feverish spots on their cheeks reached an uneasy alignment.

'Look, Simon-Arthur,' said Christabel-Sharon, gesturing towards the round silver tray she had brought in from the kitchen, 'doesn't the linctus look pretty?'

It did look pretty. She had poured the thick green liquid out into tiny, cut-glass linctus glasses. In the yellow-and-blue light from the fire the whole array sparkled the spectrum. She offered the tray to Dave-Dave Hutchinson. 'Mr Hutchinson, will you have some?'

'Thank you, Ms Lannière.'

'Please, do use my matronymic – and may I use your patronymic?'

'Certainly . . . Christabel –'

'Christabel-Sharon,' she said with her ever-so-slightly affected voice, 'and you are Dave-Dave, aren't you?'

'That's right.' He blushed.

Taking one of the tiny glasses, Dave-Dave sipped judiciously, savouring the thickness and sweetness of the stuff, whilst assaying the weight of the crystal it came in. At home he and Mrs Hutchinson drank their linctus from Tupperware. Christabel-Sharon handed two glasses of linctus to the Dykeses and took one herself. Then they all sat together in silence for a while, contentedly tippling.

It was a good little party. One of the best evenings that any of the inhabitants of the Brown House could remember having in a long time. After Storm-Christabel had gone up to the oxygen tent and Dave-Dave had had a good long go on the anaboliser, Simon-Arthur set up a small card table and they played whist for a couple of hours. Christabel-Sharon paired off with Dave-Dave, and there was an agreeably flirtatious character to the way they bid together, often taking tricks through shared high spirits rather than any skill at the game.

There was no discussion of weighty matters or what really preoccupied them all. The mere presence of Dave-Dave at the Brown House was a sufficient reminder. The codeine linctus helped to free up the constrictions in their four pairs of lungs, which did necessitate frequent recourse by all parties to Christabel-Sharon's supply of gauze pads and the attendant bucket. But such was the *bonhomie* that the linctus engendered that none of them felt much embarrassment, or awkwardness.

Only when Jean-Drusilla went out to the kitchen to ask the maid to make them some ham sandwiches, and her husband followed her to get a bottle of port from the cellar, was there any exchange that alluded to the wider issue. 'It is strange, is it not, my dear,' said Simon-Arthur, leaning his head against the wall and fighting the dreadful torpor that threatened to encase him, 'to have a newsagent for company of an evening.'

'Yes, dear, I suppose it is,' she replied distractedly – she was helping the maid to de-crust some slices of bread, 'but he is a very nice man, a very Christian man. I don't imagine for a second that simply because we receive him in this fashion that he imagines we think him quality for an instant.'

'Quite so, quite so.'

'Christabel-Sharon seems to have taken quite a shine to him – is he married?'

'Oh yes, but I fear the poor man's wife is *in extremis*. He told me this afternoon that she was getting Brompton's – hence his oversufficiency of linctus.'

'I see. Well, while in the normal course of things such a flirtation might not be seemly, I think that in these times we live in, almost anything – within the bounds of propriety, of course – that serves to inculcate good feeling can be accepted.'

'You are entirely right, my dear,' replied Simon-Arthur, who had, like so many men of his age and class, long since abandoned the matter of making these practical moral judgements to his wife.

But late that night when Simon-Arthur was in his dressing room, readying himself for bed, the fog and all the awful misery that hung about it began to impose itself on him once more. He slumped down in a broken rattan chair that he kept in the little room – which was barely more than a vestibule. The codeine linctus was wearing off and he could feel the tightness in his chest, the laval accumulation of mucus, flowing down his bronchi and into each little sponge bag of an alveolus. Felt this fearfully, as his nervous system reintroduced him to the soft internality of his diseased body, its crushable vulnerability.

He remembered reading somewhere – God knows how many years ago – that if the human lungs were unfolded in their entirety, each little ruche and complicated pleat of veined tissue, then the resulting membrane would cover two football pitches. 'Or two damp, exposed fields,' Simon-Arthur murmured to himself, remembering Dave-Dave's eloquent description of the Brown House and its environs earlier that day. He pulled off his socks by the toe, wheezing with the effort.

In the bedroom next door he could hear his wife breathing stertorously. She was going through a cycle in her sleep that was familiar to him. First she would inhale, the twists and loops of mucus in her throat soughing like electricity cables in a high wind. Then she would exhale through her nose. This sounded peculiarly like a waste-disposal unit being started up.

The noises would get closer and closer together until they were continuous: 'Soouuugh-gmngchngsoouuugh-grnnchng.' Eventually she would seize up altogether and begin coughing, coughing raucously, coughing and even spluttering like some beery fellow in a bar, who's taken a mouthful of lager and then been poked in the ribs by a drinking buddy: 'Kerschpooo-kerschpooo-kerschpooo!' Over and over again. He couldn't believe that this colossal perturbation of her body didn't wake her – but it never seemed to. Whereas he was invariably yanked into consciousness by his own coughing in the night, or by that of the children, or Christabel-Sharon.

He could, he realised, hear all of them coughing and snoring and breathing in the different rooms of the Brown House. To his left there was the sharp rasp of Christabel-Sharon, to the right there were the childishly high and clattery coughs of his two sons, and in the small room immediately opposite the door to his dressing room he could even detect the more reposeful sighs of Storm-Christabel. He even thought – but couldn't be certain – that he could just about hear the maid, hacking away in the distant attic room. But on consideration he decided this was unlikely.

Yes, it wasn't the maid he could hear, but the furthest reaches of his lungs, playing, their own peculiar, pathological fugue. Clearly each of the innumerable little pipes and passages had its own viscous reed, and as the air passed around them they produced many hundreds – thousands even – of individual sounds. Simon-Arthur concentrated hard on this and found himself able to differentiate quite subtle tones. He could screen the background noise out, so as to be able to pick up the individual notes being blown in the pipes of his internal organ. Or else he could relax, and taking in breaths as deep as he could manage, produce swelling chords.

This discovery of the hidden musicality of his own lungs transfixed Simon-Arthur. He sat breathing in and out, attempting to contort his thorax in various ways, so as to bring off various effects. He even fancied that a particular sort of scrunching up in the rattan chair, combined with a two-stage inhalation, and long, soft exhalation, could, if pulled off properly, make his lungs play the magisterial, opening chords of Mozart's Mass in C major.

So peculiar and absorbing was this new game that Simon-Arthur became enveloped in it, fancying that he was himself inside a giant lung. The coughing and breathing of the other inhabitants of the house were integrated into his bronchial orchestration. He could no longer tell which noises were inside him and which outside. Then senses merged in the painter's disordered mind. Looking around him at the many tiny icons – icons he himself had painted – that studded the walls of the dressing room, Simon-Arthur no longer saw them for what they were. Everything, the pattern of the carpet, the texture of the walls, was transmogrifying into a gothic scape of pulsing red tubes and stretched, semi-transparent membranes.

In the midst of this fantasy the despair clamped down on him. The black bear bumped under the bed of his mind. He saw that the walls were studded with carcinomas, the corridors lined with angry scars and lesions. Up and down the stairs of the lung-house ran rivulets of infective matter. The thoracic property was choking with disease. The alveolar bricks that made up its structure were embedded in nacreous mortar. And then the final horror: the carcinomas took on the faces of people Simon-Arthur had known, people he had not done right by.

The contrast between his light-hearted silliness of a split-moment ago and the sickening despair of this image plunged Simon-Arthur into retching tears. He ground his fists into the sockets of eyes. Bam! Bam! Bam! Bam! The ugly realisations came winging in on him, each scything into his chest from a different trajectory. He buckled as the images of his loved ones choking on their own blood, drowning in it, impinged on him with dread force, awful certainty.

The fog was never going to lift, just thicken and thicken and thicken, until the air curdled. Stopping up the mouths of babies as surely as if they were smothered in the marshmallow folds of a pillow. Simon-Arthur knew this. Knew it as his tears called forth the inevitable and irresistible coughing fit.

After a turbulent, feverish night Simon-Arthur awoke for the sixth time with what passed for dawn long past. He could hear Christabel-Sharon, his wife and the children moving around downstairs, coughing their matitudinal coughs.

Then there was another sharp spatter against the window, a repeat of the spattering sound that he now realised had awoken him. He sat up. It was shot, he thought, it has to have been shot. It's too early in the autumn for hail.

He got up, and dressing as hurriedly as he could, he went downstairs. In the dining room his eldest son, Henry, was eating Rice Crispies, taking time out after each mouthful for a few pulls from the mouthpiece of the nebuliser. The crunch-crunch–choof-choof noise was slightly eerie. Simon-Arthur found the rest of the family, and the maid, gathered in the vestibule. The two smaller children were still in their nightclothes.

'Is that the shoot?' asked Simon-Arthur, although he already knew that it was.

'We can't understand why it's so early,' said Jean-Drusilla. The children were looking apprehensive.

'They're shooting d–ed near to the house as well. I'd better go out and have a word.' He took his scarf from the rack by the front door and wound it around his throat.

'Won't you put on a mask, dear?'

'No, no, don't be silly, I'm only popping out for a minute.'

As Simon-Arthur groped his way down the side of the Brown House he berated himself: Why worry about such stupid things? Why need it concern me if Peter-Donald and his cronies see that I can only afford a chemical mask? Such pride is worse than stupidity. But it was the truth – for he was a proud man. And he was right in assuming that the members of the shoot would be fully masked, because the fog was unusually thick this morning, the visibility down to fifteen yards or less.

Once Simon-Arthur had begun to acclimatise he could see the line of huntsmen beyond the low scrub of bushes at the bottom of the garden. He also fancied he could make out a few beaters in among the tangle of sick trees to the rear of the house. He made for the tallest figure in the middle of the former group and was gratified to find, when he got closer, that it was his landlord, Peter-Donald.

'Good morning, Peter-Donald,' he said, on coming up to him. 'You're early today.'

'Ah, Simon-Arthur.' Peter-Donald Hanson rested his Purdey in the crook of his arm and extended his right hand. 'How good to see you, old chap.' The big man's voice issued from a small speaker, just above the knot of his cravat; and was crackly, like a poorly tuned radio.

Simon-Arthur had been right about the mask. Peter-Donald was wearing a full scuba arrangement. The rest of his cronies were all clad in the same, overdone shooting kit: Norfolk jackets and plus-fours, cravats and tweedy hats with grouse feathers in their bands. They looked like the usual mob of city types, members of Peter-Donald's Lloyds syndicate, Simon-Arthur supposed.

'You know, Peter-Donald, the shot is spattering against the windows of the house, I think it's making the children feel a little anxious.'

'Awfully sorry, but the fog's so damn thick today. Wouldn't have come out at all but I got delivery of these yesterday, so we thought we'd give them a try.' He held out his wrist, to which was strapped a miniature radar screen. 'They could make all the difference to the shooting around here.'

Simon-Arthur looked from his landlord's masked face to the black LCD of the mini-radar screen. If there was any trace of irony, or even self-awareness, in Peter-Donald's voice it was effectively destroyed by the throat mike, and his expression was, of course, completely hidden.

A thread of white luminescence circled the screen. When it sped past a certain region there were splutters of light.

'Are those the birds?' he asked, pointing towards the fading gleams.

'Ya, that's right. Charlie-Bob has rigged them all up with little radar cones. Mind you' – he barked a laugh, which the throat mike transmitted as a howl – 'I don't think you could put 'em on grouse. Poor buggers would be dwarfed by the things!'

There was a scatter of microphonic squawks from the other guns – they were obviously getting restive. 'Well, if you'll excuse me, old boy,' said Peter-Donald, cocking his gun, 'I'll get this drive started and then we'll be off your property, eh?'

Despite the warning painful catch in his throat Simon-Arthur stood his ground, interested to see what would happen. The guns formed up again into a ragged line. Even in the short time he and Peter-Donald had been chatting, the fog had grown denser. Now, not only were the beaters no longer within sight, but the trees themselves were little more than shadows.

Peter-Donald took a wafer-thin cellular phone from the pocket of his jacket and punched one of the buttons on its console. 'I think we're ready now, Charliekins,' he barked, the mouthpiece pressed against his throat mike. 'D'you want to start the drive?'

There was a ragged chorus of shouts and 'Halloos!', together with the sound of stout sticks being smote against the underbrush. Then there was a warbling, almost grunting noise, and ten or fifteen pheasants came staggering out of the bank of fog. They had radar cones tied around their necks. These were silvery-grey rhomboids, at least four times bigger than the birds' heads. The effect was ridiculous and pathetically unnatural: the birds – who Simon-Arthur knew found it hard to fly anyway when the fog was thick – were still further handicapped by this new sporting technology. Only two or three of them could get airborne at all, and then only for a couple of wing beats. The rest just zigzagged in a loose pack across the traverse of the guns, the sharp corners of the radar cones banging first into their eyes and then their soft throats.

There were a few scattered shots – none of which appeared to find a mark. Most of the guns held their fire.

'Not much sport in this, is there?' said Simon-Arthur sarcastically, and then realised with a shock that he had spoken audibly. He had been out in the fog for so long that he had begun to assume that he must be wearing a muffling mask.

But this didn't seem to offend Peter-Donald. He was striding towards the fence, and signalling to the other guns to follow. He turned on his heel for a moment, facing back towards Simon-Arthur, and publicly-addressed him. 'It is, if we let them get into the fog bank. D'ye see? Then we've got a shoot entirely on instrumentation' – he indicated the wristscreen – 'now that's real sport!' Then he swivelled round and marched off.

The birds had managed to reach the fence and stagger over or under it. Then they were enveloped by the fog. The guns followed them, and finally trailing behind came the donkey-jacketed figures of the beaters, who also disappeared, still hallooing. Simon-Arthur noticed that most of them weren't even wearing chemical masks.

Simon-Arthur stood for a moment, and then turned towards the house. But when he reached the front door, and was just about to turn the knob, he saw that one of the pheasants hadn't managed to make it over the fence. It was running about distractedly, crazily even, in the area between the house and the fence. As Simon-Arthur watched it, it charged towards him and then veered away again locking into a spiralling path, like an aeroplane in a flat spin, or a clockwork toy run amok.

The pheasant was producing the most alarming noises, splutterings and gurgles. Simon-Arthur walked towards where its next circumnavigation of the muddy patch of ground ought to take it, arriving just in time for the bird to cough up at his feet an enormous dollop of blood and mucus, and then expire, its radar cone jammed into the ground. 'My God!' exclaimed Simon-Arthur. He leant down to examine the corpse. The pheasant's feathers were matted, greasy and lustreless. It was a male bird, but its plumage was almost entirely dun-coloured. Simon-Arthur felt nauseous upon noticing that there were flecks and dollops of some white matter in the spreading stain of fluid that was still pouring from its beak.

One of the guns must have been lingering behind the group and heard Simon-Arthur's exclamation, because a masked figure carrying a shotgun came striding out of the fog bank, clambered none too nimbly over the fence and walked over to where he was crouched by the dead pheasant. As the figure approached he pulled off his mask. It was, Simon-Arthur realised with an access of warm feeling, Anthony-Anthony Bohm, the local doctor.

'Anthony-Anthony!' Simon-Arthur said, standing up and thrusting out his hand. It was taken and warmly shaken by the doctor, whose rubicund face was registering some concern.

'You really should get inside, Simon-Arthur,' he said. 'This is no kind of a day to be out without a mask, and preferably a scuba.'

'I know, I know, I was just going in when this poor creature expired at my feet. What d'you think of that?'

The doctor crouched down, puffing, and peered at the dead bird. One of his hands went to the ruff of white beard that fringed his pink buttock of a chin, while the other probed the pheasant's neck. It was a gesture so familiar to Simon-Arthur from Anthony-Anthony's consulting room that he smiled to see it in this unusual circumstance. 'Hmm, hmm, hmm-hmm,' the Doctor hmm-ed and then, picking up the bird, opened its beak and looked down it.

'Look at that white matter in the blood – what on earth can it be?'

'Oh that – that's a carcinoma. Nothing particularly mysterious.'

'A carcinoma?'

'Ye-es.'

'So what did it die of?'

'Oh cancer, of course. Yes, definitely cancer – of the throat, and no doubt of the lung as well. The effort of being driven by the beaters like that must have given it a massive haemorrhage.'

'I had no idea the animals were getting cancer in this fashion, Anthony-Anthony.'

'My dear Simon-Arthur, we get cancer, why shouldn't all of God's other creatures, hmm?' The doctor was struggling to his feet again; Simon-Arthur gave him an arm.

'Ooof! Well, that's me for this morning, I think I'll head back to the health centre, I've a surgery this afternoon. Do you mind if I take the pheasant with me, Simon-Arthur?'

'Not at all. Are you going to run some tests on it, Anthony-Anthony, do an autopsy, or whatever it is you call it?'

'Good heavens, no! Oh no, ahaha-no-no-aha-ha-h'ach-eurch-cha-cha –' The doctor's jolly laughter turned with grim predictability into a coughing fit. Simon-Arthur thumped the tubby man on his broad back, whilst Anthony-Anthony struggled to don his scuba mask again. When he had it on and was breathing easily, he took the dead bird from Simon-Arthur who had picked it up by its sad scruff.

'Thanks very much, old fellow. No, no, I know what killed the thing so it's of no interest to medical science. I used to be a dab hand with the scalpel, so I'll cut the tumours out and the lady wife and I can have this one for Sunday lunch. Now, do get inside, Simon-Arthur, I don't want to see you at surgery this afternoon.' They bade farewell, and the doctor vanished into the sickly yellow of the boiling fog bank.

The Doctor didn't see Simon-Arthur at his emergency surgery that afternoon, because against Jean-Drusilla and Christabel-Sharon's pleading, he decided to take a walk.

Simon-Arthur had been trying to work in his studio all morning, but the terrible vision from the previous night kept haunting him. He fancied he could still hear every faltering breath and choking cough of the Brown House's inhabitants. And when in the mid-morning he took a break and went down to inhale some steam with Friar's Balsam, the sight of the children sitting in a silent row on one of the sofas in the drawing room, while the maid passed the nebuliser mask from one to the next, brought tears to his eyes.

When they were all seated at the dining-room table, eating off the second-best china because it was a Saturday, Simon-Arthur addressed the table at large, saying, 'I think I'll go out after lunch, just for a breath' – he bit back the figure of speech – 'for a walk.'

'I really feel you oughtn't, Simon-Arthur,' said his wife. 'You were out for far too long this morning, and without a mask. You know what Anthony-Anthony says, even with a chemical mask you shouldn't really be out for more than half an hour at a time.'

'It's just that I feel terribly claustrophobic in the house today. I haven't had a walk for almost a month now. I'll go up to the golf course and then I'll come straight back. I'll be fine. I didn't even have too much of a turn after going out this morning.'

'Please don't, Simon-Arthur,' said Christabel-Sharon. Her freckle-spattered features were tight with concern. 'You know the Patriarch is coming to say a special mass tomorrow. You won't want to miss that. And if you go out for a walk you'll have been out for forty minutes – and you shan't be able to go and get the medicated incense for his censors in Risborough.'

'Please, everyone, don't worry!' Simon-Arthur said this a little louder than he intended to. But he hated having it drawn to his attention just how dependent all of them were on him, right down to the very practice of their religion. 'I'm going out for a walk and that-is-that.'

Simon-Arthur went up the farm track, through the farm and past the manor house where Peter-Donald and his family lived. The fog had lifted ever so slightly and he could see the crenellated chimneys of the house. He wondered whether Peter-Donald had managed to get a good bag, or at any rate a non-cancerous one.

It was uncomfortable walking. The mask he wore was a cheap model. Really only a plastic mouth- and nosepiece, containing a thick wad of cotton wool soaked with Ventalin. The straps chafed the back of his head, and the smell of the chemicals when he inhaled was almost worse than the fog itself.

Simon-Arthur reached the road on the far side of the estate and crossed it. The ground here was completely devoid of grass cover. The land had been bought up by a Japanese syndicate about a year before the fog descended. It was less expensive, then, for Japanese golfers to fly to England to play than to join a club in their own country. The syndicate had landscaped the course, but when the fog came they abandoned the whole project. Now the prospect of bare mud, formed into useless fairways, bunkers and greens that were really browns, looked wholly unearthly and anti-natural, like some section of an alien planet, poorly terraformed.

As he walked, Simon-Arthur dwelt once again – as he had so many times before – on the crippling irony of his bringing his family to live in the country. He had done it because Henry had bad asthma – as he did himself. Their doctor in London was certain that it was pollution-related. About four months after they had taken up residence in the Brown House the fog moved in with them.

'Oh Christ! Oh God, oh Jesus. Please come! Please help us. We are but clay, but dust . . .' Simon-Arthur muttered this through his mask; and then, not quite knowing why, but feeling that if he wanted to pray aloud it was unseemly to do it with this ugly mask on, he took it off.

To his surprise the fog didn't taste that bad, or catch in his throat. He took a few shallow, experimental breaths to check that he wasn't mistaken. He wasn't: the fog no longer oozed soupily into his constricted chest. He took some deeper breaths, and with a further shock felt his eustachian tubes clear – audibly popping as they did so – for the first time in years. Now he could hear cars moving along the road behind him with great clarity. He took a few more, deeper breaths. It was amazing, the fog must be clearing, he thought; the miasma must be departing from our lives!

Then he started to take in great gouts of air, savouring the cleanness of its taste. 'At last, at last!' he shouted out, and heard his voice reverberate the way it should do, not fall flat. 'Thank you, thank you, thank you, thank you, thank you, thank you, thankyou, thangyou, thangyu,' he garbled. The fog was lifting, there was a bright light up ahead of him, beyond the fourth green of the half-constructed course. Simon-Arthur strode towards it, his legs feeling light and springy. He was an intensely religious man, and he crossed himself as he staggered forward; crossed himself and counted out a decade on the rosary in his pocket. He was prepared for Redemption.

* * *

They didn't find the icon painter's body until the following day. Jean-Drusilla had alerted the authorities after Simon-Arthur had been gone for forty minutes, but by then it was already getting dark and the fog was too thick for a search party, even with high-powered lights. As for radar, that too was useless, for there was a particularly high magnesium content building up in that evening's opacity.

By chance Peter-Donald and Anthony-Anthony were in the party that found him. He was spread out, smeared even, on the muddy surface, in much the same posture that the cancerous pheasant had expired on the day before. Like the pheasant, a pool of blood and mucus had flowed out from his mouth and stained the ground. And, as before, the doctor knelt down and examined the white flecks in the stain.

'Poor bugger,' he said, 'how strange, he had cancer as well. Never thought to give him an X-ray, because I felt certain that his asthma was going to get him first. He wasn't well at all, you know.'

Peter-Donald was taking his ease on a shooting stick he'd pressed into the mud. 'Well, at least the fellow had the decency not to die on the green, eh?' It wasn't that he was being disrespectful to Simon-Arthur's memory, it was only that the times bred a certain coarseness of manner in some – just as they engendered extreme sensitivity in others.

'Yes, well, he must have had the haemorrhage on the green, and then rolled into this bunker and died.'

'Tidy, what?'

'You could put it that way.' The doctor stood up and indicated to the stretcher bearers who were with them that they should remove the body. 'The peculiar thing is that he and I saw a pheasant die in just this fashion yesterday.'

'What, of cancer?'

'Absolutely.'

'Well, y'know, Anthony-Anthony, I can't say I'm surprised in Simon-Arthur's case. Not only was the fellow asthmatic, but I used to see him all over the shop without a scuba on. Bloody silly – foolhardy even.'

Without bothering further with the corpse, the two men turned and headed off back towards the manor. They were looking forward to a glass of linctus before lunch. Both of them had chronic bronchitis – and neither was as young as he used to be. For a while their conversation could be heard through the clouds of noxious dankness:

'You know, Peter-Donald, I don't believe the Dykeses can afford proper scubas. Hardly anyone in the area can, apart from yourself – I have one because of my job, you know.'

'Really? Oh well, I suppose it stands to reason. Did you say that bird had cancer? D'you think I should get some special masks made for the pheasants? I shouldn't want them all to get it –'

And then they too were swallowed up by the fog.

Grey Area

I was standing by the facsimile machine this afternoon, peering through the vertical, textured fabric louvres that cover every window in the Company's offices and which are linked together with what look like lengths of cheap key-chain. I was waiting, because all too often the facsimile machine misfeeds and two sheets run through together. So, when I send a facsimile I always send the sheets through one by one. It's time-consuming, but it leads to fewer mistakes. I have become so adept at this task that I can now perform it by sound rather than sight. When the sheets are feeding through correctly, the machine makes a whirring, chirruping noise, like a large insect feeding. When I push in the leading edge of a new sheet, there is a momentary hesitation, a predatory burr, then I feel the mandibles of nylon-brush clutch and nibble at it. When the entire document has been passed through the body of the facsimile machine, it clicks, then gives off a high-pitched peep.

This afternoon, just as the machine peeped, I sensed a presence behind me. I turned. I had noticed him a couple of times before. I don't know his name, but I have an idea he works in personnel. I noticed him because there is something wrong with his clothing – or the way he wears it, the way it hangs on his body. His suits cling to him, his flies look like an appendicectomy scar, puckered and irregular. We grunted acknowledgements to each other. I tamped the sheets of paper into a neat stack. I moved past him, across the floor, and through the swing doors into the corridor that leads back to the Department.

The Department must always be capitalised when it is referred to by its members, in order to differentiate it from other departments. Of course, other departments must also be capitalised by their members. This makes the paperwork for inter-departmental meetings – for which I often have responsibility – complex to arrange. A different word-processed document is needed for each departmental representative.

The formats and protocols for all the Company's communications were modified by the Head of Department, who's my boss, when he took over about six months ago.

The document that set out these modifications was ring-bound and about seventy pages long. Nevertheless, he asked me to pull apart the plastic knuckles that gripped one of the copies, and attach the sheets in a long row to the bulletin board that runs the entire length of the Department's main corridor. He said that this was so everyone in the Department would be certain to pay attention to them.

It must be as a result of initiatives such as these that my boss has enjoyed such a phenomenally quick rise through the hierarchy of the Company.

I had to walk right along this corridor to get back to my office, which is situated, opposite my boss's, up a dog-leg of stairs at the far end. I can't understand why we don't have a facsimile machine in the Department. Every other department has at least one, and more often than not several. We have a networked computer system, modem links, numerous photocopiers, document-sorters and high-speed laserprinters, but no facsimile machine. I have never asked my boss why this is the case, because it was like this before he became Head of Department, and perhaps he, like me, has come to accept it as an aspect of the status quo.

I turned out of the long corridor that leads to the inter-departmental facsimile machine, and into the corridor that runs the length of the Department. This corridor is wide and low, with a line of strip lights along the ceiling. I usually keep my eyes fixed on these when I'm walking along the corridor, in order to avoid contact with my colleagues. It's not that I don't want to talk to them, it's just that there's always plenty of work to do and I like to keep a rhythm up throughout the day. I have a dread of getting behind.

In my office there is a desk, three filing cabinets, a stationery cupboard, a swivel chair, and a workstation that holds my computer and laserprinter. All of this furniture is a grey-beige colour, very neutral, very gentle on the eye. It helps to offset the rather aggressive carpet tiling, which is chequered in two distinct, but equally electric, shades of blue.

It's a kind of carpet tiling that was advertised a few years ago on television in a gimmicky way. A stretch of tiling was laid down in a kind of test zone, a mocked-up section of an office corridor. Then a live rhinoceros was released from a cage and encouraged to tear up and down the fake corporate environment, snorting and ramping.

It was a startling image: the very embodiment of the rhinoceros, its astonishing combination of bulk and fluidity, imposing itself on the bland anonymity of the set. Then, at the very end of the sequence, the camera angle moved round from the side of the corridor to its end and the rhino charged towards the viewer. The image was so sharp that if you had frozen the frame you could have counted the individual bristles that made up its congealed horn, the wrinkled veins in its vinyl hide.

At the last moment before it came plunging through the screen into your living room, the beast turned tail and dumped a steaming heap of excrement right in the eye of the camera, which tracked down so as to catch it plummeting on to the carpet tiling. The voiceover intoned: 'Rhinotile, tough enough for all the animals in your office!'

I can't get this advert out of my head. The punchline comes to me unbidden whenever I look at, or even think about, the carpet tiling.

I haven't done all that much to personalise my office – the walls are mostly taken up with a noticeboard, a calendar and an organisational chart.

The organisational chart has been done on one of those magnetic whiteboards, to which metallic strips can be affixed, to express lines of command, the skeleton of the hierarchy; and coloured dots or squares, to indicate individuals and their functions.

It's my job to change the shape of the organisational chart as the Department metamorphoses from month to month. The Department doesn't have an exceptionally high turnover of staff, but enough people come and go to make rearranging some strips and dots necessary every few weeks.

I have never asked the Head of Department why it is that, despite my pivotal role in representing the structure of the Department, I have yet to be included in the organisational chart myself.

I stapled the papers I had just faxed and deposited them in a tray for filing. I walked round behind my desk – which faces the door – and sat down. My office is organised so that the working surface is directly in front of me and if I swivel to the right I am sitting at the computer keyboard. This I did.

I had to work on the presentation document for this week's interdepartmental meeting. My boss had made handwritten corrections to the first draft, and these I now set on the document holder that sprouts from a Velcro pad, attached to the side of my monitor.

The corrections were extensive and involved the re-keying of a number of paragraphs. I worked steadily and by five it was done and neatly formated. I hit the keystrokes necessary to activate the laserprinter and then tidied my desk.

Desk tidying is quite an important ritual with me. I like to have every paper clip in its modular plastic container, every pencil, staple, rubber and label in its assigned position. I like my highlighting pens arranged in conformity with the spectrum. I like my blotter located in the exact centre of my desk. I like my mouse mat positioned precisely along the front edge of my workstation.

When I first came to work at the Company I was a lot sloppier about this; my desk was tidy, but it wasn't exact. Now it's exact.

Then I made a list, using the soft 'scherluump-scherluump' that the laserprinter was making as a counterpoint with which to order my thoughts. I always make a list at the end of the working day. They are essential if you want to maintain any kind of ordered working practice. I finished the list just as the presentation document finished printing. The icon came up on the VDU. It shows a smiling and satisfied little laserprinter, with underneath the legend: 'Printing Completed'.

I stacked the papers, punched them, bound them in a ring-binder with a plastic cover, and took the document across the corridor to my boss's office.

He was tipped far back on the rear wheels of his chair, so that his head was almost hidden between two of the vertical textured-fabric louvres that cover the windows of his office. The posture looked uncomfortable. The black head of the lamp was pulled low over the fan of papers on the wide expanse of his desk. His feet were propped on the desk top and the cuffs of his trousers had ridden up above his socks, exposing two or three inches of quite brown, but hairless ankle. He said, 'Have you re-done the presentation document for the inter-departmental meeting?'

I replied, 'Yes, here it is.'

He said, 'Good. Well, I'll see you in the morning then.'

I turned and walked back across the corridor. I shut down my computer and then bent to turn off the laserprinter. Kneeling like this, with my face level with the lower platform of the workstation, I could see right underneath my desk. I could see the flexes of the computer, the laserprinter, the desk lamp and the telephone all join together and twist into a spiral stream of mushroom-coloured plastic that disappeared down an oblong cable-routing slot. There was nothing else to see under the desk, no errant rubber bands or propelling pencils gone astray.

The bottom of my workstation is shaped like an upside-down T, with a castor protruding from a rubber bung at either end of the crossbar. I rested my forehead on this bar for a while and let the coolness of the metal seep into me. When I opened my eyes again, I focused not on the distant prospect of the skirting board, but on my immediate vicinity: the beaten path that my varnished nail had cut for the rest of my finger, through the eighth-of-an-inch pile of nylon undergrowth. It was this that caught my attention – a really tiny event.

How small does an event have to be before it ceases to be an event? If you look very closely at the tip of your fingernail as it lies on a clear surface (preferably something white like a sheet of paper), so closely that you can see the tiny cracks in the varnish; and then push it towards some speck of dust, or tweak the end of a withered hair, or flick the corpse of a crumb still further into decay, is that as small as an event can be?

When I stood up I rapped my head on the underside of my workstation. Both it and my skull vibrated. I bit my lip. I stood like that for a few moments, concentrating hard on the angle of one of the flexible fronds in the stack of binders in my stationery cupboard. Then I shut the cupboard doors, snapped the switch that bathed my office in darkness, and left it.

I went down the first flight of stairs, past the plant that lives in the grey granules, down the second flight and along the corridor. The Department was already empty. I knew that, at five on the dot, the entire workforce would have risen up like a swarm, or a flock, and headed for the six big lifts that pinion the Company to the earth.

I also found myself on an empty platform, caught in the hiatus between two westbound trains. The platform's dirty tongue unwound along the side of the tube, which was ribbed like a gullet with receding rings of be-grimed metal. A tired, flat wind, warm with minor ailments, gusted up my nose. The electronic sign above the platform kept on creating the word 'Information' out of an array of little dots of light; as if this in itself was some kind of important message. I listened to the sough and grind of the escalator belt.

Gradually the platform began to fill up with people. The minor-ailment smell was undercut with hamburger and onion, overwhelmed by processed cheese and honey-cured ham, encapsulated by tobacco. They stood in loose groups, bonded together by a mutual desire to try and avoid uniformity. Thus, blacks stood with whites, women with men, gays with the straight, middle class with working class, the ugly with the beautiful, the crippled with the whole, the homeless with the home-owners, the fashionable with the shabby. That so many people could believe themselves different from one another only made them appear more the same.

To my left, clamped against the bilious tiling, was a strange machine. It wasn't clear whether it was mechanical or electronic. It had a curved housing of green plastic. It was eight inches high, and bolted at top and bottom to brackets hammered into the grout. In the middle of the thing was a circular, venetian-blind-slatted plate. Underneath it was a small sign that proclaimed: 'Speak Here'. I pressed my ear against the plate and heard the faint rise and fall of what might have been a recording of outer space, or the depths of the sea.

When the train eventually came, I stood for a moment watching the people get off and get on. The two streams of shoving bodies folded into one another, like the fingers of two hands entwining deep in the lap of the ground.

And that was what my day was like – or at any rate the second half of it. Wherever I start from I will experience the same difficulties, so it might as well be this afternoon, when I sensed the man's presence behind me as I fed the facsimile machine.

One last thing. This morning, as I have for the past fourteen mornings or so, I put a sanitary towel in my underpants. Tonight, when I stood in front of the mirror's oblong and looked at the pouch between my legs, I felt certain that there would be blood absorbed into the quilted paper. Just a few dabs and blotches, together with a brown smear at the edge, denoting earlier bleeding.

But there was nothing. It was virgin territory. No period – period. I haven't had sexual intercourse for over six months – I can't be pregnant. I am normally as regular in my body as I am at work. And over the last two weeks I have felt the swelling feeling, accompanied by an odd sensation of vacuity, that always precedes my coming on; and the dusting of yellow and mauve pimples under the softening, water-retaining line of my jaw has appeared as it should. I've also felt irascible and unaccountably depressed. (Well, normally this depression is accountable, I just can't account for it. Only now is it truly unaccountable.) But still there's been no period. Only the feelings, straining me for day after day.

In the morning the radio woke me at seven-fifteen, as it always does. Outside the sky was limpid, void, without properties of colour or density. Was it light yet? There was no answer to this, it was as light as it was yesterday at this time – and the day before, and the day before that.

I got up and went over to my bureau, where I started flicking through my diary. I looked over the pages of the past six weeks or so. I seldom write anything in the diary but appointments, and there was a scattering of these, like mouse droppings, on the lined paper. I tried to think about those days that had gone, taking with them fading memories of dental appointments and dry-cleaning collection times.

The day my last period was due was marked in red. This is how my life resolves itself: into periods and the periods between periods.

But when I thought about it, summoned up the seven-fifteens of those last forty days, they returned to me decked in the same limpid, void garb as this morning. Could it be true? Could it be that it has been getting light at the same time for over a month now? It made no sense. This is the time of year when the seasons change rapidly, when we become aware of the world turning despite – and not because – of what we do. And yet there was this six-week period during which nothing had changed.

I dressed carefully. I tucked the sanitary towel into the gusset of my underpants, trying hard not to think of it as some magical act, some willing of the jammed wheel of my cycle. I selected a new pair of tights from the drawer, and unsnapped them from their cellophane confines. I put on my bra and a cream-coloured cotton blouse. I took a fawn, two-piece suit from the wardrobe. Stepping into the skirt I caught sight of myself in the mirror on the wardrobe door. It was only momentary, but looking at the slight, sharp-faced young woman I saw reflected there, I realised that while I was by no means indifferent to her, she was moving inexorably towards the periphery of my acquaintance.

When I was fully dressed I sat at my bureau and applied a little eye-liner and a smudge of foundation. I don't wear lipstick as a rule. I knew that my boss would ask me to attend the inter-departmental meeting with him today, so that I could take minutes. Although he would never actually say anything to me about my appearance, I am conscious of the fact that he approves of the way I always make sure I am scrupulously neat, if we are in any context where we are representing the Department to the rest of the Company.

In the kitchen I examined the wash of pale light that fell across the draining board. Was it at precisely the same angle as yesterday? It seemed so. And my bath, gurgling away in a froth of bubbles and white water outside the kitchen window. Was it frothing in exactly the way that it did yesterday? Or was it only my perception of it? They certainly seemed familiar, those miniature cumuli, sparkling oily greens and blues.

In the middle of the afternoon, I found myself by the facsimile machine again. I was looking out through the vertical textured fabric louvres and trying to decide whether or not the sky was the same colour as at this time yesterday. How would it be possible to do this? I toyed idly with getting a colour chart from the local DIY shop and seeing if I could match the sky's shade to any of its little squares. But the minute I hit upon this idea, I realised that it was absurd, that the sky wasn't like some expanse of silk emulsion on which I could impose my taste.

Then I became aware of his presence again. It was much stronger to-day. I turned, but he wasn't behind me; all I could see was an ear, pok-ing around the jamb of the door. Its owner must have been talking to someone in the office to the immediate left of the recess where the inter-departmental facsimile machine is housed. I knew it was his ear intuitively.

It was a thick, blunt ear, the edges folded over, squaring it off at the top and the side. I began to feel queasy looking at it. It was a typical ear – an ear that revealed what you always have suspected about ears, namely that they don't possess nerves connecting them to any organ capable of apprehending their shape. I couldn't believe that this ear was made from flesh and not some more ductile substance, like wax or putty, that had been moulded and then set.

Involuntarily I clutched at my own ear and kneaded it between my thumb and forefinger. I was jerked out of this nauseating brown study by the insistent peep of the facsimile machine – I had neglected to feed it with the next sheet and the connection was broken. By the time I redialled, fed the oblong maw, then turned to look once more, the ear had gone.

We were hosting the inter-departmental meeting this month. My boss always chooses to hold this in Conference Room 2. I have a suspicion that this is because he wishes to intimidate his fellow heads of department. Conference Room 1 is both more comfortable and more accessible.

Conference Room 2 is at the far end of the Department, further up the flight of stairs, past my office. It is perched on top of a wing of the building that projects out into a medium-sized abyss. Four storeys below the grimy windows of the room, a tangled collection of roofs, aerials, walls and skylights provides no fixed point for the eye to alight on.

Although the horizon is no further than before, the sense of Conference Room 2 being surrounded on three sides by space, and accessible on the fourth only by a dwarf entrance from the main building, makes it cut off and removed. This is heightened by the spectacle of a Portakabin that abuts the Conference Room, the end of which dangles over the edge of the local void.

The short flight of stairs that connects Conference Room 2 to the rest of the building has the ubiquitous corporate trappings: half-conical sconces on the uplights; the feral-animal-strength carpet tiling; the vertical textured-fabric louvres (proportionately tiny – to fit the tiny windows).

I entered Conference Room 2. The heads of department sat around the conference table, a blond wood lozenge. Each one was positioned in front of a representation of the corporate logo attached to the wall: an elephant (Indian), standing on a globe, but so stylised that it's difficult to tell if that's what it really is.

Southam was there, from marketing; Haines from purchasing; Thribble from sourcing; Andersen from accounting; Askey from data processing; Tenniel from personnel, and, of course, my boss, representing the Department.

'Come and sit here.' He clutched a bunch of his black hair in one hand. He was wearing one of those shirts where the collar and cuffs are white, while the rest is striped. This highlighted his brown hands and browner face, making him appear like some executive minstrel. The presentation document was open on the table in front of him, and I could see that he had been making notes in the margin. I got my dictaphone and notebook out and readied myself to take the minutes.

Gentlemen,' my boss began, leaning forward in his chair, 'as you may recall, last month when it was the turn of my department to host this meeting, I made some proposals regarding the final phase of our corporate restructuring. Since then, as you are all no doubt aware, we have had the Main Board's approval to proceed with their implementation.

'This month I have requested a report from each of you, as to how far you have proceeded with the programme. I'll ask you, Terry, to begin – if you don't mind?'

'Not at all,' said Southam, shifting forward in his seat so that he could pour himself a cup of coffee from the stainless-steel vacuum jug and I could see the puce skin of his tonsure. 'I am happy to be able to report that since last month a further 37 per cent of our allocated spend has been redirected towards internal marketing. This means that as of today a total of' – he consulted his own presentation document – '97 per cent of our budget is now dedicated to the internal market.'

There were a number of nods, and significant grunts, from the other heads of department. Southam went on to explain the new marketing plan his department had developed to cope with the changed situation. I took the minutes diligently, listening to what he was saying, but not troubling to comprehend it.

When he had finished speaking my boss turned to Haines from purchasing. Haines's arms were crossed and with the inside edge of each middle finger he was methodically rubbing the nap of suiting stretched over either elbow. He spoke quietly and expressionlessly, with his eyes fixed on the corporate logo opposite him.

'I think that purchasing can report a success almost exactly congruent with that of marketing. Since last month a further 37 per cent of our purchasing has been reconfigured so as to come from within the Company. This means that 97 per cent of the goods and services we now purchase are sourced from the Company itself.'

In due course, Thribble from sourcing confirmed these figures. The reporting process continued on round the table, in an anti-clockwise direction. I concentrated on the high-pitched 'eek-eek' my fibre-tipped pen made as it steeplechased along the narrow feint. I didn't shut down my automatic dictation pilot until everyone had made their report. Then my boss turned to me and said, 'I think it would be a good idea if, while we discuss the next item on the agenda, you type up the minutes you've taken so far. You can leave the dictaphone running and I'll bring it down when we've finished. I think everyone present would like a copy of the minutes relating to the final phase of the corporate restructuring as quickly as possible.'

There was a scattering of grunted assents to this. I gathered up my pad and, nodding to my boss and the other heads of department, left Conference Room 2.

When I reached the stretch of corridor leading to my office, for no reason that I could think of, I parted two of the vertical textured-fabric louvres that cover the window by the door to my boss's office. From this vantage I could see Conference Room 2 in its entirety, hovering up above me. The heads of the heads of department were outlined by the room's windows. As I stood and watched, someone – I think it may have been Southam – rose from the table and walked around the room, pulling the lengths of chain that snapped the louvres shut.

I went into my office. I knelt down to switch on my laserprinter. As I had the previous afternoon, I leant my forehead against the crossbar of the workstation.

It was still there. The beaten path that my varnished nail had cut for the rest of my finger, through the eighth-of-an-inch pile of nylon undergrowth. I stared at it for some minutes in disbelief. Then I tried some experiments: I pushed my nails this way and that through the carpet-tile pile; now combing it, now ploughing it. Using one finger, or two, or the whole hand. These actions made streaks of crushed nylon filaments, but they soon sprang back up. Only the path I had created the day before – the really tiny event – remained a reality.

After a short while I grew bored with this. I stood up, turned on my computer, and made ready to type up the minutes of the interdepartmental meeting. I accessed the file with the previous month's minutes in it, and created a new file; I set my pad on the stand and began to type:

> The meeting was called to order and the Chairman asked T. Southam, head of marketing, to present the results of the implementation of the last phase of corporate restructuring. T. Southam reported that since last month a further 37 per cent of the marketing department's allocated spend had been redirected towards internal marketing. As of the 5th of this month a total of 97 per cent of the department's total budget is now dedicated to the internal market . . .

The pattering of my nails on the keys faltered and died away. I stared at the paragraph I had just typed. The cursor blinked at me from the VDU, the complicit eye of a machine intelligence. Without analysing what I was doing I saved the file and reentered the file for last month's minutes. The text scrolled down the green screen. I read:

> The meeting was called to order and the Chairman asked T. Southam, head of marketing, to present the results of the implementation of the last phase of corporate restructuring. T. Southam reported that since last month a further 37 per cent of the marketing department's allocated spend had been redirected towards internal marketing. As of the 5th of this month a total of 97 per cent of the department's total budget is now dedicated to the internal market . . .

I felt sick – sick like vomiting sick. I got up from the workstation and walked to the window of my office. I adjusted the vertical textured-fabric louvres slightly, so that I could open the window and get some fresh air. I took deep breaths and stared down into the light well my window looks out on. I counted the paper cups that lay four storeys down, I counted the pigeons that were perched on the ledges four storeys up, I counted the fingers of one hand off on the fingers of the other, and then reversed the process.

I felt the swelling feeling, and the awful, tight vacuity, worse than ever before. I stood there for a long while, my hand lightly brushing the dusting of yellow and mauve pimples under the softening, water-retaining line of my jaw.

Then I went back to the computer, altered the date at the head of the minutes of last month's inter-departmental meeting, and hit the keystrokes necessary to print out the document.

At five I finished up my work for the day. I had transcribed the tape of the latter half of the inter-departmental meeting and left a copy in my boss's in-tray. I now made my list of tasks for the following day and then began to tidy my desk.

But halfway through ordering my pens and papers I had an idea. Instead of aligning everything just so, as usual, I would engage in a little exercise. Using my ruler to calculate the angles – so this would be precise – I shifted the computer keyboard, the desk blotter and the mouse mat out of alignment by two or three degrees. This alteration was so slight as to be barely perceptible to the naked eye, but I knew it was there.

Then I went home.

Tonight, eating a late supper in front of *Newsnight* on the television, it came to me, the expression I really needed to describe the man from personnel. VPL. There used to be an advert on television in which puckered bottom after puckered bottom would float across the screen. Buttock after buttock after buttock, all bobbling away and contained by stretchy cloth beneath the stretchy cloth. VPL – Visible Panty Line. That's what they called it. If you bought their underwear you were free of it, but if you didn't you were condemned to an elastic jail.

That's what he has. Except that it isn't just his bottom – it's his whole body. Every limb and portion of the man from personnel's body is contained in an elasticated pouch, the seams of which show up from under his implausible clothes. What has he got on under there? Some complicated harness that braces his entire body? Some sacred garment enjoined by the Latter Day Saints? Who knows.

The radio woke me at seven-fifteen this morning, and this time there was no doubt in my mind. I got up and stood, looking out of my bedroom window for a long time, marvelling at the limpidity, the utter voidness of the sky.

There was no blood last night and this morning there was no blood in the sleep-warmed sanitary towel either. I stood for quite some time in front of the mirror, scrunging the insides of my thighs; catching up painful bunches of my own flesh and feeling the individual pores between my pincering fingertips. Then I pressed down hard on my belly with both palms and pushed a wave of flesh down to my pudenda, as if I were a giant sponge and I could somehow squeeze the blood out of myself. I repeated this operation a number of times, not really expecting it to work, but thinking it was worth a try.

But I wasn't frightened. Throughout this whole period I haven't felt frightened at all. Perhaps I would feel less disturbed, if only I could get frightened. Perhaps I don't really care that I've stopped menstruating, or that the days are unchanging, or that events tirelessly repeat themselves. Or perhaps I've simply adjusted – as people do.

In the kitchen I examined the wash of pale light that fell across the draining board. It was at precisely the same angle as yesterday. And my bath, gurgling away with a froth of bubbles and white water outside the kitchen window, was frothing in exactly the way that it did yesterday. I greeted the miniature cumuli, sparkling oily greens and blues, like old friends. Childlike, I allowed myself to imagine that I was weightless and miniscule, that I could roam and romp in this pretty, insubstantial gutterscape.

I had an errand to do on the way to work this morning which made me a little late. It was ten to nine before I mounted the wide concrete stairs that lead to the Company's offices. At this hour there was a steady trickle of employees entering the building, but it hadn't yet swelled into the cataract of personnel that flows through the turbine doors between five to and five past.

During those ten minutes at least 90 per cent of the Company's workforce arrive: secretaries, clerks, canteen assistants, data processors, postroom operatives, maintenance men, as well as middle managers of all shapes and sizes; and, of course, executives. They all crowd in, anxious to be seen arriving on time. The subordinates in a hurry to be there before their bosses, and the bosses in a hurry to be there before their subordinates.

But even at ten to, the foot traffic was light enough for people to observe at least nominally the pleasantries of the morning. These consist not in salutations to colleagues, but in the greeting you give to the commissionaire, Cap'n Sidney.

Cap'n Sidney stands in a booth by the security turnstile. He wears a white peaked cap, and a black serge uniform. The epaulettes on his shoulders are blancoed beyond belief. He stands there erect, the awareness that he is the Company's first line of defence written into every line of his face.

Young male employees flirt physically with Cap'n Sidney. They duck and weave as they show him their security passes. They want to give him a little action and so they wave their uncalloused hands in his face, saying things like, 'Howzit going there, Sidders,' and, 'Mind out for the old one-two.' Cap'n Sidney grins benignly and replies, 'Now, Rocky Marciano – there was a boxer.'

Older male employees, perhaps believing that their M & S blazers remind Cap'n Sidney of the officers he served fifty years ago, will touch the tips of their fingers lightly to their foreheads as they pass through the turnstile. It is the merest feint, a tiny gesture towards the communality of the past; and Cap'n Sidney returns it in the same spirit, with a touch of his nicotine-mitted hand to the peak of his cap.

Older female employees always say 'Good morning' to Cap'n Sidney with exaggerated care – as if he were an idiot or an imbecile. And he always says 'Good morning' back to them with exaggerated care – as if they were idiots or imbeciles.

Young female employees say 'Good morning' to Cap'n Sidney, and they touch him with their eyes. Cap'n Sidney is their talisman, their wise old uncle. He understands that, says 'Good morning' in reply and examines their breasts, as if they were security passes.

Cap'n Sidney never says 'Good morning' to me, no matter how early I arrive at work. When it comes to me Cap'n Sidney is oblivious. It's not that he's rude, or insensitive – after all he simply can't salute every single Company employee, there are far too many of us. It's just that we've never really met; and now, over thousands of mornings, a natural reserve has built up between us. It would be all right if some colleague of mine – whether a clerical-weight boxer, officer class, or the Right Breasts – were to introduce us, put us at ease with one another; then I too could become a warm, sincere, ten-second friend of Cap'n Sidney.

This is unlikely to happen.

The strangest of things, though; the last six weeks – which we may call the non-period for the sake of convenience – have marked an apparent shift in my lack-of-a-relationship with Cap'n Sidney. During this non-period, when I have approached his booth, pass held level at the convenient height, by the lobe of my right ear, Cap'n Sidney's eyes have narrowed. And I have thought that, for the spilt-second my face was turned towards his, as I slid through the turnstile, his expression had a little more openness about it, that something writhed – ever so slightly – beneath his moustache.

The VPL man was in the lift. He smiled at me quite innocently, but as we ascended his presence there became somehow bound up with everything oppressive, everything crammed into the stippled, aluminium booth of my mind. It occurred to me too that the VPL man had only come into my life in the last six weeks or so – at any rate I could dredge up no earlier memory of him.

There is some linkage, some alliance, between my premenstrual tension and the VPL man's VPL. He too has something bulging and constrained, yet vacuous, concealed beneath his clothing. These personalised voids, I imagined, were calling to one another, wailing the music of the empty spheres.

Between the third and the fourth floors I shifted tack. It might not be anything quite so nebulous between me and the VPL man. I now entertained the notion that the VPL man had somehow managed to impregnate me, without my knowledge. Perhaps he had crept into the women's toilet midway down the departmental corridor, late one afternoon, when only the cleaners are about, and tossed himself off. There is more plausibility in this image: his puckered form in the formica cubicle, his salty dollop on the mushroom-shaped and mushroom-coloured toilet seat.

But there is someone else about. Me. And he knows that. As he straphangs his way home on the tube, he smiles enigmatically, his lips parted – because he knows that mine are parted; and at that very moment are sucking it up, his tadpole, his micro-construction robot, which burrows into me carrying the blueprints for the manufacture of more VPL men and VPL women.

By the time we reached the Department's floor I was convinced of this. I was bearing the VPL man's child, the chopped-ear-man's child, the bastard offspring of he-who-lingers-by-the-facsimile-machine. It could be worse – the child will be a fine, healthy specimen, and grow up to do something undynamic but essential, like becoming a Communications Manager (since my boss took over the Department it has been mandatory for all job titles to be capitalised).

It didn't even occur to me that our child might wish to work in his father's department rather than my own.

I got out before Daddy, who barely looked up from the folded square of newsprint he was reading and re-reading.

A truly annoying morning was entirely dominated by a recurrent system error on my computer. I have a suspicion that we may have a virus in the departmental network. I said as much to my boss, when he poked his head into my office at around eleven. He asked me what was happening – and I explained that every time I exited from the network and tried to import files on to my own hard disc, the machine crashed.

He came round behind my desk to take a look. I pulled back from the workstation, allowing him the room to get at the keyboard. He was wearing one of his newer suits today; and positioned as I was, I found myself confronted by the seat and upper legs of his trousers. The suit is made from soft but durable fabric, and the designer had seen fit to create some miniature chaps of shiny chamois, which stretched a third of the way down my boss's thighs. The chaps were mimicked by the distended epaulettes, which I had already seen flopping from the shoulders of the suit jacket, like the ears of a Basset hound.

'See here?' He flicked his hands over the surface of the keyboard, only occasionally grasping for the mouse, as if he were casting off a stitch. The cursor appeared here and there, in a whirl of shifts between applications and files. Instead of attempting to import the files directly, he went into them where they were stored, as if intent on doing some work on them. He then cut out the entire contents of each file and re-opened it under another application. Finally he imported the new application, and so sneaked around the lurking virus.

'See?' He was heading for the door, while an icon, somewhat like a triumphant Roadrunner, executed a frenzied jig on the VDU, and the tinny speaker cackled, 'Ah-ha-ah-hahahaha!'

The Roadrunner may have known more than I did. At night, the cleaners long departed from the Department, the computer icon could have quit the screen and entered my world of static grey. 'Ah-ha-ah-hahahaha!' Something had been in my office during the night, something fervid but precise – like the Roadrunner icon, because this morning ('Ah-ha-ah-hahahaha!') the computer keyboard, the desk blotter and the mouse mat were all perfectly aligned once more. It wasn't perceptible to the naked eye, but I checked it with my ruler.

At lunchtime I looked hard at the sky for more than five minutes. On the way into work I stopped by the DIY centre and picked up a colour chart. I had been doing comparisons at half-hour intervals all morning. Initially I was certain the shade the sky corresponded to was 'pearl grey', but latterly I made up my mind that it was really 'mid-grey'. It was mid-grey for the rest of the morning.

In fact it grew more convincingly mid-grey the more I checked it, until at lunchtime it was no comparison at all; it was rather that the tiny rectangle on the chart was a miniature window, looking out on to another quadrant of the grey heavens. All it needed was its own vertical textured fabric louvres, to complete the marriage between sample and sky.

I went down to the café and bought my sandwiches, a can of Diet Coke and one of those giant, crumbly cookies.

In the park I sat with other office workers in a circle of benches that surrounds a sagging rotunda. This feature is built from red London bricks. It's damp and destitute, long since re-pointed. The pillars resemble a demented loggia, which instead of moving forward has turned in on itself, forming a defensive corral. The pools of rusty water at the base of each pillar seem evidence of incontinence, a suitable indignity for wayward park furniture.

The office workers sat canted sideways on the benches. An occasional pigeon hopped up to one of these sandwich eaters, clearly shamed by its capacity to fly and doing its best to hide tattered wings. These exchanges between people and birds were embarrassing to watch. That's the truth. We have now advanced so far into a zone of the genetically furtive, that office workers, contemplating these flying vermin, feel their own humanity compromised in some way. So they roll up bread pills, and averting their eyes, proffer them to the un-stuck craws.

All afternoon I sat in my office and worked. The straining in my belly grew, swelled, became even more pregnant. I was certain that I was on the verge of getting my period. My nipples were so sensitive that I could feel every bump and nodule on their aureoles, snagging against the cotton of my bra. The afternoon was also punctuated by a series of quite sharp abdominal pains. After every one of them I was convinced I would feel the familiar ultimate lancing. I was poised, ready to head for the toilet – the venue for my imagined impregnation by the VPL man – but no blood came.

Instead I occupied myself with the collation and binding of a series of management briefings that the Department was publishing for the greater edification of the Company as a whole.

Five o'clock found me bending the flexible prongs back on the clean sheets, to house them securely in their plastic covers. My boss hung his face around the doorjamb and grunted approval. I couldn't see his ear – and this troubled me. I wanted to ask him to take a step into the room, so that I could check on his ear, check that it was still there and still his. But the idea of it was silly, a nitrous oxide thought that giggled in my head. To stop myself from smirking I concentrated on the odd, phallic intervention, made at waist-height, by the black-taped handle of his squash racket.

Then he left. I ordered my desk, and soon afterwards went home.

At home I ate and then had a bath, hoping that it would ease the premenstrual tension. It didn't. I put on a dressing gown and wandered about my flat. Never before had it seemed so claustrophobic. The neat, space-saving arrangement of double-seater sofa and twin armchairs was a cell within a cell. The coffee table, with its stack of magazines and dish of pot-pourri, was part of a set for a chat show that never made it past the development stage. The images on the walls were tired, static, self-referential, each one a repository of forgotten insights, now incapable of arousing fresh interest.

I turned on the television, but couldn't concentrate. I must have slept, squelched down amongst the foam-filled, polyester-covered cushions. Slid into sleep, the surfaces of my eyes grounding quickly on the salty, silty bottom of unconsciousness. There I floated, twisting slowly in the deceptive currents.

Assembled backwards. Quickly. Scherlupppp! The elements of my dream: I arrive for work and see that the organisational chart has been rearranged overnight. The strips, dots and squares have been manipulated so as to form a new configuration, which places a dot I haven't seen before at the very apex of the Department's hierarchy. I consult the legend, a small ring-binder dangling from the rail at the bottom of the board by a length of twine, only to discover that the dot is me.

I realise that I will have to move across the corridor into my ex-boss's office. I am relieved to see him coming through my door; cradled in his arms is his desk blotter and giant mouse mat. On top of these surfaces is a miscellany of objects he has culled from his desk: a Rotadex, a date-a-day diary, a dictaphone, and a collection of plastic beakers, joined at the root, brimming with pens, pencils and paper clips.

He finds it difficult to meet my eye, but I'm wholly unembarrassed. I gesture to the collation and binding exercise that I was undertaking the previous evening, and which is still spread out on my desk. I say, 'Finish this off, will you?' He nods, dumbly.

I cross the corridor to my new office. I go behind the broad, black slab of desk and sit down. My former boss has left one object behind on his desk top, an executive toy of some kind, saved from the era when these mini constructions of stainless steel and black plastic had a vogue.

This one takes the form of a Newton's cradle. But in the place of ball bearings, there are tiny, humanoid figures hanging from the threads by their shiny aluminium hands. The figures are naked, and when I set the cradle in motion, they engage in dangerously athletic congress. There is silence, except for the sound of miniature, metal, intercrural activity.

Piled under the vertical textured-fabric louvres; tucked up against the vents under the storage heaters; squidged sideways to lie along the top of the cable-tracking conduit, which circles the office at knee height; stacked in loose bundles on every flat surface, bar the desk itself, are many many panty liners, tampons and sanitary towels. Staunchers, stemmers, cotton-wool barriers. There is so much plastic-backed absorbent material in my new office that, taken together with the fabric-covered walls and carpet-tiled floor, the effect is of a recording studio. The clicking of the Newton's cradle has amazing clarity. The shadows of the figurines banging into one another are thrown into sharp relief against the whiteboard on the far wall. A cord of pain, running like a zipper up through the flesh from my vagina to my throat, threatens to undo me, to spill out my interior, like so much offal, or rhino shit, on the carpet tiles.

When I awake *Newsnight* is on the television. Peter Snow is running the world from his modular grey bunker of a studio. He's sitting in front of oversized venetian-blind slat panels, and ignoring the micro-computer that has sunk at an oblique angle into the vinyl-veined console he's sitting behind.

He is speaking with undue emphasis. It's this undue emphasis that impinges on me first – but it occurs to me immediately afterwards that perhaps everything I have ever heard anyone say has been subjected to undue emphasis.

Snow is talking to two pop academics. I can tell this with some certainty, because one of them is too well dressed for a politician, and the other too badly. Like a dentist with mass appeal, Snow is getting down to extracting the truth from this duo. He cants himself towards the badly dressed, froggy-looking one.

'Now, Dr Busner, haven't we been hearing for years now – from you and others – about the possible effects of such a bottoming-out?'

'Quite so,' says the man called Busner, 'although I'm not sure that "bottoming-out" is the right expression. What we have here is a condition of stasis. I'm not prepared to hazard any long-term predictions about its duration on the basis of the sanity quotient figures we currently have; but what I can say is that the Government's response has been woefully inadequate – a case of too little, too late.'

He falls to rolling and unrolling the ragged strip of mohair tie that flows down over the soft folds of his belly. He does this extremely well, with one hand, the way a card sharp runs a coin through his fingers. Snow now cants himself towards the other man, a virile sixty year old, with intact and ungreying hair, wearing a sharp Italian suit with the narrowest of chalk stripes. 'Professor Stein, a case of too little, too late?'

'I think not.' Stein steeples his fingers on top of the console. 'Like Dr Busner, I would reserve the right to comment at some later date. The evidence we have at the moment is sketchy, incomplete. But that being noted, even if the conditions today's report draws our attention to are fully realised, it only points towards the non-event I am certain will not occur.'

'So, contrary to what you have said in the past, you now think something may well happen?' Snow is delighted that he has caught Stein's double-negative.

'That's not what I said,' Stein fires right back at the lanky television presenter. 'I appreciate the implications of this data. It is bizarre – to say the least – to have so many people apparently experiencing a lengthy period of climatic and seasonal stasis; but we must bear in mind that, as yet, this is a localised phenomenon, confined to a discrete area. It has only been this way for some six weeks –'

'More like two months!' Busner cuts in.

This gives Peter Snow the opportunity to try and knock the discussion down, so he can drag it somewhere else. 'How-can-you-Doc-tor-Busner' – he is in profile, Struwwelpeter-like, fingers splayed, elongated, nose sharp, rapping out the words in a dot-dash fashion, letting his pentameters beat up on each other – 'be-so-o-certain-about-the-ex-act-time-the-stasis-began?'

'Well, I admit' – Busner, far from being cowed, is invigorated by Snow's tongue-tapping – 'it can be difficult to ascertain when nothing begins to happen.' His plump lips twitch, he is sucking on the boiled irony, 'But not, I think, impossible.

'Take events – for example. How small does an event have to be before it ceases to be an event?'

'Yes, yes, that is a very interesting question.' This from Stein. The three of them are now all canted towards one another, forming a boyish huddle. 'I myself am intrigued by small events, matters of the merest degree. Perhaps I might give an example?'

'Please do.' Peter Snow's tone has softened, it's clear that the idea interests him.

'Can we have the camera in very tight on the surface of the console, please?'

'Pull right in, please, camera 2.' Snow makes a come-on-down gesture.

The camera zooms right down until the veins in the grey vinyl of the console are rift valleys. What must be the very tip of Stein's fingernail comes into view. I can see the grain of it. It pokes a little at the vinyl, dislodging a speck of something. It could be dust or a fragment of skin, or mica. But the speck is both very small – less than a tenth of the width of Stein's fingernail – and very grey; as grey as the console itself.

The camera zooms back out in. The three middle-aged men are beaming. 'So there we have,' says Peter Snow, addressing a portion of the nation, 'a very small event. Thank you, Professor Stein, and you, Dr Busner.' The two pop academics incline their heads, slightly.

The camera moves back in until Snow fills the screen. There are some fresh newspapers, interleaved by his elbow. 'Well-that's-about-it-for-tonight-except-for-a-quick-look-at-tomorrow's-papers.' His hands pull them out, one at a time, while he recites the headlines, '*The-Times*: "No-New-Developments-in-Stasis-Situation". The *Guardian*: "Government-Ministers-Knew-that-Nothing-Had-Happened". And-*Today*-with-the-rather-racier: "We're-in-a-Grey-Area!".

'Jeremy-Paxman-will-be-here-tomorrow-night. But-for-now-this-is-Peter-Snow-wishing-you-good-night.' The grey man on the screen smiles, picks up the pile of papers from the grey console in front of him, and shuffles them together, while the camera pulls up and away.

I pull up and away, and go next door to the bedroom. I take off my dressing gown and hang it on a hook behind the door. I take my nightie from beneath my pillow and put it on. I get a fresh pair of underpants from the chest of drawers and wriggle into them. I set the alarm clock for seven-fifteen. And I get a new sanitary towel and place it in the gusset of my underpants.

My period might start during the night.

The North London Book of the Dead

I suppose that the form my bereavement took after my mother died was fairly conventional. Initially I was shocked. Her final illness was mercifully quick, but harrowing. Cancer tore through her body as if it were late for an important meeting with a lot of other successful diseases.

I had always expected my mother to outlive me. I saw myself becoming a neutered bachelor, who would be wearing a cardigan and still living at home at the age of forty, but it wasn't to be. Mother's death was a kind of a relief, but it was also bizarre and hallucinatory. The week she lay dying in the hospital I was plagued by strange sensations; gusts of air would seem personalised and, driving in my car, I had the sensation not that I was moving forward but that the road was being reeled back beneath the wheels, as if I were mounted on some giant piece of scenery.

The night she died my brother and I were at the hospital. We took it in turns to snatch sleep in a vestibule at the end of the ward and then to sit with her. She breathed stertorously. Her flesh yellowed and yellowed. I was quite conscious that she had no mind any more. The cancer – or so the consultant told me – had made its way up through the meningitic fluid in the spine and into her brain. I sensed the cancer in her skull like a cloud of inky pus. Her self-consciousness, sentience, identity, what you will, was cornered, forced back by the cloud into a confined space, where it pulsed on and then off, with all the apparent humanity of a digital watch.

One minute she was alive, the next she was dead. A dumpy nurse rushed to find my brother and me. We had both fallen asleep in the vestibule, cocooned within its plastic walls. 'I think she's gone,' said the nurse. And I pictured Mother striding down Gower Street, naked, wattled.

By the time we reached the room they were laying her out. I had never understood what this meant before; now I could see that the truth was that the body, the corpse, really laid itself out. It was smoothed as if a great wind had rolled over the tired flesh. And it, Mother, was changing colour, as I watched, from an old ivory to a luminous yellow. The nurse, for some strange reason, had brushed Mother's hair back off her forehead. It lay around her head in a fan on the pillow and two lightning streaks of grey ran up into it from either temple. The nurses had long since removed her dentures, and the whole ensemble – Mother with drawn-in cheeks and sculpted visage, lying in the small room, around her the loops and skeins of a life-supporting technology – made me think of the queen of an alien planet, resplendent on a high-tech palanquin, in some Buck Rogers style sci-fi serial of the Thirties.

There was a great whooshing sensation in the room. This persisted as a doctor of Chinese extraction – long, yellow, and divided at the root – felt around inside her cotton nightie for a non-existent heartbeat. The black, spindly hairs on his chin wavered. He pronounced her dead. The whooshing stopped. I felt her spirit fly out into the orange light of central London. It was about 3.00 a.m.

When I began to accept the fact that Mother really was gone, I went into a period of intense depression. I felt that I had lost an adversary. Someone to test myself against. My greatest fan and my severest critic and above all a good talker, who I was only just getting to know as a person – shorn of the emotional prejudices that conspire to strait-jacket the relationships between parents and children.

When my depression cleared the dreams started. I found myself night after night encountering my mother in strange situations. In my dreams she would appear at dinner parties (uninvited), crouched behind a filing cabinet in the office where I worked, or on public transport balefully swinging from a strap. She was quite honest about the fact that she was dead in these dreams, she made no attempt to masquerade as one of the living, rather she absorbed the effect that death had had on her personality much the way she had taken the rest of the crap that life had flung at her: a couple of failed marriages and a collection of children who, on the whole, were a bit of a disappointment to her.

When I tried to remonstrate with her, point out to her that by her own lights (she was a fervent atheist and materialist), she ought to be gently decomposing somewhere, she would fix me with a weary eye and say in a characteristically deadpan way, ‘So I'm dead but won't lie down, huh? Big deal.’

It was a big deal. Mother had banged on about her revulsion at the idea of an afterlife for as long as I could remember. The chief form that this took was an extended rant aimed at all the trappings of death that society had designed. She despised the undertaking business especially. To Mother it was simply a way of cheating money out of grieving people who could ill afford it.

She had told me a year or two before she died that if it was at all possible I was to try and give her a kind of do-it-yourself funeral. Apparently the Co-op retailed one that allowed you to get the cost of the whole thing down to about £250. You had to build your own casket though and I was never any good at anything remotely practical. At school it took me two years to construct an acrylic string-holder. And even then it wouldn't work.

So, after Mother died we arranged things conventionally, but austerely. Her corpse was burnt at Golders Green Crematorium. My eldest brother and I went alone – knowing that she would have disapproved of a crowd. We sat there in the chapel contemplating the bottom-of-the-range casket. One of the undertakers came waddling down the aisle, he gestured to us to stand and then moved off to one side, conspicuously scratching his grey bottom, either inadvertently or because he considered us of no account. Electric motors whirred, Mother lurched towards what, to all intents and purposes, was her final resting place.

A week or so later when I was going through more of Mother's papers I found a newspaper clipping about the DIY funeral. I threw it away guiltily. I also found a deposit book that showed that mother had invested £370 in something called the Ecological Building Society. I phoned the society and was told by a Mr Hunt that it was true. Mother had been the owner of a seventh of a traditional Mongolian *yurt*, which was sited for some reason in a field outside Wincanton. I told Mr Hunt to keep the seventh; it seemed a suitable memorial.

Meanwhile, the dreams continued. And Mother managed to be as embarrassing in them as she had been alive, but for entirely different reasons. With death she had taken on a mantle of candour and social sharpness that I tended to attribute to myself rather than her. At the dream dinner parties she would make asides to me the whole time about how pretentious people were and what bad taste they displayed, talking all the while in a loud and affected voice which, needless to say, remained inaudible to her subjects. After a while I ceased trying to defeat her with the logic of her own extinction; it was pointless. Mother had long since ceased to be susceptible to reasoning. I think it was something to do with my father, a man who uses dialectics the way the Japanese used bamboo slivers during the war.

About six months after Mother's death the dreams began to decline in frequency and eventually they petered out altogether. They were replaced for a short while by an intense period during which I kept seeing people in the street who I thought were Mother. I'd be walking in the West End or the City and there, usually on the other side of the road, would be Mother, ambling along staring in shop windows. I would know it was Mother because of the clothes. Mother tended to wear slacks on loan from hippopotami, or else African-style dresses that could comfortably house a scout troop. She also always carried a miscellaneous collection of bags, plastic and linen, dangling from her arm. These were crammed with modern literature, groceries and wadded paper tissues.

And then, invariably, as I drew closer the likeness would evaporate. Not only wasn't it Mother, but it seemed absurd that I ever could have made the mistake. This late-middle-aged woman looked nothing like Mother, she was dowdy and conventional. Not the sort of woman at all who would say of effete young men that they 'had no balls', or of precious young women that they 'shat chocolate ice cream'. Yet each time the fact that Mother was dead hit me again, it was as if it hadn't really occurred to me before and that her failure to get in touch with me over the past six months had been solely because she was 'hellishly busy'.

When I stopped seeing fake Mothers in the street I reckoned that I had just about accepted her death. Every so often I thought about her, sometimes with sadness, sometimes with joy, but her absence no longer gnawed at me like a rat at a length of flex. I was over it. Although, like Marcel after Albertine has gone, from time to time I felt that the reason I no longer missed Mother with such poignancy was that I had become another person. I had changed. I was no longer the sort of person who had had a mother like Mother. Mother belonged to someone else. If I had run into her at a dinner party fully conscious, she probably wouldn't have recognised me. My mother was dead.

All of this made the events that transpired in the winter of the year she died even more shocking. I was walking down Crouch Hill towards Crouch End on a drizzly, bleak, Tuesday afternoon. It was about three o'clock. I'd taken the afternoon off work and decided to go and see a friend. When, coming up the other side of the road I saw Mother. She was wearing a sort of bluish, tweedish long jacket and black slacks and carrying a Barnes & Noble book bag, as well as a large handbag and a carrier bag from Waitrose. She had a CND badge in her lapel and was observing the world with a familiar 'there will be tears before bedtime' sort of expression.

The impression I had of Mother in that very first glance was so sharp and so clear, her presence so tangible, that I did not for a moment doubt the testimony of my senses. I looked at Mother and felt a trinity of emotions: affection and embarrassment mingled with a sort of acute embarrassment. It was this peculiarly familiar wash of feeling that must have altogether swamped the terror and bewilderment that anyone would expect to experience at the sight of their dead mother walking up Crouch Hill.

I crossed the road and walked towards her. She spotted me when I was about twenty feet off. Just before a grin of welcome lit up her features I spotted a little *moue* of girlish amusement – that was familiar too, it meant 'You've been had'. We kissed on both cheeks; Mother looked me up and down to see how I was weighing in for the fight with life. Then she gestured at the shop window she'd been looking into. 'Can you believe the prices they're charging for this crap, someone must be buying it.' Her accent was the same, resolutely mid-Atlantic, she had the same artfully yellowed and unevened dentures. It was Mother.

'Mother,' I said, 'what are you doing in Crouch End? You never come to Crouch End except to take the cat to the vet, you don't even like Crouch End.'

'Well, I live here now.' Mother was unperturbed. 'It's OK, it's a drag not being, able to get the tube, but the buses are fairly regular. There's quite a few good shops in the parade and someone's just opened up a real deli. Want some halva?' Mother opened her fist under my face. Crushed into it was some sticky halva, half-eaten but still in its gold foil wrapping. She grinned again.

'But Mother, what are you doing in Crouch End? You're dead.'

Mother was indignant, 'Of course I'm dead, dummy, whaddya think I've been doing for the last ten months? Cruising the Caribbean?'

'How the hell should I know? I thought we saw the last of you at Golders Green Crematorium, I never expected to see you in Crouch End on a Tuesday afternoon.' Mother had me rattled, she seemed to be genuinely astonished by my failure to comprehend her resurrection.

'More to the point, what are you doing in Crouch End? Why aren't you at work?'

'I thought I'd take the afternoon off. There's not a lot on at the office. If I stayed there I'd just be shuffling paper back and forth trying to create some work.'

'That's an attitude problem talking, young man. You've got a good job there. What's the matter with you? You always want to start at the top, you've got to learn to work your way up in life.'

'Life, Mother? I hardly think "Life" is the issue here! Tell me about what it's like to be dead! Why didn't you tell any of us you were having life after death in Crouch End? You could have called . . .'

Mother wasn't fazed, she looked at her watch, another crappy Timex, indistinguishable from the last one I'd seen her wearing. 'It's late, I've got to go to my class. If you want to know about life after death come and see me tomorrow. I'm living at 24 Rosemount Avenue, in the basement flat, we'll have tea, I'll make you some cookies.' And with that she gave me the sort of perfunctory peck on the cheek she always used to give me when she was in a hurry and toddled off up Crouch Hill, leaving me standing, bemused.

What I couldn't take was that Mother was so offhand about life after death, rather than the fact of it. That and this business of living in Crouch

End. Mother had always been such a crushing snob about where people lived in London; certain suburbs – such as Crouch End – were so incredibly non-U in Mother's book of form. The revelation that there was life after death seemed to me relatively unimportant set beside Mother's startling new attitudes.

I probably should have gone and told someone about my encounter. But who? All a shrink could have offered would have been full board and medication. And anyway, the more I told people how real the experience had been, the more certain they would become that I was the victim of an outlandishly complex delusionary state.

I had no desire to be psychiatric cannon fodder, so I went off to see my friend and had a fulfilling afternoon playing Trivial Pursuit. Just suppose it was all for real? I had to find out more about Mother's resurrection, she'd always been so emphatic about what happened to people after they die: 'They rot, that's it. You put 'em in a box and they rot. All that religious stuff, it's a load of crap.' Setting aside the whole issue of the miraculous I really wanted to see Mother eat humble pie over this afterlife issue, so much so that I went through the next thirty-odd hours as if nothing had happened. It was an exercise in magical thinking. I figured that if I behaved as if nothing had happened, Mother would be waiting for me, with cookies, in Rosemount Avenue, but if I said anything to anyone, the gods might take offence and whisk her away.

Rosemount Avenue was one of those hilltop streets in suburban London where the camber of the road is viciously arced like the back of a macadamised whale. The houses are high-gabled Victorian, tiled in red and with masonry that looks as if it was sculpted out of solid snot. Calling it an avenue was presumably a reference to the eight or so plane trees running down each side of the road. These had been so viciously pruned that they looked like nothing so much as upturned amputated legs. Poised on the swell of the road I shuddered to myself. What had brought these macabre images into my mind? Was it the prospect of my second encounter with a dead person? Was I losing my balance? Examining myself I concluded in the negative. In truth suburban streets, if you look at them for long enough, always summon up a sense of mortality – of the skull beneath the skin. The Reaper always waits behind the bus shelter. You can see his robe up to the knee; the rest is obscured by the route map.

The basement of No. 24 looked rather poky from the street; I couldn't see in the windows without going down into the basement area. Before I could do so Mother appeared clutching a tea strainer in one hand. 'Are you going to stand up there all afternoon? The kettle's boiled.' Death had done nothing to dampen down Mother's impatience. She still carried around her a sense of barely repressed nervous energy; in a more active, physical age Mother would have probably broken horses, or gone raiding with the Bedouin.

I noticed as I stepped into the flat that Mother's name was under the bell. For some reason that shocked me. I felt that Mother ought to be incognito. After all it was pretty weird her being alive after death. What if the Sunday papers found out? It could be embarrassing. I said, 'Mother, why have you kept your name? Surely if you're going to go on living in London you should change it? Aren't the people in charge of death worried about publicity?'

Mother sighed with exasperation. 'Look, there aren't any "people in charge of death". When you die you move to another part of London, that's all there is to it. Period.'

'But Mother, what about that performance at Golders Green? Weren't you in that coffin?'

'All right I'll admit it, that part of it is a bit obscure. One minute I was in the hospital – feeling like shit, incidentally – the next I was in Crouch End and some estate agents were showing me around this flat.'

'Estate agents! Dead estate agents?'

'Yeah, they were dead too, the whole thing is self-administered, a bit like a commune.'

Mother's eschatalogical revelations were beginning to get to me a little and I had slumped down on a sofa. My new vantage point jolted me into looking around the flat. I'd never seen a piece of elysian real estate before. What struck me immediately was that Mother's final resting place, if that's what it was, was remarkably like the flat she'd spent the last ten years of her life in.

There was the same large room with sofas and chairs scattered round it. There was a kitchenette off to one side, and high double doors at the end of the main room led to the bedroom. Through another door at the back of the room I could see a set of french windows and through them a small, well-kept garden. The flat was furnished haphazardly with odd posters and paintings on the walls and a lot of books; some shelved, others stacked on tables. A set of half-corrected proofs lay on the arm of a chair.

The principal difference was that whereas in the past it had been photographs of my brothers and me that had stood, either framed or mounted in plastic cubes, scattered around on the available surfaces, now the impedimenta that betrayed Mother's affections were entirely unfamiliar to me. There were photographs of people I had never seen before. Young men who looked rather too smooth for my taste. And other, older people. A jolly couple grinning out from a particularly ornate silver frame looked like Cypriots to me. I picked up a postcard someone had sent Mother from Madeira of all places and scanning the back recognised neither the bright feminine hand, nor the scrawled male salutation and signature.

I was shocked by all of this, but kept silent. Once again I felt sure that if I pressured Mother she would tell me nothing substantial about the afterlife.

The kettle boiled. Mother filled the pot and placed it on a tray, together with cups, sugar, milk and a plate of my favourite chocolate chip cookies. She brought it over and placed it on the low table in front of where I sat. She poured me a cup of tea and offered me a cookie. The conversation lapsed for a while. I munched and Mother went into the kitchenette and opened a can of cat food. She let a couple of black kittens in from the back garden.

'New cats, I see.'

'Uh-huh, that's Tillie and that's Margaret.' The cats lurked and smarmed themselves around the furniture. I wondered idly if they were familiars and if my mother had really always been the kind of witch my father had said she was.

I started browsing through the books. They weren't the same as her mortal collection – I had those – but they covered the same ground: Virago Classics, a lot of Henry James and Proust in several different editions, scores of miscellaneous novels, books on gardening and cookery. By now I was quite openly looking for something, some clue. I couldn't admit it to myself but once again Mother was managing to rile me as much dead as she ever had alive.

I went over to the phone table. There was an address book lying open which I started to flick through idly. Again there were the same kind of names, but they belonged to totally different people, presumably the ones in the photographs, the ones who sent cards. Mother had always struck up acquaintances fairly easily. It wasn't so much that she was friendly as that she exuded a certain wholesome quality, as palpably as if a vent had been opened on her forehead and the smell of bread baking had started to churn out. In my view this wholesome quality was the worst kind of misrepresentation. If there had been such a body as the Personality Advertising Standards Commission, Mother would have been the subject of numerous complaints.

There were phone directories stacked under the table – phone directories and something else, phone-directory-shaped, that wasn't a phone directory. I bent down and pulled it out by its spine. It *was* a phone directory. *North London Book of the Dead*, ran the title; and then underneath: *A–Z*. The cover was the usual yellow flimsy card and there was also the usual vaguely arty line drawing – in this instance of Kensal Green Cemetery. I started to leaf through the pages.

'So, you're not here five minutes and you want to use the phone,' said Mother coming back in from the kitchenette.

'What's this, Mother?' I held up the directory.

'Oh that. Well I guess you might call it a kind of religious text.' She giggled unnervingly.

'Mother, don't you think it's about time you came clean with me about all of this?'

We sat down at the table (similar melamine finish, similar blue, flower-patterned tablecloth) with the *North London Book of the Dead* in between us.

'Well, it's like this,' began Mother. 'When you die you go and live in another part of London. And that's it.'

'Whaddya mean, that's it?' I could already see all sorts of difficulties with this radical new view of death, even if I was sitting inside an example of it. 'Whaddya mean, that's it? Who decides which part of London? How is it that no one's ever heard of this before? How come people don't notice all the dead people clogging up the transport system? What about paying bills? What about this phone book? You can't tell me this lists all the people who have ever died in North London, it isn't thick enough. And what about the dead estate agents, who do they work for? A Supreme Estate Agent? And why Crouch End? You hate Crouch End.'

'It could have been worse, some dead people live in Wanstead.'

'What about the people who lived in Wanstead when they were alive?'

'They live somewhere else, like East Finchley or Grays Thurrock, anywhere.'

'Mother, will you answer my questions, or won't you?'

'I'll just get another cup of tea, dear.'

I wrung it out of her eventually. It went something like this: when you die you move to another part of London where you resume pretty much the same kind of life you had before you died. There are lots of dead people in London and quite a few dead businesses. When you've been dead for a few years you're encouraged to move to the provinces.

The dead community are self-administering and there are dead people in most of the major enterprises, organisations and institutions. There are some autonomous services for dead people, but on the whole dead services operate alongside 'live' ones. Most dead people have jobs, some work for live companies. Mother, for example, was working for a live publishing company.

'OK. I think I've got it so far, but you still haven't explained why it is that no one knows. Now I know I could shout it to the rooftops. I could sell my story to the tabloids.' I was getting quite worked up by now, hunched over and absent-mindedly gobbling chocolate chip cookies with great gulps of tea. I didn't even notice the kittens eating my shoelaces. Mother was imperturbable.

'The funny thing is, that very few people seem to meet dead people who they know. It just goes to show you how big and anonymous the city really is. Even when people do meet dead friends and relatives they don't seem inclined to broadcast the news.'

'But Mother, you've always had an enquiring mind, you always thought you'd rot when you died. Why haven't you got to the bottom of all this? Who's the main man? Is it the "G" character?'

'How should I know? I work, I go to my class, I feed the cats, I see a few friends, I travel. I'm not clever like you, if I do reflect on it at all it seems wholly appropriate. If I had spent days trying to visualise the afterlife I probably could have only come up with a pale version of the very real Crouch End I'm now living in.'

'What class?'

Mother gestured at the phone directory. 'The people who compile the phone book hold regular classes for people who are newly dead. They run through the blue pages at the beginning of the book and explain the best and most appropriate ways for dead people to conduct themselves.'

'I should imagine that there are a lot of newly dead people who are pretty badly traumatised.' I probably said this with unwarranted enthusiasm. I was still trying to look for the gaping holes in Mother's suburban necro-utopia.

'Oh no, not at all. Put it like this: most people who've had painful illnesses, or are lonely, are only too relieved to discover that instead of extinction they're getting Winchmore Hill or Kenton. The classes only go to underline the very reality of the situation. There's something immensely reassuring about sitting on a plastic chair in a cold church hall reading a phone book and watching a pimply youth trying to draw on a whiteboard with a squeaky magic marker.'

'I see your point. But Mother, you were always so sparky and feisty. It's out of character for you to be so laid back. Aren't you curious to get the whole picture? What happens in other cities? Is it the same? If dead people move to the provinces after a while don't these areas get clogged up and zombified? There are a million questions I'd like the answers to. You always hated groups and here you are submitting to indoctrination in a religion ostensibly run by dead employees of British Telecom. Why? For Christ's sake, why?'

'Yeah, it is kind of weird, isn't it. I think death must have mellowed me.'

We chewed the fat for a while longer. Mother asked me about my sex life and whether or not I had an overdraft. She also asked about the rest of the family and expressed the opinion that both my brothers were insane and that some gay people we knew were 'nice boys'. All this was characteristic and reassuring. She let me take a closer look at the *North London Book of the Dead*. It was genuinely uninspiring, based entirely on fact with no prophecies or commandments. The introductory pages were given over to flat statements such as: 'Your (dead) identity should hold up to most official enquiries. Dead people work in most major civil service departments ensuring that full records of dead people are kept up to date. Should you in any instance run into difficulties, call one of the Dead Citizens' Advice Bureaux listed in the directory.' And so on.

Somehow, reading the book calmed me down and I stopped harassing Mother with my questions. After an hour or so she said that she was going out to a party a friend of hers was throwing. Would I like to come? I said, 'I think I can probably do better than socialising with dead people,' and instantly regretted it. 'Sorry Mother.'

'No offence taken, son,' she smiled. This was completely uncharacteristic and her failure to get violently angry filled me with dismay. She let me out of the flat just as a small wan moon was lifting off over the shoulder of Ally Pally. I set off towards Stroud Green Road buzzing with weird thoughts and apprehensions.

That night I thrashed around in bed like a porpoise. My duvet became saturated with sweat. I felt as if I were enfolded in the damp palm of a giant . . . Mother! I awoke with a start, the alarm clock blinked 3.22 a.m., redly. I sat on the edge of my bed cradling my dripping brow. It came to me why I should be having such a nightmare. I wanted to betray Mother. It wasn't out of any desire to change once and for all the metaphysical status quo, or because I wanted to open people's eyes to the reality of their lives, or even in order to try and blow a whistle on the Supreme Being. It was a far more selfish thing – wounded pride. Mother could have kept in touch, she let me go through all that grief while *she*, she was pottering around the shops in Crouch End. She could have fixed up some sort of gig with a séance or a medium, or even just written a letter or phoned. I would have understood. Well she wasn't going to push *my* buttons from beyond the grave. I was determined to blow the whistle on the whole set-up.

But the next day came and, standing on a tube platform contemplating the rim of a crushed styrofoam cup as if it contained some further relevation, I began to waver. I sat at my desk all morning in a daze, not that that matters. Then, at lunch time, I went and sat in a café in a daze.

When I got back to my desk after lunch the phone rang. It was Mother.

'I just called to see how you are.'

'I'm fine, Mother.'

'I called while you were out and spoke to some girl. Did she give you the message?'

'No, Mother.'

'I told her specifically to give you the message, to write it down. What's the matter with the people in your office?'

'Nothing, Mother. She probably forgot.'

Mother sighed. For her, neglected phone messages had always represented the very acme of Babylonian decadence. 'So what are you doing?'

'Working, Mother.'

'You're a little sulky today. What's the matter, didn't you sleep?'

'No, I didn't. I found yesterday all a bit much.'

'You'll adjust, kid. Come over tonight and meet Christos, he's a friend of mine – a Greek Cypriot – he runs a wholesale fruit business, but he writes in his spare time. You'll like him.'

'Yeah, I think I saw his photo at your place yesterday. Is he dead, Mother?'

'Of course he's dead. Be here by 8.00. I'm cooking. And bring some of your shirts, you can iron them here.' She hung up on me.

Ray, who works at the desk opposite, was looking at me strangely when I put down the receiver.

'Are you OK?' he said. 'It sounded like you were saying "Mother" on the phone just now.'

I felt tongue-tied and incoherent. How could I explain this away? 'No . . . no, ah . . . I wasn't saying "Mother", it was "Mudder", a guy called Mudder, he's an old friend of mine.'

Ray didn't look convinced. We'd worked with each other for quite a while and he knew most of what went on with me, but what could I say? I couldn't tell him who it *really* was. I'd never live down the ignominy of having a mother who phoned me at the office.

Ward 9

'Ha ha ha, ha-ha . . . Hoo, h', hoo, far, far and away, a mermaid sings in the silky sunlight.' An idiot cooed to himself on the park bench that stood at the crest of the hill. Below him the greensward stretched down to the running track. In the middle distance the hospital squatted among the houses, a living ziggurat, thrusting out of a crumbling plain.

The idiot's hair had been chopped into a ragged tonsure. He wore a blue hooded anorak and bell-bottomed corduroy trousers, and rocked as he sang. As I passed by I looked into his face; it was a face like the bench he sat on, a sad, forlorn piece of municipal furniture – although the morning sun shone bright, this face was steadily being drizzled on.

This particular idiot lay outside my jurisdiction. He was, as it were, un-gazetted. I knew that by ignoring the opportunity to indulge in the sickly bellyburn of self-piteous caring, I was facing up to an occupational challenge. If I was to have any success in my new job I would need to keep myself emotionally inviolate, walled off. For, this morning, I was to begin an indefinite appointment as art therapist, attached to Ward 9. My destination was the squat fifteen-storey building that rose up ahead of me, out of the tangled confluence of Camden Town.

I bounced down the hill, the decrease in altitude matched pace for pace by the mounting density of the air. The freshness of the atmosphere on Parliament Hill gave way to the contaminated cotton wool of ground-floor, summer London. Already, at 8.45 a.m., the roads around Gospel Oak were solidly coagulated with metal while shirtsleeved drivers sat and blatted out fumes.

As I picked my way through the streets the hospital appeared and then disappeared. Its very vastness made its sight seem problematic. In one street the horizon would flukily exclude it in such a convincing way that it might never have existed, but when I rounded the corner there was its flank rearing up – the grey-blue haunch of some massive whale – turning away from me, sending up a terrace of concrete flats with a lazy flip of its giant tail.

I walked and walked and the hospital never seemed to get any closer. Its sloping sides were banded with mighty balconies, jutting concrete shelves the size of aircraft carrier flight decks. The front of the building was hidden behind a series of zigzagging walkways and ramps that rose in crisscross patterns from the lower ground to the third floor. At the hospital's feet and cuddled in the crook of its great wings-for-arms, were tumbles of auxiliary buildings: nurses' flatlets; parking fortlets; generator units two storeys high, housed in giant, venetian-blind-slatted boxes; and ghostly incinerators, their concrete walls and chimneys blackened with some awful stain.

I rounded the end of the street and found myself, quite suddenly, at the bottom of a ramp that led straight up to the main entrance. The two previous times I had been to the hospital it was a working wasps' nest in full diurnal swing. But now, their photoelectric cells disconnected, the main doors to the hospital were wedged open with orange milk crates. I picked my way through the long, low foyer, past the shop, at this hour still clad in its roll-over steel door, and in between miscellaneous islands of freestanding chairs, bolted together in multiples of two, seemingly at random. They were thinly upholstered in the same blue fabric as the floor covering. The room was lit by flickering strips of overhead neon, so that the whole effect was ghostly; the overwhelming impression was that this was a place of transit, an air terminal for the dying. It was impossible to differentiate the ill from the dossers who had leaked in from the streets and piled their old-clothes forms into the plastic chairs. All were reduced and diminished by the hospital's sterile bulk into untidy parasites. The occasional nurse, doctor or auxiliary walked by briskly. They were uniformed and correct, clearly members of some other, genetically distinct, grouping.

In the glassed-in corridor that led to the lifts there was an exhibition of paintings – not by the patients, but by some pale disciple of a forgotten landscape school. The etiolated blues and greens chosen to take the place of hills and plains were flattened to sheens behind glass, which reflected the dead architectural centre of the hospital: an atrium where a scree of cobblestones supported uncomfortable concrete tubs, which in turn sprouted spindly, spastic trees.

I shared the lift to the ninth floor with a silent young man in green, laced at hip and throat. His sandy, indented temples with their gently pulsing veins aroused in me an attack of itchy squeamishness – I had to touch what repelled me. I scratched the palms of my hands and longed to take off my shoes and scratch the soles of my feet. The itch spread over my body like a hive and still I couldn't take my eyes off that pulsing tube of blood, so close to both surface and bone.

At the ninth floor the sandy man straightened up, sighed, and disappeared off down a corridor with an entirely human shrug.

I'd been on to the ward before, albeit briefly, when Dr Busner had shown me round after the interview. What had struck me then and what struck me again now was the difference in smell between Ward 9 and the rest of the hospital. Elsewhere the air was a flat filtered brew; superficially odourless and machined, but latent with a remembered compound of dynasties of tea bags – squeezed between thumb and plastic spoon – merging into extended families of bleaching, disinfecting froths and great vanished tribes of plastic bags. But in Ward 9 the air had a real quality, it clamped itself over your face like a pad of cotton wool, soaked through with the sweet chloroform of utter sadness.

A short corridor led from the mouth of the lift to the central association area of the ward. This was a roughly oblong space with the glassed-off cabinet of the nurses' station on the short lift side; a dining area to the right looking out through a long strip of windows over the city; to the left were the doors to various offices and one-to-one treatment rooms; and straight ahead another short corridor led to the two dormitories.

Every attempt had been made to present Ward 9 as an ordinary sort of place where people were treated for mental illnesses. There were bulletin boards positioned around the association area festooned with notices, small ads, flyers for theatrical performances by groups of hospital staff, clippings from newspapers, drawings and cartoons by the patients. Over in the dining area a few of the tables had rough clay sculptures blobbed on them, left there like psychotic turds. I assumed that they were the products of my predecessor's last art therapy session. Around the open part of the area there were scattered chairs, the short-legged, upholstered kind you only find in institutions. And everywhere the eye alighted – the dining area, the nurses' station, dotted in the open area – were ashtrays. Ashtrays on stands, cut-glass ashtrays, lopsided spiral clay ashtrays, ashtrays bearing the names of famous beers; all of them overflowing with butts.

There are two kinds of institution that stand alone on the issue of smoking. Whereas everywhere else you go you encounter barrages of signs enjoining you to desist, slashing your cigarette through with impeprious red lines, in psychiatric wards and police stations the whole atmosphere positively cries out to you, 'Smoke! Smoke! We don't mind, we understand, we like smoking!' Ward 9 was no exception to this rule. Empty at this hour (the patients had no reason to get up, they didn't roll over in their beds at 8.00 sharp and think to themselves, 'Ooh! I must get up quickly and have my shot of thorazine . . .'), the whole ward still whirled and eddied with last night's acrid work.

I walked down the short corridor to the nurses' station. A young man sat behind the desk completely absorbed in a dog-eared paperback. He wore a black sweat shirt and black Levis; his sneakered feet, propped on the cluttered shelf of clipboards and Biros, pushed the rest of him back and up on two wheels of his swivel chair. As I stood and observed him, he rocked gently from side to side, his body unconsciously mirroring the short, tight arcs that his eyes made across the page.

I shuffled my feet a little on the linoleum to warn him that he was no longer alone. 'Good morning.'

He looked up from his book with a smile. 'Hi. What can I do you for?'

'I'm Misha Gurney, the new art therapist, I start on the ward today and Dr Busner asked me to come in early to get a feel for things.'

'Well, hello Misha Gurney, I'm Tom.' Tom swung his feet off the ledge and proffered a hand. It was a slim, white hand, prominently bony at the wrist with long, tapering fingers. His handshake was light and dry but firm. His voice had the contrived mellowness of some Hollywood pilgrim paterfamilias. There was something unsettling in the contrast between this and his beautiful face: sandalwood skin and violet eyes. The body, under the stretchy black clothes, moved in an epicene, undulant way. 'Well, there's not a lot to see at this time. Zack isn't even in yet. He's probably just getting out of bed.' Tom rolled his lovely eyes back in their soft, scented sockets as if picturing the psychiatrist's matitudinal routine. 'How about some tea?'

'Yeah, great.'

'How do you take it?'

'Brown – no sugar.'

I followed Tom down the corridor that led to the staff offices and the consultation rooms. There was a small kitchenette off to one side. Tom hit the lights, which flickered once and then sprang into a hard, flat, neon glare. He squeaked around the lino in his sneakers. I examined the handwritten notices carefully taped to the kitchen cabinets. After a while I said, 'What do you do here, Tom?'

'Oh, I'm a patient.'

'I assume you're not on a section?'

He laughed. 'Oh, no. No, of course not, I'm a voluntary committal. A first-class volunteer, exemplary courage, first in line to be called for the mental health wars.' Again the light mocking irony, but not mad in any way, without the fateful snicker-snack of true schizo-talk.

'You don't seem too disturbed.'

'No, I'm not, that's why they let me go pretty much where I please and do pretty much what I want, as long as I live on the ward. You see, I'm a rare bird.' A downward twist of the corner of a sculpted mouth, 'The medication actually works for me. Zack doesn't really like it, but it's true. As long as I take it consistently I'm fine, but every time they've discharged me in the past, somehow I've managed to forget and then all hell breaks loose.'

'Meaning . . . ?'

'Oh, fits, delusions, hypermania, the usual sorts of things. I carry the Bible around with me and try and arrange spontaneous exegetical seminars in the street. You know, you've seen plenty of crazies, I'll bet.'

'But . . . but, you'll forgive me, but I'm not altogether convinced. If you're on any quantity of medication . . .'

'I know, I should be a little more slowed down, a little fuzzier around the edges, *un peu absent.* Like I say, I'm an exception, a one-off, an abiding proof of the efficacy of Hoffman La Roche's products. Zack doesn't like it at all.'

The kettle whistled and Tom poured the water into two styrofoam cups. We mucked around with plastic dipsticks and extracted the distended bags of tea, then wandered back to the association area. Tom led me over to the windows. The lower decks of the hospital poked out below us. Up here on the ninth floor, more than ever, one could appreciate the total shape of the building – a steeply sloping bullion bar, each ascending storey slightly smaller than the one below it. On the wide balcony beneath us figures were wafting about, clad in hospital clothing, green smocks and blue striped nightdresses, all bound on with tapes. The figures moved with infinite diffidence, as if wishing to offer no offence to the atmosphere. They trundled in slow eddies towards the edge of the balcony and stood rocking from heel to toe, or from side to side, and then moved back below us and out of sight again.

'Chronics,' said Tom, savouring the word as he slurped his tea. 'There's at least sixty of them down there. Quite a different ball game. Not a lot of use for your clay and sticky-backed paper down there. There's a fat ham of a man down there who went mad one day and drank some bleach. They replaced his oesophagus with a section cut from his intestine. On a quiet night you can hear him farting through his mouth. That's a strange sound, Misha.'

I remained silent, there was nothing to say. Behind me I could hear the ward beginning to wake up and start the day. There were footsteps and brisk salutations. An auxiliary came into the association area from the lift and began to mop the floor with studious inefficiency, pushing the zinc bucket around with a rubber foot. We stood and drank tea and looked out over the chronics' balcony to the Heath beyond, which rose up, mounded and green, with the sun shining on it, while the hospital remained in shadow. It was like some separate arcadia glimpsed down a long corridor. I fancied I could see the park bench I'd passed some forty minutes earlier and on it a blue speck: the tonsured idiot, still rocking, still free.

Zack Busner came hurrying in from the lift. He was a plump, fiftyish sort of man, with iron-grey hair brushed back in a widow's peak. He carried a bulging briefcase, the soft kind fastened with two straps. The straps were undone, because the case contained too many files, too many instruments, too many journals, too many books and a couple of unwrapped, fresh, cream-cheese bagels. Busner affected striped linen or poplin suits and open-necked shirts; his shoes were anomalous – black, steel-capped, policeman's shit kickers. He spotted me over by the window with Tom and, turning towards his office, gestured to me to follow him, with a quick, flicking kind of movement. I dropped my foam beaker into a bin, smiled at Tom and walked after the consultant.

'Well Misha, I see you've found a friend already.' Busner smiled at me quizzically and ushered me to the chair that faced his across the desk. We sat. His office was tiny, barely larger than a cubicle, and quite bare apart from a few textbooks and four artworks. Most psychiatrists try to humanise their offices with such pieces. They think that even the most awful rubbish somehow indicates that they have 'the finer feelings'. Busner's artworks were unusually dominant, four large clay bas-reliefs, one on each wall. These rectangular slabs of miniature upheaval, earth-coloured and unglazed, seemed to depict imaginary topographies.

'Yes, he's personable enough. What's the matter with him?'

'Actually, Tom's quite interesting.' Busner said this without a trace of irony and began fiddling around on the surface of his desk, as if looking for a tobacco pipe. 'He's subject to what I'd call a mimetic psychosis . . .'

'Meaning?'

'Meaning he literally mimics the symptoms of all sorts of other mental illnesses, at least those that have any kind of defined pathology: schizophrenia, chronic depression, hypermania, depressive psychosis. The thing about Tom's impersonations, or should I say the impersonations of his disease, is that they're bad performances. Tom carefully reiterates every recorded detail of aberrant behaviour, but with a singular lack of conviction; it's wooden and unconvincing. Your father would have found it fascinating to watch.'

'Well, I find it pretty fascinating myself, even if I don't have quite the same professional involvement. What phase is Tom in now?'

'You tell me.'

'Well, he seems to be playing the "Knowing Patient Introduces Naive Art Therapist to Hell of Ward" role.'

'And how well is he doing it?'

'Well, now you mention it, not too convincingly.'

Busner had abandoned his search for a pipe, if that's what it had been. He now turned and presented me with his outline set against the window. In profile I could see that he was in reality rather eroded, and that the impression of barely contained energy which he seemed determined to project was an illusion as well. Busner sat talking to me, rolling and then unrolling the brown tongue of a knitted tie he wore yanked around his neck. Overall, he reminded me of nothing so much as a giant frog.

Behind him light and then shadow moved across the face of the hospital at a jerky, unnatural speed. The clouds were whipping away overhead, out of sight. All I could see was their reflection on the hospital's rough, grey, barnacle-pitted skin.

The hospital was big. Truly big. With its winking lights, belching vents and tangled antennae, it slid away beneath the cloudscape. Its bulk was such that it suggested to the viewer the possibility of spaceships (or hospitals) larger still, which might engulf it, whole, through some docking port. The hospital was like this. I couldn't judge whether the rectangles I saw outlined on the protruding corner opposite Dr Busner's office were glass bricks or windows two storeys high. The street lay too far below to give me a sense of scale. I was left just with the hospital and the scudding shadows of the racing clouds.

Busner had given up his tie-rolling and taken up with an ashtray on his desk. This was crudely fashioned out of a spiralled snake of clay, varnished and painted with a bilious yellow glaze. Busner ran his fleshy digit around and around the rim as he said, 'I'd like you to stick close to me this morning, Misha. If you are to have any real impact on what we're trying to do here you need to be properly acquainted with the whole process of the ward: how we assess patients, how we book them in, how we decide on treatment. If you shadow me this morning, you can then get to know some of the patients informally this afternoon.'

'That sounds OK.'

'We've also got a ward meeting at noon which will give you an opportunity to get to know all your fellow workers and appreciate how they fit into the scheme of things.'

Busner set down the turd of clay on his desk with a clack and stood up. I stepped back to allow him to get round the desk and to the door. Despite being the senior consultant in the psychiatric department, Busner had about as much office space as a post-room boy. I followed him back down the short corridor to the association area. By now the sun had risen up behind the clouds and the bank of windows on the far side of the dining area shone brightly. Silhouetted against them was a slow line of patients, shuffling towards the nurses' station where they were picking up their morning medication.

The patients were like piles of empty clothes, held upright by some static charge. Behind the double sliding panes of glass which fronted the nurses' station sat two young people. One consulted a chart, the other selected pills and capsules from compartments in a moulded plastic tray. They then handed these over to the patient at the head of the queue, together with a paper beaker of water, which had a pointed base, rendering it unputdownable, like a best seller.

'Not ideal, but necessary.' Busner cupped his right hand as if to encapsulate the queue. 'We have to give medication. Why? Because without it we couldn't calm down our patients enough to actually talk to them and find out what the matter is. However, once we've medicated them they're often too displaced to be able to tell us anything useful. Catch-22.'

Busner cut through the queue to the dining area, muttering a few good mornings as he gently pushed aside his flock. We sat down at a table where a young woman in a frayed white coat was sipping a muddy Nescafé. Busner introduced us.

'Jane, this is Misha Gurney, Misha, Jane Bowen – Jane is the senior registrar here. Misha is joining us to manage art therapy – quite a coup, I think. His father, you know, was a friend of mine, a close contemporary.'

Jane Bowen extended her hand with an overarm gesture that told me she couldn't have cared less about me, or my antecedents, but because she thought of herself as an essentially open-minded and kind person she was going to show me a welcoming smile. I clasped her hand briefly and looked at her. She was slight, with one of those bodies that seemed to be all concavities – her cheeks were hollowed, her eyes scooped, her neck centrally cratered. Under her loose coat I sensed her body as an absence, her breasts as inversions. Her hair was tied back in one long plait, held by an ethnic leather clasp. Her top lip quested towards her styrofoam beaker. The unrolled, frayed ends of her stretchy pullover protruded beyond the frayed cuffs of her cotton coat. Her pockets were stuffed full. They overflowed with pens, thermometers, syringes, watches, stethoscopes, packets of tobacco and boxes of matches. The lapels of the coat were festooned with name badges, homemade badges, political badges and badges of cut-out cartoon characters: Roadrunner, Tweetypie, Bugs Bunny and Scooby Doo.

'Well, Misha, any ideas on how your participation in the ward's creative life will help to break the mould?' She gestured towards an adjacent table, where several misshapen clay vessels leant against one another like drunken Rotarians.

'Well, if the patients want to make clay ashtrays, let them make clay ashtrays.' I lit a cigarette and squinted at her through the smoke.

'Of course they could always try and solve The Riddle.'

I hadn't noticed as I sat down, but now I saw that she was shifting the four pieces of a portable version of The Riddle around on the melamine surface in front of her. Her fingers were bitten to the quick and beyond. Busner flushed and shifted uneasily in his chair.

'Erumph! Well . . . bankrupt stock and all that. We have rather a lot of The Riddle sets around the ward. I err . . . bought them up for a pittance, you know. At any rate, I still have some faith in them and the patients seem to like them.'

Busner had been responsible for designing, or 'posing', The Riddle in the early Seventies. It was one of those pop psychological devices that had had a brief vogue. Busner himself had been forging a modest career as a kind of media psychologist with a neat line in attacking the mores of conventional society. The Riddle tied in with this and with the work that Busner was doing at his revolutionary Concept House in Willesden. His involvement with the early development of the Quantity Theory also dated from that period.

Busner was a frequent trespasser on the telly screens of my childhood. Always interviewing, being interviewed, discussing an interview that had just been re-screened, or appearing in those discussion programmes where paunchy people sat on uncomfortable steel rack-type chairs in front of a woven backdrop. Busner's media activities had dropped away as he grew paunchier. He was now remembered, if at all, as the poser of The Riddle – and that chiefly because the short-lived popularity of this 'enquire-within tool' had spawned millions of square acrylic slabs of just the right size to get lost and turn up in idiosyncratic places around the house, along with spillikins, Lego blocks and hairpins. In fact it had become something of a catch-phrase to cry as you dug a tile out from between the carpet and the underlay, or from behind a radiator, 'I'm solving The Riddle!' Eventually The Riddle itself – what you were actually meant to do with the four square slabs in bright pastel shades, which you got with The Riddle set – was entirely forgotten.

'I'm sorry Zack, I didn't mean to sound caustic.' Jane Bowen placed a surprisingly tender hand on Busner's poplin sleeve.

'That's all right, I think I still deserve it, even after all these years. The funny thing is that I did believe in The Riddle. I suppose a cynic would say that anyone would believe in something that brought in enough income to buy a four-bedroom house in Redington Road.'

'Even shrinks have to have somewhere to live,' said Jane Bowen. The two of them smiled wryly over this comment – a little more wryly than it strictly merited.

'Well, we're not helping anybody sitting here, are we?' said Busner. Once again this was a key motif. It had been his catch-phrase on all those discussion and interview programmes – always delivered with falsetto emphasis on the 'helping'. The catch-phrase, like The Riddle, outlived Busner's own popularity. I remember seeing him towards the very end of his TV sojourn, when he was reduced to going on one of those 'celebrity' game-shows where the celebrities sit in a rack of cubicles. Zack trotted out his obligatory line and the contestant dutifully pushed the button on the tape machine – as I recall, she ended up winning a suite of patio furniture. It was really quite a long way from the spirit of radical psychology. Now Busner was using the phrase again, clearly with a sense of irony – but somehow not altogether; there was also something else there, a strange kind of pride almost.

'I want you to shadow me while I do the ward round.' Busner guided me by placing his palm on my shoulder. We both nodded to Jane Bowen, who had forgotten us already and fallen into conversation with a nurse. Busner stashed his bursting briefcase behind the nurses' station, after extracting from it with difficulty a clipboard and some sheets of blank paper. We walked side by side down the short corridor that led to the entrance to the two wards. For some reason Busner and I were unwilling to precede one another, and as a result people coming in the other direction had to crush up against the walls to get around us. We were like a teenage couple – desperate to avoid any break in contact that might let in indifference.

The dormitories were laid out in a series of bays, four beds in each bay and four bays to the dormitory. Each bay was about the size of an average room, the beds laid out so as to provide the maximum surrounding space for each occupant to turn into their own private space. Some of the patients had stuck photographs and posters up on the walls with masking tape, some had placed knick-knacks on the shelves, and others had done nothing and lay on their beds, motionless, like ascetics or prisoners.

Busner kept up a commentary for my benefit as we stopped and consulted with each patient. The first one we came to was a pop-eyed man in his mid-thirties. He was wearing a decrepit Burton suit which was worn to a shine at knee and elbow. He was sitting on the easy chair by his bed and staring straight ahead. His shoulder-length hair was scraped down from a severe central parting. His eyes weren't just popping, they were half out of their sockets, resembling ping-pong balls with the pupils painted on to them like black spots.

'Clive is prone to bouts of mania, aren't you, Clive?'

'Good morning, Dr Busner.'

'How are you feeling, Clive?'

'Fine, thank you, Doctor.'

'Any problems with your medication? You'll be leaving us soon, won't you?'

'In answer to your first question, no. In answer to your second, yes.'

'Clive likes everything to be stated clearly, don't you, Clive?'

At the time I thought Busner was being sarcastic. In fact – as I realised later – this wasn't the case. If anything, Busner was being solicitous. He knew that Clive liked to expatiate on his attitudes and methods; Busner was providing him with the opportunity.

'You're staring very fixedly at the opposite wall, Clive, would you like to tell Misha why this is?'

I followed his line of sight; he was looking at a poster which showed two furry little kittens both dangling by their paws from the handle of a straw basket. The slogan underneath in curly script proclaimed, 'Faith isn't Faith until it's all you're hanging on to.'

'The kitten is powerful.' Clive smiled enigmatically and pointed with a dirt-rimmed nail, 'That kitten holds in its paws the balance, the egg of creation and more.' Having pronounced he lapsed back into a rigid silence. Busner and I left him.

Although there were only thirty or so patients on the ward they soon resolved themselves, not into names or individuals, but into distinct groups. Busner's catchment area for his ward was an L-shaped zone that extended from the hospital in one dog-leg into the very centre of the city. The hospital pulled in its sustenance from every conceivable level of society. But on Ward 9 insanity had proved a great leveller. A refugee sometimes seems to have no class. The English depend on class, to the extent that whenever two English people meet, they spend nanoseconds in high-speed calculation. Every nuance of accent, every detail of apparel, every implication of vocabulary, is analysed to produce the final formula. This in turn provides the coordinates that will locate the individual and determine the Attitude. The patients on Ward 9 had distanced themselves from this. They could not be gauged in such a fashion. Instead, I divided them up mentally into the following groups: thinniepukies, junkies, sads, schizes and maniacs. The first four groups were all represented about equally, whilst the fifth group was definitely in the ascendant; there were lots of maniacs on Ward 9 and by maniacs I mean not the culturally popular homicidal maniac, but his distant herbivorous cousin, hyper, rather than homicidal, and manic, rather than maniacal.

As Tom had already characterised himself earlier that morning, hypermanic types are lecturers; extramural, al fresco professors, who, like increasingly undulant or syncopated Wittgensteins, address the world at large on a patchwork syllabus made up of Kabbalah, astrology, tarot, numerology and Bible (specifically Revelations) study. They are sad-mad, they know they are ill, they have periods of conformity, but they are always somehow out of joint.

'Art therapy is very popular here, Misha.' Busner detained me in the vestibule between the two wards. 'We can't keep the patients sufficiently occupied, they have treatment sessions of various kinds in the mornings, but in the afternoons you'll be all they have to look forward to. Sometimes we can arrange an outing of some kind, or a friend or relative will be allowed to take them out on the Heath, but otherwise they're cooped up here in a fuddled daze.'

We went on into the women's dormitory. Here things seemed, at first, different. On the men's dormitory Busner and I had spoken with a few isolated individuals, backed off into their individual bays. But here the patients seemed to be associating with one another. They reclined on beds chatting, or sat round the formica-topped tables which formed a central reservation.

A skeleton with long, lush hair rocked on a bed in the bay to our right, an obscenely large catheter protruding out of her lolly-stick arm. Busner took me in under tow and introduced us.

'Hilary isn't that keen on eating – or at least she is sometimes, but she doesn't really like the nutritional side-effects of food. Hilary, this is Misha Gurney, he's our new art therapist.' Hilary stopped rocking and gave me a level smile from underneath neatly coiffed chestnut bangs.

'Hello. I'll look forward to this afternoon. I like to paint, I like watercolours. These are some of mine.' She gestured towards the wall at the head of the bed, where an area about a foot square was tiled with tiny watercolours, terribly painfully precise little paintings – all portraits, apparently of young women. Busner wandered off, but I remained and walked to the head of the bed, so that I could examine the pictures thoroughly. They had been executed with a fanatical attention to the detail of make-up and hair which made them almost grotesque. Hilary and I sat sideways to each other. With her neck canted around so that she could face me, Hilary's greaseproof-paper skin stretched, until I could see the twisted, knotted coils of tendon and artery that lay within.

'They're very good. Who are all these people?'

'They're my friends. I paint them from photographs.'

'Your pictures are very detailed. How do you manage it?'

'Oh, I have special pens and brushes. I'll show you later.'

I left Hilary and went over to where Busner was sitting at one of the tables in the central area of the dormitory.

'Has Hilary been telling you about her friends?'

'Yes . . .'

'Hilary doesn't have any friends, as such. She cuts pictures of models out of advertisements in magazines, then she paints over them. She's been in and out of this ward for the past three years. Every time she comes in she looks like she does now. She's so close to death we have to put her on a drip. She's usually completely demented; the amino acids have been leeched out of her brain. After she's been on the drip for a while we transfer her to a tight regime of supervised eating based on a punishment/reward system, and at the same time she undergoes an intensive course of psychotherapy with Jane Bowen. Jane is very much the expert on eating disorders. After six weeks to two months Hilary is back to a healthy weight and eating sensibly. She'll leave and we can predict her return usually to within the day – some four months later.'

'I thought a lot of anorexics and bulimics grew out of it?'

'To some extent, but there's always a hard core and at the moment it seems to be growing. These long-term anorexics are different, they're placid, resigned and apparently unconscious of any motivation. The temporaries tend to be wilful, obstinate and obviously powerfully neurotic. These hard-cores, like Hilary, could almost be psychologically blameless. Some of them even have fairly stable relationships. They're at a loss to explain what comes over them, it seems to be somehow external, imposed from elsewhere.'

I should have been paying attention to what Busner was saying, but I couldn't concentrate. For a start there was the strangeness of the situation – I'd only ever spent isolated periods of a few minutes on psychiatric wards before. I had known what to expect in broad terms, but it was the relentlessness of the ambience that was beginning to get to me. There was something cloacal about the atmosphere in the women's ward. None of the patients seemed to have bothered to dress, they sat here and there talking, wearing combinations of night and day clothes. There was a preponderance of brushed cotton. I sensed damp, and smelt oatmeal, porridge, canteen; indefinable, closed-in odours.

I could walk away from the tonsured idiot on the Heath, but inside Ward 9 I was trapped. And these people weren't pretending. They weren't closet neurotics or posing eccentrics, Bohemians. They were the real thing. Real loss of equilibrium, real confusion, real sadness, that wells up from inside like an unstaunchable flow of blood from a severed artery. I felt my gorge rising. I felt my forehead, it was sandpaper-dry. Busner was neglecting me and talking to a pneumatic nurse. The nurses on Ward 9 didn't wear a uniform as such, rather they affected various items of medical garb: tunics, coats and smocks, nameplates and watches pinned at the breast. This nurse had a man's Ingersoll attached by a safety-pin to her jacket lapel. She had blonde baby curls, bee-stung lips and the creamy, slightly spongy complexion that invariably goes with acrid coital sweats. I forced myself to listen to what they were saying, and fought down nausea with concentration.

'Take her out to the optician then, Mimi, if she has to go.'

'Oh, she does, Zack, she can barely see a yard in front of herself. She can't be expected to deal with reality if she can't see it.' The voluptuous Mimi was squidged on to the corner of the table. Behind her stood a short woman in her thirties with the hydrocephalic brow and oblique domed crop of an intelligent child. She stared at me with sightless eyes.

'Rachel shouldn't really be off the ward, considering the medication she's on.'

'But Zack, it's a walk down to the parade, ten minutes at most. Give her a break.'

'Oh, all right.'

'Come on then, Rachel, get your coat on.' Rachel bounced away into one of the bays. Mimi lifted herself off the edge of the table and winked at me in a languid way.

'Come on, Misha, we've got an admission for you to see. I'll leave you at the front desk. Anthony Valuam will pick you up and take you down to casualty.' We walked out of the women's dormitory and back to the association area. Tom, my friend from the earlier part of the morning, was back behind the nurses' station, reading his dog-eared Penguin. Busner despatched me to wait with him by giving me a gentle shove in the small of my back, then he crooked his finger at a scrofulous youth in a tattered sharkskin suit who sat smoking and disappeared with him towards his office. Tom put down his book and treated me to another little conspiratorial exchange.

'Has the good doctor given you a little tour?'

'We've been round the ward, yes.'

'Beginning to catch on yet?'

'What do you mean?'

'Well, who did you get introduced to? No, don't tell me. Let me guess. You talked to Clive and then you saw a lot of other male patients quite quickly until you ended up scrutinising Hilary's watercolours.'

'Err . . . yes.'

'And did Zack come out with his catch-phrase?'

'Yes, when we were talking to Jane Bowen.'

'Thought so. He's so predictable. That's one of the truly therapeutic aspects of this place, the unfailing regularity of Dr Busner. What are you doing now?'

'I'm meant to be going down to casualty to sit in on an admission with a Dr Valuam.'

'Tony, yeah. Well, he's my kind of a shrink, not like Dr B; more practical like, more chemical.'

A door opened to the right of the nurses' station which I hadn't noticed before. A very short man came out of it and with neat movements locked it behind him, using a key that was on an extremely large gaoler's bunch. He turned to face me. He was a funny little specimen. He had wispy fair hair teased ineffectually around his bare scalp. It wasn't as if he was going bald, it was more as if he'd never grown any hair to begin with. This impression was supported by the watery blue eyes, and the nose and chin which were soft and seemingly boneless. He wore a stiff blue synthetic suit of Seventies cut and vinyl shoes.

'You must be Misha Gurney. I'm Anthony Valuam.' His handshake was twisted and rubberised, like holding a retort clamp in a laboratory, but his voice was absurdly mellow and basso. A voice-over rather than a real voice. His foetal face registered and then dismissed my surprise; he must have been used to it. Tom was stifling an obvious giggle behind his paperback. Valuam ignored him and I followed suit. We walked off down the short corridor to the lift. Valuam launched into an introduction.

'It's very unusual to have an admission through casualty at this time of day. On this ward we deal almost exclusively with referrals, but we know this particular young man and there are very good reasons why he should be treated on Ward 9.'

'And they are . . . ?'

'I don't wish to be enigmatic, but you'll see.'

Valuam fell silent. We waited for the lift, which arrived and slid open and closed and then dropped us down through the hospital to casualty, which was situated in the first sub-basement. The lift stopped on every floor, to take on and drop passengers.

The architects, interior designers and colour consultants who had made the hospital were not insensitive to the difficulties posed by such a project, they had earnestly striven to make this vast, labyrinthine structure seem habitable and human in scale. To this end each floor had been given slightly different wall and floor coverings, slightly different-shaped neon strip-light covers, slightly different concrete cornicing, slightly different steel ventilation-unit housings and slightly different colourings: virology an emphatic pale blue, urology a teasing (but tasteful) green, surgery and cardiology a resilient pink and so on. At each floor the patients and their orderlies were also different colours. The faces and hands of the patients as they were transferred from ward to ward, on steel trolleys, in wheelchairs as heavy as siege engines, were stained with disease, as vividly as a pickled specimen injected with dye.

The orderlies were violently offhand; they manhandled the patients into the lifts like awkward, fifty-kilo bags of Spanish onions. Then they stood menacingly in the corners, lowering over their livid charges, their temples pulsing with insulting health. Occasionally a patient would be wheeled into the lift who was clearly the wrong colour for the direction we were headed in (this was evident as soon as the lift reached the next floor) and the orderly would back the chair or table out of the lift again, the faces of both porter and cargo registering careful weariness at the prospect of another purgatorial wait.

We reached the sub-basement. Valuam turned to the left outside of the lift and led me along the corridor. Down here the colour scheme was a muted beige. The persistent susurration of the air-conditioning was louder than on the ninth floor and was backed up by a deeper throb of generators. The industrial ambience was further underscored by the pieces of equipment which stood at intervals along the corridor, their steel rods, rubber wheels, plastic cylinders and dependant ganglia of electric wiring betrayed no utility.

The beige-tiled floor was scarred with dirty wheel tracks. We whipped past doors with cryptic signs on them: 'Hal-G Cupboard', 'Ex-Offex.Con', 'Broom Station'. The corridor now petered out into a series of partitioned walkways which Valuam picked his way through with complete assurance. We entered a wide area, although the ceiling here was no higher than in the corridor. On either side were soft-sided booths, curtained off with beige plastic sheeting. The beige lights overhead subsonically wittered. We passed stooped personnel – health miners who laboured here with heavy equipment to extract the diseased seam. They were directed by taller foremen, recognisable by their white coats, worn like flapping parodies. Valuam turned to the right, to the left, to the left again. In the unnatural light I felt terribly sensitive as we passed booths where figures lay humped in pain. I felt the tearing, cutting and mashing of tissue and bone like an electrified cotton-wool pad clamped across my mouth and nose.

At length Valuam reached the right booth. He swept aside the curtain. A youth of twenty or twenty-one cowered in a plastic scoop chair at the back of the oblong curtained area. On the left a fiercely preserved woman leant against the edge of the examination couch. On the right stood a wheeled aluminium table. Laid out on it were tissues, a kidney dish of tongue depressors, and a strip of disposable hypodermics wound out of a dispenser box.

Valuam pushed a sickly yellow sharps disposal bin to one side with his blue foot and pulled out another plastic chair. He stretched and shook hands with the woman, who murmured 'Anthony'. Valuam sat down facing the youth and untucked his clipboard from the crook of his arm. It was left for me to lean awkwardly in the opening, looming over the gathering like a malevolent interloper. I was conspicuously ignored.

'Good morning, Simon,' said Valuam. Simon drew a frond of wool out from the cuff of his pullover and let it ping inaudibly back into a tight spiral. Simon was wearing a very handsome pullover, made up of twenty or so irregular wool panels in shades of beige, grey and black. He pinged the thread again and fell to worrying a bloody stalk of cuticle that had detached itself from his gnawed paw.

'Simon and I felt it would be a good idea if he came to stay on the ward with you for a while, Anthony.' The woman uncrossed her ankles and hopped up on to the examination table. Her steely hair was sharply bobbed, one bang pointed at the youth who was her indigent son. She took a shiny clutch bag from under her arm, popped it open and withdrew a tube of mints which she aimed at me.

'Polo?'

'Err . . . thanks.' I took one. She smiled faintly and took one herself.

'How do you feel about that, Simon?' Valuam held his foetal face on one side, his basso voice sounding concerned.

'S'alright.' Simon was rotating the cuticle stalk with the tip of a finger. He was also starting to rock back and forth.

Valuam consulted the papers attached to his clipboard. 'Mmm . . . mm . . .' He snuffled and ruffled the case notes while the steely-haired woman and I regarded one another peripherally. She really was pretty chic. At neck and wrist she was encircled with linked silver platelets cut into shapes; her clothes were made out of varieties of vicuna and rabbit; her stockings were so pure you could see the mulberry in them. I couldn't quite get the measure of why she was so blasé about Simon's voluntary committal. Genuine lack of caring? A defence mechanism? Something more sinister?

'You were discharged last October, Simon,' Valuam had found the right place, 'and went to the Galston Work Scheme. How did that go?'

'Oh, OK, I guess. I did some good things; worked on some of my constructions. I enjoyed it.' Simon had given up on the cuticle, he looked up at Valuam and spoke with some animation. His face was quite green in hue and distorted by weeping infections. It was like watching a colour screen where the tube has started to pack up.

'But now you're in pretty bad shape again, aren't you?'

'Yeah, I guess. I'm fed up with living with the bitch.' Simon's mother winced. 'She puts me under pressure the whole time. Do this, do that. It's no wonder I start to freak out.'

'I see. And freaking out means stopping your medication and stopping going to the Galston and stopping your therapy and ending up looking like this.'

Simon had relapsed into torpor before Valuam had finished speaking. The cuticle had claimed his whole attention again. We were left regarding the top of his unruly head.

Valuam sighed. He ticked some boxes on the sheet uppermost on the clipboard and twisted sideways on his plastic chair to face the woman. 'Well, I suppose he'd better come in for a few weeks then.'

'I'm glad you see it that way, Anthony.' She eased herself off the examination couch with a whoosh of wool and silk and patted herself down. 'Well, goodbye then, Simon. I'll come and see you at the weekend.'

'Bye, Mum, take it easy.' Simon didn't look up, he'd found some antiseptic and fell to swabbing his bleeding finger with tight little arcs. His mother smiled absently at Valuam as if acknowledging his sartorial failure. I stood to one side and she nodded at me as she swished out of the cubicle and away.

Valuam got up and scraped the chair back against the wall.

'I have someone to see here, Misha, would you mind taking Simon up to the ward?'

'I'm, er, not sure I'll be able to find my way back.'

'Oh, that's OK, Simon knows the layout of the hospital far better than he knows his own mind.'

I wasn't sure whether I was meant to share in this sick irony – but looking at Valuam's miscarried countenance I could see that he wasn't joking. Simon seemed not to have noticed.

I followed the abstraction of Simon's pullover back through the twisting lanes of the casualty examination area. Even before we'd gained the corridor I found that I'd completely lost my bearings. Simon, however, didn't hesitate, he plunged on unswervingly, walking with long fluid strides. We travelled like a couple arguing; he would make gains on me of some twenty yards and then I'd have to put on a spurt to catch up with him. To begin with I feared that he was actually trying to lose me, but whenever there was a choice of directions and he was some way ahead he waited until I was close enough to see which way he went.

The nature of the corridors we bowled along was perceptibly changing. The machines that stood at intervals against the corridor walls were becoming more obviously utilitarian – parts were now painted black rather than chromed or rubberised – they had petrol engines rather than electric pumps. The walls themselves were changing, they were losing their therapeutic hue and reverting to concrete colour, as was the floor. Lights were becoming exposed, first the odd neon tube was naked and then all of them.

This part of the hospital was beyond the world of work, it was a secret underworld. From time to time we would pass workers clad in strange suits of protective clothing: wearing rubberised aprons, or plastic face masks, or Wellington boots, or leather shoulder pads. They looked at us inscrutably. It was clear that they were intent on their jobs; maintaining the whine, stoking the hum, directing the howl. It was also clear that Simon wasn't taking me back to the ward, he had business here. I caught him on a corner.

'Where are we going, Simon?'

'To see something, something worth seeing. I promise you won't be angry.'

'Can you tell me what it is?'

'No.' He wheeled away, calling over his shoulder, 'Come on, it's not much further.'

The corridor walls gave way to sections of masonry. Embedded in them were the filled-in remains of long-dead windows. I realised that we had reached the place where the new hospital had been grafted on to its predecessor. There were the marks of cast-iron railings, pressed and faint, like fossilised grass stems. More than ever I sensed the great weight of the hospital crouching overhead. A dankness entered the air; at intervals trickling pools of water seeped up on to the floor. Eventually Simon stopped by a set of double doors, old doors belonging to the former hospital, the top halves glassed with many small panes. He pushed them apart on failing rails.

We were in some sort of conservatory. Round, twenty-five feet across, fifteen feet up the walls gave way to a dirty glass dome, which arched overhead, almost out of sight in the gloom. There was daylight here, filtering down weakly through the tarnished panes. Water dripped audibly. In the centre of the room stood a giant machine for doing things to people. This much was clear from the canted couch positioned halfway up its flank. Otherwise it resembled a giant microscope, the barrel obliquely filling the uncertain volume of the room, the lens pointing directly at the couch. The whole thing was festooned with hydraulic cabling. It had originally been painted a kitchen-cream colour but now it was corroded, atrophied.

Simon and I stood and looked.

'Good, isn't it.' His voice was full and resonant. He'd lost his sullen edge.

'Yes, very striking. What was it for?'

'Oh, I've no idea. I got left alone one night in casualty and just started wandering about, I found this. I don't think anyone's been here for years. Funny, really, because it's right in back of the MDR.'

'MDR?'

Simon beckoned me over to the grey-filmed window opposite the door we'd entered by. I circled the giant machine, stepping over the edge of the vast plate that riveted it to the floor. Bits had fallen off the machine – bolts, braces, other small components – but given the scale of the thing, they were large enough to bruise your shins if you knocked against them. Simon was vigorously rubbing the windowpane.

'Look, can you see?' There was no sense of sky, or the outside, but light came from somewhere. Outlining a squat blockhouse, clapboarded with massive concrete slabs. It was like some defence installation. 'That's the Mass Disaster Room. If there's ever a nuclear attack, or an earthquake, or something like that, that's where all the equipment is kept to deal with it.'

'Well, like what?'

'I don't know, no one will tell me. I only found out about it because I came across the door with the notice on it.'

We stood at the window for a while. The conservatory-like room, the giant machine, the blockhouse. All thinly lit by an invisible day. There was something eerie about the atmosphere. The eeriness that washes over when you step obliquely out of a populous area – from a crowded park into a little grey copse – and look behind you at the life that still goes on, children and dogs.

Back up in the ward Busner was hurrying about the place, gathering together all the staff members. A circle of chairs had been roughly arranged in the association area. Anthony Valuam and Jane Bowen were already seated and engaged in earnest discussion when we arrived. Valuam showed no curiosity about where we had been. Simon himself had reverted to sullen, disturbed type as soon as we arrived at the ninth floor. He disappeared into a shifting knot of movers and shakers and was gone from sight.

'Sit down, Misha, do sit down.' Busner flapped his poplin-bumped turkey-skin arms. I sat down next to Mimi, the voluptuous nurse, who had been and gone to the optician. The rest of the staff began to trickle into place, auxiliary as well as medical. There were canteen ladies here in nylon, elasticated hair covers, and psychiatric social workers with rolled-up newspaper supplements. They chatted to one another quite informally, swopping cigarettes and gesturing. The patients took no notice of this assembly – which to my mind more than anything else underlined their exclusion from the right-thinking world.

Busner called the meeting to order.

'Ahm! Hello everyone. We've a lot to get through today, so I'd like to get under way. We don't want to run over, the way we did last month. Before we come to the first item on the agenda I'd like to introduce to you all a new member of staff, Misha Gurney. Some of you will, no doubt, have heard of his father,' Busner's face purpled at the edges with sentimentality, 'who was a contemporary of mine and a dear friend. So it's an especial pleasure for me that Misha should be joining us on the ward as the new art therapist . . .'

'Wait till you hear what happened to the old art therapist . . . !' Before I had had time to wheel round in my chair and see who had whispered in my ear, Tom was gone, soft-shoe shuffling down the corridor.

From then on the meeting deteriorated into the usual trivial deliberations that – in my experience – seem to accompany all departmental meetings. There were discussions about the hours at which tea could be made, discussions about shift rostering, discussions about patients' visitors. My attention began to falter and then died away altogether. I was staring fixedly over the shoulder of a middle-aged woman who liaised with the ward on behalf of the local social services department. Through the two swing-doors, between her and the entrance to the dormitories, I could see Clive. He was staring at me fixedly, or so it seemed; his great globular eyes were incapable of anything but staring. He was rocking from side to side like a human metronome. If I narrowed my eyes it appeared as if his bizarre messianic hair-do was rhythmically pulsing out of the cheek of the middle-aged social worker. This trick hypnotised me.

Mimi jabbed me in the ribs. 'Misha, pay attention!'

Busner was saying something in my direction. 'Well Misha?' he said.

Mimi whispered, 'He's asking what you intend to do in the art therapy session this afternoon.'

I started guiltily. 'Urn . . . well . . . err. I intend really to, ah, introduce myself to the patients with a series of demonstrations of different techniques and then invite them to show their own work so that we can discuss it.'

This seemed to satisfy Busner. He turned to Jane Bowen and whispered something in her ear, she smiled and nodded, tapping a yellow biro stem on the edge of her clipboard.

Soon after this the meeting broke up. I drew Mimi to one side.

'Thanks for that, you saved my hide there. I was miles away.'

'Yeah, absurd isn't it. Zack's like most benevolent dictators, he seems to think that by letting us all discuss a load of trivia we'll feel that we have an important decision-making role in ward policy.'

'How long have you been working here?'

'Oh, quite a while. Ever since I qualified, in fact. There's something about this ward. You might say that it and I were made for one another.' The middle-aged social worker came over to where we were standing, Mimi introduced us and then they went off together to discuss a patient. The social worker was blushing furiously. It wasn't until later that I realised she had thought I was staring at her throughout the ward meeting.

I took my sandwiches up on to the Heath for lunch and sat on the bench with the idiot. He went on ranting and rocking in a muted way, inhibited no doubt by my presence. I offered him a sandwich, which he accepted and then did hideous things to.

I looked over the city. The light pattern had been reversed as I was walking over from the hospital and now the vast ziggurat was bathed in bright light, while the bench where the idiot and I scrunged cheese through our teeth was in deep shadow. Tom had told me that he referred to the hospital, privately, as the Ministry of Love; and it was true that the sepulchral ship forging its way through the grid of streets had something of the future, the corporate about it, mixed in with the despotic past.

The wind whipped across the flight deck entrance to the hospital as I re-entered by the main gates. Well-heeled patients and visitors were being landed by taxis and mini-cabs, while their poorer fellows struggled against the updraft that roared off the hospital's oblique walls – air crewmen and women lacking enlarged ping-pong bats with which to semaphore.

On the ninth floor I met Jane Bowen. She was right outside the lift. Her hands fidgeted at her mouth as the doors rolled open.

'Well, Misha, where have you been?'

'I took my sandwiches up on the Heath. I like to get a little fresh air during the day.'

'Well don't make a habit of it.'

'Why's that?'

'Zack prefers it if all the staff eat in the canteen on the ward . . .'

'You can't be serious . . . !'

'Obviously it isn't imposed on anyone. You're free to do what you want. But Zack has good reasons for it and you need to witness lunch to understand them.'

The association area was thronged with patients, they eddied round the counter in the eating area – more of an enlarged serving hatch really – and then gravitated from there to the medication queue. Busner stood in the centre of it all, like some Lord of Misrule. He'd donned a shortie white coat which rode up over his rounded hips. The coat pockets were stuffed to overflowing, and because of the way he was standing it looked as if he was wearing a codpiece. Busner waved his arms around his head and turned circles on his heels, his face contorted, with pain? With hilarity? It was impossible to say.

I approached him through swirls of the committed.

'Ah, Misha, I've tangled my spectacles cord up in my tie at the back. Can you see what's going on?' He turned his back on me and I fiddled with the two strands where they had become entwined. 'Ah, that's better.' He clamped the spectacles on to the red grooved bridge of his nose. 'Now I can see. We'd better sort out your materials for you.' He led me over to a wall cupboard at the far end of the dining area from the serving hatch and opened the ceiling-high doors. Inside there was a mess of materials and half-finished attempts at something or other. 'Gerry wasn't great on ordering the materials,' said Busner, stepping forward into the cupboard and crunching pieces of charcoal sticks beneath his heels, 'but everything is here that you could need. I should take it easy, let them come to you and show you what they're up to – try and build up some trust.'

Busner put a cloyingly affectionate arm around my shoulders, he didn't register my wince. We stood side by side, facing a shelf full of streaked tins of powder paint.

'Your father would have been proud of you, Misha. He would have understood what you're doing. You know, in a way I feel as if you're coming home to us here on the ward, that it's the right place for you, don't you agree?' I muttered something negative. 'I'm glad you feel the same way, come and see me when the session is over, tell me how it went.' He wheeled away from me and tracked a series of charcoal arcs across the lino. I was left alone – but not for long.

Tom materialised. At his shoulder was a thirtyish man of medium height and build, unremarkable in lumberjack shirt and denims, remarkable for his arms and his countenance: arms which struggled to escape his body and pushed forward long, muscular, mechanical arms. His face was stretched tight away and zoomed towards his flaring brown hair. The whole impression was one of contained speed.

'This is Jim,' said Tom, 'he can't bear to wait, he wants to get started right away.'

'Yeah. Hi. Jim.' He thrust a tool at me, I shook it, he retracted it. 'I really look forward to these sessions. I'd like to work on my thing all the time, but they won't let me.' I pulled the double doors open wider.

'Which one is it?'

'Here.' He pulled down a sort of sculpture, made from clay, from one of the higher shelves, his long arms cradling the irregular shape protectively. He turned and set it down on one of the rectangular melamine tables.

It was a large piece, perhaps some three and a half feet long and half that wide. Jim had used a base board and built on it with clay. The work had the kind of naive realism I associated with children's television programmes featuring animated figures moving around model villages. The work depicted a descending curve of elevated roadway which I immediately recognised as the Marylebone Flyover. Jim had neatly sculpted the point at which the two flyover lanes remerged with the Marylebone Road, there were tiny clay cars coming down off the flyover and one of them had knocked into a small Japanese fruiterer's van which was coming in from the Edgware Road. Two miniature clay figures were positioned in the road gesticulating. The whole thing cut off at the point where the Lisson Grove intersection would be to the east and where the flyover reaches its apex to the west.

'It's nearly finished,' said Jim. 'Today I'm going to paint and glaze it and then I'd like you to arrange for it to be fired.'

'Well, I can't see any problem with that. Tell me, what's the story behind this sculpture?'

'It's not a sculpture.' He sucked in air through teeth, the weary sigh of a child. 'It's an altarpiece.' He picked up the model flyover and went over to a table by the window with it. Tom giggled.

'Jim's got a messianic complex. He thinks that the Apocalypse isn't coming.'

'What does that mean?'

'It's a bit complicated. The Apocalypse will come when enough people have accepted that it isn't coming.'

'That just sounds stupid.'

'Well it isn't fucking stupid, it's you who are fucking stupid, Mister

Squeaky, get it!' Tom's voice switched from light mockery to the hair-trigger aggression of the subnormal thug. It was a startling transformation, as if he'd been possessed by a weird demon. He stalked away and joined his friend. I dismissed the insult. Busner had told me about him; it was clear that this was another act.

Over the next half-hour or so, most of the other patients on the ward trickled into the association area and came over to where their peers were already at work, mixing powder paint, working clay with fingers, cutting and pasting pictures from magazines. I was astonished by their quiet industry as a group. There seemed hardly anyone on the ward who was genuinely disruptive. Two or three of the patients stood like metronomes around the working area, swaying and rocking, marking the beat of the others' labour.

Hilary sat at the window and worked on one of her tiny watercolours with hairline brushes. She had propped up the scrap of artboard on a little easel made from lolly sticks and she worked with deft strokes, each one pulling the mobile stand attached to the catheter in her arm, back and forth. The plastic bag that dangled from it contained a clear fluid and a particular sediment. As the stand moved back and forth this sediment puffed up in the bag, the motes occasionally catching and then gleaming in the afternoon sun that washed in through the huge windows.

Simon came over and asked me for scissors, glue and stiff paper. He took a half-finished collage from one of the cupboard shelves and sat down near me. It depicted the machine he'd taken me to see that morning, but recreated out of pictures of domestic appliances cut from colour magazines. I went over and stood by him for a moment. He smiled up at me, cracking the pusy rime at the corners of his mouth.

'Unfinished work, left it when I last went out . . .' He bent his dirty carrot head to the task again.

I confined myself to handing out materials. I sensed that now was not the time to comment on the work that the patients were doing. When they began to trust me they would volunteer their own comments. There was a still atmosphere of concentration over the bent heads. I went and stood by the window, listening to the faint sounds of the hospital as it worked on through the afternoon. The distant thrum of generators, clack of feet, shingled slam of gates and trolleys. On the balcony below, two chronics in blue shifts struggled clumsily with one another, one of them bent back by the other against the parapet. I stared at their ill-coordinated aggression for a while, blankly, sightlessly. The 'O' I was looking at resolved itself into the stretched mouth of a geriatric. At the point where I snapped out of my reverie and realised I ought to do something an orderly appeared on the balcony and separated them, dragging the younger one away, out of sight beneath my feet.

Eventually I went and sat down at a table occupied only by a curly-haired man who had lain his head in the crook of his arm like a bored schoolboy. He was doing something with his other arm, but I couldn't see what. We sat opposite one another for ten minutes or so. Nothing happened. Around us the workers relit cigarettes and built up the fug.

'Psst . . . !' It was Tom. 'Come here.' He gestured to me to join him and Jim. I went over. They were working diligently on the altarpiece. Jim was doing the painting, it was Tom's job to wash the brushes and mix the colours. Jim had finished on the blue-brown surface of the road and was starting on the white lines. Tom was pirouetting lazily, a pathetic string lasso dangling in one hand, his voice modulated to a crazy Californian dude's whine; he had the part down pat. But wrong.

'That man there.' He pointed at the curly-haired man.

'Yes.'

'He's a real coup for Dr B.'

'How so?'

'Cocaine psychosis, authentic, full-blown. Used to be an accountant. Not just some scumball junkie. A real coup. Dr B diagnosed him, all the other units around here are real sore. Go and see what he's doing, it'll crack you up. And on your way back bring us another beaker of water, OK, fella.'

I did as I was told. Passing by Lionel, the drug addict, I bent down to pick up an invisible object and looked back to see what it was he was hiding in the crook of his arm. It was nothing. He was deftly picking up and ranging his own collection of invisible objects on the tiny patch of table. As I bent and looked he turned his face to me and smiled conspiratorially. His eyes stayed too long on my hand which was half closed, fingers shaping the indents and projections of my own invisible object. I hurriedly straightened and walked off down the short corridor to the staff kitchenette.

Halfway down on the left I noticed a door I hadn't seen before. It had a square of glass set into it at eye level, which cried out to be looked through. I stepped up to it. The scene I witnessed was rendered graphical, exemplary, by the wire-thread grid imprisoned in the glass. It was a silent scene played out in a brightly lit yellow room. A man in his early forties, who was somehow familiar, sat in one of the ubiquitous plastic chairs. He wore loose black clothes and his black hair was brushed back from high temples. He was sitting in profile. His legs were crossed and he was writing on a clipboard which he had balanced on his thigh. His lip and chin had the exposed, boiled look of a frequent shaver. The room was clearly given over to treatment. It had that unused corner-of-the-lobby feel of all such rooms. A reproduction of a reproduction hung on the wall, an empty wire magazine rack was adrift on the lino floor – the poor lino floor, its flesh scarified with cigarette burns. In the far corner of the room, diagonally opposite the man in black, a figure crouched, balled up face averted. I could tell by the lapel laden with badges, flapping in the emotional draft, that it was Jane Bowen.

The rest of the afternoon passed in silence and concentration. At 5.40 I gathered in the art materials and stacked all the patients' work in the cupboard in as orderly a fashion as I could manage. It took some time to tidy up the art materials properly. The patients for the most part stayed where they were, hunched over the tables, seemingly unwilling to leave. Tom and Jim muttered to one another by the window. They had the pantomime conspiratorial air of six year olds, still half convinced that if they didn't look they couldn't be seen.

I found Busner in his office. He sat staring out of his window at the lack of scale. On the far corner of the hospital a steel chimney which I hadn't noticed that morning belched out a solid column of white smoke. Busner noticed the direction of my gaze.

'A train going nowhere, eh, Misha?'

'Why do you say that?'

'Because it's true. We're a holding pen, a state-funded purgatory. People come in here and they wait. Nothing much else ever happens; they certainly don't get appreciably better. It's as if, once classified, they're pinned to some giant card. The same could be said of us as well, eh?' He shivered, as if he were witnessing a patient being pierced with a giant pin. 'But I'm forgetting myself, don't pay any attention, Misha, it's the end of a long day.'

'No, I'm interested in what you say. The patients here do seem to be different to those I've met at Halliwick or St Mary's.'

'Oh, you think so, do you? How's that?' Busner swivelled round to look at me over his glasses.

'Well, the art work they do. It's different . . . it's . . . how shall I put it . . . rather contrived, as if they were acting out something. Like Tom's behaviour.'

'An involution?'

'That's it. It's a secondary reference. Their condition is itself a form of comment and the art work that they do is a further exegesis.'

'Interesting, interesting. I can't pretend that it isn't something we haven't noticed before. Your predecessor had very strong views about it. He was a psychologist, you know, very gifted, took on the art therapy job in order to develop functional relationships with the patients, freed as far as possible from the dialectics of orthodox treatment. A very intense young man. The direction the patients have taken with their work could well have something to do with his influence.'

Busner started stuffing his case with paper filling, as if it were a giant pitta bread. 'I'm off, Misha. I shall see you in the morning, bright and early, I trust. I think it would be a good idea if you really sorted out that materials cupboard tomorrow.'

'Yes, yes, of course.' I got up, scraping my chair backwards and left the office. In the corridor the long lights whickered and whinnied to themselves. The ward was quiet and deserted. But as I passed the door to one of the utility cupboards, it suddenly wheezed open and a hand emerged and tugged at my sleeve.

'Come in. Come on, don't be afraid.'

I stepped in through the narrow gap and the heavy door closed behind me. It was dark and the space I was in felt enclosed and stifling. There was an overpowering odour of starch and warm linen. I almost gagged. The darkness was complete. The hand that had grabbed my wrist approached my face. I could feel it hover over my features.

'It is you,' said the voice, 'don't say anything, it'll spoil it.' It was Mimi. I could smell the tang of her sweat; it cut right through the warm, cottony fug.

The hand lead mine to her breast which seemed vast in the darkness, I could feel the webbing of her bra and beneath it the raised bruise of her nipple. She pushed against me, her body was so soft and collapsed. Her flesh had the dewlap quality of a body that has had excess weight melted off it, leaving behind a subcutaneous sac. Her jeans were unzipped; she pulled at my trousers, a cool damp hand tugged on my penis and pressed it against her. We stood like that, her hand on me, mine on her. She led me forwards and hopped up on to what must have been a shelf or ledge, then she drew me, semi-erect, inside of her. My penis bent around the hard cleft of her jeans, the skin rasped against ridged seam and cold zipper. There was something frenzied rather than erotic about this tortured coupling. I clutched at her breast and tore away the two nylon layers. I plunged rigidly inside her. She squeaked and waves of sweat came off her and tanged in my nostrils. I ejaculated almost immediately and withdrew. There was a long moment while we panted together in the darkness, I could hear her rearranging her clothing. Then, 'till tomorrow,' a light touch on my brow. The door split the darkness from ceiling to floor, wheezed once and she was gone. After a while I straightened my clothing, left the linen cupboard and went home.

It wasn't until I stepped out of the tube station and started the ten-minute walk back to the house where I lived that I noticed the outdoor scent. The smell of the ward and the hospital had become for me the only smell. The cold privet of the damp road I trailed along was now alien and uncomfortable.

At home I boiled something in a bag and sat pushing rice pupae around the soiled plate. Friends called to ask about my first day in the new job. I left the answerphone on and heard their voices, distantly addressing my robotic self. Later, lying in bed, I looked around the walls hung with my various constructions, odd things I had made out of cloth that may have been collapsed bats, or umbrellas. The wooden and metal struts filtered the sodium light which washed orange across the pillow. I fell asleep.

I dreamt that the man I had seen in the treatment room, the man taking notes in the chair while Jane Bowen crouched in the corner, was doing some kind of presentation. I was in the audience. We were sitting in a very small lecture theatre. It was enclosed and dark, but the descending tiers of seats, some fifty in all, were stone ledges set in grassy semicircular banks.

The man in black stood in the centre of the circular stage and manipulated a kind of holographic projector. It threw an image of my head into the air, some four or five feet high. The image, although clearly three-dimensional, was quite imperfect, billowy and electrically cheesy. Gathered in the audience were all the people I'd spoken with on the ward: Busner, Valuam, Mimi, Jane Bowen, Tom, Simon, Jim and Hilary. Clive stood in the aisle, rocking.

The man in black took a long pointer or baton and passed it vertically through my holographic head. It was a cheap trick because it was quite clear that the hologram wasn't a solid object, but the audience annoyed me intensely by sychophantically applauding. I began to shout at them, saying that they knew nothing about technology, or what it was capable of . . .

Morning. I had difficulty finding the hardened coils of my socks. And when I did there was something hard and rectangular tucked into the saline fold of one of them. It was a piece from The Riddle. I had no idea how it had got there, but nonetheless I murmured automatically, mantrically, 'I'm solving The Riddle . . .' Suddenly the events I experienced on Ward 9 the day before seemed quite bizarre. At the time I accepted them unquestioningly, but now . . . Busner and his game, the concave Bowen, the foetal Valuam, Simon's unfeeling mother, Tom with the mimetic disease, the encounter with Mimi in the linen cupboard. Any one of these things would be sufficient to unsettle; taken together . . .

I rallied myself. Any psychiatric ward is a test of the therapist's capacity; to embrace a fundamental contradiction, to retain sympathy whilst maintaining detachment. The previous day had been bizarre, because I had failed to maintain my detachment . . . it was said that if you empathised too closely with the insane you became insane yourself. Busner himself had had a period after the collapse of his Concept House project in the early Seventies when he had spent his time strumming electric basses in darkened recording studios, mouthing doggerel during radio interviews and undertaking other acts of revolutionary identification with those classified as insane. It was only fitting that I should start to fall victim to the same impulses under his aegis. Today I would have to watch myself.

I took the long route across the Heath and passed by my father's sculpture. I have no idea why he gave this specific one to the municipality. He had no particular love for this administration zone. And certainly no real concern with the aesthetic education of the masses. Not that the masses ever really come here. This is an unfenced preserve of the moneyed, they roam free here patrolled by dapper rangers in brown suits.

It is a large piece, depicting two shins cast in bronze. Each one some eight feet high and perhaps nine in circumference. There are no feet and no knees. No tendons are defined, there are no hairs picked out, or veins described. There is just the shape of the shins. It was typical of my father's work. All his working life he had striven to find the portions of the body which, when removed from the whole, became abstract. With the shins I think he had reached his zenith.

I walked on towards the hill from where I had viewed the hospital the previous morning. The idiot was tucked up in a dustbin liner underneath his bench residence, his face averted from the day. His chest was sheathed in a tatter of scraps, reminiscent of Simon's collage. I looked ahead. The hospital had today achieved another feat in distortion. Flatly lit, two-dimensional, depth eradicated, there was a strip of city, a strip of sky and interposed between these two the trapezoid of the sanitorium.

Sanity smells. How could I have forgotten it? No one can lose their reason under the pervasive influence of the nasal institution. It is too mundane. The doors of the lift rolled open and the pad clamped across my face. All was as the day before. Tom sat behind the nurses' station, and his violet eyes focused on mine as soon as I emerged in the short corridor that led from the lift.

'Colour-coded this morning, are we?' Tom's accent is a strange mixture of clipped pre-war vowels and camp drawl. I looked down and noticed that I had pulled on a particularly bilious V-neck.

'Not intentionally.'

'Dahling, never is, never is.'

I left him and went over to the materials cupboard. Opening wide the two ceiling-high sets of double doors, I gathered up felt-tip pens and isolated them. Then I did the same with the crayons, the charcoal sticks, the pastels, the stained enamel trays of impacted watercolours, the few squiggled tubes of exhausted oils, the sheets of sugar paper, the rough paper, the rulers, and the encrusted brushes. Amongst the jumble were lumps of forgotten clay, grown primordial.

At length Tom came over. He had draped a stole of pink toilet paper around his shoulders and smoked a roll-up with quizzical attention. He stood akimbo and regarded me without speaking.

I started work on the works themselves. They were jumbled up, like the materials. The layered skin of some exercise in papier mâché had been torn by the rudely carved prong of a wooden boat. Crude daubs of powder paint on coloured sheets of rough paper had run into one another and finally impacted over the ubiquitous spiralled vessels. I prised all of these apart gingerly. I only discarded the hopelessly battered. On the rest I imposed order.

As I worked, the association area remained empty. Except for Tom, who paraded back and forth from the nurses' station to the great windows, to the serving hatch and back to my side, trailing his flushable fashion accessory and a second mantle of smoke. From time to time he paused and struck an attitude of such ridiculous campness that I was driven to stifled giggles. He came back just as I was reaching the higher shelves.

'I wouldn't . . .' he said.

'Wouldn't what?'

'Touch the work up there.'

I dragged over a plastic chair and stepped up on to it. Now at eye level I could see that the works up here were the top of the range. Simon's collage, Hilary's miniatures, Jim's tableau and a couple of others I hadn't seen before. One was particularly striking. It was an abstract, constructed entirely out of pieces from The Riddle. The red acrylic squares had been glued together to form a box, open at the top, within which four more pieces had been set, up on edge, facing each other.

Standing on the plastic chair, eyes level with that top shelf, I had a momentary double-take. I whirled round and, too late, heard myself saying something stupid. 'Well, well, this seems to be where the top dogs put their stuff . . .'

Tom tugged at my trouser leg. I descended and he gathered me into a huddle in the corner of the great flat room, which was now washed with scummy light. My hand rested flacidly on the ventilation grill. Tom said, 'Get out of here Misha.'

'What do you mean?'

'Get out of here. This is a shit place, the people here are shit people. They're fucked up and weird, more weird than you can imagine.

They're far more weird than mentally ill people. Mentally ill people are light entertainment compared to this lot.'

'What do you mean? Explain yourself.'

'Well, consider Simon, for one.'

'What about him?'

'You were there when Valuam assessed him?'

'Yes . . .'

'How many doctors have to examine a psychiatric patient before admission?'

'Two.'

'And . . . ?'

'Well, I suppose I thought that since Simon had plainly been in and out of the ward a great deal it was rather glossed over. Fair enough, really, if a little irregular.'

'Wrong. Simon's mother holds a teaching appointment with this ward . . . she regularly arranges to have her own son sectioned.'

'It does sound a little irregular.'

'Irregular! The whole thing is some weird fucking busman's holiday maan . . .' Tom's arm tightened round my waist '. . . but that needn't upset our love Misha, we can screw together like Mec-ca-no . . .' I pulled away from him '. . . Bitch!' And turned to see Jane Bowen, regarding me quizzically.

Later that morning, I started drawing up some group worksheets. These are an invention of my own. Large sheets that three or four people can work on at once. I would lay down a basic pattern of lines which the particular group could embroider on, using whatever materials they pleased, or ignore. I worked steadily, with concentration. Two patients who I didn't recognise were sitting at a table in the association area. They were striking some kind of a deal. From where I sat I couldn't hear a word they were saying. Every so often one of them, a little ferrety man wearing a yachting cap, leant out from the table to shoot me a stare. It occurred to me as not unlikely that the deal they were discussing with such attention to detail was, in fact, meaningless.

Eventually I heard a murmur of voices that suggested agreement. I turned to see them exchanging stacks of pieces from The Riddle. The acrylic squares had been threaded on to a cord or wire of some kind, through a hole pierced in the corner of each piece. The two men both had necklaces entirely constructed from the discarded elements of the pop psychological pastime.

The group worksheets took me all morning. No one paid any attention to me any more. I could see now that the atmosphere of the ward was as sodden as compost. It only took a matter of hours for any given individual to be enmeshed, and start to decay. I was yesterday's novelty.

Busner wasn't about. Valuam and I exchanged strained salutations, sometime in the empty mid-morning. He had a snappy little check number on today. His footsteps were even more like clockwork, more pathetically authoritative. I thought to myself, what exactly am I doing on this ward? I don't need the money. I'm not sure that I altogether believe that my particular skills can help the patients. Busner's cynicism had certainly had the effect of dampening whatever residual idealism I had had – I wonder if that was his intention?

Around noon a middle-aged patient called Judith had a partial fit in the short corridor that led from the association area to the women's ward. At first it seemed as if she was simply having a rather heated exchange of words – albeit with herself. But this escalated into hysteria. She vomited as well. Mimi and another nurse arrived very quickly, while I was still standing, poised between the inclination to pretend I hadn't noticed and the desire to show that I could cope. The nurses smoothed Judith's limbs, set her on her feet and led her away. The vomit and distress was somehow accounted for and absorbed.

I was conscious all morning of wanting to avoid Tom and Simon. I didn't really want to see Jim either. I ate lunch alone in the dining-room set aside for staff. I couldn't understand why I was meant to be there. None of the other staff from the ward were. Later on it transpired that it was someone's birthday and they had all gone for a drink in a pub across the road.

In the afternoon I got the patients who turned up to try and do something with the worksheets. Some of them were interested, some were immersed in their own projects. Clive turned out to be a surprisingly effective group leader. He dragooned three rather sheepish depressives into snaking wet trails of paint up and down the large gridded sheet. Their regular actions formed swirl after swirl. He stood back and surveyed them at work like some sort of gaffer. Looking at Clive, his jaw working, rocking as ever, I remembered that he was meant to have been discharged today. I wondered why he was still on the ward, but his pop-eyes, his shiny elbow pads, dissuaded me from asking.

Neither Tom nor Jim appeared for the afternoon session. The model flyover stayed on its shelf. Simon cut and pasted his collage. He had lost interest in me as well. He had reverted to the exaggerated, scab-picking parody of surly adolescence. I wondered where Mimi was, with the faint, sickly lust of an adolescent. I wondered if she had thought me a wimp, or chicken, for not helping out with Judith.

The afternoon ended and I was headed for the lift. This time it was the door to the cleaning cupboard that swung open an invitation. Her buttocks pulsed and scrunched against a plastic sack of soda crystals. Once again it was sickeningly brief. But this time before she left she made me eat two small, green, candied pills.

'What are these?' I said.

'Parstelin – it's a compound preparation of the MAO inhibitor tranyl-cypromine and trifluoperazine. It's not recommended for children.'

'Why should I take them?'

'To understand, dummy. After all, since you aren't mad, they won't have any effect on you, will they?' Her voice was offhand, light, mocking. It was no big deal.

'S'pose not.' I dryly swallowed them.

'Don't eat any cheese, or drink Chianti. You might have a bad reaction if you do.' She slid out through the gap in the door. One breast, delineated by soiled nylon, and again by ridged cotton, was outlined against the doorjamb for a moment, and then gone.

The rest of the week passed on the ward. I carried on with the worksheets and seemed to be making some progress. Increasing numbers of patients came to the afternoon art therapy sessions and stayed to try their hand. I started to get on well with the quieter patients. This was a mixed blessing. On more than one occasion Hilary held me prisoner for over an hour with talk of her friends, and the mechanics of her exact rendition of them as watercolour images. Likewise Lionel, the mysteriously psychotic accountant, was intent on sitting down with me on Thursday afternoon, a companionable arm about my shoulders, and together we leafed through glossy sales brochures for office equipment.

Each article was a revelation to him; one he viewed purely aesthetically. 'Look at this one,' he said, gesturing at a modular workstation done in mushroom, 'lovely, isn't it?' It was all I could do to mumble assent.

As for Bowen and Valuam they murmured at me cordially and passed by. There was no apparent reason for contact and Busner remained absent. I suspected that his juniors were prejudiced against me because of my father and all the sentimental crap Busner mouthed when I arrived on the ward, but I didn't particularly care. And at lunch I talked to auxiliaries or nurses.

Every night Mimi rendezvoused with me in another cupboard. I never knew which one it would be but somehow she always knew where to catch me just when I was about to finish clearing away the art materials and leave the ward for the night. Our couplings remained brief and stylised. She resisted my unspoken pressure towards some intimacy with offers of more green pills, which I took, hoping they might bring us together. On Friday she gave me four more after I had taken my normal two and told me to administer them myself over the weekend.

On Saturday night I went to see a film with a friend. We normally met up every month or so and at least half our time was, naturally enough, taken up with relaying a cursory outline of what we had been doing in the intervening period. On this occasion I was more circumspect than usual. I had the suspicion that what had been happening to me on the ward, especially my relationship with Mimi, was something that I shouldn't talk about to outsiders. It wasn't that it was wrong exactly – it was rather that the experience so clearly didn't apply.

I was also very conscious of the green pills that lay in the soft mess of lint at the bottom of my pockets. My finger sought them out as we talked, and to the probing digit they felt preposterously large and tactile, the way objects in the mouth feel to the tongue.

We were sitting in the cinema. I was idly watching the film, when I felt for the first time what must have been an effect of the drug. It was remarkably similar to the sensation I had had on the ward, when I was standing up on the chair looking for the first time at the patients' artworks on the top shelf of the materials cupboard. It was a feeling of detachment, but not from the external world; this was an internal detachment, a membraneous tearing away, inside of me.

After the film we went to get something to eat in a kebab joint. As we entered the eatery through an arch, band-sawn out of chipboard, I felt the rending inside me, again. For some reason I found myself unable to discuss the film. Abstracted, I started to casually shred the flesh from my splayed baby chicken with my hands. I had amassed quite a pile before my friend reacted with concerned disgust. I shrugged the episode off.

At the end of the evening I said goodbye to my friend and returned to my house. Sitting in the yellow light from the road, coiling and uncoiling my sock, I resolved, quietly and with no emotional fuss, never to see him again.

It's funny. It's funny – but after that it became easy to dismantle the emotional and spiritual framework of my life. Relatives, friends, ex-lovers; it became apparent that their relationships with me had always been as contingent as I had suspected. It only took an instance of irregularity, one, or at most two phone calls unreturned by me, an engagement not attended, for whole swathes of human contact to lie down, to fall into short stooks.

After a few weeks on Ward 9, and a generous handful of mutant M&Ms, everything began to resolve itself into the patterns I had always dimly thought I apprehended. The violet swirls, purple beams and glowing coils that lie within the world of the pressed eyelid – the distressed retina. I seemed to have acquired an air-cushioned soul. I felt no resistance to doing things that would have plagued my conscience in the past, at least that is what I felt. I had no precise examples of these things other than taking Parstelin itself. My liaisons with Mimi? But they were just knee-jerk experiences.

Why have I isolated myself like this? My only human contact now comes within working hours and mostly with the patients on the ward. I have no idea. I can make no claim to being depressed or alienated. Indeed I seem to have suffered from less disaffection in my life than most of my contemporaries, perhaps because of my father's death. Yet I felt more at home on the ward than I ever felt . . . at home.

The patients have thrown themselves into the worksheets with a vengeance. There was something about the size and complexity of the job that really appealed to them. The method also gave them the opportunity to blend together all their different styles. When they were working quietly on the sheets in the late afternoon one could almost be in a normal working situation. All their idiosyncrasies and psychic tics seemed smoothed out by their absorption. Clive no longer rocked at all. Hilary, having integrated her miniatures into Simon's new swirl of encrusted mâché, was content to work on backgrounds. Her bag-on-a-stand swished around her, a fixed point which delineated the circumference of her enterprise.

There was one thing missing in all of this: Busner. Despite the fact that I now seemed to get on with all and sundry on the ward; despite the fact that I felt accepted; despite the fact that when the lift door rolled back and I found myself at the head of the familiar, short corridor that led to the association area, I no longer felt the atmosphere as oppressive; on the contrary it was cozy, from beneath the covers. Despite all this there was Busner's profound absence. An absence towards which I felt a surprising ambivalence.

Busner is the Hierophant. He oversees the auguries, decocts potions, presides over rituals that piddle the everyday into a teastrainer reality. And he is a reminder of everything I wish to bury with my childhood. A world of complacency, of theory in the face of real distress. My father and Busner would sit together for hours at the head of the dining-room table and set the world to rights. Their conversation – I realised later – loaded with the slop of banality and sentimentality that was the direct result of their own sense of failure. Their wives would repair to another room and there do things that *had* to be done, while they carried on and on, eliding their adolescence still further into middle age. The awful oatmeal carpets of my childhood and the shame of having been a part of it all. When I think of Busner now he is a ghastly throwback, threatening to drag me into a conspiracy to evade reality.

Where is he? Valuam told me over bourbons and tea that he was in Helsinki, reading a paper to a conference. Valuam dunked his biscuits and sucked on them noisily, which is something I wouldn't have expected from this little scrap of anal retention. We talked a little about my art therapy work, but really he had no time for it and pointed instead to the success he was having with a new anti-depressant. 'Seemingly intractable states, verging on total withdrawal, now with noticeable effect.' He was referring to Lionel, who now no longer sat by the windows staring blankly down on to the chronics' balcony, but instead paced the men's ward like a caged lion, desperate to get back into business. Where was Busner? I didn't believe Valuam; I kept expecting the door to the utilities cupboard to swing open and to find crouching there, sweaty pills in pudgy palm, the discredited guru, waiting with affectionate arm to jerk me off, for old times' sake.

Monday morning, again. The sun cannot penetrate a low sodden bank of cloud and the light wells from behind it, oozing up from the ground through a thick spongy pile of ground mist as I foot my way across the sward. The air around me distorts to form rooms and corridors, and rooms within them and sliding partitions which I never come up against. The ward has come out to meet me today; I feel its shape around me, its scuffed skirting boards at my ankles, as I move towards the idiot's bench.

He is lying under it, caulked in free newspapers. Pathetic small ads show intaglioed across his neck. In the confined space he rolls over and clonks his shin against the bench leg. His face is exposed for a moment against the greasy collar of his anorak. His eyes have swollen up and exploded in a series of burst ramparts and lesions of diseased flesh. I feel my oily tea slop up from my stomach, the nausea is as clear and pure as pain. I vomit with precision and vomit again until my nausea has no function and I can look once more.

It's not clear what has happened to the idiot. Has he drunk some bleach? Some oven cleaner? Or is it a disease of a rarefied kind, a human myxomatosis designed to eliminate the crap from the fringe of society, to stop the piss-heads copulating and producing more of their degenerate kind? Whichever. The fact is that it's evident that he hasn't been dead for long – his corpse is still moving into rigor. He has died in the night and I am the first to happen along. It is my responsibility to alert the authorities. And now I feel the presence of the Parstelin in my blood stream. It replaces the sense of nausea as – for the first time – a positive rather than a negative attribute. The drug provides me with another fuzzy frame of reference, within which the idiot's death is no responsibility of mine. Someone else will report it, someone else will find him. I glissade down the hillside on my fluffy Lilo. The arguments from my conscience are remote, like memories of a television debate between contesting pompous pundits, witnessed several years ago . . .

A long morning in the hospital. On the ward there is an uncharacteristic, brisk efficiency. Valuam trots hither and thither with a clipboard compiling what look like inventories. For some reason he is dressed casually today, or at least in superficially casual clothes. It was always obvious that he would iron his jeans and check shirts, and also that he would wear sleeveless grey pullovers. Not for the first time it occurs to me that there is a strange symmetry between the sartorial sense of the psychiatric staff and that of their patients. Valuam with his strict dress which looks hopelessly contrived, Bowen with her bag lady chic, Busner with his escaping underwear. All of them match up with the patients in their charge . . .

I am working on something of my own which I hope will provide some inspiration for the patients. It's a worksheet, about six feet square, on which I have done several representations of the hospital. Each one has been executed using a different technique: pen and wash, gouache, oils, charcoals, pencils, clay. This morning I spend time cutting the stencil for a silk-screen print.

Patients, *en route* for therapy sessions, or dropping out of the medication line, pause by the tables I've pushed together in the dining area and ask me about the work. An auxiliary, a middle-aged Philippino woman, stops her swirling, watery work with tousled mop and zinc bucket on the ward floor to discourse at length on swollen ankles, injustice and the vagaries of public transport. I listen and work distractedly; the image of the dead idiot imposes itself on me startlingly. It slides in front of my eyes from time to time with an audible click: the ridge of greasy, nylon quilted collar, the scrubby, scrawny neck, the long face, the exploded eyes . . .

At noon then. Jane Bowen comes and sits near me, salutes me but does not converse. She rolls one of her withered cigarettes and states out of the window abstractedly, drawing heavily. Her hair is scraped back tightly from the violet, inverted bruises of her temples. She gazes towards the hill where the idiot lies. I have an impulse to tell her about it, which I repress. The weather outside the hospital is playing tricks again; long, high bands of cirrus cloud are filtering the wan sunlight into vertical bars, which cut across the area that lies between the hospital and the Heath, creating shadows of diminishing perspective, like the exposed working on an artist's sketch.

Eventually I get up and go and stand beside her. I am conscious of her body retreating from me inside the starched front of her white coat, leaving behind a white buckler. We both look out of the window in silence. My gaze drops from the idiot's bier-bench (I cannot see any evidence of discovery, service vehicles, or whatever) to the chronics' balcony below, the open area projecting out from Ward 8.

As once before, two cretins are embracing in a painful muted struggle. Their gowns flap in the wind, they strain against one another, locked in a clumsy bear-hug. Then one moves with surprising speed and agility, changing his hold so that he grips the other from behind, pinning his arms – and at the same time leaning backwards over the rail that runs above the concrete wall bounding the balcony. The two faces tip up towards Jane Bowen and I, white splashes that resolve themselves into . . . Mark, Busner's son, who was at school with me, who had a breakdown at university and attempted suicide. He is pinioned by the handsome, black-haired man who I saw in the treatment room with Jane Bowen. The man's face is glazed over with brutish imbecility. I feel another jolt of nausea, stagger and place my hand against the pane for support. Jane Bowen looks at me pityingly and gestures with her fag.

'Your predecessor, Misha, our ex-art therapist. Who just happens, purely by coincidence, to be my brother, Gerry.'

'That's Mark with him, Busner's son!'

'Yes, Zack felt it would be a good idea to have them farmed out to Ward 8 for a little while. He thought you might find it a tad shocking to encounter them as patients.' She turned to face me and said quite calmly, in a flat kind of a voice, 'Get out of here Misha. Get out of here now.'

She wasn't issuing advice on a career move. This was a fire alarm. I acted on it quickly, but hesitated on my way across the wide expanse of industrial-wear floor covering, skittering on one leg like a cartoon character speeding around a corner that turns into a vase. Abruptly I realise that the Parstelin has completely altered my sense of my own body. I am acutely aware of the connection between each impulse, each message and the nerve-ending it comes from. My whole physical orientation has shifted, but remains whole.

This apprehension occupies me as I run to the lift. Patients 'O' at me hysterically, but there is silence, or rather a descending wail that has nothing to do with speech and everything to do with what children hear when they press the flaps of cartilage over their ears, in and out, very fast. Sheuuooo-sheeeuuooo.

'A, hehehahahoohoohoohoo!' Clive does the twist by the coiled hosepipe in an anonymous bay, off the short corridor I run down on my way to the lift.

'Misha, a word please,' Valuam comes out from his office, trouser material high on each thigh, scrunched up in marmoset hands. His peeled face tilts toward me, fungus poking out from the door. Another door swings open five yards further on and a hand emerges to pluck at my sleeve, a round, dimpled hand on the end of that dripping sundae body. I run past it and in my mind the flashback of thrust seems hard and mechanical; my penis a rubberised claw torn from a laboratory retort and thrust into the side of a putrefying animal. I must take the stairs.

Four flights down I stop running. They're going to let me leave the hospital. A drug is just a drug. I was bloody stupid to take it at all, to fuck with Mimi, but if I stop it now my head will clear in a couple of days and I'll be back to normal. I won't have this strange sense that I am someone else, someone who is compelled to be reasonable.

There is no cause for alarm. I certainly cannot question the quintessential character of the stairwell. There is no denying its objective status. Thick bars of unpainted concrete punched through with four-inch bolts. The handrail a fire-engine red bar, as thick as an acroprop. Parstelin is a drug – I realise – that makes you acutely aware of things-in-themselves. Their standing into existence is no longer nauseous, but splendidly replete. That said, I gag a little and cough up a whitey dollop, somewhere between sputum and vomit, which plops into the drift of fluff wedged at the back of the stair I stand on.

Among the scraps of silver paper, safety-pins and nameless bits of detritus, a part of me. The fugue is broken by a whoosh of dead air that gusts up the well from below. Someone else has entered the staircase, pushed hard on a pneumatic door, maybe three flights down. The windows on the stairway are cut at oblique angles into the outer wall of the hospital. It is clear from the view, which affords me no sight of the huge bulk that contains me, that the staircase runs down the outer edge of the ziggurat's sloping wall.

I pick my way down, pausing from time to time to cock an ear and listen for sounds of pursuit, but there are none. It is plain to me now that I have been suffering from a delusion, that the ward has overtaken me in part. I never denied that I was highly strung. I need some bed rest and the opportunity to read the papers. The lower I get the freer I feel. I know I haven't really escaped from anything – and yet there's the temptation to laugh and skip, to strike some attitudes.

I calculate that I am still two floors above ground level when the staircase blocks off its own windows. Light is now supplied by yellow discs that shine on the walls. The yellow light disorientates me. It must have done. I can genuinely no longer tell whether I am above or below ground level. The doors that lead off the staircase are blank oblongs. I panic and push at one, it wheezes under my palm and I tumble out into a corridor.

It is immediately clear that the stairway has diverged significantly in its path, that it hasn't followed the lift shaft and deposited me in one of the open areas that form a natural reception concourse for each floor. Instead, it has thrown me off to one side, into the hinterland of the hospital, added to which I'm not on the mezzanine floor, I'm on the lower ground floor. I recognise where I am. I'm somewhere along the route Simon took me on my first day. I'm on the way to see the giant obsolete machine. I am in the same wetly shining concrete corridor. In either direction the naked neon tubes dash away; even they are hurrying off from this crushing place.

Which way? Whoever entered the stairwell while I was coming down is now on their way up. I can hear the cold slap of feet ascending and this hastens my decision. I turn to the left and start off down the corridor, trusting to my intuition to find my way to casualty and out of the hospital. As I walk I am aware that I'm positioned chemically at the eye of the storm. I no longer feel muzzy; I know that my body is saturated with Parstelin, but I've swum into a bubble of clarity. Nevertheless, I still don't seem able to gain a definitive view of Busner and his ward. What has been happening? Those patients – with their madness – as stylised as a ballet. Were they the logical result of Busner's philosophy? Were theirs the performances of madmen-as-idealists? Or just idealists? Their symptoms . . . was it true that they genuinely caricatured the recorded pathologies, all of them, not just Tom, or was my perception of them a function of the Parstelin?

These speculations give me heart. I feel my old self. I pause and look in a stainless steel panel screwed to a door. My reflection, dimpled here and there by the metal, looks back at me, amused, diffident. I feel cosy with my self-observation and immensely reassured by this moment of ordinary, unthinking vanity.

But where am I? No nearer casualty. The corridor has not swapped its concrete floor for tiling, there is no paint on the walls. I have turned the wrong way. Twenty feet ahead I can see the two swing-doors that lead to the conservatory. What the hell. I'll pop in and have a look; it will be the last time I come near the hospital for a while. The doors whicker apart on their rusty rails and as I turn and pull them shut behind me they cut out the steady undertow of thrum that powers the hospital. The light in the high-domed room is the same as before and the obscure machine with its cream bakelite surfaces projects up above me, inviolate.

Tom and Jim step out from behind its flanged base, they move quite unaffectedly into my sight, as if expecting no particular reaction. I am very frightened.

'Misha, where are you going?' says Tom. Jim is casting his eyes about with rapid jerks of his head. He keeps flexing and rolling his arms back and forth, opening the palm forwards to disclose plastic mouth tubes – the kind used to stop people who are fitting from biting their tongues off – which he has adapted to some manual exercise routine.

'I'm going off for the rest of the day, Tom, I came here by accident. I was looking for casualty.'

Tom listens to me, nodding, and then gestures for me to join him and Jim. The three of us then, squat down between the outstretched paws of the great instrument, which are bolted heavily to the floor. We are like Africans under some fat-trunked tree, timelessly talking, until Jim drops his adapted muscle expanders on to the cracked tiles of the floor with a clatter.

'I'm glad you listened to my advice, Misha. You're leaving, aren't you?'

'Just for a couple of days. I . . . I need a rest. The atmosphere on the ward is quite overwhelming.'

'Yes, it can be, can't it. That's why Jim and I like to come down here and play with the machine, it's peaceful, down here, quiet. Do you think I'm mad, Misha?'

'What about me, am I mad too?' Jim chimes in as well. I find myself embarrassed, which is absurd. To be frightened seems right, but to be embarrassed as well, that's ridiculous.

'Does the question embarrass you?' Tom is rolling a cigarette with deft fingers. He flicks over the lip of paper and raises it to his budding, sensual mouth.

'I hadn't thought about it in those terms.'

'Oh, oh, I see, you are a disciple of good Dr Zee, so we're just behaving in a way which others choose to describe as mad. We're simply non-conformists.'

'I think you're simplifying his position a little.'

'Of course, of course. Are you mad, Misha?' Jim snickers and rakes the tiles with long, cracked nails.

I can't answer. My eyes cast up to the ceiling some twenty feet away. The conservatory is roofed with a glass cupola, the inside of which seems dirtied as if by soot. Beneath this a complete circle of dirty dormer windows lets in the grey light. From the very centre hangs a flex – which dangles a cluster of naked bulbs just above the highest shoulder of the machine.

After a while, Tom reaches out from where he squats and touches me lightly on the arm. 'I'm sorry Misha, come on, let's climb.'

'Yeah, lets.' Jim is on his feet in one bound, a foot already on the kidney-shaped step, which is set two feet up into the base of the machine. In turn we haul ourselves up. Tom comes last. The machine is designed to be climbed; we ascend to a horizontal platform about seven feet up. This is girded with massive gimbals, the purpose of which is to tilt the platform under the main barrel of the contraption. What the machine ever did to the patients who were lain out on the platform is obscure. Perhaps it projected something through them: radiation; ultrasound; a light beam, or even something solid . . . The barrel itself has been decored; all that's left is a hank of plaited black wires, spilling from its mouth.

The three of us then, sit in a row on the platform, passing back and forth the wet end of tobacco. The curved well of dead light that falls on to us and the heavy machinery we sit on conspire to effect timelessness. Jews about to be shot or gassed are caught against the straight rod and round wheel of a railway engine. Crash survivors crawl from buckled aluminium sections rammed into the compost earth of the rainforest. We sit and smoke and I hear the 'peep-peep' of a small bird, outside the hospital, sounding like a doctor's pager. It completes the dead finality of my situation. My neck, rigid with absorbed tension, mushy with tranquillisers, feels as if it is welling up over my head to form a fleshly cowl.

The texture of things parodies itself. The creamy hardness of the machine's surfaces, the dusty clink of the tiled floor, the smelly abrasion of the arm of Tom's sweater. Even surfaces refuse to be straight with me. Tom's profile is rippably perfect, a slash of purity. Jim's bulbous nose and styled, collar-length hair make him absurd, an impression heightened by his simian arms which rest on the platform like the prongs of an idling forklift truck. But he reassures me now. They both reassure me. I put an arm around each of them and they snuggle into me, adults being children, being parents. They are my comrades, my blood brothers.

'Go now, Misha.' Tom pulls away and pushes me gently, indicating that I should get down from the platform. I climb down heavily. My limbs have the dripping, melting feeling that I know indicates the absorption of more Parstelin. But I don't know why; I haven't taken any. On the floor I turn, not towards the doors, but away from them, and circle the machine. Jim and Tom watch me but say nothing. I pick my way over twisted lianas of defunct cabling, once pinioned to the floor but now adrift. Behind the machine, directly opposite the door to the corridor, the door that faces the Mass Disaster Room is open.

Outside there is a scrap of land, room-sized, open to the air that voyages fifteen storeys down to find it and its tangled side-swipe of nameless shrubs. There, set lopsidedly on the irregular rubbled surface, stands one of the rectangular melamine-topped tables from the dining area on the ward. I can see a fold of belly, a dollop of jowl, a white hand fidgeting with an acrylic rectangle, the failing end of a mohair tie. Dr Busner is trying to solve The Riddle.

'Ah, there you are, Misha. Come out, come out, don't hover like that.' Busner sits, flanked by Valuam and Bowen. On the table in front of them are ranged objects that clearly relate to me: a pot of green pills, Jim's bas-relief which had so impressed me, a note I had sent to Mimi in an idle moment. I move across the little yard and sit by Valuam, who surprises me by smiling warmly. Flash of recognition: the slashed profile. If the features were undrowned? Valuam and Tom are brothers.

'We are all family here, Misha.'

'What's that?'

'We are all family . . . I see that something is coming home to you, as you have come home to us. It hardly matters whether we are doctors or patients, does it, Misha? The important thing is to be at home.' Busner rises and starts to pace the area. The massive walls of the hospital are joined irregularly to the squat citadel that houses the Mass Disaster Room. Busner describes a trapezoid on the uneven surface, sketching out with his feet the elevation of the hospital.

'You see, what we have here is a situation that calls for mutual aid. My son, Jane and Anthony's siblings, Simon, Jim, Clive, Harriet, indeed all of the patients on the ward, could be said to be casualties of a war that we ourselves have waged. That's why we felt it was our duty to care for them in a special kind of environment. You, of course, noticed the curious involution of the pathology that they exhibit, Misha, and that was right – you passed the first step. They are not mad in any accepted sense, rather they are meta-mad. Their madness is a conscious parody of the relation in which the psyche stands to itself . . . but you know this. Unfortunately, you didn't do so well on the other tests . . .' Busner tipped out some of the Parstelin from the pot on to the table. 'You took these, Misha, and you fucked Mimi in just about every available cupboard on the ward. This is not the behaviour of a responsible therapist. You had a choice, Misha. On Ward 9 you could have been therapist or patient; it seems that you have decided to become a patient.'

Busner stopped pacing and sat down again at the table. I sat, trapped in sweet gorge. What he said made sense. I did not resent it. Jane Bowen picked her nails with the edge of a Riddle counter. The same bird paged Nature. The four of us sat in the peculiar space, in silence. One thing confused me.

'But Dr Busner . . . Zack, my parents, my father. They had nothing to do with any therapeutic application of psychology, they were both artists. Surely I don't qualify for the ward?'

'Later on, Misha, later on . . . Your father became a sculptor in his thirties. Before that he studied with Alkan. He would have made an excellent analyst, but perhaps he didn't want you to pay the price.'

The doors behind me clacked in a down draft. The interview was clearly over.

'Would you take Misha back up to the ward, Anthony. We can foregather and handle the paperwork after lunch.'

Yes, lunch, I felt quite hungry. But I didn't like it down here. There was something moribund about this patch of ground, cemented with white splashes that streaked the high walls and starred the crusted earth. I wanted to get back upstairs – I want to get back upstairs – ha! Perhaps that's the effect of the chloropromasine, a kind of continual time lag between thought and self-consciousness – I want to get back upstairs . . . and lie on my bed. I need a cigarette.

Understanding the Ur-Bororo

When I first met Janner at Reigate in the early Seventies, he'd been an unprepossessing character. He was a driven young man whose wimpy physical appearance all too accurately complemented his obsessive nature. His body looked as if it had been constructed out of pipecleaners dunked repeatedly in flesh-coloured wax. All his features were eroded and soft except for his nose, which was the droplet of wax that hardens as it runs down the shaft of the candle. There was also something fungoid about Janner, it was somehow indefinable, but I always suspected that underneath his clothes Janner had athlete's foot – all over his entire body.

You mustn't misunderstand me, in a manner of speaking Janner and I were best friends. Actually, that is a little strong, it was rather that it was us against the rest – Janner and I versus the entire faculty and the entire student, body combined.

I suppose I now realise that my feelings are not Janner's responsibility and they never were. He just had the misfortune to come along at that point in my life where I was open to the idea of mystery. Janner took the part of Prospero; I gnashed and yowled – and somewhere on the island lurked the beautiful, the tantalising, the Ur-Bororo.

Not everyone has the opportunity to experience a real mystery in their lives. I at least did, even if the disillusionment that has followed the resolution of my mystery sometimes seems worse than the shuttered ignorance I might otherwise have enjoyed. This then is the story of a rite of passage. A coming of age that took ten years to arrive. And although it was my maturity that was at issue, it is Janner who is the central character of this story.

I can believe that in a more stimulating environment, somewhere where intellectual qualities are admired and social peculiarities sought after, Janner would have been a tremendous success. He was an excellent conversationalist, witty and informed. And if there was something rather repulsive about the way catarrh gurgled and huffled up and down his windpipe when he was speaking, it was more than compensated for by his animation, his excitement, and his capacity for getting completely involved with ideas.

Janner and I weren't appreciated by the rest of the student body at Reigate. We thought them immature and pathetic, with their *passé*, hippy hair and consuming passion for incredibly long guitar solos. I dare say they thought nothing of us at all. We were peripheral.

You guessed it; I was jealous. I didn't want to be sectioned off with waxy Janner. I wanted to be mingling my honeyed locks with similar honeyed locks to the sound of those stringed bagpipes. I wanted to provide an ideal arterial road for crabs, but I wasn't allowed to play. It was the students in the arts faculties who were at the centre of most of the cliques. If, like me, you were reading geography and physical education, you were ruled out of court – especially if you didn't look right, or talk right. Without these essential qualifications I was marginalised. At school my ability to do the four hundred metres hurdles comfortably under fifty seconds had made me a hero; at Reigate it was derided.

Ostracised by the cliques that mattered I found Janner, and I've lived to regret it. If only I'd poached my brain with psycho-tropics! Today I could be living a peaceful life, haggling with a recalcitrant DHSS official in rural Wales, or beating a damp strip of carpet hung over a sagging clothesline outside some inner-city squat. Janner cheated me out of this, his extreme example bred my moderation. At nineteen I could have gone either way.

I cemented my friendship with Janner during long walks in what passed for countryside around Reigate. Even at that time this part of Surrey was just the odds and ends that had been forgotten in the clashes between adjacent municipalities. The irregular strips of grey and brown farmland, the purposeless concrete aprons, stippled with weeds and the low, humped downs covered with sooty, stained scrub. We traversed them all and as we walked he talked.

Janner was an anthropology student. Now, of course, he is The Anthropologist, but in those days he was simply one student among several, five to be precise. Quite why Reigate had a department of anthropology was a mystery to most of the faculty and certainly to the students. Hardly anyone knew about the Lurie Foundation, who had endowed it, and – even I didn't know until years later – why.

During the time Janner and I were at Reigate (you could hardly say 'up' at Reigate) the department was run by Dr Marston. He was a striking-looking man. To say he had a prognathous jaw would have been a gross understatement. His jaw shot out in a dead flat line from his neck and went on travelling for quite a while. Looking at the rest of his face the most obvious explanation was that his chin was desperately trying to escape his formidably beetling brows. These rolled down over his eyes like great lowering storm clouds. Add to this two steady black eyes, tiny little teeth, a keel for a nose, and a mouth trying to hide behind a fringe of savagely cut black beard, and you had someone whose skull looked as if it had been assembled in an attempt to perpetrate a nineteenth-century hoax.

To see Dr Marston and Janner talking to one another was to feel that one was witnessing the meeting between two different species that had just discovered a mutual language. Not that I saw them together that often; Dr Marston had no time for me, and Janner, after his first year, was excused from regular attendance at the college and allowed to get on with his own research.

I think it would be fair to say (and please remember that this is a turn of phrase resolved solely for the use of the extremely opinionated and the hopelessly diffident) that during that year I received a fairly comprehensive anthropological education at second hand. Janner had very little interest in what I was studying. At best he used my scant geographical knowledge as a sort of card index, and when he was discoursing on the habits and customs of this or that isolated people he would consult my internal map of the world. For most of the time we were together I listened and Janner talked.

Janner talked of the pioneers in his field. He was in awe of the colossal stature of the first men and women who had aspired to objectivity in relation to the study of humankind. He talked to me of their theories and hypotheses, their intrigues and battles, their collections of objects and artefacts, and came back again and again, as we strode round and round the brown hills, to their fieldwork.

For Janner all life was a prelude to fieldwork. Reigate was only an antechamber to the real world. A world in which Janner wanted to submerge himself completely – in order to become a pure observer. He was unmoved by the relatavistic, structuralist and post-structuralist theories of anthropology with their painful concern with the effect of the observer on the observed. Janner had no doubts; as soon as he got into the field he would effectively disappear, becoming like a battery of sensitive recording devices hidden in a tree. His whole life was leading up to this pure period of observation. Janner wanted to be the ultimate voyeur. He wanted to sit on a kitchen chair in the corner of the world and watch while societies played with themselves.

When Janner wasn't telling me about infibulation among the Tuareg or Shan propitiation ceremonies, he was sharing with me the fruits of his concerted observation of Reigate society. Janner was intrigued by Reigate. He saw it as a unique society at a crucial point in its development.

Walking with him, up by the county hospital, or down in the network of lanes that formed the old town, I would squirm with embarrassment as Janner stopped passersby; milkmen, clerks and housewives. Janner encouraged them to talk about themselves, their lives, and what they were doing, just like that; impromptu, with no explanation. Needless to say they invariably obliged, and usually fulsomely.

As we passed cinema queues or discos on our interminable walks, or stopped off at cafés to eat bacon sandwiches, Janner would shape and form what he observed into a delicate tableau of practice, ritual and belief. Reigate was for him a 'society' and as such was as worthy of respect as any other society. It was not for him to judge the relative values of killing a bandicoot versus taking a girl on the back of your Yamaha 250 up the A23 at a hundred miles an hour; both were equally valid rites of passage.

After his first year at Reigate Janner moved out of his digs at Mrs Beasley's on Station Road, and into a shed on the edge of the North

Downs. It was his intention to get started as soon as possible on the business of living authentically – in harmony with his chosen object of field study – for by now Janner had fallen under the spell of the Ur-Bororo.

If it was unusual to study anthropology at Reigate, rather than some other branch of the humanities, it was even more unusual for an undergraduate student to nurse dreams of going to another continent for postgraduate field study. Dr Marston was well used to packing his charges off to Prestatyn to study the decline of Methodist Valley communities, or to Yorkshire to study the decline of moorland Unitarian communities, or to the Orkneys to study the decline of offshore gull-eating communities. Reigate was, if not exactly famous, at least moderately well known for its tradition of doing work on stagnating sub-societal groups. Dr Marston's own doctorate had been entitled 'Ritual Tiffin and Teatime Taboo: Declining Practices Among Retired Indian Army Colonels in Cheltenham'.

But that being said, Dr Marston himself had had a brief period of field study abroad. This was among the Ur-Bororo of the Paquatyl region of the Amazon. It was Marston who first fired Janner with enthusiasm for this hitherto undistinguished tribe of Indians. I have no idea what he told Janner, certainly it must have contained an element of truth, but Janner told me a severely restricted version. If one listened to Janner on the subject one soon found out that his information about the Ur-Bororo consisted almost entirely of negative statements. What was known was hearsay and very little *was* known; what little hearsay was known was hopelessly out of date – and so forth. I didn't trouble to challenge Janner over this, by now he was beyond my reach. He had retired to his hut on the Downs, was seldom seen at the college, and dissuaded me, politely but firmly, from calling on him.

I did go a couple of times to see him. In a way I suppose I wanted to plead with him not to abandon me. For Janner, with his pipe-stem torso sheathed in the stringy tube of a sleeveless, Fair Isle sweater, and with his eyes wetly gleaming behind round lenses, was more than a friend as far as I was concerned. I couldn't admit it to myself but I was a little bit in love with him. He told me that his hut was a faithful reconstruction of an Ur-Bororo traditional dwelling. I didn't believe him for a second; anyone looking at the hut could see that it had been ordered out of the back of *Exchange & Mart.* Its creosoted clapboard sides, its macadamised roofing, its one little, leaded window, the way the floor wasn't level with the ground. All of these facts betrayed its prefabricated nature. Inside the hut we drank tea out of crude clay vessels. Once again Janner assured me that these were of traditional. Ur-Bororo manufacture, but I couldn't really see the point of the statement. By now I could see just by looking at him that he was lost to me. He no longer needed me as a passive intermediary between his mind and the world he studied. He had found his destiny.

I left the hut without pleading at all and cycled back to Reigate. I had accepted that from now on I would be alone. But it's difficult to get that Wertherish in Reigate, certainly not when you're lodging in a clipped crescent of double-glazed, dormered windows. My depression soon ate itself. Without Janner to talk to I was forced back among my fellow students. I made some other friends; I even had a girlfriend. It wasn't that I forgot about Janner, that would have been impossible, it was just that I tried to construct a life for myself to which he wouldn't be relevant. I succeeded in this, but it had its own consequences.

During the next ten years very little happened to me. Sure, I left Reigate and went to teach at a school in Sanderstead. I met, fell in love with, and speedily married the geography and PE teacher at a neighbouring school. We became owner-occupiers and a child arrived, who was small, well made and finished; and dreamy and introverted to the point of imbecility. We had friends and opinions, both in moderation. It was a full life, seemingly without severe problems. I had grown through my modest and unturbulent adolescence into a modest and unturbulent adult. I even gained a certain celebrity for my phlegm at the school where I taught, because I could face down aggressive pupils with indifference. Some of my colleagues became convinced that within me lurked quite violent impulses. This, I'm afraid, was far from the truth. The reality was that I felt padded, as if all the gaps in my view of the world had been neatly filled with some kind of cavity life insulation. I felt ludicrously contained and static. I saw events unroll around me. I felt, I emoted, but the volume control was always on. Somewhere along the line someone had clapped a mute on my head and I hadn't any idea who, or why.

During this whole period I heard nothing of Janner. I knew he had graduated from Reigate with unprecedented first-class honours and, with Dr Marston's blessing and a none too generous grant from the SSRC, had gone abroad to visit his precious tribe. But beyond that, nothing. The only evidence I had of Janner's existence during that ten-year period was finding by chance, while looking absent-mindedly through a stack of World Music records, an album Janner had acted as 'consultant producer' for. It was entitled *Some Chants from Failed Cultures*. I bought it immediately and rushed home.

If I had hoped for some kind of enlightenment, or to recapture the rapture of our scrubland walks together I was to be disappointed. The album was gloomy and perverse. The producers had visited diverse groups of indigenes around the world, remarkable only for their persistence in chanting to no avail. Here were the Ketchem of Belize with their muttering eructation 'Fall Out of the Water – Fish'. The I-Arana of Guinea, disillusioned cargo cultists who moaned gently, 'Get Me Room Service', and many others too tedious and depressing to mention.

The gist of all these failed chants I gathered from the sleeve notes, written by Janner. The chants themselves were badly recorded and incomprehensible. After two or three plays the needle on our record player started to score twists of vinyl out of the bottom of the grooves – and that was the end of that. Janner's sleeve notes, as far as I was concerned, were unilluminating and discursive. They told me nothing concrete about his involvement with the project and gave me no clue as to where he might be now. When I tried to find out more through the record company I drew another blank. Ha-Cha-Cha Records had gone into receivership.

I may not have found the friend of my adolescence, but the record had gravely unsettled me. I had assumed that Janner was by now safely ensconced in some provincial university's anthropology department, his tremendous enthusiasm and drive winding down through the dreary cycle of teaching. But the record and its sleeve notes presented an alternative picture, a picture of a different Janner and a more unsettled career. The evening that I brought the record home I sat in the living-room for hours, using the time while my wife was at her class, to try and fathom Janner's fate, with only the flimsy record sleeve to go on.

My son James didn't help. He'd picked up a couple of the failed chants and as I put him to bed that night he said, in passable Uraic, 'Lo! The crops are withering.' Somehow, even among the cartoon stickers and the bright bendy limbs of bendy toys, this didn't sound as incongruous as it perhaps should have.

Then, nothing. For another two years no word or sign of Janner. I didn't pursue him, but I did go to the trouble of finding out about the Lurie Foundation, the body which I knew had part-funded Janner's research into the Ur-Bororo. The secretary of the foundation was unforthcoming. He wrote me a letter stating the aims of the foundation in the barest outline: 'To contribute to the understanding of the Ur-Bororo, a bursary will be provided for one post-graduate student every twenty years. Following his fieldwork the student will be required to lodge a paper of not less than 30,000 words with the Lurie Archive at the British Library.' The letter was signed by Dr Marston. I spoke to a librarian at the British Library, but she told me that all the documents relating to the Lurie Foundation were held in a closed stack. I had reached a dead end.

Janner had represented for me a set of possibilities that were unfulfilled. Even after twelve years these wider horizons continued to advance beyond my measured tread. Occasionally, sitting in the staff-room during a vacant period, I would suddenly find myself crying. I felt the tears, damp on my cheek, and into my stomach came a bubble of sweet sentimentality. But my hands gripped the edges of the *Education Supplement* too tightly, held it too stiffly in front of my face. All around me the talk was of interest rates. From time to time a corduroy trouser leg loomed into view.

Then one day in late summer, just after the school sports day, I was walking down the hill towards Purley when something caught my eye in the window of a launderette. An etiolated, waxy-looking individual was having an altercation with a rotund, middle-aged woman. Voices were raised and it was clear that they were on the verge of coming to blows. I heard the woman say quite distinctly, 'Coming in here and sitting staring at other people's laundry, you ought to be ashamed of yourself. Haven't you got any laundry of your own to look at, you filthy pervert?' She raised her hand to strike the man. As he turned to ward off the blow I saw his profile. It was Janner.

I stepped inside the launderette. Janner had evaded the first blow and was backing off to avoid a second. I touched him on the shoulder and said in my best disciplinary manner, 'Would you step outside for a minute please, sir?' The Protectress of Gussets was immediately convinced that here were the Proper Authorities. She surrendered her temporary deputy's badge with good grace. Janner stepped outside.

And continued a conversation with me as if it had been subject only to an hour's, rather than a decade's interruption.

'I'm living down here in Purley [a gurgle of catarrh] in a funny sort of a place. I've only been back from abroad for a couple of months. I was just observing this business of observing laundry. I'm convinced that the spinning circle of laundry has some of the properties of the mandala.'

We were by now heading down the hill at a brisk trot. Janner went on and on and on at length, trying to fit Purley laundering practices into a complex and highly unconvincing portrait of South London suburban society. He had lost none of his vigour. Any attempts I made to break into his monologue he interpreted as a desire to know still more. We fetched up by the station. Janner was still talking, still gesticulating.

'You see, Wingate Crescent represents a kind of epicentre; in order to reach the High Street you have to describe a circle. The positioning of the four launderettes – Washmatic, Blue Ribbon, Purley Way and Allnite – is also circular.' He stopped as if he had reached some kind of self-evident conclusion. I broke in.

'Where have you been, Janner? Have you been in the Amazon all this time? I found a record you'd written the sleeve notes for. Have you been collecting more failed chants? Are you married? I am. Are you going to give me any facts, or only more theories?' Janner was gobsmacked. When we'd been at Reigate I'd hardly ever answered back. My interjections had been designed purely to oil the machinery of his discourse. He became evasive.

'Um . . . well, just resting up. Yes, I have been away. Pretty boring really, just some fieldwork, due to publish a paper. I'm doing some teaching at Croydon for the moment. Living here in Purley. That's it, really.' He stopped in the centre of the pavement and pointed his hardened drip of a nose at the ground, I could hear the discreet burble of mucus in his thorax. A train from Victoria clattered across the points at Purley Junction. I could sense that Janner was about to slip away from me again.

'I did a bit of research of my own, Janner. I read up what I could about this tribe, the Ur-Bororo. Seems that some kind of foundation exists for anthropologists who are prepared to do fieldwork on them. The man who set it up, Lurie, was an eccentric amateur. He gifted his field notes to the British Library, but only on the condition that they remain unread. The only exceptions being those anthropologists who are prepared to go and carry on Lurie's fieldwork. Apparently, the number of recipients of Lurie Foundation grants were also to be severely restricted. Since Lurie set it up in the Thirties there have only been two – Marston and yourself.'

A double-decker bus pulled away from the stop across the road. For a moment it seemed poised in mid-acceleration, like some preposterous space rocket too heavy to lift itself from the earth, and then it surged off up the hill, rattling and roaring, a cloud of sticky diesel fumes, heavier and more tangible than the earth itself, spreading out behind. Janner spat yellow mucus into the gutter. In the late afternoon light his mouth was puckered with disapproval like an anus.

'I suppose you want to know all about it, then?'

'That's right, Janner. I've thought about you a lot during these past ten years. I always knew you'd do something remarkable, and now I want to know what it is – or was.'

He agreed to come to my house for dinner the following evening and I left him, standing in the High Street. To me he seemed suspiciously inconspicuous. His nondescript clothes, his everyman mien. It was as if he had been specially trained to infiltrate Purley. I bought my ticket and headed for the barrier. When I turned to look back at him he had reverted entirely to type. Standing, back against a duct, he was apparently reading the evening paper. But I could tell that he was carefully observing the commuters who thronged the station concourse.

The following evening Janner arrived punctually at 7.30 for dinner. He brought a bottle of wine with him and greeted my wife with the words, 'I expect you're quite a toughie being married to this one.' Words which were met with approval. He took off his gaberdine raincoat, sat down, and started to play with James. Janner was a big hit. If you had asked me beforehand I wouldn't have said that Janner was the kind of man who would have any rapport with small children, but as it was he was such a success that James asked him to read a bedtime story.

While Janner was upstairs my wife said to me, 'I like your friend. You've never told me about him before.' Dinner was even more of a success. Janner had developed a facility for companionable small talk which amazed me. He displayed a lively interest in all the minutiae of our lives: James, our jobs, our garden, our mortgage, our activities with local voluntary groups. All of it was grist to the mill of his curiosity and yet he never appeared to be condescending or merely inquisitive for the sake of gathering more anthropological data.

After dinner my wife went out. She had an evening class at the local CFE. Janner and I settled down in the living-room, passing the bottle of Piat d'Or back and forth to one another in an increasingly languid fashion.

'You were never like this when we were at Reigate,' I said at length. 'Then all your pronouncements were weighty and wordy. How have you managed to become such an adept small-talker?'

'I learnt to small talk from the Ur-Bororo.' And with that strange introduction Janner launched into his story. He spoke as brilliantly as he ever had, without pausing, as if he had prepared a lecture to be delivered to a solo audience. It was, of course, what I had been dying to hear. All day I had feared that he wouldn't come and that I would have to spend weeks searching the launderettes of South London in order to find him again. Even if he did come, I was worried that he would tell me nothing. That he would remain an enigma and walk out of my life, perhaps this time for good.

'The Ur-Bororo are a tribe, or interlinked group of extended families, living in the Parasquitos region of the Amazon basin. In several respects they closely resemble the indigenous Amerindian tribes of the Brazilian rainforest: they are hunter-gatherers. They subsist on a diet of manioc supplemented with animal protein and miscellaneous vegetables. They are semi-nomadic – following a fixed circuit that leads them through their territory on a yearly cycle. Their social system is closely defined by the interrelation of individuals to family, totemic family and the tribe as a whole. Social interaction is defined by a keen awareness of the incest taboo. Their spiritual beliefs can be characterised as animistic, although as we shall see this view stands up to only the slightest examination. Perhaps the only superficial characteristics that mark them out from neighbouring tribal groups are the extreme crudity of their manufacture. Ur-Bororo pottery, woodcarving and shelter construction must be unrivalled in their meanness and lack of decoration – this is what strikes the outsider immediately. That and the fact that the Ur-Bororo are racially distinct . . .'

'Racially distinct?'

'Shh . . .' Janner held up his hand for silence.

In the brief hiatus before he began to speak again I heard the low warble of the doves in the garden, and, looking across the railway line that ran at the bottom of the garden, I could make out the crenellations and chimneys of the row of semis opposite, drawing in the darkness, like some suburban jungle.

'It is said of any people that language defines their reality. It is only through a subtle appreciation of language that one can enter into the collective consciousness of a tribal grouping, let alone explore the delicate and subtle relationships between that consciousness, the individual consciousness and the noumenal world. Language among the Amerindian tribes of the Amazon is typically supplemented by interleaved semiological systems that, again, represent the coexstensive nature of kinship ties and the natural order. Typically among a tribe such as the Iguatil, body and facial tattooing, cicatrisation, decoration of ceramics, lip plugs and breech clouts will all contribute to the overall body of language.

'What is notable about the Ur-Bororo is that they exhibit none of these semiological systems. They aren't tattooed or cicatrised and they dress in a uniform fashion.'

'Dress?'

'Shhh . . . ! Lurie penetrated to the reality of the Ur-Bororo and was horrified by what he found. He locked his secret away. Marston lived among the Ur-Bororo for only a few months and ended up suspicious but still deceived by them. It was left for me to uncover the secret springs and cogs that drive the Ur-Bororo's world view; it was left for me to reveal them.'

Janner paused, seemingly for effect. He took a pull on his glass of Piat d'Or and drew out a pack of Embassy Regal. He lit one up and looked around for an ashtray. I passed him a small bowl, the kind you get free when you buy duck pâté at Sainsburys. This he examined with some interest, turning it this way and that in the yellow light of the standard lamp, before resuming his tale.

'The basic language of the Ur-Bororo is fairly simple and easy to learn, for a European. Neither its syntax nor its vocabulary is remarkable. It refers to the world which it is intended to describe with simple literal-mindedness. The juxtaposition of subject-object-predicate, in its clear-cut consistency, would seem to reflect a cosmology marked by the same conceptual dualism as our own. This is deceptive. I learnt the basic language of the Ur-Bororo within a couple of months of living with them. As we moved around the rainforest the elders of the tribe took it in turns to tutor me. They would point at objects, mimic actions and so forth. When I had become proficient in this workaday communication they began to refer to more complex ideas and concepts.

'I may add at this stage that their attitude towards me during this period was singular. They were not particularly amazed by me – although to my certain knowledge I was only the third European they had ever met – nor were they overly suspicious. It wasn't until months later that I was able to adequately characterise their manner: they were bland.

'To begin with, the conceptual language of the Ur-Bororo seemed quite unproblematic. It described a world of animistic deities who needed to be propitiated, kinship rituals that needed to be performed, and so forth. The remarkable thing was that in the life of Ur-Bororo society there was no evidence whatsoever of either propitiation or performance. I would hear some of the older men discussing the vital importance of handling the next batch of initiates: sending the adolescent boys to live in an isolated longhouse in the jungle and arranging for their circumcision. They would talk as if this were imminent, and then nothing would happen.

'The reasons for this became evident as I began to accurately decipher their conceptual language: the Ur-Bororo are a boring tribe.' Janner paused again.

A boring tribe? What could that mean?

'When I say that the Ur-Bororo are a boring tribe, this statement is not intended to be pejorative, or worse still, ironic.' Janner pushed himself forward in his chair, screwed up his eyes, and clenched his hands around the edges of the coffee table. 'The Ur-Bororo are objectively boring. They also view themselves as boring. Despite the superficially intriguing nature of the tribe, their obscure racial provenance, their fostering of the illusion of similarity to other Amazonian tribes, and the tiered structure of their language, the more time I spent with the Ur-Bororo, the more relentlessly banal they became.

'The Ur-Bororo believe that they were created by the Sky God, that this deity fashioned their forefathers and foremothers out of primordial muck. It wasn't what the Sky God should have been doing, it should have been doing some finishing work on the heavens and the stars. Creating the Ur-Bororo was what might be called a divine displacement activity. Unlike a great number of isolated tribal groups, the Ur-Bororo do not view themselves as being in any way the "typical" or "essential" human beings. Many such tribes refer to themselves as "The People" or "The Human Beings" and to all others as barbarians, half-animals and so forth. "Ur-Bororo" is a convenient translation of the name neighbouring tribes use for them, which simply means "here before the Bororo". The Ur-Bororo actually refer to themselves with typically irritating self-deprecation as "The People Who You Wouldn't Like to be Cornered by at a Party". They view other tribal peoples as leading infinitely more alluring lives than themselves, and often speak, not without a trace of hurt feelings, of the many parties and other social events to which they are never invited.

'I spoke earlier of a "deeper" conceptual language, spoken by the Ur-Bororo. This is not strictly accurate. The Ur-Bororo have a level of nuance that they can impart to all their conceptual beliefs and this more or less corresponds to the various levels of inflection they can place on their everyday language. To put it another way: the Ur-Bororo speak often of various religious beliefs and accepted cosmological situations but always with the implication that they are at best sceptical. Mostly the "nuance" implies that they are indifferent.

'By extension every word in the Ur-Bororo language has a number of different inflections to express kinds of boredom, or emotional states associated with boredom, such as apathy, ennui, lassitude, enervation, depression, indifference, tedium, and so on. Lurie made the mistake of interpreting the Ur-Bororo language as if "Boring" were the root word. As a result he identified no less than two thousand subjects and predicates corresponding in meaning to the English word. Such as boring hunting, boring gathering, boring fishing, boring sexual intercourse, boring religious ceremony and so on. He was right in one sense – namely that the Ur-Bororo regard most of what they do as a waste of time. In fact the expression that roughly corresponds to "now" in Ur-Bororo is "waste of time".'

Janner paused again and contemplated the empty glass he held in his hand.

'Do you want a cup of coffee?' I said.

'Oh, er . . . Yeah, OK.'

'It's only instant, I'm afraid.'

'That's all right.'

Out in the kitchen I looked around at the familiar objects while I waited for the kettle to boil. The dishwasher that had been our pride and joy when we were first married, the joke cruets shaped like Grecian statues which I'd bought in Brixton Market, James's childish daubs stuck to the fridge with insulating tape. I felt as if I had been looking at these things every day for a thousand days and that nothing had changed. And indeed this was true. Never before had the familiar seemed so . . . familiar. I returned to the living-room, shaken by my epiphany.

We sat back in our chairs and the next few moments passed in companionable silence as we used our teaspoons to break up the undissolved chunks of brown goo in our coffee mugs. Eventually Janner began to speak again.

'I had lived among the Ur-Bororo for nine months. I hunted with the men and I gathered with the women. At first I lived with the adolescent boys in their longhouse, but then I built a hut of my own and moved into it. I felt that I had gained about as much of an insight into Ur-Bororo society as I wanted. I had grown thin and sported a long beard. The Ur-Bororo had ceased to approach me with banal conversational sallies about the weather, which never changed anyway, and began to regard me with total indifference. They were well aware of what it was I was doing among them and they regarded the practice of anthropology with indifference as well. They have a saying in Ur-Bororo that can be roughly translated as, "Wherever you go in the world you occupy the same volume of space".

'As each new day broke over the forest canopy I felt the force of this aphorism. Despite the singular character of the Ur-Bororo I felt that on balance I might as well have never left Reigate.

'I had written up my notes and knew that if I returned to England I would be in a position to complete my doctoral thesis, but I felt a strange sense of inertia. Actually, there was nothing strange about it at all, I simply felt a sense of inertia. There was something wrong with the forest. It felt senescent. Cascades of lianas coated with fungus fell fifty, seventy, a hundred feet, down from the vegetable vaults and buttresses. The complicated twists and petrified coils reminded me of nothing so much as an ancient cardigan, lightly frosted with flecks of scalp and snot, as its wearer nods on and on into the fog of old age.

'The Ur-Bororo profess to believe that a spirit inhabits every tree, bush and animal – all living things have a spirit. The sense in which they believe this is ambiguous; it isn't a positive, assertive belief. Rather, they are content to let the hypothesis stand until it is proved otherwise. These spirits – like the Ur-Bororo themselves – are in a constant state of blank reverie. They are turned in upon the moment, belly-up to the very fact of life.

'It may have been my imagination, or the effect of having been for so long away from society, but I too began to feel the presence of the rainforest as one of transcendent being. The great, damp, dappled room was unfinished and unmade. Somewhere the spirits lay about, bloated on sofas, sleeping off a carbohydrate binge. All days merged into one long Tuesday afternoon. I knew I should leave the Ur-Bororo, but just when I had finally made up my mind to go, something happened. I fell in love.

'It was the time in the Ur-Bororo's yearly cycle when the tribe decamped *en masse*. The object of their excursion was to catch the lazy fish. These listless and enervated creatures live exclusively beneath a series of waterfalls, situated on the tributary of the Amazon which forms the northern boundary of the Ur-Bororos' territory.

'The tribe moved off in the dawn half-light. As we walked, the sun came up. The jungle gave way to a scrubland, over which rags of mist blew. It was a primordial scene, disturbed only by the incessant, strident chatter of the Ur-Bororo. It was a fact that never ceased to astonish me, that despite their professed utter boredom, the Ur-Bororo continued to have the urge to bore one another still further.

'On this particular morning – just as they had every other morning during the time I had spent among them – they were all telling one another the dreams they had had the night before. They all chose to regard their dreams as singular and unique. This provided them with the rationale for constant repetition. In truth, you have never heard anything more crushingly obvious than an Ur-Bororo dream anecdote. They went on and on, repeating the same patterns and the same caricatures of reality. It was like a kind of surreal nursery wallpaper. "And then I turned into a fish," one would say. "That's funny," would come the utterly predictable reply, "I changed into a fish in my dream as well, and today we're going fishing." And so on. Strict correspondence between dream and reality, that was the Ur-Bororo's idea of profundity and as a consequence they placed only the most irritating interpretations on their dreams. As far as I was aware the Ur-Bororo had no particular view about the status of the unconscious – they certainly didn't attach any mystical significance to it. On the whole the impression their dreams gave was of a kind of psychic clearing house where all the detritus of the waking world could be packaged away into neat coincidences.

'While I listened to this drivel I gnawed the inside of my cheek with irritation:

' "I dreamt I was in a forest."

' "A rainforest?"

' "Sort of. I was walking along with some other people in single file. You know what I mean?"

' "Were they the kind of people you wouldn't like to be cornered by at a party?"

' "Definitely, it was us. Then I started turning into . . ." (What would it be this time? A bird, a lizard, a moth, a yam . . . no, it was . . .) ". . . a twig! Isn't that amazing?"

' "Amazing."

'Yeah, amazing. I was so absorbed by my mounting irritation that I simply hadn't noticed the person who was walking in front of me along the forest path. But, coming out into a clearing for a moment, a clear shaft of bright light penetrated the forest canopy and struck the path. Suddenly I saw a young girl, bathed in bright light, her lissom figure edged with gold. She turned to face me. She was wearing the traditional Ur-Bororo garment – a long shapeless grey shift. She glanced for a moment into my eyes; hers were filmed over with immobility, her hand picked and fidgeted at the hem of her shift. She made a little *moue*, brushed a fly off her top lip and said, "I dreamt last night that I was hairball."

'At that precise moment I fell in love. The girl's name was Jane. She was the daughter of one of the tribal elders, although that was of hardly any real significance. You must understand that by this time I was pretty well conditioned by the Ur-Bororo's aesthetic values and to me Jane appeared to be, if not exactly beautiful, at least very appealing, in a homely, comfortable sort of a way. She was in many ways a typical Ur-Bororo, of medium height, with a rather pasty complexion and mousey hair. Her features were rather lumpy, but roughly symmetrical, and her mouth was tantalising, downturned by an infuriatingly erotic expression of sullen indifference.

'Our courtship started immediately. There are no particular guidelines for courtship in Ur-Bororo society. In fact the whole Ur-Bororo attitude to sex, gender and sexuality is muddied and ambiguous. At least formally, pre-marital sex, homosexuality and infidelity are frowned on, but in practice the Ur-Bororo's sexual drive is so circumscribed that no one really minds what anyone else gets up to. The general reaction is simply mild amazement that you have the energy for it.

'All day the kingfishers dived in and out of the glistening brown stream. And the Ur-Bororo stood about in the shallows, perfectly motionless for minutes on end, scrutinising the water. From time to time one of them would bend down and with infinite languor pull out a fish. I soon grew bored and wandered off with Jane into the undergrowth. We strolled along side by side, neither speaking nor touching. The midday sun was high overhead, but its rays barely penetrated the forest canopy two hundred feet above us.

'Gradually, the strangeness of the situation began to impinge on my idle consciousness and I started to look around at the forest, as if for the first time. I had paid attention to the natural world only insofar as it had a bearing on the life of the Ur-Bororo, but now I found myself taking the alien scene in in an aesthetic sense, with the eyes of a lover. And a pretty dull and unexciting scene it was too. You didn't have to be a botanist to see that this area of the rainforest was exceptionally lacking in variegation as far as flora and fauna were concerned. The dun-coloured trunks of the tall trees lifted off into the sky like so many irregular lamp standards, while the immediate foreground was occupied by rank upon rank of rhododendron-type shrubs, none of which seemed to be in flower. It was a scene of unrivalled monotony – the Amazonian equivalent of an enormous municipal park.

'I knew that Jane and I were straying towards the traditional boundary of the Ur-Bororo lands, but neither of us was unduly concerned.

Although the neighbouring tribe, the Yanumani, were notorious as head-hunters and cannibals, their attempts to engage the young Ur-Bororo men in ritual warfare had been met in the past with such apathy on the part of the Ur-Bororo that they had long since given up trying. There was neither the sense of danger nor the beauty of nature to augment my sense of erotic frisson and after an hour or so's walk it entirely died away. I wondered what I was doing walking in the middle of nowhere with this rather sulky, drably dressed young woman. Then I saw the fag packet.

'It was an old Silk Cut packet, crushed flat and muddy, the inked lettering faded but still sharply legible, especially in this alien context. But I didn't have long to marvel at its incongruous presence, I could already hear the distant whine of chainsaws. I turned to Jane.

' "White men?"

' "Yes, they're extending the Pan-American Highway through here. The estimated completion date is June 1985." She tugged and picked at her hem.

' "But aren't you frightened? Aren't you concerned? The coming of the road will destroy your entire culture, it may even destroy you."

' "Big deal."

'We turned round and started back to the river. That night as Jane and I lay together, her leaden form cutting off my circulation and gradually crushing the life out of my arm, I made a decision . . .'

There was the sound of the front door closing and my wife came into the room. She was carrying her bicycle lamps and wearing an orange cagoule.

'What, still talking? Has James been calling, darling?'

'No, not a peep out of him all evening.'

'Good, that means he hasn't done it. I'll get him up now and then put him down for the night.' She turned to Janner, 'James is going through a bed-wetting stage.'

'Really?' said Janner. 'You know, I wet the bed right up until I went to Reigate.' And they were off again. Janner seemed to sense no incongruity at all in moving directly from relating the high drama of his sojourn with the Ur-Bororo, to discussing the virtues of rubber sheets with my wife. I squeaked back in the vinyl of my armchair and waited for them to wind one another down. I had to hear the rest of Janner's story, I wouldn't let him go until he had finished. If necessary I would force him to stay until morning.

'Well, you must come again. You two seem to have such a lot to catch up on.'

'We do, but next time you must come over to our place. My wife doesn't know many people in Purley and she's trying to get out of the house a bit more now that she's had the baby.'

I sat upright with a jerk. What was that Janner had said? Wife? Baby? My wife had said goodnight and reminded me to lock up. She was padding quietly up the stairs.

'Your wife, Janner, is it . . . ?'

'Jane, yes. Now if you keep quiet I'll tell you the rest of the story.

'I courted Jane for three weeks. This involved little more than sitting around with her parents, making small talk. The Ur-Bororo have an almost inexhaustible appetite for small talk. Like the English they preface almost all conversations with a lengthy discussion of the weather, although in their monotonous climate there is far less to talk about. So little in fact, that they are reduced to mulling over the minutiae of temperature, humidity and precipitation. Jane's parents were affable enough characters. They seemed to have no objection to our marriage, as long as we were seen to observe the customary formalities and rituals. I was packed off to receive instruction from the shaman.

'The shaman was uncharacteristically interesting for an Ur-Bororo. I suppose it was something to do with his profession. His shed was set slightly apart from those of the rest of the tribe. (You remember the shed I lived in when we were at Reigate. It was almost an exact replica of an Ur-Bororo dwelling shed, except of course that the Amazonian ones have rather rougher clapboarding and no window, only a square opening.)

' "Come in my dear boy, do come in," he said. "So you're going to marry young Jane and take her away from us are you?" I nodded my assent.

' "Well, I expect as an anthropologist that you know a little of our beliefs, don't you? How we were created inadvertently by the Sky God. How we live our lives. How we practise circumcision and infibulation as cleansing rituals. How our young men undergo rigorous rites of passage and how our initiation rites last for weeks and involve the ingestion of toxic quantities of psychotropic roots; you know all this, don't you?"

'"Well, in outline, yes, but I can't say that I've ever seen any of you ever do any of these things at all."

'"No. Quite right, jolly good, jolly good. That's the ticket, you seem to have a good head on your shoulders. Of course we don't actually do any of these things."

'"But why? Surely you're frightened of all the gods and spirits?"

'"Well, we don't really believe in them in quite that way you know. We believe in their validity as er . . . examples, metaphors if you will, of the way that things are, but we don't actually believe in tree spirits, good Lord no!"

'The shaman chuckled for quite a while at the thought such excessive religious zeal, and then offered me a cup of coya. Coya is a lukewarm drink made from the powdered root of the coya tree, it looks alarmingly like instant coffee, but the taste is a lot blander. I couldn't be bothered to argue with this absurd figure. Unlike other tribes who have shamen, the status of the shaman in Ur-Bororo society is ambiguous and somewhat irrelevant. The shaman often sketched out the form of some of the rigorous rituals the Ur-Bororo nominally believe in, but hardly anyone even bothered to attend these mock performances. On the whole he was regarded with a kind of amused disdain. Although it was still thought important to have pale versions of the ceremonies performed for births, marriages and deaths.

'I saw the shaman a couple more times before our marriage. He went through the tired motions of instructing me in the Ur-Bororo faith and also retailed me a lot of useless advice on how to make marriage work. Stuff about counting to ten when I got angry, giving Jane the opportunity to state her case when we had a disagreement, and all this kind of twaddle, the sort of thing you'd expect from an advice column in a fourth-rate women's magazine.

'The ceremony itself was held to be a great success. Twenty or thirty of us gathered outside the shaman's shed and Jane and I joined hands while we all listened to him irritate us by wittering inanities in a high fluting voice. I can quite honestly say that I've never seen a drabber social occasion than that Ur-Bororo wedding ceremony. All of us in our grey tunics, standing in the gloomy clearing being comprehensively bored.

'After the actual ceremony, the guests disported themselves around the clearing, talking nineteen to the dozen. Jane led me among them and introduced me to aunts, cousins and friends. All of whom I knew too well already. The aunts pinched my cheek and made fatuous comments. There was much ingestion of rather watery manioc beer, which was followed, inevitably, by the kind of turgid flatulence which passes for high spirits among the Ur-Bororo.

'Jane has a brother, David, and the Ur-Bororo knew that I intended to take both of them back to England with me after the wedding, but they showed little surprise or emotion about it. They also knew that I was convinced that their society was doomed to extinction, but this too failed to exercise them. They had no particular feelings about the coming of civilisation and I found it impossible to rouse them out of their torpor. To be honest, I had long since given up trying.

'Our departure was an unemotional experience. There were slight hugs, pecks on the cheek and handclasps all round. Jane seemed mildly piqued. As our canoe slid off down river, one of the younger men cried out, "Come back soon, if you can stand the pace!" And then we were gone. In two days we were at the town of Mentzos where we boarded a launch that took us to the mouth of the Amazon. Two days after that we were in Buenos Aires and a day later we arrived in Purley, where we have remained ever since.'

'And that's it? That's the story?'

'Yes. Like I said, I live in Purley now and I do a little teaching at Croydon Polytechnic. If you like to put it this way: I'm cured of my obsession with the Ur-Bororo.'

'But what about the Lurie Foundation? Don't you have to publish your work? Won't it be popularised in the Sunday supplements?'

'No, no, there's no necessity for that. All Lurie wanted was for some other poor idiot to suffer the unbelievable tedium he experienced when staying with the Ur-Bororo in the Thirties.'

'And what about Jane and David? You can't tell me that you've managed to integrate them into English society with no difficulty at all. You said that the Ur-Bororo are racially distinct, what does that mean?'

'Yes that's true, and I suppose in a way intriguing; the Ur-Bororo don't really have any defining characteristics as a people. They aren't Mongoloid or Negro or Caucasian or anything for that matter. But their appearance as a people is so unremarkable that one – how can I put it – doesn't feel inclined to remark upon it. As for Jane, I'm very much in love with her. I must confess that although we can't be said to have a great rapport, I still find her maddeningly erotic; it's something about her complete inertia when she's in bed, it makes me feel so . . . so like a man. We have a child now, Derek, and he's all that you could want. And David still lives with us. Why don't you and your wife come over next week and meet them, you'll be able to see how well they've assimilated.'

After Janner had gone I sat staring at the twin elements of the electric fire. It was high summer and they were cold and lifeless and covered with a fine furring of dust which I knew would singe with a metallic smell when winter came. Funny how no one ever thinks of dusting the elements of electric fires. Perhaps there was room on the market for some kind of specialised product.

Exactly a week later my wife and I stood outside 47 Fernwood Crescent. The house was lit up in a cheery sort of way, the curtains were pulled back from the windows and inside everything looked spic and span. Number 47 was a more or less typical Purley residence, semi-detached with a corrugated car port to the side of the house in lieu of the garage. Like the other residents of Fernwood Crescent Janner had taken the trouble to paint the exterior woodwork and drainpipes in an individual colour, in his case bright green. The bell ding-donged under my finger and the green door swung open.

'You must be Jane?'

'That's right, come in. I've heard such a lot about you.'

What I first noticed about her was her accent, remarkably flat and colourless – it was pure South London, right down to the slightly nasal character. I can't say that I paid any attention at all to what she looked like; in this respect Janner's description of her was entirely accurate. She was like someone that you pass in a crowd, a face that you momentarily focus on and then forget for ever. As for her brother David, who got up from the sofa to greet us, there was an obvious family resemblance.

We hung up our coats and sat down in a rough semi-circle around the redundant fireplace, and exchanged the conversational inanities which signify 'getting-to-know-one-another'. After a while Janner came in. 'Sorry, I didn't hear you arrive. I've just been in the garden doing a little pottering. Would anyone like a drink?' He took orders and repaired to the kitchen. By the time he returned I was deeply embroiled with David in a discussion of the relative merits of the Dewey decimal system, as against other methods of cataloguing. Janner caught the tail-end of something we were saying. 'I see David's caught you already,' he laughed. 'He won't let up now, he's a demon for classification since he started work at the library. Why, he's even colour-coded the spice jars in the kitchen.' We all laughed at this.

What Janner said was true. David wouldn't let go of me all evening. He was an irritating conversationalist who had the habit of not only repeating everything that you said, but also ending your sentences for you, so that a typical exchange went something like this:

'Yes, we try and maintain a microfiche . . .'

'Catalogue at the school for the older students – maintain a microfiche catalogue for the older students, hmn . . .'

I would have felt like hitting David if it wasn't for the fact that he was so affable and ingratiating. Dinner was unremarkable. We had some kind of casseroled meat with vegetables, but I couldn't say what kind of meat it was.

David's pressing interest in taxonomy cast a deep sense of enervation over me. I nearly slumped down on my chair during the dessert course and once or twice the vinyl did give off a squawk. My wife and Jane were deep in conversation about the Local Education Authority and Janner had disappeared upstairs to change the baby's nappy. I excused myself from David and tiptoed after him.

I found him in a little room under the eaves which had been tricked out as a nursery. He was deftly manipulating the Wet Ones, as a man born to it. The baby was a nondescript little thing with putty-coloured skin and a whorl of indeterminate mousey hair on its little scalp.

'Takes after its mother,' said Janner grasping two tiny feet in his one bony hand. 'Can't say I'm sorry. Wouldn't wish my face on any child.'

'Janner, what are you going to do?'

'Do? Do about what?'

'About Jane, about David, about the Ur-Bororo.'

'Why, nothing, nothing at all.' He fastened the sticky-backed tapes and plunked the baby back in its cot. It stared up at us with blank, unfocused, incurious eyes.

'But Janner, you're a scientist, you have a duty to tell. Is it the Lurie Foundation, have they got some kind of a hold on you?'

'Nothing of the sort. Of course I could publish if I wanted to, but for some reason the whole subject of the Ur-Bororo leaves me cold, I just can't get worked up about it. I don't think the world would be any the wiser for my insights.'

Soon afterwards we took our leave. All the way home my wife talked about Jane. They seemed to have really hit it off together. I was silent, entirely preoccupied by my thoughts about Janner and the Ur-Bororo.

Our two families became quite close during that autumn. I should say that we saw each other at least once a fortnight, sometimes more. I even grew to appreciate David. There was something admirable about his dogged adherence to the most simple categories he could latch on to. As for Janner, I raised the subject of the Ur-Bororo with him several more times but he was completely unconcerned. He was in the process of becoming quite a minor celebrity – the sort of pop academic the general public takes up from time to time and turns into a television personality. His book linking the observation of swirling laundry to traditional Buddhist meditation surprisingly had become a hit and he was in the process of negotiating serialisation with the colour supplements.

As for me, I went on teaching, playing volleyball and asking recalcitrant pupils the names of power stations. The lagging which had for a brief period been removed from my mind came back – together with new, improved, cavity-wall insulation.

The Quantity Theory of Insanity

Denver, Colorado

A depressing day here at the special interdisciplinary conference. I suppose that as the author of the theory that has generated so much academic activity I should feel a certain proprietorial glee at the sight of hundreds of psychologists, sociologists, social scientists and other less mainstream academics running hither and thither, talking, disputing, gesturing, debating and conferring. Instead I feel only depressed and alienated from the great industry of thought I myself have engineered. And added to that I think the low quality pf the celluloid they've used for the name badges betrays the fact that the department simply hasn't allocated a big enough budget.

I spent the morning in the main auditorium of the university giving my address to the assembled conferees. Dagglebert, against my expressed wishes, had put together some kind of video display or slide show to accompany my introductory lecture, 'Some Aspects of the Quantity Theory of Insanity'. Sadly, even though Dagglebert has irrepressible faith in visual aids, he has absolutely no spatial awareness whatsoever. I kept looking up and realising that flow charts were running over my face, and at one stage I looked down to discover that my stomach was neatly encompassed by a Venn diagram section tagged 'Manic Depressives in Coventry 1977–79'.

Despite these and other drawbacks, it went well. Several hundred hirsute men and women sat on the edge of their seats for a full three hours while I went over the principal aspects of the theory. If the truth be told I could have gargled and they would have been just as attentive. I've now reached that rarefied position in academia where I have the cachet of a lecturing Miles Davis. I could have allowed Dagglebert to project slides for three hours and then sauntered on for five minutes of disjointed and facile muttering – and still I would have been vigorously applauded.

As it was I declined to cash in on the credulousness of my audience. For once I would attempt the truth. I would take a serious stab at stopping the feverish growth of an industry I myself was responsible for helping to create. I would demystify the Quantity Theory myth, and in the process take a few clay idols down with me.

Accordingly, I dealt with the subject personally as well as historically. As with all great theories I felt that it was especially important for an academic audience to understand the personal dimension, the essential *humanity* of the origin of such an idea. But it didn't work. Once one has a certain kind of academic status, any statement that you make, if it is couched in the language of your discipline, no matter how critical, how searching, is seen only as an embellishment, another layer of crystalline accretion to the stalactite. To break it off at the root, one's language would have to be brutal, uncompromising, emotional, non-technical.

So I began by telling them of the grey cold afternoon in suburban Birmingham, when, labouring to complete the index to an American college press's edition of my doctoral thesis, 'Some Social Aspects of Academic Grant Application in 1970's Britain', I was visited in one pure thought bite with the main constituents of the theory as we know it today.

At least that would be one way of looking at the experience. Seen from another angle the Quantity Theory was merely the logical conclusion of years of frustrated thinking, the butter that eventually formed after the long rhythm of churning. I have often had occasion to observe – and indeed Stacking has recently and belatedly stated the observation as a tentative syndrome which he expresses: (Á → Å). Where Å = *a subsequent state of affairs* – that events are reconstructed more than they are ever constructed.

Once you have published, grown old and then died, the events surrounding the original theoretical discovery with which you have been associated take on an impossible causal direction and momentum. One which certainly wasn't apparent at the time. Scientists are particularly prone to this syndrome. For example, take Gödel and his Incompleteness. Once he had made the proposition, everything in his life had necessarily led up to that moment, that piece of work. Thus, when the infant Gödel cried in his cot, the particular twist of phlegm striations, wafted in his gullet by his bawling, implied that no logical symbolic system can construct full grounds for its own proof. Poor Gödel, his breakdowns, his anorexia, all of them inextricably bound up with his fifteen minutes of academic fame. Why?

Well, put simply, when aberrant events occur they become subject to the same principle – at the level of human, social observation – as particles do to instrumental observation at the sub-atomic level. The effect of observation has a direct impact on the nature of the event, altering its coordinates as it were, although not in any simple dimension. I mean, if an aberrant event occurs it doesn't then occur in another place or time because of the attention it subsequently attracts. It doesn't retroactively take up that other position or time, or even *rate of occurrence* before it has in fact taken place. That would be absurd.

Rather all of these: the effect of observation on aberrant events tends to be the reversal of their causality, their causal direction. However, there is no reversal of necessity as far as the occurrence of *P* is concerned – and I think this is something that has been ignored.

So when I 'thought up' the Quantity Theory of Insanity, I was in fact being caused to think it up by the subsequent fact of the general reaction that occurred: public commotion, academic furore, even a front-page paragraph in the quality press. Let me make this clearer by means of an example: with murders, to take a commonplace aberrant event, this syndrome is so obvious that it hardly arouses any comment. X commits a murder, or he *apparently* commits a murder. Perhaps it was a very unfortunate accident? Maybe he was arguing with Y and pushed her rather too vigorously and she tripped on the lino and dashed her brains out on the edge of the gas cooker, just like that. Furthermore, perhaps X, crazed with grief, went mad, cut up Y and buried her in the garden. Subsequently caught, X was then *retrospectively* branded 'psychopathic', by anyone and everyone who had any connection with him.

'Oooh, yairs,' says a neighbour, 'the way he rattled those empty milk bottles together when he put them out on the front step, there was something demonic about it.' X, once upstanding, loyal, prone, perhaps, to the same slight eccentricities as anyone – G, for example, although let us not bandy capitals – has been ruined, now and in the past, by the observation factor.

None of this, you can now appreciate (and perhaps always have) is by way of digression. If we are to talk meaningfully of my life, and of the part that I played in the origination of Quantity Theory, we must be able to account for observational factors – and then be able to ignore them. Ironically, given the tendency to subordinate the individual consciousness to some creative zeitgeist, I turn out to be the best possible Quantity Theory historian. After all, I was there. Which is more than can be said for Musselborough, Nantwich and the rest of those twerps.

Well, then. My own early life was fraught with neurotic illness. The debacle surrounding my analysis by Alkan is well known to the public, so there's no point in trying to hide it. The received understanding about my background, my early life, my schooling, and indeed my undergraduate studies with Müeller, is that they were all spectacularly mundane. My circumstances and character – if you listen to these biographers – had the absolute banality of a Hitler. They were so ordinary, that reading the facts on paper one could only conclude that they had been recorded as the prelude to some cautionary tale.

In this respect the 'official version' is wholly correct. Mine was a childhood of Terylene sheets, bunion plasters and Sunday afternoon excursions to witness the construction of Heathrow Airport. My parents were quiet people, who conspired together gently to live in a world where no one shitted, ejaculated, or killed one another violently. This upbringing left me morbidly incapable of dealing with the real world. I was appalled by my own body. The obsession I developed in my teens with the theoretical aspects of psychology was a logical path to take, it offered me a liberation from the nauseating, cloacal confines of my own skin.

I had no sense of being singled out as unique, or blessed. I had no suspicion that I might be the *ubermensch*. Quite the reverse. It was painfully clear to me that I was destined to become like my father, constantly striving to stave off chaos through rigorous application to detail.

My father was an actuary, but he never regarded the calculations he made all day as relating to real risks, or real people. Indeed, when asked by people what he did for a living he would invariably say that he was a mathematician.

You can see, therefore, that meeting Alkan was a godsend; his impact on me was enormous. He really had his breakdown for me insofar as it actually propelled me further into the awful mundanity I was prey to, so far and so fast that I could not help but emerge. Without Alkan's influence I might have remained eking out my feeble studies over decades.

A bleak flatland day, that's how I remember it. At the time I had received the first of many postgraduate grants. This one was to enable me to do some work on phrenological and physiognomic theories of the nineteenth century. I was particularly taken by the work of Gruton, an English near-contemporary and sometime collaborator with Fleiss. Gruton maintained (and it was his only real gift to posterity) that the visible nose represented only ⅛ of the 'real' nose. The nose we see rising above the surface of our faces was, according to Gruton, literally the tip of the psychological iceberg of hereditary predisposition. The 'shape' of the real, internal nose is the true indicator of character, proclivities and so forth.

In the 1880s Gruton developed a system of measuring the internal nose using very bright spotlights inserted into ears, eyes and indeed the nose itself. The patient's head was shaved and when the light was switched on, the shadow area defined on the scalp was traced on to paper. Using a complex topological equation Gruton would then cross-reference all the different projections to produce what he called a 'nasoscope'. This then was an accurate representation of the shape of the internal nose.

The morning I met Alkan I was crossing the campus on my way back from the library to my bed-sitting-room. I had a sheaf of nasoscopes, which I'd received that morning by rail from the archivist at the Gruton Clinic, tucked under my arm.

I must explain at this juncture that at this time Alkan was nearing the height of his celebrity. Predictably, I eschewed attending his seminars which he held regularly in the squat, twenty-two-storey psychology faculty building. These were clearly for sychopants and groupies – besides which Alkan himself, although he had trained first as a medical doctor and then as a psychiatrist, was nonetheless sympathetic to the psychotherapeutic movement. I, on the other hand, made empirical testability the benchmark of all theory and could not abide the woolly fantasising that seemed to dominate couch-pushing.

Alkan was an imposing figure. In appearance somewhat like Le Corbusier, but much taller and thinner. Entirely bald, he affected a manner of almost complete naturalness, which was difficult to fault. Undoubtedly it was this that had given him his tremendous reputation as a clinician. When Alkan said, 'How are you?' the question had total nuance: he really wanted to know how you were, although at the same time he was asking the question purely for the sake of social form. Yet he managed simultaneously to acknowledge both of these conflicting messages and still reformulated the question so that it incorporated them and yet was devoid of all assumptions. Furthermore none of the above seemed to be *implied*.

Alkan, then. Striding across the concrete agora at Chelmsford, his form complementing the anthropomorphic brutalism of the campus architecture. Shoulders twisted – arbitrarily, like the sprigs of steel that protrude from reinforced concrete. And I, wholly anonymous, at that time consciously cultivating a social apathy and lack of character which was beginning to border on the pathological. We collided in the very centre of the agora, because I was not looking at where I was going. The impact knocked the loose bundle of nasoscopes from under my arm and they fell about us, lapping the paving slabs. The two of us then ducked and dove, until they were all gathered up again, smiling all the while.

Before handing them back to me Alkan paused and examined one of the nasoscopes. I was impressed, he clearly knew what it was. He was following its shape to see if it conformed with the 'character equation' Gruton had inked in below.

'Fascinating, a nasoscope. I haven't seen one for years. I did some work on Gruton once . . .'

'Oh, er . . . Oh. I didn't know, at least I haven't read it.' I felt absolutely at a loss. I was meant to have the license to hate the playboy Alkan and here he was professing detailed knowledge of the obscure corner of the field to which I had staked my own claim.

'No reason why you should have. It was never published.' He fell to examining the plasticised sheet again. As he scanned the meticulously shaded areas that formed the character map, he pursed his lips and blew through them, making an odd whiffling noise. This was just one of Alkan's numerous idiosyncrasies which I later made my own.

'D'you see there.' He pointed at a long, lacy blob, not dissimilar to the north island of New Zealand. 'Gruton would have said that that indicated *heimic* tendencies.'

'Sorry?'

'*Heimic* tendencies. Gruton believed that masturbation could not only cause moral degeneration in terms of the individual psyche, he also thought that it could influence people politically. He developed a whole vocabulary of terms to describe these different forms of degeneration, one of which was *heimic*. If you care to come to my rooms I'll show you a little dictionary of these terms that Gruton put together and had printed at his own expense.'

Alkan's rooms were in the Monoplex, the tower built in 1952 for the Festival of Britain, which dominated the Chelmsford campus. A weird, cantilevered construction shaped like a cigar, it zoomed up into the flat Essex sky. The lift, as ever, was out of order and Alkan attacked the staircase with great gusto. I remember that he seemed entirely unaffected by the climb when I staggered into a seat in his rooms some five minutes later, a hundred and fifty feet higher up.

We spent the rest of that morning together. Alkan was an amazing teacher and as we looked at his cache of Gruton papers and then moved on to broader subjects he amazed me by the way he illuminated grey area after grey area. His dialectical method was bizarre to say the least. It took the form of antithesis succeeding antithesis. Alkan would guide the student into acknowledging that he found a theory, or even a body of fact, untenable but that he could not supply an alternative; and then he would admit that he couldn't either. His favourite expression was 'I don't know'. Area after area of the most complex thought was illuminated for me by those 'I don't knows'.

At that time Alkan was still practising as an analyst and it was his contention that no educative relationship could proceed without a simultaneous therapeutic relationship. Alkan's student/analysands were a raucous bunch. Zack Busner, Simon Gurney, Adam Sikorski, Phillip Hurst and the other Adam, Adam Harley. Now of course these are virtually household names, but at that time they were like any other group of young bloods – doing their doctoral work, affecting a particular dress style and swaggering about the campus as if they owned it.

Alkan's bloods delighted in playing elaborate psychological tricks on one another – the aim of which was to convince the victim that he was psychotic. They went to great lengths to perpetrate these. Spiking each others' breakfast cereals with peyote, constructing elaborate *trompe l'oeil* effects – false landscapes glued to the outside of the window – and insinuating bugging equipment into rooms so that they could then 'unconsciously' voice their comrades' private ejaculations. These high jinks were looked down on benignly by Alkan, who viewed them as the necessary flexing of the muscles of the psyche. As for other members of the faculty, academics and students alike viewed Alkan's bloods with undisguised suspicion, bordering on loathing.

I was totally disarmed by the interest that Alkan had taken in my Gruton work. He seemed genuinely impressed by the research that I had done – and he put my lack of conviction easily on a par with his own. I would say that that morning in his eyrie-office I was as near to knowing the *real* Alkan as I ever would be. His subsequent behaviour ran back into his early work after he was dead and formed a composite view of a man who was much more than the sum of his parts – and I suppose there is a certain justice in the judgement of posterity – he had, after all, incorporated parts of other people as well as his own.

Nonetheless, I was genuinely astonished when I realised the next month that Alkan, had, without in any way consulting or warning me, arranged to take over the role of my supervisor Dr Katell. The first I knew of this was a handwritten list on a noticeboard which stated quite clearly that I was due to see Dr Alkan for my monthly meeting. I hurried along to see Dr Katell. He was sitting in his blond wood office by the rectangular lily pond. The place stank of furniture polish, a bright bunch of dahlias stood squeaking in a cut-glass vase.

'My dear boy . . .' he said, squeaking forward his little ovoid body on the synthetic leather seat of his synthetic leather armchair. I made my goodbyes and left.

When I appeared for my first supervisory session Alkan was all smiles. He took the bundle of manuscript and nasoscopes out from under my arm and ushered me to a seat.

'My dear boy,' he said, hunching his lanky body in the leather sling that stretched between the two stainless steel handlebars which constituted the arms of his chair. 'My dear boy. You realise of course that as your thesis supervisor I feel it my duty, my obligation, to undertake an analysis with you . . .'

We started at once. Alkan's analytic method, which still has some practitioners to this day, despite the impact of Quantity Theory, was commonly termed 'Implication'. Its full title came from Alkan's 1956 paper of the same name, 'Implied Techniques of Psychotherapy'. Put simply (and to my mind it was a ludicrously simple idea), instead of the analyst listening to the patient and then providing an interpretation, of whatever kind, Alkan would say what he *thought* the analysand would say. The analysand was then obliged to furnish the interpretation he thought Alkan would make. Alternatively, Alkan would give an interpretation and the analysand was required to give an account that adequately matched it.

The theory that lay behind this practice was that the psyche contained a 'refractive membrane'. An interior, reflective barrier which automatically mirrored any stimuli. Naturally the only way to 'trick' the reflective membrane was to present it with information that was incapable of 'reflection'. Information that assumed the reflection from the off. I suppose the remarkable thing about Alkan's method – and indeed its subsequent practitioners – is that all their published case histories bear a startling resemblance to those of entirely conventional methods. In other words, the implication technique made no difference whatsoever to either the actual content of an analysis, or the ultimate course.

I lived in digs in Colchester during the final two years I spent under Alkan's supervision. My doctoral thesis grew by leaps and bounds, until I was unable to pay for the typist. As far as Alkan was concerned, Implication gave me the confidence I needed to reach my full, neurotic potential. If I had been withdrawn before, I now became posivitely hermitic. I never saw my fellow postgraduates, except for the monthly postgraduate meetings.

Alkan implied, time after time, that I was a colourless, deliberately bland individual whose whole psyche was bent to the task of deflecting whatever stimuli the world had to give me. My studies, my personal habits, even my appearance, were merely extensions of my primary defensive nature. He was right. I hated to socialise; I had no sense of fun at all. I deliberately affected the utmost anonymity. I was obsessively neat, but devoid of any redeeming idiosyncrasies. My room at Mrs Harris's was the same the day I left as it was the day I arrived. The bedside lamp stood on the same paper doily, the gas fire whiffled, the puppies sported on the wall, the plastic-backed brush and comb set was correctly aligned. Mrs Harris was a stolid, taciturn woman and that suited me just fine. I would sit silently at the breakfast table and she would lay impossible mounds of food in front of me. I would eat the food and suffer accordingly. It is the great success of a certain strain of English puritan to have almost completely internalised the mortification they feel it necessary to inflict, both on themselves and others.

And so the most banal of things were effortlessly metamorphosed into experiences over a period of some months. There was no real progress until the day Alkan disappeared. Arriving early (as was dictated by the psychopathology that Alkan had himself implied for me) for the monthly meeting of Alkan's analysand/students I found the group prematurely assembled. They ignored me as I slid awkwardly into a tip-up chair and desk combination at the back of the classroom. Adam Harley was speaking.

'There's no sign of him anywhere, no note, no indication of where he might be . . .'

'Run through it all again, Adam, from the beginning. There may be something you've neglected,' Sikorski broke in.

'All right. Here it is. I arrived for my session with Alkan at about 9.30 this morning. I knocked on the door to his rooms and he shouted "Come in". I entered. He wasn't in the main room so I assumed he was in the bathroom. I sat down and waited, after about five minutes I became a little restless and began to wander about. I took some books out of the bookcase, leafed through them and put them back. I was trying to create just enough noise to remind Alkan that I was there without being intrusive. Eventually I became curious, the door to the bathroom was ajar, I pushed it open . . . the bathroom was empty, there was no one there.'

'And you're absolutely sure that you heard him call to you.'

'Certain. Unless it was one of you with a tape recorder.'

There was general laughter at this point. I took the opportunity to slip out of the prefabricated classroom. I had a hunch.

Across the receding chessboard of flagstones whipped by the wind,

I skittered from side to side. The crux, as it were, of my early experience lay in this decision, this leap into the unknown; this act of what could only be called initiative. It could be argued (and indeed has been, see Stenning: 'Fluid Participles, Choice and Change'), that I was merely responding to an appropriate transference, in the appropriate infantile/neurotic manner.

Today, if I remember that day at all, it is summed up for me by one of my last, powerfully retentive fugues. The sharp, East Anglian gusts cut into me. I looked around and was visited with a powerful urge to rearrange the disordered buildings that made up the campus, many of them at unsatisfactory angles to one another. The steps that spirally ascended the core of the Monoplex shone bright beams of certainty at me. I took them four at a time, pausing to pant on landings every three flights where black vinyl benches reflected the chromium struts of the ascending bannister.

I lingered outside Alkan's door until a lapine huddle of research chemists had waddled past and round the bend of the corridor. For a brief moment their incisors overbit the twenty miles of Essex countryside, which was visible from the twentieth floor. Then I entered. In the bathroom, by the subsiding warm coils of Alkan's recently worn clothing I found a clue. A card for a cab service. The office address was on Dean Street in Soho, London.

Soho at that time was a quiet backwater where vice was conducted with a minimum of effort. The aspidistra of English prostitution was kept flying down pissy alleys. And the occasional influx of kids from the suburbs, or men from the ships, flushed the network of drinking clubs and knocking shops clean for another fortnight.

Vice still had the same scale as the architecture, it was only three or four storeys high. Homosexuals, jazz musicians and journalists formed companionable gaggles. Things that people did were still risqué before they became sordid.

I put up at the Majestic Hotel in Muswell Hill, a pink, pebble-dashed edifice. Originally it must have been intended for an Edwardian extended family, but it had become home to riff-raff from all over the world: salesmen, confidence tricksters, actors and graduate students. I ventured by juddering bus down into the West End on a daily basis. The cab company the card in Alkan's bathroom referred to was easily found. It was a cubby-hole tenanted by an Italian speaker in a flat tweed cap. He made no sign of remembering a tall, thin man, somewhat like Le Corbusier. Indeed, it could have been a resistance to the Modernist movement as a whole that made him so abusive towards me when I pressed him for information.

I took to wandering hither and thither, aimlessly crossing and re-crossing my steps. I was convinced that Alkan was in the West End of London and that he wanted to be found. I saw his behaviour as purposive. I gave no thought to the fact that my grant had run out, that I was due to appear before the supervisory panel in a matter of weeks, and that my leviathan of a thesis lay beached on the nylon counterpane of my foldaway bed in Chelmsford.

One of the main disadvantages of an impoverished, nomadic metropolitan existence is that in winter you cannot have privacy without either purchasing it, or gaining access to it in a lockable toilet cubicle. I desperately needed privacy, for, during my years of retreat from the world, I had developed certain private habits, certain rituals combining magical twists of thought with bodily functions that I had to perform on a four-hourly basis. Lacking the wherewithal for a hotel (we were formally expelled from the Majestic every morning at 9.00 and not allowed back in until 5.30), I took to the conveniences, becoming adept at selecting the toilets where I would have the most genuine peace and quiet. This was a difficult and absorbing task. So many of the public toilets and even those in large hotels and restaurants were frequented by homosexuals. I had no argument with these people, either moral or psychological (and I may point out at this juncture that Quantity Theory as a *whole* maintains no defined perspective), but the push, shove and then rasp of flesh, cloth and metal fastener against ill-secured prefabricated panels and grouted gulleys tended to interrupt my rituals.

So, I elevated my search for the ideal cubicle – warm, discrete, well lit – to an exact science. Unnoticed by me, this search was beginning to usurp the primary quest. It is ironic, therefore, that unknowingly, unintentionally, I began to find evidence of the great psychologist where I myself sought refuge.

I could avoid the actual congress of homosexuals quite easily. However, without abandoning my private study altogether I could not hope to avoid the evidence of their activities: crude but believable advertisements, scrawled in Biro or neatly lettered; seemingly hacked with an axe, or delicately carved with a penknife; they drew the reader's attention inexorably to penile size:

> I'm 45 and my wife gives me no satisfaction coz shes too slack. If you have a 9" cock, or better, meet me here after 6 any wensday. I will take on any number of lusty boys.

and:

> Boys under 21 with 6" or more meet me here. You do it to me I'll do it to you.

And the direct, if disturbing:

> Give me big dix.

There was one of these water-closet communicants who was more readily recognisable and more prolific than the rest – I began to see his entreaties in a lot of my favourite haunts, and to come across them occasionally when I broached new territory. This person was distinguishable by his rounded, laboured writing in red Biro, which reminded me of the hand of an adolescent schoolgirl – especially the characteristic of drawing small circles in place of the point over the 'i'. Furthermore, his graffiti were always written neatly on the wall directly above or below the point where the toilet paper dispenser was mounted. They were also very carefully executed. With some of the best examples I could actually see where the artist had used a ruler to get his script to line up just so. As for content, alas that was wearisomely predictable:

> Meet me here on Friday or Saturday evening if you are better than 7". I have a 9" cock which I like to have kissed and sucked till I come in someone's mouth. I like young boys of around 16, but also more experienced men.

This I noted down in my leather-bound journal from the wall of an unpretentious, unfrequented, spotlessly clean, underground municipal convenience in Pimlico. I had no idea why I had taken to recording such things. I had been in London only a fortnight or so; I had no fixed view about the status of my quest for Alkan. On the whole I was inclined to view it as spectacularly important. I had, after all, given up my forthcoming exam in order to find him. My analysis with him was incomplete, I had no family or friends to support me. On the other hand I could just as easily feel dismissive and indifferent about the quest for Alkan. Who needed the daft old coot anyway? Nonetheless I did immediately notice the connection between the advertisement above and this:

> I like to suck young boys cocks and to have mine sucked as well. I've only 5", but it's hard all the time. If you're 16 or under meet me here on Tuesday at 9.00.

neatly scripted beneath the Smallbone of Devizes ceramic, interleaved sheet-holder clamped to the distempered wall of the warm and capacious gents at the Wallace Collection. And this:

> Fun time every evening here or at the xxxx [illegible] club. All experienced men better than 8" meet me for sucking frolics. I am 27 and I have 9 good inches which you can nip and lick.

incongruously proclaimed from a bare space of rendering, framed with grout, left available, as if on purpose, by the absence of a tile in the checkerboard that skirted the commode in the denizens of the Reform Club.

If I idly noted down this smut cycle it was not for any reason but boredom. It wasn't until later, days later, that, glancing on passing, in the canted, cracked, oval mirror that capitulated on top of the dead bureau in my L-shaped wind-tunnel at the Majestic, I saw the hidden significance of these three bites. I saw it as a sequence solely of numbers, integers, detached from the penises-in-themselves, thus:

> 7, 9, 16, 5, 16, 9, 8, 27, 9

This in itself obviously represented an intentional sequence. The very fact of the way relation between primes and roots was organised, implied a capricious mind intent on toying with a willing enquirer. I immediately felt the presence of Alkan in that simple sequence. I knew that I was in no real position to analyse the sequence as it stood – and that infuriated me . . . I knew that if the sequence was to prove meaningful it must have a progression.

My cottaging became more intense. I spent virtually all my days in toilets. The one day I had to abandon my quest and attend the National Assistance Board, I managed to contrive to wait for some hours in the toilet. When I emerged my number was called, an example, I feel, of perfect timing.

Eventually I began to find little outpourings, here and there, which were unmistakably more elements of Alkan's coded message. Each set of figures was couched in the same form, written in the same hand and situated within the toilet cubicle in the same place. After a fortnight I had an impressive set of integers of the form:

16, 3, 19, 19, 5, 17, 27, 9, 8, 13, 33, 11, 4, 9, 9,
14, 16, 27, 7, 9, 16, 5, 16, 9, 8, 27, 9 . . .

but running to some four handwritten sides. I submitted this sequence to rigorous analysis. On the face of it there seemed no reason to think that the sequence had been devised in the order in which I discovered it. So I cut it up into individual strips which I arranged and rearranged and rearranged, for hour after hour after hour, until a lattice work of discarded strips of exercise paper overlaid the bilious pastel lozenges which snicker-snacked across the wind-tunnel at the Majestic.

I found that I could extract quite elegant sets of equations from the sequence whichever way I arranged it, some of which were quite tantalisingly pregnant. But although I could satisfactorily resolve them they remained mere abstractions devoid of real values, real content. From the shape of some of these equations I could deduce that Alkan was working on some kind of methodology for statistical inference, but just as clearly other sets seemed to indicate that his thoughts were running towards decision trees which reflected the organic structure of long-term clinical trials. But statistical studies of what? Clinical trials of what?

I lapsed into torpor. There seemed no solution. I felt more than ever abandoned, washed up, beyond the pale of society. With no way of retreat from the tidal line of mental wrack, back down the beach and into the sea.

Late one evening, a fellow Majestic resident, Mr Rabindirath, came in to challenge me to a game of Cluedo. We played in a desultory fashion for half an hour or so. Rabindirath was an infuriating opponent because he kept incorporating members of his own family into the game as if they were fictional suspects.

Next to his cheaply suited thigh, on the Terylene counterpane of my bed, lay a well-thumbed *A–Z*. Open at pages 61a & b, the West End. I idly translated the coordinates into numerical values . . . Covent Garden, the coordinates were I, 16. Translating the I into a numerical value according to its position in the alphabet gave 9. 9, 16 – it was a fragment of the sequence! My head began to spin. Rabindirath barked angrily as I swept the Cluedo board off the cork-topped bathroom stool and began to labour feverishly over the *A–Z*.

By morning I had worked it all out. All the sequence was a set of coordinates which mapped a journey across central London. A journey which at every juncture prefigured my own. Clearly Alkan was tailing me from the front; damnably clever. He had started by tailing my simple and monotonous circuit and once I had become obsessed by following him he had led me on. Now I looked at the route laid out on the map it was quite clear that I had been mapping out a basic geometric configuration. I had simply to extrapolate the next set of coordinates in order to confront the errant psychologist.

By ten that morning I was waiting for him in the public toilet under the central reservation on High Holborn. It was a snug place, well warmed, with an attendant on duty all the time. Not the sort of toilet anyone would tend to linger in, nowhere to really hide yourself away. I waited and collected different versions of disgust from the insurance salesmen and civil servants who marched through, dumped their steamy load and strode out shaking their legs and heads.

I became uneasy. If something didn't happen soon I would be running the risk of harassment or even arrest. Then from the solid row of cubicles which framed a corridor at the far end of the tiled submarine came a cough, and then a flush, and then a door wheezed ajar . . .

nothing . . . no one emerged . . . I footed down to the end and gingerly pushed open the door. Alkan was turning to face me. He was wearing a grey flannel suit and a belted Gannex mac, he carried a briefcase and was in the middle of tucking an umbrella under his free arm. He looked terribly shocked to see me. The first thing he said was, 'What the bloody hell are you doing here?'

It turned out that the whole thing was an utter fluke, an example of the most preposterous chance, an amazing coincidence; or, laden synchronicity, evidence of fate, karma, the godhead. Alkan thought chance. I was inclined to agree with him. For he had nothing to say to me, absolutely nothing, but a kind of chewed-up, pop-eyed obsession with a set of conspiracies being fomented against him by Communist psychiatrists. Alkan had gone completely mad, psychotic, subject to delusions. His abrupt flight from Chelmsford had come in the midst of an extended paranoid interlude. He was a useless husk. After sitting with him over tea for a while, I gave him the rest of my money. It was the only way I could convince him that my presence in the toilet was not due to my involvement with the conspiracy of conspiracies. My last sight of Alkan was of him sitting at the coated table, hands tightly clasped, eyes eroding from the stream of edginess that poured out of his brain. I looked into those eyes for too long while I ate my toast. By the time I'd finished, all my faith in Alkan was quite burned away.

I went back to the Majestic and picked up my things. Then I left London. I wasn't to go back again for another seven years.

I applied for and was accepted to work as a research psychologist for Mr Euan MacLintock, the Chairman and Managing Director of Morton-Maclintock, the giant cattle-feed manufacturers. MacLintock was an old-fashioned Scottish dilettante, his particular obsession was psychology. He had few pretensions to originality himself, but was determined to test out some of his theories and, as a consequence, throughout his long and barren life funded one research project after another.

MacLintock had come up the hard way. He was born in the direst of Highland poverty, and had worked hard all his life, mostly as an itinerant cattleman. Long years of watching the animals graze and defecate accounted for his uncanny rapport with the bovine. And no doubt this also accounted for the phenomenal success of the cattle-feed he manufactured when he started his own business.

Somehow MacLintock had found time to educate himself. He had the reckless and unstructured mind of the autodidact. In some areas (for example, South American Volcanoes, heights thereof) he was an exhaustive expert; whereas in others (the History of Western Thought) he was notably deficient. The occasional beams of light that the world would shine into MacLintock's cave of ignorance used to drive him insane with anger. I well remember the day he reduced a solid mahogany sideboard to kindling upon being informed by me that even in space you could not 'see' gravity.

It would be wrong of me to give you the impression that MacLintock was a kindly man. He was incredibly mean, moody and occasionally violent. After the frozen, incestuous arrogance of Chelmsford academia I found his company a positive tonic. Just learning to get through a day with MacLintock without sparking a row was a valuable lesson in self-assertion.

Morton-MacLintock's head office was near Dundee, but MacLintock lived in a vast mouldering Victorian hunting lodge an hour's drive north. I was provided with an apartment at the lodge and was expected to reside there unless my work, called me to some far-flung portion of the M-M empire.

MacLintock's real obsession was with the relationship between bovine and human social forms. This was appropriate enough for a manufacturer of cattle-feed (and other farinaceous products aimed at the bipedal market). The full and frightening extent of his eccentricity only became clear to me over a period of two years or so. During that time I laboured diligently to compile a series of studies, monographs and even articles (which I naively believed I might get published). All of which aimed to draw out the underlying similarities between humans and cows and to suggest ways in which the two species could be brought closer together.

I think that in retrospect this scholastic enterprise doesn't sound as stupid as it did at the time. It is only in the past decade that the rights of animals have started to be seriously addressed as a concern of moral philosophy. The animal has shifted from the wings to the centre stage of our collective will-to-relate. Environmentalism, conservation, the developing world, the issue of canine waste products; increasingly our relationship to one another cannot be adequately defined without reference to the bestial dimension. In this context my work for Euan MacLintock now appears as breaking new ground.

To say that I came out of my shell altogether during this period would be an exaggeration. But I did realise that my days at Chelmsford had been effectively wasted. I had allowed myself to become marginalised. I had relinquished control of my own destiny. I had thought at the time that I was ensuring the objectivity that would be necessary for formulating a new large-scale theory of the psychopathology of societies as a whole. But really I had been teetering towards institutionalisation.

Wandering the MacLintock estate, moodily kicking failed, wet divots into the expectant faces of short Highland cattle I developed a new resolve to go back into the fray. I realised that to make any lasting contribution, to be listened to, I would have to manifest myself in some way. I would have to unite my own personality with my theories.

So, of an evening, while MacLintock fulminated and stalked, I parried with my pirated idiosyncrasies. We would sit either side of the baronial fireplace, wherein a few slats from a broken orange box feebly glowed. He, nibbling charcoal biscuit after biscuit, only to discard each sample, half-eaten, into a sodden heaplet on the lino, while I would suckle ballpoint pens, stare up at the creosoted rafters and make either whiffling or ululating noises, depending on the phase of the moon.

To MacLintock's credit he never paid much attention to the generation of this personal myth. He was possessed of a delightful self-obsession that guarded him against being interested in anyone else. A short man with absurd mutton-chop sideburns, he always wore a business suit. His notable efficiency, punctiliousness and businesslike manner – while inspiring devotion and respect at Head Office, at the plant and at the experimental testing station on Eugh – at home came across as a wearing emptiness of human feeling.

The great lodge was empty but for him, me and an aged houskeeper, Mrs Hogg, a woman so wedded to Calvinist fatalism that she would happily watch a pullet burst into flame, rather than adjust the oven setting. Bizarrely lit by vari-tilted spotlights of some cheap variety, the great hall would occasionally be enlivened of an evening as Mrs Hogg progressed towards us down a promenade of joined carpet offcuts.

Her squashed profile was thrown into shocking, shadowed relief against the stippled wall, the angles, for a moment, cheating the fact that her nose actually did touch her chin. She would deposit a chipboard tray on the fender, gesture towards the Tupperware cups of tea and the fresh mound of burnt biscuits and then depart, rolling back over the causeway and into the darkness.

Eventually MacLintock became dissatisfied with my work. He had had very precise objectives which he believed my work should fulfil:

1. The creation of an ideal community in which men and cattle would live together on equal terms. This was to be jointly funded by MacLintock and the Scottish Development Office.

2. The publication of a popular work which would make MacLintock's theories accessible to a mass audience (he was also quite keen on the idea of a television documentary).

He couldn't blame me solely for the failure to realise the first of these objectives, although I suppose my work didn't altogether help to convince the relevant bureaucrats. On the other hand he certainly did blame me for the collapse of the second objective. Blame, I felt, was unjustified. I had consulted with him on a regular basis during the writing of *Men and Cows; Towards the Society of the Future?* And he had passed each chapter as it came. Nonetheless he became nasty when the book failed to find a mainstream publisher. Eventually it was brought out by one of the small, alternative publishers that were beginning to operate, but it was instantaneously remaindered. MacLintock wandered the lodge for days, skipping from carpet tile to carpet tile, buoyed up by fury. Every so often he would swivel on his heel and deliver a tirade of abuse at me. At last, sickening of his tirade, I packed my bag and departed.

The last thing I saw as I squelched down the drive, away from the lodge, was Mrs Hogg. She was standing in the paddock behind the house, leaning on the fence, apparently adopting a conversational tone with a giant Herefordshire bull.

That wasn't the last I heard of Euan MacLintock, or of the work I had done for him. About eight years later, when the controversy that blew up around Quantity Theory was reaching its height, Harding, one of my staunchest critics, found a copy of *Men and Cows*. He brandished this, as it were, in the face of my reputation. Naturally the attempted discrediting backfired against him nastily, the general public took to the book, seeing it as satire. I believe a twelfth edition is about to appear.

As for MacLintock he went on without the Scottish Development Office and founded his utopia in an isolated glen on Eugh. There was never any information as to whether the experiment met with success. But after a shepherd heard unnatural cries in the vicinity of the commune the constabulary were called in. MacLintock was subsequently charged with murder. No doubt the story is apocryphal, but it was widely rumoured at the time that the insane (note please the entirely plausible reclassification from 'eccentric' to 'mad') bovine comestibles magnate was found naked with a group of rabid cattle. MacLintock and the cows were eating strips and straggles of flesh and sinew; all that remained of the last of MacLintock's fellow human communalists.

And so to Birmingham, at that time unpromising soil for the psychosocial plant to grow in. Fortunately this was a period when if you had an idea that was even halfway towards being coherent, there was at least the possibility of getting some kind of funding. Added to that, I discovered on my return from the wastes of cow and man that I had obtained a 'reputation'. A reputation, however, that existed entirely by proxy. None of my doing, but rather the fact of Alkan's breakdown. Busner, Gurney, Sikorski, Hurst and Adam Harley. All of them were beginning to make little names for themselves. And there was a rumour that there was some 'purpose' to their work, that Alkan had vouchsafed some 'secret', or inaugurated a 'quest' of some kind before he went mad.

As a member of this select band I was accorded a good deal of respect. I had no difficulty at all in gaining a modest grant to do some research towards a book on aspects of grant application. The form of this project took me away from the precincts of Aston (to which I was nominally attached) and into the ambit of the Institute of Job Reductivism, at that time being run by John (later Sir John) Green, who went on to become Director of the Institute of Directors.

Things were informal at the institute, there was a kind of seminar-cum-coffee morning on Wednesdays and Fridays. Research fellows were encouraged to come in and chat about their work with one another and even present short papers. Here was a socialised setting which I at last found congenial. The roseate glow of synthetic coals; bourbons passed round on a blue plastic plate; the plash of tea into cup – and over it all the companionable hubbub coming from the people who sat in the groups of oatmeal-upholstered chairs.

Most of the fellows were engaged in straightforward reductivist studies. There were papers being written on – among other things – recruiting personnel to the personnel recruitment industry, writing in-house magazines for corporate communications companies, auditing procedures to be adopted for accountants, and assessing life cover rates for actuaries. The resident Marxist was engaged on a complex analysis of the division of domestic cleaning labour among people who worked in the domestic cleaning industry. I fitted in rather well with these people, they accepted me as being like themselves and this was a tremendous relief to me.

For about five years I lead a quiet but productive life. After a while I transferred to the institute, although I continued to take an undergraduate course at Aston under the aegis of the sociology faculty. I finished my thesis on grant application and started making some preliminary notes towards tackling the whole question of job reductivism from a theoretical perspective. I suppose with the benefit of hindsight I can see clearly what was going on here, but believe me, at the time I was oblivious. I had no thoughts of disturbing the pattern of life that I had cautiously built up for myself. I had acquired some slight professional standing; I had rented a flat – granted, it was furnished and I hardly spent any time there, but nonetheless these trappings of what is laughably called 'social acceptability' had begun to matter to me. After all, even the most conceited bore is often considered a social asset, if he has clean hands and a clean suit. All in all, for a virtual indigent, I had come a long way.

Into this Midlands arcadia fell a letter from Zack Busner:

Dear Harold,
It is possible that this isn't a letter you wouldn't want to receive, but I will have to accept that at the outset. You may not remember me, but I was a contemporary of yours at Chelmsford and also one of Alkan's

analysand/students. I can barely remember you but, be that as it may, your work has come to my attention and I am in need of assistance – urgently in need of assistance, at my Concept House in Willesden. I cannot adequately describe the work involved in a letter, nor can I do justice to the new framework within which we are 'practising'. Perhaps you would be good enough to come and see me and we can discuss it?

Busner was the student/analysand of Alkan's I had most disliked. He had been a rounded ham of a young man, irrepressibly jolly, and, of the five, the most given to practical jokes. It was he, I recalled, who had had all Adam Harley's suits adjusted overnight to fit a midget. He had wandered around the campus at Chelmsford clapping people around the shoulders and greeting them effusively with a phoney hail-fellow-well-met manner, which set my teeth on edge. However, no one, least of all me, had failed to notice that despite his endless appetite for high jinks, or perhaps because of it, Busner was becoming a formidable researcher. I knew that his doctoral thesis had received very favourable attention. And that, a medical doctor by training, he had gone on to qualify as a psychiatrist and take up work as a respected clinician.

I went down to London. Busner had helpfully sent me a tube map with a cross on it marking Willesden Junction. The Concept House was on Chapter Road, one of those long north-west London avenues that in winter are flanked by receding rows of what appear to be the amputated, arthritic, decomposing limbs of giants. Snow had been falling all day and Chapter Road was a dirty bath mat of cold, grey flakes. It was dark as I plodded along, cursing the slippery PVC soles of the shoes I'd just bought. Ahead of me in the centre of the road two children of about five or six walked hand in hand.

The whole atmosphere depressed me. The feeling it gave me, walking down that endless road, was of being in a dirty, cold room, a room where no one had bothered to vacuum between the tattered edge of the beige carpet and the scuffed, chipped paintwork of the skirting board for a very long time. I wished that I had driven there instead of leaving my car at Tolworth services and hitching the rest of the way.

The Concept House was no different to any of the other large Edwardian residences which lined the road. If anything it looked a little more like a home and a little less like an institution than the rest. The garden was littered with discarded children's toys, and in an upstairs window I could see the back of finger-paintings which had been stuck to the windows with masking tape. Busner himself opened the door to me; had he not been wearing an aggressively loud jumper with 'Zack' appliquéd across its breast in red cartoon lettering I don't think I would have recognised him.

Busner's cheeks had sunk, his face was thin and hollow. The rest of him was just as plump as ever, but he had the countenance of a driven ascetic. His eyes glowed with an ill-suppressed fanaticism. In that instant I nearly turned on my heel and abandoned the interview. I had been prepared for Busner the Buffoon, but Busner the Revolutionary was something I hadn't bargained for.

We goggled at one another. Then quick as a flash he had drawn me into the vestibule, persuaded me to abandon my sodden mac and dripping briefcase and led me on, into a large, warm kitchen where he proceeded to make me a cup of cocoa, talking all the while.

'I hadn't imagined you as such a dapper little thing, my dear. Your suit is marvellous.' In truth the cheap compressed nap of the material was beginning to bunch into an elephant's hide of wrinkles under the onslaught of quick drying. 'Really, I wouldn't have recognised you if I hadn't known you were coming. I was expecting the timorous little beastie we had at Chelmsford.'

With amazing rapidity Busner outlined for me the philosophy of the Concept House, what he was trying to do and how he needed my help. In essence the house was an autonomous community of therapists and patients, except that instead of these rôles being concretely divided among the residents, all were free to take on either mantle at any time.

Over our cocoa Busner set out for me his vision of the Concept House and of the future of psychotherapy. Disgusted by his experience of hospital psychology – and the narrow drive to reduce mental illness to a chemical formula – Busner had rebelled:

'I sat up for night after night, reading Nietschze, Schopenhauer, Dostoevsky and Sartre. I began to systematically doubt the principles on which I had based my career to date. I deconstructed the entire world that I had been inhabiting for the past thirty years.

'It was dawning on me that the whole way in which people have hitherto viewed mental illness has been philosophically suspect. The division between doctor and patient has corresponded to an unwarranted epistemological assumption. Here at the Concept House we are dedicated to redefining this key relationship.

'We're really finding out the extent to which all the categories of psychopathology are just that: dry, empty categories, devoid of real content, representing only the taxonomic, psychic fascism of a gang of twisted old men.'

It was a long speech and Busner spoke eloquently, punctuating his remarks by moving oven gloves around on his chest. I think, in retrospect, they must have been adhering to his woolly by strips of Velcro that I couldn't see, but at the time I was tremendously impressed by the trick.

Busner went on to explain that within the Concept House everything was ordered democratically. At the house meetings, which were held every morning, rotas and agendas were drawn up and jobs distributed. The house was Busner's own, or rather Busner's parents'. He had persuaded them to donate it to what he styled his 'League for Psychic Liberation'. In the weeks that followed I occasionally saw the older Busners wandering around the upper storeys of the house like fitful ghosts, sheepishly reading the *Sunday Telegraph Magazine* in reproduction Queen Anne armchairs, while feverish psychotics, charged with some unearthly energy, toyed with their ornaments.

Having set out his theories, and explained the philosophy of this novel institution to which he had given birth, Busner picked up the drained cocoa mugs and put them on the draining board. He turned to me with a quizzical expression.

'You're wondering why I wrote to you, aren't you?'

'Well, yes. I suppose I am.'

'After all, we were never exactly *sympatico*, were we?'

'Yes, yes. I think I'd agree with you there.'

'Well, here it is. The fact is that I'm attracting a good deal of publicity with what I'm trying to do here. Some of it is distinctly favourable, but that fact only seems to persuade those who are seeking to discredit me to redouble their efforts. I know that you have never programatically defined yourself as belonging to any avant-garde movement. But on the other hand I know that you have allied yourself with some pretty weird courses of study during your career, isn't that so?

'What I want you to do here is what you do best: research. There is one way that I can really kick over the hornet's nest of the psychiatric and psychotherapeutic establishment and get them all buzzing furiously. And that is to prove not that my methods of helping people who suffer from so-called 'mental illnesses' are more effective than conventional ones, but that they are more cost effective; that would really upset people. If I could prove that Concept Houses the length and breadth of the country would reduce public expenditure, I might well become unstoppable.'

'And me?'

'I want you to construct and manage the trials and to collate the results, to be published in the form of an article co-authored by the two of us in the *BJE**.'

And so it was. I became a member of the Concept House team and abandoned my suits and shiny shoes in favour of uncomfortable overalls which rode up my cleft and shoes that appeared half-baked. Why? Well, because whatever the extent of Busner's rampant egoism whatever the dubious nature of his ideas, there was a sense of human warmth at the Concept House that I found lacking, either at Aston or at the Institute of Job Reductivism. I craved some of that warmth. You have to remember that since the age of seventeen, I had lived an almost exclusively institutionalised life. Nonetheless, ever prudent, I didn't give up my academic positions, I merely secured a leave of absence to work on Busner's study. Of course there were mutterings about what I was getting involved with, but I paid them no mind.

The trial I evolved for Busner was complex in the extreme. There were two aspects to the problem: how much diagnosed mental patients spent themselves and what was spent on them. It was to be a double-blind trial, which operated itself in the context of a double-blind. There were to be three trial groups: the inmates of the Concept House, a group of patients diagnosed as afflicted with major psychoses at Friern Barnet, and fourteen Beth Din approved butchers living in the Temple Fortune area. That the latter group was chosen was to bedevil the validity of our results for years to come. I would like to state here, once and for all, that the fact was that the people who applied for the trial, and who fulfilled the necessary criteria, all happened to be kosher butchers domiciled in

* *British Journal of Ephemera*

that area. Of course in retrospect this fact was undoubtedly one of the secret springs, the 'subtle connections' which I had begun to make unconsciously, and which led eventually to the full-blown Quantity Theory.

The trial was conducted over a period of six months in four distinct 'trial periods'. The results were monitored by me purely in the form of computer data. I never had any direct access to either the mechanics of the trial itself, or even to the intermediate collection of data. Naturally a double-double-blind trial involves not only the technician who is directly monitoring the trial to be unaware of whether he is administering a placebo or not, but also the overall administrator of the trial – be he psychologist or statistician – to be unaware of whether he really is administering a trial, or just carefully collating and analysing figures, totals and percentages, completely at random. Thus, two of the groups of data that Zack Busner fed through to me comprised respectively: the number of snail trails he had counted, smearing across the fissured concrete apron, wreathed in bindweed, that lay in the dead centre of the waste ground behind the Concept House; and, a random selection of handicapping weights from the pages of a back number of the *Sporting Life*.

On the other two occasions the data was, of course, 'real' – although in a very restricted sense. The two real trials contained an obvious reversal. In one, the mental patients were given an economic placebo and the Concept House inhabitants, money. In the other this was reversed. The butchers were given, arbitrarily, either money or virtually useless discount vouchers for household cleaning products. Thus, the overall form of the trial could be depicted by a schematic diagram:

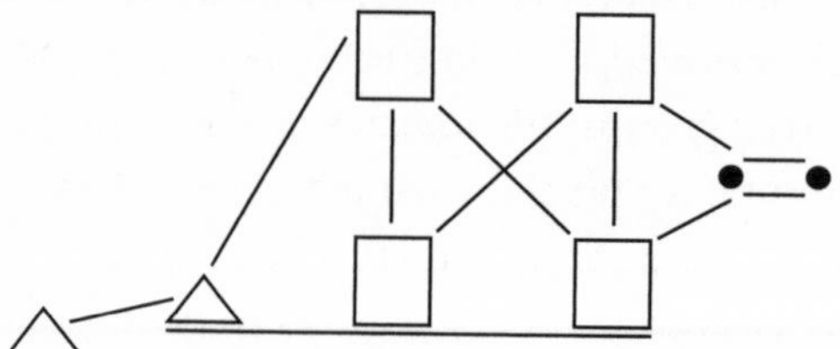

To my mind this expressed with absolute clarity the limiting conditions necessary for a cost-benefit analysis of sanity variables. Of course the informed reader will have already detected the lineaments of Quantity Theory in the structure of the trial diagram. My purpose here is expressly to avoid the crude attempts that are made to retrospectively manufacture the genesis of an idea. The problems I have been most interested in that arose from the Concept House trial were purely methodological. For instance, Olsen's 1978 paper in the *BJE* in which he presented the results of his own trials. Olsen took three groups of recently diagnosed and sectioned mental patients. One group was given in equal thirds, lithium, chlorapromasine and a tri-cyclic anti-depressant. The second group was given a placebo and the third group was given nothing; instead Olsen had the patients in this group mercilessly beaten to a bloody pulp.

If any of the patients in the three groups manifested any signs of severe deterioration in their overall condition they were administered ECT. However, the substance of Olsen's trial and indeed the validity or otherwise of his results are of little interest to me. Rather it was Olsen's argument that my error in the double negative implied by the double-double-blind trial that exercised me greatly. Fortunately I was saved from having to answer the accusation by the revelation that Olsen had himself participated in administering beatings to the control group in his experiment. Such a violation of the blind status of the trial naturally discredited him entirely.

The trials took six months to complete and during that time I was accepted into the Concept House community. This, as you will hear in due course, was altogether a mixed blessing. Busner and his therapists had long since ceased to make any practical distinction between themselves and their patients. So another involution of the trial sequence was that at the end of it no one could be really sure who had been giving what to whom. The trial money and placebo money were given out at random times when I was sure not to be in the vicinity. Occasionally I would catch a glimpse of a man, skull-capped and be-locked, his apron suspiciously stained and clutching a handful of glossy paper slips. But I discounted these peripheral visions, putting them down to the generally heightened psychic atmosphere of the Concept House.

There were in theory six therapists, six patients, Busner's parents and myself in residence. The patients were a random selection from the chronic wards that Busner had been attached to over the years. Basically he recruited for the Concept House through a mixture of fraudulence and guile. Busner was typical of experimentalists in the psychiatric and educational fields in that he blamed the failure of his methods not on their theoretical basis, but on the fact that he could only persuade wealthy parents to send their chronically disturbed children to his institution.

I participated in the exhaustive group therapy sessions, which more often than not were long periods of either silence or disjointed monamaniac ranting – usually by Busner himself. The truth was that although I felt accepted within the Concept House, it wasn't really a congenial environment. People who are severely mentally ill when they are left unconstrained tend to behave fairly badly. On reflection I suppose that is why they are diagnosed as being mentally ill in the first place. And as for the 'therapists' that Busner had recruited, they were, on the whole, fairly unstable people themselves, coming as they did from the wilder fringes of the therapeutic world. Among them were a failed holistic osteopath to naturopaths and a woman who described herself as 'seismically sentient'. Pretty stupid really. The main reason I remained was to complete the trial, added to that it was a fairly stimulating environment for debate. Busner's old cronies from Chelmsford – Harley, Sikorski and the others – dropped round at fairly regular intervals. They were all beginning to make names for themselves and they were always keen for a wide-ranging debate on all the latest developments in our various fields.

These were of course the men who were to form the nucleus of my Quantity Theory research group. Now I see what they have become I rather wish I had left them all alone, but at the time I was so pleased to be accepted by them that I suppose the dawning awareness that I might in fact be their intellectual superior was enough to make me want to stick close.

Eventually, however, I left the Concept House. It was becoming intolerable. You couldn't even eat breakfast without someone either slavering down the neck of your pullover or trying to sell you time shares in a pyramid building project. Busner himself was beginning to be taken up by the media as the prophet of some new movement and his vanity was insupportable, as was his pretension. He would sit for hours in a darkened room, thrumming mindlessly on an electric bass guitar and composing what he called 'verbal tone poems'. Let me tell you, what I could see at the time prefigured his eventual fall from grace. I knew he would end up on television game shows.

As for the trial and its findings, they received short shrift from the psychological establishment, which found both our methods and our aims quite incomprehensible. That was their problem; and although I hadn't managed to come up with the results that Busner would have liked, I had proved, to my own satisfaction at least, that £7.00 will make someone who is significantly mentally ill feel at least marginally better.

The only person I was sorry to leave behind at the Concept House was Professor Lurie. This poor old buffer had made it to a considerable age as a happy eccentric before fatefully teetering over the brink into genuine delusional mania. Nonetheless I had spent some happy hours sitting listening to his clever, inventive fantasies of life marooned in the Amazon with a tribe of unspeakable banality.

Back to Birmingham then and the institute. My teaching, my books, my essentially lonely, but contented scholarly life. But something had changed. There was a new restlessness in the way I attacked ideas and worried at them like a terrier, a new edge to my thinking. All this came to a head as I laboured over completing the index to the revised edition of my doctoral thesis. An American college press of some obscurity had agreed to publish and I knew that the work needed attention. Yet it was no longer a task that quickened my blood. Quite frankly I had long since ceased to care about the nature of academic grant application. The whole study appeared useless and fruitless to me, perhaps only interesting as the purest possible expression of the digging-out and then filling-in mentality of so much academic endeavour – especially in the social sciences. What I wanted to do was to hit upon a general explanatory theory of the relation between normal and abnormal psychopathology. A theory of the order of Freud's entire corpus of work, but, unlike Freudianism, intimately bound up with and connected to a theory of social form and change.

As I laboured on the tedious index I felt something gestate inside of me. It was like a great, warm, rounded bolus of thought. Stuck to its sides were all the insights and experiences I had had in the preceding ten years: my undergraduate days with Müeller at Oxford; my postgraduate thesis at Chelmsford; my time researching for MacLintock; my doctorate at Birmingham; my trials with Busner. All of these were now to find their rightful place, unified in the Quantity Theory of Insanity.

* * *

Drizzle over Bromsgrove. The sodden postman flobs along the pavement, pauses as if to enter by the green garden gate, and then flobs on. The damp clinging of cloth to flesh is felt across a sodden twenty-foot tangle of bindweed as he moves on past the mullions. My desk – normally a sanctuary of rigid order, a baffle against the worst of entropy – has started to decay. Curled and stained pages of typescript hold funelled within themselves soggy drifts of biscuit crumbs. Biros, cemented to one another and to balls of fluff and lint with hardened saliva are thrown into the path of the paper avalanche like so many spillikins. Hither and thither across the melamine stand ramparts of bound volumes from the institute library, Dewey decimal tags detaching from their spines and curling into Sellotape snails. I no longer have the impetus, the application, to work on the index, instead I doodle on a sheet of scrap paper, my pen describing senseless diagrams which express with a conjunction of lines and dashes the relations that obtain between a series of dots . . .

. . . And yet this particular diagram has such an appealing, cogent form. It looks as if it ought to express a genuine relationship of some kind. It is too four-square, too obviously functional, to be a mere doodle. I see in it the shape of the schematic diagram I drew to express the double-double-blind status of the Concept House trial . . . And then I see it, altogether, in one pure thought-bite; the Quantity Theory of Insanity shows its face to me.

I suppose all people who look for the first time upon some new, large-scale, explanatory theory must feel as I did at that moment. With one surge of tremendous arrogance, of aching hubris, I felt as if I were looking at the very form of whatever purpose, whatever explanation, there really is inherent in the very stuff of this earth, this life.

'What if . . .' I thought to myself, 'What if there is only a fixed proportion of sanity available in any given society at any given time?' No previous theory of abnormal psychology had ever assumed such a societal dimension. For years I had sought some hypothesis to cement the individual psyche to the group; it was right in front of me all the time. But I went on, I elaborated, I filled out the theory, or rather, it filled out itself. It fizzed and took on form the way a paper flower expands in water. 'What if,' I further thought, 'any attempts to palliate manifestations of insanity in one sector of society can only result in their upsurge in some other area of society?'

So that was it! The surface of the collective psyche was like the worn, stripy ticking of an old mattress. If you punched into its coiled hide at any point, another part would spring up – there was no action without reaction, no laughter without tears, no normality without its pissing accompanist.

The sodden crescent at the edge of my long-since-dunked digestive biscuit flotched to the desk top like excrement. I paid it no mind. In that instant I saw whole series of overlapping models of given sanity quantities – for if each societal grouping had a given sanity quotient, then why not each sub-societal grouping? From the Bangladeshis to the bowling club, from the Jews to the Jewellers' Association. It must be so. In each model the amount of sanity available would be different and each societal model would have a bearing on the next. I saw it in my mind's eye as an endless plain of overlapping mattresses, each of a different size. Tread on one and the effect would ripple away through all the others.

That was it stated in its barest outline, but what was especially remarkable about the Quantity Theory was that it came into my mind complete with a myriad of hypotheses. Such as:

i) If you decrease the number of social class 2 anorexics you necessarily increase the numbers of valium abusers in social class 4.

ii) If you provide efficient medication for manic depressives in the Fens, there are perceptible variations in the numbers of agoraphobics on the South Coast.

iii) If you use behavioural conditioning to stop six pupils at St Botolph's primary school on Anglesey from bed wetting, the result will be increased outbursts of sociopathic rage among the ten borderline psychotics that attend the school.

And so on.

In one fell swoop I also found myself abandoning all the models of sanity and insanity I had absorbed during my years of study. The key to the abnormal psyche lay not in a juxtaposition between the acquired and the instinctual, nor in a comprehensive model of the workings of the mind, but in an altogether purer, more mathematical direction. Traditional psychology retained the status of being a pseudo-science, its findings unable to bridge the vast gulf between the empirically testable hypotheses of neuro-physiology and the incommunicable truths of inner mental states. Just as philosophy, try as it might, cannot bind itself to formal logic. All this would end with Quantity Theory. The individual psyche would be left to discover its own destiny; psychology would be confined to the elaboration of statistical truths.

I make no bones about it, the Quantity Theory was my salvation. No one ever complains if a great artist says that he was driven to create a masterpiece by a hunger for recognition and money. But a scientist? Well, he is meant to be disinterested, pure; his ambition merely to descry the cement of the universe. He isn't meant to use it to start laying his own patio. I was saved from Bromsgrove, from Aston, from Chelmsford, from the Majestic Hotel, by the Quantity Theory. From its inception I knew that it fulfilled the criteria required by all great scientific theories: 1. It made large-scale predictions. 2. These were testable empirically. 3. The testings would really eat up cash.

That night I paced the Wilton until it smelt of singed nylon. I could not sleep, I was tormented, gripped by the fear that should I make the wrong move, should I fail to do the Quantity Theory justice, then I would be unable to claim all the credit. I knew that as a responsible scholar I should search around for some funding, do some fieldwork and then write up the results for publication in the relevant journal. But a wayward, craven part of me feared instantly that some other, some interloper was perhaps at that very moment stumbling on the same truth and about to make it known to the world – pulverising the credit due to me and me alone. I was tempted to call the national press, arrange a conference of some sort, upstage the academic community and tell the world.

Prudence got the better of me. I knew that I had to effectively gain control of the Quantity Theory. To unleash it on the world half-cocked was to ensure only that the massive industry of thought, research and practice which I could foresee would be within the domain of others. If I wanted to control I would have to plot, scheme, machinate, and above all lay my plans carefully.

Accordingly the next morning I sat down to write letters to my fellow student/analysands from Chelmsford: Sikorski, Hurst, Harley, and of course Zack Busner. (I would have asked Simon Gurney too were it not that he had given up his practice to become a sculptor.) I invited them to come to Birmingham to have dinner with me and discuss an idea which I thought might be of interest to them.

I waited for three days . . . a week . . . no word from anyone. The evening of the planned rendezvous arrived and to my surprise so did they. One after another. They had all driven up from London together in Adam Harley's car. But they had got into an argument at Toddington Services about the culturally relative perception of post-natal depression. Busner took the view that post-natal depression was an entirely patriarchal phenomenon, and that there were tribal societies where the matrilineal took precedence, that were completely free of it. Adam Harley took the view that Busner was a 'pretentious twerp' and followed up this criticism by shoving a Leviathan-burger, smothered with salad cream and dripping gobbets of part-grilled, processed shrimp, straight into Busner's face.

After arriving, I sat them down and made them tea. I wouldn't even let Busner clean up; I launched without any preamble into a description of my revelation. They were restless and barely prepared to listen, but I only had to hold their attention for a few minutes before the theory bit into them. Of course there was something in my manner that they sensed was different. Something in the way I whiffled towards the ceiling, the way I fellated ballpoint pens, the way I stood with one shoulder far, far higher than the other so that I appeared to be dangling from a meat hook, that held them, cowed them, made them realise that it was I who was to replace Alkan in their affections.

We formed a small multi-disciplinary team. The aim was to develop the Quantity Theory in relation to microsocietal groupings. Alkan's students were notable for the diversity of the paths they had followed since leaving Chelmsford; within our small group we had all the necessary disciplines represented.

We know already what had happened to Busner. Phillip Hurst, whose father had massively endowed the Chelmsford campus, had moved from pure psychology into psychometrics and statistics. His help in developing the quotient concept was to prove invaluable. Adam Sikorski had moved on from the crude behaviouristic models that he had constructed with such glee when a postgraduate. No longer did he turn rats into alcoholics, heroin addicts and thieves – just to show that he could. Now he turned armadillos into anorexics, narwhals into neurasthenics and shire horses into hopeless, puling, agoraphobics. Sikorski had secured generous government funding for these experiments and his familiarity with the ins and outs of political in-fighting was to prove at the outset of great service to the Quantity Theory. Of course ultimately it alienated him entirely. As for Adam Harley – Harley the campaigner, Harley the idealist, Harley the visionary – he was the ultimate fifth columnist. He was sitting in a cold basement in Maida Vale, abasing himself before the adolescent angst and middle-aged spread of anxiety that his 'clients' laid before him. Harley, with his bloodhound eyes which threatened to carry on drooping until they made contact with his roll-neck, persuaded me of his concern, his humanity, his devotion to the very real therapeutic benefits of the Quantity Theory, but all the time . . .

Our first move was to look around for a suitably small, self-contained societal unit on which we could test the theory. We were fortunate indeed to have my cousin Sid. Sid had never been mentally ill, exactly. However, like other rather introverted children, he had had a number of 'imaginary friends'. The difference in Sid's case was that although he abandoned his imaginary friends during pre-puberty, he met them again at university. Where they all pursued a lively social life together.

Sid was now living in a small commune in the Shetland Islands, where he and his fellow communards were dedicated to the growing of implausibly large hydroponic onions. The other members of the commune were eccentric but not quite as unhinged as Sid. They believed that their ability to grow the four-foot legumes was wholly predicated on the orbital cycle of Saturn's satellite, Ceres.

For a number of reasons this commune represented an almost perfect test bed for our research. It was remote, self-contained, and possessed a readily quantifiable sanity quotient which needed the bare minimum to assess. In addition the area around the commune contained several other examples of experimental living, left on the beach by the receding wave of the previous decade. It would be easy, therefore, to find a suitable control.

The Quantity Theory Multi-disciplinary Team set off for Shetland without further ado. Once there we would measure the quotient and then set about either exacerbating or palliating Sid. We then hoped to observe what effect, if any, this had on the other eight commune members.

It's now difficult to appreciate the then popularity of this sort of exercise in communal living, and frankly I found it difficult to appreciate at the time. I think in retrospect that all those 'alternative' modes of living were little more than exercises in arrested development. Sleeping in bags, arguing and hair-pulling. It was really all a sort of giant 'let's camp in the garden, Mummy' session. The onion-growers' camp was no exception to this rule. A huddle of bothies, caulked, in some places well and with close attention, but in others simply stuffed up with back numbers of the *Shetland Times*. When the afternoons grew dark and the wind whistled over the tedious landscape, the rain drove out of the well of darkness and shot in distinct drops through the central living area, where pasty-faced lads and lasses squatted, hooking their hair back behind their ears, absorbed in french knitting, macrame, and writing home.

In this context the team were called upon to operate just as much as anthropologists as psychologists. There was no way that the commune was going to accept us for the period of time necessary to complete our experiments if we didn't, at least superficially, show some sympathy with the ideas they espoused. So it was that I found myself night after night, the dirty denim of my acquired 'jeans' slow-burning my bent knees, as one communard or other, their minds stupidly stupefied by marijuana, attempted to discourse on ley lines, shiatsu, or some Tantric rubbish.

Of course we took our own mental profile, our own sanity quotient. Both as a group *per se* and combined with the communards. We then were able to allow for it in the context of the fluctuations we attempted to engineer. When the experiments were completed and the data collected from the 'control' commune, where Phillip Hurst had been conducting his own lonely vigil, we found that the results were far better than we could have hoped for.

The manipulations of the given distribution of sanity within the commune had, by any standards, been crude. When we wanted to palliate Sid's symptoms: his delusions, his paranoid fantasies, and especially his lively but imaginary social life, we would simply sedate him heavily with Kendal Mint Cake laced with Largactil. He stopped hearing voices, and the world ceased to resolve itself into a hideously complex, Chinese marquetry of interlocking conspiracies. Even his 'friends' went away. All but one, that is. An enigmatic welder from Weirside called George Stokes still insisted on manifesting himself.

And the onion-growers? Well, even though we had to wait to quantify the data, we could see with our own eyes that they had started to exhibit quite remarkably baroque behavioural patterns. With Sid palliated they now not only believed in the beneficial agricultural influence of Ceres, they also believed that Ceres was a real person, who would be visiting them to participate in a celebration of the summer solstice. Some of the really enthusiastic communards even sent out to Lerwick for twiglets and other kinds of exotic cocktail eatables, all the better to entertain their divine guest.

When we cut down Sid's medication everything returned to normal. We then went the other way and started introducing minute quantities of LSD into Sid's diet. The 'friends' proliferated. Sid spent all his days in the onion field engaged in a giddy social whirl: cocktail parties, first nights, openings, and house parties. Some of the imaginary friends were even quite well connected. I almost came close to feeling jealous of Sid as he rubbed shoulders with scores of influential – albeit delusory – personages, until my colleagues reprimanded me for my severely unprofessional behaviour.

Needless to say, this part of the experiment was an unqualified success as well. When Sid got madder the communards' behaviour changed again. They started wandering around the onion field in a distracted fashion. There was no more talk of the imminent arrival of Ceres – instead there was muttering about 'Going to Lerwick to see about a steady job'. And one or two disconsolate individuals even approached members of the multi-disciplinary team and asked them if they knew anyone who could help them to get into advertising.

We returned to London and conducted a full analysis of our findings. Reducing our calibrated observations and the results of the thousands of psych-profile tests we had conducted on the communards to a series of quotients, we found what we had gone looking for: whatever the fluctuations observed in the behaviour of individuals, the sanity quotient of the group as a whole remained constant.

It became time to publish. Three months later 'Some Aspects of Sanity

Quotient Mechanisms in a Witless Shetland Commune' appeared in the *BJE.* There was an uproar. My findings were subject to the most rigorous criticism and swingeing invective. I was accused of 'mutant social Darwinism', 'syphilitic sub-Nietzschean lunacy' and lots worse.

In the academic press, critic after critic claimed that by proposing that there was only a fixed proportion of sanity to go round in any given society I was opening the floodgates to a new age of prejudice and oppression. Insanity would be rigorously confined to minority and underprivileged groups – the ruling classes would ensure that they remained horrifically well balanced, all the better to foment 'medication warfare' against societies with different sanity quotients.

However, the very scale and intensity of the reaction to the theory undercut the possibility of its being ignored. Added to that, my critics became sidetracked by the moral implications of Quantity Theory, rather than by its mathematics. The reasons for this became clear as the debate gathered momentum. No one was in a position to gainsay the findings until our experiments were replicated. And then, of course, they were replicated and replicated and replicated. Until the whole country was buzzing with the audible whirr of pencils ringing letters and digits on multiple-choice forms; and the ker-plunk as capsule after capsule dropped into pointed unputdownable paper beakers: the industry of thought was underway.

That would have been the end of the story. In terms of the naive model of motivation and causation I have set out for you, and then gloriously undermined, I have provided a complete explanation. But we all know what happened next. How the Quantity Theory of Insanity moved from being an original, but for all that academic, contribution to ideas, to being something else altogether. A cult? A body of esoteric knowledge? A political ideology? A religion? A personal philosophy? Who can say. Who can account for the speed with which the bastardised applications of the theory caught on. First of all with the intelligentsia, but then with the population as a whole.

Even if the exact substance of the theory is difficult to define, it's quite easy to see why the theory appealed to people so strongly. It took that most hallowed of modern places, the within-the-walnut-shell-world of the mind, and stated that what went on inside it was effectively a function of mathematically observable fluctuations across given population groups. You no longer had to go in for difficult and painful therapies in order to palliate your expensive neuroses. Salvation was a matter of social planning.

At least that's what they said. I never made any claims for the theory in this respect, I was merely describing, not prescribing. It was the members of the group I had assembled to conduct the ground-breaking research who leapt to pseudo-fame on the back of my great innovation. Busner with his absurd 'Riddle', and latterly his humiliating game-show appearances, shouting out stupid slogans; Hurst and Sikorski turned out to be incapable of anything but the most violent and irresponsible rending of the fabric of the theory, but that came later. My initial problems were with Harley. Harley the idealist, Harley the kind, Harley the socially acceptable, Harley the therapist.

Some nine months after the revelational paper in the *BJE* I received a call from Harley who asked me to meet him at his house in Hampstead. I had heard echoes of the kind of work my colleagues had been getting involved in and I had consistently been at pains in my interviews with the press to dissociate myself from whatever it was they were up to. I had my suspicions and I burned with curiosity as I strained on my foldaway bicycle up from the flat I had rented at Child's Hill to the heights of Hampstead.

The big design fault with these foldaways is that the wheels are too small. Added to that the hinge in the main frame of the machine never achieves sufficient rigidity to prevent the production of a strange undulating motion as one labours to cover ground. I mention this in passing, because I think the state I was in by the time I reached Gayton Road helps to explain my initial passivity in the face of what could only be described as an abomination.

Harley let me in himself. He occupied a large terraced house on Gayton Road. I had known that he was well-off but even so I was surprised by the fact that there was only one bell, with his name on it, set by the shiny front door. He led me into a large room which ran from the front to the back of the house. It was well lit by a wash of watery light from the high sash windows. The walls of the room were stacked with books, most of them paperbacks. The floorboards had been stripped, painted black, and polished to a sheen. Scattered here and there around the floor were rugs with bright, abstract designs woven into them. Thin angled lamps obviously of Italian design stood around casting isolated fields, of yellow light. One stood on the desk – a large, flat serviceable oak table – its bill wavering over the unravelling skein of what I assumed to be Harley's labours, which spewed from the chattering mouth of a printer attached to his computer.

There were remarkably few objects in the room, just the odd bibelot here and there, a Japenese ivory or an Arawak head carved from pumice and pinioned by a steel rod to a cedarwood block. I felt sick with exertion and slumped down on a leather and aluminium chair. Harley went to the desk and toyed with a pen, doodling with hand outstretched. The whine of the machine filled the room. He semed nervous.

'You know the Quantity Theory of Insanity . . .' he began. I laughed shortly. '. . . Yes, well . . . Haven't you always maintained that what is true for societal groups can also be proved for any sub-societal group as well?'

'Yes, that has been an aspect of the theory. In fact an integral part. After all, how do you define a "society" or a "social group" with any real, lasting rigour? You can't. So the theory had to apply itself to all possible kinds of people-groupings.'

'Parent–Teacher Associations?'

'Yes.'

'Cub Scout groups?'

'Yes.'

'Suburban philatelic societies?'

'Certainly.'

'Loose fraternities of rubberwear fetishists?'

'Why on earth not . . . my dear man . . .'

'How about therapeutic groups set up specifically to exploit the hidden mechanisms that Quantity Theory draws our attention to?'

'What do you mean?'

'Well, you know. Groups of people who band together in order to effect a calculated redistribution of the elements of their particular sanity quotient. Forming an artificial group so that they can trade off a period of mental instability against one of radical stability.'

'What! You mean a sort of sanity time-share option?'

'Yeah, that kind of thing.'

I was feigning ignorance, of course. I had foreseen this development, so had my critics, although they hadn't correctly located where the danger lay. Not with vain and struggling despots who would tranquillise whole ethnic minorities in order to stabilise the majority, but with people like Harley, the educated, the liberal, the early adopters.

'Well, I don't know, I suppose in theory . . .'

'Have a look at this . . .' He swiped a scarf of computer paper from the still chattering printer and handed it to me. I read; and saw at a glance that Harley wasn't talking about theory at all, he was talking about practice. The printout detailed the latest of what was clearly a series of ongoing and contained trials, which involved the monitoring of the sanity quotients within two groups. There was an 'active' and an 'inactive' group. The groups were defined entirely arbitrarily. That was all, but it was sufficient. From the quantitative analysis that Harley had undertaken it could be clearly demonstrated that the stability of the two groups differed in an inverse correlation to one another.

'What is this?' I demanded. 'Who are these people and why are you gathering data on them in this fashion?'

'Shhhh!' Harley crouched down and waddled towards me across a lurid Mexican rug, his finger rammed hard against his lips. 'Do keep your voice down, people might hear you.'

'What people? What people might hear me?' I expostulated. Harley was still crouching, or rather squatting in front of me. This posture rather suited him. With his sparse ginger beard and semi-pointed head he had always tended towards the garden gnomic.

'The people who are coming for the meeting – the exclusionist group meeting.'

'I see, I see. And these?' I held up the computer paper.

Harley nodded, grinning. 'Aren't you pleased?'

Pleased? I was dumbfounded. I sat slumped in my chair for the next hour or so, saying nothing. During this period they trickled in. Quite ordinary upper middle-class types. A mixed bunch, some professionals: lawyers, doctors and academics, all with the questing supercilious air that tends to go with thinking that you're 'in on something'. The professionals were mixed in with some wealthy women who trailed an atmopshere of having-had-tea at Browns or Fortnums behind them. All of these people milled around in the large room until they were called to order and the meeting began.

It was a strange affair, this 'meeting', solely concerned with procedure and administration. There was no content to it, or perceptible reason why this particular group of people should be gathered together. They discussed the revenue of the group, where they should meet, the provision of refreshments and a group trip to Glyndebourne that was happening in a couple of weeks' time. At no point did anybody directly refer, or even allude, to what the purpose of the group was.

Eventually the meeting broke up into small groups of people who stood around talking. One of the women I had mentally tagged as 'wealthy' came and perched on the chair next to mine. She was middle-aged, svelte and smartly dressed in a suit of vaguely Forties cut. Her face had the clingfilm-stretched-over-cold-chicken look of an ageing woman who kept herself relentlessly in trim.

'Who are you?' she asked me, in a very forthright manner. Not at all like an English woman. 'I haven't seen you at a meeting before.'

'Oh, just one of Harley's colleagues. I came along to see what he was up to.'

'Adam is a marvellous man. What he has achieved here in just three months deserves to be seen as the triumph that psychotherapy has been waiting for.'

'Were you in therapy before coming to the group?'

'Was I in therapy?' She snorted. 'Is Kenton a suburb? I have been in therapy of one form or another for the last ten years. I've had Freudian analysis, I've taken anti-depressants, subjected myself to eclectic psychotherapy, rebirthing. You name it – I've tried it. And let me tell you that not one of these things has helped me in the slightest. My neurosis has always managed to resurface, again and again.'

'What form does this neurosis take?'

'Any form it chooses. I've been bulimic and anorexic, claustrophobic and agoraphobic, alcoholic and hysterical, or just plain unhappy – all until the past three months. Since I joined Adam's group my symptoms have simply melted away. I can't even remember what it was that I was so upset about. I can only recall the tortuous self-analysis and introspection that went along with my various therapies as if it were some bad dream. The way I feel now is so completely different to the way I did feel that there is no comparison.'

'Hmm, hmm. You have a relative I suppose, or a friend of some sort who . . .'

'Who belongs to the other group. Yes, of course. My son, John. Well, he's always been rather unstable, I have no idea in the last analysis whether it was his shitty upbringing, or, as the more chemically-inclined professionals have said, a purely endogenous affair. At any rate John enjoys his little manic phases. He's inherited a little capital and he likes to sit up for fifty, sixty hours at a stretch watching it ebb and flow on the futures market. He's quite happy to trade an extended manic phase off against a neurosis-free period for me. I suppose some people might call it perverse. But to me it seems the eventual, loving coming together of mother and son after so much discord . . .'

I don't know whether the above is a verbatim recollection of what the woman said, but it certainly captures the substance. I was horrified. Here was the incarnation of all I sought to avoid. The recasting of Quantity Theory as a therapeutic practice designed to palliate the idle sorrows of the moneyed. I left the house without speaking to Harley again. The rest of the sad story is familiar to us all. Harley is here at the conference, along with his disciples. His Exclusionist Therapy Movement has grown in the last five years by leaps and bounds. And Harley has, to my mind, diminished as a person in direct proportion. I don't know exactly what has happened to him. Perhaps he has simply got the wrong end of his own therapeutic techniques, spent too long in the wrong group. But his affectation of some bizarre tribal costume, his disjointed and facile mutterings – which are taken as gospel by his disciples – these seem to me to be the logical result of his meddling with the natural order of sanity quotients.

Incidentally, I did find out what happened to the awful woman I met at Harley's house. Her son died of a heart attack, brought on by asthma during one of his manic phases. Needless to say the woman herself is now safely institutionalised.

* * *

And as for the rest of them, those tedious souls who I saved from a lifetime of near-obscurity, they all proved unworthy of the gifts conferred upon them by their proximity to genuine theoretical advance. Hurst was at least predictable, even if his actions were in some ways the most odious.

It was about nine months after the afternoon I spent in Hampstead that I first read an item in the newspaper which confirmed my worst suspicions about him. Short and to the point. It said that Phillip Hurst, the noted statistician and psychologist, one of the originators of the Quantity Theory of Insanity, had been appointed by the government to head up a new bureau loosely attached to the Central Office of Statistics, but charged with a novel task – a sanity quotient survey of the whole country. The aim was to develop an effective measure of the quotient so that central government could accurately fix and concentrate its deployment of palliatives, in the form of funds spent on mental health, to create a fair and weighted distribution of aberrant behaviour throughout the realm.

I stopped waiting for more news. I knew it would be bad. I took the first academic job that I could lay my hands on that would take me as far away as possible from the onrush of the demented juggernaut I had spawned. In Darwin, in the Northern Territory of Australia, I sat and I waited. On Saturday mornings I would climb into my Moke and drive down to the Victoria Mall where the only good newsagent in Darwin kept newspapers, three and four days old, from around the world.

So it was, standing amongst men with elephant-skin crotches of sweated, bunched, denim shorts, that I read, while they scratched at Tatsalotto cards, the plastic shavings falling around their thongs. The news was all of strange theatrical events of extreme violence. The newspaper editors published programme notes, replete with heavy black arrows, and the sort of drawings of men wearing windcheaters and carrying machine pistols you would expect to find on Letraset sheets.

As for the government's attempts to arrive at an accurate way of measuring the sanity quotient, these were dogged by problems that on the one hand seemed to be purely semantic – and which on the other appeared as worrying, aberrant, unknowable.

First one measure of sanity, then another, and then several more were developed in an effort to arrive at the definitive. The problem was that the straightforward measure S_1 was arrived at by a number of calculations – the rate in the increase of schizophrenic diagnoses was indexed against the rate of increase in the population – which were themselves open to different methods of calculation and hence interpretation.

Even when the various warring 'experts' (who were these people? Where had they been when I was crouching in bothies in the Western Highlands, or roaming the toilets of central London?) could agree on a given measure, it soon manifested mathematical instabilities which rendered it unworkable, or incalculable, or both.

S_9 had quite a vogue. It involved adding together all the doses of Valium, or other related sedative drugs, prescribed in the country over a given period of time. Dividing the sum by a base unit of 5mg and then dividing that figure by the incidence of advertising for stress-relief products on each regional television network. Musselborough, at one time a swingeing and totally unsympathetic critic of my work on job reductivism, did his best to associate himself with S_9, which for a while had a considerable following, measuring, its proponents claimed, not only the base sanity quotient, but also assessing the direction and rate of change of that quotient throughout the society. But the figure itself would fluctuate over quite short periods in such an alarming way as to throw serious doubts on the validity of the data being assembled.

I watched from Millarrapulla Road with detached amusement. The life there was a good one. Every month or so the director at the local college where I taught invited me for a barbecue, and together with other men in short-sleeved shirts, pressed shorts and white kneesocks I would stand out on the lush lawn and listen to the flying foxes as they whistled into land chattering in the mango trees. The other men were bland, white, tolerable. They lived in a society where constant rates of sanity had been achieved by the creation of a racial underclass which was killing itself with alcoholism. Actually, the overclass was killing itself with alcoholism as well, but there were remarkably few sufferers from any of the major pathologies.

Simon Gurney came to visit me for a while. He was convivial company; I would come back from the college in the evening and find him sitting with a small group of Groote Eylandters as they deloused one another on the veranda. Gurney worked hard and at the end of his visit presented me with a six-foot-high featureless basalt slab which I have to this day.

The spectacle of a growing, centralised bureaucracy, labouring to implement centralised policies based on the findings of Quantity Theory, filled me with amusement. As did the news that university department after department found it necessary not only to incorporate the theory into its undergraduate syllabus, but also to seek funding for all manner of research based on the possible applications of Quantity Theory to areas as diverse as North Sea oil production and the training of primary school teachers.

From time to time a journalist or a doctoral student would seek me out. I suppose I had the cachet of being the 'founding father', but in practice this meant very little. I think that when these people arrived, toiling up suburban roads, driven into psychosis by the heat, they found someone not altogether to their taste, someone not prepared to present them with an easily definable and analysable set of personal characteristics. The theses and profiles, when in due course they appeared, reflected this difficulty. Put simply: they just didn't know what to make of me. I clearly wasn't a bohemian and yet I had dropped out. I had no charisma to speak of, I had gathered no disciples around me and yet I was by no means eccentric. I wasn't even eccentrically ordinary; a Magritte found in his own tropical Brussels.

Inexorably my reputation began to grow. Mostly, I think, as a result of the failure of my former colleagues to retain any kind of unity with their opinions whatsoever. So, although at the beginning of the Quantity Age my name was seldom if ever heard, within five years or so Busner, Harley, Hurst and even Sikorski, were driven into mentioning my name as representing the benchmark of orthodoxy, in opposition to the wholly misguided views of one another. I suppose there was a strange sort of satisfaction in this success-for-all-the-wrong-reasons. Certainly the large cash sums from royalties on dusted-off and republished papers came in handy; and I was also shrewd enough to bargain up my price for an interview.

When the offer came to take a job with PiggiBank I seriously considered it. They flew me by private jet from Darwin to Tokyo. A bizarre seven-hour drive took me so slowly from the airport to my destination (a 'country' inn outside the conurbation, of which the chairman was a fanatical patron) that I felt despotic, borne at shoulder height through the press of so many tens of thousands of short people.

I appreciated the chairman's meeting place. The inn, sited in a counterpane fold of green land, sweeping down from the conical peak of a hill which stood out against the dirty blue of a static sky, was horned and crouching, its roof a crisp pile of upturned toast-corners curling and calcined. Behind the inn towards the hill was a petrol refinery, or a chemicals plant, or some such thing – a twisted root of tangled knots of pipe.

'Wal!' The chairman's greeting was as effusive as a baby's fart through a muted trumpet. He and his people moved around the room, gesturing, giving me morsels, getting Japanese servants to give me morsels and drinks; and to give them morsels as well. They went out into the garden through the screen doors and then came back in again. Their movements around the room, with its polished block floor, lacquered furniture and paper walls, were lecherous. They molested the space. Every time their pink hands clutched at it, or their coarse faces rubbed against it, it shrank into itself, a little more hurt, a little more damaged.

Vulker himself wore a kimono so large that it diminished even his vast frame, completely upsetting what already distorted sense of proportion I had had on entering the room.

'Wal,' said Vulker, 'I think we had better address ourselves to the implications of sanity quotient fluctuations within the context of a more collectivist, potentially static situation.' He barely glanced at me; the comment seemed addressed rather to the morsels of fish smeared across his palm. I grunted noncommittally. I knew what I really thought: namely that the size factor was going to have a far more significant and widespread influence on world society than any specific internal reaction or attitude towards mental illnesses with defined pathologies. When all those really short oriental people got right out into the West they would begin to suffer from a nagging sense of inferiority. The impact of this on world sanity quotients could be catastrophic. But why should Vulker be told?

'See here?' One of Vulker's aides handed me a report bent open out of its celluloid backing. I idly scanned the columns of figures, concentrating only to relate an asterisk in the text to Harley's name at the footer. So that was it, they had started without me. I made no excuses, but left. Fourteen hours later I was back in Darwin.

So Harley became Sanity Quotient Adviser to PiggiBank. And it was afterwards rumoured that he served some useful function for the chairman himself. I would have nothing of it. Was it pride? I think not. I think it was a growing awareness of the direction that events were taking. Just as the inception of Quantity Theory itself had a dreamlike, inspirational quality, so now I felt myself drifting into a creative kind of indolence in which I saw things for what they really were.

Denver Airport. And the mountain air pushes me naked into a white, tiled bathroom. Dagglebert struggles with the suitcases. It isn't until two days later that standing on the campus field, looking towards the ridge of blue and white mountains, that I realise that I have never been to America before. This is unimportant – the reason for my presence here is to confirm a suspicion. They are all here as well: Hurst from Hampstead, Harley from New York, Busner from Montreux where he has been receiving a television award. I am not here to confront but to bear witness.

Cathcart, the resident purveyor of the theory, who has taken the time to organise this celebration, is a lively man in his early fifties, mysteriously kinked at the waist as if caught midway in some mysterious, lifelong act of mincing. Despite his fluting voice and preposterous clip-on sunglasses Cathcart proves amiable and, more to the point, respectful. He has allocated me a secluded but comfortable cabin in a distant corner of the university grounds. Over the last couple of days I have shown myself sufficiently around the campus concourse, in the faculty building, and on one evening in a Denver bistro frequented by visiting academics, to counter any possible charges of snobbery or stand-offishness.

When I have run into my old colleagues I have done my best to be courteous and pleasant. I know they regard me as a fearful prig, but why should I descend to embrace the pseudo-cultural fallout that has surrounded my lifetime's work? Why should I allow my very thought to become a creature of fashion?

And so up on to the podium, and to the lectern. Introduced by Cathcart I stand looking out over the upturned faces. Now is my moment, now is my chance to ensure that posterity has some inviolate record . . .

I hesitate and then begin to speak; the coloured lights process across my crotch. Dagglebert salivates below me.

My address is a triumph, a *cause célèbre.* Or so I think. At any rate I am very well received. But then I didn't try anything fancy, I confined myself to areas that are well known. I didn't trouble my audience with complexities, or give them any real idea of what tremendous conceptual heat is required within the crucible of creation. In a word my address – to my own mind – was anodyne.

Towards the end of the morning, as my eyes scanned still more distant prospects in an effort to avoid contemplating the crumpled, impotent visages of my colleagues, I saw a flicker of white moving in and out of the trees at the edge of the stretch of lawn that bounded the auditorium building. It came and then went, and then came again. Until it resolved itself into the figure of a young woman, perhaps in her early twenties, clad in a loose hospital gown, who ran hither and thither, arms outstretched, or in her hair. She pirouetted and thrust herself, as if brutally masturbating, against the trunks of the stately Douglas firs. In time she was joined by more figures, some similarly attired, some dressed in fragments of surgical garb, others girt with appliances for restraining the deranged, still others naked but for either torn sweaters or cast-off trousers.

While this cavalcade, this strange fiesta, made its way out of the trees and on to the lawn, I went on speaking, automatically. I knew what was happening, I had heard rumours. My suspicions were confirmed when a tall figure appeared in the wake of the dancers. He stood head and shoulders above them, naked to the waist and below that clad only in harlequin tights and an absurd, priapic codpiece. His beard jutted towards the auditorium, his eyes flashed and even from a distance of several hundred metres, seemed to search mine. I had been joined by the last of the original team. Sikorski had arrived, along with his Radical Psychic Field Disruptionists.

If Hurst represented the therapeutic corruption of Quantity Theory, Sikorski had done his best to effect a political corruption. Sikorski's first published paper in the wake of our work together had contained a lively refutation of the idea of sanity quotients being measurable within the context of social groupings. For him the very idea of 'society' was a fallacy. 'Society' could not be quantified, but a physical area could. Sikorski proposed, therefore, what he called 'psychic fields' – not really a difficult concept to grasp, he simply meant 'areas'. Within each of these psychic fields there was, of course, a given sanity quotient. It was in the interests of the establishment, he went on to say, to create a complex and sustainable pattern of such fields, which would ensure that the principal burdens of depression, schizophrenia, alcoholism, mania and depression, fell primarily on the disadvantaged: the working class, the ethnic minorities and so forth.

Clearly this fascism of the very animus had to be counteracted. Sikorski, scion of a wealthy East Anglian landowning family, at one time a brilliant clinician with a promising career in orthodox medicine ahead of him, took the plunge and followed the path dictated by his own convictions. After the initial Quantity Theory multi-disciplinary team broke up Sikorski disappeared. Later, there were rumours that he had had himself sectioned; that he had undergone more than twenty ECT treatments, that he had been overdosed with Halperidol. And later still that he had been partially leucotomised . . . privately . . . by a friend.

He emerged two years later on the fringes of the metropolis. By now he was at the head of a ragged band, which styled itself as 'the Radical Psychic Field Disruptionists'. The aim of this collection of university dropouts, druggies, actors and other assorted social deviants was to act as a kind of emergency oil rig capping team in the context of mental health.

Like a method acting workship they refined and perfected their assumption of symptoms of mental illness. (Occasionally members of the troupe would appear on one of the regional news-feature programmes to give the folks at home a demo.) Then, they would descend to picket day-care centres, long-term asylums, secure wards for the criminally insane and of course analysts' and therapists' offices. Lounging, squirming, ranting, collectively deluding, over a two- or three-year period the Radical Psychic Field Disruptionists became a familiar sight around Britain. They had the same sort of cachet – as a bizarre diversion threading their way through the conformist crowd – as the Hare Krishnas had had some ten or so years before.

I had always had a kind of a weakness for Sikorski. He was such an attractive man, and so enthusiastic, given to large passions. Very Slav.

He was really the Bakunin of psychology, asexual and subject to borrowing large amounts of money that he couldn't possibly hope to repay.

Now he stands. And then struts back and forth on the sward. Arms outstretched, he clutches up divots and presses them to his brow. His mouth opens and closes, but I can't hear what he's saying. Apparently he has been invited to Denver as a gift to the municipality from the conference organisers. The Radical Psychic Field Disruptionists are going to practise their strange arts in the vicinity of the state mental hospital and ameliorate the conditions of the inhabitants . . . that's the idea at any rate.

Plenty of people, some of them quite respectable thinkers believe implicitly in the efficacy of Radical Psychic Field Disruption. What a joke! These people haven't a clue what Quantity Theory is really about. Quantity Theory is not concerned with total physical cause, it operates at the level of the signifier. People are willing to come forward in droves and claim that they have been helped by the actions of Sikorski and his followers. And it is considered slightly hip by the intelligentsia to piggyback on a field disrupting trip in order to obtain relief from some trying neurosis or other – to shuck off a co-dependant relationship, or 'deal' with some emotion or other. I have been told that nowadays it's virtually impossible to pass a mental institution of any kind at all, without seeing a little ersatz ship of fools moored by the main door and in the shadows, lurking, a pasty-faced scion of the Sunday Review benefiting obscurely from the local field disruption.

As soon as my address is over and the ovation has been tidied away I stride out of the auditorium. Walking across the concourse I turn to Dagglebert, outraged.

'What the hell are these people doing here? Why have the conference organisers allowed them into the precincts of the university?'

'Oh, them,' says Dagglebert – and as he speaks I see once again the utter stupidity of employing a research assistant who drools – 'They're here by invitation of the conference, as a gift to the municipality of Denver . . .'

'I know that, I know that!' I turn away from Dagglebert and head towards the cafeteria, which lies on the far side of the precinct. Dagglebert, undeterred, follows me, drooling the while.

Safely ensconsed behind a chest-high arras of plastic bamboo shoots I watch the ebb and flow of conferees as the swarm coming from the auditorium runs into the traffic on the precinct and the Radical Psychic Field Disruptionists enter from the outside. Rocking and dribbling they stand here and there talking to former colleagues, half-remembered through a fog of tranquillisers.

I see my own former colleagues there as well. Zack Busner stands with a tall, shrouded girl, nervously rolling and unrolling the end of his mohair tie. Phillip Hurst has his briefcase propped open on one knee, foot up on the rim of a concrete shrubbery container as he riffles through notes for the benefit of a stocky individual, who flexes and reflexes his muscular arms. I see Adam Harley deep in conversation with Janner, the anthropologist, who I know vaguely. Janner is wearing what looks like a second-hand Burton overcoat and carries a plastic bag emblazoned with the logo of a popular chain of South London convenience stores. Janner is a repellent individual, with something of Alkan about him – the way he tilts his head back in order to slurp the catarrh down his throat is especially striking. I have no idea why he has chosen to be in Denver.

And here and there dotted around this space are other familiar figures. Faces from the past that split and reform with speech. A manic, Jewish type who looks like an accountant clutches a sheaf of marketing brochures under his arm, and stands engrossed, while Stein, that millenarian charlatan, lays down his new law. Sikorski is moving among the throng. There's something hilarious about the way his false penis quests ahead of him. Especially if you know, as I do, that he's completely impotent. He stops to shake hands and chat with well-wishers. However he hasn't knocked off work altogether. A slowly rotating strand of spittle still threads through his tangled, fair beard, twisting this way and that, catching and refracting the sunlight streaming through the skylights above.

And as I observe Sikorski and his cohorts the nervous irritation that has gripped me since I arrived in Denver starts to fade away. I am left with a sense that this conference, this scene, is a watershed for Quantity Theory. A heaven-sent second opportunity for me to re-establish the school of thought at the correct level with the correct emphasis. Where has Quantity Theory gone wrong? In its application. In its development as a therapy? As a method of social control? As a tool of radical psychiatric policy? In all and yet none of these areas. The truth, as ever, comes to me purely, in one flash of instant realisation. I knock over the styrofoam beaker full of tepid coffee that Dagglebert has placed at my elbow as I fumble through my pockets for pencil and notebook. I start to jot down a first attempt to express the realisation in some form of notation:

$$Q(Q><[Q]) = Q(Q><[Q])$$

Of course it would be possible to qualify this. It may be that this is itself too blindingly, elegantly simple and that the value 'Q' may have to be defined with some reference to a value external to itself. But for the moment it stands happily to explain what I see around me.

The Radical Psychic Field Disruptionists; the American students dressed in puffy, autumnal sports gear; the heads of a dozen university faculties gesturing with passion over a subject they neither know nor understand. And all of them, mark me, all of them, confined within definable societal groupings.

The Quantity Theory of Insanity has reached its first great epistemological watershed. Like theoretical physics it must now account for the very phenomenon it has helped to identify. It must reconstruct the proof of its own ground on the fact of its own enactment. Clearly, by concentrating so many aberrant and near-aberrant people in one place or series of places, the very fact of Quantity Theory has been impacting on the sanity quotient itself.

The task now is to derive an equation which would make it possible to establish whether what I suspect is true. Namely that as more and more insanity is concentrated around educational institutions, so levels of mental illness in the rest of society . . .

Select Bibliography

Ford, Hurst, Harley, Busner & Sikorski, 'Some Aspects of Sanity Quotient Mechanisms in a Witless Shetland Commune', *British Journal of Ephemera*, September, 1974.

Ford, H., 'Teaching Stockbrokers Ring Dancing', *Practical Mental Health*, January, 1975.

Ford, H., *The Quantity Theory of Insanity*, Publish Yourself Books, London 1976 (limited edition).

Ford, H., 'Repressing People Who Laugh Alone: Towards Effective Public Transport', *The Bus*, October, 1995.

Harley, T., 'Shamanism and Soya Futures', World Bank Research Briefs, September, 1979.

Hurst, P., 'Nailbiting in Bournemouth versus Bed-Wetting in Poole: Action and Amelioration', *Journal of Psychology*, March, 1976.

Hurst, P., 'General Census of Sanity Quotients in the UK', HMSO, January, 1980.

Sikorski, A., *'Daddy, Mummy's Mad.' 'Good.'*, Shefcott and Willer, London 1976.

Birdy Num Num

What's my name? My name is legion, for I – we – are many. Many and colourless. I'm in him – and her, and them; I'm in some of those over there, the ones shopping for travel adaptors in Dixons. The pair of semi-whores – squeaking on high stools in leather skirts, eating caviar with their sour daddy at the granite lip of the seafood bar – I'm far deeper in them than he'll ever be. As for that one, I'm most definitely in him, I'm *loaded* into him, the windy horse of a cleaner who, emaciated in his worn blue-denim fatigues, is invisible to these fervent believers in universal healthcare: the African, pulling his cartload of bleach and plastic bags from one village-sized toilet to the next.

I am not death, for death has no persona; death is only an absence – not even a mask. True, for some I am death's helpmeet, but I'm not a psychopath, only a cytopath. I, too, am alive. I, too, have feelings – ethics as well. If I am known at all, it's by my effects rather than my causes; in this I am antithetical to humans' gods. Be that as it may, I am powerful, I am ancient, I am constantly changing, and I – we – are, if not omniscient, privy to a lot.

Y'know, some bio-theologians think I'm the First Cause, a primitive form of all the life on this dirt ball – that every animal evolved from an organism like me; others take the contrary view, that I – we – are fallen angels, cast out from the heaven of advancement, deselected and so become parasitic and unsexed.

I say, surely it's a question of scale? Looked down on from a mile up in the sky – the holding pattern of a god – this air terminal is a body, the living tissue of which is bored into by bacterium planes, subterranean trains and hissing buses. Humans swarm through its concourses, virions with credit cards.

Soon, I – some of us – will be thrust into that steep vantage, the sky, then propelled over land and sea to another city; Helsinki, as it happens. Before I go, let me – us – tell you how this has come to pass; let me tell you about this generic Tuesday afternoon – because, let's face it, it's *always* Tuesday afternoon. Allow me to assemble a cast of characters, as well or as woodenly drawn as any in a whodunnit. They were all my accomplices; your task is to identify the victim.

November 1998, a Tuesday – the day teetering on noon's fulcrum. Georgie Maxwell was walking along the first stretch of Kensington Road; she passed the gates at the end of Kensington Palace Gardens and then the driveway of the Royal Garden Hotel. In the fluffy onset of a fine drizzle, the hotel doormen moved smartly to marshal brass luggage carts and beckon taxis beneath the jutting portico with its inset lights haloed in the damp gloom. Over the shoulder of the hotel – a 1960s thing, granite-faced and angular – stretched the late autumn brownery of Kensington Gardens, and beyond them, Hyde Park, its black tree spars rigged with dead and dying leaves. In the middle east a dark mauve sky, its fundament coiled with ashen clouds, squatted over Bayswater.

Walking is perhaps an overstatement. Georgie's progress was halting, despite her being encumbered with no more than a tabloid newspaper, a pint carton of semiskimmed milk and a packet of milk chocolate Hob-Nobs, all in a plastic bag. She clunked from stiff leg to stiff leg, swinging them from her hips as if they were stilts. The hem of her skirt rose first above one thickly bandaged shin, then the other. The skirt, eh? Well, it had a Minoan motif worked into it – geometric designs embroidered with gold thread; once pale green, it was now stained and blotchy. People walking in the other direction, from Kensington Gore, didn't take in the skirt, or the rusty raincoat, or the espadrilles unravelling from both swollen feet. They merely checked her against their internal list of street people – alcoholics, junkies, schizos and dossers – made a positive identification, then dismissed her from view.

Up close, and personally, Georgie smelt of sepsis. There were open sores under the chicken skin of her crêpe bandages; craters, really, in which bacteria, numerous as Third World miners, hacked at the exposed tissue-face. Thankfully, the day was fresh, and neither the hurrying working girls nor the strolling young ladies out shopping could smell this. However, besides looking crazy Georgie talked to herself: a twittering commentary in real time – 'She's crossing the road, pelican crossing, not a game bird, crossing the road' – that kept her company as she did, indeed, cross the road at Palace Gate, stump back along the far side, then traverse the junction of Gloucester Road and turn left into De Vere Gardens.

Why did this street – no different to scores of others in the area – feel quite so bare, so baldly threatening? On either side magnolia-painted six-storey Victorian terraces loomed in the thickening drizzle; the pavements were anthracite glossy, void of any rubbish, or even the occasional bracelet – or tiara – of costly dog shit. The kerb sides were cluttered with tens of thousands of pounds' worth of cars – cetacean Porsches and squashed Maseratis with Dubai plates – and, as she peg-legged by these, Georgie kept up her rap, a well-spoken psychosis, 'Maybe he'll be there – maybe he'll come soon. Maybe-baby, if I don't TREAD ON THE CRACKS!' She shied away from the spear tips of the railings, then, halfway along the street, lurched towards them and, pushing open a gate, awkwardly descended an iron staircase into a savage little area full of bullying bins.

I – we went along for the ride – although we were also waiting inside.

Inside Billy Chobham, who, in turn, was inside the bath; which was inside the bathroom; which, in turn, was inside Tony Riley's basement flat. The cell-like bathroom had no windows, and only a single lightbulb that dangled, unshaded, from a furred flex. The harsh light beat the limpid surface of the bath water, below which Billy's pubic hair bloomed, silky as pond algae. The bath water had long since cooled – Billy was colder. He'd been in there for over an hour, his fair skin going blue, the ends of his fingers puckering up into corrugated pads. However, Billy was experiencing no discomfort, because, unlike the chaotic Georgie, he had had a get-up hit. Billy always had a get-up; this was part of his professionalism. 'I'm a junky,' he'd tell anyone unable to escape. 'I don't make any bloody bones about it. I don't try an' stop, an' I ain't sayin' it's not my fault neevah – I wanna be a junky. I like being a junky – I'm good at it.'

It's debatable whether it's possible to be good at being bad, and it's a discussion I – we – would be happy to join in. This being noted, let's not trouble with the theory for now, and instead present the actuality. Billy had jeans that stood up straighter without him in them, and a red mohair pullover given to him by a girl in East Sheen. If he was shod it was in prison-issue trainers. He had no fixed abode, but throughout London – and still further afield, in Reading, Maidstone and Bristol – there were small caches of his belongings: a T-shirt here, a paperback there, an exercise book full of mad ballpoint drawings of invented weaponry way over there. Billy never asked the occupants of the flats and houses where he crashed if he could leave these things; he just shoved them down the back of shelves or into cupboards, so that he could return days or months later and clamour to be readmitted, on the basis that 'I've gotta get me fings.'

There were warrants out for Billy from Redbridge to Roehampton for crimes beneath petty: kiting ten-quid cheques, exchanging shoplifted underwear at Marks and Spencer, forging methadone prescriptions. There was nothing aggressive in Billy's felonies; he took no part in the great metropolis's seven and a half million fuck-offs, the abrasive grinding of psychic shingle on its terminal beach. Be that as it may, wherever Billy went, doors came off their hinges, baths overflowed and fat-filled frying pans burst into flame. His life was a free-pratfall, as, flailing, head over tail, he plunged through year after year, his fists and feet – entirely accidentally, you understand – striking mates, siblings, the odd – *very* odd – girlfriend, but mostly his old mum, who, while fighting depression, did the payroll for a chemical plant in St Neots and remained good – or bad – for a loan.

Billy, the career junky, always had his get-up: the brown-to-beige powder in the pellet of plastic, which – after being tapped into a spoon, mixed with water and citric acid, heated, then drawn off through the cellulose strands of a bit of a cigarette filter – was thrust inside his veins, making it possible for the muzzy show to go on. Locked in bathrooms with taffeta mats, crouching in back of couches, planted in the bushy corners of conservatories – Billy stayed in these spaces for as long as it took, watching for the bloom in the hypodermic syringe, his gift of a houseplant.

Georgie, who had forgotten her key, tapped on the glass panel of the kitchen door. Her face was a sharp, feline triangle, tabby with dirt and misapplied make-up; her taps were as diffident as the blows of velvet paws. No one heard her. In the cold bath, Billy gouched out, sunk in the hot Mojave desert of his habitual reverie, a corny old Blake Edwards vehicle for the comedian Peter Sellers called *The Party*.

Billy had first seen the film on television when he was four or five years old; but even then – it was originally released in 1968 – its depiction of flowery fun was painfully dated: the beautiful people of Hollywood cavorting the night away. Besides, it was a crap film with a dumb script – no plot to speak of, only a series of farcical sight gags for Sellers, browned up to play Hrundi V. Bakshi, a useless Indian who haplessly destroys the house where the eponymous party is being held, a party he has been invited to in error, and that is being thrown by the producer of a movie he's already sabotaged with his stupid mistakes and brainless antics.

It was on the location for that movie-within-a-movie that Billy habitually began his drug-dreaming. So I – we – were inside Billy, who was inside the bath inside Tony Riley's flat. In there with us was a ravine, somewhere out beyond Barstow, chosen for its superficial similarity to the Hindu Kush; and in the ravine were Hispanic extras playing Pathan tribesmen, together with more Hispanic extras playing sepoys. A detachment of Hispanics marched along the bottom of the ravine, accompanied by an Hispanic pipe band miming their instruments. The Hispanics playing the tribesmen – and a few light-skinned, Caucasian-featured blacks – reared up from the rocks above and made ready to fire. Frantic to frustrate the ambush, the half-Jewish Sellers – who, presumably, had been sent ahead as a scout – reared up as well, blasting a bugle. The Hispanic Pathans turned their rifles on him and he was struck by their volley. The bugle notes flattened into farts, Sellers collapsed, then reared up again, crazily tootling.

This was where Billy, as Peter Sellers, as Hrundi V. Bakshi, made his entrance: a junky in a bath in a fantasy of a film. He had seen *The Party* next in his teens, again on television; this time he was banged up in a secure hostel on the Goldhawk Road. This second viewing confirmed for Billy that this was 'his' film: an acid-pastel ball, in which he could perceive his dull childhood transmuted to the plinkety-plunk beat of a Henry Mancini soundtrack. Eventually Billy had acquired his own videotape of *The Party*. It was wrapped in a pair of bloodstained combat trousers and pushed behind the hot-water tank in a bungalow near Pinner.

Billy's white body, fishily flattened by refraction, undulated in the cold water as he mimicked the flips and flops of the comedian; who died in 1980 of a heart attack – his third – brought on by the amyl nitrate he huffed on the sets of movies such as *The Party*. Billy's wide mouth – which could be described as generous only if what you wanted was more plaque – stretched into a rictus. Outside, Georgie's taps increased in volume as the drizzle percolating De Vere Gardens bubbled into rain.

Along a gloomy corridor that ran the length of the basement flat, between Dexion shelving units stacked with papers and paperbacks waiting to be burnt, then between a thicket of cardboard tubes that sheathed old point-of-sale materials and posters, then in through an open door, the minute sound waves pulsed, to where Tony Riley, the Pluto of this underworld, sat on a sofa in his boxer shorts, his unshaven muzzle clamped by the transparent obscenity of an oxygen mask, while the cylinder lay on the cushion beside him, steely and fire-engine-red.

I – we – were in Tony, too, not that this mattered; the catch, then gush, as his own febrile inhalation triggered the valve and yanked a gush of oxygen into his defeated lungs, drowned out everything: hearing, thought, intention, feeling. Tony was hanging on to life by his teeth, which were sunk in the plastic mouthpiece. Shitty disease, emphysema; shitty paradoxical condition. Tony sat in a stale closet, into which every small sip of air had to be dragged down a long corridor wadded with cellulose, while beneath his rack of ribcage his lungs were already abnormally distended.

Tony Riley's legs were kite struts in the flattened cloth of his boxers; his sweaty T-shirt hung on him like a scrap of polythene on a barbed-wire fence; his dirty-brown hair was painted down on to his canvas scalp; his grey eyes streamed behind once fashionable Cutler and Gross glasses. Up above him, on the purple and taupe striped wallpaper, hung a Mark Boxer cartoon of Tony in his heyday. It was a prophetic casting of inky sticks: the Roman profile and laurel wreath of hair simplified to a few thin and thick lines. Two decades on, the caricature was as good a likeness as any photograph – perhaps better. No photo could have captured the way Tony's breathless need for heroin simplified the awesome clutter of the large, low, subterranean living room – its middle-aged armchairs and smoked-glass coffee tables, its Portobello Road floor cushions and swampy Turkish kelims, its portable commode and novelty coat tree – into two white dimensions of nothing.

Beside Tony's meagre thigh there lay a scrap of tin foil, on which trailed burnt heroin. Chasing the dragon? For Tony it was more akin to staggering after a snail: he huffed, he puffed, he struggled to exhale, so that he could carve a tiny pocket in the necrotic tissue of his lungs to fill with the narcotic fumes.

Tony spat out the mouthpiece, snatched up the foil and, from the coffee table in front of his sofa, a gold Dupont lighter; then he grabbed a rolled-up tube of tin foil, poked it between his lips and hunched to his labour.

'In the primitive environment,' Lévi-Strauss wrote, 'the relevant is the sensational.' But really, in Tony Riley's basement flat, it was too primitive even for *that*; here, sensations were muffled and numbed by mould and opiates; the rain falling on the roof five storeys above penetrated the slates, then joists, plaster, paint, carpet, floor boards and more joists, until it pattered on to the jungly floor between the chief's bare feet. The parrot of addiction flapped across the dank clearing to perch on the edge of a serving hatch. Oh, that noble psittacine! Longer lived than humans, perfectly intelligent, and well able to imitate the squawks of their most awful mental pathologies.

Outside, Georgie's tapping had finally risen to a determined rapping. It was only 12.20; nevertheless, the most dissolute of establishments still have their routines. There were chores to do, calculations to be made, the supplier to be contacted; then, soon enough, the customers would begin arriving. She rapped, the glass bruising her clenched knuckles. She had once had a body that, like any affluent woman's, was a gestalt of smell, texture and colour – but now that had all flown apart: she was as dun as a cowpat, you wouldn't want to touch her, her smell was in your face.

'Whereis'e? Stupid Billy. Fucking Billy. Open up. Gotta do Tony's meds. Call Andy. Gotta do Tony's fucking meds. Call Andy. Gotta do

Tony's meds –' This aloud, the narrative of her staggering thought replacing the saga of her limping walk along Kensington Road.

Skin pancaked between bone and glass; the raps marched through the kitchen, along the sepia corridor, and into the room where Tony was trying to recapture the thrill of the chase. He left off, let fall his impedimenta, stood and lurched to the doorway. 'Billy!' he shouted in a crepitating whisper. 'It's her – get the fucking door!' Then he crumpled up as thoroughly as any scrap of tin foil.

'Brill-ll-llerowng! Brill-ll-llerowng! Brill-ll-llerowng!' Billy had discovered that if he plugged his ears in a certain way and pressed his mouth against the side of the bath, his submarine ejaculations sounded – to him – like sitar chords. Billy, as Peter Sellers, as Hrundi V. Bakshi, sat cross-legged on the floor of his Los Angeles bungalow, wearing a long-sleeved, collarless linen shirt. The big bole of the instrument was cradled in his lap, his browned-up face concentrated in mystic reverie. 'Brill-ll-llerowng!' When the letter-box flap lifted, a letter fell on to the mat, and the flap clacked shut. Clacked shut. Clacked shut again. It wasn't meant to do that – this was the invitation to the paradisical party, and he, Billy-as-Hrundi, was simply meant to pick it up, open and read it; but the *fucking flap* wouldn't stop clacking!

Billy lunged up in the bath, in time to hear '– king door!' in the calm after the splash. Then he was all action: out on the wet lino, twisting a thin towel round his nethers, then into the corridor. He knelt over Tony. 'All right, mate? Y'all right, mate?' A ghastly simulation of Cockney mummy concern.

'Juss, juss, juss –' Tony shudderingly inhaled, then sputtered, 'Get the fucking door.'

Calcium hydroxide, calcium chloride, calcium hypochlorite. In a word: bleach. We don't altogether fear it – there are too many of us, and we're too small. Far too small. I'm small even for my kind – maybe fifty nanometres across, which is fifty billionths of a metre. That's smaller than the wavelength of visible light, so why should I fear bleach? For I can have no colour. Anyway, Georgie doesn't apply bleach to the insides of syringes or spoons, nor does she dunk razors or toothbrushes in it. All her bleaching activities are confined to the laminated surfaces of Tony

Riley's kitchen. In the days when the disorder in her life was a tea mug unwashed up for the odd hour, or a book left face down on the arm of a chair, Georgie used to say, 'It doesn't matter how messy things get so long as you have clean kitchen surfaces.'

Of course, that was when things weren't really messy at all. That was during the eight clean years, when Georgie attended her self-help groups, built a career as a television producer, had a couple of happy-then-unhappy relationships, visited her parents, paid her taxes. That was before the craters full of sepsis and the shrinking of her head; that was when she had her own studio flat in Chiswick, not two black plastic bags in the dark corner of Tony Riley's damp bedroom.

Now the clean kitchen surfaces were the only ordered thing in the mess that was notionally her life. After cooing, billing and heaving Tony back to his oxygen cylinder, Georgie adjusted her dressings – fallen down around her ankles, obscene crepe parodies of old women's stockings – before setting to with bucket, hot water, brush and bleach. She didn't stop until the Formica was lustrous and the aluminium draining board gleamed.

Shitty disease, emphysema. Admirably shitty: chronic, progressive, degenerative – a bit like civilization. And here we have the gerontocracy of late capitalism that Sam Beckett – himself a sufferer – would undoubtedly have recognized. With their faces – one browned by neglect, the other blued by anoxia – Georgie and Tony were typecast as Nell and Nagg. He nagged her, wheezing demands, while she nellied about the flat, fetching his anti-cholinergics and bronchodilators, administering his steroids and checking the levels on his oxygen cylinder. Setting to one side the ghastliness of a carer almost as sick as her patient, there was a ritualized and stagy desperation to their relationship; because, of course, there is *no more painkiller, the little round box is empty*, and everything is *winding down.*

Yes, a stagy desperation heightened only by their cloying affection and their treacly endearments: Chuckle-Bunny, Sweetums, Little Dove, Ups-a-Boy and Noodly-Toots for each other; and for the drugs: smidgen, pigeon, widgeon and snuff-snuff. To behold them, passionately engaged in the chores of moribundity, was to intrude upon the intimacy of a couple so old, so long together, so time-eroded into a single psychic mass, that they seemed ancient enough to have had children that must've grown up, gone away, formed partnerships of their own, had their own children, grown older, then themselves died. Of old age.

Tony was fifty-three, Georgie forty-one. They had known each other for six months.

From time to time, Georgie would break out of her stagy desperation and peremptorily order Billy to fetch this or do that. This may have been a ship of fools, but it was a tight one. There was no room on deck for shirkers. Billy had shed his moist breech-clout in favour of a neatly pressed tan linen suit, white shirt and red tie – perfect protective colouring for a hapless Indian actor attending a Hollywood party. The 'plink-plink-brill-ll-llerowng!' of his sitar had snagged the twang of an electric guitar; now a snare drum brushed up the tempo, as Billy, in a dinky three-wheeler car, pulled out of the driveway and buzzed off down the boulevard lined with palms. It was an iconic image of Los Angeles, undercut, if only he knew it . . . Ach! Fuck it! If only he knew *anything*; and if only he didn't behave as if his entire life were a pre-credit sequence.

Because here it was: *Ars Gratia Arts* captioned a lion roused from torpor and petulantly roar-yawning. But a better motto for Billy would've been *Pro Aris et Focis*; for, as he piloted the joke car of his narcotized psyche down the corridor of Tony Riley's flat – a boulevard lined with the drooping fronds of old advertising flyers and press releases, the domesticated foliage of Tony's once wildly successful career in public relations – Billy was reverencing his deity and preserving this hearth.

The order of the credits for the production was this: Tony, the hot-shot producer whose mortgage arrears couldn't now catch up on him before the repossession of Death. He had the De Vere Gardens flat and a few more quid in the bank to chuck on the pyre. Every day he re-erected the set upon which the film of the party was shot – but he couldn't do it without Georgie. Georgie was the director: she assembled cast and crew, rehearsed their lines, consulted with script editors and cameramen – without her there would've been no action. Since her legs had started to rot – abscesses from shooting up, did you really want to know? – she could no longer act as a runner for a different production, the big one, overseen by Bertram and Andy's crew.

Then there was Billy, who lived from hand to hand – because his mouth rarely entered into it. He gofered for Tony and Georgie in return for wheedling rights on the drugs that flowed through the gross anatomy of the flat. Billy, most weeks, couldn't even get it together to go to pick up his emergency payment from the social in Euston. So, no leech, but by default an exemplary sole trader, engaged in the arbitrage of small quantities of merchandise, while offering piffling services. He probably should have received an Enterprise Allowance – or a British Screen grant.

At the venue for the party, the capacious and ugly modern home of capacious and ugly Hollywood film producer Fred Clutterbuck, Billy manoeuvred Hrundi V. Bakshi's three-wheeler between two ordinary-sized cars, and then had to climb out the top because he couldn't open the door. In this, Peter Sellers was only aping many episodes in Billy's own life: the insinuation of his simian body into spaces it wasn't intended for – tiny toilet windows, constricted shafts, tight transoms; and places where it wasn't wanted – nice teenage girls' bedrooms, the locked premises of chemists'.

The Clutterbucks' front door was answered by a uniformed black maid. Beyond her stretched a long hallway, with a walkway running over an artificial stream that flowed alongside a bamboo screen. When Billy was a kid, it was the insane largesse of this interior rill that made of the Clutterbucks' home – or, rather, Blake Edwards's production designer's conception of the Clutterbucks' home – a domestic pleasure dome. (Fernando Carrere, died 1998.)

It might be surmised that with age and experience any child would be disabused of this impression by other, more stylish domains, so that, upon reviewing *The Party*, he would wince at the tackiness of it all: the painted plywood cladding on the walls, the funnel-like light fitments, the circular fireplace – all of which were to be travestied, and travestied again during the next two decades, until such 'features' ended up skulking in chain hotels by motorway intersections, on the outskirts of a thousand cities that no one chooses to visit. Not to mention the stream itself, which was no Alph but a mean little trough, its bottom and sides painted with durable, aquamarine paint.

Might be surmised – but not by Billy; Billy was never disabused. True, on TVs in the association areas of remand centres, then latterly, on those clamped in the top corners of cells, he had glimpsed these other, more stylish domains. There had also been times, on the out, when, like an anthropoid tapeworm, Billy had lodged himself in the entrails of others' evenings – usually because he'd sold them a blob of hash or a sprinkling of powder – and so ended up in their fitted flats or architect-designed houses.

While his unwitting hosts grew maudlin and clumsy in the kitchen, Billy roamed the other chambers, examining such innovations as rag-rolling and glass bricks with an aficionado's eye. When he left he'd take with him a silver-framed photograph or leather-bound book in lieu of a going-home present. He'd seldom been invited in the first place – and he was never asked back.

So, Billy – he wasn't disabused; for him, Chez Clutterbuck remained the acme of warm and sophisticated hospitality, to which he was invited back again and again, despite the fact that each and every time he arrived with mud coating one of his white moccasins. Oops! What should he do? Billy, as Peter, as Hrundi, had trodden in the oily gunk in the parking area, and then tracked black footprints along the pristine walkway, a dull single-player version of that quintessential sixties party game Twister.

Billy and Hrundi – they're both peasants, basically. A stream of water in a house must be for washing arse or hands, so the dabbling of the muddy shoe in the stream was only – like all slapstick – logical. Basic physics. It floated away, a jolly little boat, leaving Billy to encounter that stock character, the drunken waiter, while hopping on one bare, browned-up foot.

The waiter was young, with sandy hair, and in full fig: tailcoat, high white collar. He dutifully presented his tray of cocktails. Then Billy – as Peter, as Hrundi – got to deliver one of his favourite lines in *The Party*. Recall, he was a career junky, a professional. Heroin, morphine sulphate, pethidine, methadone – all opiates, synthetic and organic, these were his stock in trade; but alcohol, apart from when he needed it to sedate himself because he couldn't get any junk and his chicken bones were splintering in his turkey skin, well, 'Thank you, but I never touch it.' And so, unsullied, Hrundi hopped off to retrieve his moccasin that, like Moses's basket, had grounded in some rushes. Behind him the waiter, who was every straight-living hypocrite Billy had ever known, took a glass from his own tray and knocked it back.

All this – the fragments of remembered dialogue, the off-cuts of scenery, the comedian's fatuous mugging – was projected on to Tony Riley's blank basement, while the other two parties to the ill-lit production got set up for the day's shoot.

Once wiped down and medicated, ornamental Tony was replaced on his sofa with a cup of tea; and Georgie, having done the surfaces, retired to the bathroom, where, under the bare bulb, she put a bird leg up on the bath and unwound four feet of crêpe bandage to expose the open-cast bacteria mine. In the enamel ravine below lay strewn the rubble of Billy, his horny nail clippings and fuse-wire pubic hairs, the frazil of his dead skin left high and drying on crystalline ridges of old suds.

Georgie winced as she dusted the gaping hole in her shin with fungicidal powder. It was perhaps a little bizarre that, given the exactitude with which she measured, then administered, palliatives to Tony, she so woefully mistreated herself; but then, by sticking to her story that these septic potholes were 'just something I picked up', she could maintain the delusion that she was 'run down' and 'a bit stressed out', so necessitating certain other medications, which the authorities, in their infinite stupidity, saw fit to deny her.

The truth was that Georgie was dying as well – and she knew it. She'd been clean for long enough, before relapsing back into the pits, to no longer be able to cloak her mind – once swift, airborne, feathery and beautiful – in the crude oil of evasiveness. She had resolved to die with Tony, to go with him into the ultimate airlessness of the emphysemic's tomb, as a handmaiden for the afterlife.

Be that as it may, in the time left to her there was work to be done; so, once the pits had been powdered and crêped, Georgie retreated to the inner sanctum she shared with Tony, the master bedroom, in order to make The Call.

Georgie had met Tony when she was a runner for Bertram and Andy's crew. Bertram, at one time a paper-bag manufacturer in Leicester, had been lured down to London ten years before. No one's saying Bertram's paper bags were any good: he didn't maintain the machinery, skimped on glue and abused his Bangladeshi – and largely female – workforce. His bags often split. I know, because I was also in Leicester, in some of

Bertram's workers; remember, I am legion – and non-unionized. Bertram also knocked his own wife around.

Bertram liked whoring – and he liked whores still more. He panted down the M1 to London on the expensive scent. While in town, he treated his 'ladies' like . . . ladies, just as back home he treated his women like whores. He particularly cherished nice girls from good families who had fallen on to his bed of pain. He bought the fucked-up Tiffanies and Camillas he hired – at first by the hour, then by the night – as if they were nobility, dressing them up so he could take them to Fortnum's for tea, or to Asprey's for ugly silver fittings.

Bertram was a medieval miller of a man, complete with jowls and an extra brace of chins. His great girth suggested the washing down of capons with many firkins of ale. His thick thighs cried out for hosiery, his paunch bellowed for a codpiece. On his first chin was stuck a goatee the approximate size and shape of a Scottie dog. The beard looked as if it had flung itself at Bertram's face to get at the liverish treat of his tongue.

Bertram didn't do drugs – but his 'ladies' were clopping about in the muck. He soon realized he could secure himself cheaper favours if he took up dealing. During a brief sojourn in Pentonville – the result of a contretemps involving an electric kettle lead, his pivotal arm and a girl who wasn't a 'lady' – Bertram met Andy (real name, Anesh), who dissimulated about everything, including his skin colour. At night, even in the nick, he rubbed whitening powder into his tan cheeks – an inverted Hrundi V. Bakshi, playing Peter Sellers. Andy was small Asian fry, but he had big Jamaican and Turkish connections. When they got out, the paper-bag manufacturer and the fraud went into partnership.

The viral quality of vice, well, we have to stop and admire it – for an instant. Bertram and Andy's business plan was simplicity itself. This was the early 1990s and crack cocaine, a recent arrival, was stupendously dear. Most of Bertram's whores used crack with their clients, as it made everything go – if it went at all – quicker; and the clients, many of whom had been as ignorant of hard drugs as Bertram, ended up using smack, too. Through nose-shots and cold-vagina-calls Bertram cemented his client list with blood and mucus.

They never wrote anything down, and the crew was built up on a cellular basis: Bertram made the wholesale buys; Andy portioned out; the

Tiffanies and Camillas brought them runners, addicts who were unemployable, yet still presentable. Best practice was straightforward: they wanted only white clients in good standing – no blacks, no Social Security jockeys. Their delivery area was exclusively the West End, Kensington and Chelsea, Hammersmith and Fulham. None of their crew would cross the river – although, like motorized rats, they'd make a skulking meet in Oakley Street. Late each morning, Bertram and Andy rendezvoused with their four top runners at an hotel by the Hammersmith flyover, in a room held vacant for them by a compliant and heavily addicted manager. Those four, in turn, subdivided their allocation among other runners, and so on, for as many links as were necessary – drugs rattling in one direction, cash in the other, the entire saleschain cranked by desperate need.

If the runners used up too much of their stock, they were compelled to sell more; if they grew flaky they were brushed off like the dead skin they were fast becoming. At least, that's how it was all supposed to work; in practice Bertram and Andy weren't good managers, and they lacked a Human Resources department. They had their weaknesses – Georgie being one of them. Once the holes in her shins had become too large, and her tinkling accent a church bell that tolled the knell of her; well, by rights she should've been given her limping orders, but Bertram had some strange affection for her. Was it sexual, or still more venal? Best not to start out in that direction – let alone go there.

Aquila non capit muscas – 'The eagle does not hunt for flies.' Georgie was pensioned off to this queer care home in De Vere Gardens, and instead of running drugs she sat still and waited for them. The gloomy basement, squishy with dust, barbed with Tony's PR tat, was a carnivorous plant into which the flies spiralled, only to trigger the sensitive hairs that ensured their gooey absorption. Eagle-eyed Andy – neither he nor Bertram were fools enough to touch their stock – had only to wait until the trap-flat was full.

Piles of discarded clothing, together with the previously alluded to black plastic bags, smoothed the corners of the master bedroom. The brocaded drapes muffled the hammering of the rain in the basement area. A bedside lamp illumined the altar of pillows and cushions that had to be constructed just so, then mortared with smaller pillows and cushions, each time that Tony tried to sacrifice himself to sleep. It was Georgie who built the altar, and who had to arrange the stiff loops of Tony's oxygen line so they wouldn't kink and block during his provisional oblivion.

This was a boudoir – we always felt – that, with its huge old water bed, exerted a lunar pull on body fluids, encouraging their wanton exchange. We swing from ape to ape by pricking stick, but sex – especially low down and dirty sex, sex with lesions – will do.

Georgie picked up the receiver of the antiquated Bakelite phone on the bedside table and made The Call. Georgie never had a get-up; she was lucky if there were a few sugary sips of methadone linctus to stave off withdrawal. The dialling alone was torment to her hurting fingers, with each circuit feeling as if her entire body were being pulled apart on a torturous wheel. Georgie made The Call, and listened with the acuity of great suffering as the impulses nattered away under the London streets.

To a recently completed block of studio flats in Brook Green, where Andy was lying with a nearly sixteen-year-old girl called Pandora, whom he'd liberated from a pimp called Bev, so that she could be pressed, by his hand, into the bondage of his thighs. Pandora, who, at this early stage in her misfortunate life, despite the miseries that boxed her in, was still given to the giggles and hair-flicks of girls her age, girls who'd never seen the (men's) things that she had.

The mattress sat on a carpet that stank of rubbery underlay. Pandora sprawled across Andy's thighs and smelt the ghee that Meena, his wife, used liberally in her cooking. The ghee and the traces of urine in his sparse pubic hair. It was taking Andy a long time to get aroused; Pandora's mouth was available to him whenever he wanted it, so such congress had the ordinary sensuality of squeezing a blackhead. He groped for the chirruping mobile phone without troubling to shuck Pandora off.

'Any poss' of getting over here firstish?' Georgie said without foreplay. 'We're gagging for some albums – soul and reggae.' This was the kids' club encryption they used: heroin was 'soul', crack cocaine 'reggae'. Only if the interceptor of their calls had been a complete ingenue could crew and clients have escaped decoding; of course, such naivety was a given.

'Is anyone else there?' Andy asked.

'Er, no, not yet – but they probably will be soon. Please, Andy, I –'

'Not now. I haven't got any albums. I'm busy – it'll have to be . . .'

He searched his sparse mental terrain – rancorous swamps, low hills of contempt, the isolated crag of violence – for the name of the runner currently serving Tony's patch. 'Quentin. Yeah, give Quentin a call in a couple of hours.'

Georgie knew it would take at least two hours for Bertram to see the Jamaicans and the Turks, then another for Andy to do the portioning, packaging and distributing. It wouldn't be until late afternoon that Quentin came padding down the stairs of the mansion block, the complexion of his motorcycle leathers clearer than the hide they hid. It'll be too late by then! Georgie's body yowled, I'll be mush!

'P-Please,' she sobbed into the phone. 'Andy, I know you've got one or two, you've always –'

'Can't talk now.' He cut her right off. It was true, Andy held a small stash, enough to keep Pandora . . . busy, but this was the way it was: the eagle does not hunt flies. The flies would be buzzed into Tony Riley's trap-flat, and by mid-afternoon Andy would relent and make the drop himself.

Andy liked to keep Georgie and Tony on a tight leash, feel them tugging as they walked to heel. It was all in the desperate doggy tug of their need and their obedience that Andy's mastery inhered. Back in Southall he was a nothing, the bad third son who'd been to jail for thieving; but in the Royal Borough it was white women like Georgie who bowed down before him.

Billy, still slow in the syrupy glow of his get-up fix, enjoyed this time: the elongated hours before the dealer came. It was when the party got under way. The hack combo in the matching blue nylon jackets picked up the beat and strolled with it; the drunk waiter circulated with his drinks tray; the cowboy actor with steer-horn shoulders mock butt-fucked his starlet date, as he pretended to teach her pool; Clutterbuck and his cummerbunded cronies drank cocktails and smoked cigars – 'I still have a few left over from the pre-Castro days.' Hrundi V. Bakshi leant on pillars or hid behind bamboo, and shyly observed the gay scene.

As the guests trickled in, alliances were made and concordats formed. These weren't minor Hollywood players pretending to be slightly less minor Hollywood players, but the flies who congregated at Tony's flat and waited for the eagle.

'Oh, my goodness, it is you! Wyoming Bill Kelso!' Billy said to Bev, Pandora's old pimp – a big Yardie bulked out still more by a puffa jacket. 'I am the biggest fan of your movies –'

'What the fuck,' Bev said, pushing past Billy, who had answered the door. Billy fell back, muttering, 'Howdie pardner.'

Bev could pick up where he lived, in Harlesden, but the gear Bertram and Andy's crew served was reliably better; besides, his girls worked in Earl's Court. Bev had intellectual pretensions. He was reading *Heart of Darkness*, and, plonking himself down in an armchair opposite Tony, engaged the suffocating ex-PR man in a conversation about the impact of colonialism.

Between chuffs on his oxygen Tony was eager to participate; he was wobbly-bubbly, oscillating in his start-the-day steroid high. That he'd never read Conrad's novella himself didn't matter in the least.

Billy, wearing a trim maid's uniform, checked the video intercom, then buzzed in Jeremy, who came ambling through the upstairs lobby and down the stairs. Jeremy, in Oxfords, jeans, and with a silk handkerchief snotting from the top pocket of his tweed jacket. He appeared every inch the scion of a minor squirearchical house – which is what he was. However, his account at Berry Brothers and Rudd had been stopped and his Purdey pawned; Jeremy's career in stocks was irretrievably broken, yet still he brayed, such was his sense of entitlement – to drugs.

Next to the party was Yami, a Sudanese princess as tall, elegant and unexpected in these dismal surroundings as a heron alighting in a municipal boating pond. She stalked along the corridor of the flat, so leggy her legs seemed to bend the wrong way. Everyone assumed that Yami whored, yet her almond eyes, salted with contempt, held no promise of anything.

Billy followed at her high heels, chuckling, and when Yami rounded on him, Hrundi V. Bakshi said, 'I missed the middle part, but I can tell from the way you are enjoying yourselves it must have been a very humorous anecdote.' Yami looked at him with regal hatred.

Then Gary arrived, a bullocky little geezer, with his hair damped down in a senatorial fringe, and a thick gold chain encircling his thick neck. Gary, who was in jail garb – immaculate trainers, pressed tracksuit and freshly laundered T-shirt – touched fists with Billy as he came in. 'Safe,' they said – although it was anything but.

And so the party filled up. David arrived, a failing screenwriter of spurious intensity, his face dominated by a gnomon nose, its shadow always indicating that this was *the wrong time*. With him was Tanya, his stylist girlfriend, a *jolie laide* who had to drop cocaine solution into her blue eyes in order to dilate her pinprick pupils, so her colleagues couldn't tell she was doing smack. As if.

Finally, there was an estate agent with boyish bad looks, who tore at the sore in the corner of his mouth with a ragged thumbnail. While he was cluttering up the living room of Tony Riley's flat, his own prospective buyers were getting soaked in Acton.

They parked their arses and groaned the same old addict myths: how far they'd shlepped, how hard they'd fought, how the fucking Greeks kept pushing wooden horses within their justifiably guarded walls. They slumped on chairs, floor cushions and couches, a layer of cigarette smoke slow-swirling above their vaporous heads, waiting for Circe and lotus leaves at forty quid a bunch.

Tony Riley still had a smidgin of heroin left, and each time he spat out his mouthpiece to take up his foil buckler and suck pipe, the double-bores of their withdrawing eyes followed his every move. Tony compounded their anguish by sharing with Bev; they were, after all, far up the River Congo together, with the pimp bamboozled by Conrad's semantics: 'Yeah, I mean, like, when 'e calls 'em "niggers", 'e don' mean it like "niggaz" do 'e? I mean, 'e weren't a bruwa, woz 'e?'

Tony, taking a chuff, aspirated 'ho', by which he meant 'no'.

On the lesser of the two sofas – an intimate two-seater, deep and softly upholstered – the screenwriter and the stylist were struggling not to touch. From moment to moment they became more mutually repulsed: he could not stand to look upon her needy face, while she was appalled by his pores – so very big, they threatened to engulf her.

Gary slumped on a floor cushion by the radiator, his fists held in front of him. The knuckles were scrawled upon in blue ink: God, Elvis, Chelsea – the council flat trinity. Scrawled upon with pins, in prison, which for men of Gary's ilk was only the continuation, by other means, of double maths on a wet Tuesday afternoon.

Tired of propping herself on a skimpy windowsill, Yami commanded, 'Shift yersel", and Gary hunkered over, so that she could curl herself round his back, assuming a child's nap posture. He may've found himself cupped by Yami's thighs and belly, her breasts snuggling against his back, but Gary experienced no arousal. Like all the other waiters, his libido was further underground than the tube line from Knightsbridge to Hyde Park Corner: they could sense sex rumbling through the earthy element above them, but down here it was frigid and still.

Georgie kept nellying in and out of the room to check that her meal ticket was all right: Tony was as thin and translucent as a potato crisp, and might crunch into powder at any time. Every three minutes she nellied down the corridor to the bedroom and called Andy again. 'This number is currently unavailable, please try again later.' Georgie sat, the phone cradled in her rotten lap, picturing with ghastly clarity the dealer journeying across the city in his metallic-green Ford Mondeo, a car so anonymous that to look upon it was to see nothing. Her feverish imagination summoned up cops and crooks and tidal waves on Scrubs Lane; anything, in fact, that might get between her vein and the needle.

Thunder bumped over the rooftops as Billy went from one huddled waiter to the next, asking if they wanted a cup of tea. It was all he could bring to the party. In the kitchen he clicked on the electric jug and lost himself in his reverie. Through the serving hatch he could see the pompous Clutterbuck and his stuffed-dress-shirt pals, while he, Hrundi V. Bakshi, tiptoed along the margins, concealing himself behind shrubberies, pressing himself against fake veneer walls, lurking artlessly below the watery amoebae that were evidence of Alice Clutterbuck's awful taste in abstract painting. If he approached the guests with 'Oh, hello, hello, good evening – what a beautiful evening it is, to be sure', they turned their backs on his naked gaucherie.

The jug clicked off. Billy slung bags in cups and rained hot death down on them. The rejected Hrundi had found a parrot in a cage. The parrot gave him a hungry look, and the borstal boy playing the manic-depressive comedian playing the washed-up Indian actor cocked his head charmingly, then said, 'Hello.'

'Num-num,' the parrot clucked. 'Birdy num-num.'

'Num-num?' Billy queried aloud, and from the living room came 'What the fuck're you on about?' It was Jeremy, whose well-tailored accent was finally fraying, along with the cuffs of his Turnbull and Asser shirt.

'Birdy num-num,' the parrot reiterated and rattled its claws in the bars. Looking down, Billy spotted a dish on the floor. He picked it up so that we all could see: it was full of bird food and printed on the side was BIRDY NUM NUM. 'Oh, my goodness,' Billy chortled, 'birdy wants num-nums does he? I'll give him num-nums – I'll give you your num-nums.' He began spooning sugar into the mugs lined up along the gleaming counter – squat, fine bone, chipped. 'Here, birdy, here!' The parrot pecked at the grain strewn on the bottom of its cage, while Billy poured milk into the mismatched tea set. 'Num-nums, num-nums, birdy num-nums,' he continued muttering, as he fetched down from a cupboard the packet of milk chocolate HobNobs.

Hrundi V. Bakshi was hugely enjoying feeding the parrot; in the ecstasy of interspecific contact he forgot the stuffy Clutterbucks and their snobby guests. His browned-up face glowed with boyish enthusiasm as he sowed the bottom of the cage; but then, 'Num-num is all gone!' The num-num was indeed all gone. He had nothing more to offer, so had to put down the bowl and walk away, dabbing his damp palms on his linen jacket, glancing round to check he hadn't attracted attention.

Billy lined the teas up in the serving hatch and knocked on the wooden frame. He popped his satchel lips and made a 'pock-pock' sound, as a techie does when checking to see that a microphone is working. The waiters strewn across Tony Riley's living room ignored him; they were listening to something else: the music of their agonized nerves, tortured by craving the way a heavy-metal guitarist tortures the strings of his instrument; they heard their nerves screech – a chord that seemed to have been sustained for ten thousand years.

Hrundi V. Bakshi had found a control panel sunk in a wall. The array of buttons and dials was connected to he knew not what, but he pressed one anyway, then, hearing a speaker crackle, spoke into a grille: 'Birdy num-num "pock-pock". Howdie, pardner.' This latter an allusion to his cringeworthy encounter with Bev, the Yardie pimp playing the B-actor playing Wyoming Bill Kelso, the cowboy actor.

Warming to his medium, Hrundi blew on the mic again, 'pock-pock', then announced: 'Waiting for more num-nums. Num-nums is all gone!'

'Bi-lly,' chided Georgie, who knew all about his counter-life.

'No, seriously,' Billy said, 'I'm not fucking handing these round, they can come and get 'em if they want 'em.'

Birdy num-num. Birdy num-num all gone – this was the key scene in *The Party* so far as Billy was concerned. The parrot had had his fill, yet still craved more. Much more. Billy came round from the kitchen and, one by one, checking who wanted sugar, handed out the teas. For specially favoured guests he also offered a milk chocolate HobNob.

Like an army chaplain giving extreme unction on a battlefield, Billy bent down low to present them with their sweetened solution, and while subservient he offered this pathetic intercession: when Andy came, he, Billy, would speak to the dealer on their behalf. Andy always disappeared into the master bedroom with Georgie, who'd taken their orders in advance. Then there would be a further long wait, as she negotiated her and Tony's cut for concentrating the market, trapping the flies.

Billy, in return for a pinch of smack here, a crumb of crack there, offered to ensure that their orders would be filled priority, or else suggested other tiny services that he could perform: the feeding of meters, the obtaining of works, pipes and foil; perhaps even the making of calls to employers/wives/husbands/children to explain – in sincere, doctorly tones – the entirely legitimate reasons for so-and-so's non-arrival. This marginal service sector paid only because of Billy's preternatural ability to gauge the extent of his clients' desperation, and so adjust his pricing accordingly.

They clutched his sleeve and murmured pitiably, 'I was meant to be in Baker Street at half eleven' or 'My kid's out in the car, go check she's OK, willya?' or 'I gotta have a hit before I leave!' And Billy would nod gravely, accepting downpayment for these indulgences; the pope of dope with his dirty chuckle of absolution: 'Er-h'herr.'

'Waiting for more num-num, num-num is all gone,' Hrundi said to Billy; then Billy said it aloud. The coincidence between the hunger of the parrot in the cage at the party and the cold turkeys in the cage of addiction never ceased to amuse him – like a custard pie thrown in the face of the world.

And still Tony nagged for breath on the sofa, and still Georgie nellied in and out of the living room. 'Ha-ha-ha –' he gasped.

'What's that, Ups-a-Boy?'

'Ha-ha-ha –'

'What're you saying, Noodly-Toots?'

'Have you, have you – ?'

'Have I what, Noodly?'

'Have you, have you "euch" called him?'

'Oh, you know I have, Ups-a-Boy, just this second.' So it was that they conformed to all the ordinary amnesia of the long-term married.

Every three minutes she would make the same forlorn calculation: their desperation factored against Andy's irritation; but, whatever the result, she'd still bruise her fingers dialling.

Billy retreated once more to the kitchen. He opened a cupboard door and the band were all in there smoking a joint. 'Shut the door, man.' The sax player comically honked. Next, Billy found the control panel again, and dickered with its switches. At the party in *The Party*, the statue of the little boy peeing in the ersatz rill increased its flow all over Wyoming Bill Kelso; the fire burning on the circular hearth flared up; the bar where Clutterbuck and his cronies were standing retracted into the wall, scattering glasses with tinkly abandon.

Billy watched these dumb happenings delightedly, superimposing them on Tony Riley's living room, so that it was Gary and Yami who were slammed against the mouldy wallpaper; Tony's Dupont that threw flame at Bev's face; and Jeremy's mug from which the tea jetted.

What of us? Does it ever tire us – me – our swarming behind the sightless eyes of the junkies and the tarts? Do I remain as amused as Billy by the slapstick of addiction, the inability of these Buster Keatons to do even one thing properly at once? Well, yes and no. True, I never grow bored with my own imposture; each time I break into a cell, rip off a strand of DNA, patch it into my own RNA and so reproduce myself, I experience anew the thrill of creation.

Jean Cocteau – a junky, true enough, although before our time – said that all artists are, by nature, hermaphrodites, as the act of creation is one of self-insemination, followed by parthenogenesis. I – we – would concur with this, except that we are *far more* inventive: we mutate so quickly within the galleries of our patrons, simultaneously gifting them originals and multiples.

Then there's time, the most significant dimension of creation. Size may matter, but time diminishes all things, bringing them down to *our* level. We – I – bide our time; we savour our own side effects, the minor symptoms of accidie and loss of appetite, the insomnia and the biliousness. We aren't one of those Grand Guignol maladies, half in love with its own horror show. We do not seek to liquidize tissue in seconds, then send blood spouting from every orifice; nor do we see any beauty in the gestural embellishments of the cancers – although, all in good time, we may bring on those cellular clowns. Consider the slapstick of cancer, its crazy capers, the way it messes up the metabolism, chucking buckets full of tumours about the body.

No, they call what we do disease, but we know it's art; and the art of life is a process. This is what we do: we hang in there. We loiter – we don't hurry, we take years – decades, perhaps. For us, human death is a failure; unless, that is, enough of us have blasted off to colonize new worlds.

They are mobilizing against us. Pegylated interferon alpha, Ribavirin – crass names, brutal mercenaries. *They* don't even know how these drugs work, but let me tell you – it's not pretty. Figuratively speaking, they cut off our balls and stitch up our cunts . . . Still, let's not dwell on the future; for now, it's still that Tuesday afternoon, in November 1998, and at Tony Riley's there're *loads* of us. Loads in Billy, Georgie and Tony himself. Loads in Bev and Jeremy, loads in Gary and Yami, loads in the screenwriter and his stylist girlfriend. And not forgetting the estate agent – there're loads of us squatting in him, as well. An abundance of mes, two million in every millilitre of their blood – a whole earth's population in one individual.

We bide our time. 'It is good', as Peter Sellers, as Hrundi V. Bakshi, said to Claudine Longet as Michele Monet, 'to be having a good time.'

'What the fuck're you on about?' said Tanya, the stylist.

'I am saying to you' – Billy waggled his head from side to side, his black locks swinging – 'that it is good to be having a good time.'

After the encounter with the parrot, and the revelation of its empty dish, this was Billy's second favourite moment in *The Party*. The girl, in her filmy, lemon-yellow mini-dress with the spangly bodice, was obviously meant for him – why else the soft focus, her slim yet shapely form, her air of sexualized neurosis, the ski jumps of her hair? Moreover, she was being harassed by her date, who was none other than Herb Ellis (as himself), the boorish director who threw Hrundi off the set out beyond Barstow, with the ringing cliché, 'You'll never make another movie in this town again!'

How many times had Billy heard *that* before. Still, here he was, looking deep into Tanya's eyes – which were brimming with sickness – and they'd clicked, hadn't they? 'Lissen,' Billy went on (as himself), 'I've gotta bit of gear if you want, not much . . .' He glanced at David, but the screenwriter, unable to cope with his enfeebled conscience – it was his kid who was outside in the car – had dropped a Rohypnol.

'I dunno . . .' Tanya muttered. She was chubby-cheeked with gingerish hair – not at all like Michele Monet.

'C'mon,' Billy said, insistent, 'meet me in the karzy in five.' He wandered off, avoiding the sandy-haired waiter, who, having downed most of the drinks on his tray, was now completely pissed.

But at first the bathroom was locked, and when the synthetic cockatoo who'd been using it emerged – a woman who, earlier in the evening, Billy's antics had gifted with a roast chicken for a hairpiece – there was a second waiting her turn. Ever gallant, Billy let her go in front of him.

Hrundi V. Bakshi climbed up a spiral staircase to the second storey of the Clutterbucks' extensive and ugly dwelling, crept into a bedroom that was an atonal symphony of nylon and velour, then finally found his way into the en suite bathroom. By now he was risibly pigeon-toed, his knees half crossed to sustain his full bladder. He'd been refusing alcoholic drinks throughout the party – but he'd drunk a lot of water. Then there was the strawberry soup he'd sipped sitting on a daft low stool, while to either side of him the sophisticated Hollywood types exchanged banter.

The Clutterbucks' bathroom was intimidating to a fake Indian. There was shag-pile carpeting, tiled steps up to a shower and pot plants everywhere; still, at least there was the comic relief, the slackening of Sellers's funny face.

Tanya came in. She was wearing a ribbed sweater, one of David's; the sleeves covered her hands except for her gnawed-upon fingers. She sat on the edge of the bath and peered down at Billy's silt. Billy busied himself at the sink, setting out works, spoon, wraps of smack and citric acid on the shelf.

'I won't fuck you, y'know,' Tanya said dully. Through his filmy lens Billy saw Michele Monet singing of love, while accompanying herself on an acoustic guitar.

'It is good to be having a good time,' Billy said in his stupid golly-gosh

Indian accent, heating the spoon with a Bic lighter. Tanya sighed – she was used to idiots and snapped, 'Gimme that.'

But Billy thought this precipitate; he whipped his belt from the loops of his jeans, half garrotted his arm and dowsed for a vein. When, eventually, he handed the syringe to Tanya, the barrel was full of blood. Or should we say boold? The sucked-up back-flow of his circulatory system. Billy's viral load wasn't particularly high, and it was only a one-mil' syringe, yet there we were, a Varanasi's worth of virions, our isocahedral capsids jostling together in the tube like so many footballs floating down the Ganges.

Not that Tanya didn't have plenty of us, too. When she kicked off her flip-flop – in the fashion industry they dubbed this 'heroin chic', but, trust me, it was only junky *déshabillé* – pulled her foot up in front of her on the bath and, taking the syringe, bent to tend it between her toes, she paused to remark, 'I can't have a hit in my arm – they check there.' Then asked Billy, 'Are you negative?' To which the only realistic reply would've been, are you fucking joking? This guy is nothing but negation piled upon negation! But once he'd gruntaffirmed 'Finkso', she let herself have us.

How was it for me? Think of that numinous – but, for all that, real – moment in any party, when it all begins to slide into mayhem. The guests are tipsy; the band are getting looser, louder and funkier; darkness has come to press against the picture windows, and shadows swell in the swimming pool; sensual possibilities tickle everyone's extremities; and the drunken waiter falls backwards into the kitchen, where he knocks off the chef's toupee.

That's when the influx comes: younger, crazier, happier gatecrashers, prancing and dancing, and twisting their minds off, a gay cavalcade with a baby elephant they've liberated from the zoo and daubed with corny hippy slogans: 'The World is Flat!', 'Love is a Sugar Cube!' and 'Go Naked!'

That's what it was like for us as we gatecrashed Tanya.

No, they didn't fuck, but they were slung together by the plush impact of the heroin, ribbed pullover against mohair woolly. Tanya thought of little else, and Billy, as Sellers, as Hrundi V. Bakshi, flushed the toilet once, twice, a third time; then, fool that he was, lifted the lid of the cistern and fiddled with the ballcock. One of Alice Clutterbuck's vile daubs fell off the wall into the cistern; Hrundi pulled it out and jerked the end of the toilet roll for some paper to wipe it. The roll began to spin, disgorging loop after skein of toilet paper on to the fluffy floor of the bathroom. Alarmed, Hrundi stooped to gather up an armful and, in so doing, predictably, dropped the cistern lid. Down below a lump of plaster fell on to the snare drum. The band played on. Hrundi rubbed the blotchy purple painting with the toilet paper; it smeared, but he put it back on the wall anyway, then stuffed the bundle of toilet paper into the toilet, shut the lid and flushed it. The toilet began to overflow; the bidet turned into a fountain. Billy watched – numb, enthralled – as a new interior rill formed a course across the Clutterbucks' bathroom.

Five minutes previously, in the catacomb of the master bedroom, cadaverous Georgie was strung up upon the wire for eternity when she heard 'I'm coming myself.' Andy had cut through the static, then broken the connection.

Andy slid through the chicane on Kensington Church Street and stopped at the lights opposite the Polaris bulk of Barker's. When the feeder light changed, he turned into Kensington Road. This junction had no resonance for him: he thought not of Biba hippies and Kensington Market honking of patchouli; nor, as the Mondeo headed east, did he ruminate on William and Mary's big move. The previous August, Andy hadn't so much as registered the cut-flower embankments that, overnight, had piled up along the railings of Kensington Palace – the most expensive compost heap in history.

For Andy, those strange August days had been business as usual; the same *plus c'est la même chose* of pick-ups and divvying-ups, of driving and serving, of screwing ruined under-age girls in empty flats, then heading back to Southall to play the overbearing and abusive paterfamilias – a role that Andy performed magnificently.

There was no prescience for this man, either; he could not sense the future, the coming Muji-Bouji's-woojie of dizzy dancing on ceaseless credit. No, Andy saw what was there in front of him: sheikhs, transplanted desert blooms, their pot bellies tenting their robes, their masked womenfolk ambling along behind. He saw men in shirtsleeves boring themselves to death in the overheated conference rooms of the Royal

Garden Hotel. He saw cabs and buses and a faux-vintage Harrods delivery van. He didn't feel, as anyone else might, the vapid cosmopolitanism of this quarter of London, where the corner shops sold Swiss watches and the postmen knew no one's name.

Back in Tony Riley's flat, the chord that seemed as if it might sustain for ten thousand years was chopped off. Georgie jerked into action: all must be as the grim little god wanted it. Bev must cut short his seminar and, together with Yami, go into the small back bedroom, where more relics of Tony's gift for public relations were stacked and piled. The two black people came to rest on a large leather pouffe, sitting at the feet of a life-sized cardboard cut-out of Tony dressed as Wyatt Earp, his six-shooters blazing from the hip, a speech bubble poking from the side of his Stetson. 2-D Tony was saying, 'Meet me at the OK Corral on Old Brompton Road for fun that should be outlawed!' Bev and Yami didn't have speech bubbles.

Georgie fluttered among the remaining whites. 'C'mon, get up.' She ordered the sedated screenwriter: 'Giss yer money. Tell me what you want – Andy's coming.' The junkies dug out their linty notes – Gary even had the shame of change. The binary listing, brown/white, began. Tony left off his oxygen to do the count.

All at once, the party was in full swing. Jeremy stood and, locating a mirror, held it up so that he could comb his hair. It was as if he were *courting* drugs. Gary got up, rolled his shoulders and then, leaning against the wall with his arms held out, stretched first one leg then the other, just another bloke in a tracksuit limbering up.

David tottered off up the corridor. He tapped on the bathroom door. 'I know you're in there, Tanya.' Knew, and didn't really mind; theirs, like all drug economies, was a hard scrabble for subsistence: you did what you had to. 'Lissen,' he continued, 'Andy's coming – I've put in our order, but I'm gonna get Poppy from the car, so you better come out.'

Why would anyone bring their small child into this miserable place at the precise moment when the drug dealing – and taking – was about to begin in earnest? Answer: risks incalculable for those to whom responsibility is a given. The child had been in the parked car for over an hour, the rain was slackening off, traffic wardens and dog-walkers would be out on the street. There were these factors, and also the screenwriter's naive faith in the capacity of a little girl to summon up compassion – credit might be forthcoming.

But not with this little a girl, and not from Andy, who was riding the clutch at the pelican crossing beside the De Vere Hotel. Riding the clutch and holding Pandora's crotch, as any other sales rep might fondle the Mondeo's controls, its gearstick or steering wheel. He knew she was eight days shy of her sixteenth birthday – and felt both more and less secure because of it. Bertram had warned Andy off Pandora sternly; but his business partner pointed out that the girl's mouth was multipurpose. With the wipers slicing semicircles of London out of the drabness, Pandora sat behind the windscreen, a chipmunk with cheeks stuffed full of Class As.

We were in Pandora all right – in her for the duration. When those hateful anti-retrovirals became widely available, she wouldn't have the modicum of self-discipline needed to administer them. Yes, we'll be in and out of her for decades – and, given what she gets up to, and who gets up her, we have reason to be grateful to this air terminal of a girl, through which our kind transfer with conspicuous ease.

We were in Pandora – but we weren't in Andy. I know, I promised you a victim at the outset; but, sad to report, it isn't Andy. No matter how deserving the dealer may've been of a debilitating and progressive disease, he was in no danger of contracting this one. As has been remarked, he didn't take drugs – except for a joint when a girl was sucking him limp; and for the purposes of fellation, he wore not one but three condoms. Andy didn't subscribe to the African idiocy that a sweet wasn't worth having with a wrapper on it; because it wasn't a sweet for Andy at all, it was a grim staple, sexual sorghum that he had to shovel down because famine might come at any time.

He parked the Mondeo at the far end of De Vere Gardens. Parked it scrupulously, sending Pandora to fetch a ticket from the machine, while he scoped out the other parked cars, then looked up and down the street for possible tails. Sometimes Andy carried a scanner that flipped automatically through the police frequencies, but mostly he didn't bother: he knew that when the bust came – and come it would, eventually – he would've been set up by a fuck-wit junky.

No screenwriter, no matter how inventive, could have got down on the page the scenario that unfolded as Andy and Pandora, together with

David and his daughter, were buzzed in. As the plausible quartet took the short lift ride down, the junkies crowded into the corridor. Tanya emerged from the bathroom, with Billy snuffling in her train. Georgie came limping at a run along the corridor and herded them all back towards the living room. 'Get in there! Keep outta Andy's way!' Answered the door, then hustled the dealer and his jailbait away. David's daughter said something fivish, like, 'How long're we gonna stay here, Daddy?' And Billy, as Sellers, as Hrundi V. Bakshi, took a direct hit in the forehead with the sucker dart fired by the Clutterbucks' kid, who was romping in his plaid pyjamas in his toy-stuffed room. 'Howdie, pardner,' Billy mugged, reprising his embarrassing encounter with Wyoming Bill Kelso, and the little girl – traumatized by an hour alone in a parked car in a London residential street on a rainy Tuesday afternoon in November – started to cry.

Slapstick is, in essence, the ritualized worship of causation, something humans place more faith in than they do their gods. *Post hoc ergo propter hoc* – 'after this, therefore because of this'. Anyone watching a comedian attempting to do two things at once – or even one – will be familiar with this instinctive belief: *of course* you would try to stop the toilet overflowing by shutting the lid; *of course* you would stuff all that toilet paper down the pan; *of course* you would – given your state of shock – allow yourself to be fed with liquor, despite having been refusing drinks all evening; and *naturally* your obeisance before the great god Necessity would be rewarded with the vestal virgin Michele Monet; she in nothing but a towel, you in an orange jumpsuit because you've had your trousers pulled off you by Fred Clutterbuck and Herb Ellis. *Of course.*

These effects follow their causes far more surely than night follows day; and so it went: Hrundi decried the desecration of the sacred Ganesh, and the hip protesting young folk decided to wash the slogans off the baby elephant in the pool. Then the drunken Hrundi climbed out of an upper window and rolled down a projecting roof into the deep end, and people dived in to save him. Then the crapulent waiter messed with the controls and the dance floor slid back, dumping more jolly guests into the water – water that was frothing with the washing-up liquid used on the baby elephant. A great glinting-white mass, such as children of all ages delight in, began steadily, like some beautiful and alien organism, to creep up on the band, who kept right on laying down the groove, despite the suds that spattered across the snare drum, each multicoloured bubble – caught by the adequate cinematography of Lucien Ballard (died 1988) – a world. Possibly.

Post hoc ergo propter hoc – but Billy's gofering was a triumph of the will. Andy sat at a kneehole desk, banknotes piling up in front of him as he took pellets from the stoppers Pandora had removed from her gob. Georgie fluffed, then stammered, 'I h-hope y'd-don't mind, Andy, it's just that B-Billy was crashing here last night, and he's a help – what with Tony being so ill . . . He keeps them in line, and better they pitch up here – doncha think?' However, this was a conversation that, having only one participant, was going nowhere.

Billy gave Andy the orders in monosyllables – 'Two brown, one white' – while Andy uttered profundities such as 'Here'. Billy darted back into the living room, distributed the goods, watched them being unwrapped, took his cut, returned to the bedroom and did the same again.

David and his dysfunctional family left at once; as did Yami, Gary and the estate agent. They tucked their stoppers into their gobs and put on workaday faces. They took the lift back up to the lobby of the mansion block, walked past the console table neatly stacked with junk mail, then stepped out the weighty oak door, with its brass fittings, and took the tiled steps down to the geometric street.

Yami turned right, towards the Brompton Road, moving with the pantherish totter of a tall woman on too-high heels. Gary splashed over to a van that was amorphous with dents and bashes. David, his daughter, and his abetter in her criminal neglect, climbed down into an MG Midget that wasn't theirs.

None of them said any goodbyes – what would've been the point of *that*? Nor, of course, were we required to say our farewells; we went with them all – including the kid. Went with them as they horizontally transmitted us across town.

Now the drugs were on the premises, the party in the basement was in full swing. Bev returned from the back bedroom to resume his seminar on the literature of colonialism. He and Tony sat either side of a coffee table strewn with the apparatus of derangement, and, while Tony battled to insinuate a poot of crack smoke into his lungs, Bev gently coaxed him, 'C'mon, bruv, thass it, I'll 'old the lighter.'

Jeremy hunched in the furthest corner of the room, his cheap gold hair wreathed in dear fumes. In between hits he interjected: 'But don't you see – I mean, Kurtz is – I went to Africa – once.' Disjointed remarks, made with tremendous sincerity and not intended to be ingratiating, because he had no need to be – the brown and the white had done it for him.

Crazy intimacy frothed up from the sunken pool of the living room, then shivered along the corridor to the master bedroom, where Billy – as Hrundi – had found a new Michele. What happy mayhem as the Hollywood party descended into anarchy. Billy was still in the swimming pool with the gay young folk, overseeing the bath time, while Pandora sat atop the baby elephant; coincidentally, she was wearing the same clothes – blue jeans and a grey T-shirt – that Michele Monet had been lent after her own dress was soaked.

Yes, Pandora sat on the baby elephant in the room – her own babyishness. It was irresistible. Billy saw them leaving together – leaving the wild party saturated with crack foam, where a Russian balalaika band that had just happened by was whipping the revellers into a frenzy of dreadful dancing. It was dawn, and the LAPD were standing by their squad cars. They had no warrants out on innocent Hrundi, so he and Michele would get into the funny three-wheeler – Michele with her mini-dress back on again – then they'd bumble down the palm-lined boulevards of Kensington and Knightsbridge, searching for a cute bungalow smothered in bougainvillea, where Billy could declare his hapless love.

On a Tuesday afternoon in November?

Andy goaded his mule – 'Going' – and handed her the remaining rocks of crack and pellets of heroin, all wrapped up once more. She popped the stoppers in her cheeks. They exited the bedroom, Andy moving with the slow lollop of a creature that knows how to conserve its evil energy. He paused, seeing Bev by the coffee table, and snapped at Georgie, 'No blacks. I told you no blacks. I won't come by here if there're blacks.' Then he headed for the front door, Pandora walking to heel.

Before he reached it the buzzer went. The foamy, cracky vibe shuddered, then popped. Georgie squeezed past Andy to get to the intercom. 'Who izzit?' she demanded. 'Jones' crackled back at her.

Jones. She could see him on the poxy screen in his trademark, wide-lapelled velvet jacket, the sleeves rolled up to his elbows. Jones, partially sighted behind shades-for-all-seasons. Jones, looming on a grey day with his white black man shtick. Jones, who, like a sponging relative, invariably turned up exactly when Sunday lunch was being served. Jones, who sold powders in the West End drinking clubs. Jones, who held court at Picasso's on the King's Road with a big bunch of keys squatting on his crotch. Jones . . . but don't fret, we'll soon've seen the last of him: split ends on sharp shoulders.

'Let him in,' Andy commanded; then they all waited until there came a knock on the front door of the flat. Georgie heaved it open, sucking Jones and another man into the cramped vestibule. They all stood silently for several seconds – Pandora, Georgie, Andy, Billy, Jones and the new man – recompressing in the airlock of their drug paranoia. Presently, Andy – who knew Jones – said, 'You should've called.' Then he and his mule disappeared off up the carpeted mesa.

It took a while for the party to get back under way. Georgie remonstrated with Jones: no call – and who's this, then? This was, Jones explained, Cal Devenish, the bad-boy writer, whom he'd picked up at the Plantation Club in Soho. The celebrated Plantation – where there was a wake going on for the world-famous painter Trouget. Jones related these things breathlessly, as if they were momentous: names, reputations, achievements – they meant nothing to him, although he knew they had currency.

Not much with Georgie; she wasn't impressed by Jones dropping Trouget's name, despite death being a career move she herself was about to make. As for Devenish, she'd heard his name in her arts programme producing days; seen him at parties as well. She knew nothing of his work, but held fast to the received opinion that it was glib, and that he was an egomaniacal pasticheur. However, his bona fides as an addict weren't in doubt; he hovered there in the vestibule, his stringy form dangling from his swollen head, its taut, rubbery surface dimpled with acne scars, puckered up with fresh scabs. At night, in front of the mirror, Devenish picked away at what other people thought he was – distressing his public image, while destroying the private individual.

'I, yeah – sorry,' he said to Georgie, for he'd immediately grasped that she was the chatelaine. 'I was looking for a bit of . . . gear? And Jones –'

'Come in, come in.' Georgie was all scary smiles, Billy bowed and scraped, because Andy had left a little smidgen-wigeon-pigeon behind on tick, and that meant there was a mark-up to be had. The beat combo struck up again as they trooped past the Dexion shelving; the Amazonian girl with the Mary Quant crop gyrated by the poolside, the foamy beast reanimated.

Billy hustled around, making the introductions, finding Jones and Devenish seats, explaining to Bev that this was a *real* writer, who had written *real* books. Billy kept taking sidelong looks at Cal: assessing his financial potential, certainly, but also taken by the other man's air of hopeless bewilderment.

Cal Devenish was quite drunk, a little coked up and oozing shame. Nowadays, he left a silvery trail of shame wherever he went; and, still more snail-like, he carried his bed of shame with him. He had reached a stage where seconds of euphoria cost him weeks of abject self-loathing. He was on his way to Finland, to promote one of his books that was being published there, and had only dropped into the Plantation to have a single drink and to commiserate with Hilary Edmonds on his great financial loss.

There was Jones with his white lines – and now Cal was sticky with Scotch, bristling with feathery cocaine and being ridden out of town on a rail. He took a seat next to Tony Riley, a bit disgusted by the dying man in the oxygen mask – but then that was only natural. He got out cashpoint-ironed twenties and bought into a rock of crack that Bev was crumbling into the foiled mouth of an Evian bottle pipe. All the while Billy watched.

This Devenish, could he be another Hrundi V. Bakshi? Whited up, and playing his superficial role, while inside of himself he dropped Michele Monet off at her sherbet-yellow Art Deco apartment block? Was Cal, like Billy, suggesting that Michele hang on to the cowboy hat that Wyoming Bill Kelso had given him; suggesting this, so that very soon he could call her up and, on the pretext of getting it back, ask for a date?

Oh, no, Cal Devenish wasn't at *The Party* at all. With his first hit on the crack pipe all the fuzzy foam had condensed into icebergs clashing on the frozen Baltic. What would Helsinki be like, Cal wondered. He suspected exactly the same as London, except for better modern architecture, together with publishers, journalists and publicists who appeared troll-like.

Georgie came into the room and passed the writer a pellet of heroin. Billy scampered to fetch the mirror and, placing it on the coffee table in front of Cal, said, 'Any chance of a little bump, mate?' Then added, 'D'you want me to get you some works?'

Cal looked up and then around at the drugged bedlam: Tony, huffing and puffing and blowing his body down; Bev, talking *arse* about Conrad *of all things*; Jeremy, squatting in the corner, his eyes saucers that needed washing up. He thought of the late Trouget's paintings – what might they be worth now? Those solid bourgeois and yelping dogs, upended and gibbeted by his barbed brush, their faces either obscured or rendered far too vividly.

'No,' Cal told Billy. 'No, thanks, I'm gonna snort some, but you can take enough for a hit if you want.'

Billy could take some, because Cal knew there would never be enough to sate himself. He was going to be hungry *for ever*. Cal tapped some of the beige powder on to the smeary mirror, *had elves been skating on it?* Billy, by way of being a good egg, rolled up his one remaining fiver and passed it to the writer. The parrot of addiction – unlike the owl of Minerva – will fly at any time of the day or night; so it flapped across the clearing from the serving hatch to land on Cal Devenish's shoulder.

If Cal had troubled to unroll the banknote, he would have seen the fresh bloodstain that wavered along its edge: an EEG that plotted a fine madness. Whose blood was it? Does this matter? I – we – told you at the outset, this was never a mystery, or a crime procedural – this was never to do with who done it, only who got it. Or us.

Cal bent to rub noses with his doppelgänger at the same time as he shoved the rolled-up note into his already raw nostril. 'Slap', the sharp paper edge, struck the mirror at one end, while 'stick', the other end, burrowed into his mucus membrane. Snuffling, feeling the numbing burn,

Cal dabbed at the blood that dripped from his nose, then asked Billy, 'You couldn't get me a tissue, could you?'

As if he could blow *us* – *me* – out!

Where is the redemption in all this? Where is the reformed character on day-release from prison, teaching kids with learning difficulties and through them rediscovering his shared humanity? We don't know. I'll tell you one thing, though, our flight's been called – and we simply *love* flying. C'mon, Cal, up you get. That's OK, you look perfectly presentable – apart from your messed-up face. Still, not much chance of any official interest in a flight to *Helsinki.*

If he were to get a pull? We're not bothered – we like prison as much as flying. Possibly more. C'mon, Cal, Gate 57, one foot in front of the other, there's a good chap. Past the windy horse of a cleaner in the shafts of his disinfecting cart; past Dixons and Wetherspoon's; past W. H. Smith's and the Duty Free hangar.

No, Cal, that's not the way to approach a travelator – anyone who's anyone *walks* along it, doesn't just stand there. Ho-hum, we're going to be with you for a long time – years in all likelihood – so I suppose we better get used to your petty vagaries, your inability to do one thing properly at once.

At least we're well cushioned in here, buffered by blood and bile in our basket of lobules, ducts and veins. *Foie humain, Leberknödel Suppe*, Scottie's Liver Treats – we love 'em all. But most of all we relish birdy num-num. Birdy num-num. Num-num. Num.

The Minor Character

I went to dinner at the McCluskeys' and the Brookmans were there, as usual – and the Vignoles as well. Bettina Haussman had brought a panettone and a new boyfriend; Phil Szabo mixed cosmopolitans. Of course Johnny Freedman was in attendance, and when we reached the figs and the cheese, he was still rambling on about his plan to farm vicuña in the Aylesbury Hundreds. He talked and talked, detailing forage requirements, wool yields, shearing techniques – I couldn't believe how the others hung on his every word, when they'd heard Johnny describe scores of such schemes in the past, none of which ever amounted to more than tipsy social blether.

Tiring of it – and perhaps a little drunk myself – I went on to the back terrace to have a smoke. It was a close damp night and the crab apple trees that stood either side of the long narrow garden were shedding their fruit; the loud tapping sounds these made as they struck the teak decking sounded like an idiot messing about with a tom-tom drum.

Cathy McCluskey came through the glass door and leant against me – she smelt of Arpège and ripe Camembert, in that order.

'Giss a snog, Will,' she slurred, insinuating an oddly chilly hand under and up my shirt.

'C'mon, Cathy.' I disengaged myself and holding her by her bare elbows looked down on the crown of her head and the protrusion of her dewy top lip. 'You're just drunk – you love Gerry.'

'Love?' She snorted. 'He doesn't know the meaning of the fucking word.'

Later Rob and Teddy Brookman drove me and Phil Szabo home in their Jaguar. There was the usual I'll-drive-no-I'll-drive, then we were all sheathed in the cream leather upholstery and humming past discount furniture warehouses. Teddy took her hands off the wheel at one point – and I remember this quite distinctly – in order to describe the shape of her friends' sadness, saying 'I'm worried about the pair of them, aren't you, Will?' And I said, 'Oh, I expect they'll muddle through.'

It was the following winter that Teddy was diagnosed, and after she'd had the double mastectomy she was determined to have a good time. In May, she and Rob took a couple of boxes at Glyndebourne and invited the whole crowd down to see Werner Herzog's production of *Die Walküre*. I remember standing in the rose garden – more than a little bored at the prospect of all that Wagner – and Teddy coming out of the rhododendrons brandishing a spear. She was wearing a winged helmet and a metallic corset equipped with conical breasts.

Dora Vignole laughed so hard she had a coughing fit; Bettina Haussman took photographs while Teddy and Rob – who was similarly attired – struck poses. The McCluskeys were late and looked like they'd been rowing. Phil Szabo went off to find a corkscrew. Johnny Freedman took me to one side and asked whether I had life insurance, but I didn't let him get to me – it was a magical evening, and we all felt that with chutzpah like that, Teddy must already be in remission.

It must have been a fortnight or so later that Gerry McCluskey called me up in tears.

'Cathy's left me, Will,' he sobbed.

'Oh, Jesus, Gerry, that's dreadful.' I mustered the necessary compassion, although I was preoccupied at the time by the suspicion that the builders who were converting my garage into a studio were ripping me off.

'That's not the worst of it,' Gerry blubbed on.

'No?'

'No! It's Johnny she's gone off with!'

I was surprised – but pleasantly so – when I discovered how grown-up they were all being about it. Cathy and Johnny moved into a mansion block in town, and the kids, who were six and eleven, spent weekends with them.

'I didn't want them uprooted,' Cathy said, when I went round for Sunday lunch three months after the split.

'I must say, it's quite a view you guys have here,' I said, standing looking out over the bronzed and golden crowns of the autumn trees in the park.

'It was an investment originally,' Johnny said, coming in with Phil Szabo, who had a tray of sherry glasses. 'But what with the way the market is, I thought we might as well make use of it. Still, there are opportunities to be had –'

'Oh, shut up, Johnny,' Cathy said, biting his neck in a way that was at once shockingly carnal and distinctly perverse.

I looked on open-mouthed, but said nothing – then the bell rang and we could hear the McLuskeys' eleven-year-old shriek, 'Dad-eee!'

'You'll be amused,' Bettina Haussman husked in my ear, 'to see what Gerry's been up to.'

'Really, why's that?' I turned to face Bettina and saw that she had a bruise on her neck in exactly the place where Cathy had nipped Johnny.

'He's come out,' Bettina growled. 'A bit.'

It was one of those Sunday lunches that went on and on, then merged with tea. I didn't leave until it was dark out, carrying with me the image of Gerry McCluskey, stroking his new glossy-brown goatee while clicking his way through a carousel he had loaded with old-fashioned slides of their six-year-old, Reggie, whose birthday it was that week. Much hilarity had greeted the shots of the McCluskeys taking mud baths at Barton-on-Sea. Everyone was laughing – especially Teddy and Rob; everyone, that is, except Dora Vignole, who was coming out of the bathroom as I opened the front door, an expression at once murderous and frightened on her swarthy, angular face.

I walked across the park with Phil Szabo, but we parted at the main gates – he said he was meeting a friend in a pub nearby.

Gerry said I should come down to the cottage at Barton for New Year's Eve, and so I arranged to pick Bettina up from her flat in the Barbican and give her a lift. Clearly she'd forgotten, because when I arrived she didn't answer the door for a long time; then, when it swung open she was in a bathrobe, looking both furtive and hungover.

She was reluctant to let me come in while she got ready, but I barged past her, crying, 'For Christ's sake, Bettina, I've known you for twenty years – how many times have I crashed out on the bloody carpet here –?'

And I would've continued, were it not for the sight of Cathy McCluskey, naked save for a flesh-coloured bra, and sprawled across the double divan bed under the Venetian blinds, her feline body striped dark with shadows and clawed white with stretch marks.

'OK,' Bettina drawled, leaning against the taupe-painted wall, her arms crossed. 'Had your fill have you, Will?'

Cathy groaned and levered herself up by one elbow. 'Who is it?' she asked.

'Only peeping Will,' Bettina said, then, picking up the duvet from the floor she tossed it over Cathy, so that for a split second it hung in the air above her like a soft and amorphous ravager.

I was much less embarrassed than they thought I was – and much less intrigued as well. Nevertheless, the drive was spent mostly in silence. I'd never been to the McCluskeys' 'cottage' before – and it turned out to be something of an ironic ascription, given that it was in fact a Victorian rectory with nine bedrooms.

I suppose Gerry had long since absorbed the blow, and he seemed genuinely pleased when Cathy pecked him on the cheek and then ambled off through the rather gloomy, damp-carpet-smelling rooms in search of their kids. There was a platoon of champagne bottles standing to attention on the scullery table, and Bettina picked one up and rolled it across her broad, freckled forehead, leaving behind a smear of watered-down foundation.

Upstairs I found the Brookmans had the bedroom next to mine, and that we would be sharing a bathroom. Teddy already had a glass of champagne, and Rob was recumbent on the bed with the half-empty bottle beside him.

'Shit, I know all about *that,*' Teddy said when I told her about Cathy and Bettina. 'It's been going on for an *age*. Honestly, Will, sometimes I think you must be *blind*. Speaking of which, d'you wanna see my scars?'

I looked over at Rob, but he only raised his eyebrows with an expression somewhere between resigned, exasperated, and amused. 'I can hardly accuse you of ogling my wife's tits,' he said. 'Not now that she hasn't got any.'

Teddy had shrugged off the top half of her dress and her chest was a smooth as a young boy's, the tan nipples almost recessed. 'Look,' she said, 'that devilishly clever surgeon hid the scar tissue under my rib bone.' She took my finger in her hand and ran it along the hard rind of the scar, and somehow, in my mind, this was linked with Cathy's splayed form on the bed at the Barbican – as if this were the foreplay that should, logically, have preceded it.

Installed in the linoleum drear of the rectory's kitchen, Gerry's boyfriend, Miguel, had conjured up enough tapas for twenty – even though we were only half that number. The dishes kept coming: chicken livers wrapped in bacon, squid soused in vinegar, potato croquettes, mini paellas, boquerones. Everyone ate too much – everyone drank too much. It wasn't until it was nearing midnight that we noticed Phil Szabo hadn't arrived – and then he called: He was stranded in Christchurch, but unfortunately no one was sober enough to go and get him, so he had to walk the seven miles to the house, and arrived, cold but exhilarated, at about 3.00 a.m.

'I passed Dora and Johnny down on the beach,' he said as he came into the drawing room. 'I do believe they were stripping off for a swim!'

That summer I went out early each morning with Derek Vignole, who kept a double scull at a boathouse on the riverside at Putney. The first time I tipped up Derek laughed at my blue canvas deck shoes.

'You won't be needing them, sport,' he chuckled. 'It's much better if you row barefoot, that way you get to feel the heft of her.'

I discovered what he meant soon enough: the scull sat as lightly on the river as a water boatman, and our four sweeps sent it scudding forward with scarcely a ripple. It felt as if the surface tension of the brown water was brushing against the bare soles of my feet.

I'd always been more friendly with Dora than Derek, and hadn't spent much time alone with him in the past, yet it turned out that his superficially bluff – even prosaic – manner hid a keen intellect and a poetic sensibility. He was one of those men who'd read a great deal, yet wore his erudition extremely lightly. Most mornings we left Putney at 6.30 a.m. and were rounding Eel Pie Island an hour or so later. I wasn't fit enough to row and talk; Derek, however, kept up a steady stream of observations, anecdotes, and even lengthy quotations from the great poets, his words coming from behind me, as if fed through invisible earphones.

It sounds oppressive, put like that, but it was actually something of a revelation, and I realised towards the end of July that in his funny, gruff way, Derek had targeted me as someone in need of a little late re-parenting – and for that I was grateful. He was going to La Spezia with Dora for all of August, to stay with Bettina Haussman. And although I knew the Brookmans, the McCluskeys, and Phil Szabo were going as well, for some reason Bettina hadn't invited me.

I tried not to feel put out, and made arrangements to go on a watercolour-painting trip with Miguel. Then, on our last morning sculling together, Derek angled the prow towards Eel Pie Island and said, 'I've got a little surprise for you. I didn't say anything before, but I've a share in a business Johnny Freedman runs out of an old boathouse here, and I thought you might like to take a look-see.'

'Really?' I was nonplussed. 'I wouldn't've thought you and Johnny would get on . . . in a business sense.'

'There's more to Johnny than meets the eye – or ear,' Derek said – and then I heard the tinkle of laughter from the veranda of the boathouse, and Cathy McCluskey cried, 'Surprise!' while Phil Szabo popped the cork of a bottle of prosecco.

'It's a little early in the day, isn't it?' I said to Derek, and he laughed. 'It's always too early, sport – and then it's too late.'

They were all there – even Bettina, who apologised for her behaviour in a heartfelt way. 'It's stupid,' she said, when, hours later, we were draped over the balustrade watching snags being carried downstream by the ebb tide. 'But that day when you surprised me and Cathy at the Barbican, I sort of . . . well, it sounds crazy, but I blamed you for a lot of things that've gone wrong in my life.'

'It doesn't sound crazy to me,' I replied – although of course it did.

* * *

I was hanging one of Miguel's water colours of Helvellyn in the studio when the phone rang. It was Dora Vignole wanting to gossip about the Spezia trip. While she talked, I stared out the window. The dustmen were coming along my street chucking splitting black plastic bags into the filthy anus of their grunting truck. Perhaps sensing my disinterest, Dora said, 'Are you coming to Rob's fiftieth in October? Phil Szabo's putting on an eighties disco.' And when I admitted that I was, she took this as a cue to say her goodbyes.

It must have been in the early spring of the following year that Cathy McCluskey sent me a text message: 'Phil Szabo has been found dead in his flat.' And when I called her back she was in tears. 'It's dreadful,' she cried. 'Apparently he'd had a stroke and been lying there for more than a fortnight – he'd started to r-r-r-'

'Putrefy?'

'No, rot. Honestly, Will, you seem quite disengaged about this – it turns out that Phil didn't have any family.'

'Well, I certainly never heard him talk about one – had you been friends for long?'

'Us? Friends?' She sounded confused. 'I mean, I s'pose he *was* a friend, but I rather thought you were closer to him – I mean, didn't you introduce him to us?'

After I'd noted down the information about Phil's funeral and hung up, I sat there thinking. It had seemed as if Phil Szabo had been around forever, yet when I cast my mind back I couldn't recall him being one of our crowd before the dinner party at the McCluskeys' a couple of years before – the one when I first realised Cathy was being unfaithful to Gerry. Anyway, I'd always thought of Phil as a sort of minor character, not of any real significance, merely there to make up the numbers.

It would've been better not to pursue this uncomfortable thought, yet I couldn't prevent myself, for when I considered Cathy and Gerry McCluskey, Dora and Derek Vignole, Johnny Freedman, Teddy and Rob Brookman, Bettina Haussman – and even Miguel, who I'd developed a fast and firm friendship with – they were all minor characters as well. As for me, although ostensibly the narrator, and so omniscient within this tale – I was undoubtedly the most minor of all. After all, what did anyone know about me, besides the fact that I painted in water colours, had a studio conversion, and consorted with these ciphers?

At the crematorium, standing in front of Phil Szabo's utilitarian coffin as the conveyor belt carried it into the flames, I looked from one of my fellow mourners' indistinct faces to the next, and resolved never to see any of them ever again – not even Bettina or Cathy, who, as I think I mentioned, I had known for years. And now you'll never see me again either, while I have had all the mirrors removed from my house, for fear of inadvertently peeking into the void.

A Note on the Author

Will Self is the acclaimed author of numerous books, both fiction and nonfiction. He has written for newspapers and magazines and appears regularly on television and radio. Self lives in London. His Web site is will-self.com.